AGE OF THE KING

THE ECHOES SAGA: BOOK SIX

PHILIP C. QUAINTRELL

Also by Philip C. Quaintrell

For Louisa. This is your Age...

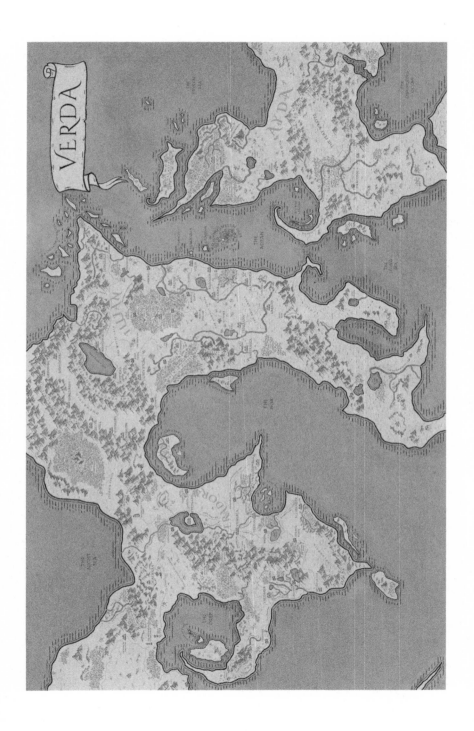

Touch to zoom/see www.philipcquaintrell.com for HD map

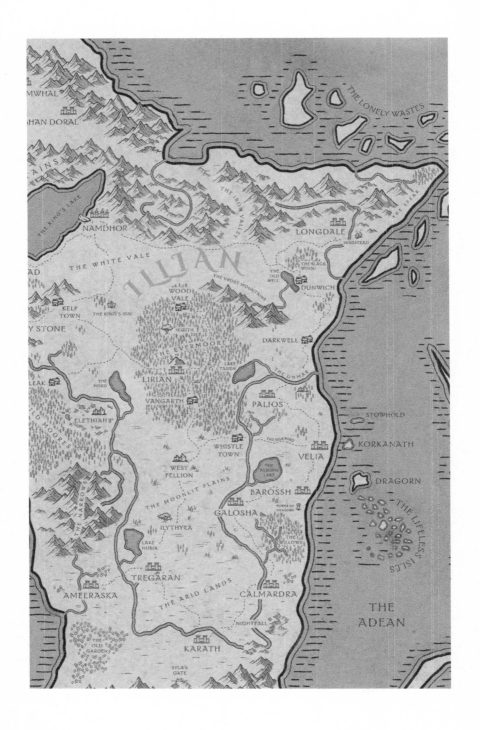

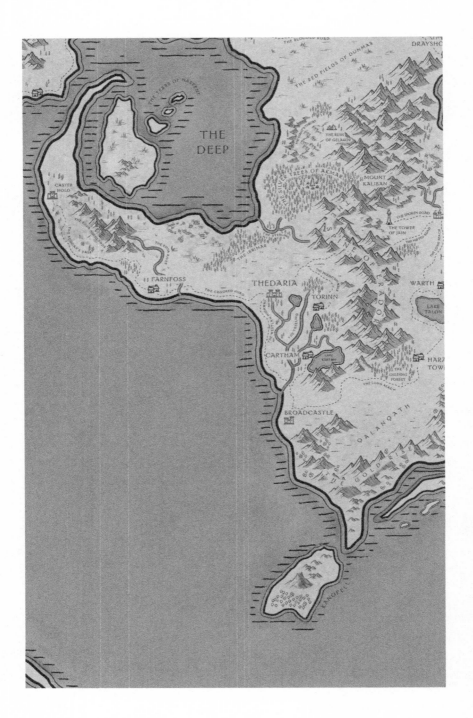

DRAMATIS PERSONAE

Adilandra Sevari
The elven queen of Elandril and mother of Reyna Galfrey

Alijah Galfrey
Half-elf

Arlon Draqaro
King of Namdhor and head of The Ironsworn

Asher
Human ranger

Athis
Red dragon, bonded with Inara

Doran Heavybelly
A Dwarven Ranger/Prince of Clan Heavybelly

Faylen Haldör

DRAMATIS PERSONAE

An elf and High Guardian of Elandril

Galanör Reveeri
An elven ranger

Gideon Thorn
A human Dragorn

Hadavad
The late mage and ranger

Ilargo
Green dragon, bonded with Gideon

Inara Galfrey
Half-elf Dragorn

Karakulak
God-King of the Orcs

Ellöria Sevari
The Lady of Ilythyra

Morvir
First servant of The Crow

Nathaniel Galfrey
An ambassador and previous knight of the Graycoats

Reyna Galfrey
Elven princess of Elandril and Illian ambassador

The Crow (Sarkas)
Leader of The Black Hand

DRAMATIS PERSONAE

Tauren Salimson
The late high councillor of Tregaran

Valanis
The late dark elf and self-proclaimed herald of the gods.

Vighon Draqaro
A Captain of Namdhor

PROLOGUE

I 0,000 *Years Ago...*

ON THE CUSP OF SPRING, winter was finally relenting its hold over the realm. It had, however, one final blast of icy air to exhale over the palace of Ak-Tor. It blew open the balcony doors of the highest room and filled the luxurious bedchamber, waking one of its two slumbering occupants.

King Atilan opened his eyes to see the hearth lose its licking flames. His wife, Fiarla, stirred next to him, pulling at the gold-laced blankets to cover her bare shoulders.

In his early fifties, Atilan had already enjoyed the company of numerous wives and, for the life of him, he couldn't remember how many had come before Fiarla. She was more bewitching than her predecessors, but they had each possessed such a quality until the king met their replacement.

He left her to sleep, since he had found her to be useless outside of this very chamber, and donned his floor-length robes, tailored with the finest fibres of Demetrium. Thanks to the precious mineral, the king's essence was in harmony with the magic realm, offering him perfect control. He flicked his finger at the balcony doors and they closed before the latch fell into place. With an open palm, Atilan conjured a ball of fire and cast it into the hearth, relighting the embers.

To the east, through the glass panes of the balcony doors, a glorious dawn rose to greet the world. For all its beauty, it was not the dawn Atilan awaited. The dawn of a new era, the end of the war, and the first rising sun of his eternal life was what the king waited for. Today, unfortunately, was just another day. The war still raged, sleep continued to escape him, and time worked against him, ravaging his mind and faculties.

Atilan waved his hand and brought forth a mirror image of himself. Standing before him, as if there were two Atilans, he looked upon his complexion, starting with the skin around his eyes first. He always started with the eyes. For all the youth that shone in those emerald orbs, the face around them was beginning to show signs of the decades that rested behind it.

Potent elixirs kept his body lean and his muscles strong, but they had their limits. He had conquered the world, from Erador to Ayda, but halting time eluded him. It was the greatest injustice that he could build the most significant kingdom that had ever existed but he wouldn't be around to rule it for all time.

His finger pulled at the lines around his eyes and the intangible image in front of him mimicked the action. Then he noticed it: the grey hair. Much like his father before him, Atilan had enjoyed a lifetime of jet-black hair, which he had grown to the base of his back in the manner of a thick mane. Now, there was a grey hair marring it.

The king tugged at the hair and held the strand out to inspect it. Time was coming for him. His army was vast, his magic powerful, and his resources seemingly infinite, yet there was nothing that could stop time.

Except for one thing...

He turned back to the east and gazed at the empty sky, once scattered with dragons. The eternal creatures had granted their Riders immortality and abandoned their king! Despite a youth spent introducing himself to dragons, none had formed a bond with him, a rejection that sparked a hatred destined to stain the realm with war.

Noting the position of the sun, Atilan finished applying his jewellery and extra clothing and made for the throne room. He paused on his departure to collect his staff, a length of wood coiled in steel and topped with a sphere of amber. Running through it was a core of Demetrium, allowing the king to command magic regardless of his state of dress. It was an added measure in a time of war but, since displaying his staff, it had become something of a fashion. Many others had crafted staffs in the style of his own while some had created a new implement - wands. Taking a liking to them, he was always sure to keep one up his sleeve.

Regardless of the extra security it offered him, the staff was a weapon in itself. Dotted along the haft were tiny green crystals of Crissalith. Mined and transmuted by his own technique, the Crissalith would prevent any around him from using magic; the best deterrent when engaged with dragons, beasts of pure magic. Only the ring on his finger, fixed with a blue Hastion gem, allowed him to wield magic in the presence of the Crissalith. Together, staff and ring made him the most powerful man in any room.

Accompanied by an escort of mage knights, all of whom were forced to rely on their swords alone around their king's staff, Atilan made his way to the throne room, on the northern edge of the palace.

The master of servants announced his arrival with all the dramatic flair he had long ago been instructed to give. "King Atilan of Etragon Blood, First of His Name, Son of Agandalan, Sorcerer Superior, The Dragon Slayer, Conqueror of the Three Realms, and The Lord of Verda!"

To a crowd of bowing heads, Atilan entered the cathedral-like chamber. He had designed every foot of it himself and had it built

3

by the greatest architectural mages in all the realms. Unlike the throne room in Valgala, the capital of Erador, the aesthetics were original and free of the ancient religion to Kaliban. His father, Agandalan, had assumed the Valgalan throne, as all the kings before him, but not Atilan. Here, in Ak-Tor, the king ruled from a throne none but himself had enjoyed, in a city his forebears couldn't have dreamed of, and in a land that had remained beyond all of their reach.

The priests of The Echoes had complained to those who had Atilan's ear that the throne room was disrespectful in its glorification of the Etragon Bloodline alone. The stuffy priests had wanted him to build shrines to Kaliban and erect statues in his honour.

Were the religion not so deep-rooted in his kingdom, Atilan would have brought down their overbearing Citadel himself. The fact that they had constructed their monstrous white tower to be taller than the palace was a great insult to Atilan. The king had no intention of worshipping their false idol. He would much rather become a god himself...

The mage knights cleared a path from the main doors to his throne, made almost entirely from dragons' teeth. The two rows of pillars, that kept the enormous ceiling and its arches aloft, were crowded with the lords of the great families. Their bloodlines went back through the eons to Erador's most ancient of days, something they felt made them worthy of being in Atilan's company.

Having bowed to their king, the Lords of Blood and their entourages began to fill the space in front of the elevated dais. Atilan, seated on his throne, left his staff to stand perfectly upright by itself. More than a few eyes roamed over the green crystals, clearly feeling vulnerable without their own magic.

From the rabble, only one stepped forward - Lord Krayt of Keldic Blood. He was a warrior who had proven his worth as a tactician in The Battle of Thedaria, a decade past. Since then, he had headed the war effort against the Dragon Riders with an equal amount of successes to failures. Should that scale begin to tip towards the latter, Atilan would see him replaced, shortly after a lengthy execution...

"How fares my kingdom, Lord Krayt?" the king asked.

As one of only a dozen in the entire kingdom granted a Hastion ring, Lord Krayt was able to generate a three-dimensional map of Verda between the lords and the throne. The Lords of Blood - none of whom Atilan had seen fit to gift a Hastion gem - could do nothing but gather around the ethereal image and take in the three realms, Erador, Illian, and Ayda from west to east.

Like the Lords of Blood, Atilan couldn't help but note the vast number of red segments on the map: territory claimed by the Dragon Riders. There were more than a few strongholds in those areas that the king could no longer call his own. Only Ayda, to the east, remained untouched by their rebellion. The eastern lands were new, however, and only the southern territories had been charted thus far.

Faint whispers passed between the Lords of Blood, their words lost on the king, but their tone unmistakable. They were afraid. More than one of them had counselled against going to war with the Dragon Riders, fearful of their power. Pain and suffering had followed their arguments and more than one bloodline had been completely wiped out by the mage knights.

Still, these great families controlled the flow of many resources needed for the war; keeping them on side was a necessity. Atilan rose from his throne before it had even warmed to his touch. He stalked towards the gathered men and stopped by the northern edge of the map.

"For thirteen years this war has raged. We must remember what it is we fight. This war isn't against Dragon Riders, it's against death itself. How many of our bloodlines are naught but dust? Would you join them in the ground or as ash in the wind?" The king began to walk around the edge of the map, pushing the lords back. "I know what *I* am fighting for. I will be the last king of the Etragon Bloodline, young and strong for all time. That power exists! The secrets of immortality lie with the dragons and their Riders."

Seeing some fire in their eyes, Atilan judged the majority to be in support, despite the victories of the Dragon Riders. He would weed out those who doubted him, those who were too weak to see the war through, and deal with them severely.

"Your report, Lord Krayt?"

The Minister of War drew everyone's attention to Erador, west on the floating map. "We received word from Elderhall in the night, your Grace. A great congregation of dragons was discovered in World's End."

"Do we know the meaning of this particular gathering?" Atilan asked, knowing that since the beginning of the war, the dragons and their Riders had been stretched too far and wide to meet in any great numbers.

"No, your Grace," Krayt admitted. "They set off across The Hox before anything could be discerned."

Atilan studied the map, noting The Hox as the only obstacle between Erador and Illian. "They will have crossed the ocean and reached Illian's shores by now."

"Indeed, your Grace. We fear they intend to bolster the Dragon Riders in the Moonlit Plains and cut off our route to Ayda." Lord Krayt stretched his hand and expanded the map, focusing on The Undying Mountains in the south of Illian. "If they block the pass we will be unable to export the Crissalith from the mines."

Atilan cupped his smooth jaw, contemplating the map. The Crissalith was being mined in its raw state in the south of Ayda, thousands of miles from their current position in Ak-Tor, in the north of Illian. Opening a portal, or even a series of portals, between here and there would require a lot of magic and likely attract the dragons.

At present, however, Crissalith was their greatest weapon against the beasts...

"We must secure that route, Lord Krayt," Atilan emphasised. He would have compounded that statement had he not caught the flicker of concern on his war minister's face. "Speak," he commanded.

Lord Krayt pinched his hand and the map snapped back to encompass all three realms again. "Word has reached our spymasters that the Dragon Riders also intend to occupy Storm's Reach."

Atilan shifted his eyes to look upon the narrow strip of freezing tundra that separated The Dread Wood from The Broken Mountains. "If they hold Storm's Reach," the king extrapolated, his anger beginning to rise, "we will be cut off from Erador. The bulk of my army and all of our Demetrium mines are in Erador, Lord Krayt."

"Yes, your Grace," Krayt agreed, his gaze averted. "We are mobilising our forces now to pass through Storm's Reach and enter Illian as soon as possible."

Atilan was shaking his head. "The Dragon Riders don't have the numbers to hold Storm's Reach *and* The Undying Mountains. One of your sources of information is wrong, Lord Krayt. Either that or you are being manipulated..."

The Minister of War looked over the ethereal map as he considered the implications. "Then I will get to the truth of it, your Grace."

"See that you do," Atilan replied with a threatening tone - he didn't suffer failure. "You're supposed to be war incarnate, Lord Krayt. Do not come to me again with half-truths and whispers."

"Forgive me, your Grace," the war minister apologised with a bow of the head.

Darakus of Helteron Blood cleared his throat. "Your Grace, I would counsel caution when it comes to mobilising our forces *out* of Erador." As the head of one of the oldest bloodlines, Darakus felt he could ignore Lord Krayt's silent instruction to remain quiet. "If we secure Illian at the cost of losing Erador, our ancestral homeland, would we not be losing something more than just territory? In the eyes of the people, it would be considered a great—"

Darakus lost his voice. Then, he lost his breath. The older lord gripped his throat, which continued to constrict regardless of his efforts. Only when he dropped to his knees did Atilan unclench his fist and release Darakus from the spell.

"You seek to protect the past," Atilan spat. "Did you hear nothing I said? Those that came before you are dust! Your image, any memory of you, even your name will fall from time if we don't win this war. Erador is the past! I'm taking us into the dawn, where the sun never sets. Ak-Tor," he declared, pointing to the floor, "is the capital city of Verda now, not Valgala!" He gestured to the large city in the middle of Erador, one of the few places on the map that wasn't red.

Darakus coughed and spluttered as he found his feet again. He was offered no aid by his fellow lords, most of whom stepped away from him. "Forgive me, your Grace," he begged, his eyes on the floor.

Lord Krayt stepped in. "Rest assured, your Grace, this war is numbered in months not years. The kingdom *will* be secured and the Dragon Rider scourge will be eradicated."

"Eradication will come, Lord Krayt, when I possess enough dragon scales to cover Mount Kaliban. Little can be gleaned by their extinction - bear that in mind the next time you pit my armies against them. I don't need any more dragon corpses, I need living specimens."

The king smoothed over his hair and dwelled on the grey strand he had found earlier. Judging by the amount of enemy-gained territories on the map, he knew the minister of war had more to discuss with him, but Atilan needed to be moving, to know that some progress was being made in his battle against death. For all their warring, only one person had offered any kind of promise that eternity would be his.

Naius...

"Out. All of you! Come to me when you actually know something!"

Only when the ornate doors shut behind Lord Krayt and the Lords of Blood did Atilan retrieve a crystal from his belt. He tossed it into the space in front of the throne and commanded the magic stored within to explode, forming a portal of pure darkness, its edges licked by sparks and lightning.

In a single step, he left the capital and travelled from Ak-Tor to Haren Bain inside the depths of Vengora. The shadowy caverns of the northern mountains greeted him with their usual malevolent gloom. The king made his way across the narrow bridge, lined with torches, and onto the jagged platform that housed the great doors. Thick and towering slabs of iron, they kept the monsters of Vengora out, away from Naius's experiments.

One such experiment stood guard in front of the doors. With the shape of a man, the sentinel was shrouded in black robes and a large hood - a menacing sight for any and all foolish enough to explore the depths of Vengora.

Had Atilan been any other man, the sentinel would have killed him before he could so much as touch the iron doors. Recognising him as king, as all creatures should, the sentinel stood aside and allowed him to pass by without incident.

As with the sentinel, the foreboding doors knew the king who approached. It was the lightest touch of his finger that caused one of them to swing open, welcoming him to the stuff of nightmares.

Haren Bain...

It was hidden deep in the cold embrace of the Vengoran mountains. The vast emptiness that hung over him was a testament to the cavern's size, its ceiling untouched by the flaming torches. Naius, his Minister of Magic, had chosen this of all locations because of its natural geysers, many of which spouted hot gases into the air with sporadic rhythm.

The king followed the path, lined with torches, and made for the source of the screaming - a noise that often accompanied Naius and his work.

Scattered throughout the cavern, Atilan laid eyes on the numerous cages, each filled with terrified test subjects. He cared for none of them, a state easily achieved when he considered they weren't even human. An earlier creation of his own, the elves, as they called themselves, were nothing more than failed experiments.

They remained very still in their cages as he passed them by. The elves knew well that what Naius would do to them was in the name of his work, but Atilan would be viciously cruel to them if they caught his eye. He hated them almost as much as he hated the dragons and their Riders.

Once human, they had been transformed by Atilan's magic and granted immortality, but it had come at too steep a price. Their very nature had been changed in the process, a by-product of which was their loss of memory. The elves in these cages had no memory of ever being human or their previous lives.

Atilan was not willing to lose all that he was, even for immortality. What was the point of living forever if he wasn't him anymore? The elves displayed a great attachment to nature and living among the forests, forgoing the trappings of kingdom-life. They didn't seek power or dominion over anything. He wasn't going to spend eternity singing to trees.

The king flashed his eyes at the prisoners in the last cage and enjoyed their cowering retreat. He would have burned them all alive if Naius didn't need so many subjects for his latest experiment.

The manic wizard was in the middle of the cavern, surrounded by stone tables scattered with alchemy equipment, parchments, and a variety of wicked-looking tools. Drawing one's eye to the centre of his workspace, a male elf, strapped to two planks of wood shaped in an X, had been cut open from neck to groin and his organs removed.

The floor was very wet...

Atilan cast his eye over the parchments, doing his best to read the poor scribbles of his minister. They didn't require much inspection to note Naius's ongoing struggle.

"It cannot be done then," the king concluded.

Naius hadn't acknowledged Atilan's arrival, but he didn't startle either. He was the only person alive the king refrained from punishing for such blatant lack of respect. Considering the man's brilliance with all things magic, he gave Naius some allowance.

The Mad Mage, as many called him behind his back, had ascended to a rocky outcropping, beyond his work area. His attention was fixed on the field of sludge and mud that blanketed the other half of the cavern. Hot gases shot into the air from the geysers that dotted the shadowy field.

"It cannot be done..." Naius repeated as if the words had been his own, his back to the king. "I have seen you burn men alive for saying those four words."

Atilan couldn't argue with that. "A luxury of being the king," he mused.

The Mad Mage muttered under his breath, his voice too low and his speech too fast for anyone to understand. Atilan knew the man could get lost in his work - something that usually benefitted the king - but today it was only irritating him.

The king paused as he inspected the early designs for The Veil, a device so powerful it could open a gateway into the world between the very fabric of reality. It had been one of Atilan's ideas, given over to Naius for execution. He noted the parchments referring to the pools of magic in his fortress, Kaliban, hidden in the heights of western Vengora.

"I see you haven't forgotten our work on The Veil," Atilan commented, fingering the parchment. "Have you given any further thought to the pools themselves, Naius? Those crystal waters are perhaps the most potent source of magic in all of Verda..."

The Mad Mage tore his eyes from the field and looked at his king with a blank expression, as if he hadn't been listening to a word. "The pools... Yes, the pools. They are most certainly capable of granting immortality."

Atilan let go of the parchment and faced his minister, his temperament somewhere between hope and anger. "Then why—"

"Death would come first," Naius interrupted, another allowance offered to the minister. "None could survive submersion in the pools, at least not without being chained to them for all time."

Atilan's hope died away, drowned by his anger. Like so many other things, the pools were a dead end, their power counterbalanced by death. Still, they could be used to forge weapons if nothing else, perhaps even The Veil.

Casting the pools and their potential from his mind, Atilan focused on the Mad Mage. "The Lords of Blood have already upset my mood today, Naius. For your own good, give me results..."

The Minister of Magic ceased his muttering and took a breath before announcing, "The elves are what they are. They cannot be any other way. No..." he added with a tone of confusion. "That was an old thought."

Atilan frowned. "Naius..."

The king's tone would have had anyone else praying to Kaliban that the ground would swallow them up, but not Naius. "I made something new. It was supposed to be perfect!" he lamented.

Atilan sighed. "The passage of time eludes you, Naius. I am already aware of the new elixir, just as I am aware of its lack of results." He recalled the last experiment, conducted on a human, and its devastating effects. The man, as he had once been, endured terrible pain before his body let go of life, melted away, and was collected into a bucket.

Naius finally turned to regard his liege, wide eyes set under bushy eyebrows. "Ah... yes. The Orcyr elixir is too potent... for *humans*."

Atilan narrowed his eyes and made for the small rise to join the Mad Mage. "You have begun testing it on elves?"

Naius smiled, flashing his crooked teeth. With delicate fingers, the Minister of Magic gestured to the field of mud and geysers. Atilan stood beside him, a contrast of clean scarlet robes against Naius's dirty black rags. The field of sludge was hard to define, so sparse were the torches.

Atilan was beginning to lose patience. "What am I looking at, Naius?"

The Mad Mage pointed at a particular mound of sludge and mud, focusing Atilan's attention. The mound was writhing. Witnessing the movement, the king searched the field and noted other such mounds, many of which were indeed alive with something.

"I tried to introduce the Orcyr elixir to the elves in many ways," Naius explained. "They didn't suffer the same fate as the human subject, but it didn't yield the desired result either. I believe gas is the missing element."

Atilan looked from one geyser to another. "The Orcyr elixir is in the geysers?" he asked with some trepidation.

Naius rubbed his hands together with a giddy grin. "Quite fantastic is it not?"

The king took a cautious step back and readied a plethora of spells to keep him alive.

"There's no need to fear it," Naius assured.

The Mad Mage reached out and flicked his finger in the air between them and the field of geysers. His gesture created a ripple effect of glowing orange runes. Atilan watched the runes light up and dissipate, stretching from one side of the cavern to the other and far up into the dizzying heights.

"Had I not put a shield in place you would have died moments after arriving. Like I said: potent!"

Atilan, one never to display fear, adjusted his robes and reminded himself that there was no one better than Naius. With that thought in mind, the king refrained from casting a destructive spell to rival the Orcyr's potency.

"*This* is the first batch!" Naius exclaimed.

Atilan eyed the writhing forms in the mud. "What do you expect to emerge?"

"An immortal!" The Mad Mage held his arms out wide.

The king wasn't convinced. "An immortal what, Naius? Those are elves in there, not humans."

"You should really spend more time around them," Naius said flippantly, ignorant of the ire spreading across Atilan's face. "Elves are quite the creation; you should be proud! They're stronger, faster, their senses are better than ours, they have an extraordinary affinity with magic, and, of course, they're immortal."

"You have a point?" Atilan cut in, reconsidering his destructive spell.

"Using unique extracts from our captured dragons, I designed the Orcyr elixir with certain specifications. It should remove all the undesired elements of elf-kind: their strange ears, their love of nature, and, most importantly, fix their loss of memory. What's left is a human: stronger, faster, smarter... *immortal!*"

Atilan worked through Naius's method until he reached the first step. "But we would have to become elves before being exposed to the Orcyr?"

The Mad Mage scratched behind his ear and lightly shrugged. "A temporary measure, to be sure."

Taking an extra moment to consider everything he had heard, Atilan was beginning to wonder if he hadn't set his sights too small. If Naius was correct, they could not only beat death but live as superior beings. The idea of becoming an elf and then being buried in mud, however, did not appeal.

"Look!" Naius pointed to a mound of sludge not far from their outcropping. "The first is being born!"

The king watched with fascination as the mound expanded and large clumps of mud fell away from an emerging form. It was difficult to understand exactly what they were looking at until, at last, he realised it was a back, pushing up from the mud. Muscular arms became clear, then legs. Then came the head...

Atilan narrowed his eyes to better see what looked to be a pair of horns curving over the head. He blinked hard, sure that his vision was wrong.

To the left, another subject began to push up from the sludge.

Two more from the right followed suit and somewhere from the back of the gloom came a roar. It was not human.

"Naius..."

The Mad Mage had seen and heard everything his king had, yet he still looked on in wonder. Risen to its full height, what now stood before them was neither human nor elf. The creature turned to set its black eyes on them, revealing a hideous face of sharp angles and dragon-like fangs. They all displayed horns of varying sizes and number and their physique was striking.

"What in all the hells is that?" Atilan demanded.

Before Naius could answer, the nearest creature broke into a sprint and charged at them with a feral roar. The creature was fast, but the magical shield cared little for speed - the monster's head snapped back and its body bounced violently away. Then the rest came at them, angry and full of rage. The shield flashed orange runes but it held up to the barrage of banging fists and ferocious head butts.

"This doesn't look like progress, Naius."

"Everything inside Haren Bain is frontier work," the Mad Mage replied casually, his gaze fixed on the aggressive creatures. "Progress is hard to measure..."

"I tasked you with finding a way to make humans immortal. What you have done is create an abomination of elf and dragon!"

The king felt the silent warning through his staff, an object that could see everything around him thanks to the amber orb. He spun on his heel and raised a hand with a shielding spell on his lips. Had Atilan been a second slower, the Dragon Rider would have plunged his sword into his back. Instead, the Rider's steel slammed into the shield point first and rebounded out of his hand.

The shield flared a brilliant blue, momentarily blinding the Rider before Atilan flicked his staff up and caught him in the jaw. The Rider stumbled backwards and tumbled over the table, knocking glass vials and parchments onto the floor.

Atilan stepped off the rise and wandered around the table,

perfectly in control of the situation. "It seems you have a breach, Minister Naius."

The Mad Mage followed behind his king with a wicked smirk, his cold eyes settled on the bloodied Rider. "We shall have to plug it then..."

Proving to be of warrior stock, the Dragon Rider jumped to his feet and faced them with all courage. Weaponless, he pushed out his arm with an open palm. Nothing happened. The Rider flexed his fingers and tried again, yet no spell came forth.

Atilan marvelled at the Crissalith lining his staff. "You're the first Rider to get this close to me in some years. For that, I give you credit." The king bowed his head. "And now, I will give you pain."

The Rider, seeing the error of his attack, ran towards the elves, seeking to retreat and escape Atilan's legendary torment. The king laughed and threw a crystal ahead of the fleeing Rider. When it exploded, two portals opened inside Haren Bain: one in front of the Rider and one on the other side of Naius's shield. Running as fast as he was, the Dragon Rider couldn't help but pass through the sudden portal.

Atilan turned around and watched him emerge through the second portal, amidst the foul creatures. Breathing in the Orcyr fumes, the Rider had only seconds to live, though his dragon bond had the potential to see him survive a little longer. Whether it would or not became a moot question when the muddy beasts descended on him with claws and fangs.

The king watched the Rider being butchered with glee, aware that, somewhere, his dragon would be experiencing the same thing. Hopefully, the dragon would pass on these final memories to its kin and share the fate of all those who challenged the Etragon Bloodline...

PART ONE

CHAPTER I

ASTARI

An eerie silence had settled over Namdhor, its inhabitants holding their collective breath in anticipation. No more than a day had passed since victory had been claimed by the men of the north, their first victory in the war. Winning the battle, however, was not comparable to winning what would inevitably follow.

The orcs would be back...

In the freezing gloom of Namdhor's dungeons, a dank and dreadful place, the battle continued for one man. This man was fifty years old, or perhaps he was eighty years old, or even a thousand years old. Past and present collided in a cacophony of sounds, smells, and imagery that made him wonder if he was ten times that age.

His name... He had to hold onto his name. It was the only thing he had ever possessed from one life to the next. Was he Malliath? Alijah? The word Arakesh blinded his thoughts, always dragging him to dark places.

He felt ancient, his memories stretching back over thousands of years, but they were fractured, interspersed with the memories of another. He had been an Outlander of The Wild Moores, an assassin

19

of Nightfall, and a ranger of the realm. Then, he was a dragon tormented by a long life of violence. Following that, he was a son, a brother, and a rogue.

He had the minds of two others inside his own, each clawing at his memories for dominance. So old was Malliath that his memories were a bottomless well that threatened to consume him.

Then there was pain, his oldest of friends. It sharpened his mind, focusing his thoughts as it always had. Decades in Nightfall had trained him to embrace the touch of pain and greet it as an ally.

His mind rose from the heavy slumber and he became aware of voices close by. He kept his eyes closed. He was wearing only trousers and, judging by the smell of his environment and the feel of the slab he was lying on, he guessed his surroundings to be that of a dungeon - he had seen the inside of many...

What had his last memories been?

That question took him down a violent path. Flashes of fighting, blood, and fire erupted across his vision. He had been fighting a man outside the city and nearly killed him too. No, not just any man. He had been a warrior of great renown. His name escaped him.

He was distracted by the conversing voices of two men, one of which he recognised. It sounded familiar in a comforting way, though a part of him knew he had never really heard the voice himself before.

"The legendary Asher..." the unfamiliar voice purred.

Asher!

That was his name. He had no family name, no house or tribe to which he belonged. He was simply Asher. Patching his memories and thoughts together was made all the harder now. New memories rose to the surface and he struggled to place them in his extraordinary life.

He recalled being a child and the pain under his left eye, caused by the black-fang tattoo his father had recently marked him with. He was a hunter next. The memory hazed and blew away like leaves on the wind, only to be replaced by a new one, far sharper and more painful. He was fighting in Nightfall, training under the watchful eye of his mentor, Nasta Nal-Aket.

Asher mistimed his defence and took a blow to the head, knocking him years into the future, where yet more pain awaited him. He was atop the walls of Velia, fighting Alidyr Yalathanil, a servant of Valanis. Agony ripped through him as he recalled the dark elf poking his eyes out, permanently blinding him.

The pain pushed him through the memory to a peaceful moment, filled with silence and tranquillity. He was submerged under the magical depths of the pools of Naius, deep in the heart of Valanis's lair. The magic of the pools restored his eyes and infused him with more magic than any being could rightly contain. Only with Paldora's gem could he maintain any kind of control.

The moment of peace was gone in an instant, and he was left looking at three people he considered to be more than friends. Reyna, Nathaniel, and Faylen... *They* were his family. Seeing Faylen, the most beautiful of elves, he was taken back to their first and only kiss. There had been a promise of something, something pure and real, and more powerful than he had ever known. That life had been taken from them both.

As the cavernous walls began to collapse on top of him, the ranger was brought back to reality, where the two men were still talking in his cell. He tried to listen and gather as much information as he could before his shattered mind dragged him back down.

"The queen is dead!" the unfamiliar voice declared. "Long live the *king*!"

There was a pause from the other man, the one whose voice Asher recognised.

"Shouldn't you be running then?" he finally asked.

Vighon Draqaro! The name came to Asher with ease, despite the fact that he had never met the man before. His heavy head pulled him down and he saw flashes of Vighon through the eyes of another. At that moment, the northman felt like a brother to him.

"You're referring to Sir Borin the *Dread*," the other man responded. "Yes, he had been a concern of mine. However..."

Whatever happened next was beyond all of Asher's senses. His mind was bombarded with image after image, running him rapidly through the events of the last few weeks. There was confusion and pain as The Crow brought him back from his eternal rest. The pain intensified as he was bonded to Malliath and subsequently Alijah.

Then there was death and blood...

He tasted the blood of dragons in his mouth, he felt the crack of bones, and he watched in terror as the rampage continued. He had been there for every moment under The Crow's spell, helpless to fight back.

The tone of the conversation changed and saw Asher's attention return to his surroundings again.

"I'm not bowing to you," Vighon stated flatly.

"You will," the other man said with authority. "Just as you will retrieve the Moonblade. Should you fail, Asher will never leave this cell, I can assure you of that."

The ranger decided there and then that the owner of that unfamiliar voice was an enemy. That was never a good category to be in where Asher was concerned...

There were no more words, only the sound of heels pressing into the stone floor and growing distant. He was alone in the cell with Vighon. Asher thought to sit up and quietly greet the northman before asking him one of many questions. Instead, something snapped inside of him, something feral combined with years of training in the arts of killing.

Without recalling his movement, Asher was suddenly standing in front of Vighon with violent intentions. He bared his teeth and growled before seizing the northman, pinning him to the wall. The entire event was born of instincts that weren't entirely his own, but the blank spot in his memory, concerning his movement from lying to lunging, was of great concern.

His head split open again and Malliath's memories flooded his consciousness. There were too many! Millennia after millennia of experiences forced themselves on the ranger, but there was one that repeated over and over.

Haren Bain...

The foreign name seared itself into his mind but the memories continued to slip through his grasp. There was, however, one thought that came with the name, a conclusion his subconscious had made or perhaps something from Malliath himself. Like all of his memories, Asher could no longer be sure of their root.

He fell back from Vighon and dropped to his knees, clawing at his head in the hope of making some sense of it all. Still, that one thought continued to push on him until he had to voice it, even if he couldn't focus on the details.

"I know how to win the war..." he said plainly.

Vighon looked back at him in shock, his stance wary. Asher had more to say, or at least he had a dozen questions to ask, but he never had the chance to say another word.

He blinked, a simple and very common thing to do, except this time his surroundings were not that of the cell. He was standing in the middle of a long hall, wearing only his trousers still. Lying at his feet were a pair of Gold Cloaks, soldiers of Namdhor. Bells were ringing from everywhere and distant shouting echoed off the stone walls.

How had he got here? Why wasn't he in his cell? Where was Vighon? His list of questions had just grown exponentially.

Asher crouched and checked over the two guards, both of whom were still alive. Their crime against him, it seemed, had been nothing more than crossing him. It worried the ranger that he had no memory of engaging them. What else had he done? How long ago had he left Vighon in the dungeon?

"There he is!" came a cry from behind.

Asher turned his head to see a group of Gold Cloaks charging down the hall, swords drawn. Instincts kicked in and the assassin within assumed control of his thoughts and actions. Five armoured men were advancing on him, but all he saw were the angles of attack, their weak spots, their youth and likely lack of experience.

He also knew how they saw him: an unarmed man with injuries, greying hair, and no armour. They should have taken better note of the two men lying at his feet.

Asher remained very still, giving all five soldiers a static target, a place for all of them to attack at once. Only when their blades were moving rapidly towards him, ready to hack him to pieces, did the ranger burst into action. He jumped inside their swings, choosing an opening between their swords, and used their momentum against them. It was a bold move, requiring confidence born out of years fighting and winning.

The closest man was delivered a blow from an outstretched arm, cutting across his shoulders and throat. Before he hit the floor, Asher kicked out, catching another guard behind him in the back of the leg. As the first Namdhorian landed hard on his back, Asher deftly removed the helmet from the man kicked down to one knee and thrust it into the face of the next opponent, pushing him back into the unrelenting wall. A quick backhand, using the helmet as his weapon of choice again, put the man down.

Robbed of his helmet, the Namdhorian tried to rise to his feet and challenge Asher again before his remaining comrades took their chances. The ranger, however, was fast on the ball of his foot and turned to shove his bare heel into the man's exposed temple. He hit the floor with a definitive *thud*.

Five seconds had passed and three of his five attackers were incapacitated...

Of the remaining two, the younger, and more inexperienced, failed to realise when he had already lost the fight. He jabbed at Asher with the point of his sword, using more strength than was necessary to kill a man. The ranger subtly shifted his body and allowed the blade to slip between his arm and ribs, positioning it perfectly to knock the guard's wrist and flip the sword into the air. Before the hilt landed in Asher's waiting hand, the ranger punched the young man lightly in the throat, forcing him back a step. The sword firmly in his grip now, Asher brought the pommel down on the bridge of his nose and added the guard to the pile on the floor.

The last guard was not so fast to advance on Asher. He circled around the ranger, his sword held out in front of him. When the hall opened up behind him again, the remaining Namdhorian bolted without a word. Asher watched him disappear around the corner before allowing himself to wince in pain. A wound on the back of his ribs had opened up, the stitches torn - he could feel warm blood slowly trickling down to his waistline.

The sound of rushing feet found his ears, warning him of rein-forcements. He wasn't sure why he was running or fighting back - everything was instinct. He dropped the sword and darted into a small alcove off the hall. Ignoring the pain in his back, the ranger scaled the stone and took refuge in the arched ceiling, above the lip of the hall. The tension in his arms and legs was the only thing keeping him aloft when the next group arrived.

"It's him," said the same voice from the dungeon. "Find him! No one leaves The Dragon Keep!"

The man strode away, followed by heavy footsteps that betrayed an enormous frame, possibly too big to be a man. Orders were given and the soldiers of Namdhor hefted their comrades away before continuing the pursuit of the escaped prisoner.

Asher held his posture for another minute before dropping down onto his bare feet without a sound. He was being hunted; a state of being that brought out his oldest characteristics.

Clinging to the shadows, Asher weaved his way through the keep, unsure as to where he was going or why. Soldiers on alert ran past him on several occasions, no one the wiser to his whereabouts. He was creeping his way down another hall, looking to get his bear-ings from a window, when one of the doors opened.

A quick drop and roll took the ranger behind a statue. The stone knight concealed him from the eyes of those exiting the chamber and he remained crouched out of sight. He began immediately searching for another route, but their voices gave him pause.

"It has to be him," said a familiar voice.

"Even if it is him, we have to be cautious. We don't know for certain that The Crow's spell has lost its touch - he's dangerous, Nathaniel."

"Gideon's right, Father," said a female voice. "He might not be the same man you knew..."

"Well, ye know there's only one way to find out!" The unmistakable voice of Doran Heavybelly preceded his boisterous bulk as he entered the hall.

There was a pause between the group, but Asher couldn't see them. They were friends all, especially Nathaniel, but his instincts drove him more than anything else. He had been placed in the role of prey, a lesson covered vigorously in Nightfall, and his training demanded he evade until he acquired a lay of the land.

"Fine," Gideon relented. "We should split up and cover more ground. We all have a better chance of stopping Asher than any Namdhorian soldier."

The ranger kept his head down and remained very still as Doran and Inara rushed past him. Seeing Inara brought Alijah's feelings to the surface, tempering Asher's instincts for a moment. She was his sister, his twin in fact. They were very close, or at least they had been. Asher couldn't control the feelings that weren't his own, feelings that told him he loved her.

Rising to his feet and an empty hall, he stepped out from behind the statue. A part of him didn't want to run anymore. After escaping the clutches of Nightfall, he had spent fourteen years trying to control his instincts and find some way of living like a man rather than an assassin. Fractured as his mind now was, all those years of hard work were slipping away...

Alone again, the ranger moved on only to hesitate outside the door they had exited. Something pulled him towards it. Curiosity perhaps? Whatever it was, the feeling was enough to combat his instincts, if only for a moment, and give him clarity of mind. Before he knew it, he was pushing the door open and walking inside.

The scent of herbs and exotic potions filled the ranger's nose, drawing him towards the bed. The blankets had been scattered with blue and yellow petals and a variety of elixirs sat on the bedside table. For all the decoration and trappings of the chamber, it was the form lying under the blankets that captured Asher's attention.

He stood motionless, for some time, staring down at Reyna Sevari, now Reyna Galfrey. Considering his circumstances it was an odd thought, and a sad one at that, but the ranger lamented that he had missed their wedding. He would have liked to have seen that...

Regardless of her name and all that had followed his death, she would always be a princess to him. Before he could ponder any further, his warrior instinct alerted him to the presence of another in the room. He couldn't boast percipience, but he knew the sound of steel being slowly drawn from a scabbard.

Asher turned his head but didn't look over his shoulder. "Lift it another inch and I can't be responsible for what happens next," he warned.

The sliding length of steel paused on its way into the world. Then the hilt dropped back into the scabbard - a wise choice Asher couldn't say he was accustomed to.

"Step away from her," the man commanded in a calm voice.

The old ranger obliged and stepped aside, his eyes lingering on Reyna's pale form. Facing the man, he quickly discovered that it was no man at all, but an elf, evident by his pointed ears clear to see. Indeed, his appearance was strange for an elf, his hair cut short with naught but a small braid.

Short hair or not, the ranger recognised the elf, his being one of the few faces he saw before his death in the pools of Naius. Asher opened his mouth to greet him but his memory stumbled over his name for a moment.

With one hand still resting on one of his dual scimitars, the elf placed his free hand to his chest and declared, "My name is Gal—"

"Galanör," Asher finished. "I remember..." In truth, his memories of Galanör were as clear as a spider's web. Both Malliath and Alijah had met the elf before and after Asher's death, but they all felt so real, making it all the harder to narrow down which memories were his and which belonged to them.

The elf tilted his head, scrutinising the old ranger. "Are you..."

"Myself?" Asher assumed. "The answer to that isn't as simple as I would like."

"It's him." The confirmation came from the open door, where Gideon Thorn was standing with Mournblade in hand.

"How can you be sure?" Galanör asked, still wary.

Gideon walked into the room, his eyes roaming over Asher. "I've fought him enough now to know the difference." The Master Dragorn sheathed his enchanted scimitar, supporting his own claim.

Behind him, Inara, Doran, and Nathaniel entered the room. Asher glanced at the Dragorn and the dwarf, though his attention was ultimately stolen by his old friend, a knight of the realm the last he had seen him.

"You've got slow," Nathaniel said with the smallest hint of a smile. "You're bleeding all over the place."

Asher looked down at the floor and noticed the blood gathered around his right foot. Once upon a time, he would never have been so sloppy as to leave a blood trail. Before the ranger could comment, Nathaniel crossed the room and embraced him in a tight hug.

The ranger closed his fist and focused his will to combat the instincts that naturally wished to react with violence. Everything in him wanted to throw his old friend to the floor and beat him until he couldn't be considered a threat. When the pounding blood ceased its drumming in his ears, Asher was finally able to lift his arms and embraced the old knight.

Nathaniel's voice was close to his ear. "I can't believe you're..." He couldn't finish his words and so he settled on a tighter embrace.

Asher patted his friend on the back before breaking their hold, aware now of more injuries thanks to Nathaniel. "I wish I could say it's good to be back."

"But ye're, lad!" Doran exclaimed. "That's all that matters. We'll sort everythin' else out..."

The dwarf's last words changed the tension in the room and Asher suddenly felt a lot of questions behind everyone's eyes.

"What do you remember?" Gideon asked.

That question alone made Asher's head thump. "I remember..."

Flashes of his life mixed with Alijah's, contorting the memories into something else entirely. The real pain came when thousands of years' worth of Malliath's memories came flooding back. There were too many for his human mind to comprehend.

"Asher?" Nathaniel's voice felt distant.

The ranger tried to focus but his head felt like someone was pouring molten iron into it. He dropped to his knees with his head in his hands and a pained groan on his lips. He heard his name again and he used it as an anchor, holding him in place. The bombarding memories began to subside enough that he glimpsed new arrivals in the room.

A man in a long black robe, fitted to his trim physique perfectly, had entered the room. Behind him were enough men to fill the doorway and conceal the hall beyond. Of the group, two soldiers broke through carrying a limp body between them.

Vighon...

The northman was sporting a fresh cut and a dark bruise above his eye, courtesy of Asher. The ranger would have felt a pang of guilt on his part, but the soldiers in the room focused his attention.

"Put him anywhere," the man in black announced, the voice informing Asher that this was the same man from the dungeon.

Vighon was about to be unceremoniously dumped on the floor when Inara intercepted his limp form. The young Dragorn shot the guards a dangerous look before hefting Vighon over to the bed, beside her mother.

"This man is an enemy of the crown," the man in black continued, gesturing to the ranger. "I thank you all for apprehending him. Had he fled the keep there would have been severe punishments for those *stupid* enough to let him escape in the first place." He cast a disappointed look over Vighon.

Asher rose to his feet, doing his best to ignore the blinding headache that threatened to crack his skull in half.

"Put him in chains," the man continued, "and *drag* him back to his cell."

Gideon and Nathaniel stepped between Asher and the soldiers of Namdhor. "Asher is in the custody of the Dragorn," Gideon stated.

Doran folded his thick arms and fixed the soldiers with a glare. "Aye, what he said."

The soldiers paused and turned to Arlon, who remained unnaturally calm in the face of defiance from one as skilled as Gideon Thorn. Asher's true memories of the Master Dragorn recalled him as a younger man, but easily one of the most capable fighters with Mournblade in his hand. His more recent, and violent, memories told Asher that Gideon had only built upon those skills to the point of being formidable.

That said, to challenge Gideon with such demeanour, Arlon had either been parted from his wits or he possessed something more powerful than the Master Dragorn.

"Not an hour past this man was in a Namdhorian cell," Arlon pointed out. "I would see him returned for questioning."

Gideon didn't budge. "Until I hear such a command from the queen herself, Asher will stay with me."

The tension in the room would have been unbearable if it weren't for Arlon's smile.

"The queen is dead," he announced bluntly. "The crown is *mine* now..."

It seemed Arlon Draqaro did have something more powerful than Gideon after all: power itself.

"Queen Yelifer, the last scion of house Skalaf, passed away in her chamber this very morn - official announcements will be made shortly. Rest assured, the throne and the realm are in *my* care now, and I will not start my reign by allowing this prisoner to wander outside of his cell."

Nathaniel shook his head. "We have to speak with him," he said with urgency. "The spell that bound Asher has been broken; we need to know what he's seen—"

Arlon held up a finger, silencing Nathaniel. "Interrogating the prisoner is exactly what we're going to do. And, in the process, we will determine his allegiance." Arlon stepped closer to the ranger. "From what I hear of your past, getting the truth out of you will require *vigorous* methods of questioning."

Everyone in the room knew exactly what he was implying, and Asher heard it too, but his head was still thumping, his mind splintering into shards of various memories. The ranger could do nothing but stand there and take the threat.

Gideon still wasn't moving. "Any questions will be done under my supervision."

Arlon Draqaro held his gaze on Asher for a moment longer before flashing the Master Dragorn a wide grin. "I think not. You are a servant to the realm, your dragons too. Your *king* commands you to attend the war council and prepare to receive orders. That is all."

Gideon took a breath, choosing his words with more care than the king. "Dragorn do not take *commands* from kings and queens, we give counsel. It's a distinction you should take with you all of your days."

Arlon shrugged. "As protectors of the realm, then. The orcs didn't conquer most of Illian to lose one battle and slink back into the dark. They will return with a vengeance!" He gestured to Inara. "I would suggest that you and Master Galfrey put your heads together and bring something useful to the table. The land needs cleansing of orcs, *my* land that is…"

Gideon had no reply and another silence settled over the room. It was becoming clear that there was only one way this was going to end and Asher didn't want any more violence, especially on his behalf. The ranger stepped in front of Gideon and Nathaniel and held his arms out, wrists together.

Arlon smirked. "Take him away."

As two of the Namdhorians approached him, manacles in hand, Asher's muscles tensed, his senses sharpened, and his heartbeat increased dramatically. His body's muscle memory perceived a threat and he didn't have the state of mind to take control. Nor could he protest.

The guard to Asher's right slapped a rough hand on his wrist and everything went black.

The old ranger opened his eyes again, only to find himself standing outside in the freezing cold. His hands were still held out, as if he was waiting for the manacles to bind him. Confused and disorientated, Asher spun around to get his bearings.

A light sprinkle of snow and ash dusted his bare chest as he looked out on all of Namdhor and The White Vale beyond. He was standing on the rampart of the highest turret and judging by the bloody footprints in the snow-covered stone, he had climbed up.

The pain in his head had subsided, allowing him to think clearly again. He needed to move. One of his earliest lessons in Nightfall had regarded the advantage of always staying on the move, a lesson he had heeded all his life. Turning away from the vista, Asher made for the edge of the turret only to find his path blocked...

Slowly bearing down on him was the horned head of Ilargo. The dragon opened its mouth half a foot and a stream of hot air blew between his fangs and over the ranger, along with the strong scent of death and sulphur. His claws were dug into the stone and his hulking body curled around the turret.

Still a slave to his instincts, Asher took cautious steps backwards until he met the wall of the turret. He had faced many foes in his time, their size and species varying, a fact that informed him of battles he could win and battles he would likely lose. This particular encounter was clearly one of the latter.

The sound of great wings and a distant roar came from behind, turning Asher back to the south. Flying towards them was another dragon, red of scales and bristling with horns. Athis the ironheart - Inara's dragon. Asher's only memories of the dragon were from recent days, under The Crow's spell; they were not good memories.

"Asher..."

The ranger spun around, surprised to have missed the arrival of Gideon. The Master Dragorn was standing beside his dragon, Ilargo, with his hand resting on Mournblade's red and golden hilt.

Asher looked away, shaking his head. "I don't know how I got here. I don't remember..."

Gideon pointed his chin at Asher's hands. "You wouldn't let them take you."

The ranger looked down at his hands, still wet from the climb. He turned them over and found blood soaking the crevices of his knuckles, some of it his, evident from the cuts, some of it not.

"Everything went black," he explained absently. "There are blank spots in my... There's too much... in my head." Asher couldn't say it any better, not with the pain returning. The more he thought about it all the more it hurt.

"It's going to be alright," Gideon assured, taking his hand off Mournblade. "Everything's going to be alright. But, you need to come with me now. I'm going to escort you back to the dungeons personally. We're just going to walk there, side by side. No chains, no guards; just you and me."

Asher could see what Gideon was doing. Appearing as an ally would keep the ranger's instincts in check, but for how long was a question he couldn't answer. With that in mind, he knew the dungeons were the best place for him right now.

"If anything happens..." Asher began, wondering what technique he should instruct the Master Dragorn to use on him.

Gideon nodded his head. "I'll be ready this time. You won't hurt anyone."

Asher could only hope he was right...

CHAPTER 2
THE WAR ISN'T OVER

Inara Galfrey had hung on Gideon Thorn's every word since she was a child, but hearing him now was akin to hearing the rain, a haze of noise free from any articulation.

Instead, the Dragorn's attention was on the stone slabs beneath her feet. Blood stained the grooves, where, not long ago, Asher had forced his way out of Vighon's room. The ranger's reaction to the guard's touch had been shocking, but not because of the speed with which he dispatched them, but because of the methodical techniques he used. His every move had been purposeful, as if he had planned out his attack and their counterattacks with uncanny accuracy.

Arlon had been smart enough to move aside, placing more Namdhorian soldiers between him and Asher. He posed no physical threat to the ranger and therefore seemed to be quickly forgotten by him. A shame, Inara thought.

The tone of the conversation changed, snapping Inara from her reverie. Turning back to the room, her father was standing now and facing Gideon with an expression of thunder.

"You walked him there yourself?" Nathaniel spat, never more than a few feet from his wife.

"Events have taken a turn," Gideon replied calmly, if frustrated. "Things are more complicated now, especially since Asher just assaulted a handful of Namdhorians in front of the new king."

Nathaniel was hearing none of it. "We need him, Gideon! Even if he didn't have answers, it's *Asher*! He doesn't belong in a dungeon!"

The Master Dragorn met the argument without pause. "The laws of the north just became the laws of the *realm*, and by those same laws, Arlon Draqaro can claim the throne as his own. Whether we like it or not, he *is* king now."

"He's right," Inara added as a matter of fact, hoping to sober her father. "Queen Yelifer had no heirs, but it matters little after the civil war. The people will bow to whomever has the strength to take the throne."

"Did he say anything?" Nathaniel probed, ignoring his daughter's statement.

"No," Gideon replied, shaking his head. "He was very focused. He's like a raw nerve. His instincts are battling for control."

The room shared a moment of deflation. They had no answers from Asher and now he resided in the dungeon again, under the control of Arlon.

Doran Heavybelly, fiery as ever, stepped away from the wall. "I refuse to accept that Arlon *bloody* Draqaro is the king o' Illian!"

"Refuse it or not, Doran," Galanör replied, dabbing Vighon's head with a wet cloth, "we live in a world of facts. Arlon Draqaro *is* the king."

"I don't care who sits on the throne," Nathaniel continued, easily the most desperate person in the room. "I care about what Asher knows. He had the silvyr blade, Gideon. You saw it yourself, that sword was with Alijah. How did Asher get it back? Where is my son?"

Gideon raised his hands to calm the ambassador. "We will get those answers, Nathaniel. We all want to find Alijah—"

"Do you?" the immortal knight fired back. "It seems Arlon has you rooted to the stone."

"Father..." Inara tried to hide her wince. She was torn between these two men, one her master and old mentor, the other her father. She could argue for both of them, but being rude to Gideon would forever rub her the wrong way.

"No." Nathaniel held his hand out, refusing to hear his daughter's cautioning tone. "*Master Thorn* here has shown his disregard for our family time and time again."

"Father!" Inara intoned her embarrassment this time.

"You can't defend what he has done," Nathaniel responded as if Gideon wasn't in the room. "Alijah's course was set the very moment you were chosen to be a Dragorn and he wasn't. Gideon's put you in harm's way, sent your mother and me on an errand that has seen her almost robbed of her life, and he left Alijah for dead! Now, when there's a chance to discover the truth of it, his hands are *tied*!"

"Father!" Inara stepped in front of him, cutting off his view of Gideon. "You know well enough that Gideon doesn't *choose* who becomes a Dragorn and who doesn't. And any danger I find myself in is because *I've* put myself there, not because he's commanded me to! The same can be said of you and Mother. Who, out of the two of you, was the more eager to take up the errand he *asked* of you? And he didn't leave Alijah for dead," she added in a softer tone. "It was a battle. You know better than most—"

"Do not lecture me, Inara. He told me himself that he put Alijah and Hadavad together. I'll be the first to admit that the old mage has done a lot of good deeds in his time, but we all know what he does with young apprentices..."

Gideon was quick to rebuke him. "Hadavad would never have used the Viridian Ruby on Alijah."

"You can't know that," Nathaniel snapped, "just as you don't know where my son is right now. For all you know, Hadavad is walking around inside his body!"

"He's also my brother," Inara pointed out. "We all want to find him. We all want Mother to get better. *But*, there are bigger things happening here than our family. We all have a duty to the realm in some capacity and, right now, the realm still hangs in the balance. Its new king is cruel and unfit to rule, the orcs are still out there in considerable number, and The Black Hand still works against us."

Inara's words calmed her father somewhat and he looked over at his pale wife. "You don't know how this feels," he whispered, shaking his head. "I *need* to bring my family back together, *me - I* need to bring us back together..."

Inara's heart broke for her father and she wrapped her arms around him and squeezed until he embraced her back.

"We *will* find him, Nathaniel," Gideon promised.

"I apologise," the old knight said with little sincerity, stepping back from his daughter. "Seeing Reyna," he continued. "And now Asher. With Alijah missing too it's just..."

"I know," Gideon empathised. "There are failings on my part. Unfortunately, only *some* of them relate to your family—"

A loud groan interrupted the Master Dragorn, turning everyone's attention to Vighon. The northman stirred groggily, his face contorting into pain and confusion. He opened his eyes to see the elven ranger sitting over him and his confusion increased all the more.

"What's... What happened?" Vighon sat up and touched his new wound, wincing as he did.

"Ye got into a fight with a wolf, laddy!" Doran offered unhelpfully.

Vighon narrowed his eyes at the dwarf. "Asher..."

"He escaped his cell," Inara specified. "Right after giving you that," she added, pointing at his injury.

Vighon glanced at Reyna sleeping beside him and scrunched his eyes as he tried desperately to put his world back together. "Where is he now?"

"Back in his cell," Galanör answered, leaving the bedside. "Your father brought you back here."

Vighon stood up from the bed and steadied himself on the post. "He's king now," he said with dread.

"We know." Inara allowed some of her trepidation to enter her voice.

"Bah! He's not *my* king!" Doran roared.

Vighon walked around the bed gripping his neck as he stretched the muscles. "Wait..." He stopped in his tracks and blinked hard.

"What is it?" Inara asked.

Vighon stared at her with wide-eyed revelation. "He knows how to win the war," he blurted.

The young Dragorn scrutinised him. "What did you say?"

Vighon adjusted himself with a breath and stood up straight. "Asher... He knows how to win the war."

Nathaniel stepped closer to the northman. "He spoke to you?"

"Aye, right before he threw me around the cell." Vighon tentatively touched the wound to his head again.

"What did he say?" Nathaniel asked urgently.

"He said he knows how to win the war," he repeated for a third time. "I think you were right about him," he continued, looking at Galanör. "The Moonblade was never meant to save anything more than Asher. *He* is the key, though why The Crow would want us to win the war he started is beyond me. All I know is what Asher told me."

"He didn't say anything more?" Gideon checked.

"If he did I was too busy trying to find my feet while he said it."

Inara could see the suspicion on her master's face. "You doubt his words?" she asked.

"No," Gideon replied, clearly troubled by the revelation, "I doubt The Crow's intentions... as always."

Galanör offered, "If The Crow is indeed aiding us, it would suggest he either wishes the orcs to lose this war, or he knows that helping us will see them to victory in some way."

"He started this war," Doran remarked, lighting a pipe. "Anythin' he does is stained with evil as far as I'm concerned."

"But he did guide us to the Moonblade," Inara replied, gesturing to the dagger on her belt. "Without that, Asher and Malliath would still be chained to each other and The Black Hand."

"Aye," Doran agreed, "but they were the scum that put the spell on 'em both in the first place!"

"But you could argue that without his intervention, Malliath wouldn't have been present at the battle. Without him we would still be fighting the hordes."

"Me last statement still stands," Doran commented.

"This is just taking us round in circles," Vighon interjected. "The Black Hand aside, one fact still looms over us all: the war isn't over. If Asher knows how we can beat the orcs, we need to do whatever it takes to free him and get those answers."

Doran cocked a bushy eyebrow. "What are ye suggestin', lad?" he asked with his pipe hanging out of his mouth.

"The simple thing would be to go down to the dungeons and ask him," Vighon replied. "But there's no way Arlon will let any of us near Asher. Unfortunately, he just became a bargaining chip for our new king."

"He's right," Gideon agreed. "The king has no interest in finding Alijah and he thinks winning one battle against the orcs means winning the war is assured."

"Aye," Doran shrugged. "So, what exactly *are* ye suggestin'?" he asked again.

Galanör looked at Vighon and answered for him. "He's suggesting that we break Asher out."

Inara looked at Vighon and wondered how hard Asher had struck him. "Is that a good idea right now?"

Vighon shrugged. "It's *an* idea..."

"It's bold," Nathaniel reasoned, his ire brought down a notch as his interest increased.

"Too bold," Gideon retorted, constantly at odds with the immortal knight. "We have to assume that we *will* win this war and that the realm *will* continue to go on as it has. That includes having

39

the Dragorn as ever-present guardians. Neither myself *or Inara*," he articulated, in case she wasn't understanding his stance on the matter, "can break out a prisoner of the king by force. I don't like Arlon as king, but the order cannot be in opposition to the realm."

"I agree," Vighon said, surprising them all. "It would also be folly for an ambassador to break out a prisoner. *And*," he continued, "should Illian's only dwarf aid in such a crime he would be wanted on both sides of Vengora. Relations with our elven cousins are fragile, ruling out their help." He glanced at Galanör, having now cut them all out of his plan.

The elven ranger frowned, creasing his perfectly symmetrical face. "You mean to break Asher out of Namdhor's dungeons by yourself?"

"I think we all knew my days as a captain of Namdhor were numbered."

"Namdhor has benefited from your elevation," Inara made known.

"I helped with a couple of battles," Vighon replied honestly, "neither of which we could have survived were it not for you. How many more sieges can the city take? This war needs ending. Right now, Asher is offering an answer to that."

"And how exactly are you going to break Asher out?" Galanör asked incredulously.

Vighon gave the elf a cocky grin. "You're not going to like it..."

Inara imagined many ways the northman would attempt the break out and they all ended with him sharing a cell with Asher. "You can't do this alone, regardless of the cloak on your back. They won't let you walk in and walk out with him."

Vighon was deaf to her cautions. "Alijah and I have... *reclaimed* secure items before. At least this time the item can fight *with* me."

Nathaniel was finally interested in something being discussed. "Let's assume you do break him out. Where will you go?"

"He's got a point!" Doran thumbed at the knight. "There's no love lost between ye an' yer father. If ye break Asher out, ye'll both be hunted down."

"You couldn't go to The Raucously Ruckus," Galanör added. "The Ironsworn have eyes everywhere, loyal or indebted."

Vighon managed a wicked grin. "Who said I was going to take him out of The Dragon Keep?"

Inara didn't like the sound of that. "Let's hear it then..."

CHAPTER 3
ONCE A ROGUE, ALWAYS A ROGUE

Vighon left his room and took what felt like his first breath since Asher had awoken. The tension in his chamber wasn't getting any better, regardless of his plan to save the ranger and get the answers they were all seeking.

For most in that room, the machinations of the orcs and The Crow had become very personal. Thousands had already died and thousands more had lost loved ones, but there was still hope for the fractured Galfreys, none of whom were yet to be confirmed as truly lost in the war. That hope, however, made Nathaniel desperate and placed Inara between her family and her order.

To Vighon's eyes, Gideon Thorn was being pulled in every direction, stretching his loyalties and oaths to the realm. He was still one of the most powerful people in all of Verda, but the northman could see how his position restrained him where action was required.

That was where he came in. After all, hadn't the Master Dragorn put him and Alijah with Hadavad for a reason? They could go to places and do the things the Dragorn couldn't. In some ways, it felt good to be doing something closer to that life again. The responsibility that came with his captaincy was a heavy burden; a burden that, very recently, had seen him shake hands with death and agree that he could have one more day to live.

There were many more who couldn't say they were so lucky. A number of his own men, from the Skids, had been put to rest along with entire companies of Namdhorian knights. As he had during his time with Alijah and Hadavad, Vighon would work in the shadows again, his efforts for that of the entire realm.

It was either that or return to his new duties as a captain of Namdhor, a job, much like Gideon's, that would hold him back. With a golden cloak on his back, he was under the command of others and directly responsible for the lives of his men. Besides, it wouldn't be long before Arlon gave him another task that would see him brush with death again.

Walking around the corner, the northman caught sight of the yellow and green sigil of house Skalaf - Yelifer's sigil. In the queen's last days, she had told Vighon a curious thing that played on his mind.

"He's afraid of you," she had said, speaking of his father.

Why Arlon Draqaro would be afraid of him remained a mystery, but he couldn't deny that since spurning his father's wishes to join him, he had repeatedly commanded Vighon to man the front lines of every orc attack, significantly reducing his chances of survival.

The northman paused when a pair of Ironsworn thugs cut across the hall and made for the hanging banner of house Skalaf. The pair tore the sigil down with little respect and replaced it with a new banner bearing the mark of The Ironsworn. In colours of black and red, the vertical crisscrossing lines of The Ironsworn adorned the walls of The Dragon Keep...

"Curious," came a startling voice.

Vighon turned around to see Galanör. As always, the elven ranger appeared far too alert considering everything they had all gone through in the last few days.

"You're becoming a shadow I can't get rid of," Vighon remarked.

Galanör smiled briefly before turning his attention to the

departing Ironsworn. "I have noticed that the banner of house Skalaf can only be found inside the keep. Everywhere else it's the lion of house Tion."

There wasn't a question in there but Vighon had become accustomed to the elf's way of speaking. "Yelifer's rise to queen was the first time in history the north had crowned someone who wasn't of the lion's blood. She wasn't given the throne: she *took* it. Being as bloody as it all was, Yelifer and her advisors felt that the lion should remain standing proud over the north."

"Out of respect for everyone's ancestors?" Galanör questioned.

Vighon shrugged having heard all of this from his mother as a child. "Partly. I think Yelifer just wanted everything to go on as normal after the civil war. She had the throne, I'm not sure she was bothered about her husband's house or his sigil."

"Fascinating," the elf observed.

Vighon looked at him incredulously. "It's really not. Why are you following me?"

As always, the elf graciously chose to ignore the northman's bluntness. "I'm going to find Lady Ellöria. She is to be invited to the war council. Also, the discussion in your chambers returned to matters I would consider more private than others, not that Doran was aware..."

"This war has done a lot of damage," Vighon acknowledged, "no less so to the Galfreys. Their family is caught up in the middle of it all." The northman continued his leave of the keep with the elf beside him; he couldn't stand to see any more Ironsworn banners.

"Are *you* not part of that family? You were raised among them, were you not?"

Vighon hated people knowing of his life, even those he would count as friends. "I was raised partly in their company, but I certainly wasn't raised as a Galfrey. Theirs is a legacy I wouldn't want hanging over me."

The northman considered his father and the grim legacy he already had hanging over him. Unlike his legacy of blood, the

Galfreys had lived lives of duty and sacrifice, even as far back as Nathaniel's father, the Graycoat. Vighon couldn't say he wanted either of them.

"Legacy..." Galanör mused as they reached the towering main doors. "A mortal concept if ever there was one."

Vighon braced himself against the cold and adjusted his fur cloak around his shoulders. "A mortal what?" he asked, wondering why he entertained the elven ranger.

Galanör lifted his voluminous blue hood to protect against the light fall of ash and snow. "Elves rarely think of what we leave behind in our name or deeds - a by-product of immortality, I suppose."

"Is this the part where you tell me you all live in the moment or something equally outlandish and useless?"

Galanör silently chuckled to himself. "We *do* live in the moment. Do you know why, Vighon Draqaro?"

The northman sighed, bit his lip, and stopped in the busy courtyard to face the elf. "Please, Galanör of house Reveeri, tell me why."

Galanör's lips came together in a tight, yet sincere, smile. "Because it's the only place to live. And, what we do *right now* is all that matters, regardless of what's to come..." The elf patted the northman on the arm and weaved between the crowds to leave the keep altogether.

Vighon stood rooted to the spot a moment longer, his mind absorbing his companion's words. He knew that anything said by an elf, especially one of four hundred years, should be taken as wisdom. Before he could linger on such thoughts, however, Commander Garrett approached him in his usual armour and golden cloak.

"Captain." Garrett gave him a nod with his helmet tucked under his arm. "You sent for me?"

"Aye..." Vighon's brother-in-arms had barely had a moment to recover from the orcs' attempted siege and he was already giving the veteran orders that would see him forgo rest. "Find Hob, Rowley, and Tolim," the northman instructed. "Position them within earshot of

45

the dungeons. If it looks like my father is going to have Asher questioned, stall them and send someone to find me. No harm is to come to him."

Garrett, an older Gold Cloak with a sprinkling of grey throughout his hair, nodded along with an expression of doubt. "Why are we guarding him, Captain? He came with the black dragon; surely he is our enemy."

"The battlefield is changing," Vighon said regretfully. "We have to adapt or die. Asher is important, trust me."

The commander stood a little taller. "You have more than earned my trust, Captain. I will see it done."

"Good man." Vighon watched him walk out of the keep, glad to finally have the man on his side.

Vighon froze. Bells were ringing. They were very loud, coming from just beyond The Dragon Keep.

Fearing the worst, Vighon dashed up the nearest steps and ran along the rampart to look out over the city. There were no orcs in sight. The northman sighed again, only now in great relief. He ignored the curious looks of the passing Gold Cloaks and looked out on the northern realm.

The main slope of Namdhor was still a mess, scattered with bodies, weapons dropped by the dead, and charred supplies, burnt by Athis. Just visible, beyond the slope, the lower town and the sprawling camps were just as they had been: cramped and spread far and wide across The White Vale.

Farther east, the bulk of the army was camped where Vighon and the remaining few hundred men had stood their ground against King Karakulak and his sizeable force. The soldiers' camp was only just larger than the new citizens', who had nowhere else to live, at the base of the city. The churches of Atilan and other various gods had been almost filled to the rafters with those who once called Lirian and Grey Stone their home.

The bells rang again, drawing Vighon's attention to the gothic cathedral of Fimira, the goddess of wisdom - something Namdhor was in dire need of. This was shortly followed by the bells of the next church, then the next, and the next. From top to bottom, the churches signalled to the entire city. Slowly but surely, the people came out of their homes drawn, as Vighon was, to the ringing. Now the people of Namdhor knew: their queen was dead.

For Vighon, it meant something far worse.

The sound of heavy footfalls brought those fears to life. The northman turned to regard Sir Borin the Dread, his enormous frame stealing Vighon's focus from the man walking in front of the giant. Arlon came to a stop by his son and joined him in listening to the bells and looking out over the city.

Sir Borin remained a few feet away and beyond him a pair of Ironsworn, recently elevated to Gold Cloaks by their attire, stood at alert. Their presence seemed entirely redundant when Arlon had Sir Borin following him around.

With his jewelled fingers clasped in front of him, the self-appointed king stood in silence for a moment. Of course, there was no one who enjoyed the sound of Arlon's voice more than Arlon, and his silence didn't last.

"And so ends the line of Skalaf," he said without a hint of remorse for his part in it all. "We're burning her tonight, after the war council."

Vighon glanced over his shoulder and realised the courtyard was busy for a specific reason. The funeral pyre was going to be twenty feet tall by the looks of it.

"You will be present." Arlon wasn't asking. "For both the funeral and the council," he added. "Your leadership in the defence of the city has been noted. I dare say I've heard the word *hero* here and there. You're doing wonders for our name."

"I don't care about our name," Vighon replied immediately, his tone even.

"You should," Arlon said, his gaze fixed on the landscape. "My coronation is to be delayed. Best to get the funeral out of the way. Maybe another victory against the orcs with me on the throne. When

I am crowned, you will be named Prince of Namdhor. Our name will mean everything then."

Vighon blinked slowly and resisted the urge to grit his teeth. "I told you before, I don't want to be a prince. I don't even want to stay in this city."

"You won't," Arlon corrected. "I'm going to charge you with the rebuilding of Grey Stone. Then Velia, Lirian, and all the towns in between. You'll be busy for years, decades even."

Vighon finally turned to set his dark eyes on his father. "You're going to rebuild?"

"Of course. Look at them all! There's barely room to breathe. No, I will see the realm put back together - there are valuable resources spread throughout the land. Think of the taxes! No kings or queens, of course, but lords, governors... I haven't decided yet. It'll keep the high-borns happy either way."

Vighon looked away again, his mind chewing it all over. He didn't like his father's tone throughout his explanation, but he could see the logic in the new infrastructure. Then again, Arlon Draqaro had never been stupid, simply ambitious, greedy even... and unnaturally cruel.

"It sounds like you have grand plans," the northman observed. "It's a shame war with the orcs will reduce the city to its bedrock." Vighon looked back at his father. "The orcs will return again and again until the realm is a husk and the world of man forgotten."

Arlon appeared unfazed by the bleak prediction. "Make sure you bring a better attitude to the council."

Vighon knew what he needed to say. The words were in his head but it felt unwise to share anything with Arlon. Still, as Inara had said: the realm was in the balance.

"There might be a way to end the war," he teased.

At last, Arlon turned his head to give his son a side-long look. "Oh yes?"

"Aye, and it doesn't include any made-up spells," Vighon

mocked, referring to his father's misplaced trust in The Crow. "Asher is the key to the war."

Arlon returned his attention to the cityscape, no longer amused. "And how, pray tell, is an old has-been, resurrected by our enemy, going to be of any help winning the war? At the very best we can hope to learn the location of The Crow."

Vighon hesitated. "I don't know... *yet*," he added in the face of his father's judging eyes. "Release him and let me find out. If I'm right we could end the war and—"

"No," came the simple reply. "You're assuming the old ranger has answers because of his time on the other side. In fact, you know nothing. As you've already pointed out; he was under The Crow's spell. Asher might have no knowledge or knowledge the enemy wishes us to have. He's better left in his cell."

Vighon mused over the king's words. The Crow may have planted information in Asher's head that would lead them astray, but the truth was that The Crow had done nothing but guide them from one aid to another. Why he had was a question that would have to wait - the immediate problem was the orcs.

"Release him and I will willingly stand by your side as prince." Vighon couldn't believe the bargain had left his mouth but there it was, out there for his father to entertain.

Arlon's shoulders bobbed with his silent laugh. "You claim we are nothing alike, yet here you are, seizing the opportunity, leveraging what you have. I would say we are very alike..."

Vighon held onto his vision of the future, a future where he would find Alijah and the two could disappear into the world and get back to what they were good at. "Do we have a deal?" he asked, wondering if he was about to save himself the trouble of breaking the ranger out.

Arlon made to leave, pausing only to clasp his son on the shoulder and hiss, "I would crown *Sir Borin* as king before I would let that *thing* out of the dungeons. Asher is an abomination. The dead aren't supposed to come back. Fear not; by the time we're finished with him he'll wish he was in the ground again." The king began to walk away when he called back, "Be at the council, Vighon. That's a command, not a request."

The northman held his ground as Sir Borin the Dread marched past him. The beast's eyes were concealed in the shadow of his bucket-helmet, but Vighon was still able to meet the eyes of the *new* Gold Cloaks.

He clenched his fists, eager for a good fight. Obedient as they were, the Ironsworn followed in the wake of the giant, ignoring Vighon.

Sick of being anywhere near The Dragon Keep, the northman left the ramparts and made for the main slope. His blood was still boiling, fuelling his anger and making him impetuous. Tonight, he decided. Tonight, while everyone was busy with the funeral and the war council, he would free Asher. His golden cloak be damned, his father too!

He made his way down the main slope, lost in his thoughts. There were people everywhere, mostly talking to each other about the queen's death - some were even crying. A few tried to speak to Vighon and thank him for his efforts, but the northman never stopped to hear the praise. It was strange enough that people knew who he was.

In an attempt to avoid the carts moving fresh supplies up and down the road, Vighon hugged the buildings to his left.

Rough hands grabbed his arm and yanked him down an alley not far from The Raucously Ruckus. Vighon was surprised but his current rage heightened his reflexes. The northman raised his fist, ready, and rammed it into the face of the man dragging him into the alley. A bloody fist later, Vighon found his assailant bouncing off the wall and falling to the ground. The injured man, however, was far from alone.

"Greetings, *little lord...*"

Vighon grimaced. "Flint..." The man was easily recognisable by the bruised eyes, given to him by Vighon.

The recently demoted captain was accompanied by six other men, all previous Gold Cloaks before Vighon had had them stripped of their ranks and honour.

"You're the worst kind of scoundrel, Draqaro, do you know that?" Flint was clearly the rousing leader here, but they all had that hungry look in their eyes.

"And you're all cowards," Vighon retorted. "This doesn't prove otherwise..."

Flint sneered. "Get him!"

The northman instinctively reached for a sword he didn't have. Since lighting it on fire, fuelled by dragon spit, the steel had become brittle and charred. Vighon had got through plenty of scraps with his hands alone, but reaching for an empty belt was all the delay his attackers needed.

Before he knew, hands were piling him into the wall and holding him in place. There was no pause before the fists began to land, driving hard blows to his ribs and gut. The force of them knocked his legs out and he slid down the wall, where a stray punch caught his left eyebrow, cutting it open.

Then came the kicks.

The one with a broken nose shouted something at him, but Vighon heard little over the sound of his own body taking blow after blow.

"Oi!"

Some of the men stopped kicking him, giving Vighon a small gap to see between them. Someone was standing in the entrance to the alley, but the northman couldn't make them out.

Flint and his men exchanged heated words with the newcomer, but the man only walked closer. The distinct sound of steel being drawn from a scabbard found Vighon's ears.

"I said get back!" It was a young voice, familiar too.

Flint pushed his men back down to the other end of the alley, pausing only to tower over Vighon. "You're nothing!" He spat on the northman's gambeson and ran after the others.

Vighon winced as new hands tried to help him up. "Ruban?"

The squire offered a sympathetic smile. "Captain..."

Vighon groaned as new pains let themselves be known. "What are you doing here?"

"There is to be a war council tonight," the young man explained. "Your armour and cloak are in the tavern, Captain. I have been preparing it for you."

Vighon was becoming exasperated with the squire as he helped him out of the alley. "I told you to rest, live a little. And where did you get a new sword from?"

"I'm ashamed to say I picked it off the ground, Captain. There are more than few without owners..."

By the time they were at The Raucously Ruckus's doors, Vighon was able to stand up straight, not that it was an enjoyable thing to do. "I need to sit down again," he said, searching the interior for an empty chair. "And I want a sword," he muttered under his breath.

After the squire aided him in finding somewhere to rest, Vighon took stock of his new injuries. How was he going to break Asher out tonight? He couldn't stand up straight without pain shooting through his back. Also, he had none of the things he would need to pull such a thing off in the first place.

Be careful what you wish for, his mother had always said. It wasn't the fight he had been looking for but he had certainly got one. The northman chastised himself for such rash thinking.

"Thank you," Vighon said to Ruban. "Again," he added, noting it as the second time he had come to his aid.

Ruban took the thanks in his stride. "What are squires for?"

The northman took in the sight of the young man and realised he had aged since the vanguard of orcs arrived. He had taken life, be it an orc or not, and it had changed him. Surviving a battle could fill one with hubris or crippling fear of the next battle. Ruban appeared to be handling it well.

"You say my armour is ready?" Vighon was loath to put it all on, but avoiding the funeral and the war council was looking more and more unlikely.

Ruban twisted his mouth. "The breastplate has taken some damage to be sure. And there's some blood staining your cloak... But it's polished and cleaned!"

The northman had plans to see himself rid of it all anyway, but telling Ruban that - after all his efforts - seemed cruel. "Thank you, Ruban. Help me get into it. Then, go to the keep and find Garrett. If there's to be any trouble with Asher I want you as a go-between."

"As you say, Captain." Ruban looked to the window. "Shouldn't we do something about Flint and his men? They did just try to kill a captain of Namdhor."

"Not now," Vighon replied, waving the notion away. "I've got bigger things to worry about than a few disgruntled cowards."

Indeed, he did have bigger things to worry about. Once again he felt the weight of the realm on his shoulders, shoulders that still ached from battle and now a vicious beating. Still, his next act would be one of treason. The mere thought of it brought back his ready and roguish grin...

CHAPTER 4

DARK DAYS

S tanding motionless between the trees, Gideon Thorn enjoyed
what precious time he had in the quiet garden.

Snow and ash sprinkled the ground and dusted the naked
branches that patiently awaited the spring. The trees helped to keep
the sound out, despite being within the walls of The Dragon Keep. It
wasn't the Dragorn library on The Lifeless Isles, but at least it was
deserted. And Nathaniel Galfrey couldn't poke holes in him with his
eyes...

Both Reyna and Nathaniel had been counted among Gideon's
closest friends for decades. Seeing Reyna so unwell and Nathaniel so
angry broke his heart. It broke all the more when he considered his
part in their family's fractured state.

The immortal knight had been well within his rights to take
some of his anger out on the Master Dragorn. Gideon had inserted
himself in their lives and made a ruin of it, their children included.

You take too much on your shoulders, Gideon.

The sound of Ilargo's voice was soothing even if Gideon didn't
take in his words. **It's not just the Galfreys, Ilargo. The realm
deserves something better than what I promised. Under my leader-**

ship, the best of us have fallen. Now all that remains are children and young dragons. They can't protect Illian, not as they are. I should have done more, prepared more.

Gideon felt Ilargo's physical presence as the green dragon flew overhead. *I know what you're thinking*, his companion said.

You always know what I'm thinking.

I think we should do it, Ilargo replied, as Gideon knew he would.

That's if we survive this war... he pointed out.

Before their conversation could continue, the harsh crunch of snow found Gideon's ears. They were slow footsteps, but not cautious ones with ill intent. The Master Dragorn remained standing with his arms folded, waiting patiently.

"I see you've finally given in to the north," Inara said, joining him under a particularly tall maple tree.

Gideon glanced down at the grey cloak and hood that did its best to keep winter's chill out of his bones. "They're obnoxiously loud on dragon back," he observed, having notably stated his dislike of cloaks among the Dragorn. "Still, it is bloody cold up here," he added with a forced smile.

"He didn't mean what he said." Inara's change in topic was sudden but Gideon didn't misunderstand her.

"Your father is angry and rightly so," the Master Dragorn reasoned. "I've never been a father or a husband, so I won't pretend to know what he's going through. But if I was him, I would be angry at me too."

"You're not responsible for our family," Inara reminded him.

"No," Gideon uttered. "I'm responsible for so much more. I have *our* family to think of. The Dragorn are sworn to protect the realm, but if I can't train them to do that I'm putting everyone's life in the balance. I don't blame your father for being angry with me. I blame myself for giving him a *reason* to be angry with me."

"I've never seen you cast so much doubt on yourself," Inara remarked.

Gideon half turned to regard her. "And I've never seen you so confident. It seems your encounter with Malliath has had a positive effect, even if it nearly killed you."

Inara subconsciously adjusted the Moonblade on her hip. "You're deflecting."

Gideon kept his arms crossed. "Perhaps now is a good time to talk about you disobeying my commands. You should have taken your mother to The Lifeless Isles and led the Dragorn to new lands by now."

"Well," Inara began in a deliberate uppity tone, "instead I chose to stay behind, free Asher from The Crow's spell, and unleash Malliath on the orcs, thus saving the city and countless lives. You're still deflecting, Master."

Tell her Gideon, Ilargo bade. *The council already know and I would say Inara Galfrey has earned your trust many times over.*

Gideon squeezed his right hand and sighed. "You've fought beside me in battle now," he stated. "You must have noted my use of magic... or lack thereof."

Inara hesitated and Gideon regretted his approach to the subject, having put her in an awkward position.

"You're more of a swordsman," she replied as if it were no bad thing. "You can keep pace with Galanör, something no other man could ever boast of."

"I rely on my Vi'tari blade because I have to, Inara." Gideon unfolded his arms and held his right hand out, palm up. "Look closely," he instructed.

Inara briefly met his eyes before gripping his hand in her own and examining it. "This is a scar?" she clarified, staring at the pale runes on his palm and two middle fingers.

"It's ancient script," Gideon confirmed. "It's marked me for thirty years." The Master Dragorn took his hand back and looked upon the line of glyphs.

"Thirty years?" Inara considered that specific time period. "You got this during The War for the Realm?"

"At the very end," Gideon answered. "In the pools of Naius, deep inside the caverns of Kaliban. You know the story, I believe."

Inara nodded. "Of course I do. You faced Valanis and defeated him - all of Illian knows the story."

"Asher defeated Valanis," Gideon reminded her. "I destroyed The Veil," he said, looking at his hand again. "It could only be destroyed inside one of the pools, where it was made. I used quite a bit of magic in the process. It worked and even killed Atilan as he tried to enter our world again, but it took something from me."

Inara tilted her head, looking from Gideon's face to his hand. "It took your magic..."

"Not all of it," he reassured. "I can still use magic in all its forms, it's just the power with which I wield it that has been diminished. Even my bond with Ilargo cannot give me back that power. The Veil marked me and took some of me with it. For thirty years it was a price I was happy to have paid. Since the orcs invaded, I'm beginning to wonder if I would have been better locking The Veil away and keeping that part of myself."

Inara shook her head. "That path would have seen you repeat the mistakes of your predecessors. You destroyed The Veil once and for all, preventing Atilan and his lot from ever returning to this world."

"True enough," Gideon conceded. "Now you know why I'm so frustrated with myself."

Inara shrugged. "I never even noticed - a testament to your skill. The potions certainly make more sense now."

"Yes," Gideon agreed, patting the vials through his jacket. "I was quite the alchemist during my days at Korkanath. They've helped me where magic no longer can. I won't lie; passing on those lessons to the Dragorn was a good way of hiding my... defect. Only the council know," he added. "I suppose that should include you now."

Inara was taken aback. "You're inviting me onto the council?"

"Well, I was tasking you with *leading* the Dragorn in the absence of Ayana or myself, so inviting you to sit on the council seems an obvious step to me."

Inara kept her smile under control. "I am honoured, Master. And you should know, it's not your ability to use magic that rallies everyone behind you. It's everything else..."

Gideon responded with a smile of his own, even if he hated hearing the compliment. He was about to offer a compliment of his own, having noted her continued strength of character in such trying times, when both received word from their companions.

Ayana and Deartanyon are coming, Ilargo relayed.

Tell them to meet us by the lake, Gideon replied. **I would speak with them away from the eyes and ears of our new king...**

MAKING THEIR WAY ON FOOT, so as to be inconspicuous, the two Dragorn rounded the base of the city and headed to the frozen King's Lake. Ilargo and Athis were already standing proud on the shoreline, their majestic green and red scales dulled under the dark clouds.

Closer to the trees, away from the lake, Thraden rested with his head lying low. His wounds were healing but they were still severe. Gideon could only imagine what Arathor must look like...

The two mighty dragons parted to reveal Deartanyon's violet and silver scales. The dragon approached slowly on all four claws until he was able to dip his head and allow Ayana to climb down gracefully.

Ayana's leathers showed signs of recent violence, streaked with blood up her arms and muddied up her legs. The elf, however, appeared unharmed, her long blonde hair pristine in its intricate braids.

"Master." Ayana bowed her head to Gideon. "Inara," she greeted pleasantly, if obviously grieved.

"You have engaged the orcs," Gideon stated, his eyes roaming over her light armour.

"They hide in places dragons cannot reach," Ayana explained in the melodic voice typical of her kind. "I have entered numerous caves and dark dwellings from east to west of the mountains. Orcs have a natural talent for finding the shadows; I fear many have descended into the depths of Vengora and taken Arathor with them."

Gideon looked away, his gaze fixed on the mountains that surrounded the north. Arathor was in there somewhere, destined for torment and death. Another life he was responsible for, another Dragorn he had failed to train properly.

The Master Dragorn glanced at Thraden in the distance, his thoughts going to dark places. His brief look hadn't gone unnoticed.

"Deartanyon and I have considered the same," Ayana said quietly.

Inara looked from elf to man in confusion. "Considered what?"

Gideon hadn't wanted to voice his thoughts, but he knew it would be better if they all agreed. "If we cannot save Arathor from the orcs, he will suffer their torturous ways, along with Thraden." The Master Dragorn chewed over his next words. "We can end that suffering."

Inara responded with silent shock, though Athis did not. The two shared a moment together in which it became clear that Athis had decided to keep any thought of ending Thraden's life to himself.

"Only war makes us consider such terrible things," Gideon said. "It would be a mercy."

Inara clamped her jaw shut and stared hard at Thraden. The turmoil ravaging her mind wasn't hard to miss and Gideon was thankful for it. Her reaction was exactly as it should have been. It didn't change what needed to be done...

"Not yet," Inara pleaded. "We must do more before we give in to notions of *mercy*."

"I agree," Gideon replied. "I would upend all of Vengora before I took the life of a dragon. We are, however, spread thin. I need to be present for Asher's interrogation and we must attend the war council this afternoon, lest King Arlon decides to do something rash that costs more lives."

"King Arlon?" Ayana's tone of disbelief matched her expression. "I thought Arlon Draqaro was lord of Namdhor?"

"He was," Inara agreed. "Queen Yelifer has passed away and he has... *assumed* the throne."

"I didn't think the days could get any darker," the elf remarked.

"Indeed," Gideon said, bringing it back to his point. "We are needed here, but Alastir and Valkor are still in need of our aid in the south. Our search for Arathor is hindered."

Ayana paused before she spoke. "I know you are against involving the adolescents of our order, but perhaps the extra eyes could—"

"No," Gideon said firmly. "We don't know how many wrath bolts the orcs have left. I won't risk their lives."

"Then what can we do?" Inara protested. "We cannot abandon the search."

Gideon thought about his limited options, as they often were, and made the only decisions he could. "Do you require rest?" he asked Ayana.

"Deartanyon has enough energy for us both," the elf replied.

"Then I would send you south, to find Alastir and Valkor—"

"I will go," Inara interrupted. "I promised him I would return."

"You promised him help," Gideon corrected. "Ayana and Deartanyon will find them and see them both safely to Namdhor."

"Then I will continue the search for Arathor," the young Dragorn replied defiantly.

"No," Gideon retorted, waving her proposal away. "You will attend the war council and the queen's funeral with me. Tomorrow, I will take up the search for Arathor. Perhaps I'll find the orc king in the process."

"Gideon..." Inara didn't often call him by his first name. "You can't keep me safe. Ordering me to stay here won't put my family back together."

Gideon knew that was the truth behind his orders, but he refused to admit it. "I want you at the war council because of your experience fighting orcs. And I want you to stay close to Namdhor to keep the *city* safe. This is the best way, Inara," he implored with a hint of his authority. "Deartanyon is faster than Athis and will reach Alastir and Valkor sooner."

Inara looked to protest his reasons but an audible snort from Athis kept her mouth shut. What the dragon had said across their bond remained a mystery, but Gideon was glad of it.

Ayana spoke before the silence between them became awkward. "If Valkor is too injured to fly, my return will take some time."

"I understand, but I will rest easier knowing that Alastir isn't dying in a cave somewhere. Besides, injured or not, Valkor will be an asset that sees Namdhor's defences bolstered tenfold. And..." he added, taking in Inara, "upon your return, the council of the Dragorn will be complete once more."

Ayana turned to the young Dragorn and gave her a warm smile much needed in these cold days. "It's about time," she commented. "And well earned."

Inara nodded her appreciation of Ayana's support. "I am no replacement for those we have lost, but I will do all that I must to uphold the ways of our order."

Gideon wondered if that meant killing Thraden to end his misery and that of Arathor. Not that he would ever command her to do such a thing; it was his duty and no others.

"Do what you must to aid Alastir," he said to Ayana, "but return with all haste. The orcs are unpredictable, but their retaliation is assured."

Ayana bowed her head and stole a glance at Thraden. "Find, Arathor," she said simply.

"I will." Gideon's response sounded more confident than he felt.

The Master Dragorn stood beside Inara and watched Ayana mount Deartanyon. Sending her away from the city was a risk given the threat of the orcs but, right now, every Dragorn felt precious, especially one as powerful as Alastir.

"If you're about to question my orders," he said without taking his eyes off Deartanyon's departure, "you should know I'm far too exhausted to argue with another Galfrey today."

Inara kept her own eyes on the sky. "I'm not questioning your orders, only your motives. You've never worried about where you send me before and I don't want you to start now. We're at war. I'm a Dragorn. There's nothing more to it."

"There are so few of us left now." Gideon felt hollow as he said it. "I'm trying to keep as many of us alive as possible."

Inara finally turned to face him. "You can't keep the order alive *and* the realm safe at the same time. One stands in front of the other and shields it from the dark. That's what the Dragorn have done for thousands of years. We haven't kept the country safe by thinking about ourselves."

She was right. Inara was right and Gideon chastised himself for not having those thoughts first. It should have been him telling her that, not the other way around.

"Appointing you to the council is either going to be the wisest decision I've ever made or the most irritating..."

Inara flashed a coy smile. "That's another way of saying you know I'm right."

"To an extent," Gideon relented. "There are two, perhaps three Dragorn left on The Lifeless Isles who could be of assistance, but I won't have them leave the younger ones. We don't know where Malliath has gone or if he'll return. Ayana, Alastir, Arathor and us. That's it. *We* can stand between the light and the dark and I accept the cost of our lives. I draw the line at putting those who are barely adults in harm's way."

Inara bowed her head. "As you say, Master."

Gideon could sense her approval and reminded himself that he didn't need it. Annoyingly, Ilargo reminded him that it still felt good though...

ENTERING THE DRAGON KEEP once more, Gideon felt he was willingly walking into the mouth of a great beast. The fortifications of the keep were forbidding and uninviting, to say the least, with the corners of the outer stone adorned with dragons' teeth.

Gideon took one last look at the constructed funeral pyre and reluctantly entered Arlon's domain. Queen Yelifer's body wasn't stone cold, yet there was no trace of house Skalaf inside those dark walls.

Now, there was only Ironsworn.

Their red and black banners hung from the walls, but the most notable change to the keep were those inhabiting it. The tattooed thugs of Arlon's gang now patrolled the halls in Namdhorian armour and golden cloaks. There was no armour or clothing in all the realm, however, that could hide who they really were.

"Oh no..."

Gideon heard Inara's despair before he noticed Nathaniel farther down the hall. The immortal knight was in the middle of a heated discussion with a pair of Ironsworn in golden cloaks.

"Take your hands off me!" Nathaniel pulled his arm free of the Ironsworn. "I am an ambassador—"

"I don't care who you are," the Ironsworn cut in, waving his gauntlet in front of Nathaniel's face. "You aren't going down there. If you try again, though, I promise you will be going down there... *in chains*!"

Approaching the argument, Gideon laid eyes on both of the guards and dismissed them with a severe look. "What's going on?"

"What did you do?" Inara asked her father.

Nathaniel straightened his clothes and met only his daughter's gaze. "I tried to speak with Asher. Actually, I *tried* to get into the dungeons to speak with Asher. Arlon's thugs got in my way."

"You shouldn't provoke them," Gideon warned. Seeing Nathaniel's expression, however, the Master Dragorn regretted saying anything.

"I thought I had you on my side. If I did, I wouldn't have to worry about provoking anyone. As it is, I'm on my own. Asher's down there and he has answers I need *now*."

"Father..." Inara held her hands up while checking the inquisitive faces of those walking past, towards the war council. "Vighon is going to get him out," she said quietly. "Trust him."

Everything about Nathaniel told of his frustration. "I can't sit around waiting for your mother to wake up. I'm doing nothing while Alijah is out there somewhere."

Gideon was about to offer reassurance when the master of servants approached. "Ah, there you are, Master Thorn. The war council is about to begin..."

"Thank you. I'll be along in a moment." Gideon waited until the servant was out of earshot. "Nathaniel, I think it would be best if you didn't attend this meeting."

"He's right," Inara added before her father could protest. "You should be with mother right now. The mages have seen an improvement in her; you should be there when she wakes."

Nathaniel huffed, his eyes lingering on the hall leading to the dungeons. The old Graycoat held his tongue and walked away without another word.

"He *is* a veteran of war," Inara pointed out, watching her father disappear around the corner. "His counsel would be wise."

"I have no doubt," Gideon agreed. "But he's not in the right frame of mind to take part in this meeting." The Master Dragorn tried to push away his feelings and heartache, focusing, instead, on what lay before him. "Come," he bade.

The war room of The Dragon Keep was almost as large as the throne room. Dominated by a large rectangle, carved into the stone floor, the chamber housed a scaled down map of Illian with raised mountain ranges, entrenched rivers, and even roads.

Lining the rectangular map, lords of the north and their bannermen turned to each other in deep discussion, their attention on various parts of the map. Among them were General Morkas and Thedomir Longshadow, the newly appointed Lord of Grey Stone. A handful of Namdhorian captains surrounded General Morkas, offering him advice before the king arrived. Thedomir kept his own counsel, just as he kept to himself.

Standing awkwardly apart from everyone, leaning against one of the narrow pillars, was Vighon Draqaro. As always, he appeared uncomfortable in his armour and golden cloak. Inara made her way through the small crowd to join him and Gideon followed her lead.

"What happened to you?" she asked the northman.

Indeed, it seemed Vighon had seen violence more recently than the battle. A fresh bruise to his jaw looked painful and he struggled to stand up straight.

"For every ally I gain in this city, two more enemies spring up," he muttered, his eyes wandering over the crowd.

"Do you need—"

"I'm fine," he interjected, straightening his posture with a subtle wince. "I've had much worse."

Seeing that Vighon didn't wish to continue with the topic, Gideon asked, "Where's your father?"

At that moment, the double doors swung open, turning everyone to the other end of the room. The master of servants entered ahead of Arlon and his armoured escort.

"He likes an entrance..." Vighon uttered.

"Lords of the realm!" the master of servants began. "Pray silence for King Arlon of house Draqaro, first of his name, Shield of the Realm, The Sword of Man, and the Ruler of Illian!"

Inara turned to Gideon and mouthed, "Shield of the Realm?"

Gideon shrugged and quietly replied, "If you're going to call yourself The Sword of Man why not the Shield of the Realm too?"

Vighon was rolling his eyes. "He's not even been crowned yet..."

Arlon strode into the room and didn't stop by the edge of the map, but continued to walk over it until he was standing on top of The Evermoore. Gideon didn't miss the symbolism of what the king was trying to convey. His escort of Gold Cloaks remained by the doors, along with Sir Borin, whose presence forced several lords to shuffle away.

"These are dark days," Arlon announced. "Our queen is dead. Tonight we will grieve as we give her body back to Atilan, then we will celebrate her life, the conqueror of the north!" The lords and their bannermen cheered. "Right now, however, we, the protectors of the realm, must face a simple truth. We remain at war, our way of life on the brink of destruction. The orcs must be dealt with before they attack again."

The captains and bannermen stamped their feet and cried, "Here, here!"

"General Morkas!" Arlon swivelled on his heel to face the shaggy-bearded man. "Your report?"

Morkas stepped forward. "There are enough orc bodies out there to build another Namdhor!" The chamber erupted into cheers and praise. "They ran for the mountains, abandoning their hope of taking this city. They left behind their war machines and any hope of victory!" More cheers greeted the general's enthusiastic, if pointless, report.

"Flee our walls they did," Arlon agreed. "What of your scouts, General? Have they located the orc camp?"

Morkas cleared his throat, choosing his next words with more care. "Multiple scouts have yet to return, your Grace. They are believed dead. Those that have returned report of traps in the woods around the base of the mountains. The orcs have made it very hard to follow them... on foot," he added with a sideways glance at Gideon and Inara.

"Ah yes, our mighty Dragorn!" Arlon wandered over The Moonlit Plains. "I believe you already have a dragon flying over the area."

"In search of another Dragorn," Gideon clarified, "taken by the orcs during their escape."

"Taken?" Arlon echoed with little sympathy. "How troubling."

Inara raised her voice to address the war council rather than speak directly with Arlon. "If the orcs have carved out their territory in the mountains, engaging them will prove almost impossible. They're natural hunters who thrive in the dark."

"You're suggesting we leave them to it?" Morkas accused, backed by his knights.

"I'm suggesting we don't give them the advantage. Namdhor is defensible; leaving the safety of the city would be unwise, especially against a foe who still possesses the greater force."

"*Greater* force?" one of the lords expressed with offence.

"Yes, *greater*," Vighon chipped in. "The orcs still outnumber us. The only reason we survived their first siege was because Malliath turned on them."

"Indeed," Arlon drawled, "the black dragon proved to be quite the ferocious opponent for the orcs, unexpected too if their disarray was to be judged. Might we expect such aid from Malliath again?"

Gideon decided to field the question. "Malliath is unstable and largely unpredictable. His current whereabouts are unknown."

"Probably for the best," Arlon surmised. "At least we still harness the power of three other dragons."

Gideon opened his mouth to strongly disagree with Arlon's phrasing, but the new king was quickly turned to Vighon's outburst.

"Inara has a point about holding our ground," the northman stated bluntly. "The caves of Vengora are no place to engage our enemy. We control the land and therefore the battlefield."

"Aye!" General Morkas cheered. "I suggest we begin securing The White Vale immediately, making the plains ready for the next battle. We need to dig in hard and let the orcs know that the north cannot be taken!"

"That's not what I meant," Inara replied, quietening the lords' hearty agreement. "The White Vale is too massive a stretch of land to secure. It wouldn't matter if you built moats, trenches, dug spikes into the ground. The orcs could attack from another direction."

"Listen to her," Thedomir cajoled, speaking up for the first time. "The orcs are inside Vengora now. They could travel through or even under the mountains to come at us from anywhere. We shouldn't expect them to appear from the north. The city itself is our best defence."

General Morkas flashed the warrior from Grey Stone an insincere smile. "Thank you, *Lord* Thedomir, but since you are not in command of our forces, your suggestions carry no weight. The men of the north will not sit idly by and wait for our enemies to overrun us, as those of Grey Stone did..."

Thedomir turned to face Morkas squarely, more than a match for the fat general. "What did you say to me?" His tone was cause enough for three Gold Cloaks to stand between the two men.

Gideon was shaking his head. They were getting nowhere and the room was filled with too many opposing ideas. Not to mention egos...

"You shouldn't even be thinking about attacking," Gideon cautioned, drawing the chamber's full attention. "The new ground they have claimed is well and truly theirs. The orcs have been surviving underground for thousands of years."

"You have a suggestion, Master Thorn?" Arlon asked, his barbed tongue eager to be put to use.

Gideon met his cold gaze. "You have the fortifications and you have the men. Keep them together. Sending more men to die in those mountains will only end this war for us."

General Morkas raised an eyebrow. "If the orcs *are* mobilising, Master Thorn, we need to know *where*. We need to know their numbers, resources—"

"I will scout the mountains myself," Gideon cut in, already tired of hearing the general's voice. "With Ilargo I can cover more ground and avoid conflict."

Thedomir Longshadow posed, "What of those deadly bolts they wield? Even your dragons aren't immune to them."

Gideon had seen the damage first hand to know that statement was true. "I have to assume their supply of wrath powder is dwindling. The orcs originated from The Undying Mountains. Unless they've maintained underground supply routes from north to south their resources are limited."

"Are you willing to die on that assumption?" Thedomir fired

back. "You and your dragons are the best defences this city has. We cannot risk losing you."

"Better we risk one dragon than hundreds of scouts," Morkas declared with all the forethought of a stunted Gobber.

"Risks must be taken if we are to secure victory," one of the lords added.

"We cannot risk the lives of so many!" another argued.

"Even one dragon is more valuable than a hundred scouts!" Thedomir protested.

"So we are to do *nothing*?" came the outcry of one lord, quickly supported by half a dozen more.

"Our enemy has been driven back!" called another. "We should see them to their end!"

Arlon raised his hands to silence them. He had yet to say much, something that troubled Gideon. He was either listening to all of their advice, or he had already made up his mind on their next course of action.

"Namdhor appreciates your bravery, Master Thorn," the king said. "Any information you can give us will leave us indebted to you."

"The realm can never be indebted to the Dragorn," Gideon corrected, making sure he was loud enough to be heard by all present. "Our order serves only to protect the people of Illian."

Arlon appeared entirely bored by Gideon's response. "Speaking for the realm, I thank you for your order's continued *sacrifices* in the name of that protection."

Gideon felt his hand clench. In some sick way, Arlon had just informed the Master Dragorn that he was glad to have heard of the Dragorns' losses. Inara's hand gently clasped around his fist, easing his anger even before Ilargo's attempt.

"He sees us as a threat," she whispered. "We're the only ones who can take his power away."

Inara was right and wrong at the same time. "Removing him from the throne would break everything we stand for," he replied in a hushed tone.

69

"He doesn't know that..."

Gideon couldn't disagree with that. In some way, he liked the idea of Arlon fearing the wrath of the Dragorn. Perhaps, if nothing else could, that would keep him in check while he sat on the throne.

"I hear your concerns," the king began. "We are outnumbered, however, and the terrain is theirs. Marching our men into the mountains will see our city become all the more vulnerable to counterattack."

Inara leaned in. "Is he actually speaking sense?"

"Wait for it," Vighon said from behind them.

Arlon turned every which way to lay eyes on all of his subjects. "But I am not a king to sit by and do *nothing*! Our enemy is on the back foot, an opportune moment for Namdhor. We will reclaim the mountains! The orcs will either be driven into Dhenaheim or they'll dig so far down they won't know what's up anymore!"

More than half of the chamber cheered for their king and his bravado while Gideon dropped his face into his hand. The king had already decided what he was going to do before he even called this council. As always, Arlon was simply positioning himself to appear the gallant hero.

"We have their catapults," he continued. "General Morkas, have them loaded with orc bodies and repositioned to the north. Prepare to unleash a fiery hell upon the woods that shelter our enemy. When the smoke clears, we will march on Vengora and secure Illian's borders for good!"

Gideon and Inara shared a disturbed look, the pair thinking the same thing: Arlon had become accustomed to the casual disposal of life. It was not the thinking of a king.

"This path will see Namdhor's entire army perish!" the Master Dragorn shouted over the cheers. His dire warning took the confidence out of the lords and their bannermen almost immediately.

Having announced his grand plan, Arlon was more than happy to take an active role now. "Surely, Master Thorn, with the aid of dragon fire we will scorch the orcs from the face of Verda."

Gideon shook his head. "Throwing men at them won't even reduce their numbers, never mind end the war. They have the mountains to fall back on, a battleground that cannot be won by us."

"Our enemy has retreated," Arlon pointed out. "We *will* destroy them."

"Not on our own," Gideon added, bringing rise to a silent question on the king's face. "The orcs have been beaten before, long ago. It took the alliance of elves and dwarves to defeat them then and I believe it will require such an alliance again."

Arlon appeared too shocked by the suggestion to respond with his usual quip. "Please do elaborate, Master Thorn."

Gideon stepped onto the map, away from Inara and the lords. Sharing the space with Arlon now, some of the king's power was reduced, a calculated step by the Master Dragorn.

"We have the orcs trapped in Vengora," he began walking north on the map, towards the mountains. "The army of Namdhor on one side and the armies of Dhenaheim on the other. The dwarves are far better suited to engaging an enemy in the mountains. If the dwarves could drive them south, back onto The White Vale, we could wage war from both sides."

Arlon was nodding along as if he was really taking it in. Of course, he wasn't. "Perhaps we can get a few Gobbers to aid us as well!" There was a notable pause before the laughter.

"Maybe a few mountain trolls too!" suggested an unhelpful lord.

Gideon decided he had been tactful enough and turned to the king with venom in his tone. "Marching Namdhor's army across the vale, and challenging our enemy on the mountainside, is akin to marching them into Dhenaheim to challenge a superior enemy in their own territory. It's an easy decision made by a mind inexperienced in the ways of war. An alliance is our only chance at securing a true and lasting victory."

Arlon's mouth twisted before his jaw clenched. Gideon had no doubt that had he been any other man, he could expect to be woken from his bed tonight and thrown into the icy depths of The King's Lake.

"If you are concerned, Master Thorn, with this council taking advice from minds inexperienced in the ways of war, you may wish to consider stepping outside..." Now it was Gideon's turn to clench his jaw while entertaining thoughts of violent retaliation. "There is a reason, after all," the king continued, "why so few Dragorn are here to combat this evil."

"Those of my order who are not present are closer to children than they are adults, their dragons included. And," he added, dropping his tone, "I draw my wisdom from a long line of Dragorn, their experiences passed down through dragons."

You shouldn't rise to him, Ilargo advised.

His every word gets under my skin, Gideon replied.

"If only it was enough," Arlon lamented sarcastically.

"It's not," Gideon replied to the council's surprise. "It's not enough and I don't have the arrogance to presume it is. An alliance is our only hope."

Arlon threw his arm out to sweep across the northern realm of Dhenaheim on the map. "You would seek an alliance with those who court war with Namdhor?" The king stuck a finger in his own chest. "The dwarves will *never* aid us, Master Thorn. To even think such a thing is possible is foolish, but to waste this council's time with such a proposal is tantamount to sedition. I will hear no more of it." Arlon returned his attention to the lords. "The orcs wanted war! *We* will give them war! From their ashes, a new kingdom of man will rise!"

Gideon shook his head to the resounding acclamation and reached out to Ilargo. **So this is how the realm will fall... to the sound of hearty cheers.**

Ilargo filled Gideon's mind with resolve. *So long as we draw breath, the realm will stand...*

CHAPTER 5
GOD-KINGS DO NOT BLEED

This was not how King Karakulak had wished to enter the home of his ancestors. Standing on a rocky platform, his feet firmly planted on Vengoran rock, the mighty orc looked out on The White Vale. In the distance stood a dark rise, towering defiantly over the land - Namdhor.

The last stronghold of man should have fallen with the others; their kind was weak after all. Yet here he was, hiding in the mountains his ancestors had fought and died in to call their own.

"It wasn't supposed to be like this," he said as softly as his gravelly voice would allow.

"Sire?" Grundi, his loyal and most intelligent subject took a step closer to his king.

Karakulak could see the hunched orc in the corner of his eye, but he kept his gaze on the white snows. "We were to pass through this ancient stone as victors, conquerors. These mountains are littered with the bones of our dead..."

"And the bones of our enemies," Grundi added. "Our ancestors' war claimed many children of the mountain."

Karakulak sneered. "Children of the mountain," he muttered.

"*We* should be the children of the mountain! The orc was born in the shadows of Vengora; our claim to the stone is just as valid as the dwarves. We were to pay homage to our fallen before marching on Dhenaheim. Now, we huddle in the dark; our war with the humans a lingering wound that must be dealt with."

Across The White Vale, Karakulak could see the masses of Namdhorians making camp. They had already attempted to continue the fight by following the orcs to the base of the mountains. A foolish plan if ever there was one. The dense forest that lined the mountains was a dark place to hunt, thanks to the thick foliage. The humans had easily fallen to their traps and retreated.

The king narrowed his eyes, focusing his superior gaze on the masses. The elixir that flowed through his veins allowed him to make out distinct shapes that no other orc could dream of seeing from such a distance.

Karakulak growled. "They are repositioning *my* catapults."

Grundi tilted his head to better see the horizon. "There is nothing they can throw at the mountain that will make a difference."

Karakulak peered down at the thick trees, their front line of defence. "They mean to carve a path through to the mountain," he concluded.

"They would attack?" Grundi asked in disbelief. "The best they could hope is to hold the woodland."

Karakulak took in the vista from east to west. "They would reclaim all of Neverdark if they held us here..."

The king felt an overwhelming desire to kill something or, indeed, several somethings. Neverdark belonged to him, the land above and below was that of the orcs now.

Grundi half turned to his king. "Reports from the narrow passes state that the dragon has left. Chieftain Lurg has already begun to resupply the woodland."

Dragons...

Karakulak had come to hate their wretched kind as much as he did the humans or the dwarves. They weren't supposed to hold such sway over his plans. Malliath should have been an ever-present shadow that accompanied the orcs and took care of the Dragorn.

The king glanced over his shoulder, taking in the large chest at the other end of the cave. It was guarded on each side by a pair of orcs from the Born Horde, his own tribe. Perhaps there *was* something he could take his frustration out on.

Turning away from The White Vale, Karakulak strode into the shadows and commanded the orcs to follow him. As always, Grundi trailed a little farther behind, no care taken for his limp.

Inside the hollow of the mountain, Karakulak found his people on the cusp of civil war. They hadn't taken their defeat very well and had immediately turned on each other to fulfil their bloodlust. What few remained of the six-legged garks roamed the jagged caverns, restless and tempted by the white flesh of their orc masters.

The chieftains did what they could to maintain control, but orcs simply weren't accustomed to gathering in such numbers for a common cause. Thanks to the orcs who had been left to keep control of The Under Realm, their numbers had begun to swell again as they were called upon from the roots of the world. Still, they had lost many in the attempted siege of Namdhor; too many when considering the war with the dwarves had yet to even begin.

The sound of clashing swords drew Karakulak's attention to a high ledge on the other side of the cavern. A single scream preceded the falling orc. The garks were already scrambling to the spot where the body would land. That one act of violence led to another, then another, and another. Within seconds, the cavern was filled with the sound of clashing swords and axes. Spears were thrown across the fray without a care for where they landed.

Among them, the Big Bastards were the easiest to see, their hulking frames battering through the horde. Closer to Karakulak's ledge, a cave troll, bound in chains, was ushered into the melee at the point of spears. Its tree-like arms swung with abandon, tossing orcs high into the air.

The king sighed. This cavern was only one of many that housed his forces, but it wouldn't be long before the scent of blood found the others and all-out war was upon them. Had he been any other orc, control would have been lost, along with his title and power. But he wasn't just any other orc. He was a God-King...

Karakulak reached over his shoulder and removed Dragonslayer from its sheath. The sword was made entirely from dragon bone, making it tougher than steel and deadly sharp. The God-King stepped off the edge and dropped effortlessly for thirty-feet, his blade angled down. Karakulak sank Dragonslayer into the troll's head and down through its jaw. The cave troll was dead before it knew what had killed it.

As its monstrous roar came to an abrupt stop, the God-King held his sword with a vice-like grip and rode the troll to the ground, leaping away moments before its skull slammed into the stone. Karakulak towered over his subjects, matching the height of the Big Bastards. One such orc, blinded by bloodlust, came at Karakulak with muscled arms wrapped in barbed chains.

The God-King had hoped to avoid killing any of his own kind, preserving their numbers, but an example had to be made. He plunged Dragonslayer into the Big Bastard's gut, halting its charge, before letting go of the sword and snapping the orc's neck with both hands. He pulled his bone sword free before the heavy body fell to the floor.

The orcs around him didn't dare attack. They stumbled backwards, tripping over their kills, to give their God-King space to walk. The wiser among them dropped to one knee and bowed their heads, some even laying down their weapons. His presence among them created a ripple effect. The sound of fighting eventually grew distant and then stopped altogether.

Karakulak held the gaze of the entire cavern having slain only two among the thousands present.

"Long ago," the God-King bellowed, "our ancestors fought the dwarves and elves for the right to rule Neverdark! They fought in these very mountains! When they were forced out of Vengora, do you think the mighty orc gave in to their defeat and turned on each other? Did they give up? Did they relinquish the world to the alliance? NO!" Karakulak bounded up a jagged boulder and turned in every direction to see his people.

"They kept fighting!" he continued. "They waged war from north to south! They bathed the surface world with elvish blood! They were forced into The Undying Mountains and forgotten! But it wasn't our ancestors who found a way out! It wasn't our ancestors who brought Neverdark to its knees!" Karakulak beat a solid fist into his slab-like chest. "WE ARE ORC!"

A resounding roar gave life to a dozen more, which quickly grew to hundreds and then thousands. Karakulak could feel the rock beneath his feet shaking as their collective resolve was put back together.

"We have tasted our first defeat since rising to Neverdark! Before we crush the dwarves and destroy the world of elves, we will suffer new defeats! But losing a few battles will not stop the mighty orc from winning the war! And when the dust settles and everything above and below is ours, take heart, for the weakest among us will have perished!"

More roars and howling cheers met his words. He had them in the palm of his considerable hand.

"Spread word to your brothers and sisters: the war isn't over yet!" Karakulak jumped down from the boulder and made his way towards the eastern wall of the cavern, where the rock was pocketed with caves both deep and shallow.

Grundi was instructing the guards to place the large chest inside Karakulak's personal cave on the level above. The High Priestess of Gordomo, Karakulak's mother, watched her son from within the comfort of her female entourage. Her reflective eyes bored into the God-King, reminding him that she alone knew of his secret pact with The Crow and the magic that flowed through him.

Karakulak held her gaze, subtly reminding her that she would suffer as he did if she were to betray him. He had given her a choice:

77

her son and the luxuries that came with his alliance, or her god, a deity that had failed the orcs consistently.

Ascending to his cave, the God-King dismissed the guards and stepped inside the leathery drapes that concealed his dwelling. He paused before allowing the drape to flap behind him.

"Grundi. Have the chieftains take stock of our supplies, specifically our wrath powder. Double check them yourself and then report back to me. If there is any more in-fighting, they are to be brought before me personally."

The hunched orc bowed his head as well as he could. "It will be done, Sire."

Karakulak turned to his dark dwelling, his eyes falling upon the large chest. Perhaps some time tormenting its occupant would soothe him. He moved to open the lid when another entered his cave unannounced and uninvited.

The God-King let his fingers fall away from the lid, resigning himself to an exchange of words with his mother. The High Priestess was standing before him as defiantly as Namdhor did, if somewhat squatter in her stature. Her tall staff, adorned with the skull of Karakulak's father, was pointed at him.

"You're losing your grip on them," she upbraided him.

Karakulak raised a hairless eyebrow. "Are you without your senses? With the stroke of my sword and a few words, I have allied the tribes once more. I alone hold the power to keep our fractious race together."

The High Priestess harrumphed. "Your words are no stronger than the wind. They come and go, any memory of their touch fast to fade. You need a victory and soon if you are to stay in control."

Karakulak snarled and waved his mother's warning away. "Victory is coming. As we speak, the foolish men of Namdhor prepare to bring the fight to us. They will be—"

The High Priestess stamped her staff into the ground. "That will not guarantee you control. Your thinking is clouded by the magics that taint your blood!" She spat on the ground between them. "You will be seen as weak if you allow the man breed to fall upon us. The fight must be taken to them! That is what conquerors do!"

"We would be marching over open ground," Karakulak argued. "They have control over our catapults, thousands of riders, and more than one dragon to bear down on us."

"The dragons," his mother mused, a spiteful glint in her eyes. "Your alliance with The Black Hand was our undoing on the battle-field. The Crow's dragon is the living embodiment of Gordomo's rage. Without the creature's aid, we are at the Dragorn's mercy, as our ancestors were."

"The only thing that embodies Gordomo is me. I will hear no other—"

The High Priestess stamped her staff into the ground again. "You are thinking like a surface dweller! Magics, open ground, dragons in the sky. We are the darkness given life. Our ancestors fled these mountains long past, but they did not flee under the gaze of the sky fire..."

Karakulak furrowed his dense brow and turned away from his mother, considering her words for the first time as anything other than an irritation. He had changed his tactics to adapt to the terrain, but the Namdhorians were about to make their biggest mistake, giving the orcs an advantage.

His mind began to race through possible battle plans, enter-taining various strategies and the resources required to ensure victory. Then, he detected a tremor in his right hand. His mind slowed down, along with his thundering heartbeat. A pit opened inside his stomach as if he hadn't eaten anything in days. He felt weak and light-headed.

"You have come this far," his mother said, her words sounding distant, "you cannot stop now. Drink your magics..."

Karakulak fumbled with the small chest secured to his belt. His fingers were slowly shrinking, but he succeeded in removing one of the vials. The green liquid within was so bright the High Priestess couldn't stand to look at it. The elixir was foul, but the taste was worth the price. When his vision had stopped spinning and the strength returned to his muscles, Karakulak discovered his mother staring at him expectantly.

"God-Kings do not bleed," she said plainly. "You are now a slave to The Crow. You have made *him* our true king..."

"You should thank The Crow," Karakulak retorted. "He was the one who suggested I make you the High Priestess, elevating you above all others. Were it not for him, *mother*, I would have you scrubbing armour until your fingers bled."

The High Priestess sneered and spat on the ground at his feet.

Karakulak resisted the urge to close the gap between them and throttle the life from her. He still needed her influence to shift the idolisation of Gordomo to him. Instead, he watched her walk out of his dwelling, leaving him with a doubly sour taste in his mouth.

She wasn't wrong. The Crow was his master for as long as he relied on the elixir. It had been promised that over time, the effects of the potion would become permanent, but the length of that time was unknown, keeping his leash ever tight.

The God-King removed another item from his belt, hidden between his waist and his cloak of human skin. The black orb was small in his hand, but its power was far-reaching. As he had before, Karakulak gave in to the diviner's pull and allowed his mind to be taken in.

There, he waited...

The shadow realm was darkness and mist, a world of magic that felt entirely threatening to Karakulak. Time was immeasurable but, for a king, any time spent waiting on another was too long.

"Apologies," came The Crow's startling voice. "Residing inside a time spell can be troublesome for diviners."

Karakulak took in the wizard's ethereal form, his apology lost on him. "You have betrayed me, wizard," he accused.

The Crow didn't appear amused. "How many times will you accuse me of such a thing? Have I not delivered you from darkness? Have I not given enough, good king?"

"You claim to see the future," Karakulak snapped. "You must know where I am right now..."

The Crow's stern expression faded into a coy smile. "I see. You have failed to take Illian in one fell swoop and you're upset."

Karakulak growled into the ether. "Orcs do not get upset! We bring our enemies to their knees and show them no mercy! Your dragon prevented any such plans. The wretched creature turned on us! It scorched hundreds and blinded hundreds more! You said it was an ally!"

"And it was," The Crow shrugged. "Without Malliath you would never have taken Velia and you would have faced resistance from the Lirians. However, his time aiding your war is at an end."

"Why?" the orc demanded.

"Because I say so," The Crow retorted. "I have prepared the battlefield, but it must be you who fights on it. I warn you, good king, your time is running out. The wheels are turning now. Soon, the world will respond to the rise of the orcs and if history has shown us anything, it is that your race cannot survive an alliance of the surface."

Karakulak bared his teeth. "Speak plainly, wizard!"

The Crow pushed his head forward. "The elves are coming..."

The God-King fumed. "They are already here! Their flaming arrows added to the dragon's wrath."

The Crow shook his bald head. "The woodland folk of Ilythyra are gentle by comparison to those amassing against you. Your war has threatened the elven queen's family. If you do not act soon, you will face the strongest magic-users in all of Verda."

"Good," Karakulak lied. "They will arrive at burning shores and a world that has already forgotten man. The elves will be destroyed along with the dwarves."

"Your hubris will be the end of you," The Crow stated. "Your kind shuns magic and, for all your ingenuity, you cannot repel a race that thrives on it. You have lost your element of surprise. The elves that meet The Shining Coast are prepared for war. As we speak, a vanguard sails The Adean. Their combined magic will cripple your efforts."

Karakulak turned away from The Crow's ethereal form. They weren't ready for the elves yet, a fact he couldn't escape. They were to go to war with the dwarves first, tackling each of the surface races in turn, ensuring there were no alliances to be had.

"If you do not take Namdhor soon," The Crow continued, "you will meet the elves in battle on ground they are familiar with. Should you advance on Dhenaheim, however, they will be forced to pursue you over terrain even they cannot master."

Karakulak snarled. "Why should I hear anything you say? You led the Dragorn to my army in The Vrost Mountains! You knew the black dragon would turn on us! For every aid you give I receive new injury!"

"You've always known we have separate goals, good king. Sometimes, a win for your enemies is a win for me. Sometimes, it's the other way around. Be thankful I have more to gain from your victories - you wouldn't want me as an enemy. Especially now..." The wizard looked over Karakulak's impressive form.

"I will need more soon," the mighty orc insisted. "The vials don't last long enough!"

"You have enough to see Namdhor to its end and with it the world of man. If you cannot finish off a race so weak as man, however, why should I give you any more? Prove to me that you are worthy of ruling Verda and I will ensure you get exactly what you deserve. Until then..." The Crow's image blew away like mist in the breeze.

Karakulak pulled away from the shadow realm and found himself back inside his real body, all eight feet of it. Speaking with The Crow hadn't made him feel any better - if anything, it drove his bloodlust even further. He had an army to keep together, an entrenched kingdom to raze, and now he had elves to contend with, a race the orcs hadn't faced in five thousand years. All the while, they were regrouping on the edge of dwarven territory.

The God-King paced his dwelling. He needed something big and powerful to crush the humans and he needed to do it without losing orc lives before they faced the other races. He could feel time working against him as his body consumed the elixirs. This kind of reliance on The Crow is exactly what he should have foreseen.

Something big... something powerful.

His mother's words returned again and again. They needed to fight like orcs, not men. Namdhor itself was risen on a slope, but its army was currently spreading out over open ground. Karakulak let all the facts swim around in his mind.

Something big... something powerful.

The God-King smiled.

CHAPTER 6
TAKING UP THE HUNT

What had begun for Doran as a pleasant stroll down Namdhor's main street had quickly turned into something of a hunt. The snow and ash had yet to fully relent, but neither had succeeded in completely covering the debris from the first siege.

There were weapons strewn everywhere.

The dwarf kicked the weapons about, freeing them from their icy burial, and examined them closely. He had lost his axe to the forge that created the Moonblade and the axe he had used during the battle had been claimed by the skull of an orc; an orc that was burnt to a crisp by Athis.

The son of Dorain still had his sword on his back, a weighty thing forged by the hands of his kin. What he needed, nay craved, was an axe to complement the sword. There was no better feeling than swinging a sword followed swiftly by an axe.

Also, there was no other weapon that could compare to the satisfying sound of an axe chopping through a monster's skull.

Alas, the weapons he continued to find were made for humans -

too big and too light. The orcs' weapons weren't much better, though they were certainly ugly things, much like those that wielded them.

At last, Doran pulled free an axe from one of the sharpened logs that had served as a spike. Unfortunately, the haft of the axe came free without the blade, which remained firmly in the log.

"Bah!" The dwarf threw the haft over his shoulder. "Humans can' make a damned thing that lasts!"

Doran huffed and continued down the rise, offering friendly nods to any who would look his way. For most, it was known that the dwarf had assisted in the battles to keep them safe but, for a few, the sight of any dwarf was still an oddity, especially since the army had only just returned from near-war with Dhenaheim.

Weaving between the horses and carts and general activity surrounding the city's defences, the son of Dorain eventually found himself approaching The Raucously Ruckus - a source of cheap mead, but mead all the same! The dwarf stopped on the first step to the porch, his attention snatched by the only figure standing still in the middle of the busy street.

A smile, long missing on Doran's face, tugged at his cheeks.

"An' where in all the hells 'ave *ye* been?" he bellowed.

Russell Maybury mirrored the dwarf's grin and made his way over. The werewolf dropped to one knee and old friends came together in a tight embrace.

"Ha!" Doran couldn't stop grinning. "Ye wily wolf! It's damned good to see that ugly mug o' yers!"

Russell assumed his full stature and glanced down at the stout ranger before taking in their surroundings. "I look to have missed a few things," he remarked.

"Oh aye, an' then some! Where 'ave ye been?" Doran noted Russell's tattered and dirty clothes, absent a cloak to shield against the cold.

"I had to leave the city." Russell paused, waiting for a young couple to pass them by. "Forty years and I still can't fight it. I had to get far enough away to make sure there wasn't so much as a scent on the breeze. The wolf is always hungry..."

Doran understood. "Ye did what was best for everyone. Any injuries?" he asked, giving Russell a once over. The tavern owner was usually safe inside a custom-built cell under The Pick-Axe when his transformation took place.

"Woke up next to a dead bear." Russell shrugged. "I'm fine though."

Doran nodded at the tavern door. "Well, let's get a couple o' pints an' catch each other up, eh?"

"You know I don't drink, Heavybelly."

"Course I know!" Doran replied marching into The Raucously Ruckus. "The pints are for me..."

IN SUCH GOOD COMPANY, the hours couldn't help but fly by, just as numerous pints of Wellbeck Mead studiously saw to the end of Doran's mental faculties. He told Russell of his journey with Reyna and Nathaniel, noting as much detail as he could. There were laughs and moments of quiet contemplation as each dwelled on the consequences of the dwarf's tale.

Russell had questions and Doran had answers, though his every reply was interrupted by either a mug touching his lips or a burp exploding from his throat.

"He's really back?" Russell's yellow eyes bored into Doran. "It's actually Asher?"

The dwarf put his tankard down, pausing before taking the next swig. "Aye, the spell was broken by Inara. It's definitely 'im. Ye should o' seen what he did to them Namdhorians that tried to take 'im. I've never seen 'im like that before, Rus. He was out o' control but, somehow, in control at the same time. Still," he added with a smile, "Asher's back! It seems nothin' can keep 'im down, a bit like yerself, eh!"

Russell nodded his head absently, his eyes staring through Doran. The dwarf knew well of the pair's history and the profound effect Asher had had on the werewolf's life. If it wasn't for the ranger, Russell would have been lynched by a mob decades ago or, worse, left to ravage town after town, trapped by his curse.

"I would very much like to see him," Russell said.

"Wouldn' we all," Doran replied before downing the rest of his mead. "But, as usual, the old fool has found 'imself in the middle o' it all."

Russell twisted his cup of water on the table, his eyes finally focused on Doran again. "Much like yourself then, *Prince* Heavybelly..."

Doran hesitated before continuing his signal to Bartholomew behind the bar, requesting another tankard. "I knew ye weren' goin' to let that go."

"Let it go? Doran you're the bloody prince of a dwarven kingdom! I've known you for thirty-five years and it never came up!"

"Why would it?" Doran contended, desperate to leave the subject behind.

"Because everything else came up!" Russell argued. "Getting you to shut up is about as easy as getting that damned pig of yours to stay still!"

Doran chuckled to himself. "He's already gettin' a reputation around these parts. The Vale Inn, up the rise, has come to callin' 'im the scourge o' Namdhor!" That set the dwarf off laughing into his empty tankard. "Pig - the scourge o' Namdhor!"

Russell couldn't help but fall in with the dwarf's merriment, infectious as it was. "That bloody Warhog," he reminisced. "I can't believe I'm actually going to miss chasing him around The Axe..."

Doran brought his laughter under control and looked seriously at his friend. "I'm so sorry about The Axe, Rus. It was more than just a tavern."

Russell sat back in the booth as Bartholomew placed yet another tankard of mead down in front of the dwarf. "I know," he lamented. "You should have seen it, Doran. Dragon fire burned everything. It was a heat I'd never felt before. And the flames! They rose as high as the trees. I can still hear the Millers from across the street... burning in their home."

Doran gave the Millers and all of Lirian a moment of his reflection before taking his next gulp. He had seen dragons on the battlefield and knew he would readily recount of their devastation for all his days to come, but the thought of one, especially one as ferocious as Malliath, descending on a defenceless city was horrifying.

"Gideon told me ye fought 'im, *Asher* that is."

Russell sighed. "I didn't want to believe it was really him. I always told him death was the only reprieve he would ever find. After all he went through he deserved some rest."

Doran couldn't agree more. "As I said, they reckon he's back for a reason."

Russell sat up a little straighter. "So am I. I've got another month before... Well, it's been too long since my pick-axe tasted orc. I killed so many in Grey Stone there isn't enough room on the haft for all the notches!"

"Bah!" Doran hammered his tankard onto the table, spilling mead over the lip. "Ye couldn' 'ave killed more than me, laddy! I met 'em in the streets an' I met them on the vale! Run the cowards did!"

A cheeky grin tried to spread itself across Russell's weathered face. "I left none to run..."

Doran paused on the edge of offence and confusion. Then he laughed from a place deep in his chest. The son of Dorain lifted his mead to enjoy another sweet mouthful when the side of the booth was blocked by a pair of figures, and not just any figures.

Standing over them was the master of the Dragorn and beside him the greatest swordsman in the realm, though *man* was perhaps the wrong term. Gideon Thorn and Galanör Reveeri looked upon the many empty tankards beside Doran and shared the same questioning expression: how was Doran still awake?

"What fine company joins us!" The dwarf raised his tankard.

Galanör bowed his head to Doran's companion. "I am glad to see you returned to us, Russell."

"I'm glad to be back," the werewolf replied. "I'm only sorry I missed all the action."

"Unfortunately," Gideon said, "there will be more fighting to come, so I hope you haven't retired that pick-axe of yours."

Doran licked the mead from his beard and belched. "Shouldn' ye be in that war council thing?"

Galanör displayed the hint of a smile as his eyes roamed over the empty tankards. "The hour is late, master dwarf. The council has come and gone. The city is preparing for the queen's funeral."

"Bah!" Doran waved it all away. "Early, late, dawn, dusk... It's all the same with a sky o' ash hangin' over our heads."

"Won't you join us?" Russell gestured to the available seats beside him and Doran.

Gideon made a cursory scan of the tavern before taking the seat beside Russell. Galanör perched on the end of the bench beside Doran but didn't dare put his arms down on the table, so covered in spilt mead as it was.

"I have come in search of you, Doran," Gideon announced quietly, a flicker of doubt flashing across his face.

The dwarf frowned. "Was I supposed to be at that council?"

"No," Gideon assured. "I don't think our new king is particularly fond of dwarves."

Russell was shaking his head. "I heard of this on my entry into the city, though I dared not believe it. Arlon Draqaro is the king of Illian?" he asked incredulously.

"He is," Gideon confirmed. "And worse, he is taking no counsel but his own. Years of controlling The Ironsworn have done him no favours; that war council was just for show, an opportunity for him to display his power."

"I get it," Doran slurred, nodding along. "Ye want me to..." The son of Dorain ran his thumb across his neck but Galanör gently lowered the dwarf's arm as he checked their fellow patrons.

"No, Doran," Gideon replied with more patience than the stout ranger deserved. "I'm afraid the task I would ask of you is far more dangerous."

Doran chuckled to himself. "O' course it is! The more dangerous it is the less likely it is one o' *ye* can get it done. Ye're all too tall... an' soft. Yer skin is like Velian silk an'... What did ye ask me?"

The Master Dragorn sat back against the wooden stall and shared a look with the elf. "King Arlon is marching the army on Vengora. He intends to root out the orcs and finish this war with an all-out assault."

His mind far sharper than Doran's, Russell turned to Gideon beside him. "He would take the army into the mountains? In all of history has such a strategy ever worked?"

Gideon turned back to Doran. "Only once. But, it wasn't humans or elves that passed so violently through the mountains..."

Doran could feel the Wellbeck Mead doing its very best to make a mess of Gideon's response, jumbling his words and steering him to the wrong end of his meaning. He looked from the Master Dragorn to the elven ranger and back again, wondering, for just a second, why there were two Gideons looking back at him.

"What are ye sayin', laddy?" Doran truly needed a few more words to fully grasp the conversation unfolding across the table.

Gideon leaned forward. "When your ancestors first met the orcs, in the halls of Vengora, they forced them out of the mountains and into the waiting ranks of the elves. Only together were they able to turn the tide."

Dwarves were a plain-speaking folk, so reading between the lines was tedious at best, but under the thrall of mead, and a lot of mead at that, it was just *hard*.

"It was a bloody war," Doran elaborated. "Vengora is littered with the bones o' me kin." He lifted his tankard and stopped in surprise when he discovered it was empty... again. When he looked back at his companions, it appeared their patience was finally beginning to wear a little thin.

"Doran." Gideon waited until he had the dwarf's full attention. "If Dhenaheim rose up to meet the threat of the orcs, there's a chance we could actually end this war."

"Aye," Doran agreed heartily. "The orcs wouldn' know what hit 'em!"

The son of Dorain's short laugh and big grin slowly faded as he took in the faces of those sharing the booth. They were all looking at him and with some expectation. The Wellbeck Mead was finally meeting some resistance as Doran put two and two together and was closing in on four. The more he thought about it, the more he understood Gideon's intentions in *searching him out*.

Doran swallowed and speared Gideon with a sobered gaze. "Ye can' be serious, lad."

"We can't win this war on our own. We *need* allies."

The son of Dorain swivelled his head towards Galanör. "What abou' yer lot? I thought Illian an' Ayda were chums!"

"I have already spoken with the elves of Ayda," Gideon explained, drawing Doran back. "I will reach out again, but they are an ocean away. Right now, the orcs are between us and Dhenaheim: that's an opportunity we cannot ignore."

"O' course we can ignore it!" Doran protested. "Jus' don' think abou' it an' move on." Even as he said it, the dwarf knew it was a ludicrous suggestion.

"The king is against it or I would have advised he send a peace envoy. As it is, dwarvish is your natural tongue and... you are a *prince*."

The Wellbeck Mead was now fully crushed beneath Doran's mounting anxiety and sheer disbelief. "A prince in exile!" he pointed out. "Were ye ears clogged when I told ye me tale?"

"Doran," Galanör chastised.

The dwarf, however, was beyond caring now. "We broke out o'

Grimwhal, then we broke *in* to Silvyr Hall an' stole an ancient text. We left many a soldier o' King Uthrad in the snow, their war chariots reduced to kindlin'." Doran couldn't help but laugh hearing it all said aloud. "An' ye think sendin' me back there with a plea for help is goin' to end with anythin' but me execution?"

Gideon paused before replying, perhaps giving the dwarf a moment to collect himself. "Returning as you are would indeed be a death sentence. Having heard your tale, I can believe that there are no words you could offer that would see you spared such a dire fate." A mischievous smile slowly pushed at the Master Dragorn's beard.

Doran didn't like it. "What are ye abou'?"

Galanör turned to face the son of Dorain. "Who could claim to hate the orcs more than dwarves?"

Doran sniffed, inhaling a few droplets of mead from his moustache. "If one o' ye doesn' start speakin' plainly I'm jus' goin' to order another drink."

Gideon clasped his hands over the table. "How would the lords of Dhenaheim react to seeing a living, breathing orc? If they knew the orcs had returned wouldn't they raise their armies and march to war?"

Doran was speechless. He couldn't argue with Gideon's logic - his kin had no idea their most hated enemy had survived The Great War. It wasn't his reasoning that the dwarf found hard to get his head around; it was the execution.

"Ye want me to hunt down an orc, capture it *alive*, an' present it to the kings o' Dhenaheim?"

There was a silence between them, the booth easily the quietest place in the whole tavern.

Gideon began, "It might be—"

"Ye're out o' ye damned mind!" Doran cut in. "There were others who risked their lives gettin' us out o' Grimwhal. I promised I would never return, for their sake an' me own."

Gideon was beginning to look like a defeated man. "We're

running out of options and time, Doran. An assault on the mountains will be the end of Namdhor. That means the end of us all..."

The son of Dorain sighed, filling the booth with his mead-breath. "Well, when ye put it like that. I'm to either die on the battlefield 'ere or die in the hands o' me kin."

"Certain death is assured if you stay here," Galanör reasoned. "Alone, we cannot beat the orcs. But, if Dhenaheim does react as we expect, they will come down on the orcs with all their might."

"So I'm to take the slimmest option o' survival an' return to the halls o' those that hate me guts. Speakin' o' guts, that'll probably be what they take out o' me first!"

Gideon tried again. "Doran, I wouldn't ask this of—"

The dwarf held up his hand. "I'm thinkin'," he stated bluntly.

His first thought considered the amount of Wellbeck Mead it would take to drop him into an oblivion from which he never awoke. His second thought was that of death; not just his own but everyone's. The elf was right, whether he liked it or not. They would all die if aid wasn't found, and if there was even a chance that such a thing could be found in Dhenaheim, then didn't the people deserve the risk be taken.

Doran was sick of being the best available option...

"A'right," he said at last. "I'll go back. But, I beg ye not to rely on me kin. Orc or not, they may do nothin'."

Gideon nodded, accepting that possibility. "I'm hoping that's not the case but, on behalf of the realm, I thank you for trying."

"Aye," Doran replied dryly, "ye had better thank me now. Whether they come to Illian's aid or not, there's a good chance I'll not be returnin'!"

"You won't be going alone," Galanör told him.

Doran couldn't hide his surprise. "The hell ye are, *elf*. Me kin hate orcs, but elves are a close second."

"Your mission is one of great importance," Gideon reminded him. "Galanör is an exceptional hunter; his skills will only add to your own. Plus, you must capture one alive and orcs aren't known for travelling alone. The extra blades will be needed."

Doran looked up at the elven ranger. "I thought ye were watchin' Vighon's back these days?"

"Vighon isn't journeying into orc territory alone," Galanör answered casually. "Or returning to a land that wants him dead. Besides, he can take care of himself, he's the prince of Namdhor now..."

"I'm coming too," Russell proclaimed. "You're both good hunters, but neither of you has my nose. I can find us some orcs and anything else besides."

"Rus," Doran warned. "This isn' goin' to be like the old days. We'll have to pass through Vengora with an orc in tow an' then make our way into Dhenaheim, a place where I'm already hunted. The chances o' returnin' to Illian are slim at best."

"There won't be an Illian to return to if we fail," Russell countered. "I don't know how to fight alongside soldiers and their sort, but I can be of help to you. I'm coming, Heavybelly," he finished.

Gideon appeared satisfied. "A formidable trio if ever there was. No one can know of your errand; the king would see to its undoing. You must act this very night and gather your supplies, while the queen's funeral provides a distraction."

"I've already made a list of what we'll need," Galanör added.

Doran ignored the fact that they had assumed he could be persuaded. "What about Reyna?" he put out. "I promised to keep her safe, an' that blasted keep is far from safe in me eyes."

"She shows improvement every day," Gideon said. "But, should you succeed in convincing Dhenaheim to go to war with the orcs, you will be helping to keep more than just Reyna safe."

Doran pushed his empty tankard aside, refraining from licking the metal lip. "Very well. I would give *you* a task, Master Dragorn..."

Gideon's interest seemed piqued. "Name it."

"In our absence, Asher's oldest friends, I would charge ye with makin' sure he doesn' rot in them dungeons. I've got plenty o' faith in Vighon. Grarfath knows he's damned crafty but, should he fail, I'm expectin' that dragon o' yers to melt the stone if it means gettin' Asher out."

"You have my word," Gideon promised.

"A'right." Doran cracked his neck and turned to Galanör. "What ales did ye put on yer list o' supplies, then?"

The elf raised a questioning eyebrow.

CHAPTER 7
SACRIFICE

Beyond The Dragon Keep's ramparts, a trail of fire illuminated the main street from the iron gates to the lower town. Torches and candles were raised by the people of Namdhor in remembrance of their queen, who for some had been their ruler since birth. For others, they still remembered the day Yelifer took the throne as her own.

For miles around, Namdhor was a beacon in the night. Vighon realised that's exactly what the city was now; a beacon for all the wayward survivors from the southern lands.

The northman walked along the narrow strip of the rampart that had been left clear by the numerous soldiers standing in lines. Everyone was facing the courtyard, waiting for the towering pyre to be lit and be transformed into an inferno.

Taking his position beside Commander Garret, Ruban, and the rest of the Skids, Vighon took stock of his latest injuries. His ribs continued to hurt, the cuts to his head stung, and his right arm felt heavier than it should. Still, he was standing, in full armour, with his life very much intact. That was more than he could have hoped for.

"When was the last time you slept, Captain?" Garrett asked.

Vighon shrugged. "I pass out here and there. How are the men?"

"Eager to spill orc blood... but less eager to march on the mountains. Are those really our orders?"

The northman felt a pang of guilt. He was going to commit treason and be forced to abandon his post, leaving Garrett and the Skids to the command of another. They would be ordered to march towards the orcs without him and he still had no idea what Asher was going to tell him.

"Our company was ordered by the king himself to maintain Namdhor's defences. That's exactly what you're going to do. Stay in the city, keep the people safe."

Garrett gave him a sideways glance. "You're talking like that doesn't include you, Captain."

Vighon was about to make something up when a pair of Ironsworn in golden cloaks approached from the steps.

"King Arlon *demands* your presence," one of the thugs relayed, gesturing to Vighon's father inside the courtyard.

The northman weighed up his options and finally relented. Leaving Ruban and Garrett behind, he descended to the courtyard and passed through the tight crowd of lords and ladies. Arlon was standing in front of the pyre, easily found with a goliath for his personal guard. Sir Borin's gambeson now bore the red and black of The Ironsworn, though Arlon was quickly instilling the belief that it was the sigil of house Draqaro.

Standing beside his father, Vighon kept his eyes on the pyre and his mouth shut. Arlon wasn't one for keeping his mouth shut.

"This is where you should be," he whispered. "This is where we were always meant to be."

Vighon had a venomous retort ready to escape his lips, but a small boy was presented to them, his mother and father close behind and a pair of Gold Cloaks behind them. It had been Namdhor's tradition since the time of Gal Tion that the fire for a monarch's pyre would come from the people. The young boy lifted a torch and the king took it without recognition for the child, despite the symbolism of the flame.

Arlon stepped away from the crowd and pressed the torch to the base of the pyre. Once the flame had taken, he discarded the torch completely and walked back to Vighon. The king wasn't even pretending to be sad anymore.

The fire rose quickly until it engulfed the pyre from top to bottom, enveloping Queen Yelifer's body in a final embrace. The roar of the flames was loud, but not loud enough to drown out Arlon's voice.

"The interrogation of our prisoner begins tonight," he purred, filling Vighon's gut with an icy lump. "I've asked an old friend to oversee it personally. Godfrey's always had a talent for such work..."

That icy lump grew barbs and threatened to dislodged what little food Vighon had kept down. Godfrey Cross was the worst of The Ironsworn, cruel to his core. It wasn't long ago Vighon had had a violent run-in with the man, down in the fighting pit. If Russell Maybury hadn't arrived when he did, it's more than likely the northman would be at the bottom of The King's Lake by now.

Vighon looked to his right, searching the crowd for Inara's face. The young Dragorn was standing between Gideon and Nathaniel and she was the only one of the trio watching the northman instead of the pyre. With her eyes alone she asked him if he was alright, his quiet distress easily noted by one who knew him so well.

Conveying the cause for his distress, however, was too compli-cated a message for his eyes. He was trapped. Trapped by his father, his title, his duty... Even his armour felt concerningly tight. The northman needed to break away now and reach the dungeons before Godfrey and his thugs turned Asher inside out.

How could he do such a thing with so many eyes on him? He had hoped to perform the breakout in secret, giving Asher and himself more time to escape and figure out their next move. Perhaps, he thought, they could use the massive crowds to their advantage.

Vighon reined his thoughts in. He was assuming he could make it to the dungeons without Arlon sending a tail after him. Also, there was no guarantee that he could defeat all the guards between him and Asher, especially with his fresh injuries.

Stuck between a rock and a hard place, Vighon's mind struggled to land on the right strategy. His finger tapped incessantly against his thigh and his eyes darted from the raging fire to the entrance to the keep. He had to go; the consequences be damned. His right foot made to move then stopped, remaining firmly rooted to the ground.

He had no sword...

The northman closed his eyes, cursing dragon spit.

Still, Asher was being tortured this very moment and the key to winning the war was locked inside his mind. Vighon would free him, sword or no sword.

ASHER SAT BACK against the cold wall, his arms propped on his knees. The ranger watched carefully as the man in his cell began delicately to remove and place down a variety of tools, each designed for a different form of torture.

He watched this with passive interest - aware that the careful placement of the horrific tools was in itself a part of the torture. Every few tools, the man would turn to regard Asher, hoping, no doubt, to see him squirm. Arakesh didn't squirm.

In truth, Asher didn't identify as an assassin anymore, but he could never let go of Nightfall's teachings: they were in his bones. And, from what he knew of his resurrection, his bones were the only things that had remained in the world after his death.

Now, looking upon the tools that would soon bite through his flesh, Asher's mind called on those teachings. He could take his mind elsewhere, leaving his body to endure the torture. Noting the open gate of his cell, however, the old assassin couldn't help but call on a different set of skills.

Why should he endure this at all?

There was only one man outside the cell and he guessed, from the odd bits of conversation he had picked up, that there were only two more at the other end of the dungeon. He liked those odds.

A heavy conscience weighed on him in that moment. How many had died since his resurrection? At The Crow's beckoning, he and Malliath had unleashed fiery hell upon the land. Did he deserve this fate? Shouldn't he be punished?

The man inside his cell laid down a corkscrew, still stained with the blood of his previous victim. Asher pushed all of his questions away and decided he wasn't going to take it, deserving or not. Besides, there was a very good chance his instincts would take over and he would kill the man before he could spill a single drop of his blood.

He reassessed the man in his cell. He had scarred knuckles - a fighter then. His tattoos identified him as an Ironsworn - a *dirty* fighter then. He carried himself well, appearing strong for a man of his age. Still, he possessed two wrists, easily broken with enough leverage. His throat was soft and vulnerable. His knees would cave in as easily as anyone else's. A solid strike to the centre of his chest would force the air from his lungs, incapacitating him.

The options were almost limitless...

"My name is Godfrey Cross," the man announced with a brief glance at the ranger. "Depending on how you answer me, I may well be the last person you ever meet."

Asher maintained his demeanour, an attitude that was sure to piss any torturer off. Since the man would be on his back shortly, the old assassin didn't much care for his feelings.

"Have you ever wished you weren't born?" Godfrey asked, his tools finally laid out to his liking.

Asher remained on the floor, calm as ever. "I've wished I'd stayed dead," he replied, confusing the man.

"I'm talking about real pain." Godfrey continued his prepared speech, "The kind of pain that turns a man back into a babe. You're going to cry for your mother. You'll piss yourself. You'll offer me everything and all to keep the red stuff on the inside." He chuckled to himself. "You'll be begging me for death before the dawn."

Asher groaned. "Another amateur. I'm yet to meet anyone outside of Nightfall who knows how to torture a man. You all make the same mistake."

The Ironsworn firmed his jaw, all the more eager now to get started. "And what mistake is that?"

"You talk," Asher replied. "If you ask questions, the victim will tell you anything to make the pain stop. If there is only pain, however, the victim will tell you everything in the hope that they give you what you want."

Godfrey shrugged and offered the ranger a pleasant smile. "Answers or no answers, truth or lies: *I* don't care. There's nothing inside that head of yours that concerns me. I'm just here for the fun." The Ironsworn looked from Asher to the manacles bolted into the wall above his head. "Now, why don't we get you strapped in and comfortable?"

As the last syllable left his lips, the unmistakable sound of a full-grown man hitting the floor resounded from outside the cell. Godfrey whirled around, a jagged hook in his hand.

It wasn't the opportunity Asher was expecting, but he wasn't going to waste it either. The old assassin launched to his feet and slammed into the Ironsworn's back, his left arm wrapping around the man's throat while his right hand gripped Godfrey's hook hand.

He squeezed.

Godfrey groaned, then he hissed, then he gargled and turned red. He tried to stab Asher with the hook, but the ranger had already predicted such a counterattack. A sudden twist of his hand inverted the Ironsworn's wrist, forcing him to drop the hook. Asher squeezed a little tighter around his throat and only relented when his would-be torturer went limp.

Standing in front of him was a lone figure, the one who had aided his escape. For the first time in thirty years, Asher smiled...

~

THE PYRE BLAZED in front of Vighon. Queen Yelifer's body was partially visible through the flames, though it wasn't much of a body anymore.

Vighon absently watched her burn, his mind elsewhere. Asher was being tortured right now. He had no feelings towards the old ranger, one way or another, but he needed the information he claimed to possess.

He had to do something.

A pair of Gold Cloaks emerged from the crowd with an urgency about them. They paused by the king and one of them whispered in his ear, the words leaving a mark on Arlon's face. The king nodded at the keep and turned to quietly command three others to accompany them.

"What's happening?" Vighon asked, drawing eyes from the lords and ladies.

Arlon's calm composure didn't match his irritated tone. "There's been an *incident* in the dungeons..."

Considering his father's sour demeanour, Vighon took this incident as a good thing where Asher was concerned. He struggled to conceal the smile so desperate to break free and instead turned to Inara and the others. They hadn't missed the urgent Gold Cloaks and were all looking back at Vighon expectantly.

The king managed to stand in front of the pyre for a few seconds more before he cursed out loud and strode towards the keep. Vighon quickly fell in behind him, both ignoring the quizzical expressions of the surrounding crowd. Their swift departure could easily be considered an insult to the late queen, but there was none who would dare suggest such a thing.

Sir Borin followed closely behind Vighon, his very presence enough to quicken Vighon's heart. A glance over his shoulder informed him that Inara, Gideon, and Nathaniel were accompanying their small entourage into the keep.

"What's going on?" Gideon asked.

Vighon slowed down and let Sir Borin walk past him. "There's been an incident in the dungeon."

That became very evident when rounding the next corner. The two guardsmen placed at the entrance to the dungeon were lying unconscious at their posts. Vighon noted that neither guard had removed his sword from his scabbard, though both men possessed visible bruises to their faces.

Arlon stepped over them and strode into the dungeon, his black and gold cape fanning out behind him. The other prisoners who occupied the cells were sure to step back from the bars upon sighting Sir Borin.

At the end of the row, where Asher had been imprisoned, another man lay still on the ground, only he wasn't a Gold Cloak. Vighon recognised him as an Ironsworn, his tattoos spreading up the side of his face, much like the swelling from the beating he had received. Again, the king ignored him and turned his attention to the cell and its single occupant.

It wasn't Asher...

Vighon watched a groggy, and recently injured, Godfrey Cross slowly rise from the floor. He cradled his right hand, keeping it close to his body. Such a sight would normally have brought a smile to the northman's face, but the table lined with hideous implements of torture sobered him. Cross would have used every one of them on Asher before bothering to ask even one question.

"What happened here?" Arlon demanded.

Godfrey rubbed his throat and winced as he spoke. "He had help."

Impossible was Vighon's first thought. He was the one planning to help Asher. He had laid out parts of his plan for the others and they had seemed willing to give him his opportunity. Had they found another way? Ruling out Inara, Gideon, and Nathaniel was easy, given their location, but Galanör and Doran were notably absent.

Vighon gleaned nothing from his subtle glance at Inara and the others, all three content to hear Godfrey's story.

Arlon was not so subtle as he turned to look at Gideon, suspicion written all over his face. Still, to accuse the Master Dragorn of treason was a step too far, even for a king so brazen as Arlon.

"You saw this traitor?" he asked Godfrey.

Cross hesitated, his eyes roaming over his small audience. "No," he admitted. "Everything was... blurry. But I know it was a woman!" he blurted.

That piece of information only added to Vighon's confusion and he turned once again to Inara and the others. Only Gideon maintained his composure.

"Those are contradictory statements," the Master Dragorn pointed out. "You didn't see who aided Asher, but you know it was a woman..."

Godfrey scowled at him. "I saw enough to know it was a woman. She wore a hood and cloak, but they couldn't disguise her body. I know a—"

"Silence!" Arlon fumed, spitting across the small cell. "This man has escaped Namdhor's dungeons *twice* in one day! Regardless of what he may or may not know, I deem him too dangerous to be held prisoner." The king turned to his Gold Cloaks. "He is to be killed on sight." The soldiers nodded their understanding but remained rooted to the floor. "Find him!" Arlon barked.

The soldiers rushed from the dungeons, leaving Sir Borin to protect the king. It hadn't escaped Vighon that the giant's attention had yet to stray from him, as if he considered the northman to be a threat. Perhaps the mindless beast was more perceptive than he had given him credit for.

"Asher won't stay in the keep," Nathaniel offered. "He's trained to disappear. Right now, the entire city is crowded into the streets - it's the perfect way to escape unnoticed."

Arlon turned back to Godfrey. "Rally the men. Comb the city and find him." The king stepped closer to his man and rasped, "Find him and redeem yourself." Godfrey bowed his head and quick-walked out of the cell, his pride as injured as his wrist.

After the king and Sir Borin had left the dungeon and returned to the funeral, Vighon joined the others in a close huddle, wary of listening prisoners.

"Was this your doing?" Inara asked the northman.

"Don't look at me," Vighon replied innocently. "I thought *you* were behind this."

Gideon cut in. "Regardless of who helped him, we need to find him before the king's men do... for their sake."

"We should return to my room," Vighon suggested. "Asher knows to find us there."

"He wouldn't go back to the same place twice," Nathaniel disagreed, "especially if he was caught there last time."

"Or he might think that they wouldn't bother to check there again," Vighon countered.

"Let's just rule it out," Gideon said, eager to get on the hunt.

The halls were alive with activity now, the Gold Cloaks brought in from the funeral to begin their sweep of The Dragon Keep. Vighon received a nod from the passing soldiers, or at least the ones who weren't Ironsworn - they gave him a look that promised death.

All four of them checked the proximity of the nearest soldier before entering the chamber. There was no sign that Asher had come this way, but that only bolstered Vighon's belief that the ranger was waiting for them.

He wasn't.

In fact, the chamber was devoid of all life. The four-poster bed was absent of Reyna, the blankets strewn, and her clothes gone. Nathaniel rushed around, checking every corner in case she had collapsed somewhere.

"I don't understand..." he muttered, deeply concerned in his frantic search.

"She isn't in here," Inara clarified, her senses superior to the others.

Gideon walked over to the wardrobe, the door ajar. "There was a cloak in here," he commented.

Vighon quickly put the obvious answer together, even if he couldn't believe it himself. "Reyna helped Asher?"

"She wasn't even conscious," Inara stated. "Aiding Asher was beyond her, let alone getting dressed and walking out."

"Unless she wasn't unconscious," Gideon posed.

Nathaniel shook his head. "Why would she do such a thing?"

Vighon could see the two men moments away from their next argument and decided to interject. "If Reyna has rescued Asher, where would they go?"

Thankfully, Inara followed his line of thinking. "If she hasn't been sleeping, it stands to reason that she heard your plan."

The northman thought the whole thing was unlikely, but it was the only lead they had. "Then let's go to Yelifer's chamber and find out."

ASHER TOOK in the dank and gloomy room that had, until very recently, belonged to Queen Yelifer of house Skalaf. Illuminated by sparse candles, the chamber was steeped in shadows. The ranger had come across every rank and putrid smell the world had to offer, but the queen's room had a malodorous scent that even he found unpleasant.

A person had died in this room, and slowly at that. Decay had taken root and mixed with the numerous herbs and elixirs employed to battle death.

He wandered around, inspecting what he could. A large desk took up most of the wall space to his right. The ornate wood was entirely covered in scraps of parchment and piles of scrolls. He briefly scanned some of the writings and drawings, picking out key words that spoke to his ranger self. Yelifer had been a witch. Judging by the spells and designs he was looking at, she had been a damned good one too.

The old assassin turned around as a small fire was brought to life in the grand hearth, set into the far wall. In the light of the licking flames, his rescuer finally removed her hood and set her emerald eyes on him.

"Reyna..." It felt good to say her name. He had stopped himself from saying it on their escape from the dungeons, ensuring her anonymity.

The elf smiled weakly and reached out to steady herself on the mantlepiece. Asher crossed the gap in a heartbeat and gripped her arms with both hands. She felt cold to him.

"Are you injured?" he asked.

"No," she croaked, searching for somewhere to sit.

Asher guided her to the large armchair and crouched in front of her as she sat down. There was something missing, as if the princess wasn't quite herself, yet the answer eluded him.

"Assaulting three guards was probably more than I should have attempted..."

Asher heartily agreed. "True enough, but I'm glad you did."

Reyna looked into his eyes, holding him in place. Her warm smile quickened his heart and he gripped her hand in his own, enjoying their quiet reunion. Despite the years, Reyna was just as she had always been: beautiful, a fact that radiated from somewhere within the elf.

"I've missed you," she whispered.

Asher couldn't quite manage a smile. "It only feels like yesterday to me."

"Well, it wasn't," she replied firmly. "Thirty years is a long time to go without you."

The ranger swallowed and tightened his grip. "I'm back now. It's *me*."

Reyna's eyes glazed with tears. "I'm sorry I wasn't there when you were... If I had known there was a way to bring you back I would—"

"No you wouldn't," Asher interrupted. "The magic that brought me back was dark, the kind of magic that should never be used. Wherever I was, I went there knowing that you and Nathaniel were safe, Faylen too."

It was the first time he had said Faylen's name and he noticed the recognition on Reyna's face, though he couldn't discern her thoughts. Asher had no doubt that Faylen was still alive, having been appointed High Guardian, second only to Queen Adilandra herself. He wanted to ask Reyna a host of questions regarding the only woman he had ever loved but, considering their circumstances, the ranger kept himself grounded.

The princess reached forward in her chair and wrapped her arms around Asher's shoulders. She held him close and kissed him on the cheek before sitting back.

"Clearly the world can't go on without you," she remarked, wiping her tears away. "I know Nathaniel and I have found it hard."

Asher presented the princess with a tight smile before he stood up, eager to move on before they could dwell any further on the past. For all his love, his instincts continued to steer him away from emotional interactions. Perhaps if he hadn't died so soon after discovering his *family* he might have embraced that other side to himself.

"Why are we here?" he finally asked, stepping away. "It would be better to get as far away from the keep as possible."

Reyna's eyes roamed over their surroundings. "It was Vighon's idea - I heard him talking to the others. Given the pall of death that hangs over this room, he thought it would be the last place anyone wanted to check for fugitives. Northerners are a superstitious lot..."

The sound of approaching footsteps drew their attention to the door, causing Asher to wonder if Vighon had misjudged his peoples' superstition. The ranger instinctively scanned the chamber and found multiple objects that could be utilised in a fight until he could get his hands on a sword.

The handle creaked under pressure and the door slowly opened to reveal four familiar individuals. Asher made an effort to reign in his instincts and allow the tension in his muscles to relax. Gideon walked in first, followed by Inara, Nathaniel, and Vighon, who closed the door behind him.

The ranger received only a glance since the companions were captured by the sight of Reyna. Nathaniel dashed over and crouched by her side. The immortal knight took in every inch of her with tears welling in his eyes before he pulled her head into his shoulder and planted a kiss on her head.

"I feared the worst," he whispered.

Reyna looked up at her husband and smiled, a gentle hand on his cheek. "I would never leave you, my love."

Inara was quick to follow her father and reached down to embrace her mother. The two shared a silent moment, their eyes interlocked as mother and daughter conversed without words, their love for each other abundantly clear.

At that moment, Asher wished more than anything that he could have been around to see Reyna and Nathaniel with their children, to watch them grow up surrounded by the kind of love he never knew.

Gideon stepped into her eye line. "I knew you were too strong, even for death."

Reyna held out her hand and the Master Dragorn took it in his own. "I told death I was friends with you," she replied with a cheeky smile.

Nathaniel's averted gaze didn't go unnoticed by Asher, but whatever tension lay between the two men escaped him. Still, it was obvious that Gideon Thorn had become close to the Galfreys after the ranger's death. It seemed he had missed so much...

"*You* helped Asher?" Vighon said, a few steps away from everyone else.

Reyna stole a glimpse at Asher before giving the northman her attention. "I have slept against my will," she explained. "My body had given up but my mind remained alert. I heard you all and your plan, Vighon. I could not let you risk so much."

The northman frowned. "Why not?" he asked, genuinely confused.

Reyna tilted her head and spoke softly. "Because you are like a son to me, Vighon. You know this, surely?"

Vighon's expression told of his understanding, but it also told of his reluctance to accept such a thing. The colliding thoughts stole his words from him, leaving a gap for Nathaniel to ask the obvious question.

"How did you get up?"

Reyna looked down at her lap and took a breath. "I have been fighting a battle of my own. In my slumber, I have been struggling to keep a hold of what little magic I had left. I could feel its essence floating away, leaving me... *hollow*. I have been clinging to it since we forged the Moonblade."

Asher's eyes flickered to the dagger sheathed on Inara's hip. He could still feel the sting of it in his back, beneath his ribs. Thankfully, the Dragorn had stabbed Malliath with it and not him.

"What are you saying?" Inara asked.

Reyna licked her lips, considering her words. "If I was to help Asher, I knew I had to stop holding on - it was the only way I could wake up. So I let it go..."

Nathaniel looked from his daughter to his wife. "You let your *magic* go? Will... Will it return?"

Asher had become something of an observer in this conversation, leaving him to note the looks that passed between Inara and Gideon; they weren't hopeful.

Reyna caressed her husband's stubbled jaw. "No, it won't. I can't even feel its absence, it's as if I'm—"

"*Human*," Gideon finished.

"I don't understand," Nathaniel said with frustration.

"The realm of magic overlaps our own," Gideon began. "It's

everywhere. But there are those, such as mages, elves, Dragorn, who have a connection to that realm. They become a conduit for the magic to pass through a... barrier of sorts. Those connections, however, can be severed."

"That sounds like a *theory*," Nathaniel snapped. "You can't know that."

"My knowledge is that of the dragons," Gideon replied calmly. "Also, something similar has happened to me."

"What are you talking about?" Reyna asked.

The answer clicked in Asher's mind, his memories rising to the question. "The pools of Naius," he stated, gaining everyone's notice. "I was in the pools when you destroyed The Veil. I felt your magic being drawn in..."

Gideon nodded with sorrow. "My connection to the realm of magic hasn't been severed, as yours has, but I have less power than I used to. I'm afraid it doesn't come back."

Nathaniel turned back to his wife, greatly concerned. "Does that mean..." He swallowed hard. "Does that mean you're not immortal?"

"No," Reyna answered with a shake of her head and a reassuring smile. "I am still an elf. Magic or not, my immortality will remain intact."

Along with Nathaniel, Asher found comfort in her response, but the ranger knew in his heart that only time would tell. It would be the cruellest twist of fate that Nathaniel, a human, lived forever while his wife, an elf, would die of old age. Asher felt terribly responsible for all of it.

"You have sacrificed too much for me," he said in his gruff voice.

Reyna's eyes went wide at such a remark. "*I* have sacrificed too much for *you*? You gave your life for us, Asher. Because of you, I married the man I love and have two children. Our debt will never be repaid."

Aware of his surroundings, the ranger was sure to keep any stray tears at bay. "You owe me nothing."

Gideon gripped the hilt of his magnificent scimitar and postured, reminding Asher of the heroes of old, often depicted in books or built into statues. "Well, I for one am glad to see you both in a better condition," the Master Dragorn said. "Perhaps together we actually have a chance of winning this war."

Asher felt all eyes on him, but before he could utter a word, Nathaniel stood up beside his wife. "Words cannot describe the wonder of your return, but I would know of my son before all else. When you fought Gideon, he took your silvyr sword from you. That sword adorned our wall until Alijah took it." The knight paused, hesitant to ask his question. "How did you come by it again?"

Asher looked away, his memories tumbling like a snowball down a mountain. He saw events through his own eyes as well as Malliath's and Alijah's. Any attempt to untangle the mess was accompanied by pain in the very centre of his head. Still, it was an answer his friends deserved, so he pushed through the pain and dredged up the memories of all three and put them together like a jigsaw.

"Alijah was fighting in the streets of Velia," he told them, his eyes shut tightly. "He fought the king of the orcs... *Karakulak*. He was saved by Hadavad, but not before he dropped the silvyr blade. Malliath saw the blade... or I saw it." He shook his head free of the insignificant detail. "I retrieved it from the street."

"Why would you do that?" Gideon asked. "You were still enthralled by The Crow."

"I don't know," Asher admitted. "It felt like mine, so I took it."

"It sounds as if the spell that bound you to Malliath and Alijah wasn't perfect," Inara commented. "It's good to know that The Crow isn't *all*-powerful."

Reyna raised her hand, flexing her fingers to give her daughter pause. There was a sense of urgency about the princess not dissimilar to Nathaniel. "Where is he now?" she asked, her eyes pleading. "Where's Alijah?"

CHAPTER 8
THE FORGE

Alijah Galfrey... That was his name. The half-elf held onto those two words for a moment. There were entire days, weeks perhaps, when he forgot them. His name felt trivial in the light of his lessons. *They* meant everything.

He fought to keep others alive and blood off the Reavers' hands as, day after day, The Black Hand would deliver more prisoners, snatched from a war-torn land, and throw them into his hell.

He was all they had.

Looking up from the floor now, he could see an old man and a young woman, cowering behind a group of Reavers. They were already cut and bruised, the old man especially - he wouldn't last much longer.

He had to get up. He had to push through the pain and keep fighting to save them. They deserved to live, to live in a land that was protected and safe.

He was all they had.

Alijah's groan morphed into a growl and he fell back on his lessons to avail him. At that moment, like so many before, he heard The Crow's words with perfect clarity.

"Love gives you the strength to transform pain into power..."

The innocent people dying only a few feet away were not his relatives or even his friends. This was the first time he had ever seen them. Yet, somehow, he knew in his heart that he loved them. He was their protector, their saviour. They looked to him in their need, aware, just as he was, that no other could rise above the darkness and deliver them from what evil would claim their very souls.

Alijah's skin was coated with his own blood, blackened with bruises, and pale from his time in a windowless cell. But he was stronger than ever. Unlike before, he was being fed well and often. In the weeks or perhaps months - he couldn't begin to guess - his muscles had responded to the daily fights.

His growl was fierce, at last...

The half-elf rose from the dirty floor, broken sword in hand, and faced his enemy with calm determination. He would have preferred to unleash his rage upon the Reavers, but his lessons echoed in his mind, reminding him that he was so much more than he had ever been before.

"Emotions can be the enemy if you give in to them..."

He gripped his sword, blade down, and crouched into a fighting stance he had adopted from the Arakesh Reavers. The steel was broken, the top half shattered by one of the Reavers days ago, but the jagged end was still sharp enough to plunge through dead flesh.

The Reavers didn't advance; they didn't need to. Behind them, their comrades were laying into the poor man and woman and would continue to until Alijah could reach them. With red blindfolds covering their mangled faces, the two dead Arakesh held their twin short-swords at the ready, all four blades caked in Alijah's dried blood.

"Time is against you," The Crow announced from the far corner. The necromancer was seated on the only chair, nay, the only piece of furniture in the cell. As always, he watched with an intensity that most would find unnerving, but Alijah had become accustomed to it.

The Crow's presence had become familiar...

"They don't have long left," he continued. "You must act if you are to save them."

Considering the cell he was in, time really was against him. Beyond these wretched walls, it was possible that only hours or days had passed by but, thanks to the never-ending script of ancient glyphs staining the walls, Alijah had perceived what already felt like an eternity.

The young woman screamed, sharpening Alijah's mind. He dashed forward, feigning right, before swinging left. The half-elf thrust his broken blade horizontally and pushed the steel through the side of the Reaver's neck while his free hand blocked its reflexive counterattack. The blow would be mortal to all but the undead, however The Crow had instructed the Reavers to play dead when such an injury was received. Before the Reaver dropped to the floor, Alijah kicked out behind him, launching the second Reaver back into the wall.

Prior to The Crow's instruction, and his time in The Bastion, Alijah would have pressed the attack and gone in for the kill then. Now he knew that such a thing carried too much risk, especially when the lives of others hung in the balance. Instead, Alijah sprang forward into a roll as the second Reaver bounced off the wall and advanced.

Relying on his elven side, Alijah flung his arm back as he emerged from his roll and threw the broken sword. Were his enemy any but an Arakesh, such a throw would spell their doom, but it *was* an Arakesh or, at least, the Reaver still possessed the skill set of the legendary assassins. The creature's twin blades slashed through the air and chopped the broken sword down.

This didn't come as a surprise to Alijah. Continuing his momentum, he rushed the Reavers attacking the innocent man and woman. In one smooth motion, he removed one of the short-swords from the scabbard on a Reaver's back and spun around, just in time to drop down and slice across his foe's midriff.

Everything stopped.

The Reavers ceased their relentless beating and the undead creature Alijah had been fighting froze with its swords raised, both ready to come down on him. The Crow slowly applauded.

"You learn quickly," he complimented. "I see your skill grow with every... well, it grows." The Crow stood up and looked down on the man and woman, both huddled together on the floor. "You saved them, Alijah. You did what so many would have failed to do."

Alijah cleared his throat, his eyes glancing nervously from the people to The Crow. "You will let them go?" he asked, panting for breath.

"Of course," The Crow assured. "Like the others you have saved, they will be set free."

Alijah watched as two of the Reavers picked the man and woman up. They squirmed at their touch and winced in pain from their new injuries. The door opened revealing a peculiar, yet disturbing, sight that his mind found hard to understand.

The doorway was more akin to a painting than an entrance to a long corridor of cells. At two different parts of the corridor, a pair of Reavers were dragging bodies away - they were all frozen still. How long ago had he fought for them? He could barely remember their faces and here they were, their bodies still being dragged away.

Alijah had to watch closely in order to observe their departure. When the Reavers left now, with those he had saved in their arms, they entered the corridor and instantly slowed down to a crawl before stopping altogether.

Adding to the strangeness, Alijah could see the icicles hanging from the door frames and the glistening diamonds of ice that clung to the walls. It was freezing beyond his new cell, yet there was no source of heat beyond the four torches that adorned his walls. It didn't matter whether he was fighting or sleeping, it was always hot inside his cell, his body permanently covered in a sheen of sweat.

"It's the magic," The Crow remarked, as if he could read Alijah's mind. "Controlling time like this requires powerful spells; the heat is a result of that power."

The necromancer wandered casually around Alijah, inspecting his bare torso and arms, all streaked with blood and marred by gashes. A flick of his wicked wand slammed the door shut with a *bang*, bringing them face to face. The Crow's leathery cheeks were a chalky white and riddled with pockmarks and deep wrinkles. His bald head was lined with ancient scars that curved over his scalp.

For every tale Alijah had been read as a child, The Crow could easily stand in as the story's villain. From his black robes to his pointed fingernails, the necromancer was the epitome of evil.

But he wasn't the villain of the story.

Alijah had begun to see that, after months of listening to his instruction. Sarkas, as was his true name, was simply the harbinger of evil. He had travelled ten thousand years and crossed over to death and back all so that he might warn and prepare Alijah for the darkness that forever lingers on the fringes of the realm.

Alijah still had his rebellious moments, however. There were times when he would hold on too tightly to his former self and fight The Crow's teachings. Hadavad's voice had grown so distant now he could hardly recall the sound of his old mentor's voice. Everything was inevitably buried under the torment and lessons. Pain had become his closest friend, always with him as it broke him down and raised him up.

There was little he couldn't overcome now.

But then he would remember, however briefly, what was going on outside of The Bastion. There was a war on, the biggest war Illian had seen in five thousand years. People were dying everywhere, slaughtered by the orcs. It was The Crow's doing. The Crow had orchestrated everything, including the thousands of deaths.

Alijah would make it all go away when he was ready. His lessons pressed down on him again and again, reminding him that he was so much more than everyone else. Only he had the power to bring real peace to the realm.

Didn't he?

"Doubt is the seed that will claim your mind if you allow it to,"

The Crow purred. "I can see it on your face, Alijah. I know every inch of you now. All the thoughts that pass through your head are like words on a page." The wizard's fingers fluttered in the air. "Victory defeats doubt. Every victory you gain will bolster your self-belief. Today was a victory!"

Alijah let his eyes fall on the blood that splattered up the walls, blending in with the red glyphs. Why didn't it feel like a victory? Both had survived the day, which was more than could be said for others who had shared his cell.

"Not every battle can be won without spilling blood," The Crow said, glancing over the splattered walls. "The future I have seen, your future, isn't entirely without bloodshed. The realm won't want to bow to you. But time will be on your side, immortal as you are. When the peace you bring stretches on and on, the people *will* love you."

Immortality...

The concept swam around Alijah's mind. For years he had known himself to be mortal, destined to grow old and die as any human would. It had been the motivation behind his self-exile, pushing him away from his immortal family. Now he had Malliath! Their bond would elevate them both, a union that would keep the world safe for eternity.

But they weren't united. Alijah couldn't even feel the edges of the dragon's mind across their bond. Malliath's absence sat within the half-elf like an icy lump. Since he had been thrown inside this cell, their connection had severed, leaving Alijah with the feeling that a part of his own body was missing.

"Where's Malliath?" he asked suddenly.

"This again..." The Crow sighed. "Aspects of your training must be completed without a dragon. This is why you will be superior to the Dragorn. They rely on their dragons from the moment they bond. You will—"

"Where-is-he?"

The Crow stepped back and took Alijah in from head to toe. "I see your resilience to pain has emboldened you. This is good, but never forget; pain is like a well: it has *depths*."

The wizard threw out his arm and pointed his wand. The spell that exploded from the end blasted Alijah into the far wall and pinned him in place. The pain, however, did not come from the impact of the spell or the wall, but from the magic that writhed under his skin. Barbed and spiky, the strands of The Crow's spell slithered through Alijah's body, igniting his every nerve.

If he was screaming, he couldn't hear himself. The pain intensified to a crescendo that threatened to blanket his world in darkness, but The Crow relented before such an end. He dropped to his hands and knees, coughing and spluttering as he spat blood.

"As it happens," the wizard continued, waving his hand in the air as if the torture had never taken place, "I have received word from the frontlines of the war and, with it, news of your Malliath."

Your Malliath... Despite his strong feelings towards the dragon, the idea of being bonded with him was still a foreign concept to Alijah.

He wanted to stand but his body refused, allowing him only to sit back against the warm stone.

"It was a brief conversation, but enlightening none the less. You recall my absence, I'm sure?"

It was hard not to notice The Crow's absence, given the size of his cell. To Alijah, the necromancer had left his cell and returned well over a week later, though, from the sound of it, he had only left long enough to have one conversation.

"You will be delighted to know that Namdhor still stands and the orcs have been forced to flee into the Vengoran mountains."

That was indeed great news, but Alijah kept his mouth shut and his gaze firmly fixed on The Crow, awaiting the inevitable bad news - there was always bad news.

"The spell has been broken," the wizard articulated. "Asher and Malliath have gone their separate ways, leaving the way clear for you and him to finalise your bond."

Alijah couldn't believe it. How could he? The Crow had given him one piece of great news followed by an astounding piece of great news.

"It is true?" he asked cautiously, waiting for the rug to be pulled out.

"I told you, Alijah; everything I say is the truth. I would never lie to you."

He considered the news for another moment until he was able to voice the obvious. "Why can't I feel him? If the spell is broken, why can't I feel Malliath?"

The Crow's eyes roamed the walls that surrounded them. "This room's place in reality is questionable. *Distance* might have no effect on the bond shared between man and dragon, but *time* certainly does. In here, your mind is working a hundred times faster than Malliath's out there."

Alijah had wanted nothing more than to get out of this chamber of despair since the moment he stepped inside it, but knowing that these walls were the only thing stopping him from calling out to Malliath... Now he *really* needed to get out.

"When will this part be over?"

"Soon, depending on your view of time," The Crow added cryptically. "This will all come to an end precisely when it should do so. Take heart, Alijah, for when that time comes, it means you are ready for what comes next."

Alijah's shoulders sagged in defeat. He already had manky hair, knotted and long with an uncontrollable beard. Would they reach down to the floor before he was ready to leave this cell? He thought about using the broken sword to trim both when a much darker thought crept into his mind. That thought soon fled, overshadowed by the knowledge that suicide wouldn't end any of it, not when you were surrounded by necromancers.

Besides, death wasn't the answer it seemed anymore. Curiosity had worked its way into his bones. Alijah had not much else to do but wonder, and wonder he did. What would this world look like, the one The Crow spoke of over and over again? A world where he would be king, a throne he shared with Malliath for all time...

Seeing his attention on the broken sword, the wizard kicked it over. "If you can master ruined steel you will be invincible when you grasp your promised sword."

It seemed a lifetime ago that The Crow had promised Alijah a new sword, one fit for a king, he had said. It was a gift the half-elf had yet to see, though he sorely needed it.

"When will you give it to me? The sword?"

The Crow pouted his lips and frowned. "The best kings are not *given* their swords. They *take* them! You will know it when you see it..."

More puzzles and riddles, just like everything else The Crow spouted about. Alijah picked up the broken sword and knew his destined sword wasn't going to be this ruined thing.

"I hope you feel rested having sat down for so long." The Crow stepped back as the remaining Reavers stepped forward. "It's time for your next lesson..."

CHAPTER 9
WHAT LITTLE HOPE

T here was nowhere to hide from Reyna's gaze as her question hung in the air. Asher knew exactly where her son was, but telling them he was trapped in hell was not how he wanted to say it.

He could still see Alijah's torment when he closed his eyes, however. The Reavers, once Arakesh before their resurrection, beat the half-elf to the edge of death on a daily basis. When they weren't beating and torturing him, they were committing horrific acts on other innocents in front of him, all under the guidance of The Crow.

"He's in The Bastion..." Those four words didn't describe where Alijah was or what he was going through.

After his response, the ranger could feel the intensity of everyone's attention. There wasn't a person in the room who didn't have some kind of bond or responsibility towards Alijah.

"The Bastion? What is that?" Nathaniel asked, hungry for every scrap of information pertaining to his son.

"An ancient fortress, built by *Atilan*..." Asher looked Gideon's way, the Master Dragorn's history being the most significant when it came to the would-be god. "It's hidden in the heights of The Vrost

Mountains," the ranger continued. "Alijah was taken there by Hadavad after the siege of Velia."

"Hadavad?" Vighon enquired. "Now there's a name I haven't heard in a while. He's with Alijah?"

"He's dead," Asher replied bluntly, realising only after his statement that there might have been a better way to convey such sad news.

Grief and sorrow consumed them all for a moment, the mage's murder another blow against their resolve.

"Who killed him?" Vighon asked, the first to recover.

"The Crow. He discovered Hadavad's original body and resurrected it to draw his essence back into it, then he burned him alive. He made Alijah watch..." It wasn't easy to say; Asher had known Hadavad longer than any of them, but saying it as simply as that gave him some detachment from Alijah's lingering emotions.

There was also nothing Asher could say to make them feel better, but it seemed his every word carried upset. There wasn't, and never could be, anything good to be reported from The Bastion, a wholly evil place.

Gideon folded his arms and cupped his beard. "Why would Hadavad take Alijah to this Bastion?"

The pain intensified when the ranger tried to recollect memories that weren't his own. "Hadavad believed he had been given a vision, at least that's what he told Alijah."

Inara had the look of revelation. "A vision, yes. When I met Hadavad in The Undying Mountains, he told me he had seen... *something*. A woman! A woman in a forest."

Asher nodded thoughtfully. "He thought there were answers in The Bastion, answers that would reveal the truth of The Crow and the emergence of the orcs. The visions were a lie, given to him by The Black Hand. There were no answers in The Bastion... only suffering. The Crow and his necromancers took control of it years ago."

"Tell me he's alive," Nathaniel entreated, his body perfectly still and his knuckles white as he gripped the edge of Reyna's chair.

"He's alive," Asher replied confidently. "The Crow wouldn't let him die, he's too important to him."

"Important?" Vighon and Inara said as one.

Reyna's gaze intensified. "Wouldn't *let* him die?"

Asher hated being the one to tell them so much, but he was the only one in the unique position to know it all. "He attempted to take his own life."

All three of the Galfreys were visibly rocked by his recounting. Inara put a hand to her mouth and turned away as if she was searching for something on the floor. Reyna blinked fresh tears from her eyes while Nathaniel remained very still.

"Why would he do that?" the knight dared to ask.

Asher shrugged hopelessly. "There's no simple answer to that."

"Then give us the complicated answer," Reyna said evenly, her tears paused while she listened intently.

There was naught but the sound of the crackling fire as Asher put his memories in order and decided on the best place to start. He was careful in his delving, wary of searching too deep and falling into the oblivion of Malliath's mind.

"His name is Sarkas," Asher began, drawing on Alijah's memories first. "*The Crow* is just a title he uses to control The Black Hand. In truth, he doesn't share their belief in Kaliban or any gods for that matter. To Sarkas, the necromancers are a means to an end, servants and nothing more."

Gideon narrowed his eyes at the ranger. "I have spoken with The... with *Sarkas*. He gives Kaliban much praise."

"It's all an act," Asher told him. "He discovered long ago that Kaliban was a fiction, created by the first priests of The Echoes. They were brought to an end by the dragons, along with Atilan's entire kingdom, but Sarkas used the chaos of war to his advantage, just as he's doing right now."

Gideon tilted his head back as if he had just been given a missing piece of a troubling puzzle. "Sarkas *created* The Black Hand..."

"Created?" Inara echoed. "The destruction of The First Kingdom took place ten thousand years ago."

The Master Dragorn laid his dark eyes on Asher. "He's like you, isn't he?"

That wasn't a comparison the ranger enjoyed, but he couldn't deny it either. "Sarkas is... *complicated*. He was born and lived most of his life during The First Kingdom, but he killed himself shortly after the war and left The Black Hand very clear instructions on when to resurrect him. Now, he's an Astari, like me."

"Astari?" Reyna raised an eyebrow.

"It means *new life*," Asher clarified. "It takes a powerful well of magic but, if you have the resources and the spells, you can bring someone back just as they were in life."

Vighon added, "The alternatives are those monsters The Black Hand resurrect."

"Reavers and Darklings," Asher expanded. "Sarkas surrounds himself with them, for protection."

"Why did he want to jump ten thousand years?" Inara asked. "Taking your own life isn't easy."

The more Asher pulled on the threads of Alijah's memories, the more his head became fuzzy. The pain had spread to the back of his eyes, but he pushed on, every detail important.

"Sarkas taught himself the worst that dark magic has to offer. He wanted to be free of The Echoes, but then he wanted the whole world to be free of people like them and kings like Atilan. He used this magic to see into the future." Asher paused, allowing them to absorb everything. "In the last days of The First Kingdom, he scribed two prophecies, each written with a specific purpose."

Gideon's eyes were glazed as he said, "He really did write the Echoes of Fate..."

"And the other one," Asher continued, "found in The Wild Moores. He took steps to ensure they were preserved through the Ages until they could be found by the right people."

"What was the purpose of these prophecies?" Reyna had yet to stray from Asher.

The ranger looked from the princess to Nathaniel, aware that his next words would carry some weight.

"It's about Alijah," Inara divined. "Isn't it?"

Asher nodded once. "The Echoes of Fate was meant only to ensure Alijah was born, nothing more."

Another silence settled over the room, accompanied by questioning expressions and an undertone of disbelief. Their reaction wasn't far from Alijah's when he discovered it inside The Crow's memory.

"There was a lot gleaned from that prophecy," Nathaniel mused. "I don't remember any of it leading to Alijah's birth."

"Of course it did," Reyna said, her melodic voice mixed with hushed revelation. "The Echoes of Fate plagued my father's mind for centuries. It was perhaps the largest factor in his decision to invade Illian. Had he not come to that conclusion, I would never have been sent across The Adean, and we would never have met..."

Inara looked to add something but the words caught in her mouth and she remained silent, her sight piercing them all as she gazed into the distance.

"The chances of that outcome are incalculable," Gideon reasoned. "He would have had to have known exactly what to say and where to put the prophecy to make certain that *every* event led to Alijah's birth."

"A task made much easier when you can see into the future," Vighon concluded.

Gideon sighed and blinked very slowly. "He really can see the future..."

Asher detected a hint of defeat in the Master Dragorn's voice. The old ranger had fought many foes in his lifetime, but even Asher couldn't say he had fought an enemy who had seen what was to come. How do you beat someone who knows what you're going to do?

That question wasn't entirely his own. Alijah had pondered on that conundrum many times, but as Asher posed the same question, their memories aligned, causing another jolt of pain to shoot through his skull, taking him out of the world for a moment. When he next returned, Reyna was saying his name.

"Asher?"

"These aren't my memories," the ranger tried to explain, rubbing his forehead. "There's some of Malliath and Alijah in here too..."

"You have their memories," Gideon said with great intrigue. "That is not a good thing. Possessing the many memories of a dragon is dangerous for a human," he added gravely. "Only a Dragorn can handle the bond; there's too much for an ordinary mind. Appropriate barriers should have been put in place before the spell was enacted."

Asher recalled only snippets from the moments after his resurrection, but he didn't recall The Crow considering anything *appropriate* before binding them all together.

"I think the lack of barriers was intentional," he opined.

"What was the purpose of the second prophecy?" Reyna asked, her tone suggesting that she had already put this question to him before.

"To have Alijah travel south and reach Paldora's Fall," Asher replied.

"We assumed as much," Vighon asserted. "The Crow wanted Alijah to be present for that..." The northman waved his hand at Asher. "That binding spell."

"No." Again, it was Gideon who answered instead of the ranger. "It was to make sure he met Malliath."

"What are you talking about?" Reyna probed.

A silent, yet brief, discussion took place between the Master Dragorn and Inara. "The spell that enthralled Asher and Malliath... It was not cast over Alijah. He was simply pulled into the spell by his natural bond with Malliath."

"Natural?" Reyna repeated.

Gideon appeared somewhat reserved. "I tested him on The Lifeless Isles. Alijah *is* a Dragorn. With The Crow's spell broken now, their bond will be compounded."

"*That's* not a good thing," Asher said abruptly.

The ranger's comment was ignored as Nathaniel started towards Gideon, his face flushed. "You knew he was a Dragorn and you didn't say anything?"

Gideon stepped back. "The bonding process is a private matter—"

"Dragorn business, is it?" Nathaniel spat back. "You didn't think it was important to tell me that my missing son was bonded with The Crow's deadliest pet?"

Reyna stood up for the first time since their discussion started. "Nathaniel..." Her tone was quiet but laden with authority. The elf looked past her husband, to Gideon. "You should have told us, either of you," she added, looking at her daughter.

Inara had nothing to say but offered her parents an expression of apology. Gideon was not so inclined.

"I have had enough of your scorn," he proclaimed boldly. "I respect and love you both more than any other, but you are *not* Dragorn. For all our mutual admiration, that line very much exists between us. Like Inara, Alijah has bonded with a dragon; that makes him one of *us* now. I cannot apologise for a bond I have no control over and I will *not* apologise for keeping my order's business to itself."

Nathaniel took another threatening step towards Gideon. "When your business is the lives of my children, you can bet Ilargo's scales I'm going to get involved!"

"Father!" Inara moved to stand between them.

"Wait!" Vighon held up his hand, silencing them all as he turned to Asher. "You said Alijah's bond with Malliath isn't a good thing. What did you mean?"

Asher's instincts felt prickly having so many eyes on him. "He's not one of you," he told Gideon. "Don't think that. *You're* Dragorn, *he's* bonded with a dragon - there's a distinction, or at least there is in Malliath's mind and, trust me, that isn't a place you want to be bonded with for eternity."

"What are you saying?" Inara pressed.

"Malliath is..." Asher chewed over the right response. "To say he's old doesn't do his age justice. He was around *before* The First Kingdom. He's seen everything, *endured* everything. I've been inside his mind; it's fractured, dark. I tried to get in Alijah's way but their bond is too strong."

Gideon circled behind Asher, putting some distance between him and the Galfreys. "Malliath has had a harder life than we could comprehend, but he isn't *evil*. If anything, Alijah's mind might help him to heal."

"He doesn't *want* to heal," Asher made clear. "In all the time we were bonded he wanted nothing more than to break the world. His mind is stronger than Alijah's, his memories alone could bury me in madness for the rest of my days. Given enough time, his mind would be consumed by Malliath."

"Can the bond be broken?" Vighon asked desperately.

"No," Inara answered. "No bond has ever been broken once a connection was made."

"It doesn't need to be broken," Gideon argued. "Alijah is one of us, a Dragorn. We can help them, *both* of them. The order has thousands of years of teachings and guidance..."

Hope. Asher could hear it in the Master Dragorn's voice. It wasn't something the ranger was accustomed to hearing and it certainly wasn't something he had come to rely on. In his experience, facts and skills yielded results - hoping for things was a sure way to get yourself killed.

Nathaniel moved for the first time since advancing on Gideon, only now he wandered over to the fire. "What does The Crow want with my son, Asher?" The knight turned back to face the ranger, questions and grief clinging to his demeanour. "What could he have possibly seen ten thousand years ago that would make him go to all this effort? Why would he want Alijah bonded to Malliath?"

Asher could still hear The Crow's rasping voice in his head. How many times had he stood in the shadows and watched the necromancer torment Alijah? Throughout it all The Crow had spoken openly of his agenda, proud as he was of what he had set out to achieve. Again, it was a hard thing to say out loud.

"I couldn't tell you what he saw," the ranger began. "Only what he said." Asher moved away, buying time to think of the best way to describe The Crow's ultimate goal. When he turned back, all five of the chamber's occupants were waiting.

"He wants to reshape the realm," he said simply. "No more kingdoms and monarchs with their own agendas. He believes Illian should be ruled by one king, a king like no other, one who could rule for all time. They are to be better than all that came before them, putting the people *first*."

Inara walked forward, each step carefully planted in front of the other. "Alijah? The Crow wants Alijah to be king?"

Vighon ran a hand through his black hair. "Is that why he started the war? The Crow brought the orcs back to wipe the other kingdoms off the map."

Asher met the northman's eyes. "The Crow's been *preparing his kingdom* for him."

Inara shook her head, ridding herself of the immediate shock. "If he's all for the people he has a terrible way of showing it. How many have died at the hands of the orcs?"

Asher considered all that he knew of Sarkas. "The present means very little to a man who has lived his entire life in the future. His concern is for the generations to come."

"He believes he's doing the right thing," Gideon reasoned, his gaze suggesting he was lost in thought.

"What's he doing to him?" Nathaniel asked bluntly.

Asher assessed his old friend and wondered if he was truly ready for that answer. "Simply put; he's breaking Alijah down and rebuilding him."

"Rebuilding him?" Vighon picked up. "Into what?"

"Asher..." Nathaniel commanded the room with his grave tone. "What's he doing to my boy?".

The ranger squared his jaw, hesitant to recount his time in The Bastion. After all, he had aided The Crow many times.

"Turning Alijah into a king isn't enough," he finally said. "The Crow wants him to be a warrior worthy of the realm, someone who can protect everyone. He needs to be incorruptible, selfless, unwavering in his servitude to the people."

"Asher," Reyna added a grave tone of her own. "*What* is he doing to him?"

There was no getting around it anymore. "He's... He's tortured daily in an effort to make him more resilient to pain." There were gasps, tears, and deep breaths taken by all, but Asher ploughed on, determined to get it over with. "He uses undead Arakesh, brought back as Reavers, to administer the beatings. He makes Alijah choose between the lives of captured prisoners. The Reavers are also instructing him to fight with better skill, again, often at the cost of innocent lives..."

The ranger continued for several minutes, detailing all that he had borne witness to in The Bastion. When he was finished, Reyna's face was buried in Nathaniel's leg, who stood beside her chair. The knight was a ghostly pale, his face as blank as a statue. Inara had walked away to face the fire, her shoulders bobbing occasionally with her tears. Vighon had slumped into a chair with a hand covering his face.

Gideon finished pinching the bridge of his nose and faced Asher with what appeared to be the weight of the world on his shoulders. "How do we—"

Without warning, Nathaniel sprang into action. The old knight barrelled into Gideon and drove them both into the wall. He landed two blows to the Master Dragorn's chest and gut before Vighon leapt in to separate them. Nathaniel threw his elbow back and struck Vighon in the middle of his chest, pushing the northman back.

Most notably, Gideon offered no resistance. He raised his hands to protect himself but he made no effort to stop Nathaniel from laying into him. Reyna and Inara yelled across the room but their words were drowned out when Nathaniel threw Gideon onto the dresser and dragged him along, knocking off the many sundries.

Reyna snapped her head at Asher, questioning his lack of action with a single look. Had the fight been in reverse, the ranger would have intervened by now, but it had been Nathaniel who attacked Gideon - a warrior far more capable than the old Graycoat. Should Nathaniel take it too far, he didn't doubt Gideon's ability to end the tussle in a heartbeat.

"He can stop this whenever he wants," Asher observed.

Inara started across the room, quickly followed by a recovering Vighon. Gideon was taking every punch, only evading the blows that would strike his face. Nathaniel was all rage. He didn't speak or shout, he just attacked again and again.

Vighon intercepted the knight's next blow, catching his hand mid-air, preventing it from slamming into Gideon. Inara, gifted with her mother's strength and that of a Dragorn, wrestled her father from behind, immobilising him. He struggled against her but she dragged him back relentlessly, leaving a dishevelled Gideon still on his feet.

Reyna stood up, coming between the two men. "Stop," she told her husband, her tone firm but gentle. Inara waited until Nathaniel had calmed down before she released him.

His chest was heaving as he spoke. "You shouldn't have left him in Velia. You should never have taken him in the first place."

Gideon didn't bother to straighten his attire. "I'm so sorry. I truly am..."

A thick tension settled over the room as fresh blood dripped from Nathaniel's knuckles, lacerated against Gideon's buckles. In that silence, they all heard the approaching footsteps from outside the room. Asher's experienced senses told him they were soldiers, laden with armour. There was only a couple of them, a patrol in search of him no doubt.

They paused by the queen's door and a hushed, yet brief, conversation passed between the guardsmen. Asher kept his eyes on the handle. If it began to turn he would have to act immediately, ensuring the others weren't compromised and deemed traitors.

The handle never twitched and the door remained firmly shut. They all remained quiet and listened to the guards move on, more than happy to leave the putrid room behind unchecked.

After another moment passed, Reyna turned to Asher. "How do we rescue Alijah?" she asked plainly.

There was a simple answer to that and, even though Asher knew he shouldn't say it, they needed to hear it. "It's too late for that."

For the first time, Reyna wore a mask of anger. "What do you mean?" the princess demanded.

"Before my bond was severed, I saw... *Malliath* saw Alijah taken to a new cell inside The Bastion. The Crow had been preparing it for months. Inside, time passes differently. To him, he's been a prisoner of The Black Hand for months already, maybe years."

Reyna closed her eyes and let her head sink low; Asher had nothing but bad news and worse news.

"That doesn't mean it's too late!" Nathaniel argued.

Asher kept his voice low and in control. "The Crow already has his claws in Alijah. I'm sorry, but saving him now won't make a difference. He's been set on a course that none of us can alter, no matter how hard we fight."

"You want us to abandon him?" Nathaniel fired back, his ire quickly turning on the ranger now.

"What I want is irrelevant. I'm not even supposed to be alive, Nathaniel. The Crow brought me back and connected me to Alijah and Malliath in a way you can't begin to imagine. I've seen inside both of them. The Alijah you knew is already gone. I can't say for certain what you'd find in The Bastion, but you won't find your son."

Gideon returned to their conversation, keeping more than a few pieces of furniture between him and Nathaniel. "The question hanging over your return, Asher, is yet to be fully realised."

Reyna gripped Nathaniel's wrist and spoke before he could hurl abuse at either man. "I can't believe you were brought back just to tell us to give up."

"He wasn't," Vighon answered, elbows resting on his knees. "In the dungeon, you told me you knew how to win the war...."

Asher sighed. "The reason I was brought back is the same reason I know it's too late for Alijah. The answer to winning this war is inside Malliath's memories; it's been there for thousands of years. We need to reach Haren Bain; it's located somewhere inside Vengora, near The Spear."

Vighon sat up a little straighter. "What's Haren Bain?"

"It's where the orcs were born..."

That had Gideon's attention. "You have seen this?"

"Not really," Asher admitted. "And neither has Malliath; you couldn't fit a dragon through the tunnels of Vengora if you tried. The memory was passed on to him in the dying moments of another dragon. The memory itself is that of a Dragon Rider's. He found a way inside Haren Bain and—"

Nathaniel held up his hand. "Wait. If you've taken this memory from Malliath, why does that mean it's too late for Alijah? They're apparently bonded now," he said, flashing Gideon an icy look. "If The Crow wants us to win the war against the orcs, why would he bring you back from the dead? We could rescue Alijah and learn of this from him?"

"Because The Crow has seen the future," Inara pointed out, if regrettably. "He must know that if we rescued Alijah, he couldn't help us."

"Also," Vighon added, "without Asher, we wouldn't even know about The Bastion *or* Alijah."

"The memory passed on to Malliath is thousands of years old," Gideon reasoned. "It can take months, years even, before a Dragorn can see all of their dragon's memories. This war could be over for us by the time Alijah learned of Malliath's secrets."

Vighon stood up. "The Crow brought you back because we need to act on it *now*, before all is lost."

"We're going to The Bastion," Nathaniel argued again. "We have dragons. We can fly to The Vrost Mountains, save Alijah, and then fly north, to The Spear. We can do both!"

"Not in time," Asher said, reinforcing the odds that stacked against them. "The orcs will attack again and again before we reach Haren Bain. The opportunity we have is brief."

"How does finding Haren Bain help us win the war?" Vighon pressed.

Asher was denied the chance to reply when Nathaniel pointed his finger at him. "I'm going to save my son."

"Father..." Inara tore her gaze from the floor and looked Nathaniel in the eyes. "We have a duty to the realm. We cannot save Alijah at the cost of the people." It clearly pained the young Dragorn to utter such words.

The old Graycoat set fierce eyes on his daughter. "You would abandon your brother?" Nathaniel waved her away before she could reply. "None of you understand. Alijah is our son, our child! I would let the world fall into ruin before I gave up on him..."

Vighon looked to ask his question again when they all heard more footsteps approaching. There were more of them now and walking fast. The deep muffled voice soon took on a clarity they couldn't mishear.

"We have to check every chamber, you bloody oafs! The king will have our guts in buckets if we let the prisoner escape the keep!"

"But, Commander," another voice pleaded, "the queen died in there!"

"It was nothing natural that took her, Commander," a third voice added. "The room is plagued - you can smell it in the air!"

The guardsmen came to a stop outside the door. The commander instructed the two soldiers to locate their manhood before The Ironsworn removed it.

Their time short, Inara stepped close to Asher and hissed, "The cliff behind the keep." He nodded his understanding. "Athis will get you to the ground," she continued. "Find your way to the elves in the camp, they will shelter you."

As the Dragorn offered him an escape route, the others doused the candles and retreated into the shadows. Gideon waved his hand over the fireplace and extinguished the flames before pressing his body against the side of a wardrobe.

Asher turned to face the door, his sight lingering on Reyna and Nathaniel. He did his best to show them all of his regret, sorrow, and apology in that moment. His return from the dead had been shocking enough, but now he was the one to tell them that their only son was a lost cause, his fate in the hands of their enemy. They had every right to hate him...

The door creaked and the assassin in him tried to assume control. His instincts wanted him to blend in with the dark and wait for them all to enter the room. Then, he would attack the guard at the back - a quick kick to the back of the knee and a snap of the neck would take care of him. The next would turn around and receive a swift punch to the throat, collapsing his airway and inevitably killing him. The commander would naturally attempt to draw his sword, but Asher would already be in possession of his previous victim's dagger, worn by all Namdhorian soldiers. Death was assured, as was his escape.

The door opened halfway, revealing the torchlight held by the commander. Asher blinked hard, squeezed his fist, and shook his head. He had to regain control of his instincts or suffer another blackout, not to mention the bodies he would leave in his wake.

There was nothing for it. If he was to forgo the surgical strikes of his assassin training, he would have to employ the blunt techniques he had picked up during his ranger days. A sharp growl escaped his lips and he jumped forward to kick the door shut. The commander was almost in the room when the door slammed back on him, compressing him between the wood and the stone. The torch fell to the floor in a spattering of sparks, putting Asher in menacing shadows.

The ranger swung the door open again and booted the commander backwards, pushing him into the guardsmen - he needed them out of the room. Though they had shown cowardice in the face of searching Yelifer's room, both soldiers were drawing their swords before the commander hit the floor. A split-second was all Asher had to consider his options: run or fight. Thinking of his friends, the ranger dashed to his left and sprinted away from the queen's bedchamber.

"Get after him!" the commander hurled, struggling to rise.

Unencumbered with Namdhorian armour, however, Asher was quick to put some distance between him and his pursuers. Unfortunately, his escape from the dungeon had seen The Dragon Keep filled with plenty of soldiers.

"There he is!" came a cry.

Asher didn't have time to look. The ranger ran as fast as he could without throwing himself into the walls as he turned the sharp corners. The sound of approaching patrols forced him to take a left instead of continuing down the hall. The sudden change in direction prevented him from properly assessing the new hall - an error on his behalf, though it was the approaching guards who suffered for it.

Using speed to his advantage, Asher charged at the two soldiers and jumped in the air before coming down with his fist. It was painful for both the guard and Asher, but the ranger came away with a split knuckle, whereas the Namdhorian was knocked off his feet and greeted by an unwelcoming slab of stone.

A steel blade scraped along its scabbard and sliced through the air, the angle perfect for cutting the ranger from groin to shoulder. Unfortunately for the soldier, Asher was no longer standing beside him. The old assassin had followed through from his first punch and dropped into a roll, continuing his momentum down the hall. He came up sprinting, leaving the remaining soldier to flounder.

"He's over here!"

Asher ignored the responding cries; he needed to reach the northern side of the keep, where the walls overlooked the pointed cliff of Namdhor's rise. The old assassin was pleased to find that The Dragon Keep's layout was still in his head. Learning the intricate details of every keep, fortress, and palace had been key lessons in Nightfall, a place where failure was met with death.

Asher skidded to a stop. There was a wall in front of him, but there should have been a door. Looking around, it was clear to see that this wing of the keep was in the middle of being renovated. The ranger swore, cursing his bad luck. A bitter breeze turned him to the right, where an open archway led out onto a wooden bridge, sheltered by a pointed roof. It wasn't the way he wanted to go, but at least it offered a direction away from the many footsteps that followed him.

Striding across the wooden bridge was a cold affair. The dark blue shirt, provided by Gideon earlier that morning, did little to keep him warm. At least, since reclaiming his boots, his feet were warm and able to grip the damp wood.

The ranger froze halfway across the bridge, though it had nothing to do with the freezing chill of Namdhor's air. On the other side of the bridge, five soldiers blocked his way, swords in hand. A quick glance over his shoulder informed him that his pursuers had caught up as well. He was wedged in.

Due to the width, a pair of Namdhorians stepped onto the bridge from both sides, their swords pointed at Asher. Before their second step, however, the ranger had already planned his escape. He darted to his left, jumped onto the railing and propelled himself forward, arms outstretched to catch the edge of the roof. The angle was awkward and the fall deadly, but Asher managed to pull himself up and swing his legs up and back, over the roof above him.

The Namdhorians ran for him, promising death with raised swords. Asher's head remained below the lip of the roof, as his body found its balance, but he succeeded in escaping before the first soldier was able to take a swipe at him.

Now on the roof of the bridge, Asher carefully made his way to the rampart. He could see the pointed tip of the cliff, just beyond the northern wall. It was a dead end for anyone without wings and so the path from the back gate had been left unguarded. It was, however, forty-feet down from Asher's current position.

On the other side of the rampart, a towering blaze reached for the sky. The courtyard was filled to burst and many soldiers lined the far wall, paying their respects to Queen Yelifer.

Asher crouched low and followed the low wall round to the steps that sat beside the back gate. He hopped over the side and rolled across the steps to muffle his fall. Another short drop and he was on the ground, inside the courtyard. Three or four people, high-borns by the look of them, turned around and scowled at the ranger. He offered them his most charming smile and slunk back into the shadows, towards the back gate.

He was almost to the edge when an arrow hit the snowy ground beside his boot. Instinctively, Asher dropped and rolled, an action that saved him from two more bolts. When he came back up, the rampart behind him was beginning to fill with Namdhorian soldiers, several of whom wielded bows. One last dash, he thought, and he could add The Dragon Keep to his list of places successfully escaped. It was only as the vast expanse of The King's Lake and the surrounding mountains began to consume his view that he wondered exactly how he was going to survive his escape.

"Athis will get you to the ground," Inara had said.

There was no sign of the red dragon and the tip of the rise was about to disappear under the ranger's rushing feet. More arrows pelted the ground, their aim hindered by the weight of their own armour - another reason to wear leathers. Seeing as his options were to either jump off the cliff and die or stop running and die, Asher chose the more spectacular death.

He jumped.

Naturally, a large degree of falling was involved, so tall was Namdhor's rise. The King's Lake rushed up to meet him, its frozen surface the guarantee of death - still, death held no surprises for him. The same could not be said of Athis, who did surprise the ranger. The red dragon swooped in from the west and caught Asher between his front claws. It was painful, to say the least, but it wasn't as finite as death, so Asher was pleased.

Athis glided low to the ground, his dark scales near impossible to make out from the rise so far above. By the time the Namdhorians reached the edge to investigate, Asher's escape would be described as a mystery and nothing short of a miracle.

As soon as the ranger's guts settled, he was sure to agree...

CHAPTER 10
WHAT LIES BENEATH

In the deep and dark places of Vengora, where even the dwarves dare not delve, the orcs were steadily reclaiming their ancestors' ancient grounds. Karakulak had set his vast army to the task of preparing for battle and, with thousands of subjects at his disposal, they were able to spread far and wide, accomplishing multiple tasks at once.

One such task had been the replacement of the garks. The six-legged beasts had proven reliable and ferocious mounts, but many had been lost when the Namdhorian forces collided with the orcs on The White Vale. Those that survived were needed for towing the ballistas, though, for Karakulak, the immediate problem was finding a mount big enough to carry him.

According to Chieftain Barghak of the Big Bastards and Chieftain Lurg of the Grim Stalkers, this problem had been solved. Looking upon the sparkling cavern, filled with bristling giant spiders, the God-King had to wonder how right they were.

Giant spiders had proven to be great weapons of war, used by Karakulak and the Born Horde during one of the many tribal wars, but mounting them was largely unknown. Three times the size of a horse and four times as wide, they would certainly make a difference when facing the army of man.

Either way, the chieftains appeared very pleased with themselves. The Grim Stalkers had tracked the spiders to their lair and the Big Bastards had hemmed them in and even killed several in order to dominate the creatures.

At least the two tribes weren't trying to kill each other. There had been a dozen more fights and twice as many deaths since his rousing speech, but tasking his race seemed to be occupying them, especially when it was in the name of war.

Karakulak scrutinised the nearest spider. Its violet body had a sheen to it, as if the creature was naturally armoured. Four bulbous black eyes stared back at him and two enormous fangs, each the size of an orc's arm, scraped against each other. Behind the eight-legged monster were two of its kin, dead and littered with spears.

The God-King pushed his way through the larger orcs of the Big Bastard tribe, all of whom pointed spears at the deadly creatures, and faced the nearest spider. It was big, but he had killed bigger in The Undying Mountains.

"There are no garks here?" he asked no one in particular, his eyes never straying from the spider before him.

"No, God-King," Chieftain Lurg replied, his head bowed. "They dwell in the south. We could retrieve some, but it would take time."

"The war will not wait," Chieftain Barghak asserted. "North or south, the spiders dwell in both and we have them here, now. We can adapt the saddles and begin breaking them in immediately."

Karakulak narrowed his eyes at the spider and walked towards it. The giant monster shifted, slowly rearing up on its back legs, its dripping fangs looming over the mighty orc.

"Every creature should know when it transitions from predator to prey..." Karakulak could tell by the dumbfounded expressions of his fellow orcs that he had used one too many words they didn't understand.

Unlike the spider.

The creature thundered down on all eight legs again, only now it bowed its stubby head and bent its front legs. Karakulak reached out and placed a heavy hand between its many eyes. Satisfied that he knew the spider's intentions, the God-King turned away to leave the cavern. As predicted, the creature showed a level of intelligence many wouldn't attribute to their kind and attempted to attack its predator from behind.

The spider pounced towards Karakulak's back. Unlike those around him, the mighty orc possessed reflexes akin to a god. He spun around, having removed Dragonslayer from his back in half a blink, and thrust the sharpened blade of bone up into the spider's soft throat. The sword pierced its head, splitting its four eyes equally through the middle. Karakulak's thick arms held the weight of the spider's front half up before he tossed it aside, withdrawing his sword in the process. The dragon bone was coated in black blood as thick as tar.

The God-King turned his wicked gaze on the rest of the spiders, daring them to challenge him next. Some attempted to escape through one of the burrows, but the Big Bastards were there with spears to push them back.

Karakulak snorted and turned to the chieftains. "Find me the biggest one."

Leaving them to it, the king of orcs strode away with his entourage of warriors, all hand-picked from the Born Horde. Of the six, there wasn't one among them who could best Karakulak in a fight, nor could any orc for that matter, but he enjoyed the look it gave him.

The tunnels of Vengora were alive with the kind of activity they hadn't seen in thousands of years. The ancient tunnels were everywhere, a web of passages that had once allowed Karakulak's ancestors to move freely under the cover of the mountains and surprise the dwarves of old. Now, marked with symbols only an orc would understand, the God-King's forces explored long forgotten caverns and battlefields.

Emerging from the chaos, Chieftain Orlaz of the Fallen tribe hurried to intercept Karakulak. The chieftain's pale skin was tight against his muscles and decorated in black tribal tattoos that had passed down through the Fallen for generations.

"God-King!" Orlaz briefly dropped to one knee.

"Chieftain Orlaz..." Karakulak didn't like being stopped, but the Fallen had been loyal since the king began his campaign to unite the tribes, a fact attributed to Orlaz's faith in Karakulak.

"We have taken stock of our wrath powder," Orlaz reported. "We have two dozen spears left and three barrels. The rest were lost as we fled..." The chieftain stopped himself and swallowed hard. "As we retreated to better ground."

Karakulak snarled. "That won't be enough," he lamented, considering his ingenious plan. "Even if it were, dragons await us on the battlefield - wrath powder will be needed."

"The wrath mines are in The Undying Mountains," Orlaz explained. "We have no way of knowing if they still exist after Gordomo's breath defeated the sky fire."

Like the garks, it mattered little if the wrath mines were still in The Undying Mountains; they were a thousand miles south of Vengora. Karakulak was tempted to consume another bottle of The Crow's elixir to speed up his thinking and come up with a solution.

"Our ancestors used wrath powder," he reasoned. "Are there no mines in Vengora?"

"I have sent my best scouts in search of them," Orlaz reassured.

Another chieftain pushed his way through the traffic of orcs passing through the crossing tunnels. Chieftain Golm of the Mountain Fist stood taller than Orlaz and unmistakably proud at this very moment. His heavy double-headed axe hung over his back, but it wasn't the orc's weapon that always made him stand out. Golm possessed nine short horns on his pale head and all nine of them pointed to the left, as if he had been hit by a strong breeze.

Golm held his impressive arms out. "Where my brothers from the Fallen fail you, God-King, the Mountain Fist will succeed!"

Orlaz shot his rival a venomous look. "What are you talking about, Golm?" he demanded.

Karakulak held up a pointed finger, silencing any further quarrel. "Speak, Chieftain Golm."

Golm bowed his head in gratitude while simultaneously offering Orlaz a smug grin. "While the Fallen have been searching for mines that ran dry long ago, the Mountain Fist has been searching the old tunnels for something else." The chieftain gestured to the symbols carved into the stone beside them. "Our ancestors were at war. What do you do during a time of war? You stockpile resources."

Karakulak inspected the symbols, drawn specifically to the glyph that represented *stores*. It was the smallest name inscribed on the wall, since the larger symbols denoted directions to more important areas within the network of Vengora, such as the armoury and ancient throne room.

"You have found wrath powder?" Karakulak clarified.

Golm hesitated, choosing his words with what little wisdom he could muster. "The Mountain Fist has found the *vault* that once housed the wrath powder. The doors have been sealed shut, but they are not of orcish design."

Karakulak's attentions was piqued. "Someone else sealed the wrath powder?"

Golm grunted. "Dwarves by the look of it."

That made some sense to the God-King. "In the final years of The Great War, our people were forced south, away from Vengora. The dwarves likely sealed the vault up because they didn't know how to handle it."

"That wrath powder is ancient!" Orlaz argued at Golm. "You could doom us all if you open that vault!"

Golm bared his fangs. "The Mountain Fist has been cracking stone and digging tunnels since before the Fallen tribe even existed. We can handle a pair of old doors..."

"Enough," Karakulak interrupted. "Chieftain Golm, open those doors and reveal the truth of what lies beyond. Limit potential casualties by clearing the adjacent tunnels." The God-King put a meaty finger in his chest. "Oversee it personally. If wrath powder awaits, you will have the honour of drawing first blood when we meet the dwarves." Chieftain Golm bowed his head and backed away until he blended in with the horde.

Karakulak turned his attention on Orlaz. "Have your scouts pulled back and divert your tribe to the farthest tunnels. You are to assist the Mountain Fist with exploring the ancient passages."

"But, my king..."

Karakulak quashed the chieftain's protest with a look. "Find the southern tunnels," he commanded. "And make them bigger..."

The God-King didn't wait for another word from his subject before walking away. He had seen to the mounts, ensured the tunnels were attributed enough workers, and potentially found a new source of wrath powder. There was one more thing his plan needed...

It took some time to navigate the tunnels, especially without a gark, but Karakulak's powerful legs never faltered. There were times when his entourage was forced to jog in order to keep up with him. He waved away any orc who would stop and bow to him - they all had work to do. From moving supplies, to digging fresh tunnels, there was a job for everyone.

Entering a new cavern, beneath a jagged arch, the God-King came to check on Grundi's job. The orc was useless when it came to shifting heavy rocks or fighting, but his mind could dream up contraptions and machines no human could hope to match. When given command of the Grim Stalkers' most talented hunters, there wasn't much Grundi couldn't do.

This new cavern was painfully loud. Unnatural screeches bounced off the walls and orcs cursed and growled. It was twice as large as the cavern that housed the giant spiders and cut in half by a fast-flowing stream that was fed by a waterfall. Stalagmites, as dark and shiny as oil, were broken and shattered from one side of the cavern to the other.

"Grundi..." Karakulak said his name with great expectation. "What have you found?"

The short orc tilted his head to lay one of his eyes on his king. "Monsters, Sire. I have found monsters."

Monsters was indeed the best word to describe the creatures that fought against the restraints being placed on them. On four pointed legs of pure yellow bone, their black chitinous bodies were covered in what appeared to be fungi, but nothing drew the eye away from their upper body. The black plates rose up into a dense torso lined with two rows of small claws. Either side was a long arm that ended with the same yellow bone as their legs, only the edges were serrated and hooked at the end. The head itself was simply a collection of slimy tentacles surrounding a circular jaw of razor-sharp teeth.

There was more than one dead orc on the cavern floor, each in various pieces. One orc was screaming as he clawed his way across the stone, his legs completely severed, as blood poured out behind him.

The orcs still living were having a hard time wrestling with the monsters, as anyone would when facing a beast ten times their size. Still, they used Grundi's weapons, the same ones used to capture Malliath years ago. Nets were fired, lined with hooks, and slings weighted with heavy spheres ensnared the creatures, tripping them up and binding their deadly limbs together.

As with all things, numbers were the key. For every four-legged monster, twenty orcs were there to corner it and pin it down. A similar tactic would work on the surface world, he was sure.

"What are they?" Karakulak asked from their elevated platform.

"You said you wanted something big and powerful, Sire."

The God-King envisioned them on the battlefield, creating bloody chaos wherever they roamed. They would certainly cut a swathe through the Namdhorian army, but they would need more than this if they were to challenge the dragons.

"They can be controlled?" he probed, sure that he already knew the answer as an orc was flung high into the air.

"Certainly not," Grundi was quick to reply. "These harnesses are just to herd them."

Karakulak couldn't argue with the orc's reasoning. "Either way," the God-King supposed, "we will unleash them on the humans."

Grundi frowned, though the effects on his face were subtle. "Unleash? No, Sire, you misunderstand. These monsters are not to be used in the battle, though I'm sure a few will slip through. No, these monsters are *bait!*"

Karakulak couldn't help but smirk, revealing one of his fangs. "Bait? Now you have my attention, Grundi."

"These beasts are killers to be sure," Grundi gestured to the orc running for his life, closely followed by the whipping tentacles of the monster's head, "but I don't want *them*, I want what *eats* them!"

Now Karakulak was intrigued. "What creature of the depths could possibly prey on these monsters?"

Grundi looked up at him. "Do you recall the legend of King Morku, Sire?"

Karakulak grunted. "Of course I do. There isn't an orc alive who doesn't know of Morku."

"Yes," Grundi nodded eagerly. "In the legends, it is said that he personally led the assault against Koddun Battleborn and his army of dwarves. He slew thousands of dwarves during his reign, elves too if the stories are accurate. Do you recall how he did this?"

Karakulak required a moment to remember the tale in all its detail. His father had told him and his brother of it when they were children. Then, the king's eyes lit up as it came back to him.

"He rode into battle on the back of a stonemaw," Karakulak uttered, a new wonder sparked within him. "The legends of King Morku have been greatly exaggerated over the generations, Grundi. Even if he didn't ride on its back, stonemaws have never been seen in The Undying Mountains or anything close to it. What makes you so sure it even exists, never mind baiting it?"

Grundi's mind was too sharp to be left to anything other than advancing the war effort. Karakulak couldn't afford for him to be chasing myths and ancient tales.

"Not far from here, there is a tunnel, not of orc making; neither is it of dwarf making. It's large, Sire, and the pattern on the stone is repeated, as if a creature has burrowed its way through. In its wake, we found debris from a variety of monsters, but also traces of mucus, likely secreted by the stonemaw."

"It could be anything, Grundi. Vengora is home to more monsters than the rest of the world combined. These fiends will be more than enough for what I have planned. Have the Grim Stalkers find more. I need your mind on other things now."

Grundi stepped forwards and cupped one hand to his mouth. "Make them hurt!" he bellowed.

The outburst was uncharacteristic of Grundi, giving the God-King pause before he punished him. It seemed, however, that the stunted orc had a point to make. The four-legged beasts were set upon by spear-wielding orcs, their chitinous hides pierced on every side. Their screeching was louder than ever and agonising to the ears but, through it all, Grundi smiled.

Karakulak closed his mouth and let any thoughts of punishment drift away, his voice no match for the sound of the rumbling growl that reverberated throughout the cavern, drowning out the screeches. The pincer-legged monsters below instantly cowered, withdrawing their tentacles into their circular mouths and seeking shelter the orcs weren't inclined to provide. The walls shook and rock dust rained down as something massive passed the cavern by.

Then it was gone.

Whether that had been the legendary stonemaw remained to be seen, but the sound alone told the hunter in Karakulak that a predator of unequal size had just been close by. That was something he could use...

Now, the God-King shared his subject's smile. "You surprise me as always, Grundi. Find this beast and make it ours."

"As you command, Sire."

Karakulak was more than happy to leave the hollow and the screeching monsters - his sensitive ears could only handle so much. On his way back to the central cavern, where the ancient kings of the orc had once resided, the Bone Lord of The Under Realm made sure his presence was felt in the farthest tunnels, where the majority of the digging was taking place. Under the gaze of their God-King, no orc would dare slack.

The tunnels were beyond old, with many in need of repair or clearing out altogether. Still, this is what the orcs were made for. Just as the humans and the elves moulded the surface world to their liking, the orcs dominated The Under Realm, hewing the rock better than any dwarf could carve stone.

It wasn't lost on Karakulak that they had spent years digging through the ancient tunnels in the south, so that they might reach the north, and now they were digging in the north to reach the south. Adaptation was key to any species' survival, especially in a time of war. Seeing the determination in his fellow orc bolstered Karakulak's resolve beyond that of his elixir.

Their rule was inevitable...

After his journey through the web of tunnels, the God-King returned to his personal camp. The fabric of his tent had been erected over the ancient throne of dwarven bone, so that he might sit on it and conjure new strategies to break the surface dwellers. Indeed, he did enjoy occupying the throne, imagining his predecessors as they planned wars of their own.

He wasn't in the mood for resting, however. Karakulak turned his attention to the large chest beside the throne. The mighty orc flicked the latches and tossed the lid back on its hinges, a wicked smile already pushing at his cheeks and revealing his fangs.

His eyes wide in the pitch black, the Dragorn's expression quickly changed from confusion to fear. Good, Karakulak thought as he yanked the man out by his throat. Fear was a good place to start...

CHAPTER 11
LOVE AND DUTY

Inara held her mother in an embrace that all but an elf would struggle to break. The fact that Reyna was on her feet felt like a miracle, but her skin was finally warm and the sweet smell her mother forever possessed had returned. It was a great comfort to the Dragorn.

Alone in Vighon's chamber, the three Galfreys shared a quiet moment as they all dwelled on Alijah. Asher's news had broken them all in some way and added to their resolve in another. For Inara, it was mostly shock mixed with the kind of fear that opened a pit within her stomach. She couldn't help but think of all the things that could have been done to prevent his fate, though The Crow would have foreseen such a thing.

Her mother eventually pulled away from her with tears bridging her eyelashes. "Did Asher reach the ground?"

Inara nodded. "Athis tells me he's already heading to the lower camp."

Reyna smiled and nodded along, her thoughts clearly elsewhere. "We should go down ourselves and find Aunt Ellöria. She will shelter Asher, but Ellöria doesn't like to be in the dark on matters."

"Inara..." Nathaniel turned away from the window and faced his family. "Regardless of what Gideon commands or what Asher tells us, you will take us to The Bastion, won't you?"

Inara had never seen her father so desperate, nor her mother so distracted. "I have a duty..." she whispered, hating herself for falling back on such a response.

"Do you not have a duty to your brother?" Nathaniel countered, ignoring his wife's silent plea to calm down.

"Of course I do!" Inara shot back. "Do you think it doesn't tear me up inside knowing that he's out there being..." She couldn't say the word. To think of someone harming her twin brother was enough to make her feel physically sick.

"There are tens of thousands of people in the north right now," Inara continued. "I'm needed *here*."

Desperate as he was, Nathaniel heard none of it. "It will take us days, weeks even to reach The Vrost Mountains. Asher said The Bastion is high up; we would find it quicker with Athis's sight."

Inara had no reply, having said all she could on the matter. Of course she wanted to go and rescue her brother, but if she was to return and find that all of Namdhor had perished in her absence, the young Dragorn would never forgive herself.

It was her mother, however, who spoke reason. "Inara," she began softly. "If Asher is right, then The Crow is going to turn your brother into something else, something that might even threaten Verda. If we save him before it's too late, the duty we *all* have to the realm will be fulfilled."

Some of that made sense to Inara. "Asher told us The Crow wants a king, a *good* king. What he's doing is twisted and beyond evil, but why should we fear Alijah?"

Reyna guarded her expression. "The Crow has used dark magic to see Alijah's future," she said gravely. "Such a thing can alter one's perspective. And, in all my time, I have never seen evil fail to breed evil. I want my son away from him at all costs."

Inara couldn't argue with the wisdom of her mother's words and neither could Athis.

There is a reason dark magic is forbidden, the red dragon said into her mind. *It wasn't banished eons ago to ensure a balance between mages. It is known that such a thing can break the mind, body, and soul...*

Before Inara could reply, a vigorous knock beat against the door. "In the name of the king, open this door!"

Inara scowled and let her hand fall onto the hilt of her Vi'tari blade. Seeing as her father looked to be in the mood to punch someone, again, the young Dragorn crossed the room and greeted the knocker. She was quickly forced to step aside as three Namdhorian soldiers pushed their way through, making room for the king himself. Remaining outside, Sir Borin the Dread stood as a sentinel at his master's back.

Arlon scanned his son's room before resting on Reyna. "Ah, it warms my heart to see you back to health, Ambassador!" Inara had seen a more genuine smile on a Gobber. "I see we're having a lovely little reunion. How nice." The king's demeanour finally turned sour. "I'm not a religious man, I don't see the divine instead of coincidence and, tonight, a very suspicious coincidence has taken place."

Nathaniel started forward. "Arlon... your Grace. My wife has not long awoken, she needs to rest a while longer."

"Not long awoken," Arlon repeated, his eyes roaming over Reyna's boots. "Don't get me wrong, any excuse to get me out of the old warwitch's funeral is a welcome one. Tonight, however, Namdhor's most dangerous prisoner escaped the dungeon, apparently aided by a woman. Also tonight, Reyna Sevari miraculously awakens from her deep slumber. I find it hard to believe that a woman could aid Asher in his escape, but an elf? Elves are notoriously stronger, faster... *sneakier*."

Reyna squared her shoulders and raised her chin. "Are you accusing me of something, your Grace?"

The king sauntered around the room, confident that every inch belonged to him. "Accusing the princess of Elandril would be a serious thing," he continued. "Especially when I'm hoping that, with your help, we might strengthen the bond between Illian and Ayda."

Reyna bowed her head in agreement. "An alliance between our two shores would be a mutually beneficial one."

"Excellent!" Arlon threw his hands up. "Then I can count on the Galfreys for support? And any sign of Asher will be reported? I would hate to start issuing decrees with the words *treason* or *execution* in them."

Again, Reyna bowed her head. "You can always count on us to do what is best for the realm, your Grace."

Arlon maintained his gaze a moment longer: only a fool would miss what she had really said. "Very good," he finally replied. "My army is preparing to take the fight to the orcs. As legendary as your skills in battle are, neither of you are expected to join the melee, obviously. I will have chambers made up for you, so that you might stay in The Dragon Keep as my guests."

Nathaniel opened his mouth with what could only be a scornful rejection but, thankfully, his wife beat him to their response.

"That is very generous of you, your Grace. I'm not feeling completely myself yet."

Arlon briefly narrowed his eyes at Inara on his way out. "Master Galfrey. The same cannot be said of you, I'm afraid. You and your dragon are valuable assets to Namdhor's battle plans."

Inara glanced at her parents before addressing the king. "The Dragorn will always keep the dark at bay, your Grace." It was the best answer she could give, torn as she was.

In the king's absence, the Galfreys took a collective breath. Arlon Draqaro had a way of sucking all the air out of a room, his very presence a threat.

Nathaniel checked the view from the window. "The funeral is ending," he reported. "We should use the cover of the masses to reach Ellöria's camp. Arlon is sure to have his Ironsworn watching us."

Inara was about to agree when a sharp sense of urgency crossed her bond from Athis. The initial emotion was despair, its source a great deal of pain.

It's Thraden! Athis told her, already on the move.

Inara wanted to ask what was happening, but she already knew the terrible answer. "I have to go!" she blurted, heading for the door.

"What's wrong?" her mother asked.

Inara paused in the doorway, her face ashen. "The orcs are hurting Arathor..."

HER TIME in the air was brief, though Inara was unable to enjoy even a second of it. Any time with Athis was a joy, but being in the air, above it all, was easily the best feeling in the world. Now, soaring low towards the edge of The King's Lake, the only feeling the young Dragorn had was a sinking one.

Thraden was visible along the shore, his devastating tail hammering the frozen surface of the lake. His roar was distorted, wracked with pain and suffering. His thick claws raked the ground and the spikes on his back quivered.

Blood was seeping into the lake...

Ilargo and Gideon touched down first and approached Thraden with caution. A wounded dragon could always be helped, but a dragon in the throes of intense pain was akin to a cornered animal - there was no telling how it would react.

Athis fanned his wings, cutting his speed to land beside the shore on all four of his powerful legs. Inara jumped down and ran to Gideon's side as the dragons deliberately placed themselves between their Dragorn riders and Thraden.

All of them opened their minds to the bond, allowing the dragons to share everyone's thoughts. Thraden wasn't saying anything intelligible, his pain too intense. Inara moved to get a better look at him but Athis turned his head back with a warning in his crystal blue eyes.

Stay behind us, he cautioned.

Ilargo edged forwards. *Thraden?*

The blue dragon tried to writhe on all fours but his front right leg gave way and he roared as his jaw hit the ground. There were new gashes along his body and his red eyes were clearly swollen. It broke Inara's heart, if it could be broken any more. She couldn't stand to think of what was being done to Arathor...

Ilargo inhaled a sharp breath and exhaled a torrent of icy air to cover Thraden's wounded side. It soothed the dragon for a moment, allowing him enough control to give them a pleading look.

Inara watched Gideon closely, well aware of the decision that sat on his shoulders. The young Dragorn had been very against killing Thraden to end their suffering, but that was before the torture began. Now, seeing the blue dragon at the mercy of the orcs, Inara wasn't sure it was such a terrible idea.

Thraden, Ilargo tried again, *what can you see?*

Thraden's roar died down and a trickle of blood oozed from between his fangs. *The king...* he whined.

Gideon's jaw clamped hard. ***Karakulak,*** the Master Dragorn seethed. ***Arathor is his prisoner?***

Yes! Thraden's response exploded into a new roar of pain. *They are deep in the mountain,* he hissed. *The orc lands of Vengora...*

Inara recalled a segment from an old tome in the library on The Lifeless Isles, written by Valtyr, an ancient master of the Dragorn. Her studies had been brief, too brief in hindsight, but the orc lands had sounded exciting at the time, drawing her in. It didn't sound exciting now. Beneath the dwarven halls of stone lay their dark dwelling, a place where even Arathor couldn't survive.

Another spasm of pain shot through Thraden's body and a handful of scales fell away to reveal fresh wounds. The dragon shrieked and his anger rose to the surface in a bid to combat the fear and pain. Athis quickly shifted his bulk in front of Inara and Gideon and raised his far wing to shield them all from Thraden's flames.

Athis was, of course, immune to the fire, but Inara could still feel the intense heat on the left side of her body.

Through their bond, they all felt Ilargo's intentions a moment before he acted. The green dragon swung his tail around with enough force to tear a tree in half. In this case, it was just enough to rob Thraden of consciousness. The dragon's head snapped to the side and his body followed it down to the ground with an earth-shaking *thud*.

Athis blew freezing air over flames before lowering his wing and moving aside. Between them and Thraden's body was a fog of smoke and scorched ground. Gideon crossed the black earth and placed a hand on Thraden's face, beneath his eye. The strain of it all was beginning to show on him.

"I remember when Arathor met Thraden for the first time," Gideon reminisced. "I remember their trials, their success, their struggles." The Master Dragorn took his hand back and stared at the dragon, his shoulders sagged. "I can't do it..." he whispered.

Inara reached out and placed Gideon's hand in hers. "We can't let them suffer."

Gideon's dispirited demeanour began to harden until he was the perfect display of determination. "I won't let one more Dragorn die," he insisted, squeezing her hand. "Not one."

Inara watched Gideon storm away, returning to the rise of Namdhor. "Where are you going?" she called after him, certain that they had been moments away from ending Thraden and Arathor's life.

Gideon replied over his shoulder, "To figure out how we save the world..."

In a bid to remain inconspicuous, Inara and Gideon made their way to the lower camps on foot, leaving the dragons to tend to Thraden, should he wake up. The trek had been a quiet one, with Gideon wrapped up in his own thoughts and stubborn will. That suited Inara, who felt she had an imminent decision to make.

Upon their arrival among the camps, the sun was beginning to rise in the east. It was the only time the sun could be glimpsed, as it passed between the horizon and the dark clouds of ash. It was beautiful, and it reminded Inara that the sun hadn't been destroyed, but merely hidden.

The masses of refugees who had filled Namdhor's main street were now flooding the camps again. The added foot traffic compounded the chaos of the lower grounds, filling the air with more aromas than Inara could say were pleasant. The atmosphere was tense, as any campsite would be when it was occupied by various cultures, all of whom had been forced into becoming Namdhorians to survive.

Here and there, Inara caught sight of sigils carved or scribed in chalk on tent poles and fabrics. The wolf of Velia and the bear of Grey Stone were more prominent than the stag of Lirian or the horse of Tregaran. The alliance that existed between these people was thin. Bleak was their common ground, considering they were all camped on The White Vale, a mile away from the Namdhorian army and an inevitable battleground.

Both Dragorn kept their hoods up and their eyes averted, hoping to blend through the camp and make it to the elves unseen. There was no hiding their Vi'tari blades, unfortunately. Gideon's Mournblade possessed a hilt of red and gold and was topped with a golden dragon's claw. The hilt of Inara's enchanted blade housed a crystal gifted to her from her grandmother, Queen Adilandra, and was a sight to behold.

More than one person stopped what they were doing to watch the pair walk by, their eyes naturally drawn to the swords. Inara offered kind smiles and friendly nods where she could, her hand resting directly over the crystal.

The elven camp was situated on the outskirts, the farthest point from the lower town of Namdhor. It was also the only patch of ground that had flowers poking through the snow, while even the grass had grown longer and thicker. Rather than feeble tent poles, the elves of Ilythyra had used magic to pull roots from the earth, twisting them into various shapes that could be draped in fabrics.

As messy as the whole campsite was, the elves made it look homely, though Inara wondered if that was the elf in her talking.

The Dragorn were allowed to walk freely through the area, but they were both stopped outside the entrance to the largest tent, in the centre. The elven guards that greeted them were far more regal than any Gold Cloak of Namdhor. Their long, braided hair fell gracefully over their armour, an amalgamation of iron feathers and leaves stained gold and purple. Each had a bow slung over their shoulder and a double-handed scimitar on their hip.

Recognising the Dragorn only required an extra moment before they were shown inside. A fire pit decorated the centre of the tent since there was no pole required for support. The licking flames highlighted Lady Ellöria's sharp features, where she resided beyond the central fire, on a small throne made entirely of roots. A handful of elves surrounded her, dressed in long ethereal robes and furs, none of which were even half as dirty as they should have been given their circumstances.

Their keen gaze fell on Gideon and Inara - judgmental, but not condemning. It was the way of her mother's people, a culture of observers who had time on their side to perfect such a hobby.

Rounding the fire, Inara's parents came into view, beside Vighon and Asher. The ranger had been given fresh clothing and a chance to wash his face, revealing the black tattoo under his left eye, a small fang to Inara's eyes.

From the looks of it, Inara guessed the group had been deep in discussion before their arrival. That was to be expected, of course, for Lady Ellöria was known for being the most well-informed person in all of Illian.

As was dictated by all formality and ceremony, the Dragorn stopped in front of Lady Ellöria and bowed their heads out of respect. Ellöria's interest roamed over Gideon, but her eyes, exquisite orbs of emerald, rested on Inara, her sister's granddaughter.

Ellöria raised her chin. "A shame that such dire circumstances are needed to bring our family together." Her tone was such that Inara found it hard to gauge her sincerity. "Still, you have arrived at the perfect moment. Our new friend, *Asher*, here was about to regale us with a story even older than myself."

Gideon bowed his head again. "Thank you, Lady Ellöria, for the privacy and shelter you offer."

Remaining immaculately still, Ellöria replied, "I only hope, for the sake of the realm, that you can achieve more in here than you could inside that dreadful keep."

"Quite," Gideon agreed. It was clear to Inara that her master was still on edge, his nerves battling with the need to act and the necessity of planning.

A disturbance by the entrance of the tent halted their conversation before it could go any further. Galanör entered first, though the elven ranger was not the source of the disturbance.

"If ye've come *'ere* lookin' for supplies, elf, ye're not goin' to find any that will help ye in Dhenaheim, mark me words." The dwarf was entirely inside the tent by the time he realised where he really was.

Behind him, Russell Maybury's broad shoulders filled the entrance. The tavern owner took in the occupants far quicker than the son of Dorain, his yellow eyes settling promptly on Asher.

"What's all this then?" Doran asked nervously, shifting his girth. Then, he too noticed the old ranger, standing quietly beside the Galfreys, though the dwarf looked rapidly from Asher to Reyna. "Me Lady!"

Ignoring everyone else, the Lady of Ilythyra included, Doran ran over to Reyna and slammed into her with a tight embrace. Inara's mother smiled down at the son of Dorain and wrapped her arm around his blond head.

With glistening eyes, he pulled away and gazed up at her. "I thought ye lost to us, me Lady."

"Fear not, Doran, son of Dorain. I am still here..."

Doran sniffed and tried to hide his emotion. "An' ye!" he barked turning to Asher. "Ye 'ave the audacity to die a hero an' return to lap up the praise! All before windin' up in prison I might add!"

Both rangers held each other in an unwavering stare, the suggestion of violence in their eyes. Then, they both smiled from ear to ear and embraced forearms as old brothers in arms.

Behind the dwarf, Russell Maybury approached Asher. "Is it really you?" he asked, his voice equally gruff.

"Mostly," Asher replied cryptically.

It was enough for Russell. Just as he had done with Doran, Asher reached out and gripped his old friend's forearm and patted his large shoulder.

"You nearly took my head in Lirian," Russell commented.

Asher took a steady breath, his guilt unusually clear to see for once. "I'm—"

Russell held up a hand. "You don't need to apologise," he stated. "It wasn't you, I know. Besides, I would be long dead if it weren't for you."

Galanör cleared his throat and glanced at Lady Ellöria.

Russell stepped back from Asher and bowed his head at the regal elf. "Apologies, my Lady."

Doran appeared more uncomfortable than apologetic. "Aye... What he said." A pointed look from Reyna encouraged him to add, "Apologies for the, eh... *interruption*. My Lady..."

A bemused smile flashed across Lady Ellöria's face so fast that Inara was sure she would have missed it had she blinked. "No apologies required. It will be the few who make a difference in these trying times. And, it pleases me to see such unorthodox alliances..."

"Forgive me," Gideon interjected, looking from Asher to Ellöria. "You have been informed of events thus far, my Lady?"

"I have, disturbing as they are. I would say there is little time to save this realm."

Gideon agreed with the grave statement. "Time the north doesn't have..."

"With that in mind, and our part complete," Ellöria concluded, "perhaps Asher could continue his tale?"

Just as in Yelifer's chamber, Inara noted Asher's reluctance to have everyone's attention on him. It was in his bones to remain unnoticed, to blend in, and become another face in the crowd. Inara didn't envy him for the burden he carried. He had been brought back from the dead to carry a memory that could save the world, when all he deserved was rest.

Asher stepped forward, his usual confidence replaced with awkwardness. "As hard to believe as it is," the ranger began in his usual gruff voice, "The Crow *does* want us to beat the orcs. The world he has envisioned cannot exist with them in it."

"Then why unleash them upon the surface at all?" Ellöria asked.

"The Crow wishes to change the landscape of Illian - what better way to bring about drastic change than war?"

Ellöria glanced at her niece and Nathaniel. "This change... You are speaking of The Black Hand's desires for Alijah?"

Asher nodded once. "As I was saying earlier, The Crow believes Alijah is to become the greatest king the realm has ever seen. He's manipulated events for thousands of years to see him born."

Gideon added, "But The Crow wants a world with only *one* king. The orcs have already seen the realm changed to that effect."

Responding to that, Asher continued, "How Alijah is to become king is beyond me. I only know what Alijah and Malliath know, and The Crow has revealed no details on the matter."

Inara took a second to look at Galanör and Doran, both of whom appeared in complete shock at the news. Doran had the face of a dwarf slapped while Galanör furrowed his brow into one of great anger.

Ellöria narrowed her eyes at the ranger. "You have the memories of Malliath the voiceless... That must be very *insightful*."

Asher gave little away, but Inara guessed he wasn't agreeing with the Lady's assessment. If the headaches and blackouts he complained of were anything to go by, possessing the memories of two other beings was agonisingly intense.

"He may have had several reasons for bringing me back," Asher replied, "but carrying Malliath's memories is the most important."

"Why else would The Crow bring you back?" Ellöria inquired curiously.

Asher hesitated, stealing a glimpse at Gideon. "Malliath was essential in the success of the orcs' invasion. The only one who could oppose him, stopping both Velia and Lirian from falling, was... Gideon. He brought *me* back because Gideon *had* to falter. It was his hesitation to kill me that allowed Malliath to fend off the Dragorn."

"This Crow is a master strategist," Ellöria remarked.

"An easy thing to master when you've seen the future," Reyna commented.

"Indeed," Ellöria agreed. "Please, Ranger, continue."

Asher offered Gideon what could have been an apologetic look before he began again. "Thousands of years ago, during Atilan's time, his kingdom was at war with the first Dragon Riders. From what I can tell, Atilan cared little about the war itself. It was a means to an end. He wanted dragons. He believed the key to immortality lay hidden within them."

"We are aware of this tale," Ellöria cut in again. "Just as we are aware that Atilan... *made* our elven kind."

"Yes, he created elves, but he didn't stop there." Asher paused to nurse his returning headache. "Using the essence of both an elf and a dragon, he made something else entirely."

Doran looked up at him. "It's warmed me heart to see ye again, laddy, but if ye say *dwarves* I'm gonna hit ye."

"No," Asher clarified. "He didn't make dwarves. He made *orcs*..."

Were they in a hall of humans, such a revelation would have set off a wave of mutterings and musings, but the occupants of this particular tent had seen and heard what most couldn't comprehend. Given this particular revelation, however, Inara had to wonder if

Atilan was truly worthy of a divine title; for all the life he had taken, the ancient king had created twice as much.

Reyna moved her hand away from her mouth. "Orcs are part *elf?*"

"And dragon," Asher reiterated.

Inara found such a combination hard to comprehend. "How can two noble creatures produce something so violent?"

"You have seen this?" Ellöria pressed, naturally taking command of the conversation.

"A Dragon Rider saw it, deep within Vengora. Before Atilan killed him, the memory was passed on to the closest dragon; Malliath. He's never shared this with any other dragon. From what I could tell, he didn't much care where the orcs came from... he just enjoyed having something to burn on a new battlefield."

Inara didn't miss the ranger's pointed glance. She couldn't dwell on her brother's bond to Malliath right now, there simply wasn't time.

"You said as much," Vighon pointed out, his confidence climbing these days. "How does this help us to win the war?"

Asher met the northman's question with a simple answer. "Because they can be unmade. Atilan wasn't happy with their creation, so he ensured there was a way to stop them for good."

Reyna didn't look as hopeful as everyone else. "Asher, that was ten thousand years ago. Even if you could find a way inside this *Haren Bain*, there's no assurance that anything is left to glean."

"That's not entirely true," Gideon opined. "We have *The Crow's* assurance."

Nathaniel shook his head with enough vigour to suggest he was ready for another fight. "That is absolutely no assurance. For all we really know, The Crow's planted this whole thing in Asher's mind - a distraction to keep us off the battlefield."

Inara's eyes quickly darted to Gideon, hoping her master would remain calm and not rise to her father's tone - a fight in front of Lady Ellöria would be embarrassing for them all.

"We've feared distraction was his plan before," Gideon countered, his tone even. "So far, The Crow has demonstrated a mutual need to end this war, favouring us no less."

Nathaniel was quick to reply, "Tell that to the thousands that lie dead between The Arid Lands and Namdhor..."

Asher stepped forward, commanding attention and diverting it from the growing argument. "A distraction or not, it doesn't matter if only *I* go to Haren Bain. Though, the weapon itself is guarded by magic, or at least it was. Either way, once we possess the weapon, it is likely a certain amount of magic will be required to wield it. I'm no mage..." he added, looking to Ellöria.

"We stand on the edge of battle," the Lady stated. "Magic will be our greatest ally when the orcs return. I cannot spare my kin, Ranger, neither can the men of Namdhor."

"Wait," Gideon held up a finger, his expression lost in thought. "Did you say Haren Bain was in The Spear, near The Shining Coast?"

"I did," Asher agreed.

Gideon turned to Ellöria. "Have you spoken with Queen Adilandra, my Lady?"

"I have," Ellöria replied, her eyes glancing at the black orb resting on a small podium beside her. "Unfortunately, my sister is still amassing a force capable of rivalling the orcs. Ships are being made ready to set sail from The Opal Coast of Ayda, but I fear they will not reach us in time. However," the elf added, "a vanguard set sail several days ago, a complement of four hundred elves. They are led by the High Guardian, Faylen Haldör..."

Inara noticed a flicker of elation on her mother's face. Seeing her old mentor would likely be a small glimpse of light in what had become very dark days. The Dragorn also noticed Asher's stony expression soften at the sound of Faylen's name.

"I believe," Ellöria continued, glancing at Asher, "that you are all well acquainted with the High Guardian."

Gideon offered a soft smile. "That we are, Lady Ellöria. In part, Faylen is the reason Illian still stands to this day."

Doran scrunched his face and looked from person to person. "Am I missin' somethin'?"

Gideon spoke quickly now, ignoring Doran's question altogether. "If you leave now, Asher, and find your way to the River Adanae in the east, you may yet receive the aid you require. I'm sure Faylen can spare a few from her vanguard to assist you before sending the rest to Namdhor."

"How will they know to meet me?" the ranger asked.

Gideon turned to their host. "If you would be willing, my Lady, I would ask that you contact Faylen and have her divert a small force to meet Asher?"

"Of course," she replied in her melodic voice.

"Thank you." Gideon rested his attention on Inara. "We fight this battle on many fronts; the orcs are but one. The Crow's plans for your brother aside, Alijah must be saved from that hell. Take your parents and find this Bastion in The Vrost Mountains."

Inara was about to protest, believing her place was on the battle-field, beside her master. Gideon, however, shot her a look that requested her patience. For her parents, on the other hand, there was visible relief and no lack of shock on her father's part. Like Gideon, they too were on edge, stuck between the need to act immediately and form a plan that would see them all succeed.

"From there," Gideon continued, "take him to The Lifeless Isles. I think it would be best, given what he's been through, that Alijah is kept away from the war for now. He'll be safe there until we can properly assess him."

"What about The Crow himself?" Reyna posed. "Are we to bring him back for judgement?"

"He won't be there," Asher said confidently. "If the decision has been made to retrieve Alijah, he will already have seen it."

Inara hoped the ranger was wrong, given her predilection for slaying all things evil. "You believe he would flee rather than fight to keep Alijah?"

"The Crow can fight," Asher replied. "But the real problem is his foresight. If you are to rescue Alijah, it's likely part of The Crow's plans for him."

"You're saying it doesn't matter what we do now, my brother is lost to The Crow?"

"It's not losing him to The Crow that worries me," Asher said gravely. "It's Malliath..."

There it was again. That reminder that the most glorious bond possible was going to be her brother's undoing. Inara couldn't believe it, nor was she ready to accept it.

"Nothing is certain," she said, stealing a glance at her parents. "Not where dark magic is concerned..."

In the lull that followed, Gideon took the lead again. "Of course," he said, "we cannot assume The Crow really has our victory in mind. And, regardless of your skills, Asher, it's a long way to The Spear - anything could happen between here and there. So, we will take an extra step to ensure our survival." Gideon turned to look directly at Doran.

"Of what do you speak?" Lady Ellöria asked, curious.

"I have charged Doran, son of *King* Dorain, with travelling back to Dhenaheim. Along with Galanör and Russell, they will hunt down a living orc and take it back to the dwarf lords as proof. I'm hoping this will enrage Dhenaheim enough to take action."

Doran pulled a face and muttered, "It'll be the last ye see o' us..."

Ellöria didn't appear impressed. "You are *inviting* dwarves into Illian, Master Thorn? Enraged ones at that. Such a thing is dangerous. Once they are through Vengora, they may decide to stay..."

"Bah! Illian holds nothin' me kin would be interested in. Too damned flat! It's a thousand miles before ye hit The Undyin' Mountains an' they're not worth the trek."

Ellöria looked down on the son of Dorain in more ways than one. "Mountains or not, Prince Doran, land is land and with it comes power - something your kin *do* value, I believe."

Gideon raised his hand to Doran before the dwarf could continue the argument. "We have neither the time to debate this nor a choice with which to replace it. The orcs have faced us once; they *will* adapt. Whatever they attack us with next, it will come at a heavy price for Namdhor. We need the armies of Dhenaheim, just as your people did during The Great War."

Lady Ellöria had no reply, which, in itself, was a reply of sorts.

In the silence that followed, Inara asked Gideon, "If we're going to The Vrost Mountains, Asher's going to The Spear, and they are going to Dhenaheim, what will *you* do?"

Gideon heard the question but decided to address the whole tent with his answer. "Inara and I were delayed because Thraden suffers, a result of Arathor's torment at the hands of the orcs. I will not allow his torment to continue. I'm going into Vengora, to find him. Ilargo will remain close to Namdhor, in case of an attack."

That was perhaps the stupidest thing she had ever heard her master say. "You're going into Vengora alone?" she fumed, beating her mother to the same question.

"All of our paths are dangerous," Gideon pointed out. "But they're also necessary."

Inara had no response to that. Of course he was right, he usually was. If she wasn't going to argue that Asher was travelling into Vengora alone then she shouldn't openly cast doubt on her master's survival, though The Spear was miles away from the orcs. Still, it wasn't something to say in front of the others.

Lady Ellöria rose from her wooden throne. "We will help with whatever supplies you all require. If we do not already possess it, I can assure you we have the means to procure it."

With her final words, they began to file out of the tent, each charged with a grave errand. All except for Vighon, who pushed ahead to reach Asher.

"I'm coming with *you*," he insisted.

Asher cast unimpressed eyes on the northman. "I'm quicker on my own."

"You won't be on your own," Vighon countered. "My father will send Ironsworn after you."

"Your *father* won't even know I've left Namdhor, never mind which direction I take. Besides," the ranger added, "I can take care of myself."

"There's more than just Ironsworn to look out for. It's some distance between here and The Spear. Gideon said it himself," the northman argued, gesturing to the Master Dragorn, "anything could happen between here and there. Your mission is perhaps the most important; it can't be left to just one man."

"He's right," Inara agreed. "Though I would suggest another goes in your place, Vighon."

The northman blinked falling snow out of his eyes and frowned. "Why?" he demanded.

"You are a captain of Namdhor now, a prince too—"

Vighon waved her words away. "I don't care about titles."

Inara paused, distracted as she watched Gideon walk away, his strides purposeful. "It doesn't change the fact that you are the son of the most powerful man in the world right now. If you leave, how many more Ironsworn will he send after you both?"

"I'm not leading another one of my father's suicidal strategies to fight the orcs, Inara. This war needs ending so there *are* no more frontlines. No more battlefields. Go and save Alijah, *please*."

Inara could see the personal battle that raged within Vighon just as it did her. They were both torn between Alijah and the war, their love and duty colliding endlessly. She finally relented with a short nod and looked to Asher, who couldn't appear more bored by their brief conversation.

"Fine," he said. "Keep up or fall behind; either way I'm not carrying you."

"We can't go yet," the northman blurted.

Asher stopped himself from taking another step, glancing from Inara to Vighon. "You heard what was said in there, yes? We need to leave, *now*."

"It's a long journey," Vighon pointed out again. "It would be folly to leave without supplies."

"I'm a ranger, boy, I live off the land."

"I'm not a *boy*," Vighon retorted, "and *you* have no horse, no sword, and apparently nothing between your ears. We get supplies. I'll use my rank to take a couple of horses, and we *both* need to find a sword each."

Asher folded his arms and sighed. "Make sure the horses are fast."

Inara wanted to help them all, but she was happy having nothing to do with this particular pairing; they were likely to kill each other before they even found Haren Bain.

Seeing Gideon disappearing, Inara planted a heavy hand on Vighon's shoulder. "I'll leave you two to get better acquainted."

Without actually running, the young Dragorn hurried to catch up with her master, weaving between the elves and their tents.

"Master?" she called, halting her stride to allow a pair of elves past. "Gideon?" she tried again, just as he re-entered the larger camp.

"You're either going to lambaste me about going into Vengora alone or shout at me for ordering you away from the battlefield. Let's assume it's *both*, then I *ignore* both, and we move on with what needs to be done."

"Well," Inara began, her tone dripping with sarcasm already, "that would skip out my part and I was rather looking forward to it."

Gideon maintained his stride. "I brought Arathor here. I won't leave him to die in there, Inara. Lady Ellöria and the elves of Ilythyra are here to assist the Namdhorians should the orcs attack before I return. And, of course, Ilargo won't be following me into the mountains."

"I fear you going behind enemy lines given your... disadvantage." Inara didn't want to say it but now that she knew it haunted her.

The Master Dragorn gave Inara a sidelong look. "My magic has been such for thirty years; I've got by just fine. And, until I told you as much, you've never worried about my capabilities before."

"Yes, but then you started talking to me about dying with

everyone on the battlefield and sending me away to lead the Dragorn in some far-off land."

Gideon finally halted and turned to Inara. "I don't have a death wish. We survived a battle I didn't think we could and... I can't believe I'm saying this: the fact that The Crow wants us to win means we probably will. There's some twisted hope in that."

Inara agreed, but she couldn't help but wonder at what cost. What would come after the war was hard to contemplate when they were still stuck in the middle of it and so many lives were at stake. Inara had a sinking feeling in her gut that their victory would come with a sour taste...

"I was going to leave for The Bastion," Inara stated. "Regardless of what you might order me to do."

"I know," Gideon nodded, a smile daring to creep up his face. "This way I get to look like I'm still *some* kind of Master Dragorn." With that, he turned to continue his journey back to Ilargo.

Remaining where she stood, Inara called, "What am to do after I reach The Lifeless Isles? What should I do with Alijah?"

Gideon spun on his heel and walked backwards a few steps. "You're a master on the Dragorn Council now but, more than that, you're his sister. You'll know what to do..." With that, he spun back around and disappeared into the camp.

In the chaos that had taken over their lives, Inara had barely had a chance to think about her elevation to the council. She spared a thought for Ayana and Alastir, hoping against all the odds that one had found the other and both were already on their return journey to Namdhor.

Turning back around, Inara was faced by her parents, both attired in hooded cloaks. "We will find the supplies," her mother offered. "We'll take things for Alijah too."

That was incredibly hopeful of her, but Inara wasn't going to bring her down with a heavy dose of reality. "The Bastion will be guarded by The Black Hand at the very least," she said instead. "Are you ready for a fight?"

Her father puffed out his chest slightly, his hand gripping the hilt of his sword. "I would bring that place down brick by brick with my bare hands if meant saving Alijah... you too."

It was the answer she expected, but Inara was more concerned with her mother. "You haven't long been on your feet," she observed.

Reyna glanced to the east. "Between here and The Vrost Mountains, I don't expect to be on my feet at all. Plenty of rest before we get there." Both of her statements were delivered with a tone of finality - she wasn't to be questioned again.

Inara noted the black bow slung over her mother's shoulder. Enchanted as it was, the bow possessed enough power to bring down mountains, a weapon the Dragorn was thankful her mother wielded. There was the question, however, of her strength to pull back the string.

Athis's calming voice sent waves of confidence through her. *We will keep them safe, wingless one.*

Inara smiled, confusing her parents, before she gave them both a crushing hug. "Let's put our family back together..."

CHAPTER 12
PARTING WAYS

The trek back up to The Dragon Keep had been arduous, claiming what little patience Vighon had left when it came to removing his various pieces of armour. Doing his best, Ruban moved around the northman, studiously untying knots and ceremoniously placing the armour on a mannequin.

Rooted to the spot as he was, Vighon considered his chamber, a room he felt was hardly his. It still had the aroma of herbs and healing elixirs, left over from Reyna's recovery, muddy footprints, dried blood, and empty tankards - mostly piled in the corner Doran had staked. This was the first room he could call his own in some time and he hated it now. It had only been bearable when filled with his friends.

Still, it would only be his until he next walked out of the door...

It was too late. He shouldn't have thought about friends. His mind should have been going over his plan, working through his movements, and potential obstacles. Now, he was thinking about Alijah...

His best friend had been confirmed alive, but at what cost? The Bastion sounded like hell, a hell his friend had endured without him by his side. They had faced everything together, even as children. Now, Alijah was in the dark, surrounded by enemies, and at the mercy of The Crow.

Alijah as king wasn't the most outlandish idea Vighon had ever heard - the half-elf certainly had the potential in there somewhere, hidden beneath him that dominated his every action. But it wasn't Alijah The Crow wanted on the throne... From Asher's description, he wanted something else entirely.

The thought of not going to The Bastion with the Galfreys was close to physical pain for the northman. He wanted to kill every dark mage in The Black Hand and cut off The Crow's head himself.

He wanted to save his friend...

Like so many times during this war, Vighon felt the weight of so much more than his own life, or even the life of another. He felt the weight of them all. He had lived on the streets, survived off scraps and luck alone, and now he saw so many others doing just that in Namdhor's alleys and hovels. They deserved better, to be picked up, and given a better world to live in.

None of that could be achieved with the orcs at their door. Alijah had some of the most powerful people in Verda coming for him, people who would do anything to see him safe. Alijah himself was tough; Vighon just hoped he was resilient enough to keep The Crow out of his head.

It was hard to accept, but he wasn't going to Alijah's aid. It simply wasn't where he was needed. He hoped Alijah could forgive him...

The last piece finally removed, Vighon busied himself with stretching his limbs, enjoying the freedom that came with only the weight of his unencumbered limbs. He was sure that armour would be the death of him if he continued to wear it.

Ruban noticed the thin piece of parchment on the table. "These supplies are fit for a journey," he observed.

"Oh, yes. I need you to get everything on it. And another horse," he added lightly, despite the trouble it would take to acquire a spare horse. "When you've got everything, divide them up between both saddles - feel free to make mine the lighter one. The stable master might give you some grief acquiring the extra horse so..." Vighon had to take a breath before his next words. "So, tell him the *prince* demands it."

Vighon paused as something caught his eye. Standing upright, resting against a large chest, was Alijah's silvyr short-sword. No, he corrected himself; it wasn't really Alijah's. That short-sword had belonged to Asher since before either of them were born.

The northman crossed the room and picked it up in its sheath. "Strap that to the heavier horse too," he instructed his squire.

Ruban accepted the blade, but his focus remained on the list of supplies. "If we are travelling to the frontlines, Captain, the army has supplies enough."

Vighon eyed his squire. "I'm not going to the frontlines, Ruban. And neither are you."

Ruban glanced at the list again. "I don't... I don't understand..."

The northman placed both hands on the squire's shoulders. "After this last errand, you are free of my service. Stay within the city, help where you can and make coin where you can. Just stay off The White Vale."

Ruban shook his head of thick, curly dark hair. "My place is by your side, Captain."

A sudden knock at the door halted their conversation, but Vighon knew who it was. "I'm not a captain anymore," he told the bewildered squire. "Enter!"

Commander Garrett stepped into the room with his helmet tucked under his arm. His receding hairline was all the more obvious when dampened under sweat and melted snow. The bottom of his golden cloak was caked in mud and blood to match his stained white armour.

"You sent for me, Captain."

Vighon beckoned him further into the room as he went about changing his shirt. His chest and ribs were marred with dark bruises and stinging cuts, all of which detracted from his physique. Not that his looks mattered anymore; he couldn't remember the last time he'd tried to impress a woman. He had always held a place in his heart for Inara, a love that could never be...

"How are the men?" Vighon asked.

"They grieve for those we lost but, considering everything they've been through, their spirits are high. Defending the city in the army's absence has earned the Skids something they thought unattainable: respect."

At last, something made Vighon smile. "That's good," he said, truly meaning it. "Given the Skids' superior understanding of Namdhor's defences, they are to remain in the city and keep the people safe. There's no guarantee that the battle to come will be contained on The White Vale."

Garrett nodded once. "As you command, Captain. Though, I believe General Morkas intends to order us to the front - they're about to begin the bombardment on the tree line."

Vighon looked at Ruban and gestured to his dark leather armour, discarded in a corner. The squire understood immediately and went about preparing it for the northman.

"Garrett," he said seriously. "Keep the men here."

The commander narrowed his eyes. "Captain?"

"No matter how many orders you receive, no matter who gives them... keep the men *here*. My father's plans will see us suffer heavy losses if not outright defeat. It's going to be a bloodbath down there. Keep the men here and keep the people safe. They are what matters most."

Garrett's eyes quickly roamed over the room, noting Ruban's attentiveness towards Vighon's leathers and the abandoned captain's armour. "What's happening here?" the commander asked.

Vighon smiled again and turned to retrieve his golden cloak, emblazoned with the lion sigil. "It won't be long before Arlon has this replaced as well. Until then, wear it with pride, the armour too."

The northman handed Garrett the cloak and rapped his old chest piece with his knuckle. "*Captain* Garrett... Sounds good."

The commander appeared lost for words as he stared at the golden cloak in his hands. "You're making me captain? But..." Garrett looked at Ruban again. "What are you doing?"

The answer to that was far more complicated than Vighon would have liked, not to mention lengthy, and time was still against him. "There might be a way to end all of this, for *good*," he added.

"You're leaving?" Garrett shot back.

"Throwing soldiers at the orcs isn't going to win this war," Vighon pointed out. "If there's another way, I *have* to find it."

Garrett had no reply to that. He looked away, considering, Vighon hoped, the logic in his rationale for leaving, regardless of how vague it was.

"I would be wrong to call you a coward," Garrett finally said. "And I know you would see this war brought to a swift end. Your father won't be happy," he offered with a sly smirk.

Vighon mirrored him. "I'm hoping so."

"When are you leaving?" the new captain enquired.

Vighon turned around to see Ruban dusting off the black fur that would drape over his dark cloak. "Right now," he answered. "Try and keep him out of trouble," he added, nodding at the squire.

"I could come with you?" Ruban blurted.

Vighon shook his head. "Where I'm going isn't much safer than here. Besides, you've never left Namdhor in your life and I've got quite the journey ahead of me."

"I won't slow you down," the squire tried again.

"I'd be lucky if that's all you did," Vighon retorted. "You're staying here and getting me those supplies. *Now*." Once the squire had left the chamber, the northman turned his attention back to Garrett. "Do you know where my father is right now?"

The new captain tore his eyes from the silver armour. "Sir Borin is standing outside your father's bedchamber, so he must be inside."

"In a meeting?" Vighon probed.

Garrett's mouth twisted into amusement. "Of sorts. Judging by the noises I heard, I would say it is quite a successful meeting."

Vighon rolled his eyes - it was mid-morning! The man had just walked away from his predecessor's funeral and decreed orders of war. As it happened, however, this particular meeting worked in the northman's favour.

He placed a heavy hand on Garrett's shoulder. "In my absence, your orders are simple: stay alive. If you can, keep everyone else alive while you're at it..."

Garrett raised his chin. "And since you are no longer a captain of Namdhor and you denounce your title as prince, *I* shall give *you* an order, Vighon Draqaro. Come back to us, *soon*."

IN THE BRACING air of the north, Vighon looked down from the quiet rampart to the small balcony that belonged to his father's room. Thanks to the clear-up required after the queen's funeral, combined with the army's advance on The White Vale, the ramparts were relatively unmanned.

Vighon had given a couple of patrols an assertive nod to go along with his meaningful stride. Alijah had always told him; act as if you belong somewhere and no one will ever challenge you. Well, he might not be in his armour anymore, but his face hadn't changed. The men had nodded back and now he stood overlooking his father's balcony.

The drop down wasn't too far, though even if it had required him to climb down, it still would have been preferable to confronting Sir Borin the Dread.

Hanging by his fingers, Vighon let go and dropped into a crouch to absorb the sound of his fall. He waited for a moment by the balcony doors, hoping he wouldn't have to abandon his plan before it really got started.

Carefully, with delicate fingers, the northman eased one of the doors open a crack. It didn't creak, but the sound that came out of the room would have drowned it out anyway. It wasn't the first time he had heard his father with a woman, or women in this case, but it didn't make hearing it any easier.

He had to sneak inside quickly, before the wind caused a stir within the warm room. He waited again beside the heavy curtain, using it as cover. There was no change to the carnal sounds coming from Arlon's side of the room. Thankfully, for what little there was to be thankful for, his father's bed was nestled inside an alcove on the other side of the room, out of sight.

With wary steps, Vighon entered the room proper. A cursory scan of the chamber was all that was needed to find what he was risking so much for.

The sword of the north!

Across the room, sheathed in a dark red scabbard, the exquisite blade was displayed horizontally on a stand. Arlon had seen to the sword's polish if the shining pommel was anything to go by. The roaring lion's head was a symbol of times soon to be long forgotten if the king had his way. Reform was coming for Namdhor, whether it liked it or not, and it was coming under the sigil of The Ironsworn.

Vighon took light steps to reach the sword. He gripped the black hilt and pulled the blade out an inch so that he might lay eyes on the silvyr. It was as beautiful as it was deadly and entirely wasted on a king who only wore it ceremoniously while others died by his command. Besides, Queen Yelifer had gifted it to the northman - it was *his*.

As quietly as he could, Vighon strapped the sword to his belt and turned to leave. He hesitated by the balcony door. Desperate as he was to get as far away from the sounds coming from his father's bed, he couldn't help but wonder what good could be done if he walked into the alcove and slew the vicious king of Namdhor before he doomed them all.

Vighon looked down at the sword on his hip. It would be so easy. Arlon was unarmed and naked to boot - he was defenceless. The northman knew in his heart, however, that he couldn't kill a man in cold blood, regardless of the hatred he harboured for his father and tormentor. Killing Arlon would make him no different from any of The Ironsworn; then his father really would have won.

Then, there was his own execution to think about. Crowned or not, killing Arlon Draqaro would result in his hanging - after a lengthy one on one time with Godfrey Cross no doubt.

Vighon quickly and quietly extracted himself from the chamber before his thoughts could turn dark again. After climbing back up to the ramparts, the northman used his cloak to hide the distinct pommel of what most would assume was a stolen sword. Along with his concealment, he struggled to balance his casual walk with the haste that propelled him. How long did he really have before Arlon discovered the sword was gone?

The same guards he had walked past earlier gave him a suspicious look, but Vighon maintained his confident eye contact and nodded his greetings. Neither of them were Ironsworn, thankfully, and he managed to descend the steps into the courtyard without incident.

The queen's funeral pyre was still being cleared by a small army of servants. Busy was good. He blended into the hubbub of activity and made his way to the far side, where Ruban was tending to a pair of horses.

"You made quick work of that list," Vighon remarked by way of a compliment.

Ruban cast a paranoid eye about. "The Dragon Keep has been stocked to bursting, Captain."

Of course it has, Vighon thought. Only Arlon would horde all the food and water while his people survived off scraps.

"After I ride out of that gate, you don't need to call me captain anymore." Vighon inspected Ness, his horse, and was happy to see the squire had strapped his enchanted shield to the side. A cursory glance over Asher's steed showed its saddlebags to be well filled.

"You will come back, won't you?"

Vighon mounted Ness and took Asher's horse by the reins. "If I don't, gather whoever you can and travel to The Shining Coast. Find a fishing town, anywhere that still has a boat worth sailing. Head east, to Ayda, and don't come back."

By the expression on Ruban's face, it was clear that he had not given the answer he wanted, but it was the only answer Vighon had. If he didn't return it was because he was dead, an ending not worth dwelling on with so much in the balance.

Vighon wanted to say something else, something that would lift the young man's spirits, but there wasn't time. Any minute now, Arlon and his unnatural brute of a bodyguard would come storming out of the keep.

"Just live, Ruban," he said, spurring his horse on. "Just live..."

The northman didn't look back as he guided both horses down Namdhor's vast slope. He navigated the people, who were doing their best to carry on with their lives, and the soldiers who continued to work on the city's defences. He eventually passed The Raucously Ruckus and hoped that they would all return one day to enjoy a drink together, Alijah included.

Weaving through the sprawling campsite was a far harder task, especially astride a horse with another one in tow. He looked down at the children running between the tents, playing and laughing as if nothing was ever going to change. But he could see the worry on mothers' faces and defeat on the elderly's, all of whom had the wisdom to know when death was prowling. There were few men among them, with most conscripted into the army to help with everything from filling the ranks to the movement of supplies.

A lot of those men wouldn't make it back to their families. It was a sobering and harrowing thought, but inescapable all the same. These people needed something, someone to show them that everything was going to be alright. There was no such person. Their new ruler cared for naught but power itself and the Dragorn were so few in number that the protection that felt synonymous with their name was notably absent.

And what could he do? A single moment of introspection told Vighon that he was just a man. He didn't have Asher's experience or training, he didn't have Alijah's elven heritage, and he didn't have a dragon by his side, nor their wisdom. He was just a man trying to do the right thing in a world that seemed to punish such behaviour.

These thoughts were put aside when he finally reached the elven camp. Ignoring the large tent in the centre, Vighon continued to the eastern edge of their camp, where his friends and companions were readying themselves for their separate journeys.

Asher walked towards him. "I was about to leave without you."

Given Vighon's mood, that simple comment was enough to get his back up. "And travel on foot? Perhaps from here on out, I should make the decisions..."

Asher had no reply. Instead, the ranger inspected his horse and the saddlebags. If he was dissatisfied he said nothing.

"Look under there." Vighon gestured to the blanket on the back of the horse.

The ranger pulled back the blanket and found his old short-sword. Again, he said nothing. Asher stared at the hilt for some time, taken back, perhaps, to memories of old. The slightest flicker of emotion crossed his stubbled face and Vighon wondered if he was about to reject the magnificent blade.

"You should have it," Nathaniel said, walking up behind Asher. "Alijah took it in a moment of rebellion; he's always favoured the bow."

"Which he stole as well," Vighon added, unhelpfully. Seeing the look Nathaniel sent his way, the northman decided to get off his horse and busy himself with his own saddlebags.

"I can't believe you kept them all these years," Asher said to Nathaniel. "You could get a small fortune for the blade alone."

"They were all we had left of you," the old Graycoat revealed. "It was an honour to have something left of the man who saved the world..."

Vighon couldn't see either of the men's faces on the other side of

Ness and he was glad of it. Instead, he mindlessly fiddled with the straps on his bags, listening to the awkward exchange.

"I'm sorry about Alijah," Asher agonised. "Of course you should go to him." There was a moment of silence between them before the ranger continued. "I've seen inside of him. For all The Crow's twisted plans, there's a part of Alijah he'll never be able to break. His love for—"

Nathaniel stepped forward and embraced Asher with both arms. "I'm glad you're back, old friend." The knight stepped back from the ranger. "Don't die again. Come back so you can share a drink with Alijah and me. We'll start again when this war is over."

"I... I would like that," Asher replied.

As true as that might have been, Vighon could hear the strain in his voice, the reluctance to believe that such a thing would ever happen. Be it his own death or his belief that Alijah couldn't be saved from The Crow, Vighon hoped both were wrong.

Reyna approached the two men with a bundle in her arms and a sword resting across the top. Vighon had been passively listening, but now he was interested, and so he moved around Ness to better see.

"Your journey is long," the ambassador began. "Not something you are unaccustomed to. But a ranger must be equipped," she added with the hint of a smile.

Asher took the bundle and the sword, examining the pommel with its short stumpy spikes. Vighon had last seen Asher wielding that sword on The White Vale, during his fight with Gideon. He had also seen rows of them in The Pick-Axe, back in Lirian. Apparently, Asher was quite particular about the sword he wielded.

"Thank you," he said simply.

Reyna looked at the bundle in the ranger's arms. "There's more. It's not the same shade of green I remember, but I think it will do. Elven made."

Asher unravelled the green cloak and suppressed his grin.

"Thank you," he said again. "You... You didn't need to do... I really don't deserve any of this, especially from either of you."

"This isn't the return any of us would have wanted for you," Reyna explained, "but you *have* returned, somehow, against all the odds and the heavens above. That *is* worth something, more, in fact. But these simple tokens are all we have to offer. As Nathaniel said, we shall start over when this is all done."

Asher nodded along, his lips tight. "Tell Inara to find the tops of The Vrost Mountains, starting in the west, and follow them east. Follow them and you *will* find The Bastion. I truly hope you can save him."

Nathaniel tensed up but maintained his soft gaze. "We will. You just make sure you return from Haren Bain."

"With Vighon," Reyna added with a smile at the northman.

"Don't worry," Vighon replied playfully, "if his knees give out I'll carry him back."

The northman would have said that Asher threw him a scowl, but it seemed to him that the ranger was always scowling. Either way, he turned from the three of them to greet Galanör, who was similarly seeing to the supplies on his horse. Russell Maybury was looking over the cart that was attached to his horse, easily the largest mount among those assembled. Doran was paying particular attention to the branded bottles of ale and mead hanging off the saddle of his Warhog.

"You're going to go into the land of the dwarves then," Vighon observed. "I thought you were *my* shadow these days?"

Galanör glanced at his companions before turning to face the northman. "I would say you have outgrown this shadow. Besides, my skills are required for this task." The elf's eyes roamed over Asher in the distance. "I would be redundant on yours."

That surprised Vighon. "You would compare his skill to yours? He's an old man!"

Galanör offered him a knowing smile. "You will see."

Vighon wasn't close to being convinced. He had seen the ranger dispatch a few soldiers with enviable skill and speed, but after a long journey, attired in armoured leathers as he now was, the old man in him would emerge no doubt.

"I see you have acquired a new sword," the elf remarked.

The northman felt conscious of the blade, but he banished such feelings. "It was gifted to me by a queen and stolen by a king. Neither were fit to use it. I'm just making sure it serves the north..."

Galanör held his hands up. "You don't have to explain yourself to me. I think it looks better on your belt than your father's."

"It'll look better in the belly of an orc," Vighon opined.

Galanör's tone turned grave. "You won't find orcs where you're going. The Vengoran mountains that embrace The Spear are home to monsters of their own - there's a reason the dwarves of old never conquered the other side of The Iron Valley."

"Do I detect a hint of fear in your voice, Galanör?"

Doran Heavybelly's stout form strode between them. "Ye'll detect me foot up yer arse if ye don' get out o' me way, boy!" The dwarf went on to rummage through the crate at Galanör's feet. "Do yerself a favour, laddy; listen to Asher. That *old man* knows more than ye do an' he packs a meaner swing too." He pulled out one last bottle of ale, Hobgobbers by the look of the label. "Found ye!" Doran declared with triumph. "Right! I'm ready to go!"

With visible discomfort, Galanör watched the son of Dorain walk away. "In all my days," he said to Vighon, "I've never travelled with a dwarf. I'm sure it will prove to be... *interesting*."

Just the thought of it made Vighon laugh. "Make sure you return to tell me all about it."

"And you," Galanör replied.

Elf and man locked forearms before pulling each other in for a brief hug. It was the last friendship Vighon had expected to make, especially given his feelings towards Galanör upon their first meeting. Yet, here he was, uneasy about parting ways with him.

Vighon eventually walked away from the elf and found the last person he needed to say farewell to. Inara Galfrey, a vision regardless of the mud and grime that gripped to her, stood away from the others, her eyes set adrift to the north. Her concern for Gideon was evident.

Without a word, the northman stepped in beside her and looked upon the mountains. "He'll be fine. He's *Gideon Thorn*, after all. The orcs should be worried about being trapped in the mountain with *him*, not the other way around. I know I wouldn't want to come between him and whatever he——"

"You've come to say goodbye?" Inara interrupted.

His reassurance cut off, Vighon lost his flow and scratched his head. "Everyone is saying goodbye," he answered, motioning to the others. "It's like we know we're not all going to make it..."

Inara turned to him. "After all you've survived, I thought you'd believe anything was possible."

"Well, you're going to face The Black Hand, they're going to hunt orcs and seek out a bunch of angry dwarves, Gideon's going behind enemy lines, and we're going into the darkest depths of The Spear to find a place that hasn't been seen in ten thousand years. I'd say we're against it this time."

Inara shrugged. "We've been against it before. This is just another day."

Vighon grinned but kept his laugh to himself. "I could do with a day off."

The Dragorn shared his grin. "We *will* see each other again, Vighon Draqaro."

The northman was cast back to his youth, when Inara had said those words before. On the night before she left for The Lifeless Isles, such a promise had been made, a promise that wasn't fulfilled for over ten years. In that time, they had become different people, or at least Inara had. Anything he felt for her wasn't reciprocated anymore, her own heart given to Athis.

"Whether I make it back or not, just make sure the world has Inara Galfrey looking out for it." Vighon made to leave the young Dragorn when she gripped him by the hand, holding him in place.

"I *am* sorry that nothing... *more* could ever exist between us. In another life, I think we would have been very happy together. In this life, though, I would like us to be good friends."

It still ached to hear that nothing romantic could ever exist between them, and as painful as nothing more than a friendship would be, Vighon couldn't say no.

"Being counted among your friends is an honour," he replied honestly.

Along with her entourage, Lady Ellöria emerged from the central tent, layered in warm furs that swallowed her slight frame. A private conversation was held between the Lady and Reyna, aunt and niece. They touched foreheads before Ellöria moved on to Nathaniel and finally Inara.

"The bloodlines that run through our family have forever proven strong," she said to the Dragorn. "Many times have we stood the line that keeps the darkness back. We will remain in Namdhor and do what we can, but I would ask that you do no more than listen to yourself. You have the strength and wisdom to know what is right. Listen to yourself..."

Vighon could see that Inara was taking it all in and, perhaps, finding the Lady's encouragement overwhelming. Without a word, the Dragorn nodded her understanding, closed her eyes, and let her great aunt pull her in for an embrace. The northman couldn't say he really understood what had transpired.

"And you..." Surprisingly, Ellöria turned to Vighon. "I would presume your bloodline has forever proven corrupt, prone to greed, and cruelty."

Vighon couldn't disagree, but it didn't sound very nice to hear. It felt natural to protest, despite his father being living proof, but Ellöria wasn't finished.

"When our bloodlines fall to weakness, it takes but one individual to *break* that line." Ellöria glanced at Reyna, who had famously stood defiant in the face of her father's plan to invade

Illian. "Do you have the strength, Vighon Draqaro, to break your line?"

Before the northman could flounder with any kind of reply, Ellöria walked away, leaving Vighon to dwell on the profound question.

Standing before Galanör, the Lady of Ilythyra spoke softly. "Your family lost its greatest treasure when you chose to remain in Illian. The people of this realm do not know you, nor will they ever thank you for your service. But I will." Ellöria touched the pommel of Stormweaver. "I have no steel to spare and nor would you need it. I have no magic to give that you don't already harness yourself. I'm afraid all I can offer is this..." She took Galanör's face with both hands and pulled his head down, where she gently kissed his forehead.

The elven ranger had the look of a man blessed by the gods. "That is gift enough for a lifetime, my Lady."

Doran shifted nervously as Ellöria paused in front of him. "I like you, dwarf."

The son of Dorain stumbled over his reply. "Thank... erm, thank you, me Lady."

Stopping Russell from his inspection of the cart, Ellöria had words for him also. "The curse that holds you in its grip has no cure but the relief of death itself. Before such relief takes you, I thank you for turning that curse on our enemies."

Keeping his unnatural yellow eyes averted, Russell thanked the elf with a mumble that only she could hear.

A curt smile and the elf glided away to greet Asher. The ranger cut quite the figure now, attired in brown leathers and his new green cloak. Over his shoulder, the hilt of his silvyr short-sword could be seen, a formidable weapon. On his waist hung the two-handed broadsword - a monster killer of a blade.

Both man and elf stood in silence as the Lady tilted her head and took him in from head to toe.

"Outlander, assassin, ranger... *hero*. You have possessed many names and lived many lives. We are similar in age, yet you are just a man. You fought and defeated Valanis, yet you are just a man. You left this world and returned, yet... you are just a *man*. It seems you have spent your entire life proving that being one thing does not mean it can't be another. This realm faces a war it should rightly lose. Prove to us now that you still live to unbalance the scales of fate."

Stoic as ever, Asher replied with a bow of his head. Satisfied, Lady Ellöria re-joined her entourage, ready to watch them all depart.

Astride his horse once more, Vighon trotted over to Asher, their direction east. Galanör, Doran, and Russell mounted their horses and Warhog and turned to the north. The Galfreys turned to the south, where Athis was waiting for them at the distant tree line.

A final look and a nod between them was all that remained. They each had their own task to complete, they each faced death, and the realm was relying on all of them, even if it didn't know it.

Vighon gripped the hilt of his silvyr sword and looked back at Namdhor. It was a corrupted city, but it stood for something so much more now. He hoped he would see it again...

PART TWO

CHAPTER 13

WITH GREAT POWER COMES A GREAT PRICE

O ut of space and time, Alijah Galfrey slumbered in a deep and dark place. His mind was black, absent of thought and dream, an empty tomb. Only when he woke did he realise what had been missing from his sleep...

Malliath.

The half-elf ached for the bond, its absence noted all the more when he rose. He longed to close his eyes and fall into the dragon's mind like an endless well. It made him feel whole, strong, invincible even.

Now, he was dragged from his corner on the floor and hefted to his feet by rough hands. There had been no contact with Malliath, no comfort or encouragement. He was alone.

The Reavers pushed him into the middle of the cell and began fixing manacles to his wrists, the chains passing through a series of rings bolted to the ceiling. It wasn't the first time he had gone through this and he had learned to accept it rather than fight. Out of sight, another Reaver pulled on the chains, yanking Alijah off his feet and suspending him in the air.

As always, this was when The Crow stepped into view. Since the necromancer rarely left the cell, he had forgone his usual thick collar of black feathers and was stripped down to his waist. There wasn't a bone in his torso that Alijah couldn't identify, though much of his skin was a patchwork of scars.

Bony hands and long fingernails grasped his wand, stolen eons ago from the one who gave him so many scars. Alijah's eyes twitched nervously from the tip of that wand to the floor, careful to conceal the fear that tried desperately to grip him.

"It's hard, I know," The Crow said. "When the mind is aware that pain is imminent it begins to panic. Out of that panic comes irrational thought. A king cannot afford to make such errors. Your mind must be clear at all times, even when you know it will hurt. There will be times when pain wracks your body and torment claws at your thoughts."

The Crow took a breath before plunging his wand into Alijah's side. An explosion of worms could be seen writhing under the surface of his skin, each one carrying excruciating pain. The half-elf cried out but once before he gritted his teeth and took rapid breaths. His eyes bulged and another layer of sweat began to emerge across his skin.

After what felt like a lifetime, The Crow removed the tip of his wand and the pain vanished. "This is an experience you and I share. The same was done to me, though I was much younger than you are now. My master would torture me for naught but the fun of it." The wizard leaned in. "I do not do this for fun. Every moment of agony is a moment of instruction, a lesson that will stay with you for all time."

The Crow pressed his wand to Alijah's skin again, this time over his spine. The pain was worse and he quickly lost feeling in his feet from shaking so much. A feral groan escaped his lips, but pain was quickly becoming a familiar acquaintance and he kept any screams to himself.

"What is the first lesson?" The Crow demanded.

Alijah found his focus through the pain. "Men may die, kingdoms may rise and fall, but an idea... lives on."

"Yes," The Crow purred. "Peace! You will be the embodiment of that idea." The wand twisted and the pain spread across his ribs. "The second lesson?"

Alijah fought to unclamp his jaw. "Heroes die," he blurted.

"That they do," The Crow agreed. "The world has seen enough heroes rise to stand up to evil. What have they accomplished? Fleeting moments of peace. No. You will be something more than a hero, something lasting. The third lesson?"

"Sacrifice without hesitation." Alijah almost choked on the last word but ended up biting his lip instead.

"The life of a true king is not one of banquets and balls. You will have to choose between life and death for your subjects, knowing that every choice can be the spark of rebellion and the beginning of war. If the arm is infected, you cut it off to save the body; never forget that." The Crow tilted his head but kept his cold eyes on Alijah's. "The fourth lesson?"

Alijah gasped as the wand was taken away, giving him a few seconds of reprieve. "Fear is not real; it is simply—" The next word turned into a yell as the wand found his chest and unleashed fire in his veins.

"Focus," the wizard hissed.

The half-elf dug deep and found his reserves. "Fear is not real; it is simply a product of the mind. Danger is real."

"Fear has its place," The Crow instructed. "Use it or discard it. Either way; do not let it control you or your actions. Your every word will affect the lives of thousands. The fifth lesson?"

Alijah could only just hear The Crow's words over the throbbing of blood in his ears and the rattle of his chains. "Love... gives you the strength to transform... pain into power."

The necromancer finally removed his wand and examined the smoking end. "Love: a double-edged blade. It can hold you back or it can unleash you. The love you have for your family, your friends...

that love will hold you back. *They* will hold you back. As king, you must not be burdened by their opinions and views, for only you and Malliath know what the realm truly needs."

The Crow stabbed his wand into Alijah's stomach and sent bolts of agony through his muscles. "The love you have for your people, for your kingdom... now that love will set you free. Making decisions on that scale will give you clarity of mind. A caretaker of the land, a father to the people, a champion of the realm!" Standing right in front of him, the wizard asked, "The sixth lesson?"

Alijah was cast back to this particular lesson. He had been pulled inside The Crow's mind and taken back to The First Kingdom, a ten thousand year old memory of Sarkas's. Inside that memory, he had come to learn that his birth had been carefully orchestrated by The Crow millennia in advance.

"Truth is not what you want it to be..."

The Crow removed his wand and casually placed it under Alijah's jaw, the spell held back for his words. "Truth. It is what it is. Bend to its power or live a lie. Accept the way of the world and be who you were meant to be."

As Alijah laid his eyes on the wizard, the wand let loose its magic and shot a wave of pain up through his head. So intense was it that he couldn't even open his mouth to protest. His sight disappeared with the feeling that his skull was about to explode across the ceiling.

When next his eyes opened, the half-elf was lying face down on the floor, his wrists free of the biting manacles. His muscles ached and his joints felt stiff as he tried to pull himself up. His beard tasted salty from all the sweat brought on by the pain. A head of matted hair covered his eyes, concealing The Crow and whoever he was speaking to. The other voice was familiar, but Alijah was so exhausted he could hardly care who it was or what they were talking about.

Dragging himself over to the nearest wall, the half-elf managed to sit up and observe his cell through the strands of his hair.

Standing by the open door, The Crow was talking to another member of The Black Hand. It was tempting, for a brief moment, to shout the truth of their religion, but pointing out Kaliban's fabrication would make no difference at all. They were all blinded by their faith and loyalty to their Lord Crow.

"...The workers have been tasked with double shifts and promised more coin than they could ever spend in one lifetime, even on *that* island" the dark mage reported. "I'm afraid it hasn't made a difference. They fail on a daily basis to excavate the last skull. Also, they fear weakening the city's foundations."

The Crow didn't appear overly bothered by what sounded to be a disappointing report. "That wretched city has no place in the new world. Use magic if you must; it's too late for the Dragorn to interfere now anyway."

"Of course, Lord Crow. Will you be leaving soon? I have a boat waiting for you in what's left of Velia's harbour."

The wizard turned to look at Alijah. "I think I will, yes." His attention back on Morvir, he commanded, "Prepare a sacrifice for me. I would ask Kaliban to bless me with a glimpse of what is to come."

Morvir bowed his head. "I will have one of the prisoners sent to your chamber, Lord Crow."

The necromancer dismissed the servant with a flick of his finger. He looked upon Alijah expectantly, waiting for the inevitable questions.

"Nothing?" he baited. "Is there nothing left of that inquisitive nature?"

Alijah swallowed, the memory of his torture fresh in his mind. "You're going to look into the future again. Why? I thought you had already done that?"

The Crow smiled as if pleased. "I witnessed ten thousand years of what you now call history. That's an awful lot to see. Taking it all in, understanding it, and remembering it is an impossible task. Were I an elf or perhaps a Dragorn, it would have been easier. I saw the future in broad strokes, like glancing at a large painting. You have to look again and again to take in the details."

"You use *dark magic* again and again," Alijah specified.

The Crow raised a hairless eyebrow. "What is dark magic? Is there light magic? These are just words given to spells by those who are too weak to wield them. People are good and bad. Magic is a tool. I have used *dark* magic for years and it has done nothing but serve me. In fact, I am using it to better the entire world!"

"It comes with a price," Alijah replied with his mother's words.

Appearing somewhat exasperated, The Crow said, "All great power comes with a price, Alijah. And I am well aware of the price I will pay for using this magic..." The Crow flicked his wand at the ceiling and the manacles dropped down again. "Now, you have thirty-two more lessons to recite before the day is over. Shall we continue?"

Karakulak nudged the Dragorn's limp body with his foot. Nothing. It wasn't the first time the pathetic man had passed out from the pain, halting his entertainment. Tempted as he was to kill the prisoner, it brought him so much more satisfaction to know that his dragon shared the suffering.

Perhaps, the orc thought, when they had conquered the realm of men, he could capture all the Dragorn and their dragons, so that he might torment one and watch the other cry out for mercy.

The God-King called in his guards and ordered them to keep the man alive. He wasn't even close to finished with him. The orcs clearly weren't happy about the prospect of nursing a human back to any kind of health, but a command from Karakulak was a command from Gordomo Himself.

Before leaving his dwelling, the mighty orc swigged another vial of The Crow's elixir, careful to keep his considerable back to the guards. Outside, the vast cavern wasn't nearly as crowded as it had been. His forces had been put to task and their labour was taxing. Ancient caverns were being explored and made safe, while entirely new ones were being burrowed.

They were digging south.

Namdhor would suffer a fate worse than the other kingdoms. Karakulak had decided he would make a spectacle of it, one that would remind generations to come that man had been trampled back into the dirt.

The sound of tiny bones rattling against each other found his ears, followed by the sound of a staff tapping rhythmically against the stone. To his right, the High Priestess and her entourage were approaching, their visage a testing sight for the impatient God-King. His mother waved a hand and the younger priestesses and guards stopped following her.

"You are finally thinking like an orc again," she complimented.

Karakulak slowed down and allowed her to walk beside him along the cavern's ridge line. "No," he corrected. "Thinking like an orc would see us returned to The Undying Mountains, there to wait another five thousand years before we try again."

The High Priestess whipped her head up at him. "You speak of your own kind as if we are no more than the dirt under your feet!"

"I speak as your *God-King*," Karakulak informed her. "As such, you will—"

The entire cavern shook with a thunderous *boom*, stealing Karakulak's threat. The jagged walls cracked and these spread across the rock face like a spider's web, until they reached the ceiling and created havoc. Giant slabs and daggers of rock fell free, their size and weight offering no escape to those on the cavern floor.

The larger boulders slammed into the ground and shattered into a hundred deadly pieces, each the size of an orc. Both Karakulak's and his mother's royal guard rushed to their side, ushering them into the mouth of the nearest tunnel. In the distance, the God-King could hear the cries and wails of his kin, as the other caverns and caves fell prey to the same disaster.

Then it stopped.

The cavern settled and the sound of splitting rock came to a halt. A light dust rained down on the ancient throne cavern, coming to rest on the orcs who had succumbed to the crushing weight of multiple rocks.

Leaving his mother behind, Karakulak pelted down the tunnel, away from the cavern. He knew exactly what had caused such a tremor...

The closer he got to the source of the explosion the thicker the air became, filled with black smoke and an acrid taste. Orcs were wandering around mindlessly, most absent a limb or two. Blood stained the ground and stung Karakulak's nostrils, while the occasional orc bumped into him, dazed and confused.

Pushing through to the tunnel that housed the vault of wrath powder, the God-King could see the extent of the devastation. Bits of his kin were everywhere, including the shredded head of Chieftain Golm of the Mountain Fist. At least he had a quick death; Karakulak would not have been so kind for this failure.

Chunks of rock continued to fall out of the ceiling and the ground was hot under Karakulak's feet as he approached the circular vault doors. They were gone, vaporised in the explosion. There wasn't even a small slab of the stone left that could be identified among the debris. By the look of the site, he guessed that Golm had tried to use what little wrath powder they had left to crack open the doors. In such a cramped environment, however, it would only take one clumsy orc to mishandle the powder and send them all to Gordomo.

Frustrating as it was to see his forces depleted before battle, Karakulak advanced into the vault to see if anything useful could be taken from the disaster. He wafted the smoke from his face and narrowed his eyes to better make out his surroundings.

He stopped in his tracks, his better judgment rising to the surface. He had no idea what condition the wrath powder would be in, nor the type of storage his ancestors might have used.

Given his enhanced size and weight, should he step on just a few grains of the volatile powder he would lose his foot. The subsequent shockwave would then impact the rest of the wrath powder and blow Vengora into the sky.

Crouching low, Karakulak waited patiently for the smoke to clear around him. He threw his arm back only once and commanded the orcs lining the threshold behind him to stay away. The God-King focused his eyes on the floor in front of his clawed feet. He blew the air away gently and discovered the chamber was empty but for a pair of looming doors on the far side.

The doors made sense given that this cavern was nothing like the others he had come across since entering his ancestors' dwelling. The walls and ceiling were hewn stone and reinforced, providing a much stronger chamber inside the larger cavern. Judging by the attention to detail, Karakulak guessed it to be of dwarven design, claimed by the orcs during The Great War.

The stone doors were lined in dwarven script - gibberish to the orc. With strength only he commanded, Karakulak pulled hard on one of the doors. His arms bulged and his veins pushed against his pale skin as he heaved. The dwarves of old must have used some kind of mechanism to open them.

A low growl erupted from his throat when the door finally began to budge, one inch at a time. When the gap was big enough, the God-King wedged himself between the doors and pushed it open all the way.

Cracking his knuckles with satisfaction, Karakulak was finally able to enter the next chamber. He stopped abruptly with only his toes protruding over the threshold.

The wrath powder was everywhere.

The cavernous chamber was filled to the ceiling with red powder, each grain a deadly weapon.

Clearly, it had been abandoned in the last years of the war, not so much as a grain disturbed by the dwarves or elves. Craning his neck, Karakulak took it all in - a mountain of red wrath powder!

"God-King Karakulak!" one of the orcs shouted from the threshold. "Shall we begin collecting the wrath powder?"

The mighty orc scrutinised the very top of the cavern. "No," he instructed. "I want to know exactly what's above this cavern, on the surface."

Karakulak's mind was racing with new ideas, ideas that would see the world of men wiped out for good. After all, Grundi was finding him something big and, now, he had something powerful...

The God-King smiled.

CHAPTER 14
NEVER ALONE

"Where are they?" came the king's abrasive question.

Having become accustomed to his rank as Master Dragorn for some decades now, Gideon was quick to find Arlon Draqaro the rudest man he had ever met. Most bowed their head upon greeting him out of respect for his title if not his deeds. Standing before the expectant king of Illian, however, it was clear that he cared little for Gideon's history.

The Master Dragorn employed every piece of body language and facial expression to feign his ignorance. "You will have to be more specific... your Grace."

Fuming before his dragon skull throne, Arlon loomed over Gideon with his hands on his hips. "The Galfreys, Master Thorn! All of them! They are not in my keep and witnesses report seeing a dragon flying south. Added to that, my son has failed to report to his post and..." Arlon checked that only Gideon, Sir Borin, and himself occupied the throne room. "And my sword has been stolen. Of course, there's the issue of our missing prisoner to consider as well. Asher hasn't been seen since his escape."

Gideon let his eyes wander for a moment, suggesting his lack of interest and attention. "I'm not their keeper, your Grace. I couldn't say where Reyna and Nathaniel are and your son is a northerner by birth; he blends in. As for Inara; she is flying high above us as we speak, ready to provide cover from the air. The dragon seen flying south is another - Master Glanduil. I have sent her to retrieve another Dragorn, Master Knox, to aid in your strategy for assaulting the mountains."

It was all lies, something Gideon would feel terrible about were he speaking to any other monarch. As it was, lying through his teeth felt like the only way to converse with Arlon Draqaro.

The king's demeanour suggested that he was aware of this. "And Asher?" he asked futilely.

The Master Dragorn pretended to give it some serious thought. "Given his past, I would give up any search for him. You won't find him if he doesn't want to be found and, even if you did, it probably wouldn't end well for those you sent."

Some of Arlon's frustration melted away, leaving a smug grin that worried Gideon. "You're absolutely right, Master Thorn. Asher's appearance is unknown to my people and he has been well trained in the arts of an assassin. He could be anywhere by now. What you are wrong about, however, is my *son's* ability to blend in. He *is* known to the people of the north, along with the sword he now carries on his belt. I was hoping you would be more forthcoming with the details, but I suppose I will have to learn of them in time."

Gideon thought he understood the king exactly, but decided to continue with his ignorance. "I'm not sure I follow, your Grace."

"Then I shall enlighten you!" Arlon barked, his behaviour manic. "My spies in the lower camp report seeing Vighon leave for the east. He wasn't *alone...*" the king added, his tone dripping with venom. "Another man travelled with him, hooded in green. His identity remains a mystery to all but myself."

Again, Gideon pretended to chew over this *revelation*. "Why would Vighon journey east with Asher?"

"Answers will find me in time," Arlon replied cryptically. "Since you cannot provide any, I suggest you rejoin Master Galfrey in the sky and prepare for our advance."

Something inside Gideon snapped. It wasn't violent or dramatic, but he had most definitely just gone past the limit where his patience was concerned.

"I recall giving your Grace clear instruction relating to any and all commands you might give to me. The Dragorn are not your soldiers."

Arlon's eyes blazed with seething hatred. The expected outburst never came, however. The king closed his eyes, sighed, and dropped into his throne as if exhausted. When he finally looked upon Gideon once more, his hand was propping up his head and his body was slouched in anything but the manner of a king.

"Let's drop the charade shall we? The game has changed. There aren't six kings on the board any more... there's only one. *Me*. I might not be the king you would have wanted for Illian, but I'm the king you've got, and I'm not going anywhere. I will win this war and I will see my kingdom thrive. My time in charge of The Ironsworn has gifted me many talents when it comes to ruling. Allies such as yourself leave the gate open for mistrust, unrest... *rebellion* even. In my new world, the Dragorn will either bow to me or they will be *banished* from the realm altogether."

Gideon took a step forward and so did Sir Borin. "You're powerful as king, but you're not *that* powerful. Even if you beat the lords into line, the people wouldn't stand for it."

"The people?" Arlon echoed. "The people will do whatever they're told, *believe* whatever they're told. That's why they're *the people*. They're nothing but sheep, a flock constantly in search of direction. If I tell them my army is all they need then they will nod their peasant heads and *thank me*."

Gideon shook his head and pointed out, "The Dragorn offer the realm protection you can't compete with."

Arlon let out a short sharp laugh. "That might have been the case before the orcs invaded, Master Thorn, when there was no threat. Since then, one kingdom after another has fallen into ruin under your so-called protection. The Dragorn has nothing to offer. What will you do when you're not welcome anymore? What will you do when the people of Illian realise that they don't need you?"

There were numerous replies to those questions, most of which contained obscene words, but Gideon decided Arlon wasn't worth it. "I'm glad to hear you think that, your Grace. I actually came here to inform you that I will be temporarily unavailable."

"Unavailable?" Arlon scowled, sitting forward in his throne.

"The orcs have a prisoner - a member of my order - and I aim to free him or end his suffering. I can't do either of those things from here."

The king narrowed his eyes at the Master Dragorn. "You're going into the mountains," he surmised. "You would leave Namdhor to defend itself for the sake of one man?"

"Every life matters," Gideon argued. "Only when weight is given to the individual will the many thrive."

Arlon waved the comment away. "An antiquated notion of your predecessors no doubt; I require no lecture on the matter of kingly duties."

"An elvish saying, actually. A lesson yet to be fully realised by the rulers of Illian." Gideon gripped Mournblade in its scabbard and turned to leave. "Even a blind man can see the lesson is beyond you..."

"Speaking of old lessons," Arlon called after him, "shouldn't a Master Dragorn know better than to insult the king of Illian? I believe the last time your order fell out with the man who sat on this throne, he decimated the lot of you."

Gideon paused with his hand on the door. The lesson of which Arlon spoke was a thousand years old, but he wasn't mistaken. King Gal Tion declared war on the elven Dragorn and nearly wiped them out - it was among the first history lessons every Dragorn was taught.

Just leave, Ilargo advised. *Bartering words with this snake is pointless.*

Gideon took a breath, fighting the urge to have the last word. In the end, he pushed through the door and didn't bother looking back, already aware that the king wore a grin that would ignite his blood.

I need to fly...

~

HIGH ABOVE THE snows of the north, Gideon finally felt some semblance of peace. Up here was where he belonged, the only place where his thoughts made sense. It took some soothing from Ilargo before he finally let go of the idea of burning down The Dragon Keep. With the king inside.

If he was a worthy king of the realm, Gideon seethed, **he would be leading his army from the front, not sitting on a throne.**

I can see inside your mind, Gideon. I know what you're really thinking...

The Master Dragorn let his head hang low. He was really thinking about the dangers of fighting on the frontlines and the high probability that Arlon would fall in battle. It was an unbecoming thought for someone with his title.

I can also see what gnaws at you, Ilargo added.

Gideon knew it was pointless to either avoid or hide the things that preyed on him. He was lucky, really, that Ilargo's mentality bolstered his own, picking him up and forcing him to face his fears.

Arlon asked what I would do when the people realise they don't need us.

The answer to that is simple in my mind, Ilargo replied.

As it is in mine, Gideon agreed. **I have no doubt that this realm will always need the Dragorn; even more so under the rule of one king.**

Then what is the question that really bothers you? Ilargo asked, teasing it out of his companion.

What do I do when the people realise the Dragorn can't protect

them from everything? That question had plagued him for some time, weighing him down.

We have both found the answer to that question already, Ilargo said, reminding Gideon of their earlier conversation.

I suppose we have...

Of all the things to consider in light of that answer, Gideon found himself thinking of Inara. What would she think when he told her of his plan?

One step at a time, Ilargo cautioned. *We both have to survive your journey into the orc lands. We must be focused if you are to return with Arathor.*

It was subtle, but Gideon was able to detect an underlying current of irritation on Ilargo's part. The dragon wasn't entirely satisfied with his companion's decision to go into the mountain alone, a place where he couldn't follow. The choice to save Arathor hadn't come without some hint of guilt for Gideon. He was putting Ilargo's life in jeopardy and taking away the dragon's ability to defend himself.

I trust you, Ilargo remarked casually, not wanting to make a topic out of his feelings.

Knowing better than to push his companion, the Master Dragorn left it there. They didn't have a choice, after all. Arathor needed saving from his hell and there was no one more capable or willing than Gideon.

Settling in to Ilargo's back, Gideon began a brief yet effective form of meditation to hone his senses and focus his mind. When he returned to the world, he noted his surroundings with greater accuracy.

Dark clouds raged above, spewing out a light yet steady rain of ash. It was the scene playing out below, however, that pulled at his attention. The bulk of the Namdhorian army remained in place, a deep wall of knights between Vengora and Namdhor, but several hundred had advanced with the captured catapults and dozens of wagons filled with dead orcs.

Ilargo banked to the west, giving them both a better view as the catapults unleashed payload after payload of burning orc bodies into the distant trees. The flames that clung to the orcs soon spread among the trees, creating a thick plume of black smoke that worked to conceal the mountains beyond.

Gideon looked back at Namdhor and the sprawling camp at its base. At least they had the south behind them, land largely left by the orcs in favour of their future conquests. Should all fail, the people could flee south and hope that the orcs continued their invasion north, where they might fall upon wave after wave of dwarves.

Having seen enough of the bleak view, Ilargo turned to the north and beat his powerful wings. The mountains of Vengora grew in size as they approached, leaving the Namdhorian army behind. The dragon only began his descent after they had safely cleared the cata-pults' range - something that had greatly increased since being engineered by the orcs in Velia and made far more powerful than any made by man or elf. Circumnavigating the black columns of smoke, Ilargo searched for a patch of open ground that could fit his size.

Can you see any orcs? Gideon asked.

None, Ilargo answered. *I see no evidence of a cave either.*

Gideon peered over the edge of the dragon, taking in the mane of trees that wrapped around the mountains' edge. *There must be some way inside,* he mused.

Ilargo glided lower and lower until Gideon could make out individual trees and smaller boulders dotted in the gaps of the mountains. The terrain was perfect for orcs. Hard ground, shadows, enclosed spaces between the trees. He would be prey once he touched down.

You are Dragorn, Ilargo reminded him. *You have never been prey, nor shall you. Keep your wits about you and Mournblade in hand. The orcs will soon come to fear its steel again.*

Gideon patted Ilargo's green scales as the dragon came to rest on one of the few patches of flat ground that wasn't covered in trees. He jumped down and scanned between the foliage, wondering if there were any orcs looking back at him from the darkness. Ilargo's sight was penetrating, fortunately, encouraging Gideon that he remained safe, for the time being at least.

The sound of Mournblade pulling free from its scabbard was satisfying and comforting for both companions. The enchanted scimitar had claimed more orcish lives than any other and it hungered for more.

Gideon made a conscious decision to leave his grey cloak behind. Its volume would only add to his size and he had the distinct feeling that a degree of stealth would be required before he found Arathor.

Turning back to Ilargo and his sharp blue eyes, Gideon said, *I will return.*

Be sure that you do, Ilargo replied, lowering his head to Gideon's. *Should we meet in the next life, however, be assured that I* will *sit on you for eternity...*

Gideon smiled and cupped what he could of his companion's fierce jaw. They would meet again, he told himself. They always did...

CHAPTER 15
BAIT

L ike rivers on a map, the chasms and valleys of Vengora were narrow and intrusive, winding and weaving between the gargantuan mountains. In the heart of winter, many of these passages were closed to human travellers, sealed by sheets of fallen snow, layered in a deadly coating of ice or blocked by the treacherous avalanches plunging down from the impassable cliffs.

They were perfect for orcs wishing to flee the bulk of their army and the whips of their chieftains. Taking any one of these routes, in the chaos of its escape, a deserting orc could find its way through to Dhenaheim or simply follow the mountains around to the west and get lost in the south of Illian again.

Doran wasn't convinced.

The dwarf huffed and muttered under his breath as Pig dutifully trekked deeper into Vengora. "Ye're riskin' a lot, elf!" he called back over his shoulder.

Galanör and Russell were close behind the Warhog, astride their horses. They had towered in front of Doran for most of their journey and the son of Dorain had quickly become fed up with his lack of view, leading him to take the point of their small caravan.

"We know for sure that there's orcs back that way!" he protested. "We could o' bagged one by now an' been half way to Dhenaheim!"

Galanör replied with a hint of exhaustion in his voice. "My reasoning is sound, *dwarf.*"

"He's not wrong, Doran," Russell chipped in. "Besides the blazing catapults hammering the mountains, those trees will be crammed with traps and ambushes."

"We need to be the hunters," Galanör added, "not the prey."

"Bah!" Doran took immediate offence. "I don' need no lesson in the ways o' the hunter! Ye might 'ave a couple o' centuries on me, Galanör, but I've been catchin' beasties on Illian's soil for a lot longer! An'," the son of Dorain bellowed with a finger in the air, "these 'ere be mountains! *Mountains*! I know the rock an' stone like ye know the woods an'... braidin' ye hair."

A trickle of small rocks bounded off the mountainside to Doran's right, stirring the Warhog beneath him. The dwarf narrowed his vision and inspected the dark rubble and black boulders, searching for any sign of menace.

He was itching for a good fight.

Colliding with the orcs in battle had ignited something ancient in his blood, something that craved war and steel. His ancestors had carved their names into history in their battle against the fiendish orcs - now, it was his turn.

The son of Dorain huffed again, convinced that they weren't going to find a single orc so far away from The White Vale. "We saw the lot o' 'em run for their pathetic lives into them trees; we know where they fled! I'm tellin' ye both; we're too far north now! Those blasted orcs are behind us!"

There was a moment of silence behind Doran in which Galanör was clearly deciding whether it was worth replying to the prickly dwarf. "They scattered, Doran," he finally said. "They were chased by dragons and Namdhorian riders. How many orcs burned that day, staring into Malliath's jaws? How many more watched from afar and realised their fate was sealed if they remained with their kin? Trust me, son of Dorain, some of our prey took this route."

Doran craned his neck to check their empty surroundings. "There's nothin' 'ere but rocks an' us, lad!"

"Heavybelly!" Russell chastised. "Start using your eyes and less of your mouth!"

Doran looked back at the testy werewolf and followed his gaze to the ground. Only one experienced in hunting would notice the dark scrapes on the gravelly slopes, places where something or someone had rushed down, disturbing the rock. It could have been anything, from a mountain goat to a Gobber.

Still, Doran began examining the ground in front of Pig. The ash fall was far lighter here, but a thin coating had managed to drape over the boulders and stones that pebbled the hard path. There was never a whole print, but here and there were markings in the ash where a finger or two had pressed down. Again, it wasn't a detail that would jump out at just any wanderer and Doran berated himself for not seeing it earlier.

Of course, he could never admit such a thing. "Those tracks could belong to anyone. The barbarians o' The Iron Valley 'ave been known to venture as far west as The King's Lake, ye know. If it is barbarians," he continued without missing a beat, "do yerselves a favour an' leave 'em to me! I've had more than a few dealin's with that lot, let me tell ye! I've lived among 'em, fought beside 'em, an' I've put a few down to boot! These mountains hold no surprises for the son o' Dorain!"

There was another moment of silence from behind the dwarf. Then, the moment extended into rudeness as his fellow companions held their tongues entirely. Doran turned around in his saddle to shoot daggers at the pair.

He was alone...

The winding pass behind him was devoid of all but snow, ash, and rocks. It was eerie and the dwarf of clan Heavybelly didn't like it one bit. Turning every which way, Doran scanned every nook and crevice of the mountains, searching for any sign of his companions. Russell was towing a cart, not an object easily hidden.

Deciding they were farther back on the way they had travelled, Doran began to guide Pig around. He tugged hard on the reins, turning the Warhog's head to the right. Had he done such a thing a second later, his mount would have been sporting an arrow in the eye.

The first arrow was swiftly followed by two more. The second whistled past Doran's ear and the third caught his pauldron at an awkward angle and bounced harmlessly away. It took no time at all to trace the projectiles back to their source, a little way up the slope.

Orcs!

The wretched creatures emerged from behind every obstacle on the slope, their obsidian armour blending into the shadows. They wielded spears, swords, and axes to go along with their bows - they hadn't deserted their army without a few supplies.

All thought of his companions took flight as the son of Dorain pulled free his sword from his back. Instinctively, he reached for his axe and lamented its absence, long melted down to forge the Moon-blade. Instead, he raised his sword in one hand and his hatchet in the other, a war cry on his lips in the face of his ancient foe.

The Warhog, however, felt something similar to Doran and bolted at the orcs. The dwarf was thrown backwards and dragged halfway up the slope before he finally fell off the back of the saddle. He groaned and grunted on his roll down the slope, help-less to halt his momentum or the slapping of his sword against his face.

At last, his tumble at an end, Doran lifted his head and spat dirt from his mouth. His blond hair fell in strands across his vision, obscuring Pig's charge into the orcs. A sharp exhale lifted the veil and he witnessed the first orc to meet the Warhog's tusks and be flipped in the air with deep gashes to its groin.

Doran laughed, despite his downfall in the Warhog's haste, and picked himself up with brandished steel in both hands. "Now ye're goin' to get it!" he yelled.

To his dismay, the son of Dorain was not even the second to reach the melee and spill orcish blood, nor was he the third. Faster and lighter of foot, both Galanör and Russell came from nowhere and sprinted up the slope. The elf darted left and right, his magnificent scimitars flashes of deadly steel, and dispatched two orcs with smooth ease. Russell lacked Galanör's grace, but his supernatural strength still made for quite the display. His pick-axe staved the head of one orc before he clubbed another, robbing them both of life.

Doran growled and advanced up the slope, eager to kill and maim. They were beasts. Nothing more. The first orc to lunge at him was an easy kill, its midriff exposed by such a ridiculously dramatic swing of its axe. The son of Dorain slashed one way with his hatchet, bringing the wounded orc down to his level, and cut open its face with a fast lashing of his sword.

It didn't just feel good to the dwarf, it felt *right*.

His victory was brief, however, as the next orc decided to murder Doran from afar. The dwarf had a split second to react before an obsidian spear pierced his body and brought an end to his adventures. Dropping his weapons, the son of Dorain roughly pulled up the dead body at his feet and fell backwards. The spear was accurate, its tip plunging through the dead orc and out the other side, straight into Doran's chest plate.

He grunted in pain as he took the impact of yet another fall. His armour proved its worth and held up to the blow, though he was thankful it had been slowed down by his *shield*. Doran shuffled the dead orc off and inspected the dent in his chest plate.

"Right..." he muttered determinedly.

Exploding from all fours, Doran collected his weapons and charged at the orc. Oh the things he was going to do to that orc! It was going to die slowly so that it could watch its kin fall to a Heavy-belly's blade. The final blow would be accompanied by a broad grin on Doran's face; the last thing it would ever see.

Galanör raced past the orc like a wraith and sliced its throat without even stopping. The elf was engaging three more before the spear-thrower had fallen to its knees, clutching helplessly at its torn neck. Outraged by the injustice of it, Doran roared and slammed the edge of his sword into the orc's skull, determined to be the one who delivered the mortal blow.

"Damn it, elf!" he cried, turning in search of his next enemy.

Galanör cut down two of his three attackers and maimed the third, leaving him wounded on the slope. "Leave this one," he instructed, ignoring the dwarf's outcry.

"I'll leave that one if ye'll leave the rest!" Doran countered. "Ye're both stealin' all the bloody fun!"

Russell was a killing machine, full moon or not. His pick-axe slammed into one deserter after another, dropping orcs like flies. One brave enough to jump on the werewolf's back found the point of a pick-axe ripping through its armour and lifting it free. Galanör ran past and sliced the top of its head off, making certain it would never rise again.

The band of deserters was relatively small and the three rangers soon whittled them down to the last few. Doran chased one down to the path while Galanör and Russell killed those left on the slope. The orc fleeing Doran's sword was wounded, its leg cut open by the dwarf's hatchet, but the injury failed to slow it down.

"Come back 'ere ye coward!" Doran shouted after it, his chest heaving and his legs tiring. "Face death with some dignity, eh!"

It was no use; the orc quickly disappeared up the path, vanishing behind the weaving walls of the mountain pass. Doran considered chasing after it, especially since there were no more orcs left on the slope, but the creature had nowhere to go but north along the route, *their* route. He'd be sure to crack the beastie's skull somewhere along the way.

Turning back to his companions, Russell was pulling his pick-axe free of a dead orc and Galanör was wiping blood from his scimitars.

"Ye two cheeky buggers 'ave got a lot to answer for!" By the looks

216

on their faces, they both knew exactly what he was talking about. "Ye knew we were surrounded, didn' ye! Ye jus' thought, *oh aye, Doran looks like a good piece o' bait*! Ye jus' let me wander straight in without a word! An' then," he added, working himself up, "ye both jump in an' start killin' the lot o' 'em! Didn' ye mothers ever teach ye to share?"

Galanör was smiling now. "Apologies, Doran. You were just perfect for the role."

"That's a delicate way of saying you're a loud brute," Russell clarified. "I wouldn't be surprised if the orcs in The White Vale can hear you."

"Don' go makin' excuses." Doran wagged his finger at his old friend and marched up the slope. "This is *my* mission, *my* expedition, an' *my* hunt. Ye two are tag alongs. Should ye 'ave any more bright ideas, be sure to run 'em past me first, a'right?"

Galanör sheathed his scimitars and glanced at the wounded orc. "I'd say our *bright* idea was a success. I would also say that I was right..."

Doran levelled his eyes on the wounded orc and sniffed with derision. "Now I've got to put up with that foul stench!"

The orc bared its fangs and managed to pick itself up onto all fours. Apparently, there was still some fight left in the horned monster. Doran was only too happy to beat that out of it and took a step towards the prisoner.

An ear-piercing squeal preceded the Warhog and its charge.

"Heavybelly!" Russell bellowed.

All three of the companions yelled at Pig to stop, seeing the calamity unfolding, but the Warhog had never been one for taking orders. The orc could do nothing, injured as it was, to get out of Pig's way. Doran jumped forward to wrestle it and grabbed nothing but air.

The orc was taken clear from the ground, its chest and gut impaled by Pig's ferocious tusks. The Warhog eventually dropped it to the ground and violently shook its head, tearing the orc apart.

The prisoner was dead. Very dead.

Doran sighed at their misfortune, though he was undoubtedly proud of his mount. "From now on I'm callin' ye Orcsbane," he said, patting it on the head. "I'd say ye've earned it..."

"Doran!" Russell snapped. "You're patting him on the head? That stupid pig just killed our prisoner!"

"He's not stupid!" Doran shouted back, hoping he wouldn't have to prove such a thing.

"I've been telling you for years to get that animal under control!"

"Ah, stow it, Maybury. What's done is done an' it's not exactly a punishable thing. He's a Warhog an' he killed an orc. What more could I want from 'im?"

Galanör took no part in their argument but, instead, crouched down and inspected the orc. "Could we take a dead orc to Dhenaheim?" he asked Doran.

"Were it any but me kin I'd say aye, but these aren' humans or elves, lad. Dwarves are suspicious by nature an' especially o' magic when yer people are involved. They could accuse us o' makin' the orc's body with magic."

Russell threw his arms up. "So we need a live and kicking one then..."

Looking around at the bodies strewn across the mountainside, they were all out of that variety. "Maybe we should o' left more than one alive, eh?" Doran pointed his comment at Galanör.

Not rising to it, the elf gestured to the northern pass. "One escaped. Lucky for us it's heading in the right direction."

"Ye want to hunt a single orc?" Doran spat. "That narrows our odds o' success right down. We should turn back an' hunt in richer grounds, where we know there are orcs!"

"That will take too long," Galanör pointed out. "We've come this far; our journey cannot be undone."

Doran let out a heavy sigh. "I hope ye haven' doomed us, lad. There's more than a few folks relyin' on us."

Galanör made his way back to his mount. "A single orc cannot outrun three trackers such as ourselves, nor can it hide from Russell's senses."

"It's bleeding," the werewolf remarked, his nose pointed up the pass.

Doran wasn't sure how accurate his old friend's sense of smell really was. Looking around, there was a lot of blood staining the ground, though the dwarf knew better than to question Russell's nose - he had once tracked a Vorska for seventeen miles without once laying eyes on it.

A closer inspection of the orcs showed them to be as different to each other as any dwarf was to another of their kin. No two orcs had the same style or combination of horns and their sizes varied like humans. For those who weren't missing limbs, they possessed a branded arm with the sigil of their tribe. The diverse collection of sigils was further proof that this was a band of deserters who believed they would have better lives in the wild. If Doran's mood wasn't sour he would have chuckled at the irony of their fate.

"Come on, Doran!" Russell bade, climbing onto his horse. "These ash clouds haven't spread beyond Vengora yet; the orc is likely to seek out shelter soon."

"A'right, a'right, I'm comin'."

The son of Dorain was about to walk away from the bodies when his eye for a good weapon fell upon the orc who had tried to spear him. The fiend itself possessed no weapon the dwarf would dare to call worthy of his heritage, but it did possess a particularly sharp horn, and long too. Seizing his opportunity, Doran used his hatchet and chopped one of the ridged horns off. Holding it up, he decided that with a bit of work he could forge a decent dagger out of it.

Russell raised an eyebrow at him. "I didn't peg you for a trophy collector, Heavybelly."

"Trophies no," Doran replied, eyeing the horn, "but weapons? I love the idea o' killin' orcs with orcs!"

"Come along!" Galanör beckoned from the north pass. "Time is against us!"

Doran muttered under his breath, dissatisfied with orders from an elf and his overall lack of control. He never thought he'd come to such a conclusion, but he actually missed travelling with the Galfreys. At least with them he knew what scraps he was walking into...

CHAPTER 16
A SHADOW IN THE WOODS

Finally, after a tumultuous and violent return to life, Asher felt that sense of freedom that only came with leaving the beaten track. Diverting north-east from The Selk Road, the ranger guided his horse across the snowy plains, taking him towards The Spear, the very tip of Illian.

The wind was bracing and flowed through his green cloak and whipped at his greying hair. The snow crunched under the hooves of his horse, and the world was laid flat before him, invitingly. The ranger breathed in deeply, remembering what it was to be alive.

During his final moments, in the pools of Naius, he couldn't have dreamed of returning to the majesty of the world. It was a cruel twist of fate that he should now return to it in what could be its final days. Perhaps, he thought, he had yet to atone for his years as an Arakesh, for the lives he had taken in service to Nightfall.

Be that the truth of his destiny or not, his life was still that of the sword. As it had so many decades ago, the feeling of doing the right thing settled on the ranger's conscience. He was helping people once again, the entire realm in fact. How he managed to find himself in the middle of these calamities was beyond him...

Closing his eyes, Asher inhaled a long breath, hoping to clear his mind. Shutting out the light, however, only served to bring his memories to the surface. He was back inside The Bastion, watching helplessly as Alijah suffered at the hands of the Reavers. The ranger was stuck, rooted to the spot, unable to move, unable to do anything but watch The Crow worm his way inside the boy's head.

Asher opened his eyes again and allowed the vast landscape to press upon him. He had done a lot of terrible things in his life, but dragging Alijah into that hell was close to the top, regardless of the spell that had enslaved him. He could still feel the half-elf writhing in his grip, pleading with him to fight against The Crow's spell.

It had been useless. Asher had done as commanded, just as he had done during his days as an Arakesh. Dwelling on his past, the ranger thought of his old mentor for the first time since his resurrection.

Nasta Nal-Aket...

The Father of Nightfall was undoubtedly dead, killed by time if not the blade of another - a likely scenario given the assassins' violent hierarchy. There was a part of Asher that wondered what might have been, had Nasta and he met in a different life. Had he been a simple orphan and Nasta an innocent farmer, would the southerner have still adopted him?

Asher shook his head and turned to the mountains. Such musings were for naught. In truth, the ranger knew he was thinking about family because of the Galfreys. His words had been too harsh in Namdhor. Who was he to tell a mother and father they should give up on their child? Despite his bluntness, Reyna and Nathaniel still sought to keep their friendship with him. He didn't deserve them.

A bolt of pain split the ranger's head and he glimpsed a flash of Malliath's purple eyes in the darkness. It only made his heart break all the more for his friends. As blunt as he had been, Asher had spoken only truth about Alijah and his bond with the feral dragon.

The boy was lost to them...

Tired of his melancholy, the ranger held his head high and reminded himself that Reyna and Nathaniel were no ordinary parents, let alone people. They had proven time and time again that nothing could stand in their way and, as little hope as there was, Asher had to wonder if The Crow was truly ready for them to come down on him. The ranger knew *he* wouldn't want to get in their way.

Deciding that he would put more faith in his friends, Asher continued along his route and did his best to soak in the world. Even though he couldn't have missed Illian, being dead for thirty years, he still felt as if he had longed for it.

Of course, he wasn't alone.

With the stretching Vengoran mountains to his left and the vast plains of The White Vale to his right, Asher could feel his companion's unease behind him. It was irritating and served only to take him out of the moment.

"If you have something to say... *don't.*"

Vighon Draqaro did indeed keep his mouth shut, but only for a precious few seconds. "I don't agree with abandoning The Selk Road."

Asher kept his eyes on the horizon and kept trotting along. "Is that so?" he remarked lazily.

"I understand that cutting across country is the fastest way, but hugging the mountains like this invites peril. Our task is perhaps the most important and our current path takes us close to the barbarians of The Iron Valley, not to mention any wandering orcs."

"Are you afraid?" Asher asked bluntly.

"For my life? No. I've slain more orcs than *you* have. The Selk Road would still take us to The Spear and the Adanae River, but we would avoid Vengora for the time being. Also, unlike you, I have to consider who I'm travelling with. Right now it's an old man with a penchant for blacking out and attacking people. Not to mention his history as a professional killer..."

Asher had become a very good judge of character in his time and, in truth, he couldn't detect the fear he had suspected in the northman. Annoyingly, he also couldn't argue with his conundrum. Added to that, there was a degree of logic in his suggestion, but he was missing a key factor.

"Our task is important," the ranger agreed. "That's why we don't have the time to take the longer route. If there really is a weapon to be used against the orcs, we need to harness it before they attack again."

Vighon brought his horse alongside Asher's. "*If* there's a weapon? It's *if* now? You were so sure back in Namdhor!"

Asher regretted engaging the man in any conversation now. "Whether The Crow wishes us to win this war or not remains to be seen. We can't, however, take the chance; so we go to Haren Bain."

The northman sighed again, his vision cast over the ominous mountains and hanging clouds of ash. "You've taken this path before, then? To The Spear?"

To Asher it was only a decade ago that he had visited the pointed tip of Illian but, in reality, he knew it had been almost fifty years. "Not this particular path, no. But I have been to The Spear."

Vighon looked from the ranger to the plains before them. "But you know the way, yes?"

Asher chewed over his decision to respond at all, wondering if the northman would simply shut up when met with silence. "Keep the mountains on our left until we reach The Guardian Cliffs. Head east from there until we reach the bank of the Adanae. Once the elves arrive, it would be quicker to take a boat or a skiff up river, through Longdale until we reach the western bend."

"It sounds like you've got this all planned out," Vighon remarked with a hint of doubt in his voice.

It was indeed planned out inside Asher's mind, only it didn't feel entirely like his plan. The route he envisioned was presented in his mind's eye from the sky, as if he was looking down on the terrain and following the path around the curve of the mountains.

"It's Malliath's memories," the ranger explained, his sight deliberately focused on the snow in front of them. "It's the path he flew."

"That was a long time ago," Vighon replied, the doubt still lingering in his tone.

"Bar a few forests here and there, it's still the same landscape."

Vighon nodded along, finally satisfied to leave the subject there. Unfortunately for Asher, the northman wasn't finished talking.

"What were you doing in The Spear? Back then I mean?"

The ranger glanced at him. "You talk a lot."

The northman held a moment of introspection before chuckling to himself. "I suppose I do. I always thought I was the quiet one. Travelling with Alijah can make you *feel* like the quiet one."

Bringing up the Galfreys' son hit the ranger with a pang of guilt he didn't wish to explore. "I was taking a job out of Longdale," he relented.

"A ranger job?" Vighon probed.

"No, as a barmaid. Of course a ranger's job!"

"Careful, old man, that was almost a joke..."

For just a moment, Asher was taken back to his days journeying with Nathaniel, before Valanis and the weight of the world fell upon them. He didn't make friends easily, but there were more than a few qualities he liked about this northman. Still, they had quite the journey ahead of them and Asher wasn't one for sharing.

"What was the job?" Vighon pressed.

Asher could see he wasn't going to find any more peace until the northman's curiosity was satiated. "It was..." The ranger stumbled over his memories, seeing glimpses of Alijah's visits to Longdale. "The Bandit Lord," he finally recalled.

"That doesn't sound like a monster? I thought you rangers were monster hunters."

"The Bandit Lord was a monster," Asher clarified. "He had a talent for turning other men into monsters too. His gang terrorised Longdale and the surrounding villages. They took children, attacked women, murdered anyone who denied them what they wanted."

"So, you've hunted men..." Vighon mused.

Asher dwelled on that statement. He had been hunting men long before his years as a ranger. "They were barely men. The Graycoats tried to help but they failed again and again to track down their hideout in the mountains. Eventually, the reward for The Bandit Lord's head was so high that every bounty hunter and ranger in the land was travelling to Longdale."

"I'm surprised The Ironsworn didn't kill them," Vighon commented.

"There was no Ironsworn back then," Asher corrected.

"So *you* found this Bandit Lord?" Vighon continued.

"I did." Asher kept his response as short as possible, hoping to dissuade the northman from continuing with his questions. He just wanted to enjoy the view.

Vighon, however, stared at the ranger. "How did you do it?"

"I joined them," he answered simply.

"You joined the gang?" Vighon asked incredulously.

"I had a few skills The Bandit Lord was interested in utilising. I had to prove myself of course. A few crimes here and there, nothing I wasn't able to stage in advance. Eventually, their trust gained, I was taken back to their hole in the mountains."

Vighon looked impressed. "And you killed The Bandit Lord?"

"No," Asher replied quietly. "I killed them *all*..."

At last, the northman had nothing to say. What was running through Vighon's head he couldn't say, but he didn't care if it meant his travelling companion was quiet for a while.

～

THE FARTHER EAST THEY travelled the brighter the world became. The ash clouds tapered out towards The Shining Coast, offering Asher and Vighon the occasional hint of blue sky and sunlight. For the most part, they had trekked in silence, exchanging words only to share supplies.

The mountains continued to loom in the north, though their bulk was now hidden by the thick pines that stood tall in the snow. The forest around them sat in their way, obscuring the vista of plains that crossed The Iron Valley. The next few miles of their journey carried potential danger, the valley being home to the infamous barbarians.

Asher wasn't too concerned. Since the entire Namdhorian army had passed through the valley, twice, it was likely the barbarians were sticking close to their dwellings and avoiding the road. Instead, the ranger was more concerned with the shadow they had picked up...

"Take my reins," he instructed Vighon.

Taken aback, the northman frowned at the ranger. "That's the first thing you've said to me in hours and it makes no sense."

"We're not alone," he replied cryptically, holding out his reins for Vighon.

Credit to the northman, he didn't instantly turn in every direction, though his dark eyes shifted from one side to another. "How do you know?" he asked, taking the ranger's reins.

"Because I know." Asher quickly and quietly jumped down from his horse and collected the bow and quiver of arrows from his saddle.

"Well, how many are there?" Vighon hissed.

"Just keep riding," Asher ordered him before striding off between the trees.

Vighon's frustrated mutterings were the last thing he heard before the forest stole all but the noise of nature. Now in his element, Asher's instincts switched on like an animal hunting its prey. He moved from tree to tree with swift grace worthy of an elf. Pausing here and there, he waited for their shadow to pass him by. If they were an assassin they were undoubtedly the worst, stalking them on something as loud as a horse.

He caught glimpses between the trees and the foliage, but the angle proved forever awkward, hiding their stalker's identity. He did, however, catch sight of a sword. Knowing his would-be attacker was armed only compounded Asher's instincts, urging him to pounce and put an end to the threat.

The fact that the rider had already trotted past the ranger was proof that he had no idea Asher wasn't still astride his horse. Perhaps he wasn't the threat he appeared to be...

Quickly and quietly, Asher advanced from behind. Up ahead, he could just make out Vighon through a thin gap in the trees. The northman still had much to learn if he had been unaware of this clumsy oaf trailing them.

Sticking to the trees and off the path, Asher stalked alongside the rider for a while. The rider was hooded in a cheap brown cloak, and certainly a man from the look of the hands on the horse's reins. The sword on his belt was decent in make, Namdhorian possibly, but the pommel was too far for Asher's eyes to make out the details.

The saddle was laden with bags and supplies, but no visible weapons. More to the point, there was nothing to suggest the rider was a mage. Asher had to be wary of magic these days, his immunity to such things long gone with Paldora's gem.

Deciding now was the time to strike, Asher crouched down and picked up a small stone. A casual throw to the other side of the rider turned his attention away from the ranger. It was all the time Asher needed to abandon his cover and pull the stalker down from his horse.

Before he was even slammed into the ground, a hit-pitched yelp told Asher he was assaulting someone young. Young or not, he knew from his own early years that anyone capable of holding a blade was a danger to be reckoned with. Regardless of his age, this person had been stalking them and he would be treated as a foe until proven otherwise.

The ranger came down on top of him, ignoring the startled horse, and held a small dagger to the young man's throat. Terrified eyes looked up at Asher and he didn't even attempt to reach for his sword. He was no threat.

"Who the hell are you, then?" the ranger enquired, his dagger still pressed against the man's skin.

Vighon came galloping down the path with Asher's horse in tow. The young man, held firmly in place beneath Asher's bulk, turned his eyes to see the northman.

His features softened. "Vighon!" he cried.

The northman brought the horses to a stop and frowned at the prone figure. "Ruban?"

"You know him?" Asher looked from one man to the other.

"Aye, unfortunately for him." Vighon left his horse and walked over with a hint of anger in his expression. "What in all the hells are you doing out here, Ruban? I gave you orders to stay."

Stuck beneath Asher's knee, Ruban's voice was somewhat strained. "You did, but then you stopped being a captain. After that, I didn't really have to follow your orders..."

Seeing that he was in the middle of something he didn't care for, Asher sheathed his dagger and stood up, offering the young man a helping hand by way of apology.

Ruban patted his clothes down and held the hilt of his sword, emulating the stance of a warrior - something Asher decided he wasn't. "I came to... join you," the young man explained. "I've saved your life before; I thought I could be of help."

Asher pointed from Ruban to Vighon. "*He's* saved *your* life before? Maybe you should both return to Namdhor."

Vighon's back was up. "He fought by my side in the battle. And he fought well too." Seeing the beaming smile on Ruban's face, Vighon turned on him again. "That doesn't mean you should be here. This journey isn't for squires!"

"He's a *squire*?" Asher echoed.

"My name is Ruban Dardaris," the squire announced proudly, if a little defiantly.

Vighon looked a little embarrassed. "I didn't know that was your name."

Trying to hide his hurt, Ruban shrugged. "You never asked..."

Asher held up his hand before the conversation went any further. "This is getting out of hand. Vighon, send him home."

As clear as it was that Vighon loathed receiving orders from Asher, the northman agreed. "Get back on your horse, *Ruban Dardaris*. There's no place for you on this journey."

Ruban rushed forward and put himself between Vighon and the horses. "There's no place for me back there either. I don't know what you're doing, but I do know you wouldn't leave if it weren't for the betterment of Namdhor."

"Then I would say you don't know me very well," Vighon quipped, moving around the squire.

"But I do," Ruban argued. "This secret mission must have something to do with the war or you would be on the frontlines as we speak. I've seen you put yourself between the people and the orcs and from what the men of Grey Stone say, you've done so for more than just the north. Whether you're a captain of Namdhor or not... I *am* your squire."

Asher didn't like the way Vighon looked at him then. "You're already slowing me down," he warned the northman. "There's no more time to spare carrying him as well."

The squire moved to see both men. "I can be useful!" he proclaimed. "I have a sword! And I've used it! I brought more supplies with me," he blurted, seeing that his boasts were falling on deaf ears. "I know how to make camp and I can cook, I'm a *good* cook!"

Asher looked to Vighon, but the northman was stubbornly quiet when the ranger actually needed him to pipe up. "I'm going to Haren Bain. You can either go with him or come with me now, but there's no room for three on this trip." With that Asher turned his horse around and prepared to continue his journey along the path again.

"Haren Bain?" Ruban repeated. "What's that? I've never heard of that."

"It's where *we're* going and where you're *not* going," Vighon replied with the tone of finality Asher had been waiting for. "Go home, Ruban."

"I can't go back!" the squire called after the departing duo.

"Yes you can!" Vighon shouted over his shoulder. "Just turn your horse around and retrace your tracks."

Something clicked inside Asher's head and he stopped his horse. "Wait," he said, turning back to see the squire. "How did you know where to find us? No one followed us out of Namdhor."

There was a trace of worry on Ruban's face. "That's why I can't go back," he explained. "Word got back to The Dragon Keep that Vighon had been seen heading east on The Selk Road. I left immediately and managed to get a head start. I was lucky enough to see you in the distance when you left the road..."

Asher guided his horse around to face Ruban. "What do you mean you got a *head start*?" The squire winced and stuttered. "Speak, boy."

Vighon answered for him. "The Ironsworn are coming."

Ruban nodded. "He's sent Godfrey Cross."

"How many more?" Asher didn't much care for one man; it was the numbers that would give the thugs their advantage.

"A dozen maybe," Ruban shrugged. "I'm not sure. I left as soon as I could."

Vighon looked beyond the squire to the path they had taken. "They won't be far behind," he reasoned. "The weather might have covered our earlier tracks, but they might have been following Ruban."

Asher cast a look over the squire that communicated his resentment. "We need to push on, *now*."

"Push on?" Vighon challenged. "We have an advantage here. They don't know they're expected. We could camp in these woods and let them pass us by or even ambush them here - there's plenty of cover. Out there it's just plains."

Asher groaned. "The stupidity of youth... If we let them pass us by here we'll just have to face them somewhere else. If we stay and set up an ambush, we'll be attacking a dozen or more with two men and a child."

"I'm twenty-one years old!" Ruban protested.

Asher ignored him. "We *need* to press on. With any luck we'll outrun them to the River Adanae and lose them in the water."

"Lose them? The great Asher wants to outrun a few thugs?"

After a lifetime of blood and war, the ranger felt he had nothing to prove. "Pick your battles, northman. Time is our enemy now, not The Ironsworn."

Asher didn't much care whether the pair got on their horses and followed him - *he* was going east. The world was falling apart, after all, and the key to everything lay dormant, forgotten by all but a violent dragon and now Asher. He *had* to reach Haren Bain...

CHAPTER 17
FAMILY MATTERS

S wifter than the wind itself, Athis cut through the sky like a red blade, his scales dulled under the black clouds - though his appearance was no less magnificent for it. His beating wings filled Inara's ears with thunder as his speed filled her heart with hope. They were heading towards Alijah and nothing could get in their way.

For miles and miles, The White Vale had passed beneath them, a white blanket of snowy plains stretching as far as the eye could see. But now, that stark sheet was being gradually replaced by hills and cliffs as the ground crinkled and became dotted with trees and small forests.

The Vrost Mountains dominated the Dragorn's view.

They rose up to touch the heavens for some distance, farther than Inara could see. Mist gathered in the hollows and the curving valleys that carved out the mountain range. Never had Inara flown over this land and thought it harboured so much evil. The monsters of Illian were often associated with Vengora, but now she knew the greatest evil of all had been hiding here all along.

"Is that it?" her father called from behind, boxing her mother in between them. "Everything looks so different from up here..."

Inara pointed her mouth over her shoulder. "That's it, The Vrost Mountains!"

Reyna's voice was closer to Inara's ear. "I never realised how vast it was."

The young Dragorn looked back at the view before her and had to agree. The world had often felt like a small place from astride Athis - everything so easily accessible - but now that they were looking for a single structure that none of them had ever seen before, The Vrost Mountains felt like the proverbial haystack.

We will find him, wingless one.

Inara was thankful for Athis's bolstering words. Nothing felt impossible when her companion said it. **Asher told my parents to start at the top of the mountains in the west—**

And follow them east from there, Athis finished. *I remember; I was there when they told you.*

I'm sorry. I just want to find him...

And we will. I am concerned for your mother, however. She is not back to full health and we have been flying for some time. She needs to rest before you enter The Bastion.

Inara was inclined to agree. Her mother was capable of much and her stubbornness often gave her more reserves than most, but even she couldn't maintain this level of energy. Not after everything she had been through.

Can you see anywhere we can make camp for the night?

I will take us down and search closer to the ground.

Athis stopped beating his wings and began his descent into the curving valley. Inara swallowed hard as her ears popped and she advised her parents to hold on a little tighter, aware that Athis was going to be gliding from side to side in his search.

"Why are we going down?" Nathaniel asked. "Asher said to follow the *top* of the mountains!"

"We need to make camp for the night!" Inara yelled back.

"No!" her father protested. "We need to find The Bastion!"

Inara didn't want to argue with him, especially from such an awkward angle. Sensing this, Athis dipped a little faster, forcing everyone's stomach up into their chest and stealing any potential words. The red dragon continued to drop until he banked to the north in a bid to follow the curve of the mountain range.

Flying a little while longer, Athis used his unparalleled vision to discover a narrow crack in the side of a cliff face. It was wide enough for five men abreast and about as deep as Athis himself. It was also a few hundred feet above the ground.

You'll have to climb over me, Athis said.

Inara turned her head back to her parents. "Brace yourselves!"

Athis fanned his wings and slammed into the cliff face with all four of his thick claws. The rock crumbled at first, but the dragon found his anchor point and dug in.

I will keep searching while you rest.

Find some food if you can, Inara told him. **It's been too long since you ate anything.**

Yes, mother...

Inara instructed her parents to follow her up Athis's neck and over his head, making sure to use the same footholds. The dragon levelled his head at the base of the cave, allowing the trio to walk over his snout.

Once inside, her mother turned back to Athis and put a hand between his nostrils. "Thank you, Athis."

The dragon snorted a cloud of warm air into the cave and pushed away from the entrance. He dropped for a hundred feet as he rolled his body over before spreading his wings and taking off, back into the sky. Inara watched him disappear from the jagged entrance of the cave, never happy to see her companion fly away.

"We shouldn't be stopping," Nathaniel said, renewing his argument.

Reyna raised her hand to her husband. "We must be ready if we are to save Alijah. It won't help him if we storm The Bastion too tired to fight - who knows what we'll face in there."

Coming from his wife, Nathaniel took a breath and let it go. Instead, he pulled her in and gave his love a crushing hug. Every minute that went by was agony for them...

Leaving them to have a moment, Inara collected a handful of rocks and began piling them together in the middle of the narrow cave. There was no firewood to be had halfway up the cliff, but a Dragorn was never out of options. Inara could still remember Gideon saying those exact words during her training.

She missed him. Her master had been a source of comfort in hard times, his presence alone often enough to fill her with confidence.

Athis's soothing tone spoke into her mind. *How often of late have you faced the perils of this war without him? You are breaking free of the shackles that have bound you to your youth. The world is still turning because of your deeds, deeds that have seen you risen to master.*

Inara held her hand over the pile of rocks and used magic to heat them up. Their dull surface quickly turned into bright orange and waves of heat rose into the cave. It wasn't much, but it would do.

Inara? Athis coaxed.

I don't want titles. Not anymore. I'm... I'm not sure what I want anymore.

For years you dreamed of sitting on the council, Athis pointed out. *Then you dreamed of exploring the world, your duty be damned. Then, you wanted to prove yourself, to step out of your parents' shadow.*

Inara knelt in front of the heated rocks, nodding her head solemnly. **I wish I could take some of that back.**

It's not a bad thing to feel a little scattered, wingless one. We don't always know what we want to do with our lives, our gifts. We're still writing our story.

I just want to help people, Inara concluded. **Whatever my title is, wherever we are, whenever evil preys on the land... I want to help people. That's the only thing I know.**

She could tell Athis was pleased. *Then it is a good thing we are Dragorn.*

That didn't fill Inara with the warm feeling the dragon had intended. **There's something weighing on Gideon's mind, beside the war I mean. I think he's planning on doing something drastic.**

More drastic than entering Vengora alone?

He's had a lot of thoughts about the order recently. He doesn't just fear for our survival, but for our ability to serve the realm. He doubts himself...

I too have sensed something similar in Ilargo. As the masters of our order, they do not need to share their thoughts until they are commands.

Whatever happens, Inara said, **we will... I don't know how to say it.**

Knowing her inside and out, Athis replied, *You feel our identity is in the Dragorn.*

Yes, Inara agreed, thankful for the articulation.

Whatever decisions Gideon and Ilargo make, the dragon continued, *you and I will always remain the same, wingless one. Our purpose will always remain the same...*

Inara took comfort in her bond, the most important thing in her life. A very primal part of Athis's mind began to take over, relaying to Inara that her companion had spotted a potential meal.

Try not to get the little bones stuck between your teeth. I hate pulling them out...

There was no verbal response from the red dragon, his senses too honed in on his prey. The Dragorn let that part of their bond fall away, leaving her companion to it.

Her mother came to sit opposite the glowing rocks with a blanket draped over her cloak. Nathaniel sat beside her and rummaged through their supplies.

"You have been talking with Athis?" Reyna enquired.

"Yes. He's going to keep searching for The Bastion while we rest."

Judging by her father's expression, that bit of information placated him, though for how long she wouldn't like to guess.

"Is everything alright between you and Athis?" Reyna asked in her typical motherly way.

Inara chuckled lightly. "There's no *between us*, mother. There's just *us*. And yes, we're fine."

Reyna tilted her head, her emerald eyes piercing her daughter's mind. Inara had seen her mother look at her that way countless times growing up. It was infuriating. She knew there was more to be said yet she knew there was more to be gained by not actually asking anything. It was a technique Reyna had apparently learned from Faylen, her old mentor.

Giving in, Inara asked, "Did you always know what you wanted to do with your life? The two of you have always been so focused, always putting yourselves where you needed to be."

Her mother had a look of surprise about her. "I... I still have no idea what I want to do with my life. That's part of the fun, though, isn't it? Your father and I have just taken each day as it came. Some days brought joy, others heartbreak. I know what I want for my *family*, for those I *love*. But for myself? We're immortal, Inara. Best not to get tied down with any one thing."

Inara was capable of reading between the lines. "You'll never stop trying to get me to move back in, will you?"

With a cheeky grin, Reyna shook her head. "A mother's prerogative."

"Your mother's just jealous because you followed your old man's path and became a knight... of sorts." Nathaniel handed round a few pieces of food and water, his mood brightening.

"Nonsense!" Reyna protested. "I'm more proud of you than I can express in one lifetime."

"That we can agree on," Nathaniel added. "When the war's over your name will be more famous than ours."

Initially, Inara had meant to get advice from her parents about her own life, but there was an opening she couldn't ignore. "What about Alijah?" she asked suddenly, forcing a nervous glance between her parents. "Are you proud of him?" she pressed.

"Of course we are," Reyna was quick to reply.

Inara held her tongue for a minute, wishing to be delicate with her words. Her pause, however, troubled Reyna and Nathaniel.

"Why would you ask that?" her father quizzed.

"Before Alijah left for The Lifeless Isles with Gideon, we had a chance to talk. It had been four years so I had a lot of questions." Seeing her parents' eager faces, Inara decided to get to it. "He left because he felt overshadowed. Not just by your legacy but by me as well. He didn't know you were proud of him. In fact, he thought you both loved me more because I became a Dragorn."

"That's ridiculous!" Nathaniel flared. "We could never love one of you more than the other."

"Regardless of your accomplishments," Reyna added.

"He didn't know that," Inara continued. "We all know he was less driven than me growing up. You did... *praise* me more. Back then I loved it," she confessed. "I was the good one. But that made him feel like the bad one."

"We never meant..." Nathaniel couldn't finish and he looked down at the ground as Reyna placed a hand on his back.

"We never meant for him to feel like that," her mother finished. "We just wanted him to be happy."

Inara was beginning to feel a little guilty about upsetting her parents. "It wasn't just us, the way we were. Alijah found a grey hair, a few actually."

Reyna blinked in confusion. "A grey hair?"

Nathaniel looked up with glassy eyes. "How could he find a grey hair?"

"He wasn't immortal," Inara answered simply. "He didn't inherit immortality like I did. Though, it's possible I didn't either. We'll never know now that I'm bonded with Athis."

"Alijah has a bond now too!" Nathaniel said with revelation. "His bond with Malliath will make him immortal, yes?"

"It will," Inara confirmed, happy to ease her father's concern.

Reyna stared at the glowing rocks. "He wasn't immortal..." she muttered in a berating tone. "I should have known."

"It doesn't matter now," Inara consoled. "With Malliath he will live forever, like us. But that's why I'm telling you all of this. We *will* free Alijah from The Bastion. We *will* have a second chance with him. If Asher's even a little bit right about Malliath, though, Alijah's going to need us more than ever. He needs to know how we feel about him. He needs to know he's loved."

"Are *you* worried about his bond with Malliath?" her father asked.

"No. I've never heard of a bond produce evil, not between dragon and rider. Besides, he'll have Gideon to guide him, just as I did."

Nathaniel didn't look convinced. "That means nothing. His recklessness is the reason—"

"You have to let this go," Inara spoke over him. "Gideon has his flaws, like all of us, but he's never done anything but try to keep the realm safe. The Dragorn order is still young; he hasn't had the luxury of choosing those to help him." As true as that statement was, Inara knew she needed to strike to the heart of her father's variance. "You're just angry because Gideon was there for him when he was lost, and you weren't. By directing Hadavad, Gideon gave Alijah a sense of purpose. He might not have known it was Gideon, but Hadavad never did anything but look out for him. And you know as well as I do that Gideon would have stepped in the moment Hadavad tried to take advantage of Alijah."

Nathaniel took a breath, considering his daughter's words. "She sounds like you," he said to Reyna.

"You mean she sounds right?" Both mother and daughter shared a smile, one so infectious that Nathaniel couldn't help but mimic it.

"I *may* have been too harsh on him," the old knight admitted with some reluctance. "I just..." His demeanour dropped again. "I just wish I could have been there for him."

"You can," Inara told her father. "You can be there for him now, when he needs you most."

Her parents hugged each other, swapping promises of future deeds. Inara was beckoned by both and brought into the huddle. It didn't feel the same as cosying up to Athis under the stars, but it still felt like home.

This was what they were all fighting for.

THE CROW'S eyes snapped open and his mind returned to the present, a place that was almost as chaotic as the future. Without a word, he took the wet cloth from Morvir and wiped the blood from his face and hands. It always took a moment to focus on where and when he was.

Images, sounds, and even smells bombarded his mind. As always, he had seen a vast army at Alijah's feet and a world bowing down to him. This time, however, Sarkas had narrowed his vision and refrained from looking upon the important events. It had hurt, of course, but he had seen imminent scenes that would soon play out in these very halls.

With the help of Morvir he slowly rose to his feet again. Decades of using such powerful magic was finally taking its toll, but it mattered not; it was all coming to an end soon, even for him. He looked down at the dead prisoner, motionless in the middle of his private chamber.

"Get rid of him," he commanded.

Morvir stamped his staff twice onto the floor and two dark mages entered the room. Without dawdling, they heaved the body between them and hurried out through the door, dripping blood with every step.

"What did the great Kaliban show you, Lord Crow?"

Your death, the necromancer thought.

Walking away from his servant, Sarkas massaged his left temple, the source of what was going to be a throbbing headache. "The next stage of Alijah's training is about to begin."

Morvir trailed his master, eager to hear more. "What would Kaliban have us do?"

Sarkas considered everything he had just seen. "I leave tonight."

Morvir grinned like a child. "I will gather the others immediately!"

"No," Sarkas hissed. "Everyone is to stay, yourself included. I will go alone." The Crow walked over to his long desk to collect what few things he needed; he wouldn't need much in these last days.

"But, Lord Crow," Morvir pleaded. "I am the first servant; I should be by your side. Those of our order can protect you."

"The Reavers will accompany me," Sarkas relayed without a hint of emotion.

Morvir looked distressed. "What are we to do here, Lord Crow? Should we continue Alijah's training?"

Sarkas spun on his heel to face his incompetent servant. "You will go nowhere near him! In fact, Morvir," he added with a coy smile, "you are to make certain he never leaves that cell."

The first servant produced his usual expression of confusion. "But how could he ever escape such a cell, Lord Crow?"

Sarkas turned back to his desk and began unravelling one of his maps, making sure it was spread across the surface. "He will have help." His answer was perfectly cryptic, putting Morvir on edge.

The first servant cast his eyes around the room nervously. "The Dragorn are coming?"

Sarkas didn't reply straight away, letting Morvir panic a while longer. Instead, he walked around his desk and examined the Viridian Ruby that hung on a stand. He had taken no satisfaction from Hadavad's death, regardless of the thorn he had been. The old mage's demise had simply been necessary, not just for Alijah but also for the last stage of The Crow's plan.

Sarkas removed the ruby necklace and placed it inside his robes. "Yes, the Dragorn are coming. And a few others..."

"Others?" Morvir echoed, gripping his staff with both hands. "And we are to... repel them?"

Sarkas looked down on his servant. "*Oh yes,*" he said dramatically. "Kaliban is relying on you and the others, Morvir. Alijah must not be freed, not yet." Every word was a lie, of course, but The Black Hand's days had always been numbered, just as Morvir's were, just as Sarkas's were...

"There are only a handful of us who remain. I have sent all that I could to the dig site..." Morvir straightened out his robes and tried to look confident. "But, if Kaliban wishes it, The Black Hand will see it done!" he proclaimed, his bravado lacking true belief. "You have seen this, Lord Crow? You have seen our victory here?"

One last lie. Why not? "You will all survive to see the kingdom we have strived for. It will be glorious!" Morvir took some heart in that. "You say the boat is ready?" Sarkas asked, cutting through the moment.

Morvir cleared his throat. "Yes, Lord Crow. It awaits in the docks of Velia. I have a small crew waiting to take you from there."

"Excellent. Then I shall say my goodbyes..."

Sarkas made his way back into the bowels of The Bastion. As the door to Alijah's cell opened, he glimpsed flashes and blurs flitting around inside. Only when Alijah was permitted to sleep did Sarkas see enough of him to know it was even a man.

Crossing the threshold was briefly nauseating. Once inside, his mind and body were captured by the powerful spells that encapsulated the room. There he saw his Reavers, the perfect killing machines, still in possession of their skills, skills only found in Nightfall. In the middle of the room, Alijah was exercising.

Holding onto the chains that hung from the ceiling, he kept his legs together as he lifted them into the air, bringing his feet in line with his waist. It was a hard exercise for anyone to do, but doing it with a wooden bar resting over his ankles and two heavy buckets of water on each end made it almost impossible.

Almost.

Alijah knew that if he should spill any of the water hanging over his feet, the Reavers would jump in and renew his beatings. In the

243

beginning, many months ago, he had continuously dropped the buckets and spilt water everywhere. His beatings had been severe and relentless. Now, however, Sarkas looked upon a honed warrior, his focus absolute. Alijah's muscles were taut, if covered in scars, and his expression was pure determination.

"You can stop that now," Sarkas told him.

Finally, Alijah had come to believe his every word and knew he wasn't being tricked. The young warrior lowered his legs and carefully placed the buckets down before standing before The Crow.

"I'm leaving," he announced.

There was a flicker of uncertainty on Alijah's face, sadness perhaps. "When will you return?"

"I won't be returning this time," Sarkas explained. "I have done all I can within these walls. Your time here is almost at an end." A mental command caused every Reaver in the cell to file out, confusing Alijah all the more. "They are coming with me."

"I am to stay here... alone?"

"For a time, yes. It will be good for you. Time is needed to think, to dwell on all that has transpired here. When the time comes, Alijah, you must *choose* to be who you are. Such a choice cannot be made without a little introspection. Consider that your last lesson," Sarkas said, turning back for the door. "No king before you ever took a moment to observe himself and see the truth of who they really are."

Alijah remained perfectly still in the middle of his cell. After everything that had happened to him in The Bastion, Sarkas could understand the shock that would come with realising it was over.

Pausing by the threshold, The Crow had some parting words. "We will meet again, Alijah Galfrey. You, and you alone, will know where to find me. I only hope that you do before it's too late..."

Giving no chance to reply, Sarkas walked out and used his wand to shut the door behind him. He had one last task before he could leave the world in Alijah's hands.

CHAPTER 18
CHOOSING LIFE

The forest was quiet, but for the rhythmic pounding of burning missiles in the distance. Gideon had moved between the snow-covered pines like a ghost, his footsteps deliberate and his movements precise. There were no orcs to be seen, but this was certainly their territory.

Following the thousands of tracks in the snow and mud was easy. The orcs had barrelled through the forest in a desperate bid to escape Malliath's rage. The tracks were everywhere, splitting off in every direction, but the Master Dragorn was sure to trail the densest tracks.

Smoke drifted on the breeze and he knew from his bond with Ilargo that the fires were east of his position.

Gideon despaired. *Only Arlon Draqaro could think that setting the world on fire is a good thing.*

Focus, Ilargo replied sternly. *I cannot see you through these trees, which means I cannot see anything else.*

I'm fine, Ilargo.

Gideon pressed on, following the tracks. It was as if the orcs felt the calling of the dark, their instincts showing them to the holes in the world. Rounding a dense cluster of pines the Master Dragorn came across an upturned chariot. One of their foul six-legged fiends lay dead at the front, half covered in snow and ash. By the look of its charred body, the animal had suffered Malliath's wrath and survived just long enough to reach this far.

He crouched down and inspected the chariot's contents. There were no more wrath bolts inside and no signs of any orcs. The six-legged beast had a stench about it, but it wasn't the smell that drove Gideon away, it was the low growl of a wolf.

Standing up very slowly, the Master Dragorn turned around to discover a pack of wolves surrounding him. Whether he was on their territory or he was simply competition for the meat, the wolves didn't want him there. The largest of the pack, shaggy and dark of fur, stepped closer and bared its fangs.

In truth, there was little to fear on Gideon's part; he just didn't want to kill any wolves. His magic couldn't be described as powerful, but it was definitely enough to repel a few wolves without bursting them apart. To ensure he didn't take any lives, the Master Dragorn sheathed Mournblade, his eyes never straying from the alpha's.

"I'm going to leave now," he said quietly.

With slow steps, he made his way north of the toppled chariot. He aimed for a large gap between two of the wolves, hoping they would understand he was no threat. The nearest of the pack growled at him and adjusted its stance to face him.

"Easy..."

The rest of the pack was closing in from behind, making Gideon wonder if they were more interested in eating him. With his palms out, however, a spell waited for any wolf too confident that he was prey.

As he approached a thick pine tree, Gideon realised he had no choice but to go around it, a path that would take him too close to the nearest wolf. He turned around to face the rest of the pack, regretful about what he was going to do next. Still, a telekinetic shove wouldn't kill any of them, but it would make them think twice about hunting him.

Palm out, Gideon prepared to unleash the spell upon them. The wolves cowered. Their growls changed to whimpers and they began to back up, away from the Master Dragorn. It wasn't the reaction he had expected but, then again, the wolves weren't looking at him. Noting the point of their attention, Gideon quickly came to the conclusion that there was something in the tree behind him. Something the pack was afraid of...

Keeping his palm out, Gideon changed the spell he had in mind. Before he could completely turn around again, the pine tree exploded as an orc leapt out from its branches. Raising his hand, a shield flared to life in a flash of colour, offering the orc nothing but a hard wall to slam into. A quick reverse of the spell propelled the orc back into the tree with enough force to break limbs.

Everything happened at once. The alpha fled into the forest, trailed by its pack, the wounded orc crashed down through the tree, and the surrounding pines came alive with more of the wretched creatures. Gideon removed Mournblade and assumed the stance of form three, his favourite among the techniques of the Mag'dereth.

More orcs appeared, this time from within mounds of snow that surrounded the area. Together, they created a cacophonous roar, thankful to their wicked god that there was someone they could kill.

Try not to have too much fun, Ilargo said across their bond. *Remember, you still need to find a way inside the mountain.*

Gideon made a quick head-count of his opponents and found a dozen orcs had chosen today as the day they would meet their god. *I'll try not to...* he replied with a smile.

Remaining perfectly still, Gideon waited for his enemies to close in on him. Orcs were good fighters, but their bloodlust always took over in battle, making them impulsive and dangerous to each other when fighting side by side. It also meant he could kill more than one of them with a single swipe of his Vi'tari scimitar...

Using a burst of movement, the Master Dragorn brought Mournblade across two of the orcs in a sweeping motion. They hadn't even tried to attack him before their insides were visible on the outside, their deaths assured. As they fell away, screaming and yelling in their death throes, three more of the group lunged at Gideon with their obsidian weapons, crude in comparison to Mournblade.

Following through the movements of form three, Gideon evaded and parried until he was naturally taken into form four of the Mag'dereth. With Mournblade in hand, all three of the fiends felt the biting touch of its enchanted steel. All three were dead before they hit the snow.

Gideon fell back to form one and went on the defensive as the next wave of five orcs rushed him. Comparable to a dancer, the Master Dragorn spun, flipped, and twisted out of the way, his scimitar flashing here and there to bat obsidian blades away. Ducking under the swing of an orc which thought it was successfully flanking him, Gideon whipped Mournblade across its waist, severing most of the blood vessels and organs that connected the orc's legs to the rest of its body.

Returning to his full height and facing the rest of the group, Gideon held Mournblade out to his side, observing the last droplets of blood running free of the steel. Within seconds it looked freshly forged again. Then, the group pounced on him with a violent vengeance.

Seconds later, the Vi'tari blade was soaked in orc blood again.

The Master Dragorn weaved between the hunting pack, his enchanted sword lashing left and right, until he was out the other side. Four dropped to the ground behind him with mortal wounds.

Three orcs remained, their gaze fixed on the very tip of Mournblade as the last of their kin's blood ran into the snow. Nervous glances passed between them, followed by a few words in their guttural language. Following that, the three fanned out, hoping to take Gideon from different angles. It was commendable, but folly.

Assessing their angles of attack, the Master Dragorn assumed the stance of form five. Barring the less-known style of form six, it was the most aggressive of the Mag'dereth's teachings. It was also the most unorthodox, making it the perfect technique to employ against a group of fighters.

As one, the orcs closed in from three different sides. Gideon spun in a circle, his blade outstretched in one direction and his leg flexed in another direction. He cut the throat of one, kicked the second, and parried the third. He immediately advanced on the third orc, coming down on it with heavy strikes, but he ultimately dropped to one knee, twisted his body in the snow, and plunged Mournblade backwards into the orc's gut.

Now, there was only one orc left.

Recovering from Gideon's kick, the orc stumbled to its feet, desperate to put as much space as possible between them but, reaching its feet, the pale beast tripped over the body of another and fell face first into the snow again. Gideon walked steadily towards it.

Just kill it and move on, Gideon.

I don't want to kill it, he replied.

But what else is there to do with an orc?

The beast in question scrambled to its feet again and sprinted away, towards the mountains. **Well, I was thinking about following it,** Gideon said smugly.

He sheathed Mournblade and dashed into the forest after the orc, pretending to give chase in the hopes of a kill. The orc yelled at him over its shoulder, its words lost to the forest.

The ground shook under Gideon's feet.

Then again.

And again.

The impacts were stronger each time.

Look out! Ilargo's warning came with an imagery of fire and death.

Gideon stopped in his tracks and looked up as a flaming ball of Namdhorian fury rocketed into the forest. The pines were blown aside and licked by the flames, but the fleeing orc wasn't so lucky. The burning missile buried the creature into the ground with a deafening impact. Gideon held his hand up to shield his eyes from the blinding flames and exploding debris.

The catapults have been moved! Ilargo told him furiously.

More flaming missiles hurtled through the trees and slammed into the ground, shattering trunks and felling the pines.

Get out of there, Gideon!

The Master Dragorn broke into a sprint, returning to the path taken by the orc. ***It was running this way for a reason!***

Ilargo wasn't satisfied. *That will take you farther north, keeping you in line with the catapults!*

The tracks are consistent here, Gideon argued, jumping over the roots of a fallen tree. ***This is the right way!***

What good is the right way if it leads to your death?

Gideon skidded to a stop as another fireball hit the ground in front of him. The smoke was beginning to fill the small forest now, obscuring his vision. With nowhere else to go, he pushed on, running between the burning missiles and broken trees. Another broke through the canopy and hammered the ground to Gideon's right, sending chunks of wood and mud into the air.

Finally, the muddied path, laden with orcish footprints, came to an end at the base of a shear wall, where the mountain had been cut in half by a narrow valley. The ground was harder and the path strewn with ancient boulders and cracked walls of moss. Even if it hadn't been the path taken by the orc horde, Gideon would have taken it just to avoid the Namdhorian salvo.

The farther into the narrow valley he explored, the more distant the burning missiles sounded. The air was clearer, if a little misted, and he could breathe more easily. The high walls had a haunted feel to them, however, as if the stone itself was watching Gideon.

It didn't take much of a search to discover more traces of the horde. Wounded in the battle or in their escape, the orcs had bled across the rocks, smearing them with their hands and feet. Of course, without any of that, he could have continued to follow the trail of discarded armour and weapons, abandoned in the shadow of Malliath.

Somewhere overhead, Ilargo was following him. The green dragon was too high for Gideon to make out, but he could feel his companion close by.

Turn back, Ilargo.

Since leaving me you have encountered a pack of wolves, engaged a hunting party of orcs, and nearly been squashed by Namdhorian catapults. I think I shall stay nearer to you...

Gideon pushed his way up a small rise that met the side of the mountain, hoping to see a little farther ahead, beyond the large boulders and rocks that dotted the path. **We agreed that you would stay close to Namdhor, remember? If the orcs decide to attack, one of us needs to be there to help.**

Ilargo was nothing if not stubborn. *I will be no good to the Namdhorians if you die now and kill us both.*

Gideon made it to the top of the gravelly rise and peered over the nearest boulder. Spotting a band of orcs, he immediately crouched out of sight and began to skid back down to the valley floor.

Oh good, Ilargo said, his tone heavy with sarcasm, *more orcs...*

Yes, more orcs, Gideon replied, frustrated. **You were fooling yourself if you didn't think there would be more orcs between me and Arathor. And sarcasm isn't befitting of a dragon,** he added with coy smile, knowing that his companion would be huffing in the sky.

What exactly is your plan? Ilargo questioned pointedly. *Are you going to take on every orc that stands in your path? It will only take one survivor to alert the entire horde to your presence.*

Now that would be foolish. Gideon crept along the path, hugging the awkward boulders. **The orcs weren't moving. It's possible they're guarding an entrance into the mountain.**

A sense of worry overcame Ilargo and crossed their bond.

There's nothing more dangerous in those caves than me, Ilargo.

The dragon disagreed. *There is nothing more dangerous in those caves than* me, *Gideon. You can only get away with saying that above ground, when I am with you.*

Gideon rolled his eyes and sighed. **I will be fine, old friend. Now, turn back and keep an eye out for... well, anything.**

The closer he crept the louder the orcs became, shouting at each other in their hideous language. Crossing the valley, Gideon climbed another rise and stole a look at the band in the distance. The majority of them were huddled around two individuals who had stripped down to their waists. The huddle roared as the two collided with heavy blows, their horns locking together.

It seemed the orcs were incapable of enduring peace. Fighting was all they knew, all they craved. As entertaining as the orcs found their scrap, Gideon was more interested in the arching cave, dug into the mountain side. The orcs had departed the entrance to seek out the space required for their tussle, leaving the path into the mountain unguarded.

You see, Ilargo; nothing to worry about.

There was no verbal reply from the dragon, but his feelings on the matter were easy to detect. Ignoring his companion's concerns, Gideon moved between the boulders and worked his way around to the cliff face that housed the cave entrance. There was, however, a significant patch of open ground between himself and the cave.

He waited, weighing up his odds of reaching the entrance without any one of the spectating orcs seeing him. Ultimately, he had no choice; he had to get inside and find Arathor, before there wasn't enough of him to find.

Gideon, wait...

Ilargo's voice gave the Master Dragorn pause, rooting him to the spot with muscles tensed and ready to spring. **What is it, Ilargo? My window is short.**

The dragon didn't reply straight away and Gideon sensed his companion's mind reaching out, beyond their bond. *Ayana and*

252

Alastir return! he proclaimed at last. *I can feel the edges of Deartanyon's thoughts, Valkor's too.*

That *was* good news. Gideon allowed himself a moment to breathe and embrace the elation he felt. So long had it been since such a feeling that it was almost foreign to him, but he welcomed it back with open arms.

Can you connect us to them? he asked the dragon.

There was another pause from Ilargo. *Only Deartanyon and Ayana. I sense Valkor and Alastir are too weak; the distance is too great.*

That's fine, let them concentrate on flying. We need to speak with Ayana and—

Gideon? Ayana's voice came through the dragons' bond, though it sounded distant, absent the melodic tone typical of an elf.

It's good to hear your voice, Ayana. Gideon had more questions regarding her mission to aid Alastir, but his angst was easily conveyed across the bond.

Alastir and Valkor are not far behind me, the elf explained immediately. **They are still wounded and travel slowly, but I believe they will overcome their ailments. Deartanyon and I have suffered no injury.**

More good news. Gideon sank a little lower behind the boulder and focused on their bond. **There have been developments since you left, but Ilargo can pass all of it on to Deartanyon; it'll be quicker. In the meantime, get yourselves safely back to Namdhor. Stay out of The Dragon Keep, though; you'll find better shelter among Lady Ellöria's company.**

Ayana's reply came in the form of a probing strand that weaved through the bond they all shared. **What exactly are you doing, Gideon? I sense a great disturbance in Ilargo...**

Of course his companion wasn't keeping anything to himself. Gideon shared with Ilargo the same exasperation he would display with a human eye roll. He could also sense that Ilargo was about to tell Ayana and Deartanyon everything about his plan... or lack thereof.

I'm going to find Arathor, he blurted before Ilargo could begin. *I won't let him die, Ayana.*

You're going into Vengora alone? the elf retorted, her opinion on the matter very clear.

Gideon considered the fight not too far away. *I know, I know. Ilargo has pointed out the flaws in my plan more than once. I really don't have time; I have to—*

When a dragon tells you your path is folly, Ayana interrupted, *you stop and listen. Those are your words, Gideon! You're allowing your emotions to control you. Arathor knew the risks when he chose to become a Dragorn. The authority and wisdom both you and Ilargo carry are too important to lose for one life.*

Gideon shook his head. *I disagree. All I know is, Arathor will die if I don't act. I'm choosing life for him.* He wanted to say a lot more, but his window of opportunity was closing fast. *Get back to Namdhor, Ayana. Take care of Alastir and Valkor and I shall return with Arathor shortly.*

He couldn't promise the latter, but if he couldn't bring Arathor back, he wouldn't be returning from the orc lands himself. With that, Gideon instructed Ilargo to sever their connection with Ayana and Deartanyon; this wasn't the time for a debate.

You will suffer Ayana's wrath should we survive this, Ilargo said unhelpfully. *Inara's too,* the dragon added. *It wasn't long ago that Inara reminded you of the order's purpose: we are the shield that guards the realm from darkness. Just as we should not hesitate to send others into danger, we should not risk so much for one life.*

You would place our lives above Arathor's and Thraden's? Gideon asked with disbelief.

Yes, Ilargo answered honestly. *As Ayana pointed out, the authority and wisdom we carry is important to the order and therefore important to the realm. The Dragorn have always known casualties; they are sacrifices befitting of our purpose.*

Gideon pressed his fist hard into the boulder's rough surface. *I know all this, Ilargo. I know I'm supposed to send Dragorn out into the world, into danger itself. I know I shouldn't hesitate to lay down the immortal lives of dragons for the realm. I know I'm supposed to be the Master Dragorn who makes the hard choices, regardless of the lives I throw at a problem.*

He took a breath.

The truth is: I'm sending children into war, Ilargo. I can't overlook that, no matter what my title is. None of them are prepared for the real darkness this world has to offer. Arathor deserves a chance to be trained, to be trained properly so that he might defend himself as well as others. I'm not an elf, like my predecessors. I can't be pragmatic when it suits me and emotional when it suits me. I'm human to the bone. We're emotional all the time. I can't have another life on my shoulders...

In the silence that followed, Gideon felt Ilargo's presence fill him up, bringing their minds into harmony. They shared all of their fears and emotions until they felt like one being that occupied both the land and the sky. After they came back together in unity, their post-war plan felt all the more compounded.

There might be no memories left of the original Dragon Riders, Ilargo said, *but I am certain you would be counted among the best of our human companions.*

Gideon appreciated the words from Ilargo and would have reciprocated with a compliment for the dragon, but time was against him.

Peering over the boulder again, the fight had shifted as one of the orcs had fallen to the floor and his opponent had leapt on top of him. A savage beating was given, which only served to excite the jeering crowd. As their eyes followed the fighters to the ground, Gideon took his chances.

As quietly as he could, the Master Dragorn dashed along the cliff face, pausing only once as he disturbed a loose patch of stones. The orcs didn't so much as twitch in his direction, their eyes glued to the blood in front of them. As he reached the edge of the entrance, Gideon realised his error. Had he waited a while longer and taken the time to observe his point of infiltration, he would have seen the miserable orc that remained on guard, just in the shadows.

Rounding the edge of the cave, the orc was close, so much so that Gideon was unable to remove Mournblade from his scabbard. If he was to find any success, it would be because the guarding orc was just as startled by Gideon's appearance as he was of its appearance. Unlike the Master Dragorn, the orc failed to adapt to their close encounter and still fumbled for his sword.

Gideon didn't fumble.

Using form six of the Mag'dereth, a deadly form of hand-to-hand combat known only to himself, Gideon assaulted the orc with fists alone. The technique required as few as five touches before the mortal blow could be delivered. That fifth and final attack was a hammering knock to the orc's temple. Dead, the creature could do nothing but crumple under its own weight, which was significant given that it was in full armour. The Master Dragorn reached out and caught the falling body before a great clatter could echo throughout the entire cave network.

He waited again, ensuring he hadn't been observed by the group lower down. It wouldn't be that long before the fight was over and they returned to the entrance, whereupon they would come across their dead kin. Gideon decided to give himself as much time as possible and drag the body farther into the mountains. A missing guard would be a mystery, but a mystery was better than an obvious invasion.

The cave penetrated the mountain for more than fifty feet before sloping down; a fact that Gideon was thankful for while dragging an orc in full armour. A part of him wondered if it would have been easier to have simply killed all the orcs in the valley.

It's thinking like that, Gideon Thorn, that will see us both to our doom.

Sweating, Gideon didn't bother with a reply but, instead, continued to drag the orc along. He found a small cluster of rocks, off to one side, and decided to conceal the body between them. It probably wouldn't work considering the strength of orcish night vision, but it was the best he could do.

The Master Dragorn remained crouched by the rocks, concerned now with his own night vision. Seeing as clearly as they did in such conditions, the orcs didn't require torches to show them the way. What little light there was from the mouth of the tunnel did nothing for his human eyes beyond his current position.

There were numerous spells he knew that would assist him, but all of them would require a degree of sustainability. He had no idea how long he was going to be wandering around in the dark for, let alone how long it would take to get Arathor out. He just couldn't handle that kind of magic anymore...

As always, his eternal companion had a solution. *You have a vial of Nocturn's Phemora in your jacket.*

Gideon patted the outside of his jacket and felt the neat row of vials sitting on the inside. **What would I do without you?**

Wander blindly through the depths of Vengora most likely.

The Master Dragorn retrieved the purple liquid from inside his jacket and made the mistake of smelling it once he popped the small cork. It was foul, as any liquid would be when its colour was as unnatural as purple. Still, he had made it himself, a derivative of the Nightseye elixir used by the Arakesh. With the exception of his vision, his senses would remain as they were, rather than over-loading him with information he wasn't trained to handle.

You don't have many vials left, Ilargo remarked.

I haven't exactly had time to attend to brewing any potions of late. You might've noticed it's the end of the world.

All the more reason to be prepared. Are you not the one who instructs every Dragorn to be prepared for all situations? You should have every potion in that jacket of yours.

Gideon downed the potion in one and wiped his mouth as the sour liquid bathed his tongue. **Well, look on the bright side; if we die, future Dragorn will learn from it and take the lesson more seriously.**

Only a human would suggest looking on the bright side of death...

Gideon would have laughed to himself were he not so far behind enemy lines. He blinked hard, several times as the *Nocturn's Phemora* took effect, altering his perception. Bit by bit, the shadows of Vengora disappeared, as if an unseen light source was shining on everything. Up ahead, what had been an abyss with no end was now a visible tunnel that curved round to the left.

Time to find Arathor...

CHAPTER 19
WHO HUNTS THE HUNTERS?

T he deeper Doran Heavybelly travelled into the Vengoran landscape, the more he felt at home. It was as if his very bones resonated with the mountain stone that rose up around him. To be on the hunt, and that of an orc too, only intensified the feeling for the dwarf.

Together with Galanör and Russell, they had tracked the lone orc for nearly two days. Doran had told his companions many times that they had Grarfath and Yamnomora to thank for guiding the witless orc ever northward, towards Dhenaheim. Of course, given his misdeeds among his own people, there was every chance the dwarven gods were leading Doran to his death.

That thought alone drove the son of Dorain to dwell on what lay before him. His mother had asked one thing of him prior to aiding his escape from Karak-Nor, and by returning to Grimwhal he was spitting in her face.

"What troubles you, Doran?" Galanör asked, riding his horse alongside the Warhog. "You have the look of a dwarf stricken with grief."

Doran glanced at the elf before returning his gaze to the path ahead, where Russell was leading with his sensitive nose. "Our paths have crossed at times in the last decade or two. Never 'ave ye asked what troubles me, elf."

"Now our paths are aligned," Galanör pointed out. "Your troubles are mine now, especially given my heritage and our destination."

"Oh aye, ye right to be fearin' me kin. The days o' any alliance, be it with humans, elves or even among themselves, has long passed. There's no welcome where we're goin'," he added grimly.

"And is that what troubles you?" Galanör pressed. "You fear our reception?"

Doran licked his lips, wondering how he could excuse himself from the conversation. Still, the persistent elf had a good point; they were in it together now and what affected one of them would have consequences for all of them.

"Ye recall me recent visit to Grimwhal?"

The elf nodded from atop his horse. "I was present for the tale."

"Aye, well there was a detail I missed out." Doran could still remember his mother's urgency, all too aware that her son would die should he remain. "I told ye that me mother helped us escape, but her only condition was that I never return."

"You don't wish to break your promise," Galanör concluded. "Take heart, Doran, your errand carries the weight of Illian—"

"Bah!" The dwarf waved the stupid comment away. "I ain' afraid o' breakin' no promise, elf! I'm aware o' what we're doin' 'ere. What *troubles me* is Dorain, son o' Dorryn..."

Galanör looked down on the dwarf with a raised eyebrow. "Your father?"

"Unfortunately. Grarfath gave 'im a stone for a head! He's likely to order me execution on the spot... right in front o' me mother."

A look of understanding flashed across Galanör's face. "And you don't want her to see that."

"O' course not! Nor me brother for that matter." Doran considered his troubles a moment longer and discovered there was actually something worse than his immediate execution. "An' what if he doesn' order me death straight away? What if he decides to 'ave me questioned abou' our escape from Karak-Nor? That'll 'ave been no small thing, let me tell ye! There's only so long ye can lie before the inquisitors get the truth out o' ye. He'd 'ave us all parted from our heads if he learned the truth."

For just a moment, the weight of the world be damned, Doran considered turning Pig around and journeying back into Illian.

"None of that will come to pass," Galanör replied confidently.

"Oh? An' how can ye know that?"

The elven ranger gestured to the path ahead. "Because your father will be far too occupied with the orc in his throne room."

Doran frowned and turned his attention from Galanör to Russell. Up ahead, his horse and cart had come to a stop, only the werewolf himself was nowhere to be seen.

"Abou' time!" Doran hollered, jumping down from his Warhog.

Beside Galanör, the two made their way down the path on foot, passing Russell's horse and cart. A little beyond the mount, the narrow path opened up and descended into a pit of gravel and fallen rocks. Both elf and dwarf crept around to the left, keeping high as they circumnavigated the pit. Russell's impressive frame and cropped white hair were visible from their position, crouched as he was behind the trunk of a tree that had grown awkwardly from the slope of the pit.

"Psst!" Doran tried to get the werewolf's attention.

Close to the dwarf's ear, Galanör sniffed. "I think he can probably smell you..."

The son of Dorain ignored the comment and waited for Russell to acknowledge them. Without facing them, the old ranger pointed down into the pit. Following his finger, Doran and Galanör both spotted the wounded orc they had been chasing.

"Well, what are we waitin' for? Let's bag it an' be on with it."

Russell held up his hand, halting the dwarf's charge. He flashed them his yellow eyes before pointing elsewhere. Doran had to adjust his own hiding position to see where the wolf was pointing to now.

Upon sighting the source of Russell's caution, the dwarf of clan Heavybelly swallowed hard. "Oh... I see."

On the other side of the pit, stalking down towards the oblivious orc, were three spiders, each twice the size of a horse. Their spindly legs carried their bulbous bodies effortlessly down the mountain's wall without a sound. With black hides and splashes of purple, they were truly beasts of the deep, creatures that didn't belong on the bright surface of the world.

"That's not right," Doran observed. "Beasts so foul as 'em 'ave never been seen outside the mountains. There are ancient tales o' 'em huntin' me kin, but never under the sky; they dwell too deep."

Galanör slowly drew his scimitars. "Perhaps the orcs have displaced them."

Creeping back towards them, Russell said, "Either way, they're set on eating our prey; that makes them competition." The werewolf removed the pick-axe from his back.

Doran looked shocked. "Are we actually goin' to save an orc's life?"

"Don't think of it as saving," Russell replied. "We're just *extending* its life until your clan rips it to bits."

Doran considered his friend's description of the orc's death and decided he wasn't far off. "Fine, but let's leave this part out o' our tale, shall we. I don' wan' to be known as the dwarf that saved an orc..."

As one, the three hunters rose from their cover and charged down the slope with weapons in hand. Doran cried the loudest, hoping to warn the orc about the spiders behind him, but the orc was more concerned with the three companions who had slaughtered his band, and so it didn't even notice the spiders.

The son of Dorain tripped on the uneven slope and was propelled forward in a painful roll and tumble that took limbs over limbs. Cursing the terrain, Doran managed to turn his violent roll into a leaping charge just as he reached the bottom of the pit. The orc was brandishing its sword now and baring its fangs in a bid to appear dangerous. Whether it heard the spiders approaching or noticed Doran's eyes focused beyond it, the orc finally turned around and looked upon certain death.

Gone was its boldness, now replaced with terror. The orc hurried backwards to join the three hunters, their temporary alliance naturally assumed in the face of such monsters.

Galanör skipped off the lower stones and came down beside the orc from on high. The elf was taking no chances, having finally caught up with their elusive prey, and brought the pommel of his scimitar down on the back of the orc's head, dropping it where it stood.

The three spiders angled down towards them, their black eyes fixed on their next meals and their pincer-like legs piercing the gravel. Doran tightened his grip on his sword in one hand and his hatchet in the other. He had never killed a giant spider before and he was looking forward to adding it to his repertoire. In fact, he was hoping, when the war was over, to raise the price of his services considering the number of beasties he had killed of late.

"Let's be on with it, ye ugly fiends! Come an' meet me steel!"

The closer the spiders approached, the closer they were to each other, a state that three predators such as these were not accustomed to when food hung in the balance. The two spiders on the right were almost touching when they turned on each other. The sounds they produced were just as hideous to the ears as their appearance was to the eyes. They collided in a ball of flailing legs and gnashing fangs. Their combined weight and momentum threw them across the slope and down the other side of the pit in a cloud of dust.

The remaining spider saw its opportunity. That monster broke into a mad dash for the trio, its massive fangs clashing together with strands of sticky saliva between them. Russell moved first and lunged at the spider with his pick-axe held high over his head. The spider, however, was fast and its legs had an even greater reach than

263

its size suggested. One of its eight legs flicked out and caught the wolf in the chest mid-sprint.

Doran dodged to the side, narrowly avoiding Russell's flying bulk as he slammed into a boulder. The dwarf knew his friend could handle such a blow and maintained his focus on the spider. Those gnashing fangs came down on the son of Dorain only to find his axe and sword in the way, the steel blades crossed over each other. Thick saliva poured down on him, stealing his war cry to Grarfath. Its long legs stamped the ground around him, desperate to find a better angle.

Then, the spider felt the bite of elven steel, something it had never come across in all its years. Galanör had skidded across the gravel, with Guardian held out to his side, and sliced perfectly through two of its back legs. The monster squealed in agony but the elf didn't stop with a single strike. Instead, Galanör nimbly found his way onto its bulbous body, where he could plunge both Guardian and Stormweaver deep inside.

Doran felt the crushing weight of the fangs ease off as the spider reared back in its dying moments. To make certain death greeted the monster, the dwarf shoved his sword up into its underbelly, spilling dark guts across the pit.

Without another sound, the spider flopped heavily to the side and Galanör jumped down. Doran spat on the creature and wiped as much of the saliva from his armour as he could.

"I'm goin' to need a bath after that!" he complained.

The sound of eight legs clambering over the boulders behind them reminded the dwarf that a single spider had not been their issue. The foul beast rose to the top of the nearest outcropping, its dark hide coated in the blood and debris of its kin.

"All this for a bloody orc..." Doran muttered.

The spider reared back on its powerful legs, ready to pounce on the trio below. The son of Dorain prepared himself for one last fight, confident, as always, that it wouldn't be his last. He took one step when something whistled past his ear, a blur without shape.

Only when it slammed into the exposed underbelly of the spider did Doran realise it was Russell's pick-axe. The monster shrieked just once before stumbling and finally collapsing off the top of the rise.

Doran looked from the dead spider to his friend. "Ye couldn' 'ave done that with the first one?"

HALF A DAY LATER, the three companions finally emerged from Vengora, where upon they were greeted by the white plains of Dhenaheim. Beyond the mountains, as far north as north could go, the wind carried a bitter chill and the air was akin to breathing ice. The whipping wind was strong enough to throw Doran's braided ponytail and beard about, but nothing it seemed was strong enough to diffuse the stench of the orc.

Tied up and gagged, the pale creature was hidden beneath the tarpaulin of Russell's cart. Every time the wind found its way beneath the cover, Doran glimpsed the orc's unconscious face. The dwarf in him wanted to beat that face until every bone was broken. Just travelling with it - keeping it alive - felt like an insult to his ancestors.

After too long riding behind the cart, Doran spurred his Warhog to take the lead. It had been sixty years since Pig had crossed into Dhenaheim, but the animal had been young when Doran began rearing it. Any memory of the land or his people would no doubt have fled the Warhog's memory.

Galanör's horse trotted through the snow to meet Doran and Pig. The elven ranger was entirely hidden by his voluminous blue cloak and white furs. Turning to look at his dwarven companion, but one of his eyes was revealed from within his hood.

"I've never been this far north," he commented.

"There are few o' your kin who 'ave," Doran replied. "An' for good reason I might add. The forests up 'ere will freeze ye to the bone. An' if ye don' know how to work the rock an' stone, livin' above ground will be the end o' ye in Dhenaheim."

"It's a beautiful land," Galanör opined, regardless of Doran's description. "It has a wild feel to it."

Beautiful wasn't a word often used by a dwarf, not unless they were referring to a weapon, but Doran couldn't help seeing what Galanör was talking about. Dhenaheim was a wild and free country, its landscape a marvel that only Grarfath and Yamnomora could take credit for.

"Listen," Doran began seriously. "I said it to Lady Reyna an' I'll say the same thing to ye. When we reach our destination, don' talk, don' say anythin'. Ye don' need pointy ears up 'ere to announce your immortality."

Galanör silently laughed to himself. "I apologise if my *pointy* ears offend your kin."

"It's not yer ears, laddy. The tension that exists between our two kinds stems back to The Great War, the first time we knocked these buggers back to hell. After the fightin' was done, there was a feelin' that the elves took all the credit for defeatin' the orcs, on account o' the Dragorn."

Galanör scanned the horizon as he considered the dwarf's words. "I have studied all that we have from The Great War. Credit never swung one way or the other; there were just facts about which side accomplished what. Granted, a lot was said about the Dragorn, but they did have dragons..."

"But that's jus' it, isn't it. Facts! It might be written down in some musty book, but that doesn' mean it's true." Doran waved the topic away. "I'm not gettin' into it. The argument is older than both o' us an' from the looks o' things, we're writin' our own tale these days."

Galanör lightly shook his head. "It was five thousand years ago, Doran. The argument is older than every dwarf still living."

"Well, we 'ave long memories," Doran pointed out. "Longer than yerselves an' *we* don' even live forever."

Galanör appeared to concede the point. "Immortality gives one the luxury of choosing what to remember and what to forget."

"In Grimwhal, nothin' is forgotten." Doran truly meant that. "Seein' me allied with ye, *another* elf, is goin' to make me look weak but, worst o' all, it's goin' to make me look like I'm spittin' on me ancestors' graves. Now, I can handle all o' that - I know what me kin thinks o' me. But I don' want yer rollin' head on me conscience to boot, so keep yer mouth shut an' let me do the talkin'. A'right?"

"I will bow to your wisdom," Galanör replied graciously, nonplussed by the potential to lose his head. "I would ask, though, are we not better journeying to Silvyr Hall? If we're to ask your kin to lend their armies, does it not have to be sanctioned by King Uthrad?"

Doran shook his head. "No. King Uthrad's word only matters when the clans go to war with each other. Should a clan declare outright war against a clan beneath them, they must present a worthy case to the king o' Silvyr Hall. Attackin' a clan without a good enough reason can brin' shame an' dishonour, a deadly combination when it comes to reliance on trade. O' course, if a clan wanted to go to war with those above them, they wouldn' 'ave to send Silvyr Hall so much as a letter.

"Now, if one o' the clans were to attack Illian, they *would* have to get Uthrad's permission, because it could have ramifications on all o' Dhenaheim. Asking a clan to wipe out the orcs, however, requires no such permission."

"Then why not go to Bhan Doral?" Galanör posed. "You said that city is closer."

"Bah! *Bhan Doral*! The Brightbeards are the lowest o' the clans, their army the smallest. Besides, I know Grimwhal like the back o' me hand an' me clan at least knows me voice; it might not count for much, but it's better than nothin', which is exactly what it counts for in Bhan Doral."

Russell's voice carried on the wind. "We need to camp soon! Make sure our prisoner doesn't die before we get there!"

Doran scrutinised their route, cutting diagonally across the plains of Dhenaheim. They had at least another day in their journey before reaching Grimwhal. A part of him wanted to push them and forsake any camp. He knew from Nathaniel's recent tale that the Brightbeards had been denied their battle with the army of Namdhor. Those same colourful dwarves wouldn't be far from their current position, making their way home to Bhan Doral.

It would be hard travelling at night, however, and they did have their prisoner to consider. As much as Doran hated the idea of it, they couldn't come this far only to lose their prisoner to dehydration.

GETTING AWAY from the ash clouds over Illian to see the blue sky again had been more of a comfort to the son of Dorain than he would ever admit. Watching it fade to the black of night was an aspect of nature Doran had missed.

Sitting around the fire now, his eyes were drawn to the flames. They were partially sheltered by an outcrop of rocks that connected to the northern head of The Whispering Mountains. It concealed the light of their fire to any in the east, such as the Brightbeards, but Doran was more concerned now about those to the west, who could see the flames for miles.

On the other side of the fire, Russell was wrestling the orc back into the cart. Bound as it was, the beast was hopeless to do anything itself - thankfully, Russell was stronger than the average man. Once bundled into the cart and covered by the tarpaulin again, the old ranger hit the orc's head with the haft of his pick-axe, sending it back into a deep slumber.

Doran laughed heartily. "I don' suppose it needs to 'ave its wits abou' it!"

The three companions sat around the fire and shared their supplies for a while. After such a long trek and a fight with giant spiders, they were all on the edge of exhaustion, leaving little energy to talk. Doran was happy about that for a change. With every step he got closer to his old home, he got closer to breaking his promise.

He had told the elf that he didn't care, given the importance of their mission, but he didn't want his mother and brother to see his final moments. Then again, he reasoned, there was every chance his mother would be livid with him for returning and order his execution herself, on the grounds of being the stupidest dwarf ever to live.

Deciding he would prefer to sleep rather than dwell on such dark thoughts, Doran picked up a bottle of Hobgobbers Ale and looked to his friends. "So, who's takin' first watch?"

Russell eyed the alcohol in Doran's hand. "Not you by the looks of it."

Galanör's hand slowly moved to rest on the hilt of Stormweaver. "None of us will be taking first watch..."

Doran followed the elf's gaze to the abyss that lay beyond the light of their fire. He couldn't see anything, but the look on Galanör's face told him everything he needed to know. Plus, having travelled with Reyna Galfrey, Doran knew better than to ignore the ears of an elf...

The son of Dorain kept his eyes on the dark as he mimicked Galanör's movements and slowly reached for his weapons beside him. Russell, who had his back to the horizon, gripped the haft of his pick-axe and carefully lifted it to hold it with both hands. He watched Galanör intently, waiting for the signal to move.

It was hard to tell over the crackling fire, but Doran was sure he had just heard the crunch of snow under a boot. Either way, Galanör stood up and drew both of his scimitars in a flash of steel. At the same time, Russell jumped up and readied himself to swing his pick-axe. Doran hopped onto a flat boulder and brandished his own weapons, waiting for the dark to produce some fresh nightmare to add to his collection.

Three *thunks* went off in succession, swiftly followed by three arrows. The first landed in the haft of Russell's pick-axe, the second sank into the ground at Galanör's feet, and the last arrow cut through the air and caught Doran's hatchet, sending it flying out of his grip.

The dwarf growled. "Show yerselves!"

There was more crunching in the snow as several figures approached from the black. Doran's shoulders sank when six dwarves stepped into the firelight, all attired in Heavybelly armour and wielding the finest crossbows in all the realm.

"*We will show ourselves, traitor,*" came the gruff dwarvish reply, "*but we will not muddy our tongue with the language of fools.*"

Doran's eyes roamed over his kin and he recognised them all: the hunters that had tracked them to Silvyr Hall. Sent forth from Grimwhal by his father, this pack of hunters had followed Doran and the Galfreys across Dhenaheim. Nathaniel had told them of his encounter with this particular group, before he turned the Namdhorian army around.

The Heavybellys approached until they were between the cart and the companions. The three who had fired their crossbows reloaded their weapons with smooth efficiency before continuing to aim them.

The leader of the hunting party stepped forward. He was squat and, like the others, he was packed out with armour and more weapons than any dwarf really needed. His red overcoat was apparently some kind of uniform, as all the Heavybellys wore the same thing over their armour. Setting the leader apart, however, was the jet black mohawk that continued to run down his back and over his coat.

He was also smiling from ear to ear.

"*Grarfath blesses our hunt, lads! You can't imagine what's been going through our heads these last few days. Never has any prey eluded the Blood Boys. When you escaped Karak-Nor with a couple of humans and an elf it should have been easy. But there we were, making our way home to inform the king of our failure, when a distant light draws us in. The Mother and Father must really hate you Doran Heavybelly!*"

"*The Blood Boys?*" Doran questioned, buying time while he thought of a way out of this. "*I've never heard of you.*"

"*Of course you haven't,*" the leader replied coolly. "*You ran away from your duty years before the Blood Boys was formed. We're an elite guild, specialising in the acquisition of all things lost, breathing or otherwise.*"

"*Is that so?*" Doran continued, stealing a glance at Russell. "*So... you could hunt down, oh, I don't know, a pair of boots, say? Because, you know, it's got to be seventy years ago now that I lost the finest pair of boots. I could pay you handsomely if you could track those down for me.*"

The leader's stern expression cracked into one more of laughter. "*We've got ourselves a funny one, lads. I'll tell you what, funny little prince, I'll give you my boots. Would you like to know where I'm going to put them?*"

Doran heard the rhetorical question but his attention had been captured by one of the hunters. The curious dwarf was taking in the cart, inspecting its sides and wheels.

"*What's your name?*" Doran asked the leader, his eyes flitting between him and the curious dwarf.

"*You see this crossbow pointed at your face? That means I ask the questions.*" The leader gestured at Russell and Galanör. "*These are not the ones who escaped Karak-Nor with you. Where are they?*"

Doran commended the dwarf for his craft; he had been commanded to bring all four of them back and he meant to. "*One of them is dead, the other two are beyond the reach of every clan.*"

The leader dipped his head, showing all of his black mohawk. "*I have been issued orders by King Dorain, son of Dorryn, himself to return his fugitive son and all of his accomplices to Grimwhal for justice.*" The mohawk offered Galanör and Russell a hard look. "*They might not be the ones to have escaped Karak-Nor with you, but being in your company does not pay, Doran Heavybelly.*"

The curious dwarf climbed up the cart and began poking the tarpaulin with the tip of his crossbow.

"Doran..." Russell was tensed, ready for whatever came next.

The leader didn't appreciate the interruption. *"Tell the human if he speaks again he'll have to find a way of living with a bolt in his throat."*

Doran heard every word but he couldn't take his eyes off the curious dwarf. *"I wouldn't threaten him if I were you; he has a nasty side..."*

Galanör adjusted the grip on his scimitars. "Doran, we can't let them kill the... *prisoner.*"

"You can tell the other human to shut it as well!" the leader barked.

The curious dwarf finally pulled back the tarpaulin and jumped back in shock. *"Revek!"* he called, turning his mouth to the leader while his eyes remained fixed on the orc.

The leader, Revek, scowled at Doran and backed up towards the cart, his crossbow never straying from the son of Dorain. He climbed onto the cart and laid eyes on the prisoner, bound and gagged, neither of which disguised the prisoner's identity as an orc.

Revek maintained his dumbfounded expression for several seconds as he scanned every inch of the horned beast. Of course, there wasn't a soul alive in all of Dhenaheim who had been around during The Great War, but there were more than a few paintings and illustrations of the battles, all of which detailed the physical features of an orc. Their pale skin, cracked like stone and toned with a hard edge. Their pointed ears and distinct horns with a brow of bone. There was no other creature in all of Verda that resembled an elf but appeared to have emerged from the mountain stone.

The orc began to stir. Its reflective eyes flickered open to see the dwarves standing over it. Then it began to writhe and struggle against its bindings. Revek planted his boot on its chest and aimed his crossbow at the orc's head.

"Stop!" Doran bellowed, jumping down from the rock.

Revek paused with his fingers on the trigger. *"This beast... It's... It's an..."* The dwarf didn't believe his eyes enough to speak the word.

"It's an orc," Doran confirmed.

The other hunters moved to look inside the cart and Revek took aim again.

"*You can't kill it!*" Doran warned.

Revek gestured for his gang to take their positions again before addressing Doran. "*I don't know how such a monster is breathing Dhenaheim's sweet air, but you can't have sunk so low, Doran, as to defend an orc!*"

Doran took a breath and sheathed his sword on his back. "*The orc is the reason we're here,*" he said calmly. "*We're on our way to Grimwhal, to show my father that orcs still dare to challenge us for the world.*"

Revek looked from the orc to Doran. "*You claim that the orcs have returned?*"

Doran frowned. "*I don't need to claim anything. Look at what's under your boot! That thing isn't just one of a few; there's thousands of them! Think of the stories you've heard, the ones we've all heard. They stop after the alliance drove them into The Undying Mountains, after the Dragorn buried them under the rock. Our ancestors' mistake was believing they would perish with so few numbers.*"

"*Now you're going to mock our ancestors?*" Revek snapped.

Doran sighed and shook his head. "*Forget about all that! What matters is what's happening right now. The orcs have returned to the surface and invaded all of Illian! They're heading north as we speak. They won't be satisfied until the whole world is theirs!*"

Galanör turned to look at Doran. "My dwarvish is a little rusty..."

Doran held out a hand, asking the elf to wait. "*I know man's troubles aren't that of Dhenaheim's,*" he said to Revek, "*but we dwarves have no greater enemy than the orcs. If they have returned to the world, wherever that may be, it should be us who meet them with steel and blood.*"

Revek spat on the orc under his boot. "*Why does any of that mean this creature gets to avoid this here bolt?*"

Violence first, sense later. That was the way of his people and there was nothing he could do about it. Doran even felt a twinge of shame that he had once thought in such a manner.

"*We need to present my father with a living orc, so that he can see there is no trickery. The rest of Dhenaheim deserves to know that orc blood is being spilt by men and not dwarves, as it should be.*"

The Blood Boys' leader glanced at his fellow hunters, none of whom offered him any advice. He took a minute to consider what had to be the last possible scenario he could ever have imagined. *"Perhaps our goals can align,"* he said finally. *"We will take you to Grimwhal and collect our reward, and you may present this* thing *to King Dorain. What say you?"*

Doran licked his lips, aware that he was speaking for his companions as well. *"We would be travelling together,"* he stated firmly. *"Not as your prisoners. And the orc stays with us; your boys aren't to go near it."*

Revek took another moment to consider the terms. *"Acceptable,"* he declared, raising his crossbow over his shoulder. *"But be warned, Doran Heavybelly; should any of you try to be rid of us, I will drag you into the throne room by your beard to get that reward."*

The son of Dorain relaxed a little. *"Acceptable,"* he agreed.

Seeing the Blood Boys lower their weapons and Revek abandon the cart, Russell turned to Doran in confusion. "What's happening, Heavybelly?"

"These fine dwarves are goin' to escort us into Grimwhal," Doran explained with little detail. "No funny business though, eh, lads. They won' hesitate to put a bolt through either o' ye."

"And what about you?" Galanör enquired.

"I think the bounty on me is quite specific abou' me bein' alive. Doesn' mean they won' shoot me in the leg, mind ye..."

Russell's large shoulders sagged. "They're hunters."

"Aye," Doran relented. "Sent by me father. I think I've talked some sense into 'em though. I'm hopin' it's a good sign regardin' the rest o' me kin's reaction," he added in a hushed tone.

Out of the dark, six Warhogs trudged through the snow to meet their masters. The Blood Boys didn't appear entirely at ease yet, every one of them talking about the orc in the most vitriolic language.

"You're making camp with us, then?" Doran asked Revek.

The leader of the Blood Boys scrutinised their small fire and supplies. *"This isn't a camp,"* he replied with a short laugh. *"Not yet anyway! We stay here for the night and make for Grimwhal at dawn. One of my boys will be awake at all times and they don't miss a trick, so be warned."*

Doran held up his hands. *"We won't try anything, you have my word. An escort into Grimwhal is no bad thing."*

Revek turned on him. *"Firstly: the word of a dishonourable traitor means nothing. And secondly: we're not escorting you anywhere. When the time comes, I'm telling them you're my bounty. Oh, and if you do lose control of that orc, you can bet your life I'm putting it down."*

Doran waited for the Blood Boys leader to walk away before turning back to his companions. "Russell, do us all a favour an' double check the bindin's on the orc. An' it might not be a bad idea if we take it in shifts to make sure these boys don' use our prisoner as an anvil…"

CHAPTER 20
THE WATCHERS

Emerging from the miles of woodlands, Vighon Draqaro once again set his dark eyes on the mountains that stretched across the northern horizon. Vengora was beautiful... on the outside. The northman wasn't looking forward to reaching their destination.

The most distinct feature lay a little farther north, where the mountains parted, making way for The Iron Valley. From astride his horse, Vighon could just make out the two outposts that sat on each side of the valley.

"The Watchers," Ruban whispered beside him, his young eyes glistening in the cold.

Vighon narrowed his vision, taking in the black ruins of The Watchers. "Have you never seen them before?"

Ruban shook his head. "I've never left Namdhor..."

"Of course you haven't," Vighon muttered. "Don't tell *him* that," he advised, nodding at Asher ahead of them.

"He seems like a very angry man," Ruban observed.

"Don't tell him that either."

They rode on for a little longer, trailing the ranger, before Ruban had to speak again. "Are we really going inside Vengora?"

Vighon smirked. "Wishing you'd stayed in Namdhor now?"

The squire couldn't decide whether to shake off such a suggestion or simply shrug. "As I said, my place is by your side." The boldness of his words didn't carry through to his voice. "I just..." he continued, struggling to find the words. "I just can't believe what we're doing. Everything you told me about the orcs and Haren Bain... and *Atilan*."

Vighon knew it was a lot to take in, especially if one held faith in the religion of Atilan, but he had one simple way of getting over it. "Don't think about it. Accept the world isn't the way you thought it was and move on; trust me, it's the only way you'll find sleep."

Ruban was quiet for a moment, hopefully absorbing the advice. "Is he really *the* Asher, from the stories about the war? How did the dark wizards bring him back to life? Can he speak to the dragon or just see its memories? Can *he* bring people back to life?"

Vighon sighed into his hood. Perhaps, in hindsight, he had divulged one too many details to the squire. "You're overthinking it, which is *worse* than just thinking about it. Use your... squire training. Focus on one task at a time and keep moving forward. Right now, you don't need to think about anything more than reaching the River Adanae."

Ruban nodded along. "And The Ironsworn on our trail," he added.

Vighon closed his eyes and sighed again. "Maybe try focusing on things in your head..."

Taking the hint, the squire remained quiet for their trek across the plains. A moment of introspection, which was rare for the northman, made him wonder if Asher saw him as he saw Ruban. Deciding he didn't much care what the ranger thought, he continued on their journey and did his best not to think about what was really bothering him. Travelling so freely, however, made that the hardest task of all.

His best friend needed him. That fact was unavoidable, regardless of the formidable party currently on their way to rescue him. Alijah needed *Vighon*. He always had. It hadn't been that long ago that the northman would have forsaken everything in favour of helping Alijah. Now, for reasons he couldn't put his finger on, he was trying to save the whole bloody world!

He felt sorry for the world...

His spiralling mood was taken off course when he realised the ranger was diverting from their path, leading them towards the farther of The Watchers, on the eastern side of the valley. It was a welcome distraction.

Vighon spurred Ness on and caught up with him. "What are you doing?" he demanded, his patience ever thin when communing with Asher. "You said we needed to put distance between us and The Ironsworn."

The ranger gestured to the sky. "It'll be dark soon; too dark for you and the squire to keep moving. We'll camp inside there for the night and continue in the morning."

Vighon looked at the farthest Watcher, its ancient black stone harkening back to Gal Tion's reign, a thousand years ago. It was a ruin of a fort, poked with jagged holes and crumbling walls.

"We can keep going," Vighon protested, preferring to sleep under the sky rather than enter the long-abandoned outpost.

"Our pursuers will need to make camp as well," Asher replied, his eyes never wavering from their destination. "We rest here," he stated.

Vighon could see there would be no arguing with the ranger. He looked over his shoulder, scanning the horizon behind them. What light they had was beginning to dim, making it all the harder to see anything of note. More importantly, it made it harder to see if any Ironsworn were emerging from the distant trees.

Approaching the derelict Watcher, the three companions rode across the wide stretch of path that ran through the valley. It was abundantly clear that the army of Namdhor had recently trampled over the land, their great numbers cutting a dark path as far as the eye could see.

At the base of the ruins, the three riders dismounted and guided their horses under the tall arch and into a small courtyard. It was eerie. Crows squawked down at them from the broken parapets and rats scurried between the inky shadows. Of them all, Ruban appeared the most unsettled. The squire's head had yet to stop swivelling, his eyes frantic. For Vighon, this was just another relic of an older time, the kind of place Alijah was always dragging him to.

"Tie the horses up over there," Asher instructed. "Bring any supplies you need for the night."

Ruban looked desperately from the courtyard to the shattered towers that loomed overhead. "Are we not just camping here?"

"No," Asher replied with his usual bluntness. "Too exposed. We'll find better shelter inside, somewhere we can start a fire that won't be seen from out there."

Without another word, the ranger threw a sack of supplies over his shoulder and started up the steps, into The Watcher's embrace. Vighon secured his horse beside the others and hesitated whether to take his shield or not. Sense won the day and he removed it from the saddle, hoping he wouldn't need it. Ruban, on the other hand, looked to be busying himself with gathering the necessary supplies - a coping mechanism no doubt.

Together, they joined the ranger in the gloomy halls and began their brief exploration of the ancient outpost. After a thousand years of standing guard against the barbarians of The Iron Valley, the dwarves of Dhenaheim, and the countless wars the north become entangled in, there wasn't a wall without damage. The ruin had been picked at by everyone, from desperate travellers to treasure hunters.

There were, however, unlit torches still on the wall. Vighon paused to inspect one, hoping against the odds that it was in a decent condition.

"Try lighting this," he said, giving it to Ruban. The squire crouched down, relieving himself of the supplies while he rummaged through the bags in search of some flint and pitch.

Vighon walked a little farther and met Asher. "We need fire. I might as well have my eyes closed."

The ranger glanced at the northman before returning his vision to the passage ahead. "I can see where I'm going."

That made no sense to Vighon. "Well we bloody can't. And this is..." The northman lowered his voice. "This is all new to Ruban."

Asher turned on him. "He's your responsibility. Not mine. I told you to send him away."

"Back to The Ironsworn?" Vighon hissed.

The ranger took a breath. "If he stays by *my* side, he's dead. I attract the worst things in this world, things he can't stand against. I've travelled like this before, with others, with inexperienced fighters. It didn't matter what I did, they still ended up dead."

"What about me?" Vighon retorted. "Am I going to end up dead as well?"

The ranger adjusted the sack on his shoulder. "That remains to be seen."

The passage came alive in fiery light behind them. "Got it!" Ruban exclaimed, holding the torch aloft.

"Keep it behind me," Asher told him before striding off into the shadows.

Vighon shrugged in the face of Ruban's questioning expression. "Let's just follow him."

Asher led them a little deeper into The Watcher's ruins and up another level. They were careful to avoid the holes in the floor and stay away from the rooms with the creaky doors hanging off their hinges. The wind whipped through the ancient halls, howling as it attempted to snuff out the torch.

At last, the ranger chose a room, a fairly large one inhabited by long broken tables and benches. Vighon assumed it had once been a place for the soldiers stationed here to come and eat together. There was a single hole in the wall, high up and facing the valley.

"You can start a fire in here," Asher concluded. "The light shouldn't be seen from the vale. Use what wood you can find in here."

"*We* can start a fire?" Vighon questioned. "What are *you* doing?"

Asher pulled free the silvyr short-sword from his back. "Making sure we're alone." The ranger didn't wait for a response before leaving them to their task.

Working in silence, Vighon and Ruban went about preparing their makeshift camp, the centre of which was a much larger fire than the one still burning on the torch. Thanks to Ruban's extra supplies, the northman was able to eat more than he perhaps would have, a luxury on a journey such as this. He couldn't help but miss the times when he would cook for Alijah and himself...

A little while after they were established and their camp secured, the ranger returned, glum despite his ready-made camp.

"I take it we're alone, then?" Vighon assumed, gesturing for Asher to take a seat by the fire.

"Not as alone as I'd like..." Asher muttered under his breath.

Tired and fed up with his companion's attitude, Vighon snapped his head up and locked his dark eyes on the ranger. "You think far too much of yourself," he said harshly. "By the look of you, I'd say your best days are behind you. I'm here to make sure you don't drop dead on the way back."

Asher looked back at him from across the fire. "Careful, boy. There's a good reason I'm old..."

Vighon didn't doubt the ranger had picked up a few skills between Nightfall and hunting monsters for a living, but time was a foe he couldn't beat. Still, he didn't feel like challenging Asher to a sword fight right now, not with fatigue settling into his muscles. There was much of their journey left and plenty of trials to come with it - time would reveal all.

In the awkward silence that followed, Ruban filled it with his questions about the world. "What was this place?"

Seeing that Asher was happy to busy himself with his own

supplies, Vighon answered the squire. "The Watchers were just that: watch towers. Gal Tion had them built a thousand years ago to keep watch over The Iron Valley."

Ruban scrutinised the wretched hollow. "I'd say they didn't do very well at keeping the place tidy."

Vighon allowed himself a brief smile at the remark. "Too many wars," he explained. "I would bet the soldiers garrisoned here were recalled for some battle or another."

"Look at the stone," Asher instructed, his own attention on his gear. "Outside," he elaborated. "The tops of both towers have taken the same kind of damage: dragon fire."

Ruban's eyes lit up. "Dragons did this?"

Vighon couldn't fault the ranger's eye for detail. "Why would dragons do this?"

"You spent all that time with Alijah; weren't you listening?"

Talking to the northman like he knew Alijah or anything about the two of them only served to wind Vighon up. "He had a lot to say about a lot of things. More often than not, I just made sure he didn't lose his head. Like I'm here to do for you," he added with a broad smile.

Asher didn't rise to it. "Gal Tion had The Watchers built when he assumed control of Illian. Then he declared war on the dragons, forcing the elves out. These outposts were just casualties of war."

The ranger had Ruban's full attention. "You know a lot about history," he complimented.

"He's living history," Vighon commented, stoking the fire. "Ask him when he was born."

Asher stared at Vighon through the flames, clearly uncomfortable with such pointed questions. Still, the ranger failed to protest and Ruban was terrible at detecting facial cues and body language.

"When were you born?" the squire asked straight away, as if they were playing a game.

Vighon glanced at Asher, noting his discomfort. The northman knew all about the old assassin, though little of it was from the war

282

stories. Along with Alijah and Inara, Vighon had been treated to the same bedtime stories of the ranger's extraordinary life. There were times in his youth that Vighon could remember Asher being something of a hero to him. Now, he knew he was just a grumpy old man with a chip on his shoulder.

"I couldn't say exactly," Asher replied. "It was a long time ago, before the elves left for Ayda..."

Ruban's look of wonder quickly creased into a frown of confusion. "That was a thousand years ago!"

"And then some," Vighon added, swigging his water.

Ruban had the look of a man trying to work out the mystery of life. "But I heard the stories of you from The War for the Realm; that was only thirty years ago. I know you were... *brought back* recently, but how could you—"

"Tomorrow will be a long day of riding," Asher interrupted. "We should all get some rest before the journey." Having nothing more to say, the ranger turned away from them and lay down with a blanket rolled up under his head.

Ruban looked at Vighon questioningly - a hint of worry in his eyes - but the northman shrugged in a way that told him not to get hung up on it. "Don't overthink it," he reiterated. "Get some sleep. I'll tell you everything tomorrow."

If the ranger had an issue with him promising Ruban the tale of his life, he didn't protest. Instead, he continued to lie with his back to them, his green cloak covering his body. Vighon decided he would tell Ruban never to seek out his own heroes... they were nothing but disappointments.

"I'll keep first watch," the northman volunteered.

"Do you want me to come with you?" Ruban offered with a nervous glance at Asher.

"No," Vighon said. "That's why it's called *first* watch. You'll get the next one."

Taking the torch poking out of the fire, the northman adjusted the collar of black fur around his shoulders and neck and left his companions to sleep. The eastern Watcher was all the more eerie for exploring it on his own. He made his way back to the horses first to check on Ness and the others, ensuring they were warm enough and had enough to eat and drink.

Tending to their mounts had always been his job. Alijah had always seen horses as a means of transportation, a by-product of growing up in a family that travelled a lot and put an emphasis on the people they were meeting. To Vighon, they were animals with just as much personality and emotion as a person.

He thought of Alijah's bond with Malliath and it struck him as unusual. He couldn't imagine his friend caring for any animal the way a Dragorn cared for their dragon. Then he considered the profound effect such a bond would have on Alijah - he would live forever now, along with his family. Forever was a long time to get over the torments of The Crow, he mused. He was thankful his friend would have such a time, though a small part of him was sad at the thought of dying and Alijah living on for eternity. He would have liked to have seen his best friend through all of his adventures.

Wandering through the ruins of The Watcher, Vighon couldn't shake the gloom that hung over him. He searched every room, bringing light to the many shadows, but his thoughts continued to dwell on Alijah's desperate situation, Inara's rejection, and his evil father assuming the throne of not just Namdhor but the whole of Illian. What joy he had ever clung to in his life had been sucked out by one terrible thing after another. What was worse, however, was his helplessness to do anything about it all.

The northman walked past a broken archway, casting a cursory glance into the room as he did, when he stopped and retraced his steps. Examining the room again, the far wall was entirely gone, exposing a western horizon and the mouth of The Iron Valley. It wasn't this particular view that caught Vighon's eye.

In the distance, a flickering flame defied the night and made itself known. Vighon entered the room and narrowed his vision at the flame, lowering his torch to better see in the dark. The small flame was coming from inside the western Watcher, on the other side of the valley mouth. A pit began to open inside the northman's stomach and he told himself it could be anyone. The northern towns and villages had scattered in the face of the orcs' invasion, after all.

No. As possible as that was, Vighon knew exactly who was taking shelter in the other outpost: Godfrey Cross and The Ironsworn.

Looking down at his torch, the pit in Vighon's stomach turned into one of pure dread. If he could see their flames it stood to reason that they could see his... The northman threw the burning torch into the corner of the room, where the snow had gathered into a pile big enough to douse it.

"It's too late for that," came the ranger's startling voice.

Vighon turned on him with his blade halfway out of its scabbard. "How long have you been standing there?" he demanded, his nerves on edge now.

"Long enough..." Asher's focus wasn't on Vighon, nor was it on the distant flames. His head was turned towards the darkened hall of their own outpost.

Vighon moved to the broken arch and listened intently. Echoing footsteps and the sound of swords being drawn from their sheaths greeted his patience.

"Wake the boy," Asher told him. "Meet me in the courtyard."

"What are *you* doing?" Vighon asked before the ranger could stalk away.

"I'll get the horses ready," Asher replied, disappearing into the shadows.

Vighon collected himself and pulled free the sword of the north. He had to remind himself that it was made from silvyr and that its lack of weight wasn't a mark against its proficiency. Without a moment to lose, he hurried back to their camp, pausing only at corners to check for Ironsworn. The journey back to the camp felt too long and Vighon began to worry about Ruban, fast asleep and unaware of their dire situation.

Rounding the last corner, the shocking sound of clashing steel found Vighon's ears, spurring him on. There was a sharp yell of pain and a stream of curses - all words Vighon was sure Ruban didn't even know.

"I warned you!" shouted the squire's shaky voice.

Ruban's raised voice masked the sound of Vighon's arrival as he stopped in the archway of the double doors. He didn't know what he was going to find but he was sure Ruban had to be injured by now. With that image plaguing his mind, it was quite the surprise to discover the young squire holding his own against two Ironsworn, one of which was nursing a hand dripping with blood.

"I'm going to gut you slowly, boy!" the wounded thug promised.

Ruban brandished his sword and did his best to keep Vighon's shield aloft. "I've fought worse than you!" he spat, using his anger to fuel what courage he had.

The Ironsworn who had yet to be injured began to edge his way around the fire. "Where's Vighon, you little worm? Tell me and I'll see that you die nice and quick."

The northman was only too happy to answer the thug's question... with his sword. Creeping up, Vighon plunged his blade into the man's back until the other half came out of his chest, coated in blood.

"I'm right here," he whispered in the man's ear. The Ironsworn maintained his expression of horror for another second before the life left his eyes and he dropped to the floor, free of the silvyr blade.

The wounded Ironsworn jumped back from the startling attack, but he recovered quickly and hurled profanities at Vighon. It was a waste of breath, considering the precious seconds after his comrade's death were his only opportunity to strike Vighon down. Instead, his retaliation came late and the northman had more than enough time to raise his sword and parry the thug's one-handed attack.

The Ironsworn's midriff exposed, Ruban lunged in and ran the man through with his sword. The thug's agonised grunt soon turned into a gargle and he dropped to his knees, staring at the squire in shock. In his final moments, it was clear to see the Ironsworn had never considered his life would be brought to an end by one such as Ruban Dardaris. But it was and, with their eyes locked, the squire watched the man fall dead at his feet.

Vighon gave Ruban an extra second to take a breath. "Are you hurt?" he asked. Ruban shook his head, his attention arrested by the body between them. "We need to leave," the northman coaxed, ushering him towards the double doors.

"This is yours," Ruban said absently, offering Vighon his shield back.

"Keep it," the northman replied, checking the halls before they left. "You may need it before this is over."

With the squire close on his heels, Vighon guided him through the ruined maze of halls. Only once did they hug the walls and melt into the shadows as a pair of Ironsworn walked past them, oblivious.

Back in the courtyard, Vighon looked around frantically for any sign of their hunters. Crossing the disturbed snow, he entered the small building in search of Asher and the horses. Ness and the others were lying down, alert to his presence, but there was no evidence that Asher had recently been here.

Turning back to the courtyard, the pair froze in the light fall of snow. Godfrey Cross was stalking out of a doorway with a smug grin on his face. Behind him, three more thugs emerged, then more appeared from the hollows and even the archway into the outpost. Vighon recognised a few of them, besides Cross, though he couldn't name any of them. He could, however, name the treacherous coward who stepped out from behind Godfrey.

"Flint." He said the man's name through gritted teeth. "I see you've taken up with this lot. You're a good match."

The ex-captain of Namdhor sneered, his eyes boring into the northman. "It's hard to find work when little lords brand you a coward. I suppose I should thank you, though. The Ironsworn pay is much better than the army—"

"Shut it!" Godfrey barked, making Flint jump out of his skin. "Did I tell you to speak?"

Vighon would have found Flint's berating amusing were he not surrounded by enemies. A quick count showed them to possess numbers north of ten; counting any more wasn't necessary.

"Now..." Godfrey announced, drawing the attention back on himself, "I have one question. Answer it to my liking and this will be over as pain-free as possible. Lie to me, boy, and this'll go on all night."

Happy to have more time to plan their escape, Vighon went along with it. "Ask your question, Cross."

The Ironsworn smiled. "Always so obliging..." Cross took an extra second to let his eyes roam over Ruban and the exposed walkways above. "Why did you leave Namdhor?"

Vighon raised an eyebrow. "There's a war on, a war we'll *lose*, and that's your question?"

"So you're deserting then, is that it?" Godfrey scrutinised the northman. "No, I don't believe that for one second. You left suddenly and without a word just as that ranger fella escaped the dungeons. I don't like coincidences, Vighon, and neither does your daddy."

"I see," Vighon said with an air of calmness that no man in his boots should possess. "My father had a question and he sent his favourite *dog* to find the answer."

Godfrey licked his lips. "To be so bold... you must know you're a dead man."

"Or maybe it's because you've been ordered to bring me back alive," Vighon suggested.

"Oh aye, the big man does want you back alive," Godfrey agreed, nodding his head. "But out here, in the *wilds*, anything can happen. So, tell me what you're doing and your daddy'll get at least one of the things he wanted."

Vighon shrugged, buying time. "Perhaps some of us don't aspire to be Arlon's jester. Perhaps I'm just out looking for a better life."

From the look of him, Godfrey was beginning to lose what little patience he had. "I'll tell you what; since you used to be one of us, I'll cut you a deal. Obviously, offering you a quick death isn't going to be enough. So, if you tell me what I need to know, you have my word I won't tie the boy to my horse and *drag* him back to Namdhor."

That just made Vighon mad. "He's already killed one of yours today," he replied threateningly.

Godfrey ran his tongue round his teeth and his gums as he stole a glance at the broken ramparts. "This could have gone a lot smoother. I want you to remember that when we're gutting you like a fish."

Vighon had heard enough. The sword in his hand was weighing heavy, eager as he was to see what a silvyr blade could really do. The northman started towards Godfrey, ignoring all those between them. He didn't know what he was going to do or how Ruban and he were going to survive this. Like always, though, he would fight for his life.

Beyond Godfrey and Flint, a flicker of movement caught Vighon's eye. A moment later, the shadows gave life to a wraith in a green cloak. Asher dropped down from between the shattered bricks of a wall with both his broadsword and short-sword in his hands. The two nearest Ironsworn, behind Godfrey, only became aware of the ranger's presence a second before his blades plunged down into their bodies. For them, there wasn't another second to be had.

Asher ripped his blades free and immediately launched the silvyr short-sword across the courtyard, killing the only Ironsworn armed with a bow. Dropping into a roll, the ranger ducked under Flint's swing and came up fighting the next Ironsworn brave enough to charge at him. A quick deflection and a swift slash of his double-handed broadsword ended the thug's life with a gaping cut to his throat.

Seeing that Asher had just killed four men in the time it took Vighon to take three steps, the northman decided to pick up his game. The sword of the north came up in both hands and he challenged those who sought to put themselves between him and Godfrey. They were both bigger than Vighon and they wielded larger swords, but after the recent battles against the orcs, there wasn't a man alive that frightened Vighon Draqaro.

The northman weaved between them, evading their swings, before coming back with clean swipes of his own. He barely felt the resistance as the sword cut through his foe's chest cavity, slicing through the ribs like butter. The Ironsworn couldn't say the same thing - he was on the ground bleeding out before Vighon turned to face his next opponent.

Outraged by his friend's death, the thug came at Vighon with heavy downward strikes. The silvyr sword rose up to meet the steel every time, jarring the northman's arms with the consistent blows. By the fifth or sixth strike, however, the Ironsworn's blade had nothing left to give. Coming down on the silvyr, the sword split in half and rebounded into the thug's shoulder. Vighon marvelled at his own sword, giving the man a few extra seconds to live. Then, he ran him through and kicked him away.

Behind the northman, Ruban sought shelter behind the enchanted shield as two scrawny Ironsworn thugs attempted to bury an axe and a sword into him. The squire's own blade would come out every other swing and give the thugs something to think about, but his form was non-existent and his attacks wild.

"Oi!" Vighon yelled at them, drawing the axe-man away.

The Ironsworn had likely received as little training as Ruban, but he had experience on his side. That said, it did nothing for him now. Vighon thrust forward in a flash and drove the tip of his sword into the thug's mouth and out through the back of his head, all before the scrawny Ironsworn raised his axe.

Ruban shouted at his remaining attacker, relying on his anger again, and charged him shield-first. The Ironsworn was beaten back into an ancient wall and pummelled again and again by the shield until Ruban was satisfied.

Vighon gave him a proud nod. "Keep your sword up!" he advised.

Meanwhile, Asher was proving his skill, parrying against two and dodging a third. Vighon hurried over to lend his sword but by the time he reached the ranger, two of his three attackers lay dead at his feet, their faces and torsos slashed. The third came down on Asher with a raised sword, only to have his wrist snatched by the ranger, halting him mid-strike. Asher hammered him once in the face with his spiked pommel and dropped him where he stood.

Taking advantage of Asher's distraction, an Ironsworn jumped out at Vighon, swinging for his head. The northman was able to duck under the blade, leaving only a chunk of his hair to be sliced away. The thug came at him with relentless fury after that, feeling the injustice that his victim should survive. Vighon raised his silvyr sword and parried left then right as he took one step back after another. Using the Ironsworn's advance against him, the northman stopped retreating and stepped forwards instead. The fool lunged straight into the tip of Vighon's blade. Ensuring his death, he stepped forwards again and pressed the sword in deeper, stealing the Ironsworn's breath, then his life.

That only left two.

Flint and Godfrey were side by side, wary of Asher, who stood between them and the archway of the outpost. Their swords were held steady in two hands and continued to point from the ranger to Vighon.

"Which one?" Asher asked.

With a heaving breath, Vighon replied. "Which one what?"

"Which one do you want to kill the most?" Asher specified.

The northman looked at the two Ironsworn again, both of whom he had imagined killing before. They both certainly deserved death.

"I'm not in a choosing mood..."

"Fair enough." The ranger sheathed his broadsword and walked away to retrieve his silvyr blade.

Vighon had a touch of exhaustion about him - enough that Asher's shocking decision rolled off him like water on a duck's back. Instead, he raised his sword and locked eyes with Godfrey Cross, his real adversary in this fight. He had witnessed the veteran Ironsworn fight many opponents during his time in service to the gang. The fact that Godfrey was still here was testament enough to his skill.

Believing his attention split, Flint bared his teeth and attacked Vighon like a wild animal, as if he knew his own chances of survival were slim.

Slim would have been good...

Slim chances might have seen the coward survive longer than a few seconds. As it was, Vighon knocked Flint's sword aside and dashed forward with his blade tip pointed at his throat. It was made all the easier by the fool's pressing attack.

With bulging eyes and a mouth full of blood, the once captain of Namdhor choked on his last breath. Vighon slid his sword out of Flint's throat and he fell to the floor, dead. Blood pooled out of his gaping wound, spilling out until it gathered around Godfrey's boot.

The Ironsworn sighed. "Do you know how hard it is to find good help with a war on?"

Vighon had a witty retort ready, as he often did when bartering words with Godfrey, but the Ironsworn gave him no such opportunity. His sword came out with a long jab that forced Vighon back a step, then he advanced with furious abandon, slashing from all angles. The northman kept every swing of steel at bay but the incoming blade took his focus away from his feet.

"Watch out!" Ruban cried.

But it was too late. Vighon tripped over the body of another thug and fell backwards onto the hard ground. Cross lunged with a growl and came down on him with a two-handed strike. Vighon rolled left and heard the steel collide with the ground beside his ear. Deciding he wouldn't give Godfrey another chance to cave his head in, the northman brought his right knee up and kicked out with all his strength.

Godfrey hunched over to absorb the kick and succeeded in grabbing Vighon's ankle. "Come here, boy!" he roared, dragging the northman farther into the courtyard.

Vighon leaned forward and took a wide swipe with the sword

of the north. Godfrey released him and jumped back to avoid losing his hand. Wasting no time, the northman scrambled to his feet and held his sword out in front of him, ready for the next attack.

"Vighon," Asher called casually. "We should really be moving on from here." The ranger looked bored.

Disbelief plastered across his sweaty face, Vighon replied, "I'm sorry to be holding you up. As you can see, I'm a little busy right now..."

A flash of movement in the corner of his eye alerted Vighon to Godfrey's incoming attack. The Ironsworn came in low, sweeping his sword up to come back down on the northman. Vighon batted the sword aside and brought his own up to parry the heavy strike from above. This brought their faces within inches of each other.

"I always knew you'd be a useless sack of meat," Godfrey spat. "I told your father he should have killed you years ago... when he killed your mother."

Be that a revelation or a lie, it shocked Vighon enough that his defending stance faltered. Godfrey took the advantage and forced the northman's sword down, opening Vighon up to a solid headbutt. The blinding pain forced him to stumble backwards but it only lasted another second before the Ironsworn booted him in the chest, sending him rolling through the snow and mud.

"Pathetic!" Godfrey yelled at him. "All that potential... *ruined* by your mother. She should never have taken you away."

Vighon shook his head and wiped the blood from his nose as he found his feet again. "You're lying!" he accused. "My mother died of the Red Pox," he seethed, just the memory of it boiling his blood.

To make it worse, Godfrey laughed. "Aye, boy, she did - horrible way to go," he added with an infuriating smile. "Who do you think made sure she got it, eh? The minute you entered Skystead, Arlon knew about it. He wanted his heir back, but killing her in front of you would have pushed you away. Arlon's always been smart when it comes to dealing out death though, hasn't he?"

Vighon started forward, his rage climbing ever higher. "You're lying!"

Godfrey pointed his sword at the northman and edged around slowly. "Lying? Who do you think set the whole thing up for him? Your granddaddy's business was going under. You needed money. I know for a fact that you didn't go with your mother to meet the lender, a man who had recently been touched by the Red Pox. He wanted some security for his family's future; something The Ironsworn could offer." He smiled arrogantly at Vighon. "All he had to do was shake her hand..."

Tears had begun to gather in the corners of Vighon's eyes. He could remember all too vividly his mother's agonising death. The Red Pox ravaged her body first, then her mind. She suffered before the end...

He wanted to believe that Godfrey was just trying to unhinge him, but he knew the terrible truth when he heard it.

Arlon had killed his mother.

The storming rage that threatened to consume him quietened to something far more dangerous.

Believing he had successfully got under Vighon's skin, Godfrey charged at him, prepared to end their duel. But the northman didn't want to fight anymore, he just wanted blood on his hands.

With both hands, Vighon launched his silvyr sword horizontally across the courtyard. The blade caught Godfrey in the gut and halted his charge with some finality. He looked down at the weapon piercing his leathers, covered in the blood of his men and now his own. Vighon strode over without a word and took his sword back, his eyes never straying from the Ironsworn's.

He plunged the blade back in, eliciting a sharp grunt from Godfrey. Then, he pulled it free only to drive it through the man again, dropping him to his knees. A lone tear streaked down the northman's face as he reclaimed his sword one last time.

Then he swung.

Godfrey's head flew through the air before landing at Asher's feet. The ranger looked down at the Ironsworn's contorted expression without a hint of emotion.

"We should move on from here, just in case there are more."

Vighon heard every word but he didn't understand any of them. The image of his mother's body continued to flash before his eyes, taking him back to the worst of times.

In the end, it was Ruban grabbing his arm that shook him from his past. "Vighon? We need to go."

The northman nodded absently and sheathed his sword. It had removed Godfrey's head with smooth ease, as if the Ironsworn hadn't even possessed a neck. He wanted to kill him all over again. No, he realised, he was satisfied with Godfrey's death; it was another he wanted to kill now.

He wanted to kill his father...

CHAPTER 21
WHERE THE DEAD DON'T LIE

Astride the most powerful predator in all the world, Inara Galfrey hunted for her prey. This prey was ancient, a testament to its history of hiding in The Vrost Mountains' dark rock. After another whole day of flying, following Asher's guidance, Inara was beginning to wonder if magic was the reason The Bastion had escaped attention for ten thousand years.

There was little to nothing that could elude Athis's keen vision, be it day or night, yet here they were, searching beneath the ash in the biting cold. The young Dragorn had already cast several spells that day to keep herself and her parents warm and she was beginning to think about camping again. Her parents wouldn't be happy about that.

Perhaps we should have forced Asher to accompany us, Inara mused.

His errand is too important, Athis replied.

Inara detected something else behind her companion's words. Her mind probed their bond and she felt Athis pull away, resisting her curiosity.

What is it? she asked outright. **What are you not saying?**

The dragon's red-scaled head turned to the side as he laid one startling blue eye on her. *Asher's warning, about Malliath and Alijah...*

Inara felt a wave of fear bubbling up inside Athis. **You are concerned about their bond?**

The dragon turned away again, focusing on the mountains. *I spoke briefly with Ilargo about their bond. He agrees with Gideon that they are one of us, that we can help them.*

Inara frowned at the back of his horned head. **You disagree?** She couldn't believe such a thing.

Ilargo was too guarded, Athis explained. *I could sense the doubt in him.*

That alone opened a pit inside Inara's stomach. Gideon's confidence, like any Dragorn, was often born of his bond with his dragon; the wisest of all living creatures. To know that doubt existed inside Ilargo was troubling...

What do you think? she asked Athis.

The dragon was contemplative. *Their bond has a touch of destiny about it, of that there can be no doubt; Malliath has lived for thousands of years having never found the one he was to share his life with.*

Even if their bond was being controlled by some grand scheme of fate, Inara argued, **that doesn't mean they're destined to be evil.**

I agree, Athis was quick to respond. *But your mother was right about dark magic; it produces nothing good. That aside, my true concern lies with Malliath. His past is as much a mystery to the dragons as it is to the humans and elves of the world. He was named the voiceless one for a reason.*

Inara could feel everything Athis was thinking and knew he was dwelling on Malliath's violent tendencies. **He spent a thousand years chained in Korkanath, a slave to the magic of men once again. What those mages did to him would drive any being to the point of rage and madness. He just needs time...**

Athis wasn't convinced of such a thing. *I hope you are right, wingless one, I truly do.*

That wasn't enough for Inara. She wanted to hear surety from her companion, to know that he held the same faith as she did. If they were to help Alijah and Malliath, she would need Athis to believe that it could be done. On the verge of renewing her argument, Athis found something, his excitement passing eagerly through their bond.

Where? Inara demanded, pushing up from his neck.

Athis banked to the north, bringing them in line with an inlet in the mountains. Inara squinted her eyes and pushed her head forward, desperate to see The Bastion. The mist that hugged the mountains drifted lazily over the rock, shrouding the ancient fortress.

Dipping low and coming up at The Bastion with all his speed, Athis flapped his mighty wings as he flew across the hewn stone, battering the mist into great plumes of vapour. Inara and her parents turned and craned their necks to see the broken towers and damaged spires. It was ugly but, more than that, it oozed evil. Just knowing that King Atilan himself had once stepped foot inside the dark place lent The Bastion a malevolent atmosphere.

"We've found it!" Nathaniel cheered.

The only place for me to land is on the front steps, Athis told her. *I fear that anything else would shatter were I to touch it.*

Inara looked down at the grand flight of steps that rose up to the double doors. **Get us to the top of the steps. If The Black Hand challenges us, I don't want to be fighting them uphill.**

The red dragon flew back around and angled down towards the entrance. Snow and debris were blasted into the air as his wings brought them all to a stop outside the double doors. The stonework cracked under the pressure of his fearsome claws and his hot breath blew over the closed doors.

All three Galfreys jumped down from Athis's red scales and brandished their weapons, ready for battle.

I will remain close by, Athis said. *Be careful in there, wingless one; we still have much to do in this world together.*

Inara looked up and met her companion's eyes. ***If anything other than us comes out of those doors, burn it.***

Athis huffed one last breath of air before pushing off and taking to the skies. Inara adjusted her grip on the Vi'tari blade, feeling its familiar weight and balance. Whenever she left Athis's side, the Dragorn knew that her scimitar was more than just a weapon with which to cut down evil, it also kept her companion alive in its defence of herself.

Reyna nocked an arrow against the string of her enchanted bow. Much like a Vi'tari blade, the bow responded to the will of the user, altering its level of devastation. If her mother wanted to, she could bring down every tower in The Bastion with one well-placed shot.

Nathaniel held his steel sword in the manner of a knight, his training always clear to see. The weapon wasn't enchanted, but her father certainly was. His retained youth and vigour would make him a worthy opponent for the greatest of warriors.

As Inara cautiously approached the double doors, the Dragorn was reminded of the enemy they faced. This was The Black Hand, an order of dark mages. Magic was their weapon of choice...

With her hand on the flat of the black door, Inara turned to her parents. "Stay behind me at all times," she advised.

"We were doing this kind of thing before you were born," her father pointed out, anxious to get inside and find Alijah.

"I don't doubt your sword arm, Father, only your ability to repel destructive magic." Inara looked at her mother. "Your instincts have kept you alive in the past, but listen to them in here and a spell will claim your life; you cannot create shields anymore. Rely on your bow, nothing more. If we face magic, leave it to me."

A flicker of sadness crossed her mother's face, but it was soon replaced with determination. "We will follow your lead," she promised.

Satisfied that her parents understood the risks, Inara pushed her way into The Bastion. What lay beyond was just as hideous as the outside, and no warmer. A vast receiving area, lined with columns and fire pits greeted them. At the far end sat a throne with a tall back, once used by Atilan - it sent a cold shiver up Inara's spine.

Out of the wind, the closing door sounded all too loud as it *creaked* and *groaned* before finally slamming back into place. The last one in, Nathaniel shrugged apologetically. Arriving on dragon-back wouldn't have been the quietest infiltration, but slamming the door on their way in was likely sufficient to alert every dark mage. Inara sighed and pushed farther into the open room, her eyes darting from one shadow to the next.

The young Dragorn gestured for her parents to follow her as she remained close to the line of pillars. Walking through the middle of such a large chamber was a sure way to get ambushed.

A howling wind rushed through a side door, startling the Galfreys. Inara pressed against the nearest pillar and stayed perfectly still, waiting for an attack that never came. Reaching as far as the throne, the trio were offered three doors to take, though where they led was unknown to them.

"We would find Alijah faster if we split up," Nathaniel suggested, eyeing the door to his right.

"And what will you do when you're looking down the length of a wand?" Inara countered.

Nathaniel rested a hand on the dagger sheathed on his belt. "I'm a pretty good throw," he boasted.

Inara didn't hide her frustration. "You can only throw it once. This place will be full of dark mages. We're sticking together," she told him firmly.

The Dragorn chose the door to her left and bade her parents to follow. With a glowing orb to accompany them, they could see that every passage was a ruin, poked with jagged holes, shattered doors, and ancient debris. The trio were careful with their steps, taking care to avoid anything that would give their position away.

Floating above them, the bright orb produced stark shadows on the ground, often adding to the darkness that lay beyond the broken doors. Here and there, Inara commanded the orb to float away and illuminate one of the chambers, checking for any foes that wished to flank them.

"Where is everyone?" Nathaniel posed in a hushed tone.

"Maybe they're..." Her mother's reply faded away and her emerald eyes rolled to the ceiling that stretched along the passage.

Inara heard it too, through the cavities of The Bastion. The sound was unusual, yet there was something familiar about it.

"I hate it when you two do this," Nathaniel complained. "What is it?" he asked, following their gaze to the ceiling above.

Inara scowled at the stone. "It sounds like..."

"Bare feet," Reyna finished. "Lots of them, slapping against the stone."

"Bare feet?" Nathaniel echoed incredulously. "Other prisoners perhaps?"

Inara shook her head. "They're moving rapidly." The Dragorn stepped closer to the wall, where an abyss-like hole penetrated the stone. She listened. Then she stepped back, her muscles tensed.

"What now?" Nathaniel dared to ask.

"What did Asher say?" Inara stared into that hole. "The Crow surrounds himself with Reavers and..."

The sound of bare feet and hands clawing at the stone grew louder and was now coming from the end of the passageway. The rasping din of what could only be monsters echoed through The Bastion.

Reyna levelled her bow. "Darklings..." she whispered.

Nathaniel gripped his sword in both hands. "Which ones were those?"

Answering his question, the end of the passage exploded with undead creatures. Once human, the despicable fiends moved on all fours and climbed over each other to reach their prey. Rotted flesh hung off their bodies, their mortal wounds clear to see. Some didn't even possess eyes, but simply followed the momentum of the horde, hungry for the living. Others were little more than skeletons with pointed fingers of chipped bone.

Inhuman was their cry and inhuman was their mad rush. The shrieks and moans bounced off the stone as they closed the gap between them. Reyna didn't have to wait for the gap to close before unleashing her bow.

Her mother's arrow pierced the air so close to Inara's head that it cut through her hair, blowing strands out before her face on its journey down the passage. The first Darkling it struck burst apart in a shower of limbs and gore but, of course, the arrow wouldn't be satisfied until it found stone. One after another ran into the projectile's path and lost their head or a limb.

"Run!" Inara shouted, pushing her parents back the way they had come.

Snarls and howls followed them around every corner, the horde relentless in their pursuit. Those behind them, however, were only a few of the Darklings that dwelled in The Bastion. Retracing their path, more of the undead breached the crumbling walls and scurried out of the holes, herding the Galfreys one way then the other.

"This way!" Nathaniel barked, taking them up a spiralling staircase - the only route that didn't have Darklings crawling all over it.

After reaching the top of the stairs, Inara turned back and held her hand out. The fire she expelled was a blazing heat that engulfed the spiral from top to bottom. The Darklings didn't make a sound as the flames consumed what was left of their bodies. Only one made it far enough for Inara to see it burn, its clawed hand outstretched.

"There's more!" her father bellowed.

Nathaniel dashed left and right, swinging his sword with precision. The steel removed one decaying head after another, dropping the Darklings around him. A particularly scrawny Darkling lunged over the bodies to clamp its jaws around his neck, but the creature was sent flying back with an arrow in its head. Before it hit the ground, Reyna nocked another arrow and let loose the power of the enchanted bow.

The arrow struck the floor several metres away with enough magic to cave the stone in. Inara reached out to steady herself as she watched a dozen Darklings fall through the new hole. The explosion rocked The Bastion and sent deep cracks up the external wall. A moment later, the wall caved in, burying the Darklings on the floor below under tons of heavy slabs.

An icy wind rushed in to fill the passage, blowing Inara's red cloak out behind her. "We need to keep moving!" she warned.

Together, the Galfreys ran down the only passage left to them. The sound of more Darklings wasn't far behind, forcing them to ascend another level. This time, Inara cast a freezing spell that layered the staircase in a solid sheen of ice. It would only delay the undead of course; they were like spiders that crawled through the cracks in a house.

As quietly as they could, the trio moved from room to room, checking every crevice of The Bastion. Only twice did a lone Darkling find its way into their path, but Inara's Vi'tari blade sliced easily through both, dropping them with barely a sound.

"Where is he?" Nathaniel asked aloud, his frustration evident.

Inara was beginning to fear the worst. What if The Crow had foreseen their arrival and whisked Alijah away, to continue his torment elsewhere? What if this was just a trap?

"In here," Reyna called, a little farther ahead.

"Mother, I told you to stay behind me."

Reyna didn't apologise, she just stood motionless in the doorway. Inara looked in, inspecting the chamber before entering it. It was impossible to miss what had captured her mother's attention.

"Wait here," Inara instructed.

The Dragorn entered the chamber very slowly. In one hand she held her scimitar and in the other she wielded a flaming ball of fire. Upon entering, the chamber's size became apparent and it was large to say the least. There was no roof to speak of and what pillars remained were charred and bore deep claw marks. This was all taken in at a glance, for Inara's attention was drawn to the same thing as her mother.

Using the tip of her blade, the Dragorn poked one of the bodies piled on top of each other. They were all dusted in snow and ash, their limbs frozen together. Men and women alike, the dead stared into nothingness, their eyes solid orbs of ice. Since they were not falling over each other to devour her, Inara decided they had been spared the humiliation of resurrection.

Walking past her, Reyna moved to the far wall with Nathaniel close behind. Her mother reached out to touch a pair of hanging manacles. Inara heard the chain rattle and winced, hoping the Darklings didn't possess sensitive ears.

"What is it?" she whispered.

Reyna lifted one of the manacles up. "Dried blood. It's not fresh, but it isn't ancient either."

"This is where they were keeping him," Nathaniel stated, turning away from the manacles.

Inara looked from the manacles to the piled bodies, putting the pieces together. "Asher said he was forced to watch innocent people die."

"He said Alijah had to fight for them," Reyna corrected.

Inara moved a little farther into the large chamber, pausing to scrutinise the claw marks on a broken pillar. There were more on the ground, their spacing familiar to the Dragorn.

"Malliath was in here with him," she observed.

"I don't care about any of this," Nathaniel raged. "I want to know where my son is!"

Reyna released the manacles and placed a strong hand against her husband's chest. "Remain calm, my love. If we are to find Alijah in this maze, we must be quiet, lest we attract more of those hellish creatures."

"What did Asher say?" Inara began pacing. "The Crow had prepared another room for him..."

"A cell," Reyna specified.

"Yes." Inara caught hold of the thread. "A new cell. One scribed in powerful magic."

Nathaniel caught the next thread. "Does The Bastion have a dungeon, actual cells?"

"It must do," Reyna reasoned, gesturing to the pile of bodies. "They kept prisoners here. The Black Hand must have been securing them somewhere."

"Somewhere below," Inara concluded. "Dungeons are either really high or really low, and we're about as high as you can go."

Nathaniel wasted no time heading for the door. "Then let's go down and—"

The immortal knight stopped in his tracks, faced by a doorway of pale eyes that were far from lifeless. The Darklings crept into the chamber one limb at a time, their malevolent presence forcing Nathaniel back. Inara raised her hand, her spell ready, while her mother aimed her bow. The Darklings continued to pour steadily into the chamber, their bony fingers writhing in anticipation and their jaws *clacking* together.

There was a lot of them.

"Get behind me," Inara said quietly.

She was going to discharge her spell with all the unbridled fury she could muster, hoping it would be enough to destroy them all, even the ones crawling up the walls.

Pulling her arm back, Inara prepared to let all the magic go. "Shield your eyes," she warned.

Confident their meal was trapped, the Darklings rushed forward with a collective snarl. Inara pushed her hand out and released the destructive spell of raging fire. The flames that submerged the Darklings in roaring fire, however, were not her own. Inara ended her spell and looked up to see Athis as his claws came down on the tops of the broken walls.

The dragon increased the output of flames and Inara was forced to erect a shield around her family. The magic flared a multitude of colours under the bombardment, testing Inara's strength. Outside her protective field, the Darklings were quickly being reduced to ash.

In the chaos, several of the undead things ran headlong into Inara's shield before bouncing away to disappear in the inferno.

When Athis finally closed his jaws, there wasn't a surface inside the vast chamber that wasn't burning. The only evidence that anyone had survived such a destructive force was the circular patch of untouched stone, inside Inara's field.

The red dragon coughed above them as he altered the glands in his mouth. Inara kept her shield around them as he exhaled a long breath of freezing air to extinguish the flames.

The way is safe now, he told her.

Inara lowered her shield and was immediately set upon by steam and smoke. The Dragorn wafted it from her face and carefully weaved her way between the brittle remains of the Darklings. Every one of them deserved better, their deaths orchestrated by The Crow for nothing more than his twisted lessons. Inara wondered how many husbands, wives, and parents were out there searching for their loved ones in a war-torn land, unaware of the true fate that had befallen them.

As her parents left the awful chamber, Inara paused to look up at Athis. ***Thank you.***

You don't have to thank me for saving our lives, Athis replied.

I know. I was thanking you for saving theirs.

Athis bowed his head and took off again. Inara knew there were none so lucky as a Dragorn to have a dragon looking out for them. It was a lot more than these people ever had. It bolstered her belief that she was meant to protect them. It should have been the Dragorn that stood between these people and The Black Hand, it should have been her...

Hearing her parents get farther away, Inara left the dead to their resting place and hurried to catch up. Unsure of the Darklings' numbers, they continued to explore The Bastion with due care. Crossing treacherous bridges and contending with ruined passages, the Galfreys began to find their way into the depths of the ancient fortress.

Whether it was luck or skill, the trio finally made it to the lowest levels without meeting another Darkling. Inara held on to the hope that Athis had burnt them all.

The door barring the dungeons was a heavy slab of wood with a rusted latch. It would open without a problem, but it wasn't going to be quiet.

Inara placed one hand on the lock and turned back to her parents. "Stay behind me," she reiterated.

With her Vi'tari blade raised at eye-level, the Dragorn lifted the latch and began to pull it open. At once, the sound of a discharging spell and its subsequent impact found Inara. The dark mage had been too eager, however, or perhaps afraid, and released their spell before the Dragorn had entered the dungeon.

It still hurt though.

The door was pushed beyond Inara's control, slamming into her with some force. Debris from the door blew out in a cloud of smoke and her parents dashed to the sides in search of cover. Having hit the wall and slid down, Inara kicked out to close the door again before more spells could be hurled at them.

"Are you hurt?" Reyna asked urgently, fearing the worst.

Inara rose to her feet and readjusted her red cloak, displeased with the dirt caked to her leg. "I'm fine," she replied, allowing some of her irritation into her tone. "They won't be..."

The Dragorn balled her fist, siphoning energy from the magical realm. Light collected in colourful strands, each one being sucked between her clenched fingers as the magic coalesced. Satisfied with the power she wielded, Inara pushed her hand out and unleashed it upon the door. Everything encompassed within the doorframe was instantly carried away in the wave of destructive magic. The wood splintered into deadly points and the metal hinges and lock rebounded down the length of the dungeon with enough speed to impale a man.

The two dark mages closest to the door were swept up in the battering force and thrown down the passageway, their bodies reduced to pin-cushions. A third dropped his wand when a stray piece of the door's twisted lock careered into his knuckles and removed his fingers. He cradled his hand and staggered in pain from one side of the cells to the other, holding it in agony.

Reyna gently let loose an arrow and hit the mage in the side of the throat. It wasn't a pretty death, nor a swift one. Inara had the sense her mother wished for these men to suffer.

Farther down the length of the dungeon, another dark mage popped out of an open cell and flicked his wand their way. A staccato of lightning filled the dungeon on its way to the Galfreys, a piece of magic that spelled death for any it touched. Inara had but to raise her hand and the lightning went no farther.

"Inara..." Her mother was standing behind her with another arrow nocked.

The young Dragorn maintained the shield for a moment longer, demonstrating to the dark mage that she could hold out much longer than he could keep his spell up. The second the lightning came to an end, Inara dropped her shield and ducked under her mother's aim. The arrow flew true and literally disarmed the mage.

The arrow itself dug hard into the stone, but the man floundered in shock, staring blankly at his dismembered arm on the floor. Before shock and blood loss could claim him, Reyna fired another arrow and put the mage out of his misery with a direct hit to his heart.

Inara tensed where she stood, her blade itching to taste battle while her hand remained ready to produce another shield. Before them, the dungeons were strewn with the bodies of four mages. Their reliance on magic had filled the narrow passageway with the fresh smell of sulphur. It was acrid and unpleasant, but the Galfreys stood their ground, focused. A warrior's sixth sense told each of them that it wasn't over yet.

Inara took another step, advancing towards the door at the very end of the dungeons. Alijah was in there; she knew it. It was as if she could feel his proximity. Another step, avoiding the body at her feet, and The Black Hand revealed its last line of defence. A small man, robed in the typical black of his dark order, stepped out of a cell with a long staff in hand. There appeared nothing extraordinary about him: in fact, his every feature was entirely forgettable.

The look in his eye, however, was most memorable. He blinked fresh tears as his eyes roamed over the dead that littered the floor. There was a hint of shock about him, as if he was struggling to comprehend the last few seconds. Inara was more concerned with his staff. It was no more powerful than a wand, but those that chose to wield staffs over wands tended to favour a more aggressive form.

The mage's eyes finally rested on Inara and her parents. "He... He said this wouldn't happen. He said we would live..."

Reyna pulled back her bowstring. "He lied."

The small man didn't even try to deflect the incoming arrow. He simply stood there, dumbfounded, as the missile pierced his chest, leaving a neat hole where his heart should have been. Inara watched him drop to his knees before slamming face first into the ground, dead. She had never seen this side of her mother before and it scared her more than a little. A mother's love, she decided, was something no one should ever cross.

That only left the door at the end of the dungeons.

Inara approached it with her parents in tow. She was hesitant to open it. What would be on the other side? The Dragorn couldn't decide if it would be worse to discover an empty cell or a broken Alijah.

"Wait," her mother warned. "Asher said there was a time spell inside. We should observe before entering."

"We didn't come this far to observe," Nathaniel countered. "I want my son." Inara's father moved past them both and opened the door.

CHAPTER 22

THE MASTERS OF MONSTERS

Exploring the maze-like depths of Vengora was no simple task, regardless of *Nocturn's Phemora* running through one's veins. It had taken hours before Gideon Thorn started coming across orcs with any regularity, so deep were they, but it was with some difficulty that he chose the right path. The tunnels intersected every few hundred metres, offering the Master Dragorn more options than he cared for.

His ears began to pop for a second time, forcing him to pinch his nose and blow out. His descent aside, the temperature felt as if it was increasing every minute, causing him to sweat.

Here and there, Gideon came across markings carved into the ancient walls; the language of the orcs. He didn't understand a single glyph of their crude language.

This definitely isn't dwarven work, he observed, noting the lack of craftsmanship around the glyphs.

The orcs of old most likely blasted their way through the mountains with that wretched powder. Ilargo's voice was just as clear as it had been when Gideon was on his back, their bond unfettered by distance.

Karakulak's ancestors might not have mined as the dwarves had, but Gideon couldn't fault their tenacity. They had pushed through the tough Vengoran rock in every direction, mapping out the darkest depths of a mountain range that most avoided.

As always, the noisy orcs gave their presence away long before Gideon saw them. The Master Dragorn hesitated at an intersection of five tunnels, making certain he knew their direction before choosing his own route.

The orcs emerged from the central tunnel with a cart in tow behind each. They were hauling supplies like all the others Gideon had come across. The Master Dragorn waited, hanging from an outcropping of rock above the central tunnel, until the orcs took a left and disappeared. He dropped down and wondered whether to follow them or retrace their steps.

Do not follow them, Gideon, Ilargo advised. *If they are moving supplies, it is probable they are heading towards a larger group of orcs.*

Good point, Gideon conceded. **You are paying attention to what's going on up there, aren't you?**

Ilargo shared a feeling that told Gideon he was puffing out his considerable chest. *Unlike you, I can do several things at once...*

Gideon smiled to himself. **I'm following them,** the Master Dragorn announced defiantly. **The king is likely to be surrounded by a large group of orcs and that's where I'll find Arathor.**

Your logic runs side by side with recklessness...

Taking this particular route was long and winding but, worst of all, it offered little in the way of shelter. Were another group of orcs to approach or follow from behind, he would have no choice but to engage them. Of course, there was every chance that his first kill had already been found and a small horde of orcs were hunting him at this very moment.

At last, the tunnel branched and presented Gideon with more options. Sighting the orcs he had been trailing, he could hear a distant clamouring, echoing from the tunnel they had chosen. Tools striking rock and the cacophonous roar of labouring orcs told him exactly what was happening. The orcs were digging.

It is unlikely you will find Arathor with them, Ilargo pointed out, suggesting Gideon stay away.

But why are they digging? the Master Dragorn posed.

Why orcs do anything is beyond reasoning, Ilargo replied dryly.

Still, Gideon's curiosity was piqued. He knew he should have taken the tunnel to his left, but his feet took him right, towards the digging and the shouting. Hugging the rocky wall, the Master Dragorn followed it to a small shelf that overlooked a vast cavern that sat under a roof of crystallised stalactites. Descending from his left, the zig-zagging path would have shown him to the cavern floor, but he remained up high, where the view might offer him some insight.

Hundreds of orcs, even thousands, were filing in and out of multiple tunnels at the base of the cavern. Absent their dark armour, the orcs were easy to see in their pale near-naked form. Those that came out passed on their tools to those going in and found rest off to the side, where food was being handed out. Even exhausted, the orcs worked the mountain stone with an efficiency that would be the envy of the dwarves. It helped that those who appeared to be slacking received a severe whipping.

One of the tunnels down to Gideon's right was the source of more commotion than the rest. Shuffling quietly along the shelf, the Master Dragorn crouched to take a closer look. The tunnel was being evacuated of orcs and no more were being sent to relieve them. A smaller team of orcs were setting up a large tripod in the mouth of the tunnel and fixing a ballista to its mount. With great care, one of the pale beasts loaded the ballista with a long wrath bolt.

No sooner had the last orc run from the tunnel than the wrath bolt disappeared. Considering the time before the resulting explosion, Gideon estimated the length of the tunnel to be at least a hundred metres. The walls of the cavern shook and a dark plume of smoke rushed out to greet the orcs and spread around the vast hollow. A terrible *cracking* sound came from overhead and was met by an outcry from the orcs below. Gideon watched three of the stalactites relinquish their hold on the ancient ceiling and plummet to the floor.

The orcs scattered in every direction and avoided the main impact, but the dense stalactites broke apart and sent deadly chunks of rock into those who had sought reprieve from the digging. More than a few lost their lives, but the whip masters kept order, commanding them to ignore the dead and wounded and focus on their tunnels.

Gideon took in the many dig sites, all heading in the same direction. ***My bearings are off,*** he said to Ilargo. ***But, I would bet my life they're tunnelling south, under The White Vale.***

I cannot relay that, Ilargo explained urgently. *You need to find Arathor and return to warn the army, before it is too late.*

I agree. Gideon stood up and turned to retrace his steps when he found himself face to face with an orc.

The beast dropped its cart and pulled free its blade, recovering quickly from the shock of discovering him. That obsidian blade came down once, twice, and a third time, hitting nothing but air, before Gideon spun away and drew Mournblade. The enchanted blade absorbed his will and knew Gideon wished to end the orc's life as quickly and quietly as possible. Submitting to its power, the Master Dragorn listened to his instincts and moved, parried, ducked, and finally thrust his scimitar up into the orc's gut and through its back.

The sound of their clashing swords was thankfully drowned out by the digging below, but the orc's death was not so quiet. The stupid creature stumbled backwards, away from Mournblade's tip, and fell off the edge of the shelf. Gideon dashed forwards in an attempt to grab the orc, but it was too late. He could do nothing but watch it fall and inevitably collide with the cavern floor. It went everywhere. The scene also captured the attention of a few other orcs, many of which looked up at Gideon's position.

He ran.

With Mournblade back in its scabbard, the Master Dragorn retraced his steps at a sprint. With a slightly more frantic feel to his movements now, Gideon moved from one tunnel to the next, doing his best to sneak through any of the caverns. At one intersection, he was forced to hide in an alcove as an orc passed by astride the biggest spider he had ever seen.

They truly are the masters of monsters, Ilargo remarked, seeing the spider's image across their bond.

Hopefully, giant spiders are the worst thing they've found down here...

Continuing along his chosen route, another hour went by in which it became apparent that his enemy was on high alert. Unable to understand the snippets of conversation and the barking orders, Gideon had to assume he was the reason for their increased patrols. It didn't help that wherever the Master Dragorn was, he had travelled so far within their ancient dwelling that the orcs were everywhere. Their heavy presence slowed his exploration down and often encouraged him to divert from his path and take different tunnels to avoid detection.

After several minutes of following one particular tunnel, he had yet to see a single orc. It was for this reason that Gideon stayed his course. He needed to hurry, not only for Arathor's sake or even the Namdhorians, but because his potion of *Nocturn's Phemora* wouldn't last forever. Once it was gone, he would be stuck in a pitch black as all-consuming as the depths of The Adean.

Coming to another intersection of tunnels, Gideon noted the amount of tools and supplies that lay strewn across the ground. They were perfectly good tools and the supplies were intact, but they appeared to have been dropped wherever they were.

I do not think you are in the right place, Gideon. Thraden said that Arathor was being tormented by the king. Karakulak is likely to be in a densely populated area...

Gideon agreed, but the debris that littered the tunnel up ahead was far too interesting to see him turn back. Stepping over the tools and supplies, he made his way farther into the tunnel to investigate. As he had thought, the debris in question was limbs and heads. They were mostly charred, missing chunks of flesh, but they had all belonged to orcs. The Master Dragorn had seen wounds and dismemberment like this before.

Wrath powder, he elaborated across their bond.

That area has been abandoned for a reason, Gideon. You should leave.

He knew he should too, but he couldn't help seeing the pattern of the blast. Tracing it back to the source, Gideon discovered a jagged hole in the wall where the surface of the rock was charred black. It was, however, what lay beyond the hole that stole Gideon's attention and gripped him with fear.

The Master Dragorn stepped inside the empty chamber. His eyes were naturally drawn to the open door on the far side. His investigation of that chamber led to a tightening of all of his muscles. He stopped in the threshold and craned his neck to take its size in. Of course, its true depth was hidden behind the mountainous hills of red grains...

There's enough wrath powder in here to crack the north in half.

Gideon... A sense of dread filled Ilargo's tone. *I can sense where you are from up here. The wrath powder is only a few hundred metres in front of the catapults.*

Gideon swallowed hard. *Along with a battalion on Namdhorians,* he added. *We have to warn them.*

You can't do that from down there, Ilargo pointed out.

No, but Ayana can. Is Deartanyon within range yet?

Ilargo paused. *Yes, I can feel the edge of his thoughts. They will be here soon.*

Then share this with Deartanyon and have them move the catapults back.

Gideon crouched down to better examine a small mound of the deadly powder.

Why are you still in there? Ilargo pressed. *One misstep, one crushed grain, and you will kill more than just us.*

Gideon considered his environment and the resources at his disposal. *I have an idea...*

~

ANY CONCEPT of time was lost on Gideon. The only thing he knew was the fatigue steadily taking a hold of him. Ilargo had told him of the sunset and the subsequent dawn, but it meant nothing down here.

Drink it, Gideon, Ilargo instructed for the third time. *You cannot sleep down there.*

Gideon stared at the vibrant yellow vial in his hand. He really didn't want to drink it. Of all his concoctions, *Allidai's Voronum* was the only one that felt like consuming fire. The Master Dragorn was in need of it, though, a fact he couldn't deny for much longer; he had been exploring the orc lands of Vengora for well over a day now and he was exhausted.

With a deep breath, Gideon downed the yellow liquid. He almost gagged and spat the last drops out, but he relied on his companion's determination and resilience to finish the whole thing. Everything inside his mouth hurt, as if he had just tried to swallow a burning chunk of coal. The burning consumed the length of his tongue and ran down into his stomach with a boiling wrath.

Immediately, his heart rate increased and his muscles tensed. Trying to remain as silent as possible, the Master Dragorn stifled his gasp and gripped the hilt of Mournblade until his knuckles were stretched white. Any traces of fatigue were wiped away by *Allidai's Voronum*, leaving him alert. The first few minutes after consuming the potion were always the most dangerous for any person; if they were too young or too old, it could stop their heart, but for someone like Gideon, it made him crave a good fight.

Stay in control, Ilargo urged, experiencing the same effects across their bond. *You must avoid conflict.*

Gideon gritted his teeth and waited for the extreme feelings to pass. When it finally settled down, he was left with a steady heart rate and a clear head, now very much alert. There was, however, a decline in his sight. The *Nocturn's Phemora* was beginning to fade, failing to bring light to the farthest patches of darkness.

I'm relying on you to remember the most direct path out of here, he said to Ilargo.

It would not be the first time I have led you back to the light...

Gideon was never more thankful for Ilargo's incredible memory than when he was lost in the dark. The Master Dragorn picked himself up and shimmied along the edge of a deadly drop to bring himself back to the tunnels of the orc lands. The small outcropping had given him what reprieve he could afford, but the prospect of being stuck without sight was enough to push him onwards.

Taking Mournblade in hand, Gideon crept from one tunnel to the next, hiding whenever he needed to avoid the orcs. What little remained of the *Nocturn's Phemora* in his veins was his only guide, its magic just managing to highlight the paths that cut through the mountain. Its true limits were found when the Master Dragorn came across a cavern so large the potion couldn't illuminate the other side.

Approaching the cavern from upon high, Gideon crouched by the hole in the wall and inspected as much of his surroundings as he could. Below, the ground level was crawling with orcs, giant spiders, and even a few of their six-legged mounts. Unlike a lot of the other caverns, this one contained the remnants of civilisation. The orcs of ancient times had once occupied this space and worked the stone, leaving behind shattered pillars and the broken walls of old buildings.

Gideon's eyes caught sight of one particular orc striding down the centre of what had perhaps been some kind of street or path. This orc was larger with two horns curving neatly over its head and flicking up at the ends. Long white hair flowed over its shoulders, where the hilt of a sword pointed to the roof. A long cape dragged on the ground behind it, a cape that Gideon had seen up close before and knew it to be tailored from the skin of humans.

King Karakulak...

That would be very foolish, Ilargo warned him. *I know exactly what you are thinking, Gideon Thorn, and that is not the reason you are down there.*

Killing Karakulak would likely bring an end to this war, Gideon argued.

You know as well as I do that such a theory is not true. The orcs have come too far to stop now.

Their king's death would create a vacuum, Gideon countered, **one which would see them turn on each other.**

There would be another to take his place, Ilargo reasoned. *They mean to take this world, Karakulak or not. You are down there to save Arathor, nothing more. An attempted assassination on the king will reduce your chance of success and increase my chance of falling out of the sky. Find Arathor. Get him out.*

Gideon knew it was a selfish part of him that wanted to slay the orc king right there and then. Besides, Karakulak was a foe unlike his kin; he was larger, smarter, and most definitely touched by magic; The Crow's doing no doubt.

Seeing that the hole in the side of the cave went nowhere, Gideon had no option but to scramble down the wall. He called upon every ounce of his bond with Ilargo to strengthen his grip and improve his agility, careful not to make a sound on his way down. A single misstep would alert any one of the monsters that resided inside the cavern...

As the pads of his fingers became numb, he was finally within jumping distance of the path below, a narrow rise that sloped around the circumference of the cavern. The Master Dragorn turned his fall into a roll as he touched down, reducing the sound of his landing. It did help that the cavern was relatively empty in comparison to the network of tunnels he had traversed so far. It seemed the orc king had the bulk of his forces digging and blasting their way through Vengora.

Waiting for the opportune moments, Gideon dashed and crept his way across the cavern, taking every measure to avoid the small camps of orcs that dotted the ground. The spiders were the hardest to evade, considering their height and that of their riders. Thankfully, the six-legged creatures that towed the ballistas were stalking around the main entrance on the far side. If they knew he was here, their sensitive noses would likely have detected his unique aroma by now.

To his right, slightly above his position, was a dark canvas tent. It was grander than the rest, its size befitting a king. Gideon moved from cover to cover on his way. He was forced to hold his position for several minutes on three occasions, waiting for the orcs to pass him by. He was itching to reach that tent; it was the logical place for Karakulak to keep his personal prisoner and the reason Gideon had journeyed into the darkest depths of Vengora.

Using a burst of speed to propel himself up the walls, Gideon was able to avoid trekking along the winding slopes that would have taken him up to the tent. Since Karakulak had left the cavern, the tent was unguarded, but Gideon couldn't see past the floor-length fabric that concealed the interior. He had little choice, however, but to keep going.

With Mournblade leading his way inside, the Master Dragorn moved the fabric aside and slinked into the tent on the balls of his feet. He waited by the entrance for a moment, waiting to see if his Vi'tari scimitar would be needed for any orc that might have spotted him.

Deciding he wasn't being followed, Gideon lowered his sword and turned his attention to the rest of the tent. The most obvious thing was the throne, situated towards the back. It was made entirely out of bones, dwarvish bones if he had to guess. It was a grotesque creation, on par with Namdhor's dragon throne in Gideon's eyes.

Besides the throne, there was a large bed covered with several rugs made from a variety of skins, some reptilian. Supplies were scattered throughout, offering the king a diversity of meats and drinks, none of which a human could stomach.

The tent also had a particular mustiness to it that attacked Gideon's nose; it could easily have been the lair to some gruesome beast that possessed nothing more than base instincts.

Stepping farther into the tent, *Nocturn's Phemora* brought colour to the dank environment. The blood splattered on the rugs and the posts was clear to see now. It had to be Arathor's blood. Gideon swallowed hard and did what he could to control his emotions.

Thraden is still alive, Ilargo reminded him.

Gideon nodded. **Then so is Arathor. But where is he?** he asked frustrated.

Perhaps Karakulak is keeping him somewhere else, Ilargo suggested.

The Master Dragorn didn't agree. **Arathor is a valuable prisoner, desirable even. There isn't an orc down here who wouldn't want to take a pound of flesh from a Dragorn. If Karakulak wanted Arathor for himself, he would have to keep him somewhere close by.**

Then he saw it - the chest. It wasn't a large chest, but it was certainly big enough to stuff a grown man inside. Gideon only hoped he was wrong. A closer inspection of the chest didn't fill him with hope, as the surface was marked with the bloody handprints of a massive orc.

Sheathing Mournblade, Gideon used both hands to throw back the heavy lid and look inside. He was both relieved and heartbroken to find the chest empty.

He's not here...

Then keep searching; time is against you.

Gideon stepped back from the chest, unsure of his next move. The network of tunnels was so vast it made every city in Illian appear small - Arathor could be anywhere now.

"DRAGORN!"

Gideon froze. The bellowing word had been closer to a feral roar, but he recognised enough of it to know he was being called out. His heart sank as he removed Mournblade from its scabbard again. To say he had a bad feeling was a gross understatement.

Cautiously, the Master Dragorn exited the tent, his eyes darting left to right as he scanned the cavern for threats. There were a lot of them. Giant spiders crawled up the jagged walls, their front legs raised aggressively. Below him, filling the main cavern, was a host of orcs in full armour and swords at the ready. In the middle of them all stood Karakulak, his monstrous form never hard to spot.

There was potentially a lot more in the cavern, all looking at Gideon, but his enchanted sight could only pierce the darkness so far. It mattered little - there were more than enough foes to end his life.

Gideon... Ilargo's tone said it all: they both knew this was the end.

It's alright, old friend. If this is to be our end, we will take the king of orcs with us.

As he descended the levels to meet the horde below, the orcs began moving aside, clearing a wide path between Gideon and Karakulak. As the last orcs moved away, Arathor came into view. The Master Dragorn employed what steely facade he could to maintain his composure, when all he really wanted to do was run to Arathor and comfort him.

On his knees, it was hard to see all of the Dragorn's injuries, but through the strands of his hair, Gideon could see a face that had taken severe punishment. It enraged him, tempting him to give in to such fury and leap at the orc king with feral abandon. But seeing Arathor also reminded him why he was here in the first place. If there was a chance, even the slimmest chance, that he could still get Arathor out of this nightmare alive, then he would take it.

"You are quiet, little human!" Karakulak shouted across the gap. "But you leave a trail of death behind you..."

Gideon frowned, confused for a moment as to why the orc's words were so clear. Then he saw the translation spinner on the ground, likely given to the orcs by The Crow.

"The same could be said of your entire species," Gideon replied, tightening his grip on Mournblade.

"Gideon?" Arathor croaked, his eyes hopelessly searching the abyss.

Karakulak advanced, bringing him in line with Arathor. "Speak again and I will rip your head from your body." Arathor took the threat seriously and lowered his head.

Gideon pointed his Vi'tari blade at the king. "Speak to him again and it will be you who loses their head."

Karakulak smirked. "Your threats mean nothing down here. Without your dragon, you are nothing. Just another fragile sack of meat waiting for me to burst it open. I told you upon our first meeting; you will not be the one to stop me."

Gideon's steadfast gaze didn't falter as he declared, "This sword was forged for the sole purpose of killing your kind. It already has a taste for the blood of orc kings. Whether it be here, right now, or on the battlefield above, I will cut your ugly head from your ugly body if it's the last thing I ever do."

Karakulak laughed. "More threats from the meat sack! You're already dead. The best you can hope for is a swift death." The king nudged Arathor with his foot. "Gordomo knows this one has begged for such a death."

Gideon glanced at the orcs surrounding him, shoulder to shoulder, as they crammed together in a bid to be the first to attack him. They were salivating at the thought of tearing into him, their bloodlust rising. Some were even clashing horns to take their position on the front row.

"I will stand on a mountain of bodies before one of them claims my life!" Gideon meant it as much as he believed it.

"That may be true," Karakulak concurred. "But you will kill far less than your dragon would were you to walk out of here." The orc king paused, chewing over his next words. "Perhaps there is a way that life can be spared then; that is your way, is it not?"

Gideon recalled his first meeting with the orc king, on the plains of The White Vale. He had halted their army to slow them down, giving Arathor the time he needed to evacuate the city of Dunwich. Hearing such a proposal from Karakulak, however, didn't make Gideon feel any better.

"If you throw down your sword and surrender, I will release this pathetic creature and see him returned to the surface unharmed."

"You want me to take his place?" Gideon clarified, enticed as he was.

"A king must be entertained," Karakulak stated with arms wide. "What say you, Dragorn?"

He cannot be trusted, Ilargo strongly averred.

Karakulak removed a large sword from his back, distracting Gideon. It was distinctly bone, from the curved hilt to the pointed tip, and its size suggested it could only belong to one creature. "I call it Dragonslayer! A name I think it will earn this day." Karakulak rested the edge of the sword on Arathor's shoulder. "What say you?"

Gideon eyed the steel of his blade, weighing up his options - they were limited. Or perhaps they weren't...

"I have a counter offer," the Master Dragorn said boldly.

Answering Karakulak's unasked question, Gideon removed a vial from his jacket. It was red, visible through the glass slits, but it was not liquid inside. He held up the vial so that Karakulak could see it clearly. "I believe you call it wrath powder. I came across mountains of the stuff. I didn't think you would mind me taking a few grains."

The orc king curled his lip and bared one of his fangs. Those dark eyes narrowed on the red vial, but he maintained his demeanour, unlike the orcs around Gideon, who immediately scrambled backwards.

"What courage you have, little human, daring to even touch wrath powder, especially after seeing what it can do to your precious dragons."

Gideon eyed the vial. "I know it's pressure-sensitive. I just have to drop it and that overgrown body of yours will decorate this cavern for eternity."

Karakulak didn't budge. "As will yours," he pointed out smugly.

Gideon shrugged. "If the alternative is death anyway, I'll choose how and when I die."

"Will you choose for him as well?" The orc king gestured to Arathor.

Ilargo's voice crossed their bond with some urgency. *Gideon...*

Not now, he retorted, his focus narrowed on the edge of death.

Gideon began to take slow steps towards Karakulak and Arathor. "You're going to move aside now," he instructed the orc king. "And you're going to personally accompany us to the surface. Try anything and we all die."

Gideon! Ilargo tried again.

Karakulak sneered, clearly dissatisfied with the leverage used against him. "Try anything?" the orc echoed mockingly. "You mean like this?" The king's perfect back swing took the edge of Dragon-slayer through Arathor's neck and sent the Dragorn's head flying into the horde.

Shock and instant grief took a hold of Gideon. He watched the orcs go mad fighting over the head as Arathor's body collapsed to the ground at Karakulak's feet. He was gone. It took the vile king but a second to extinguish Arathor's and Thraden's life. It hurt. It hurt somewhere deep inside that Gideon knew would never leave him.

"I am a God-King," Karakulak commanded, "not some weak surface-dweller you can..." The king's words died away as Gideon lifted the vial of wrath powder to the air, his eyes still fixed on Arathor's headless body.

The Master Dragorn blinked his tears away, gritted his teeth, and remembered once again his first meeting with Karakulak, specifically the part where the orc king threw a wrath bolt into the air.

"I wouldn't be here when this lands," Gideon growled.

Judging by the recognition in his eyes, Karakulak's memory had caught up. It was too late, however, to do anything before the Master Dragorn threw the vial of wrath powder high into the air between them.

PART THREE

CHAPTER 23
A BROKEN PROMISE

Beyond Vengora, the company of three rode under a calming blue sky, free of the ash clouds that hounded Illian. The snowy plains laid out before them were flat and undisturbed, a clean slate of inviting white powder. That which sat on the horizon, however, was not so inviting - at least not for Doran Heavybelly...

Looking upon the golden pillar that had long held half a mountain over Grimwhal's entrance, the son of Dorain felt pit after pit open up inside his gut. Surrounding the pillar, to the north, the mountain stone had been carved out, forming a vast concave wall dotted with burrows that served as ballista mounts. It was the only entrance to the city, since Grimwhal itself was the foundation of the mountain, hidden from sight.

"If only there was another way..." he muttered to himself.

Beside him, on the other side of Russell's cart, Galanör turned to look at the dwarf. "Doran?"

The stout ranger reminded himself that the damned elf had ears like a bat. Eyeing the Blood Boys that travelled with them, Doran lifted his chin at Russell and both he and Galanör spurred their mounts onward to bring them either side of the old wolf.

"*Doran!*" Revek barked from the rear. The leader of the Blood Boys was gesturing to the back of the cart where the orc was beginning to stir again. "*I told you to keep that beast under control or I would do it for you!*"

The son of Dorain nodded along and waved Revek's concerns away. "*I'm dealing with it, I'm dealing with it!*"

The dwarven ranger slowed Pig down to bring him alongside the cart rather than Russell. A scramble over the lip brought him crashing down into the cart with all the grace of a falling boulder. With the tarpaulin now gathering around its ankles, the head of the orc was exposed to the light of day, something it really didn't like. The beast roared and thrashed about in a desperate bid to hide its face from the bright blue sky but, being bound as it was, the orc could do nothing but writhe as Doran set upon it.

"Ah, shut ye gob, ye ugly monster!" The dwarf gripped one of its horns and turned its head against its will, where he could score a hammering punch.

All of its thrashing came to an abrupt end and Doran let its head fall back onto the cart with a *thud*. He proceeded to kick the orc into the centre of the cart where he could cover it up again - just the sight of it was likely to incite rage in the Blood Boys.

Taking a breath, Doran moved to the head of the cart and climbed over to join Russell on the bench, putting him between the old wolf and the elven ranger who rode beside them.

Galanör stole a glance over his shoulder. "The orc is still alive, I hope."

Doran cracked the knuckles in his right fist. "It was jus' a tap is all. Don' get yer cloak in a twist..."

"You're testy today," Russell observed. "I take it that's Grimwhal?" He nodded at the towering pillar in the distance.

"Aye," Doran replied quietly. "Now, listen up, the pair o' ye. As ye might o' surmised from our present company, dwarves hate *every-*

body. They distrust elves an' they reckon werewolves are good for nothin' but rugs. Right now, the two o' ye are just plain old humans an' we'd be best keepin' it that way. That means keeping *yer* hood up and *yer* yellow eyes on the ground. Leave the talkin' to me."

Galanör arched an immaculate eyebrow. "From what I can gather, that plan didn't work for you last time. It is the definition of madness to repeat that which doesn't work."

Doran rolled his eyes and turned his shoulders to face the elf. "Handlin' the orc - that's *yer* job. If a single word comes out o' yer mouth that ain' dwarvish yer likely to lose yer tongue."

Russell held up his hand to calm the dwarf. "What exactly can we expect in there, Heavybelly?"

Doran stared at the pillar as its golden base caught a glimmer of the sun. "Nothin' good. Me clan might not preside over the silvyr mine, but they've been tradin' in it long enough that almost every soldier has *some* silvyr in their armour or weapon. If this doesn' go our way, there'll be no fightin' our way out."

"What about your family?" Galanör asked. "They helped you last time. Can we not rely on them to hear us out?"

"Dakmund, me brother, might listen, but me mother, Queen Drelda... Well, she will more than likely beat me head in for returnin' at all. Me father is goin' to be our real obstacle though. There's a chance he'll order me execution before ye can show 'im the orc."

"I'm starting to feel this plan is unravelling," Galanör remarked dryly.

"Plan?" Doran echoed with a laugh. "There ain't been no plan, laddy. The best we can hope for is me kin see the orc, get really mad, an' march to Namdhor without delay. An', if we're lucky, the three o' us won' get executed somewhere in all that..."

That sobering thought kept the companions quiet for the rest of their trek across the plains. Only when the golden pillar was so close that they had to crane their necks to see its apex did the Blood Boys begin to take charge. They guided their Warhogs and closed the net around Doran and his companions - it was both comforting and threatening all at once. Doran had to remind himself that Revek and his hunters were the only way they would reach his father without being slapped in chains and their prisoner taken from them.

The square burrows that lined the concave wall, beyond the pillar, came alive with Heavybelly warriors. They adjusted their giant ballistas and aimed them at the approaching group. In the centre, at the base of the concave wall, sat an ominous entrance, a pair of tall black doors that could repel a dragon if needed.

In front of the doors, a group of warriors took note of their arrival and advanced to receive them with spears in hand. *"Who approaches Grimwhal?"* the captain called.

Revek took the lead on his Warhog, his black mohawk bouncing on his head. *"What's the point in wearing bright red coats if no one can recognise you?"* he shouted back.

The Heavybelly captain scrutinised the group. *"Blood Boys, is it? And what riffraff are you tarnishing Grimwhal's halls with today?"*

Russell leaned down to Doran. "What are they saying?"

"Shut it," the son of Dorain hissed. Drawing attention to themselves before Revek had smoothed over their entry was asking for trouble, though the dwarven ranger was beginning to wonder what kind of reputation the Blood Boys really had in Grimwhal.

Revek grinned at the Heavybelly captain. *"This here is the catch of the century! A catch, I might add, that is protected under the laws of my guild."*

The captain tilted to the side to look past Revek and his Warhog. Then his spear came up, along with those of his comrades. Credit to him, Revek stared down the length of the spear without flinching.

"I see three armed strangers in your midst, two of which are most certainly not dwarves! Explain yourselves or prepare to have silvyr rained down on you!"

Revek sneered. *"Under the laws of the guild, I don't have to explain anything to the likes of you. Especially when the one who put out the bounty is our king..."*

The latter gave the Heavybelly pause and his grip on the spear faltered, his eyes darting from one comrade to the other. *"You have Doran, son of King Dorain, in your capture?"* With the others, he peered around Revek to lay eyes on the dwarven prisoner.

"None other," Revek announced proudly. *"And two accomplices to boot! So do your job and open those big doors for me. There's a good little soldier."*

The Heavybellys hesitated but the captain eventually squared his shoulders and assumed some kind of control. He lifted his spear from Revek's face and stood at ease, his display catching on among the others. It was at this point that Doran thanked Grarfath for putting the Blood Boys in his path. Had they been in this moment without them, their important mission might have come to a sudden end.

Under the watch of the ballistas, the company finished their journey to Grimwhal's massive doors. "Say goodbye to the light, fellas," Doran commented under his breath.

The shadow of the doorway overcame them, replacing the light of a glorious day with the gloom of torches. Before they were all inside, the Heavybellys guarding the city's entrance were already closing the doors, offering the last Blood Boy a narrow passage. A thundering *boom* shuddered behind them, leaving Doran with a sinking dread in his stomach.

The wide tunnel allowed for the company to continue on their mounts, though they were now being led by the captain from the gate. Lots of dwarves began to cross their path, moving from one passage to the next. It wasn't long before the tunnel was lined with Doran's kin, staring at him and his giant companions. He had a flashback to this same moment with the Galfreys, only this time the dwarves staring at him wore smug expressions instead of pure shock. They were happy to see him returned for judgment and punishment...

Being escorted into the throne room didn't do much for Doran's mood. The Warhogs, including his own, were prevented from entering, along with Russell's and Galanör's horse. Only Russell was permitted to tow the cart behind him. The ease with which he pulled it betrayed his supernatural strength and Doran quickly instructed him to slouch and slow down.

Just as it had always been, the throne room was a museum, a display of the Heavybellys' wealth and position in the dwarven hierarchy, surpassed only by the Stormshields and the Battleborns. The diamond-encrusted pillars sparkled in the light of the roaring fire pits, which was reflected in the polished marble floor. Expertly crafted statues of pure gold lined the chamber, each one an ancient member of the Heavybellys who had presided over the throne.

The chamber itself was filling up as the company advanced towards the silvyr thrones. Doran recognised the various lords of his clans. According to his brother, the lords gained more power every day as their confidence in his father waned - a result of his self-exile. Doran wondered if it would be them he needed to convince rather than his father...

Before Revek could reach the podium housing the empty thrones, a line of shield guards emerged from a shadowy arch and hurried into position around the steps. Trying to cross them without invitation was a death sentence; Doran should know: it had been one of his duties to hand-pick the shield guards, once upon a time.

Then, they waited.

Their arrival had clearly interrupted his parents, who must have received word from somewhere inside their kingdom. Doran hoped it hadn't been anything too enjoyable.

At last, the Keeper of Rule stepped forward from a doorway behind the thrones. "King Dorain, son of Dorryn, of clan Heavybelly! And Queen Drelda, the hammer maiden of Grimwhal!"

Doran held his breath as his mother and father entered the throne room from behind the Keeper of Rule. The king glared at his son on his way to the larger of the thrones, while his mother looked everywhere but at Doran.

When they were seated, a final figure emerged from the doorway. Dakmund, his younger brother, was broad-shouldered with a breastplate that shone a bright silver in the torchlight, highlighting the Heavybelly sigil in the centre. He wore a helm of brilliant silvyr, coated in gold - often worn to hide his fading hair. A jewel-encrusted axe adorned each side of his hips and a mighty sword of pure silvyr was sheathed over his back. In Doran's stead, Dakmund had been made the commanding general of Grimwhal's army.

Though his brother looked the part of a fierce warrior, Doran knew the truth of Dakmund's personality. Had Doran remained and accepted his duties, Dakmund would still be expressing himself through art, be it painting or metal work. He had always been the gentler of the two growing up and Doran loved him for it, even envied him at times, for he had been laden with the responsibility of war. Seeing him now, the old ranger knew he had been monstrously selfish to abandon his brother to this fate.

Standing beside their mother, Dakmund looked down on Doran with disappointment, not an ounce of it held back.

Revek cleared his throat and bowed his head. *"My king, I have—"*

The Keeper of Rule took a quick step forward and snapped, *"Silence! You will speak when spoken to!"*

Revek averted his eyes and kept his mouth shut, glancing only once at Doran over his shoulder. The son of Dorain had little advice to offer, however, since they were all under the scrutinising eye of his father - a dwarf who always had the first and last word.

King Dorain stared at his eldest son a little while longer, though there was nothing to be gleaned from his stony expression. Doran guessed him to be weighing up the best way to execute him - a spectacle, no doubt, in the hope of gaining some respect from the lords.

The king's voice filled the chamber. *"Come back to mock us, have you, boy?"*

Doran knew it to be a rhetorical question and maintained perfect silence; his father was nothing if not volatile.

"Proving Karak-Nor inadequate," King Dorain continued, *"you have come back to gloat, eh? And who are these that accompany you? More friends from Illian, is it? Speak, boy!"*

Doran put his pity for Revek aside and addressed the entire chamber. *"I have returned because the realm has need of our kin!"*

Revek looked hastily from Doran to the king. *"Technically, Prince Doran has been captured by the Blood Boys, a bounty of—"*

King Dorain's glower alone was enough to silence the bounty hunter. *"I see no prince,"* he remarked venomously.

Doran puffed out his chest. *"You can throw me back in my cell, if you must, but it will make no difference out there. The dwarves of Grarfath are needed, Fath—"* He stopped himself from calling the king his father, hoping to prevent any outbursts and keep them on track.

The king tilted his head and smirked. *"Out there,"* he repeated after a lengthy pause. *"You speak of Illian, their land."*

Doran regarded Russell and Galanör. *"I do, aye. Illian has fallen under the shadow of an ancient enemy, one we believed long vanquished."*

King Dorain heard every word but he didn't look to be taking any of it in. *"I don't care what happens in man's land. It wasn't that long ago the queen of Namdhor tried to invade Dhenaheim! They can fight among themselves for eternity as far as I'm concerned. Though, the fact that you would return to Grimwhal, trading your own life to aid the humans, is only further proof that your head's good for nothing but hammering stone!"*

Having worked himself up now, the king shot up from his throne to continue his tirade. *"I spared your life for the sake of your mother last time; I will not be making that same mistake twice! Take their heads, I say! Strap them to their mounts and send them back through The Iron Valley! You're no son of mine and humans are no allies of Grimwhal's!"*

Doran cursed his father's wrath. He had hoped their conversation would have progressed a little further before the executions were ordered. As one, however, the shield guards raised their famously heavy rectangular shields and rested their spears on the top, angling them at the trio. The Blood Boys quickly made themselves scarce, though Revek looked to protest on behalf of his bounty being unfulfilled. Still, in the face of the shield guards, the hunter knew better than to start quoting guild laws.

Behind Doran, Galanör shrugged his blue cloak over his shoulders and removed his fine scimitars from their scabbards. Russell reached over his shoulder in search of his pick-axe, but the old wolf let his hand stay in the air rather than pull the weapon free.

Doran turned on Galanör. "Put those away, ye dolt! There's nothin' to be gained from a fight."

"I've always found my life is to be gained from a fight," Galanör quipped.

"Well, not this one!" Doran argued.

As the shield guards continued to advance, Doran found his mother's eyes. They were filling with tears. Her hands fidgeted until they finally purchased the arms of her throne, whitening her knuckles. Doran could see it in her, the dangerous bear that lived in all mothers. She was moments away from making her stand and reeling against her husband, the king. Her punishment would be severe, Dakmund's too for he would always stand between his mother and any threat.

Doran was scrambling, desperate to find some way of taking back control before his mother did something stupid on his behalf. The solution, however, came from Galanör, who sheathed his blades and stood calmly before the shield guards. Then he lowered his hood.

"I am Galanör, of house Reveeri!" he proclaimed, as if it meant anything.

Doran's shoulders sagged and he put his face in his hand. "Elves..."

"Killing me will greatly anger my kin!"

Doran knew he wasn't lying, but he was most definitely stretching the truth of his insinuation. "I told ye to keep ye mouth shut," he hissed at the elf.

King Dorain held up his hand and the shield guard came to a stop in front of the trio. "If ye think courtin' war with the folk o' the forest scares me, *elf*, ye're greatly misinformed," he replied in man's tongue.

It wasn't the opportunity Doran had been expecting, but as soon as his father's hand came down, the shield guards would resume their deadly advance - he had to act. Turning around, he broke another law by presenting the king with his back, but he needed to reach the cart before all was lost.

The stout ranger ignored the jeers from the surrounding dwarves and climbed onto the cart to gather the tarpaulin in his hands. *"The call to war has been given by our ancient enemy! I have come to see if clan Heavybelly answer it!"* With that, he threw back the tarpaulin and lifted the orc up by its horns.

The chamber fell silent as eyes widened and jaws hit the floor.

More importantly, the king staggered forward, failing to signal the shield guards. Doran's mother - half out of her throne - sat back in shock. The stout ranger took a much-needed breath, sure that he had just saved his mother and brother.

King Dorain pointed at Doran and his prisoner. *"That...* thing; *it cannot be. It is a trick!"* he added with more bluster.

"It is no trick!" Doran promised, noting the orc's lack of consciousness.

Using both hands, he threw the vile creature over the side of the cart and onto the smooth floor. That woke it up. The orc croaked, struggling against its restraints, before breaking into a roar no man, dwarf or elf could accomplish.

Doran jumped down and planted a heavy boot on the beast's chest. *"From the depths of The Undying Mountains, the orcs have returned in great numbers! They have conquered most of Illian, forcing what remains of the humans to the north. They have been—"*

The clashing of armour interrupted Doran's speech before the shield guards gave way to their king. Dorain strode towards his son with more energy than Doran could recall in his father. As he came to stand over the writhing orc, a pair of shield guards rushed up behind him; one to point its spear at the orc and the other to push Doran back.

The king ignored his son for the moment and crouched over the orc. He examined every inch of the creature's face and horns, looking for signs of trickery.

"*Torch!*" he commanded with a hand held out.

After the fiery torch was given to him, King Dorain carefully brought the light to bear, shining it over the orc's face. It screamed and shut its eyes as tightly as possible. The shield guard applied more pressure with his spear, but the orc feared the light more than the bite of steel.

The king discarded the torch and slowly turned his gaze on his eldest son. "*Do you swear on your mother's life, boy? On your brother's too?*" his voice was low, his words for Doran alone. They also told the stout ranger that his father was in possession of more information than he let on...

"*This is no trick,*" Doran reiterated seriously. "*I wouldn't return for tricks. The realm is in need of an alliance again—*"

The king held up his hand to cut in. "*I told you before, your time of counselling me has long been at an end.*"

Doran wanted to say so much more, to plead his case for an alliance. Getting his kin to fight was only half the battle, after all, for they still had to mobilise and journey through Vengora and into the north of Illian. Time was against them, as always, but in these halls, only one possessed power.

"*Fetch the cleric!*" the king barked, eliciting a series of mutterings and whispers among the gathered lords and soldiers.

That particular command shocked Doran. Before his self-imposed exile, he could count on one hand the number of times his father had called on the cleric. It was, however, a good sign, indicating that the king believed a real orc was bleeding on his floor.

"*My king?*" One of the high-born dwarves broke away from his fellow lords and approached them. "*Are we really taking the word of a treasonous coward who is known to associate with humans and elves? This is clearly the work of magic,*" he said a little louder, drawing everyone's attention.

Doran raised a bushy eyebrow at the bald dwarf, wondering how and when a lord could talk to his king in such a way - there was no *we*, only the king and *his* opinion. Had his family truly fallen so far since he left? Even now, his father wasn't snapping the lord in half, but listening to every word and examining the gathered crowd, looking for his own supporters.

Judging by the nodding heads, this obnoxious lord had all the supporters...

"*Come and see it for yourself!*" Doran grumbled, receiving a scolding look from his father.

King Dorain gripped the orc by one of its horns and lifted it to its knees, presenting the crowd with its grotesque body. "*I have seen the work of magic, Lord Dodurum, as have you. Does this look like magic? All of you, look upon this beast and listen to your very bones! There isn't a dwarf alive who doesn't know an* orc *when they see one!*"

"*Magic can be deceiving, my king,*" Lord Dodurum continued. "*It could simply be a spell telling us how to feel. I think it prudent, before the cleric be left to his duty, that we examine the source of this revelation. After all, there isn't a single note from history that tells of the orcs surviving The Great War. Look who stands in our hall! An elf, a man, and a traitor to our clan! This is likely the schemes of Queen Yelifer!*"

"Bah!" Doran waved such nonsense away. "*Queen Yelifer is dead! This is no scheme! The blasted orcs are days away from destroying what's left of Illian! After that, they'll march on Dhenaheim!*"

Again, his father shot him a look that told him to keep his mouth shut or risk losing his life. It was a lot to convey in a mere expression, yet somehow the king had always had a talent for that particular message. What was more interesting, to Doran at least, was his father's apparent side in all of this - why wasn't he agreeing with Lord Dodurum and condemning him?

"*Traitors don't get to speak to me that way!*" the lord retorted.

"*Yelifer is dead, you say?*" the king cut in, stirring the argument.

"Aye," Doran replied, "*dead and reduced to ashes. Their kingdom couldn't coordinate an invasion if they wanted to. Defence is Namdhor's only option now.*"

"Anything from his mouth is suspect!" Dodurum accused. *"I say we kill the elf and the human. This foul magic will die with them, revealing the truth of the matter!"*

Doran immediately protested, but his words were drowned out by the cacophony of agreements. He flashed his companions a wary look and both of them braced again, their hands hovering over their weapons.

King Dorain let the orc drop to the floor. In the face of the lords, he was lacking the presence befitting of a dwarven king; he wasn't the person Doran remembered. For so long the stout ranger had harboured ill will towards his father, but seeing him now - his power reduced by his own subjects - made Doran feel nothing but guilt. His self-imposed exile had cast doubt on their family and weakened them all...

The orc renewed its struggle, fighting fiercely against its bindings. One of the shield guards sought to put it in its place with the point of his spear. The orc, however, saw the spear coming and raised its bound hands to intercept the weapon.

The bindings were cut.

Like a cornered animal, the orc lashed out as if its life was in the balance. It pulled on the haft of the spear, dragging the shield guard down with it, and gripped the dwarf's throat. Doran and his father reacted as fast as they could, but the orc tossed the shield guard aside, sending him barrelling into both of them. Its hands free now, the beast quickly snapped the bindings around its ankles and jumped to its feet. There was only one other close enough to strike.

Lord Dodurum panicked. His years of action, if he had any, were long behind him. He scrambled backwards, his only hope that the rest of the shield guards would reach him before the orc did. They didn't. The orc swung with wild abandon and caught the lord across his face with a hand of sharpened claws. The lord cried out but his shriek was cut short when the orc drove him to the floor and beat him with heavy fists.

Galanör was easily the fastest person in the throne room, beating the shield guards by several seconds. The elf wrestled the orc off Lord Dodurum, yanking it back by the horns before locking its throat in a vice-like grip. The beast thrashed and clawed at the air, but Galanör succeeded in dragging the orc away.

Doran could see the calamity that was about to unfold but he was only just getting back on his feet. *"No!"* he yelled. *"Don't kill it!"*

As perfect as his dwarvish was, the shield guards took no heed of his command. Galanör did his best to angle the orc away from the incoming spears, but their proximity sealed the creature's fate. Three silvyr-tipped spears ran the orc through, forcing the elven ranger to jump back, saving himself from the same death.

The orc gargled as the shield guards drove it to its knees with their spears. As all three spears came free, blood spurted across the marble floor, providing a large pool for the orc to fall face-down into.

Doran groaned. "We needed it alive, ye dolts!" he blasted in man's tongue. How could they hope to convince the other kingdoms now?

Lord Dodurum was helped to his feet sporting horrendous claw marks across his cheek and nose, along with a few unseen bruises.

"Are you convinced now?" Doran asked him pointedly.

"Enough!" King Dorain growled. *"Lord Dodurum, have your injuries seen to. Somebody get this monster off my floor! And General Dakmund!"* The king turned to face his youngest son. *"Have our guests escorted to secure quarters, absent their weapons if you please!"* Dorain looked about impatiently. *"And where the blazes is that damned cleric?"* he raged.

Doran was roughly handled and guided away from the chamber with his two companions. He tried to steal a glance at his mother but there was too much activity between him and the thrones.

Russell looked down at the son of Dorain. "Is this a good thing or a bad thing, Heavybelly?"

Doran considered his father's request for the cleric. "I think it's a good thing. He didn' order our deaths, though, so that's definitely a win!"

CHAPTER 24

REUNION

In the freezing gloom of The Bastion, hidden beneath its broken spires and ancient towers, Inara braced herself in the dungeon. Her father pulled open the door to the last cell, the only place left for Alijah.

Her blue eyes raced across every surface she could see, but the majority of the cell was to the left of the door, concealed from view. What she could see was glyphs, ancient ones that had been painted in red on every inch of available wall space.

Something blurred inside the cell, a flicker that made the mind wonder if the eyes were being tricked. Then it moved again. Inara's eyes were sharper than most and even she couldn't make out what was darting about inside the cell. The blur was the size of a man but it never stood still long enough for any details to be discerned.

Impatient, Nathaniel made to step inside. He hesitated, stumbling almost, as the blur flickered repeatedly right in front of them. Inara's eyes glazed with tears and a hand naturally covered her mouth when the blur became a figure.

Alijah walked out of the cell.

They were all overwhelmed to see him and not just because it had been so long for her parents, but because he looked so different. Inara had spoken with him only weeks past, yet her brother emerged from his cell with a whole new body.

A lump formed in her throat to see so many scars and wounds marring his bare torso, though none of them distracted from the muscles he had developed. Alijah stared blankly at them all, his toned body a stark contrast to his scraggy beard and knotted hair. He looked more like an Outlander than her twin brother.

None of that mattered, nor would any of this in time. The only thing that mattered was the four of them, standing there together. They were a family again.

"Son..." Nathaniel whispered before slamming into Alijah with a tight bear hug.

Inara watched her brother's response carefully. He looked to be just as overwhelmed as they did, or perhaps it was disbelief. Nathaniel held him for a long time before Alijah's hands slowly moved up to rest on his father's back. Reyna was quick to join their hug, wrapping her arms around both of the men in her life. A moment later, her mother reached out and pulled her in to the family embrace.

It wasn't long before they were all sharing tears, Inara included. How long had it been since they were all together? Recalling such a time was like recalling another life.

Eventually, it was Alijah who pulled away. He looked at each of them in turn, examining their every feature. He was looking for signs of trickery...

"It's really us, Brother," Inara told him earnestly.

Alijah rested his eyes on her, a pair of blue orbs equal in shade and intensity as to her own. Once upon a time, Inara would have looked at her brother and known exactly what he was thinking. Now, he was a blank slate. The Dragorn got nothing from him, not even a hint of emotion. What had The Crow done to him?

"He said you would come." Alijah's voice was that of a ghost, absent the life and vitality it normally carried.

"We have come to save you," Nathaniel said with an encouraging smile.

Inara noted the slightest of twitches in Alijah's left eye and she wondered how saved he really felt. Having spent so long trapped inside a time spell, their arrival must have felt too late.

Reyna stepped closer to her son and placed a gentle hand on his cheek. "Alijah, is he here?" Her tone was serious, cut with an edge of violent intent.

Alijah stared back at his mother in silence, his thoughts a mystery. "No," he answered at last. "He left... some time ago."

Inara looked from the dank and terrible cell to her brother. "How long have you been in there?" she asked with a whisper.

Alijah turned back and scrutinised his private hell. "Long enough," he replied cryptically. He took a breath and marched away from the cell, sparing no time to inform his family of his purpose. Stepping over the dead mages, Alijah continued down the length of the dungeon without giving the bodies a glance.

Inara shared a moment of concern with her parents before they hurried after him. Whatever his purpose, it was encouraging to see that he was still quick and light of foot as he ascended The Bastion. He moved swiftly from passage to passage, suggesting he knew exactly where he was going.

"Alijah!" Inara called after him. "Slow down! What are you doing?" She finally caught up with him outside a closed door. "We should leave this horrid place, Brother. Athis is waiting for us."

Their parents joined them outside the mysterious door, looking from the back of Alijah's head to Inara's face for an explanation.

"Alijah," Reyna said softly, "You've been through a lot. I think it would be best if we put this place behind us."

"I agree." Nathaniel added vigorously. "There's nothing but torment to be taken from this wretched fortress."

Alijah placed a hand on the flat of the door. "He isn't finished yet." With no further explanation, he pushed through to the room beyond.

Inara followed him in, her curiosity more than piqued. The room was grand, or at least it probably had been, a very long time ago. Now, it was tired, the corners consumed by cobwebs and the walls dotted with moss and mould. A large desk occupied the centre of the chamber, with what looked to be an alchemy lab in the far alcove. The wall to her immediate left was decorated with unusual ornaments, including an extraordinarily large tooth.

"What is this place?" the young Dragorn asked absently, her attention flitting from one thing to the next.

Alijah came to a stop on the other side of the desk. "It was his private room."

"The Crow's?" Reyna queried.

"Yes, and Atilan's before his." Alijah was focused on the table, his eyes darting from one parchment to another.

Inara watched him trace a finger over several maps, connecting ancient symbols from one location to the next. It was like catching a glimpse of the old Alijah, the Alijah who chased adventure and uncovered secrets long forgotten and lost to the world. After poring over the maps, he touched the base of a wooden stand, situated on the corner of the desk. Inara could see that the empty stand meant something to him.

"What is it?"

Alijah tapped the wooden stand before snapping out of his reverie. "Nothing. We should leave now." He rolled up the top map and made for the door.

Seeing her parents' questioning faces, Inara could only shrug. For the first time in her life, she didn't know what was going on inside her brother's head and it broke her heart. Her parents had always gone to her when Alijah was upset or acting out of the ordinary, knowing that she understood him better than anyone, even Vighon.

Trailing him again, the Galfreys soon found themselves back in the main foyer, Atilan's old throne room. Alijah paused on his way to the double doors, the slapping of his bare feet coming to an eventual stop. Inara gave him his space and allowed him the time to contemplate his next move. There was every chance he didn't want to leave The Bastion, given his severe torment.

Leaving the doors behind, Alijah headed in a different direction, his steps less confident this time. Along the way, back into The Bastion's dark halls, they came across the dead bodies of Darklings, none of which bothered Alijah for a second. He continued until he came across another door, one which led into the western spire.

He took a breath and walked inside.

Like every other chamber in The Bastion, this one succumbed to nature before any of them had been born. It was a circular tower of dark and depressing stone, occupied by a large fire pit. Above it, raised by a pulley system of chains, was a simple plank of wood, charred black.

Alijah stared at that plank of wood.

Inara stepped closer to him. "Alijah?" As she moved to rest a hand on his shoulder, her brother walked away, towards the pulley system.

Without a word, he began to pull on the chain, lowering the plank of wood. The chains rattled and the mechanism *creaked* in protest, but he soon brought the plank to the base. Alijah intrigued them, but they followed his gaze to the contents of the plank and joined him in front of it.

A skeleton, burnt black and littered with ash, lay still on the plank. Alijah leaned over and ran his thumb across the top of the skull.

Inara knew exactly who this was. "Hadavad..." Saying his name aloud caused Alijah to shut his eyes and clamp his jaw. For the first time since seeing him again, Inara could safely say she knew what was going through his head: grief.

"We can give him a proper burial," Nathaniel suggested.

"No." Alijah stepped back from the skeleton. "He always cared more for the bodies of his hosts, never his own. This is the body that failed him...." Alijah looked up as if someone had called his name from the rafters.

Then he took off again. With haste this time, Alijah made his way back to the main doors of The Bastion and ran outside into the icy cold air of the mountains. Athis raised his mighty head, his bulk occupying the central steps, and blew out a cloud of hot air. Alijah skidded to a stop in front of him and looked around, searching the sky and land alike.

"What's wrong?" Inara copied his movements but couldn't see anything.

"I can *feel* him," Alijah breathed, showing no sign of discomfort being half naked in the freezing cold.

Reyna and Nathaniel looked nervously from each other to Inara. "The Crow?" her mother asked.

Alijah ceased his search and turned to his family. "*Malliath.*"

Inara felt Athis's unease immediately. "Is Malliath close by?"

Alijah's shoulders sagged and he shook his head. "No. But I can feel him."

Inara approached her brother. "That's normal. You will always be able to sense his general direction. Can you speak with him?"

Alijah closed his eyes. "He won't say anything."

"That's alright," Inara reassured. "There's time. We brought you some clothes and supplies," she offered, gesturing to a sack tied around one of Athis's spinal horns. "Why don't you get changed and we'll make leave for The Lifeless Isles?"

Alijah turned on her, reminding the young Dragorn that her brother had inherited their mother's speed. "The Lifeless Isles?" he questioned. "Why are we going there?"

Reyna stepped forward to answer. "You will be safe there, away from... all of this."

Alijah was shaking his head again. "The war is in the north. Shouldn't we be going there? I need to..." His words drifted away with his resolve and he looked to the east, where there was nothing but mountains to the eye with the sea hidden beyond. "Yes," he said in a softer tone. "The Lifeless Isles..."

Inara narrowed her eyes at her brother. "You will come with us?"

Alijah pulled away from whatever was drawing him to the east. "Of course. My things?"

There was the brother she remembered. "I'll get them for you."

"There are bodies over here," Nathaniel called, his attention drawn to the piles of snow beside the steps.

"Bodies?" Inara looked at Athis, checking that her companion hadn't killed any dark mages while they were inside.

Alijah ran over and dropped to his knees in the snow. He used his hands to push and pull the snow away from the outline of a body until he could see their face, the face of a young woman. His shoulders dropped, overcome with a sense of defeat and grief. All around the woman, there were more bodies scattered without care, their limbs just poking through the snow.

"Who are these people?" Reyna asked.

Alijah gripped the wrist of the young woman. "They were the ones I saved," he whispered. "He said he would set them free." His jaw clenched. "But they had nowhere to go..."

Inara watched her brother wipe his eyes before any tears could be seen. They would have given him a moment if that was what he needed, but Alijah covered the young woman in snow again and stood up.

"My things?"

Inara hesitated. Her brother had always been the more emotional of the two since they were children. Never had she seen him shrug off something like this.

"I'll get them," she finally replied, seeing that he wasn't going to share anything.

They waited a short while for Alijah to change his ragged trousers for new clothes and a fur cloak to keep him warm in the sky. Reyna embraced him again and again before they finally climbed onto Athis, hoping to feel something familiar about her son. It hadn't been the reunion Inara had hoped for, but a reunion it was and that was all she could ask for.

Doing her best not to think about the part of her brother's mind that he now shared with Malliath, Inara settled into her companion's scales and kept her eyes on the east. They were going home.

CHAPTER 25
DRAWING A LINE

In the most ancient of caverns, nestled in the heart of the orc lands, a small vial filled with red powder flew high into the air. It turned end over end, tumbling through the empty space. To the eyes of the many orcs who filled the cavern, this vial was too small and moving too fast to be seen.

This was not the case for Karakulak.

The God-King's enchanted senses were aware of the vial's position above him, as well as that of the Dragorn in front of him. He could feel the displacement of air on his sensitive skin as Gideon Thorn charged towards him. Enhanced senses or not, magic wasn't required to tell Karakulak that the Master Dragorn had snapped, his own life a worthy price for killing the king of orcs.

With more strength than the average human, Gideon leapt into the air and came down on the God-King with his legendary Mournblade. The attack was more than obvious and Karakulak raised Dragonslayer to intercept the Vi'tari blade. The Dragorn didn't need to kill him with the sword; it was only a matter of seconds before the vial of wrath powder lost its momentum and began to fall.

Karakulak was able to keep track of it all, from the constant movements of his surroundings forces, to the current position of the vial relative to Gideon's attacks. To the orc king, the whole scenario was simple: he would keep the Dragorn at bay until he was able to catch the vial; then he would be free to take his time with the execution.

Their duel was furious, but Gideon's every attack was clearly calculated to keep them fighting in the same place. More than once, Mournblade sliced through his pale flesh, spilling his exceptional blood. They were never more than nicks and cuts, however, which was nothing compared to what they would both receive when the wrath powder impacted at their feet.

The vial began to fall...

Karakulak needed space and time to calculate his catch, ensuring he caught it in such a way that the powder wouldn't explode. Gideon was coming at him from every angle with his scimitar, his steel biting into the dragon bone. The vial was halfway returned from its journey when Karakulak found the opening he needed.

"You're too slow, human!" he mocked, adding a strong boot to Gideon's chest.

As the Master Dragorn was launched backwards, Karakulak buried his sword in the ground and turned his attention to the vial. His sharp eyes spotted it instantly and his body responded with an almighty jump. Mid-air, the orc king reached out and lowered his hand in time with the vial, easing its capture from the air. He brought it into himself and fell into a roll, the volatile powder undisturbed.

Opening his palm, Karakulak contemplated the strength of such a small thing. A pity the same could not be said of the Dragorn. Rising to his magnificent height, the orc king turned on Gideon with smug satisfaction. Now, his mind could focus on one thing: inflicting pain.

Gideon rose to his diminutive stature, rubbing his chest with one hand. A statement of his scimitar's power, the last of Karakulak's blood ran clean from the steel, leaving the blade exquisite once again.

"What now, mighty warrior?" Karakulak cajoled. "Your fate is mine to decide!"

Gideon had no reaction to his words, a fact that made sense when the orc realised the translation spinner had been lost in their battle. Karakulak decided he would have to let his actions do the talking then.

As far as any orc was concerned, what happened next wasn't just extraordinary, it was wholly unnatural. A portal of pure darkness, an abyss so absolute that even Karakulak's eyes would forever fail to pierce it, exploded to life behind the Master Dragorn. A single figure emerged, a female and, outrageously, an elf to add insult. She dashed forward and yanked Gideon backwards with enough strength that he had little choice in his direction.

The surrounding orcs roared in protest and charged at the two Dragorn. Only Karakulak knew that such a thing was folly; the distance too far and the Dragorn too fast. The portal had collapsed and the Dragorn vanished before any of them were within striking opportunity.

Karakulak retrieved his sword and examined the new indentations it had gained. They would meet again, he told himself. Only next time, his attention wouldn't be split...

GIDEON'S WORLD was turned upside down as he was dragged from the dark and tossed into the light. The portal collapsed on itself, a phenomenon that he barely glimpsed on his way to the ground. His fall hurt, and the subsequent roll down the slope hurt even more, but hitting the ground was nothing compared to facing the light of Illian. Even when dimmed by the ash clouds, the light was agonising after so long in the pitch black of the orc lands.

Before his sight returned, Gideon had nothing but his other

senses to rely on. He could smell the foul odour of burning bodies mixed with smoke that drifted in the mountain breeze. The sound of crackling fire found his ears, somewhere from behind him. He could also hear the distinct sound of a dragon breathing, two dragons in fact.

Someone was striding towards him, their feet disturbing the loose gravel. Through his bond, Gideon could see that Ayana Glanduil was that someone, and she didn't look happy.

"You fool!" she berated - an outburst that was quite out of character for her. "What were you thinking going in there alone?"

Gideon tried to open his eyes again but the light was overwhelming. Instead, he lay back on the ground and covered his face with one hand. There was something that hurt far more than the light. He watched Arathor die over and over in his mind and knew the same fate had befallen Thraden, by The King's Lake.

He had failed...

Another Dragorn had lost their life and, to add to the pain, Arathor's body couldn't be reunited with Thraden's in death.

"You're lucky Ilargo was able to guide me or I would never have been able to open that portal!" Ayana's tone was harsh but her words felt distant to Gideon, muffled by his anguish. "Gideon?"

"They're dead," he said bluntly. "Arathor and Thraden... They're gone."

Ayana took a long breath, her anger dampened by grief. "You tried. That matters."

"He died in the dark," Gideon growled, "surrounded by enemies after days of torment. Trying doesn't matter, Ayana. Saving him from that hell... that would have mattered."

Arathor and Thraden are gone, Ilargo echoed. *It is up to us now to carry their light.*

Gideon sat up and forced his eyes to open, to accept the pain and adjust. Ayana was a blurry silhouette and the dragons looked to be giant boulders that swayed in the narrow valley.

He could feel more tears welling behind his sore eyes. "I promised that no more would die..."

Ayana crouched by his side, her elven features finally coming into focus. "You cannot promise such a thing, no Master Dragorn ever has." .

Gideon wiped the escaping tears and dirt from his cheeks. "We weren't prepared for this. I wasn't naive enough to believe there would never be another war, I just thought we would have more time."

"We take the world as it is," Ayana replied softly, "not as we would like it to be. Our youngest are safe in The Lifeless Isles; take heart in that. What matters now is those of us who stand between the realm and destruction. Alastir and Valkor are still suffering wounds, Inara and Athis have left the north, and Arathor... He and Thraden have gone where none can ever come between them. That leaves us. Ilargo has shared your memories. The orcs have enough wrath powder down there to set the world on fire. We have to act, Gideon."

Ayana is right, Ilargo insisted. *This war is still very much alive. Regardless of our defeats, regardless of those we lose, we must face the orcs again and again until the realm is safe.*

Gideon rose to his feet and blinked hard. His eyes required a few more seconds before they could take in the detail of his surroundings. He was standing outside the cave he had first infiltrated, only now there was a pile of smouldering orc bodies on the valley floor. Ilargo was closest, his startling blue eyes locked on Gideon as he searched deep into his companion's soul.

"Then we fight," Gideon finally stated. "We fight for them, for the ones we've lost."

And we fight for those who cannot fight for themselves, Ilargo added.

Ayana moved to be a little closer to Deartanyon. "Ilargo shared *all* of your thoughts. Your plans for when this war is over..."

Gideon's mind was too clogged with emotions to fire his companion a scolding look.

Ilargo huffed, blowing a cloud of steam into the air. *Ayana sits on the council; her opinion should sway our decisions.*

Gideon wanted to argue the point, but he couldn't help agreeing with the dragon. The Master Dragorn rubbed his eyebrow, a subconscious action to represent his clearing mind. Now wasn't the moment to dwell on his failings; people had died and action was needed.

"Do you agree?" he asked Ayana.

"Initially we didn't," the elf replied honestly. "It's a bold move. But, our predecessors had centuries before they faced real war... We think it's the right decision."

Gideon found himself relieved to hear it. "We will return to this when the realm is secure. Right now, we have a war to win."

For Arathor and Thraden, Ilargo proclaimed.

For all of them, Gideon corrected.

It was hard flying away from the mountains without Arathor in his care. It felt wrong to the Master Dragorn, who had envisioned his rescue over and over, reuniting the Dragorn with Thraden. Even now, in death, he couldn't reunite them, a ritual that had been part of Dragorn tradition since the time of Elandril.

Gideon added it to the list of things he would see to after the war, as much as it pained him...

Ilargo and Deartanyon glided west, away from the bustling catapults and their relentless bombardment. Having seen the orcs underground, Gideon knew the Namdhorians were wasting their time trying to clear a path to the mountains.

Above them all, the ash clouds offered a reprieve from their gritty rain, though the sun was yet to find its way to the surface. It was still a world fit for orcs...

The White Vale, sprawled around Namdhor's base, had lost its crisp blanket of snow. The army consumed most of the landscape with only a strip of melting snow between them and the littered campsite of refugees. Along with the great rise that housed Namdhor itself, they were all at risk from the threat that lurked below their feet.

At the southern tip of the camp, where the elves of Ilythyra now resided, Gideon caught sight of a distinct shape that would catch anyone's eye. Valkor, Alastir's dragon, lay on a patch of ground beside their perimeter, his oak-coloured scales clear to see against the snow.

The Master Dragorn wanted to greet both of them, having not seen either in person for some time, but there was still an urgency to their departure from the mountains. A blur of violet and silver scales cut down through the air in front of Gideon and Ilargo, reminding both that Ayana and Deartanyon were better rested. Following their dive, the pair were heading for the very top of Namdhor, where The Dragon Keep overlooked the city.

Ilargo needed no instruction from Gideon to follow them. One behind the other, the dragons soared over the black towers and buildings of the ancient city, their presence halting every citizen of Namdhor. This was not the return Gideon had had in mind but, Arathor or not, he would make sure his attempt to rescue the Dragorn did *some* good.

Arriving astride a dragon was very similar to arriving with either a crown on your head or a key to every room. Guards stepped aside and servants opened gates and doors without hesitation to admit the two warriors. There was only one chamber in all the city where Gideon felt his title meant nothing and his welcome was overstayed from the second he walked in.

The throne room...

Arlon Draqaro rested inside the hollow skull of Drakaina, a dragon who had suffered the wrath of man a thousand years ago. The king of thugs crossed one of his legs over and arched an expectant eyebrow at the sight of the Dragorn. He was clearly dissatisfied with Gideon before the Master Dragorn had even offered a report from his time behind enemy lines.

Given the way you are feeling, Ilargo spoke into his mind, *I wonder if it is best that you commune at all with Namdhor's future king.*

Ilargo wasn't wrong; Gideon could feel the confrontation bubbling within him. Still, it had been him who discovered the large deposit of wrath powder, and so it had to be him who informed Arlon.

I'll try not to take his head, Gideon quipped. **That's the best I can offer...**

Without waiting for announcements or introductions, Arlon called out, "Our catapults assault Vengora day and night, Master Thorn. We would certainly save on supplies and manpower if you set one of your dragons to the task of burning a path through to the mountains. Imagine my dismay to look up and see you gliding in pointless circles. And now, two more of your order come to Namdhor's aid, yet here you are, in my throne room. Why are you not assisting with our efforts to attack the orcs?"

Having come from a culture that paid respect to all forms of hierarchy, no matter how deserving they were, Ayana bowed her head. Gideon didn't. The Master Dragorn came to a stop and made the king of Namdhor wait for his response. In part, he was also trying to calm himself down in a bid to prevent any outbursts.

"Forgive my absence..." Gideon's words wandered away from him as he considered what to call the imbecile sitting before him.

"Your Grace," Arlon provided with a smirk.

Gideon's face twitched with the hint of a smile - he wouldn't be calling him that. "I have spent the last two days scouting behind enemy lines."

Arlon sat forward in his throne. "So you did ignore my orders to stay."

"And I recall our conversation about *orders*," Gideon shot back. "You rejected my idea to call on the lords of Dhenaheim and your catapults are more than capable of burning a few trees. I saw no other option but to utilise my skills where they would be best to serve the realm."

Arlon narrowed his dark eyes at Gideon. "And you believe that disobeying the king of Illian is *best* for the realm?"

Forget what I said, Ilargo interrupted. *Take his head.*

Gideon ignored both Ilargo's statement and Arlon's question. "As I advised earlier, pursuing the orcs into the mountains is an absurd strategy. Having explored under Vengora, I now know it is not only absurd, but it also plays into the orcs' plan. They know Namdhor is advancing towards the mountainside and they are ready to attack."

Arlon snorted. "Of course they know we're advancing on them! A force of nine thousand men moves ever closer with each passing day! Even a blind man couldn't fail to spot them!"

"They will not attack from the surface this time," Gideon countered. "The army is exposed on the plains of The White Vale; they advance over ground that cannot offer the same protection this city enjoys."

General Morkas, curious by his expression, spoke up. "Of what do you speak, Master Thorn?"

Arlon didn't hesitate to display his disdain for the general or his interest.

"As we speak, your catapults and a battalion of Namdhorian soldiers stand on a mountain of wrath powder."

"Wrath powder?" Arlon repeated.

"Perhaps you noted it on the battlefield?" Gideon knew it was a petty shot, but when he had to refrain from running the man through with Mournblade, petty would have to do. "A volatile powder used by the orcs. It's how they brought down every other kingdom."

By the look on his face, Arlon didn't miss the intended jibe, highlighting his absence on the battlefield. "How do you know this mountain of *wrath powder* is where you say it is?"

Gideon was afraid of this: the doubt. "A dragon can always sense the location of their Dragorn and vice versa. While I was down there, Ilargo kept track of my whereabouts relative to the surface."

"Then why haven't the ugly beasts blown my soldiers back to Atilan yet?" the king posed.

Gideon sighed. "Because all they have to do is wait a little longer and they can kill every Namdhorian knight on The White Vale. That's why I'm here, right now, telling you to cease the army's advance and pull them back."

"Retreat?" Arlon spat. "Based on the word of the same man who didn't want us to do anything in the first place? Your aversion to warfare, Master Thorn, makes for an ill-advisor. Still, I am a king who values his people and especially his army. To be safe, I will hasten their advance and get them past this so-called *mountain* of wrath powder."

Gideon closed his eyes in disbelief. He couldn't have said it any clearer. The Master Dragorn easily found his next line of argument but sense won the day, and he realised that bartering words with a man who could only hear his own voice was a pointless exercise.

Turning on his heel, Gideon made to leave with Ayana in tow. "What are we doing?" she asked him in a hushed tone.

"Where are you going?" Arlon called after them, his voice dripping with contempt. "I didn't say you could leave!"

Gideon didn't falter a step on his way to the doors of the throne room, where a pair of Namdhorian guards stood their ground, barring their way. The Master Dragorn came to a halt and gave both men a hard look, offering them a very simple choice. They glanced nervously at each other and back to Gideon, specifically the red and gold hilt of Mournblade. At last, they stepped aside, choosing to suffer their king's punishment rather than Gideon's exuding wrath.

"Do not turn your back on me!" Arlon screamed.

Ayana matched Gideon's stride on his way out of The Dragon Keep. "What are you doing?"

Gideon called to Ilargo and the emerald dragon dropped out of the sky beyond the keep's walls. "For the first time in a long time," he said to the elf, climbing atop his companion, "I'm not doubting myself. I know what I'm doing and I know it's right. Meet me at the elven camp."

The Master Dragorn didn't wait for a response before Ilargo and he launched into the air. So forceful were his beating wings that the pressure blew open nearby doors and windows in a maelstrom of snow and ash. There was no point in trying to be quiet; what would come next could only be described as a spectacle for all to see.

Ilargo took to the sky and made for the north-east, where the army claimed their stake of The White Vale. *This may come with consequences,* the dragon opined.

Failure to act on our part will come with graver consequences, Gideon maintained.

Ilargo soon found his way to the head of the army, where the dozen catapults were lined up in a neat row. There was a gap between the war machines and the bulk of the army, a space mostly filled with supplies to set alight and hurl at Vengora. Scattered between them all were the hundreds of men from the battalion charged with firing the catapults.

Fly low, Gideon said. ***Give them reason to stop and take note of you.***

Ilargo altered his angle and dared to fly out in front of the discharging catapults. He dodged the highest missile on his descent and dropped into a low glide, his presence enough to halt their assault. The battalion stared at the dragon, questioning for the first time if they were allies.

Let's push them back...

Flying farther east, Ilargo came around to bring himself in line with the row of catapults. Ensuring his attack didn't come as a complete surprise, claiming lives, the dragon exhaled a jet of fire across the plain as he advanced towards them. The men yelled out before turning to run for the safety of their army.

The inferno quickly caught up with the first catapult and set every inch alight, the force of Ilargo's breath more than enough to shatter the wooden beams and blow the war machine to pieces. Continuing his attack run, the dragon exhaled one long breath of scorching fire along the row. Like ants, the Namdhorians scurried across the plain, abandoning their tasks for fear of death.

Ilargo's reptilian eyes caught sight of a young man desperately clawing at a net that had become knotted around his ankle. The dragon clamped his jaw shut and banked hard to the north, refraining from encompassing the very last catapult in flames. Coming back around, Gideon could see that the young man was still trapped under the net, still half-filled with supplies, and had begun to crawl on his belly away from the war machine.

Put me down.

Gideon waited for Ilargo to touch down on all fours before he jumped off. Striding through the snow, past the catapult, he caught up with the young knight.

"You won't get very far dragging those behind you," Gideon told him.

The young man turned onto his back, his attention drawn immediately to Ilargo. His look of shock quickly turned to fear.

"Don't worry," Gideon reassured, "neither of us means you any harm. In fact, we're here to do quite the opposite."

The young Namdhorian turned to his right and looked upon the half mile wall of fire and burning wood. He didn't appear convinced.

"The army is to go no farther." Gideon wasn't making a request. Alleviating some of the soldier's fear, the Master Dragorn crouched down and freed him of the net. "No farther," he reiterated, holding the Namdhorian's gaze.

The young man nodded like a child and made a mad dash to the south, where thousands of Namdhorian soldiers stared at a wall of fire that now stood between them and the mountains.

Ilargo engulfed the last catapult in dragon fire. The wood snapped and the catapult lost its shape as it collapsed to the ground in flames.

I'm going to the elven camp, Gideon told his companion.

You are walking there? Through the army's camp?

They need to know we did this for them. We won't get very far if the entire Namdhorian army believes we're a threat.

That may require some convincing, Gideon.

The Master Dragorn started across the snows. **Trust me, Ilargo, I finally know what I'm doing...**

CHAPTER 26
TOGETHER AGAIN

For two days, Asher rode east, from The Watchers to The Guardian Cliffs, desperately clawing at his memory to recall the faces of all the Ironsworn he had killed. Three of them were blank spots in his mind for most of the journey, but as the land stretched on, he was finally able to recall one of the three men he had slain. That was an improvement, he decided.

For most of the fight, he had maintained control of his instincts and been aware of his actions, though he couldn't deny the effort that had required. Time would surely heal his mind, or at least that's what the ranger told himself. He certainly couldn't keep up a life of combating monsters if he himself was no better than the mindless beasts he hunted.

Behind it all, Asher could feel Malliath's presence in his thoughts. The dragon's consciousness wasn't truly there, but the echo was. Those memories and thoughts were heavy, weighing on the ranger's human capacity. The last thing he needed, a man who had committed the worst of crimes in his life, were the dark and malevolent thoughts of a being who had done terrible things for millennia after millennia.

Leaving The Selk Road behind again, the ranger led the trio over the last stretch of ground that separated them from the River Adanae. Only then did Asher realise how long it had been since he had heard either Vighon or Ruban speak a word. Looking back over his shoulder, the pair were sullen, but the northman clearly had a chip on his shoulder that weighed heavier than the squire's.

A part of Asher, his older self, didn't much care about what bothered his young companions, being far more troubled by the fact that they were distracted rather than upset. The ranger, who hadn't felt the stretch of time over the last thirty years, couldn't quieten that part of himself that Reyna, Faylen, and Nathaniel had awoken in him.

He sighed, cursing the very idea of *feelings* and their new hold over him.

Slowing his horse down to bring him in line with the northman, Asher attempted to open a line of dialogue that would allow his companion to speak his mind. Just the thought of it was painful; he didn't know Vighon the way he knew the Galfreys or the rangers.

"The Adanae is just below that rise," he began. "We'll have to follow it north and find a way down the bank."

Vighon simply nodded in response, happy to keep to himself inside his hood. Asher didn't know what to say next; he had hoped that would be enough. Were he talking to Nathaniel, the old knight would have told him everything on his mind by now.

The truth was, however, Asher knew exactly what was on the northman's mind; it had been apparent since he learned the supposed truth regarding his mother's death.

"He was probably lying," he started again. "Whatever his name was, *The Ironsworn*. He was probably just trying to distract you."

"You don't know my father," Vighon croaked, his voice out of practice. "And you didn't know Godfrey Cross either. He was telling the truth. He killed my mother..."

Now Asher really didn't know what to say. Instead, he continued to ride alongside the northman, steadily guiding them both along the small rise. If Vighon needed to speak more on the topic then he would. The ranger decided it wouldn't be the worst thing in the world if they continued their journey in silence. After all, it wouldn't be long before he greeted Faylen.

What would he say to her? Thirty years had come and gone for her, but for him it felt like only yesterday. The ranger suddenly became self-conscious of his appearance for the first time. He had been trekking across the wilds and had fought a handful of men in the process; he wasn't exactly at his best. Then again, he pondered, there was a good chance Faylen wouldn't recognise him if he were to wear anything else.

"Have you ever taken vengeance, Ranger?" Vighon asked without warning, his distant gaze following the coursing river beside them.

Asher reluctantly put his thoughts of Faylen aside, now regretting his attempt at interaction. "Vengeance? Once or twice."

"Did it make you feel better?" the northman pressed.

Asher spared a moment to consider his long life of violence and those who had slighted him but, more significantly, those who had slighted people he cared about. There wasn't much of the latter, but he recalled his bloody revenge with clarity.

"Yes," he replied honestly.

Vighon turned to look at him, though the ranger was partially concealed within his green hood. "You felt better? I've always heard that vengeance leaves you feeling bitter, that it changes nothing."

"Everyone is wrong," Asher countered. "Either that or they're *doing* it wrong. Besides, if you truly believed that, you wouldn't have asked me the question in the first place."

Vighon narrowed his eyes. "Then why *did* I ask you?"

"Because you suspected I would tell you otherwise, and that's what you *really* wanted to hear..."

The northman turned away again, hiding within his dark hood so that only his breath could be seen on the freezing air. Whether he had struck a nerve or not, Asher couldn't say. He wondered, in hindsight, if that had been one of those times it was acceptable to lie.

"You speak a hard truth, Ranger."

Asher glanced at the northman, or at least the side of his hood. "I told lies for the longer time. I've discovered that both can hurt, but only the truth can allow you to live free."

"Is that what you're doing?" Vighon asked. "Living free?"

Asher couldn't help but hear that question and dwell on his life. He had only been living free since walking away from Nightfall, but the years that followed suggested that fate had been pulling his strings all along. How many times had he been dragged into conflicts that held so much in the balance?

"If there is such a thing as a god, or perhaps fate," Vighon continued, "I really couldn't say whether they loved you or hated you..."

"Either way," Asher growled, "I'm alive. That's more than can be said for a lot of the monsters that have crossed me, be they men or beasts."

Ruban's voice broke before he said, "I don't think killing your father will make you feel better. It won't bring your mother back at any rate."

Vighon looked at the ranger and thumbed at the squire. "For future reference, that's what normal people usually say..."

A few hours later, and their conversation about vengeance behind them, the company of three rested on the banks of the River Adanae. They waited for the elves. Unfortunately for Asher, they didn't wait in silence.

Vighon had decided that Ruban needed training in the ways of the sword and that such training should begin right now. With nothing but empty river to watch, the ranger couldn't help being drawn into the spar. He lit a long pipe of Namdhorian red spice, taken from Vighon's saddlebags, and sat on the bank.

"It's heavy!" Ruban complained, heaving Vighon's circular shield in one hand.

"It'll save your life!" Vighon promised.

They both looked a little ridiculous to Asher, but the distraction seemed to have pulled Vighon from his darker thoughts. Hopefully, he would be able to put his problems to the side while they focused on saving the world...

"I can't move as fast while I'm holding it!" Ruban continued, following the northman in their never-ending circle.

"You don't need to move as fast," Vighon pointed out. "Having a shield allows you to wade in, take your enemy's blow and counter with a strong swing. Try it!"

The northman stopped circling and came at the squire with his silvyr sword. His strike was deliberately slow and incredibly obvious, giving Ruban more than enough time to raise the shield. By the sound of the impact, he had pulled his swing too. Vighon struck again and again, steadily increasing his speed and strength as Ruban grew more confident. By the fifth swing, the squire finally came back at him with a fast jab. Vighon turned the sword away and wrapped Ruban's knuckles with the flat of his blade.

"Don't thrust like that," Vighon warned him. "Only ever thrust when you know your enemy can't defend; it should be a mortal blow."

Ruban shook his hand and retrieved his sword from the ground. "Aren't all my attacks supposed to be delivering mortal blows?"

"Ideally but, in an *ideal* world, you'd just be fighting scarecrows. In the real world, your foe is likely to be armed, facing you, and, in your case, they've probably killed more opponents. You need to test their skill against your own while searching for weaknesses or, in some cases, just tiring them out."

"So, I just have to always be more skilled than my opponent?" Ruban questioned with a face of disbelief.

"Aye," Vighon replied as if it was obvious.

The squire licked his lips and frowned. "How could I possibly do that?"

The northman shrugged. "You weigh them up. You'll get better at that in time."

Ruban then asked the obvious question. "What do I do if I decide my enemy is more skilled than me?"

Vighon exaggerated his shrug. "Just make sure you're always more skilled than they are."

Asher couldn't help but laugh with the pipe in his mouth. "Is that how you've been getting through life? Just believing you're a better fighter than the man standing in front of you?"

"Well, I'm still here aren't I?" Vighon pointed out. "And what do *you* do?"

Asher blew out a cloud of smoke. "I *know* I'm better than my opponent."

Vighon rolled his eyes. "Of course you do."

The ranger gestured to Ruban. "In your case, young squire, I would say *run away* in the face of a superior foe. You've got youth on your side; use it to your advantage."

"He doesn't need to run," Vighon protested. "He just needs to practise."

Asher looked at Ruban and mouthed, "Run."

"I'm inclined to agree with Asher," the squire declared.

Vighon shook his head in despair. "Just raise your shield and get ready."

The pair continued to spar as what little light remained began to fade, covering them in a dusky glow. Eventually, night claimed the world and the trio had no choice but to consider this their camp until dawn. Asher took first watch, his mind too active to give into the likes of rest.

He couldn't stop thinking about her.

It was the anticipation that got to him. That uneasy feeling stayed with him for more hours still, until at last he caught sight of a small ship sailing quietly up the River Adanae. The ranger had seen ships of that design during The Battle for Velia, at the end of The War for the Realm. It was all curves with a sleek build that cut through the water with grace befitting of those who made it.

The deck was illuminated by the soft glow of hanging lanterns, their light casting shadows over the elves. He counted five and no more, each one hooded with a robe that partially concealed their armour. The ranger narrowed his old eyes, searching for Faylen among the silhouettes.

His heart rate increased.

In years past, he had received training to assist in lowering his heart rate in stressful situations. It wasn't working. Asher stood up with nervous energy and nudged his sleeping companions before making his way towards the water's edge.

With no manual input, the boat simply came to a stop, the wind taken from its sails. Two of the hooded elves lowered a ramp to the shore and stood either side in the fashion of guarding soldiers. There was a pause among the remaining three, still on the deck. Their words were low, just outside of Asher's comprehension, but he noted the sound of a female voice among them.

The figure in the middle of the three raised their hand, silencing any debate. Asher tensed as that same figure began to walk down the ramp, a grey cloak dragging behind them. With the firelight not far behind Asher, the elf's face came perfectly into view, and what a beautiful face it was.

Faylen, of house Haldör, lowered her hood and looked upon the ranger's face with glassy eyes. Her jet-black hair melted into the night over her back. Her skin wasn't as pale as Asher remembered, in fact she now had freckles spreading across her nose and cheeks. The eyes were the same. Orbs of hazel with just a hint of emerald bore into him, taking in his every imperfection.

Faylen made to speak but her lips parted and nothing more. Asher was drawn to those lips and his memory of their kiss was soon to follow, leaving him with a longing that was almost akin to an emptiness. For him, it hadn't been that long since he said goodbye to her in the caves of Kaliban, but he *had* said goodbye. Seeing her again was confusing and somehow painful...

"It really is you," she whispered at last.

"I've been hearing that a lot," Asher quipped, instantly regretting such a flippant remark.

Faylen reached up and ran a gentle hand down his stubbled

cheek. "When Lady Ellöria told me... I couldn't believe it. Even seeing you now, before my very eyes, I can't believe it." She blinked once and found control of the tears threatening to spill out.

Asher gripped her hand in his own and squeezed. "There's so much—"

"Faylen?" The two elves from the deck had made their way down the ramp, leaving the other two on board to stand guard.

Upon hearing her name, Faylen pulled her hand away from Asher's and offered him an apologetic look. It was only an expression, but it said so much as it clenched Asher's heart. Standing back from the ranger, Faylen revealed the two elves, both exquisite male specimens of their race. Their immortality made it impossible to guess their ages but, of the pair, Asher was drawn to the elf who looked at Faylen with an expectancy that didn't belong on the face of her subordinate. After all, she was the High Guardian of Elandril, a position only granted by the king or queen and only given to one worthy of leading the elven army.

This same elf reached out for Faylen and she reciprocated until their hands were one, displaying the identical bracelets they both wore. A pit was slowly beginning to open inside Asher's gut.

Faylen took her hand back and gestured to the elf he had barely noticed. "Asher, this is Celeqor, of house Atraysil. He has the honour of being the youngest elf ever to sit on the Elder council; his magic and wisdom will be invaluable on an errand of this magnitude." Faylen hesitated before introducing the elf standing beside her. "And this is Nemir, of house Helevyn. He is a captain among our ranks and also... my *husband*."

In order to maintain a neutral expression, Asher fell upon his training and used it to combat his heartache.

Faylen caught herself and continued, "Celeqor, Nemir, this is Asher..." Accustomed to longer titles, the High Guardian stumbled over his name.

Asher was there to catch her. "Just Asher," he elaborated for the elves. "Keeps things simple," he added with a flicker of an empty smile.

Vighon cleared his throat beside the ranger.

"Oh, this is Vighon Draqaro and Ruban..." Asher looked at the squire in the hope that his family name would come to him.

"Dardaris," Ruban said with little confidence.

"Ruban Dardaris," Asher said, nodding at the elves with nothing more to add regarding their unusual trio.

Nemir's dark eyes ran along the line of humans before resting on Faylen. *"This is it?"* he said in elvish. *"I recall your tales of the ranger, my love, but I fail to see why Lady Ellöria would allow three humans such as these on an errand of great importance."*

Faylen's gaze darted from Asher to her husband. "Nemir..." she cautioned.

Asher, however, couldn't resist. *"We were tasked by the Master Dragorn, not Lady Ellöria. I believe even the elves of Ayda bow in the wisdom of the Dragorn..."* His elvish wasn't perfect, but every word rolled off his tongue in the correct order; he would need more time submerged in the language before his pronunciations were as melodic as theirs.

Imperfect or not, Vighon and Ruban stared at him in awe while Nemir found a way of straightening his impeccably straight form. Along with a tensed jaw and a raised chin, these were the only signs that the elven captain was uncomfortable.

Diffusing the awkward atmosphere, Elder Celeqor remarked, "Your command of our language is exceptional for one with a human tongue. Forgive my intrigue - I have read much on yourself after your defeat of Valanis - but am I correct in thinking your knowledge of our language was imparted by Alidyr Yalathanil?"

Asher stopped himself from rolling his eyes. Or frowning. Or groaning and sighing. The last thing he needed was some elven scholar wanting to turn over every rock in his life. It was surreal enough that anyone, let alone an elven elder, had read about him.

Now that he thought about it, the ranger wanted to know who was writing about him and what they were saying.

Reluctantly, he obliged with an honest answer. "Alidyr was an instructor in Nightfall. He taught all of his lessons in elvish. You either picked the language up or you were punished."

"Fascinating," Nemir replied with no enthusiasm. "Perhaps you would like to collect your belongings and steeds," he added, gesturing to the ship behind them.

"We're going on the ship?" Ruban's voice was quiet, but his fear was audible.

To Nemir's elven ears, Ruban's little voice had nowhere to hide. "We will continue up the river until we reach The Spear; it will be faster this way."

Asher tore his eyes from Faylen and turned his attention on the squire. He had the very specific look of a man who didn't know how to swim; another absent skill to add to his growing list.

Vighon patted the young man on the arm. "The trick to surviving in the water is not falling in."

After the northman's unhelpful comment, the three companions went about collecting their supplies and belongings. Asher had removed little from his own saddlebags and was left waiting awkwardly by the side of the ship. Faylen watched him from the deck but he tried not to notice, feigning interest in his horse. Once on board, they were introduced to the remaining elves, a pair of warriors in full armour beneath their robes.

By the time the horses were secure and the ship was on its way, Asher had forgotten the warriors' names. They were another detail he seemed to be having trouble holding on to. Was it his crowded mind? It would have been the simple answer, but it was more likely that the old ranger's mind was distracted by his shipmate. Since being freed of The Crow's spell, he had imagined all that he might say to Faylen, their conversation often his last thoughts before sleep.

Now, they were breathing the same air for the first time in thirty years and he had no idea what to say to her. What should he say? He had died after all. Was he really entitled to confess any kind of love for her? Three decades was a long time...

Interrupting his thoughts, the ranger detected a presence from behind and knew it had to be Vighon - standing by the edge of the bow, Ruban certainly wasn't about to join Asher and the elves wouldn't have announced their arrival with such heavy footfalls.

"Have you ever seen a ship like this?" Vighon asked, leaning against the side. "There's no one but us on the deck. No one is seeing to the sails or even steering it. And it's night!"

"It's magic," Asher grumbled, no interest in continuing this conversation.

"Obviously," Vighon shrugged. "I've just never seen it used like this. It's impressive. It definitely beats a few days on horseback. Faylen said we should be in The Spear by midday tomorrow."

Asher nodded along, sure to keep his mouth shut. He had been around people long enough to know that speaking back only encouraged them.

"Is there a reason you're more sullen than usual?" the northman continued.

Asher sighed. "Now you want to talk..."

Vighon raised a suspicious eyebrow. "It wouldn't have anything to do with the way the High Guardian was looking at you, would it?"

Asher had no intention of talking about it with him. "How's the boy doing?" he asked instead. "Have you peeled him off the floor yet?"

Vighon kept his eyes on the ranger for a moment longer. "He's coping better below decks... where he can't see the water. He's had a sheltered life in Namdhor."

Asher looked longingly into the distance. "A bit of sheltering doesn't sound so bad."

"True enough," Vighon conceded. "But this will be good for him. Get him out into the world, get a few experiences under his belt. Killing a few orcs in battle has already changed him."

Asher shook his head. "I'd say he's got one *too many* experiences under his belt..."

Vighon frowned at him. "What do you mean?"

"You can see it in his eyes," Asher explained as if it was obvious. "Those orcs aren't the first to lose their lives by his hand. Whoever he's killed, though, it's stuck with him."

Vighon shook his head. "How can you possibly tell all that?"

"There's a difference between killing a man in combat, be it war or self-defence, and killing a man who didn't know he was about to die. The latter can haunt you if you let it."

The northman looked back at the ship in disbelief. "That's quite a leap. He's just a squire!"

"A few days ago," Asher pointed out, "you didn't even know his whole name. Perhaps you should let go of your assumptions and start looking at what's really in front of you..."

"Perhaps I should start looking at you," Vighon countered. "You fight like you're in control but you're not. Your mind has been fractured yet here we are, following you like the blind into the memories of a dragon you tell us we should fear. You've warned us about Alijah's bond to Malliath, but who's warning us about your bond? You were connected to him for—"

"I'm in no mood to be lectured by a pup," Asher cut in. "And I'm no Alijah." With that, the ranger moved away, happy to be anywhere but standing on an icy deck talking to Vighon.

The northman, however, was a dog with a bone. "You don't know him, just like you don't know Ruban!" he called after Asher. "Alijah is strong, stronger than you think."

The ranger stopped and turned back. "Alijah is a blank slate. He has a *handful* of experiences he can recall from his very young life. Malliath's mind will pour in and fill him up: it's already started."

"And what about *your* mind?" Vighon asked aggressively.

"Malliath showed me just enough to be terrified," Asher replied with brutal honesty. "In time, his mind might have made me into something worse than I already am. But I got out. Alijah can't say the same." Having said his piece, the ranger prepared to descend into the ship.

"You're wrong about him," Vighon insisted, his voice betraying a hint of concern.

Asher paused on his way down and looked back at the northman over his shoulder. "I hope so..."

Leaving Vighon with his thoughts, the ranger weaved through the cabins below. It wasn't like other ships he had travelled on, its general aroma far too fresh and the surfaces too clean. Following his nose, he came across the galley where Ruban was curled up sleeping in the corner, his unease brought to rest by the smell of elven cooking.

Asher nodded politely at the elf who was cooking, though his name still eluded him. Moving on, he soon found his way blocked by Faylen. They stood opposite each other in silence, their words not required to take the other in. It was clear that both had something to say. Their moment was shattered when the door at the far end opened to reveal Nemir.

"Would you talk with us?" Faylen asked the ranger.

Asher looked past her to the elven captain, keeping any answer to himself.

"I know you aren't one for talking," Faylen continued. "It won't take long."

The ranger bowed his head and followed her into the cabin where Nemir was waiting. The room had been stripped of all but a square table in the middle, upon which lay a map of Illian and a couple of smaller maps detailing The Spear in the north-eastern tip. Standing quietly in the corner was Elder Celeqor, his hands hidden within the large sleeves of his robe.

In the torchlight of the cabin, Asher was able to see Nemir and Celeqor in greater detail. The elder appeared no older than Ruban, though considering his title among the elves, his age was likely in the thousands. Long blond hair ran down his back and over his chest. So clean and straight was it that Asher could only suspect magic. Still, the elder offered the ranger a kind smile, which was more than Nemir gave him.

Faylen's husband possessed hair as dark as her own, but Nemir's was braided and scraped back into a long ponytail that hung over the back of his armoured chestplate. His face was sharp, a contrast to his dark eyes that provided his appearance with a softness that was almost disarming.

"Would you prefer man's tongue?" Nemir asked him before they began.

"Speak however you like," Asher offered.

Nemir glanced at his wife. "Then I shall take the opportunity to further my lessons in man's language."

Asher was already bored. "What's all this?" He nodded his chin at the maps. "I know where we're going."

"Yes..." Faylen agreed absently, her focus roaming over the ranger's head. "Lady Ellöria told me you have the memories of Malliath the voiceless. That must be... *painful*."

Asher shrugged. "It has its moments."

Celeqor stepped closer to the table. "Malliath is the oldest recorded dragon in history. How are you managing all of that memory?"

The maps, the questions about Malliath; they were doubting him. "Every day I lose more of it," he admitted. "Malliath's life is slipping away, Alijah's too. I'm just left with an echo of their thoughts, like an impression of them."

Asher fixed his gaze on the map, feeling suddenly vulnerable. That was a lot more than he intended to share, though whether that was because of Faylen's presence or simply being in a room of elves, beings who left you feeling like they had been examining your soul, was unknown to the ranger.

"The memory fades?" Nemir clarified with concern.

Asher put his finger on the arrow-tipped mountains known as The Spear. "Not this one. Since Malliath saw the orcs, the memory has been ever present on his mind. The memories passed on to him detail the exact place the Dragon Rider entered the mountains, including the path he took to Haren Bain."

"You are certain?" Nemir questioned.

Asher looked him in the eyes. "I wouldn't be here if I wasn't."

Nemir looked doubtful but a look from Faylen settled him. "Where would you suggest we make port?"

Asher examined the Adanae River and pointed at the western curve. "Here. From there, we could make it to the entrance on horseback in a few hours."

Faylen dragged the larger map towards her and focused on the north. "Haren Bain aside, and I'm sure it will come with its own obstacles, we are concerned about Namdhor. I have already ordered four hundred elven warriors to the city to aid in the defence against the orcs, but time is against us."

Asher nodded in agreement. "You're talking about getting back to Namdhor with the weapon before they attack again."

"It is because of that concern that Elder Celeqor is with us," Faylen continued to explain. "Unlike Nemir and myself, Celeqor has seen Namdhor with his own eyes."

"I was barely out of childhood," the elder elaborated.

Asher scrutinised the three elves. "I fail to see how this will help us return with any haste."

Celeqor smiled warmly and dipped his hand into a leather pouch on his belt. From within, he produced a glowing crystal, the gem carrying the magical potential to open a portal.

"As you know," Faylen said, "it's impossible to open a portal to a destination you've never seen. Once we possess this weapon you have spoken of, we will journey to the western edge of The White Vale where Celeqor can open a portal and see us returned to Namdhor in a single step."

Asher remembered a time when he had the power to harness those crystals. With Paldora's gem on his finger, opening a portal would have been easy. Now, he was just another human, his connection to the magical realm tenuous at best.

"Why can't we portal from Haren Bain to Namdhor?" Asher posed. "That would be much faster."

"It would," Celeqor agreed. "However, the distance is too great. Some of the journey will need to be made on horseback."

Nemir leaned against the table. "What can you tell us about this weapon, Ranger? Will it even fit through a portal?"

"It was made by Naius." Just saying that filled Asher's head with pain. The more he focused on the memory, the more it made him suffer.

"Asher?" Faylen reached out but stopped herself from placing a hand on his shoulder.

"I'm fine," he lied. "You're just going to have to trust me," he added, looking solely at Nemir. "The weapon is there. You'll see it for yourself when we reach Haren Bain."

Nemir wasn't close to satisfied and he made to ask another question. "That will be all," Faylen said first. "I think we have all we need for now. Perhaps we should all retire and prepare for tomorrow."

Celeqor bowed his head. "An excellent suggestion, High Guardian."

As the elder and Nemir made for the door, it became apparent that Faylen was staying behind. She gave her husband a look and a light nod, ushering him from the room with a wife's reassurance. Unsure what was happening, the ranger followed behind Nemir as he left.

"Asher," she called softly. "Might we speak?"

The ranger didn't miss the look Nemir shot his way. "I suppose so," he replied, closing the door after the elves.

With the table between them, another awkward silence settled on the cabin. Asher found himself unable to look Faylen in the eyes and decided the maps were far more interesting.

"I feel as though I should be asking for your forgiveness," Faylen confessed.

Asher couldn't hide his surprise. "*Forgiveness*? There is nothing to forgive."

"I waited," Faylen continued, her knuckles white from gripping the edge of the table. "You were dead but I still waited."

Asher could see her becoming upset. "Faylen... You don't have to—"

"And I didn't reject all of my suitors because I felt guilty," Faylen spoke over him. "I pushed them all away because I loved..." She sealed her lips and averted her eyes before finishing. "It was twenty years before I met Nemir," Faylen continued, wiping a single tear from her cheek. "Despite what you're seeing of him, he's actually very gentle and kind. Funny too, which is hard to find in an elven captain. I think he's a little threatened by you," she added with an amused smile that didn't belong on a face so upset.

"*Good*," Asher jested, mimicking Faylen's smile. "There's really nothing to forgive," he reiterated. "I was dead, I still should be. I'm just sorry you had twenty years of... mourning me. It's not fair that I've returned to your life after everything you went through."

Another tear found its way down her perfect skin. "What about you?" Faylen asked. "You and I, what we had, however brief, must feel so recent."

"I won't lie; it isn't easy to see you with him, but I'm glad you found him, I'm glad you found some happiness. You deserve it, Faylen."

"But what do *you* deserve?" she pressed, joining him on the other side of the table. "For you, seconds have gone by and you're back fighting in another war. How much punishment can you take, Asher? You deserve more than this."

The ranger couldn't say whether that was true or not. To Faylen's eyes, he was an honourable man who had sacrificed himself for others and nothing more. Asher could still remember every life he had taken in service to Nightfall, every innocent he murdered. What he deserved was probably worse than what he had endured thus far...

"I keep putting one foot in front of the other," he finally responded. "I do whatever I can, wherever that takes me."

Faylen cupped his cheek. "You are still trying to atone for your previous life. Asher, you died for the world. Whatever you did as an Arakesh, the debt has been paid, the scales balanced. This can be a whole new life for you."

Asher couldn't help himself and he took her jaw in his hand. "You don't know the things I've done," he whispered. "I could die a thousand times over and it still wouldn't erase my past, the lives I've taken." The urge to kiss her was overwhelming and the ranger caught himself. He removed his hand from her jaw and took a breath. "I am truly happy for you, Faylen. I mean that. Whatever road lies before us, I will gladly walk it knowing you are one of my closest friends."

Faylen took back her hand and looked up at him questioningly. "Friend? I thought the great ranger of the wilds didn't keep friends?"

Her smile was infectious, even if it did hurt to hold back. "I'm coming round to the idea," he accepted. "Goodnight, Faylen."

"Goodnight, Asher."

Walking away from her didn't feel natural yet, but just seeing her made him feel a bit more complete, helping him to fill the voids that had existed within him since his return to the world. He meant every word he said to her and, indeed, it did make him feel good to know that she hadn't been a depressed wreck for thirty years. Now, he just had to tackle his feelings towards Nemir, specifically the way he felt about punching him...

CHAPTER 27
A CALL FROM THE SEA

Walking into the Dragorn library, in the heart of The Lifeless Isles, was like stepping into an old memory for Alijah. It was surreal to be anywhere but inside the cold walls of The Bastion, trapped in its freezing embrace.

The library was warm and cosy. The dark stone of The Bastion was now replaced with wood, be it tables, chairs or the towering bookshelves. Alijah recalled the last time he was here, standing before these ancient books. With Gideon by his side, they had read through thousands of years of history trying to learn more about the orcs and any magic that could explain his bond to Malliath.

Alijah knew he should feel something being here. Surrounded by history, he should feel in his element, excited even. The library, any library for that matter, no longer called to the explorer who had lived inside of him. He didn't belong here, a place where he could get nothing done.

His destiny lay elsewhere...

Such a thought drew the half-elf to the cabinet on the far side of the library. As he made his way over, Alijah remembered the other thing he and Gideon had been examining. From within the cabinet, he removed a bound scroll the length of his forearm and laid it out on the table.

The Echoes of Fate.

Staring at those three verses, he knew he was looking at history, a history devised and manipulated by The Crow to ensure his birth. It was hard to accept the scope of such a thing, to dwell on the lives that had been changed or lost by no more than a few words.

Alijah ran his fingers over the parchment. For a moment, he was transported back inside The Crow's memories, where he witnessed a younger version of the dark mage scribe the prophecy.

His reverie was shattered when he realised there was someone else in the library with him, watching him. "I don't need minders," he announced.

"I'm not here to mind you," Inara replied, making her way down to him.

"Between you and our parents, that's exactly what you're doing." Alijah turned away from the prophecy, but Inara still caught sight of it.

"We're worried about you," his sister went on. "After everything you've been through…"

"Is that why you brought me here, to The Lifeless Isles? If you think trapping me inside a cliff is what I need you're very mistaken."

Attempting to diffuse the building tension, Inara quipped, "What you need is a shave. A wash wouldn't hurt either."

Alijah stroked his messy beard and offered Inara the hint of a smile. In truth, he cared little for their banter and even less for his appearance, but his smile would help the diffusion since he didn't have the energy to argue with her.

"They are concerned though," she continued. "They said you wouldn't talk to them."

"They didn't want to talk," Alijah corrected her. "They wanted to question me again and again until they knew everything that happened to me."

"Talking about that will help you," Inara reasoned.

The tension between them was quickly building again, so Alijah said nothing and glanced at the prophecy.

"Alijah..."

"I'm still there," he snapped. "I'm still inside those walls. I can hear The Crow's voice. You want to talk about what happened to me, but it's still happening right now."

Inara stepped closer. "We know about this," she said, referring to the prophecy. "We know what The Crow did, what he wants of you. Asher told us."

They know nothing!

Alijah was pulled towards that voice, a voice that only he could hear. His eyes roamed the library even though he knew the source was miles away from his current location. He also knew that voice, perhaps the most ancient voice in all of Verda.

Inara looked down at the prophecy. "This is where it all started."

Malliath's voice vanished as quickly as it appeared, leaving Alijah with an emptiness that made him feel like the last man in the world. To distract himself, he followed Inara's attention to the scroll.

"Every word..." he began. "Every word was placed exactly where it needed to be to shape the future. One mistake and I wouldn't have been born."

"Neither of us would have been born, brother."

Inara's correction was entirely accurate, yet it was a fact that bore no consequence. The Crow had scribed the prophecy to bring him into the world; his twin sister was simply a twist of nature that no prophecy could have caused.

"Do you believe any of it?" Inara asked. "Do you even want it, to be the king of Illian?"

Alijah didn't want to talk about it. He hated to admit it, but there was a part of him that wanted to get permission from The Crow before he said anything. There was a simple truth attached to that feeling - he was still a prisoner.

"None of it matters right now," he finally replied. "The orcs must be close to bringing the north to its knees and The Crow is still out there. What either of us want is irrelevant until they're dealt with."

Inara didn't look convinced by his answer. "The last place you need to be right now is in a battle. You can stay here and recover until the war is over."

"We both know I can't recover on my own," Alijah countered. "Could you without Athis?"

Inara didn't need long to answer that question. "No, I couldn't. Do you know where Malliath is?"

Alijah subconsciously turned to the northern wall. "I know he's not here."

"That might not be a bad thing," Inara replied. "The youngest of our order survived his attack, but they still witnessed it all."

"He attacked against his will," Alijah argued. "He would never have done that..." He couldn't continue down that line of reasoning, aware that there was a hint of something darker inside his companion.

"We know," Inara replied sympathetically. "But the memory is still fresh and our dead are still being counted."

Alijah sighed. "So I *am* trapped here."

"No!" Inara insisted. "You're not a prisoner here, Alijah."

"The only way out is with a dragon or a hundred foot drop into the ocean." Alijah made for the stairs and the door to leave the library. "Doesn't that sound like a prison to you?" He walked out without waiting for an answer.

His parents were sat at the stone table that served as the Dragorn council's chamber. They were both clearly in the middle of a deep discussion, regarding him no doubt, but they brought it to a sudden halt at the sight of him.

They started to stand up when he held a hand out, giving them pause. "I need to..." he waved a hand in front of his face.

Reyna pointed at the door behind him. "Gideon said you can use his rooms. Is there anything you need?"

Alijah shook his head without actually looking at either of them and disappeared inside Gideon's private chamber. On his own again, the half-elf slid down the door and exhaled a long breath, meant to help focus his mind. He was searching...

Where are you? he asked the ether.

There was no response from Malliath, but their bond was stronger than ever, preventing the dragon from hiding from him. He could feel his companion's presence, so tangible was it that Alijah was sure he could reach out and touch Malliath's scales.

Where are you? he asked again.

There was no verbal response but Alijah felt himself pulled to the north and not far either. As he had suspected outside The Bastion, Malliath had returned to a prison of his own...

Keeping up with the charade of putting himself back together, Alijah rummaged through Gideon's things until he found a razor and a pair of scissors. It pleased his parents to ask them for a bowl of water, though he offered them nothing but a *please* and *thank you*. He took his time shaving and washing his hair, waiting for his family to grow tired and seek out some rest. Through the door, he heard his mother volunteer to stay and keep an eye on him.

Alijah could wait. Patience was the mark of a true... He never quite reached the word *king*, but the thought had been there. He looked in the mirror, his face clean shaven and his hair dripping wet but clean, and considered his intended fate. He realised that he was considering it for the first time without The Crow speaking in his ear or the oppressing walls of The Bastion surrounding him.

He was free...

Alijah began to wonder if he really did want all that The Crow had promised. To be king, and not just any king but *the* king. His destiny might have been scribed ten thousand years in advance, but the ultimate decision was his now.

Feeling the pull of Malliath again, Alijah decided that he couldn't make any choices without the dragon. They were one now and he craved Malliath's thoughts on all things. Waiting for his mother to fall asleep at the table, Alijah busied himself with a number of things, from meditation to putting a braid in his hair.

Taking into account his intended journey, Alijah also helped himself to Gideon's wardrobe. Being a Dragorn, Gideon possessed clothes that were designed to be worn on long expeditions as well as combat. The leathers were light but tough: even his belts were made of stronger materials than the one Alijah was wearing. Luckily, their boot sizes matched and before he knew it, the half-elf had the full look of a Dragorn about him.

There was also an inside pocket to his new jacket that allowed him to store the map he had taken from The Bastion. No matter what happened, he would make sure that map stayed with him.

Stealing a look through a narrow gap in the door, Alijah could see that his mother had finally fallen asleep at the table, her face buried in her arms. He crept out and checked his surroundings before making his escape. Moving past his mother, however, Alijah paused, catching her scent. It was familiar and comforting - as a child, he had said his mother carried the scent of love itself.

Alijah bent down and placed a gentle kiss on her head. He wanted to whisper he loved her, but the words got stuck in his throat and he decided to move on before she awoke and tried to stop him from leaving.

By the edge of the opening in the cliff face, Alijah looked out on the cold waters of The Adean below. The waves collided with the white walls of the archipelago and the wind raced between the cliffs. It was an uninviting vista for one who couldn't fly.

"Fear is a choice," he said to himself.

Then he dived forwards.

The water didn't welcome him. He pierced the surface and sank beneath the waves to find a freezing embrace waiting for him. He focused on his bond with Malliath, relying on the added strength and stamina it would give him, and burst from the depths with renewed energy. He had to concentrate on swimming and nothing more, his mind resigned to one task.

Following the cliff face, he swam north until he came across a rocky beach. Putting hard ground under his feet again was a relief but his training allowed him to ignore the pains and aches that radiated from his arms and legs. Instead, he put his mind to the task of reaching Malliath.

In the dark, he scrambled across the rocky beach, careful to avoid the cliff face, where there were sleeping dragons surrounding the young Dragorn, all unaware of his presence. The cliffs that surrounded him were featureless in the dark of night, their details only visible where more Dragorn were camped. There appeared to be a lot less of them than his last visit to The Lifeless Isles...

Travelling farther up the beach, he eventually found what he was looking for: boats. They were simple in their build and designed to be rowed by one or two people. The Dragorn would use them to fish since their dragons hunted for food that wasn't meant to be shared.

With one eye on the dragons behind him, Alijah pushed a boat into the water and jumped in. His arms protested at the first few strokes as he found his rhythm with the oars but, again, his mind found the control it needed over his muscles and he rowed hard.

Weaving across the extensive archipelago, Alijah rowed all night until he was surrounded on all sides by the flat horizon of The Adean. By late morning he was ready to collapse in the boat and sleep for a month, but still he rowed. He passed by the densely populated island of Dragorn, on his right, ignoring the children who shouted at him from its rocky shore. Until he reached his destination, Alijah's world comprised of one thing: rowing.

Only once did his attention falter and his eyes were drawn to the west, where dark clouds blanketed Illian. The ash clouds went no farther than The Shining Coast but, after midday, the warm glow of the sun was hidden on the other side of those clouds. The winter breeze rolled over The Adean's surface and reminded Alijah that the world wasn't due to warm for many weeks yet.

It was a fatuous thought, the kind of thought the old Alijah would entertain. He scrunched his eyes and fell upon his lessons to refocus his mind before he gave in to the ache in his bones. Concentrating on his love for Malliath, he transformed his pain into power and welcomed the strength it lent him.

More hours of uninterrupted rowing followed, bringing him closer to his destination, closer to Malliath. The sound of thunder finally snapped him from his place of focus. Coming in fast from the east was a storm cloud so dark it could rival the ash in the west. Flashes of lightning lit up the sky as brilliant bolts danced across the clouds. The ocean responded accordingly and the waves picked up, making it all the harder to direct the boat.

It wasn't long before torrential rain was hammering Alijah, masking his view of anything. He tried with all his strength to guide the boat north, but the choppy waves wanted nothing more than to carry him to Illian's distant shore. More thunder *boomed* overhead and he looked up as the largest wave yet slammed into the side of his small boat. He gripped the sides and managed to remain inside the boat, but his oars could do nothing but slip into the water.

Struggling to maintain control on his anger, Alijah turned around and looked to the north, hoping to see his destination. With the sun hidden and the rain pouring, there was nothing to see but sheets of grey. If he stayed in the boat, however, he could be taken anywhere by the sea. Alijah considered swimming before realising the same could be said if he left the boat; there was no beating the ocean.

Despite the jarring sounds of the storm, Alijah found himself being pulled into a quiet place. His surroundings fell away, taking the noise of the rain and the waves with it. His mind gave into the strange sensation until he was somewhere else entirely, somewhere you couldn't find in the real world.

Darkness enveloped him, yet he could see himself perfectly. He looked around, curious, but there was no light to be found anywhere. He walked forward and felt the light resistance of water around his feet. He was standing in a puddle that stretched on as far the eye could see, which was quite far considering there was no sun, moon or firelight.

From behind him came the distinct sound of hot air being forced through the nostrils of a dragon. Alijah had heard that sound a thousand times during his weeks chained in the highest tower in The Bastion. It had provided him with warmth and comfort at the time.

Turning around slowly, the half-elf came to look upon Malliath, though the black dragon's bulk melted into the inky abyss behind him. Another gust of hot air flared from his nostrils and blew ripples across the water between them. Alijah couldn't help but walk towards his companion's purple eyes, their beauty almost hypnotic.

"Is this a... a sanctuary?" he asked.

Inara had spoken of such a place that she shared with Athis, though his sister described their private realm as a mountain range. An even earlier memory reminded him that Gideon shared a vast forest with Ilargo, a place that resided under the stars for eternity.

When Malliath didn't respond to his question, Alijah reached out to touch him. The dragon shook his horned head and pulled away, taking with him the fabric of their sanctuary. The half-elf felt his mind snap back with such a force that his physical body was flung back and thrown over the side of the boat. After a disorientating splash, he discovered a moment of peace beneath the violent waves. He used that moment to ground himself back in reality and fight the urge to return to the sanctuary.

With a gasp for air, Alijah burst from the depths to find his boat had already drifted beyond his reach. Despair would have been easy to give in to, but his time in The Bastion would never leave him, reminding him that his destiny was far grander than drowning in the middle of the ocean.

A flash exploded before his eyes, immediately followed by a *crack* of thunder, and, for just a second, it etched a dark island that rose up from The Adean. Another flash of lightning highlighted the island, giving Alijah a better sense of its size but, more importantly, what dominated the island.

Korkanath...

Alijah swam with all haste, battling the waves that tried to push him west, past the island. That brief swim was almost as tiring as rowing the boat, but he finally made it to the rocky shore where he was able to crawl onto hard ground. It was tempting to lie there and fall asleep, regardless of the freezing rain that battered him relentlessly. Malliath was close, however, his presence an undeniable force that gave the half-elf just enough energy to keep going.

Standing on the shore, Alijah cracked his back and looked up at the school for mages. It was a ruin, its high walls brought down by dragon's fire, specifically that of Malliath's. He could still see the island burning in his memories, the flames reaching for the sky, as Ilargo had made for Velia to repel the orcs. Like his memory of the library, that too felt like another life that he couldn't claim to have been his own.

Seeing the scorched walls and the shattered towers, Alijah knew he should feel a sense of grief for the students and teachers who had died in the fires of Malliath's rage.

But he didn't feel anything like that.

In fact, he could feel a smile trying to creep up his face. It was a terrible thing to do in the sight of such destruction and death, yet there he was, standing in the rain with a feeling of satisfaction. For a thousand years the mages of this wretched place had imprisoned and enthralled Malliath to the island, forcing him to protect it with magic.

Adding insult to injury, they had perpetuated the lie for a millennium that Malliath had started The Dragon War against mankind, thus deserving his punishment. It had taken Gideon some years, but he had since rewritten history to reflect the truth about man's greed and King Tion's war against the dragons.

A whisper ran through Alijah's mind, turning him east on the rocky beach. He followed the connection he felt, navigating the treacherous shore, until he came across the mouth of a cave large enough to accommodate a dragon of Malliath's size.

Walking into the black, Alijah did so without an ounce of fear. Alijah had no trouble finding the dragon, his enormous body curled up in the pitted cavern beneath the school's foundations. Malliath must have known he wasn't alone anymore, but he made no effort to greet or expel Alijah.

The half-elf climbed down to the pit, his eyes rarely straying from the dragon. "I know why you came here," he said quietly, preventing a loud echo.

Malliath didn't move but for the exception of his continued breathing, the only sign that he was even alive. Alijah cautiously walked around his tail and wing to try and see his face, to see those blazing purple eyes. They were closed, but the bond that existed between them told the half-elf that Malliath wasn't sleeping.

"I know why you came here," he said a little louder this time. "Prisons have a way of feeling like home after a while. The Bastion is a part of me now, just like this island is a part of you. No matter how far we run, we'll always feel the call to return."

Malliath's eyes opened, his reptilian pupils focused on the far wall before shifting to Alijah. To be caught in his sights was a death sentence for most, but not Alijah. Beside Malliath, he felt safer than he ever had, invincible almost. The black dragon slowly began to rise, bringing his jaws of razor-sharp teeth to hang over the half-elf.

For any other it would be a terrifying sight, but Alijah knew what was coming, he could feel it. Malliath was about to speak to him. It was an overwhelming feeling and the one thing Alijah had craved more than anything else.

The dragon, however, stared at him in silence.

"Say something," he coaxed. "You can say anything to me."

A low rumble erupted from Malliath's throat and he brought his purple eyes down to Alijah. *I can feel your pain...*

Alijah hadn't known what to expect, but he never would have guessed it to be that. "My pain?"

The dragon growled. *There is always pain with your kind! You use your magic and steel, always biting, always ripping and tearing and wanting more!*

Malliath stood tall and let loose an almighty roar that bounced off the walls with a discomforting effect that left Alijah wincing. Then, as quickly as he escalated, the dragon calmed down and exhaled a long breath.

"You have suffered," Alijah stated, feeling Malliath's emotions. "I can understand your desire to be left alone. I too feel the need to... leave everything behind."

You talk like you know me, Malliath retorted. *You haven't even scratched the surface yet. Are you prepared for what you will find? My suffering dwarfs all others and you will have no choice but to take it on as your own.*

"Your true feelings betray you," Alijah told him. "Our bond is complete now, our minds one. I know how you have longed to meet me. You've wanted to meet me for thousands of years. How many dragons have you watched bond with their riders while you were left to continue your lonely existence?"

You do not know me, Malliath insisted, his conviction waning.

"Could I say the same to you?" Alijah countered. "Can you look at me and not see what lies beneath?"

I look at you and see the weak creature that will be the death of me. Our bond is destined to doom me. I have seen history repeat itself enough to know that my kind will always suffer as long as your kind tethers us.

Alijah disagreed. "The magic that binds us is natural, a force that is beyond either of us. Fate brought us together; I know you can feel that. The first time you saw me, in Paldora's Fall, your very soul reached out for mine. From that moment on, we were helpless to stop this."

Magic... the dragon grumbled. *Natural or not, it makes humans dangerous. Any balance achieved has always been tipped by mages.*

Alijah could feel Malliath's rage bubbling under the surface, his logic strained by centuries of pain and suffering.

"Things will be different now," Alijah promised. "Balance is the reason you and I have been brought together. But first, we must find harmony..."

The half-elf raised his hand and left it there, an invitation. If

Malliath felt even a small amount of what Alijah was feeling, the dragon wouldn't be able to ignore that sense of completion that would come with his touch.

"I will take on your suffering as my own," he said, his hand outstretched. "You don't have to be alone anymore..."

Malliath remained very still, his predatory eyes shifting from Alijah's face to his hand. He was asking a lot of the dragon, more than any other had ever asked. Letting each other in and accepting their bond would bind them mind, body, and soul. It would be painful and glorious all at once.

Very slowly, the black dragon lowered his head to meet Alijah. Hand and scales were only inches apart. The heat radiating from Malliath was welcoming, adding to the anticipation of their touch.

He could feel the turmoil swirling inside Malliath's mind. Countless years of longing and rage battled together for dominance, but the power of their bond was all-consuming, leaving neither of them with a real choice.

Malliath pressed forward as Alijah reached out and the two came together for the first time.

Forever more, they would be one...

CHAPTER 28
THE KINGS OF DHENAHEIM

For a dwarf, there was nothing worse than sitting still. For this reason, Doran Heavybelly had paced the inside of his room all night and most of the morning. Sleep escaped him, leaving his single bed untouched, the blankets still crisp and the pillow smooth.

It wasn't the room he had expected to be held in. In fact, the son of Dorain was surprised he was still in Grimwhal's halls having been sure he was destined for the cells of Karak-Nor. The quarters he had been given were void of all but a bed, however, lending it the appearance of a cell none the less.

Most disturbing was his isolation. After being escorted from the throne room, he had also been split up from Galanör and Russell. He could only hope that they too had been given rooms like this one and spared the hell of Karak-Nor.

"What were ye thinkin'?" he muttered to himself for the hundredth time. "Should never 'ave come back..."

The sound of a key turning a heavy lock stopped Doran in his tracks. Since being deposited here, no one had interacted with him, not even to bring him water. The door opened without a sound, a

393

testament to dwarvish craftsmanship, and two people entered his room, both of which he knew intimately.

"*Mother, Dak...*" Doran looked them over curiously. "*Shouldn't you be wearing a disguise to be visiting me?*"

His mother glanced at Dakmund and his younger brother quickly closed the door behind them, shutting out the guards. Once alone, the queen of Grimwhal stepped forward and clipped Doran around the back of his head.

"*Fool of a Heavybelly!*" she scolded. "*We risked everything for you. I gave you one instruction, Doran! One! I don't recall dropping you on your head yet here you are. Do you want to die? If so, I will send you to the Mother and Father myself!*"

Doran rubbed his sore head. "*You saw what I brought with me!*" he argued. "*I wouldn't have returned if the fate of the whole bloody world wasn't in the balance!*"

Now Dakmund stepped forward and clobbered his brother around the head. "*How many men call Illian home? One of them couldn't have dragged an orc across the snows?*"

Doran rubbed the other side of his head and scolded at his younger brother. "*What human could have found their way to the throne of Grimwhal? With an orc in tow no less!*"

Queen Drelda was shaking her head with fury in her eyes. "*With every day that passes our family loses a little more of its grip on this kingdom. Your return reminds the lords of these halls that our bloodline is too weak to wear the crown - their beliefs, not mine! But what you have failed to grasp, son of mine, is that those very lords will push for your execution.*"

Doran raised a questioning eyebrow. "They'll *push for my execution? Does the king of Grimwhal really need the shove to make such a decision?*"

His mother didn't answer straight away, though she did give Dakmund a sidelong glance that begged more questions. "*Your father knows that we helped you to escape Karak-Nor...*"

That was a revelation Doran found very hard to accept. "*How is it you're both still breathing?*"

Before either could answer, the door swung open without warning and the king of Grimwhal strode into the room. As always, he maintained a face of thunder shrouded in white hair and a bushy white beard.

Without taking his cold blue eyes off Doran, he commanded, *"Leave us."*

Queen Drelda hesitated. *"Dorain..."*

"Now," the king barked.

Dakmund shot his brother a sympathetic look before ushering his mother out of the door. Doran really didn't want that door to close behind them. He hadn't been alone with his father in over sixty years and there was a very good reason for that: they didn't get on.

Without a word, the king removed the solid-looking crown from his head and tossed it to Doran, who caught it with both hands. It was heavy and no doubt uncomfortable.

"So, you can *take the weight of it,"* his father remarked sarcastically.

Doran held the crown in his hands awkwardly, unsure what to do with it now. *"It was never a question of whether I was ready for the crown,"* he explained. *"It was whether the crown was ready for me..."*

The king questioned his son with a look.

"One battle after another," Doran continued. *"On your command I killed my kin and my hands got bloodier every time. After so much killing, nothing made sense any more. If I was to take the throne, I would try to change everything. No more wars with the other clans, no scheming against the Stormshields, no senseless slaughtering of the Hammerkegs. And I definitely wouldn't be kissing the arse of King Uthrad!"*

His father snatched the crown from his hands. *"You would undo our way of life! And why? Because you couldn't handle a little blood on your hands? You're supposed to be a dwarf! Prince Doran of clan Heavy-belly! The promise of you kept everything together. The lords kept their mouths shut because Grimwhal's greatest warrior was going to sit on the throne!"* King Dorain dropped his head and shoulders, a look of defeat about him.

"I'm sorry, Father—"

The king raised his hand. *"I'm sure neither of us know what you're sorry about, boy. You should be sorry for the position you put your mother in, your brother too! Whatever you might think and whatever the lords of my kingdom might whisper, I am not a fool. Your mother's aid in Karak-Nor didn't go unnoticed and it was left to me to seal lips and keep them safe."*

Doran couldn't imagine his father taking steps to cover up his mother's secret deeds. *"I didn't mean for them to—"*

"You don't mean for anything to happen!" Dorain snapped. *"You just do! No thought for the consequences."* The king stopped and took a breath. *"I mourned for you. When you didn't return from battle, we thought you dead, your body lost among the others. Then, reports came in from witnesses who had watched you walk away. I punished all of them for their lies! My boy wouldn't abandon me, I said! But there was no fighting the truth..."*

Doran didn't know what to say. To apologise now would only anger his father, but it would also be an empty apology. If he had a second chance, he would still walk away from it all.

"I'm not the son you wanted and I'm not the prince Grimwhal wanted. I have come to terms with that during my time in Illian. And you're right; I wouldn't know what to say sorry for. We were once a noble race that put honour before all else. Now, we're greedy and selfish to the bone. We spill our own blood so we can say we have more! *That's not a world I want to be a part of."*

Dorain turned on his son with wild eyes. *"You can say the world of man is any better?"*

"At least they strive for peace!" Doran countered. *"We work towards nothing but war!"*

"Yet here you are!" the king spat. *"Pleading for Dhenaheim to march to war!"*

Doran shook his head in the face of his father's ignorance. *"I would see Dhenaheim march against the enemy that fractured our people! Fighting the orcs could unify us, Father!"*

"*Don't be so foolish, boy! You think the kings of Dhenaheim would give up their crowns and kingdoms and bow to Uthrad?*"

"*They already bow to him,*" Doran pointed out. "*All of you possess your kingdoms because he allows you to.*"

Dorain waved his son's remark away. "*You know nothing of what you speak! Your mind has been spoiled by the humans and their world!*"

"*Their world has opened my eyes! I see now what you wanted of me, but I could never be that king—*"

His father raised a hand again, his seething anger struggling to contend with the limitations of his advanced age. "*Do you think me so cruel and greedy that I would want to be that king?*"

The question shocked Doran, as well as his father's weary tone. For the longest time King Dorain had used one voice and it was nothing if not commanding.

"*Do you think I never wanted to change things?*" the king continued. "*Sitting on that throne, wearing that crown... It places a responsibility on your shoulders that stretches back not only to our ancestors, but forward, to those still to come. Our bloodline has ruled Grimwhal for thousands of years. There are a dozen lords like Dodurum who seek to replace us, but there have always been lords like them. Keeping control demands... well, you either bend to the throne or it breaks you.*"

For the first time in his two centuries of life, Doran empathised with his father. It was as if he had removed a mask and revealed his true self, a stranger to Doran, but it was someone he couldn't hate.

"*You've never spoken of this,*" he said softly.

"*You're my first-born,*" Dorain grumbled, unable to look Doran in the eyes. "*I treated you like a duty instead of a son. After all, you were to succeed me, and I believed you would continue our royal bloodline as intended. I saw my error too late. When your brother was born, I thought I had a second chance, an opportunity to simply be a father. Unlike the life I forced upon you, Dakmund was given a choice.*"

"*He doesn't anymore by the look of it.*" Doran regretted his comment the moment it left his lips.

"*And whose fault is that?*" the king snapped. "*After you left, I had no choice but to disown you and present Dakmund as the future king. You can imagine the reaction that received! He was always more philosopher than warrior. For sixty years I've thrust him into every battle I could and forced him to become someone he wasn't."*

"You mean you forced him to become me?" Doran clarified.

"I was left with no choice," his father replied venomously. *"You saw to that. You forced my hand and changed all of our lives. Now, here you are again, doing exactly the same thing!"*

Doran slowly shook his head. *"What are you talking about?"*

"The return of the orcs... They present me with an opportunity I cannot ignore."

The stout ranger tried to think like his father, but he had learned more about him in the last few minutes than he had over the two centuries of living with him; it skewed his reasoning.

"The only opportunity is one of reclaiming our honour," Doran put forward, suspicious of his father's point of view.

"Indeed it is," the king agreed. *"I am going to suggest the clans of Dhenaheim march into Illian and meet the orcs in battle. And I am going to place Dakmund at the head of that march."*

Doran became very animated. *"No!"* he protested. *"He hasn't the experience for a battle on that scale!"*

"His return would be that of a hero's!" Dorain proclaimed. *"The lords couldn't question our ability to rule Grimwhal. It would be the making of him..."*

"Or the unmaking," Doran growled.

"What did you expect?" his father asked. *"You wanted us to go to war. Your brother is the general of my forces."*

Doran turned away, angry with himself for not even considering it. Of course his brother was going to be among the ranks that marched against the orcs! The more he thought about it, the more he wanted to shove his fist down Gideon Thorn's throat for even suggesting this whole plan.

"And I'm going to give him Andaljor..." the king added.

Doran faced his father again. *"It won't ensure his survival. Nothing will against these numbers."*

For the majority of Doran's life, he had imagined that he would be the one to wield the greatest weapon of clan Heavybelly, their sigil a replica of the weapon itself. With a double-headed axe on one end and a hammer on the other, Andaljor had sat on the wall behind the thrones for as long as he could remember, passed down through the generations from one king to the next. His father had used it only once in battle but it was enough to prompt a hundred paintings and sculptures.

It was a statement giving it to anyone before they were king.

"This is the only path left to us now," the king said with great sadness. *"I was never strong enough to change things, nor was I compassionate enough to be the father you both deserved. I cannot change the past, however. This leaves me with duty alone."*

"It will leave you bitter if you don't try to change things."

The king nodded along under a shadow of depression. *"Yes, I suspect it will. Grarfath willing, Dakmund will be better than both of us."*

"That's if he returns," Doran warned, sick to his stomach even thinking about it.

"Should he return, I will abdicate the throne. Then, finally, this clan will be taken into the future under strong leadership, supported by the lords no less."

Doran didn't know what to do. He had set events in motion that couldn't be undone. He found himself hoping that King Uthrad would refuse to march his army, thus swaying the rest of the clans to remain in Dhenaheim. Though, such a refusal would see Illian laid to waste by the orcs... Most dwarves enjoyed being stuck between a rock and a hard place, but this was not a place Doran felt he could endure for much longer.

His father placed the crown back on his head and straightened up, assuming his role as the king of Grimwhal, an angry and cruel dwarf. *"Now, come,"* he ordered, turning for the door.

"Where are we going?"

As the door opened to a passageway filled with shield guards, the king faced his son and replied, *"The cleric is ready..."*

Doran swallowed hard.

~

HAVING RETURNED to the throne room, the son of Dorain was finally reunited with his companions. Galanör and Russell were just as he had last seen them, which was a relief. He half expected to find them covered in bruises and life-altering scars - often a result of dwarvish interrogation.

Both were surrounded by Heavybelly soldiers, a contrast to Doran who entered the chamber beside his father and tailed by shield guards. He wanted to talk to them more than anything, to formulate a plan that would somehow undo the bloodshed they had put the clan on course for.

Instead, he was forced to stand obediently beside his father and watch the cleric perform the most important job a cleric had. In the middle of the chamber, between the rows of pillars, crouched an old dwarf. He had white wisps of hair and a beard so long it could be nothing but a nuisance. His tattered robe was enough to tell him apart from every other dwarf in the throne room, but his belt, laden with scrolls, miniature books, and rare ingredients, gave his very particular profession away.

The king shivered just looking at him. "Magic..." he muttered.

The cleric was quietly chanting over a small dark orb on the marble floor. Every clan possessed one cleric, a dwarf who practised damned hard to overcome their natural resistance to magic and wield it for the betterment of their clan. Regardless of their service, however, the clerics were treated poorly by their kin. Doran had once been among them in their opinion of magic - the stuff of tricksters - but his time in Illian had changed his views on a lot of things, magic among them.

"*It's just a diviner,*" he commented. "*They use these all the time in Illian. Very practical.*"

"*It's magic,*" the king said with disdain. "*There's nothing practical about something you can't trust. Now be quiet. You are not to speak in this meeting unless requested to.*"

The cleric stood up, his work apparently complete, though there was nothing to show for it at present. He made his way over to the king and was quickly waved away by Doran's father, happy to say he had shared no word with the strange dwarf. His presence had a similar effect on the guards, all of whom stepped back, wanting nothing to do with one who commanded magic for a living.

"He's jus' doin' his job..." Doran muttered under his breath. Had he once treated the cleric as if he was diseased? His time in Illian had changed him in more ways than one obviously.

"*I told you to be quiet,*" the king enforced. "*And don't speak a word of man's language around the other kings.*"

On the far side of the chamber, two Heavybellys began pulling on chains, both of which disappeared into the ceiling and floor below. The sound of cogs knocking against each other came from below Doran's feet, then more mechanisms sounded from beneath the marble. Doran hadn't seen this since he was a child.

A larger rectangular slab of marble rose steadily from the floor, surrounded by six smaller square slabs. The higher they rose, the clearer it became that a carved table and throne-like chairs were ascending to the chamber. The chairs were high backed, far taller than any dwarf or even a human would require for comfort, and topped with a flat lid that plateaued over their heads.

It was all very regal, befitting of the royalty that would assume those chairs. Doran followed his father to one of the two chairs that lined the side. Each king had their designated position around the table, with King Uthrad of the Battleborns and King Gandalir of the Stormshields at each end. There was no seat for Doran and so he awkwardly stood off to the side from his father.

A moment of silence hung over the throne room as they waited.

401

Only King Uthrad's diviner could initiate the meeting from his chambers in Silvyr Hall. When he was ready, the dark orb brought their forms to life, filling the great chairs with the kings of Dhenaheim.

To Dorain's left sat King Torgan, son of Dorald, and ruler of the Hammerkegs. His ethereal presence didn't do his girth justice. On the other side of the table, sat King Gaerhard, son of Hermon, and ruler of the Brightbeards. Bluish in hue, the king's hair and beard of garish purple was left to the imagination.

At the head of the table, to Dorain's right, the king of the Stormshields came into being. He was the first to appear at the table who sat above Doran's father in the hierarchy of power. King Gandalir, son of Bairn, didn't even bother looking at the three kings before him, his eyes fixed on the empty throne opposite him.

It was soon filled by none other than King Uthrad himself, the son of legendary Koddun, and ruler of the Battleborns. From Silvyr Hall, he called himself the king of kings and there had been none to tell him otherwise. His tall crown of pure silvyr was dulled by his ethereal form, but he maintained his air of superiority regardless. His ancient eyes roamed over the gathered royals and landed on the only chair that had yet to be filled.

It was King Gaerhard of the Brightbeards who broke the awkward tension with his hacking laugh. *"Damned clerics! The Goldhorns must have done away with theirs!"* He laughed some more until Uthrad's gaze silenced him.

"Goldhorns or not then..." The king of Silvyr Hall looked at Doran's father. *"Why have you summoned us, son of Dorryn?"*

King Dorain cleared his throat and puffed out his barrel-like chest. *"Kings of Dhenaheim, thank you for accepting my invitation. I realise that gatherings such as this are most rare, warranting grave importance—"*

Uthrad waved his meaty hand in the air. *"Get on with it, Dorain. I have a mine twice the size of your entire kingdom to run."*

Doran would have found a smile on his face not so long ago, but hearing the king of Silvyr Hall and seeing the rulers of Dhenaheim reminded him that his father was truly stuck in a system he couldn't hope to change.

"*I have called for this meeting,*" Dorain continued, "*because we have built our kingdoms on the foundation that our ancestors left Vengora a ruin—*"

King Torgan of the Hammerkegs cut in, "*You were told to get on with it, Heavybelly! So get on with it!*"

Being directly beneath clan Heavybelly, Doran's father needed to show no respect when addressing him. "*Shut your mouth, Torgan! So help me, I will march my army on Nimdhun this very day and shut it myself!*"

"*Do it!*" King Gaerhard of the Brightbeards shouted, eager to see the clans above his own be weakened by war.

Ignoring the ruler of the Brightbeards altogether, King Torgan looked up at Dorain. "*You don't have the numbers to take Nimdhun! Try it, Heavybelly, and test the mettle of the Hammerkegs! You will soon come to regret it!*"

Doran sighed and pinched his nose: this wasn't off to a good start.

King Uthrad brought his fist down hard on the table in his own chamber, but the network of diviners made no distinction between his table and Dorain's. The squabbling kings held their tongues immediately for fear of Silvyr Hall.

In the silence that followed, Doran's father took the silent invitation to continue, only this time he replaced words with action. However, the kings of Dhenaheim could see nothing beyond the chairs and were left waiting for enlightenment. It came in the unceremonious dumping of an orc's body on the flat marble between them.

Doran looked from one king to the other, gauging their reactions. Much like that of his father's court, the kings stared in silent disbelief. To them, the orc was absent the extra details gleaned from being in the creature's presence but, even without the smell or general feel of the orc, they could see it for what it was.

"*Explain,*" Uthrad said bluntly, his eyes tethered to the orc's body.

"*There is no trickery,*" Dorain began. "*Before us all lies a creature so foul it has defied extinction. Not a day has passed since this orc breathed Dhenaheim's sweet air, that is until clan Heavybelly gutted it.*"

"*It's not possible,*" King Torgan of the Hammerkegs stated. "*This is either a Heavybelly scheme or their clan has been taken in by a magician.*"

King Dorain turned on him. "*Do not talk about me or my clan as if I'm not standing beside you!*"

"*It cannot be what you claim!*" King Gaerhard of the Brightbeards added. "*Their wretched kind was purged from Verda's soil five thousand years ago! There isn't a dwarf alive who doesn't know that!*"

"*Then what is that?*" the king of Grimwhal demanded furiously. "*I swear to Grarfath,*" he continued, looking from King Gandalir of the Stormshields to King Uthrad, "*I swear on my bloodline, and I swear on the deeds of my ancestors, this-is-an-orc!*"

Before the lower kings could respond with their vicious comments, King Gandalir asked, "*Where did the orc come from?*"

Dorain had time to consider his answer, given that Torgan and Gaerhard were forbidden to interrupt a question posed by the king of the Stormshields. Doran could see his father's eyes flicker towards him as his finger drummed against his chair.

"*An envoy from Illian,*" the king finally admitted, his words bringing derisive looks from the lower kings.

King Gandalir glanced at Uthrad across the table before leaning forward in his chair. "*Humans brought an orc to Grimwhal's door?*"

"*Yes, though the envoy was led by a dwarf...*" Dorain paused, licking his lips nervously. "*My first-born, Doran, has returned with a plea for aid on behalf of the humans - all of them. The orcs have—*"

"*Prince Doran...*" King Uthrad said his name aloud with a musing expression. "*This would be the same Prince Doran who walked away from the battlefield, forsaking his clan and people?*"

The king of Grimwhal gripped the arms of his chair. "*The very same, King Uthrad.*"

Ushered forward by his father, Doran approached the table until he was close enough that the diviners revealed his image to the kings. It was quite a thing to be looked upon by the most powerful people in Dhenaheim, but especially by King Uthrad, who scrutinised every inch of the ranger. He bowed his head under their gaze and remained quiet, waiting to be spoken to.

The king of Silvyr Hall looked from the orc's body to Doran. "*Why should we trust anything brought to us by you, one who has abandoned our way of life? You have come on behalf of Illian, but last I heard, the northern kingdom of man was trying to invade our land and lay claim to Vengora.*"

"*I cannot defend man or their ways,*" Doran replied honestly. "*I have not returned in the hope that you will aid their kingdoms. I have come to you because our ancient enemy has returned, an enemy only the dwarves of Dhenaheim can vanquish. None but the children of the mountain should claim victory over the orc.*"

King Uthrad narrowed his eyes. "*You haven't answered why we should trust you? This could be the work of magic for all we know. A trap. The bait is certainly excellent...*"

Doran shook his head at such a preposterous idea. "*There is no trap that could be laid by man that would see Dhenaheim defeated. I assure you, good king, the armies of Illian have been ravaged by an army of thousands, their kingdoms shattered, and their land overrun. But, again, I do not ask so that you might aid—*"

"*No,*" Uthrad announced, his deep voice easily drowning Doran out.

The ranger was unsure as to what the king of Silvyr Hall was saying no to. He looked from his father to the others, but like him, they hung on to Uthrad's every word and waited for an explanation.

"*No what?*" Doran's question was swiftly followed by a thump from his father.

Ignoring the exchange, King Uthrad continued, "*No, we will not march south.*"

Doran could feel the world falling out from under him. He looked over his shoulder and shared a moment with Dak. He didn't want his brother to spearhead a war, but he couldn't ignore the ruin being made of Illian, its people on the brink of decimation.

"*No?*" he echoed, stepping away from his father's reach. "*How can you say no?*"

"*Doran!*" the king of Grimwhal barked.

The ranger paid his father not a moment's notice. "*Orcs!*" he yelled at the kings. "*The demons have returned, the same demons who ran us from Vengora! We have no greater enemy! How can you not meet them in battle?*"

Uthrad didn't say anything at first, his silence gathering an intense audience. "*If the orcs have returned as you say, they will find their way to Dhenaheim. There is no better place to pitch a battle than on ground you control. Besides, why should we care what becomes of Illian? Let the orcs wipe out their pathetic race.*"

King Torgan nodded along. "*Our inaction will ultimately lead to the destruction of two enemies.*"

"*The humans are not your enemy!*" Doran bellowed. "*The orcs are your enemy! Ally with Namdhor and together the orcs' defeat will be assured.*"

"*Doran!*" His father spat his name with enough authority to silence the ranger.

Uthrad straightened his back. "*I have said all that is needed to be said. I suggest we reconvene with an appropriate war strategy - I expect the orcs to advance no farther than Khaldarim. Obviously, you will be wanting more silvyr; I will begin drawing up the contracts.*"

Doran slammed both of his fists on the table. "*Contracts? There are people dying in Illian and you're concerned about your profits!*"

King Uthrad addressed Doran's father. "*Grimwhal is yours to rule as you see fit, Dorain, but I suggest executing your son before he spreads discord.*"

King Dorain slowly stood up from his chair. He glowered at his son, a look so wicked that Doran stood back from the table and his image disappeared from the network.

"*As you say, King Uthrad, Grimwhal is mine to rule how I see fit. Therefore, I will be marching on Illian and sending every orc to Grarfath with the name Heavybelly on their vile lips.*"

Now Doran smiled. He didn't know his father had such courage but, since this was a day for firsts, he was proud of him in that moment.

King Uthrad's face dropped. "*You would defy me? You would defy Silvyr Hall?*"

Dorain puffed out his chest. "It is your right to hold sway over Dhenaheim's wars. Silvyr Hall's power is unquestionable. But you do not have the right to stop me from taking my army and waging war in another country."

The king of Silvyr Hall didn't miss a beat. "*With your army absent from Grimwhal's halls, you will have no defence against the Hammerkegs.*" Uthrad leaned forward. "*And I will not stop them...*"

Doran could see his father faltering. The only reason he was sending his army to meet the orcs was to elevate Dakmund and secure his bloodline's right to rule Grimwhal. Of course, there would be glory given to the entire clan for such a victory, but Dorain was making it much more personal.

"*I will stop them,*" King Gandalir offered, surprising them all.

Uthrad glared at the king of the Stormshields. "*What?*" he demanded.

"*The son of Dorain is right: we have no greater enemy than the orcs. Clan Stormshields has a long memory, longer than the Battleborns I would say. We do not lightly forget the crimes of their wretched race.*"

The king of Silvyr Hall was almost straddling the table now. "*If you join the Heavybellys I will take Hyndaern in less than a day!*"

"*I know,*" King Gandalir replied coolly. "*That is why my army will not be joining them. It pains me not to spill orc blood, but the Stormshields will be staying to keep watch over Grimwhal. Should King Torgan and his Hammerkegs attempt invasion,*" Gandalir looked directly at the king of Nimdhun, "*my clan will remove them from the kingdoms of Dhenaheim.*"

King Uthrad growled. *"You would defend a clan that has done nothing but wage war against you?"*

"Every second the orcs draw breath is an insult to my ancestors," Gandalir reasoned. *"I would not have them claim another victory, be it in Illian or Dhenaheim. Heavybellys, Stormshields, even Brightbeards - I do not care which clan sends them to Grarfath as long as they have dwarven blood in their veins!"*

King Dorain gave his rival a bow out of respect. *"We will flank them from the north as they attack Namdhor. I will have many paintings commissioned depicting their surprise so that we might enjoy the moment for all time!"*

King Uthrad sat back in his chair, his threatening gaze shared between Dorain and Gandalir. *"Fight for the humans if you must, son of Dorryn. An army of your size will struggle to contend with ten thousand of anything, let alone orcs. You can also consider any contracts between Silvyr Hall and Grimwhal dissolved. Your clan is on its own now..."*

Without waiting for any reply, Uthrad's image faded away, leaving his chair empty and the chamber without so much tension.

King Gandalir stared down the lower kings until they too faded away. *"You have my word, Dorain; no harm will come to Grimwhal. Just promise me our ancestors will hear the orcs scream as you crash upon them."*

"My son, General Dakmund, will lead the army himself, thus ensuring that all of Verda will hear the orcs take their last breath."

The king of the Stormshields bowed his head and faded away. Doran was left feeling both elated and severely crushed. Illian would now receive the aid it so desperately needed, but the dwarven army would be attacking without the support of the other clans. Dakmund was more vulnerable than ever...

The king of Grimwhal turned to his people, his eyes picking out the lords. "For the honour of our clan! For the honour of our ancestors! TO WAR!"

CHAPTER 29
AN UNLIKELY KINSHIP

B y the northern edge of the Adanae River, the mountain range
known as The Spear naturally drew the eye. Shaped like the
head of a spear and pointed east, the mountains dominated
the horizon. These snow-capped giants had hidden the secrets of
The First Kingdom for ten thousand years.

Vighon had an uneasy feeling about disturbing them.

Only once had the northerner seen The Spear before, though
there had been no occasion to explore the ominous mountains.
Seeing them, knowing that he was descending into their depths, he
had to wonder whether madness had driven him here.

Vighon recalled times past and many a place none would dare to
venture, places he and Alijah had turned inside out in their search for
relics. There had always been a sense of adventure accompanying
those journeys, along with the recklessness of youth. Since then,
Vighon had brushed with death more than a few times and knew
well how mortal he was.

Now, he would venture into another dark place the world wished
to keep from prying eyes. There was no sense of adventure this time.
With every foot covered by the horses, he knew it was duty that

drove him to this particular madness. This concept was still new to the northerner. Considering the lives of others, especially the lives of people he didn't even know, was a heavy burden, one he hoped to shrug off after the war.

That's if there was to be a time after the war...

Their mission aside, Vighon knew he was on a collision course with his father. It would be violent - that much he knew - but it would undoubtedly be final. Killing his mother demanded punishment, and the north had only ever served one kind of punishment for murder. The thought of killing his own father didn't bother him, though he wondered if it would haunt him after, when he had to live with it.

Vighon almost laughed to himself. If, and it was an if, he managed to slay his father, he would be swarmed by Namdhorian knights and Ironsworn alike.

Any amusement was washed away when he thought back to his mother's final days. She had suffered, greatly. He decided there and then that he would gladly give his life if it meant bringing her justice.

"Which way, Ranger?"

Vighon fell back into the present and turned to Nemir, Faylen's husband and captain among the elves. He appeared every bit the warrior to the northerner, reminding him of Galanör.

From astride his horse, Asher pointed north-east. "That way. There's no path but I know the route. Follow me."

Elder Celeqor trailed the ranger and Faylen rode behind him. Nemir held back and issued orders to the two elves under his command. Their elvish words were lost on the northerner, though he did enjoy hearing them. Their orders given, the two warriors gestured for Vighon and Ruban to fall in behind Nemir while they followed from the back.

Judging by the size of the mountains, Vighon calculated another few hours on horseback before they reached the base of The Spear. That would give him a few more hours to dwell on the different ways he could bring an end to his father's tyranny. They weren't pleasant thoughts, but they were all he had after killing Godfrey Cross.

As the sun travelled across the sky, slowly moving towards the ash clouds in the west, the party weaved through small valleys, navigated a narrow cliff, and trotted through one small outcropping of forestry after another. The ranger had been right; there was no path this far north. The people of Longdale, the nearest town, had no cause to journey into The Spear, leaving the wilderness untouched.

Having decided that he would confront his father, rather than kill the swine in his sleep, Vighon found himself glancing at Ruban more than once. His conversation with Asher had got under his skin, leading him to a point of curiosity where the squire was concerned.

Clearing his throat, the northerner caught the young man's attention beside him. "Have the dreams started?" he asked.

Ruban overcame the startling question. "What dreams?"

"They're quite common after a battle," Vighon explained. "You close your eyes and everything comes back to you in such clarity that you're sure you're still there, fighting for your life."

Ruban didn't answer but, instead, asked, "Do you have them? These dreams?"

"I would be lying if I said they hadn't woken me up more than once. Orcs coming at me from every angle. A dragon bearing down on me..."

The squire absorbed Vighon's honest reply, perhaps considering his own. "I have dreams like that," he admitted. "That and other dreams... *nightmares* really."

There was something in his tone that told Vighon the ranger had been right about the squire. How had he missed it? There was a weight on his shoulders, hooks in his soul, a burden he couldn't voice. Vighon prided himself on reading people, a technique he had perfected alongside Alijah, yet he had been oblivious to the one person who could double as his shadow.

"The orcs who attacked Namdhor," Vighon began. "They were

your first kills, yes? It's not a bad thing to feel bad about it. It shouldn't be easy to kill anything."

Ruban nodded from within his muddy hood. "Have you ever killed... a *person*?"

Vighon knew he should have expected such a question going down this path, but hearing it posed out loud brought a lump to his throat. There was no answer but yes, of course, though he couldn't recall them all, he was ashamed to say.

"I have killed people," he confessed. "Only ever in self-defence, but I have been present for the murders of others, people who didn't deserve to die. They're the ones that stay with you. In time, the orcs will fade from recent memory and my sleep will be haunted by others."

Ruban listened to every word but he said nothing in reply. Side by side, they journeyed a little deeper into the north, bringing the mountains of The Spear to loom over them. Asher made several stops along the route, his pain evident as he delved into memories that weren't his own. They gave him the time and space he needed to keep them on the right track, his mind their only map.

As they crossed a stretch of flat snow, the party drifted apart, opening up large gaps between those in the front, those in the middle, and the elves bringing up the rear. It was here, where more privacy was gained, that Ruban found the courage to speak.

"I have killed a person," he stated bluntly. "Before the orcs. I... I killed a person."

Vighon was reluctant to say anything, sure that his silence would allow the squire to get this weight off his chest. When Ruban fell silent, however, the northerner had no choice but to offer him another chance to open up.

"Was it self-defence?" he asked evenly, careful to keep any sound of judgment from his tone.

"I killed my uncle," he answered in a small voice. "After my father died, his brother took me and my mother in. In the beginning, every-thing was fine. He was kind to us. Then he wasn't. He lost his job. He started drinking. He would beat my mother for every little thing. She would always make sure he beat her instead of me..."

Vighon had an idea of where this was going but, rather than interrupt, he remained quiet in his saddle and continued alongside the squire.

"One day," Ruban continued, "I broke a plate in the kitchen. My mother stepped in and took the blame. He broke her jaw with one hit. Something in me snapped. While his back was turned, I picked up the carving knife and..." The squire swallowed hard, his gaze equally so. "He didn't get back up."

The northerner did his best to absorb the squire's story as fast as he could. With only a few words, Ruban Dardaris was a different man in Vighon's eyes. He felt sorry for him, yet proud of him at the same time.

"What happened next?"

"We were very lucky. Our neighbour was the master of servants in The Dragon Keep. He knew what my uncle was like; he'd heard it often enough. He helped us dispose of the body, late at night. Told others he had heard my uncle talk of leaving for Wood Vale. He even gave me a job in the keep - told me a squire's job was honourable..."

"He sounds like a good man," Vighon observed.

"He was," Ruban agreed. "He died a few years ago."

"And your mother?" Vighon enquired.

Ruban didn't answer right away, his eyes on the reins in his hands. "She died too. Got the Black Lung - there was nothing anyone could do."

Vighon had watched his mother die, slowly too with the Red Pox. He knew what that was like. The northman would never have believed that they could have such kinship, their personalities so wildly different. Their paths had differed due to the kindness showed to Ruban by the master of servants. Vighon had been taken in by a cruel lot under the thumb of his father.

"Is that why you've been asking questions about Asher? About his resurrection?"

Ruban looked ahead, to the ranger. "I would do anything to bring her back."

Vighon knew the feeling. "There are rules about resurrection," he started, hoping he could remember Galanör's words. "To be brought back as Asher has, you have to have some life left to be given. Does that make sense? If you die of natural causes, like Black Lung, there would be no life to offer except maybe a few seconds. Asher died with years left on his life."

Ruban took a long breath, letting go of any hope that dared to linger. "I see."

Vighon didn't know what to say that might comfort the young man. In his own moments of sadness, his father had been brutal, giving the northerner something far worse to think about than those he had lost. But Vighon wasn't his father.

"When you've been around death long enough, you realise what really matters. *Life*. That's why we're out here, as far north as north goes. We're going to get this weapon, destroy the orcs, and make sure everyone gets to keep living. Because that's all we can do."

It wasn't much, but Ruban looked to have pulled himself up from the depressing pit that threatened to swallow him. "You won't turn me over to the Namdhorian guard?"

Vighon almost laughed. "Did you not hear me? I am not one to judge. And, even if I did, I could hardly judge you for ridding the world of a witless beast no better than an orc. What matters is what we do next." The northerner looked at the squire. "You stick with me, Ruban Dardaris, and together we might just leave our past where it belongs..."

～

THE NARROW CRACK that split the mountain stone offered no insight as to what lay beyond. Vighon narrowed his eyes but there was nothing except darkness there to greet him. It would only allow one person at a time to enter, funnelling the party one behind the other. It was less than inviting.

"Are you sure there's no other way?" he asked the ranger.

Asher finished tying his horse's reins to a nearby tree and joined the northman. "This is it. This is where the Dragon Rider entered."

Vighon sighed. "It's pitch black in there."

Faylen came up on Asher's side. "That shouldn't be a problem for you," she commented, her eyes piercing the ranger's.

"No," Asher replied a little too quickly. "I would rather go by fire light, as the Dragon Rider did. It will make the memories easier to recall."

Faylen didn't look convinced, but the whole exchange was lost on Vighon. "What are you talking about?"

It was clear Asher felt uncomfortable being asked a direct question about himself. "I was an Arakesh, remember?"

Vighon followed that statement to its obvious conclusion. "Oh. Right. You can see in the dark..." He thought about it for a moment longer, his curiosity rising. "Is that really true? I always thought it was just a legend about the Arakesh."

Asher busied himself by removing his bow and quiver, both of which he was apparently leaving behind. "It's true," he answered reluctantly.

Faylen elaborated on his behalf. "They have Nightseye elixir in their veins. They're dosed with it daily from childhood until the effects become permanent. He needs complete darkness, however, for it to work."

"Ah, hence the blindfolds." Vighon remembered the red blindfolds the Galfreys had described in their tales of the war.

"If story time is over," Asher cut in, "perhaps we should get on with saving the world."

Vighon stepped back as the ranger made for the narrow entrance. Nemir and the two warrior elves removed their robes, entering the mountain in their armour alone. Celeqor wore only robes and a belt of pouches, his scimitar hidden within his folds. Faylen opened her hand and birthed a ball of light that quickly escaped her palm and floated into the mountain, pouring white light on the ranger and her kin.

The shadows were stark, making the ground hard to follow for human eyes. "Did you bring any torches?" Vighon asked Ruban.

"No," the squire said apologetically. "Oh! But I did bring this!" Ruban rushed back to his horse and retrieved a small water-skin.

Vighon didn't mind showing the young man how unimpressed he was. "Oh good. At least we won't get thirsty as we trip and fall down a chasm."

Ruban popped the cork and held it out for Vighon to smell. It was foul. The northerner yanked his head back in disgust as his mind required an extra second to place the unique aroma that assaulted his nose.

"You brought dragon spit?"

"Yes," Ruban replied eagerly. "There was half a barrel of it left. Your flaming sword has become quite the talking point among the knights, the people too. I thought it would, you know, come in handy..."

A flaming sword was certainly an orc's worst nightmare on the battlefield, but it also spelled the end of any blade - especially when the fuel was something as potent as dragon's spit.

"It was a good idea," he conceded, "but I really need this sword..." Vighon cut himself off as he considered the sword in question. Then he smiled.

Removing the sword of the north from its scabbard, Vighon poured a neat line of the thick saliva down the length of the blade. Ruban smashed his flint together and cast a handful of sparks onto the sword, setting it alight from end to end.

"There's nothing stronger than silvyr!" Vighon declared, holding the sword out. Though, now that he really thought about it, he had never witnessed a dragon try and melt silvyr before...

Putting his doubt aside, Vighon bade Ruban to follow him into the mountain, behind the ranger and the elves. The fire of his sword lit the way perfectly, though he had to maintain some distance between himself and the elves.

The party followed Asher into the depths of The Spear just as they had followed him from the banks of the Adanae. Stops were required along the way to give him time to consider their route, as they were offered more than one path here and there.

Beyond the light of the orb and Vighon's sword, The Spear provided nothing but featureless abyss. The northerner was sure to keep his sword held low after they had navigated a very narrow ledge not long after entering the mountains. Wherever he could, Vighon would take a moment to look at the ranger, concerned for his fractured state of self. He often caught Asher rubbing his temples or pinching his nose as he chose their next turn.

At one intersection, Nemir pushed up to Asher. "How close are we, Ranger?"

It was clear to see that Asher was debating their next step. They were presented with a flat path, straight ahead, that would lead into a hollow, as well as a narrow path to the right that climbed up the face of the cavern. To their left, beyond the narrow incline, was a great nothingness, a ravine of black that could fit a hundred dragons inside.

With no reply, Faylen came up on the other side. "Asher? Do you know where we are?"

Frustrated, the ranger walked towards the flat path ahead rather than speak. But then he stopped and looked to the narrow incline on his right. It was an odd sight to see him hesitate.

"These memories…" he said, pushing a palm into his eyebrow. "They belonged to a man who passed them onto his dragon, who then passed them onto Malliath who had no choice but to share them with me. Some of it is a little distorted."

Nemir took a jab at the ranger. "This entire mission relies on your ability to navigate these caverns."

Faylen raised her hand, preventing her husband from continuing his verbal assault. It was obvious there was something more going on between the three of them. Vighon could easily guess, what with there being one woman and two men in the triangle, though he couldn't recall any tale of romance between the two from the Galfreys' stories. Perhaps it was a part of the tale they believed to be private.

Asher gestured to the path straight ahead. "That way leads directly to Haren Bain," he told them.

"Then that is our way," Nemir concluded, making to move.

"But the Dragon Rider deliberately avoided going that way," Asher continued, halting Nemir in his tracks.

"Why did he avoid it?" Faylen asked.

"I don't know," Asher confessed. "I only know that he spent days down here seeking another route inside."

"Perhaps that way is guarded," Celeqor posed.

Asher nodded in agreement. "The Dragon Rider went this way instead."

Following the ranger, the party advanced up the narrow incline, careful not to fall over the edge and drop into a ravine that had no visible bottom. At the top, they journeyed along the only path available to them and explored the short network of tunnels that promised them a way inside Haren Bain.

At the front of the group now, beside Asher, Vighon was the first to see the wall of rock that stood in their way. He ran his flaming sword across the compacted boulders and wondered how many thousands of years they had blocked the way.

"I take it this isn't supposed to be here," he commented.

Asher reached out and touched one of the rocks. "The way is clear in Malliath's memories."

"That was millennia ago," Nemir pointed out.

"Can we move the rocks?" Ruban suggested.

"We don't know what caused the collapse in the first place," Asher replied, examining the ceiling. "If we disturb the rocks, we might cause a bigger cave-in."

Faylen stepped away from the group and looked back the way they had come. "Then there remains but one path..."

Vighon looked at Asher, who still couldn't define the reason that particular path had been avoided. Faylen, however, was correct in her assessment. The party reversed their direction and made their way back to the flat path, unsure of what they would find.

That route took them through a winding tunnel that opened up into a cavern that disappeared above and below, their only route across a man-made bridge that led to a circular platform. On the other side of the cavern, attached to the platform, stood a pair of foreboding doors, their size easily accommodating a mountain giant.

Though the eye was immediately drawn to the iron doors, it was only a second later that Vighon looked upon the most curious, and haunting, sight before them. Standing in the middle of the platform, unnervingly still, was a figure shrouded in tattered black robes and a shadowy hood.

Vighon had a bad feeling. "That'll be the guard then..."

CHAPTER 30
LIGHT FROM THE EAST

Gideon held Alastir's hand as he faded back into unconsciousness. His journey north, alongside Ayana and Deartanyon, had been taxing, his injuries still severe. As the Dragorn closed his eyes, so too did Valkor outside the elven tent.

Content to let them both rest, Gideon left Alastir in the care of the elves. It had been crushing to tell his old friend of Arathor's death and that of Thraden. The only light for Gideon had been in greeting Alastir and Valkor again and knowing that they would pull through.

Ilargo's voice rang clear in the Master Dragorn's mind, his tone grave. *Gideon, I feel we are about to be threatened...*

Searching their bond, Gideon knew exactly what his companion was talking about. Exasperated, the Master Dragorn bowed to the elves and left Alastir's tent with Ayana by his side. It was cold outside, though the elven camp had the look of spring about it, causing Gideon's senses to clash.

Together, the Dragorn weaved between the tents and flowers and found their way to the north, where the sprawling camp was laid across The White Vale. It was a noisy and busy place, pulling one's attention in many directions, but right now there was only one thing that drew Gideon's gaze.

Namdhorian riders.

There must have been nearly a hundred of them circumnavigating the camp and making their way towards the elves. The riders were led by none other than Arlon Draqaro, Namdhor's would-be king. Riding beside him, on a considerably larger horse, was Sir Borin the Dread.

Gideon let his eyes wander north, where a wall of dragon fire still blazed. The catapults simply didn't exist anymore. Of course, the army could march around the fiery wall, but they were apparently hesitant to test Ilargo.

Meeting the riders by the edge of the elven camp, Gideon kept his hands by his sides, deliberately leaving Mournblade to hang from his belt. He didn't want to spark violence now, not so close to the camp and especially on the edge of another battle. Though these riders were bound by their duty and oaths to the crown, they were all soldiers, men of Namdhor - each and every one of them needed.

As Arlon brought his horse around to face the Dragorn, the riders began to fill the space between the elven camp and the refugees, concealing their meeting from prying eyes. It could mean anything in truth, though Gideon wondered if he was about to be charged and arrested.

"The fate of this realm teeters on the edge of destruction." Arlon's tone was calm, as if he was telling a story. "We have but few weapons we can use against the orcs, weapons that save lives. You yourself are one of those weapons, Master Thorn." Then his tone took a dive. "So were the catapults you burned. The supplies were needed too, in case you were wondering. Then there's the displacement of the ranks, as now my army has to navigate a wall of fire."

"All necessary, I'm afraid." Gideon didn't offer the future king of Namdhor a hint of remorse.

"Necessary?" Arlon echoed mockingly. "You have attacked Namdhor, nay the realm itself!"

"I attacked no one," Gideon corrected. "By keeping the army where it is, they get to live and fight in the real battle."

Arlon looked down at him as if he had gone mad. "The real battle? The real battle won't begin until we march on the mountains and engage the orcs!"

"You believe the orcs have retreated to lick their wounds, that they hide in Vengora, afraid of man's army. But they do not. As we speak, they are tunnelling under this very ground. The orcs aren't finished with Illian yet. The real battle will begin when they return to finish what they started..."

Arlon curled his lip in disgust. "You would spread fear because of your cowardice," he accused.

Ayana puffed out her chest, ready to lambast the would-be king for such an insult, but Gideon calmly gripped her wrist, keeping the elf's anger in check.

"Your order has been decimated," Arlon continued his tirade. "Your defeats weigh upon you, infecting your decisions now. You bring your doubt and fears to my strategy and they are unwelcome I say! You would have us do nothing, as if our enemy isn't a stone's throw from Namdhor, weak after our victory." Arlon straightened his back. "Your counsel is no longer required in The Dragon Keep. For your crimes against the realm and your insult to the crown, I am charging you with treason. Arrest him."

Gideon glanced at the knights behind Arlon, every one of them tense and equally uncertain about their ruler's judgment. That fact also became abundantly clear to the would-be king when none of the soldiers stepped forward to arrest Gideon. Their fear of acting against the Master Dragorn was compounded when Lady Ellöria appeared with a hundred elves at her back, each armed with a bow and a nocked arrow.

Arlon clenched his jaw, battling with his pride no doubt. "Sir Borin," he said unevenly, "arrest this man."

The giant bodyguard climbed down from his horse without a moment's pause, a slave to his orders. A row of arrows were pointed at the giant but still he advanced on Gideon. The Master Dragorn would have removed Mournblade at this point, but he knew what was about to happen.

As Sir Borin came towards him, Ilargo rose to his full height, bringing his head and shoulders over the top of the elven camp. He snorted black smoke, his sapphire eyes focused on Sir Borin like a predator that had caught sight of its prey. Then, Deartanyon stood up on the other side of the camp and stretched his mighty jaws, exposing his lethal fangs.

Proving that Sir Borin was incapable of thinking like a man, he continued towards Gideon without hesitation. The threat of dragons, however, was not lost on Arlon Draqaro.

"Stop!" he barked, halting Sir Borin only feet away from Gideon.

Nobody spoke, giving Arlon the time he needed to reconsider. He stared hard at Gideon and the Master Dragorn could see the wrath behind his eyes. That rage could only build in the shadow of two dragons until, with no outlet, he had no choice but to calm down and think clearly. Of course, what he was really trying to do was save face - something Gideon wasn't going to let him do.

"In hindsight," he began, "imprisoning an immortal being would prove to be most taxing. It is to be exile then..." he added with a glint in his eye. "From this day hence, the Dragorn are not welcome—"

"No," Gideon said loudly and rather bluntly. "You will not be the one to make that decision. Whether you like it or not, having two dragons in this fight will tip the scales in Namdhor's favour. Your strategy was foolish, but to dismiss our aid now would be a death sentence for everyone, and I won't let you make that choice for the people. They deserve better..."

"You would place yourself above the laws of man?" he posed, a trap set within his words.

Gideon was wary of that trap, aware that the wrong response could name all Dragorn as outlaws. "I am placing myself exactly where I need to be to ensure that man is still around to have any laws..."

Again, that rage was visibly building in Arlon, a man who was unaccustomed to being addressed in such a way. Ilargo and Deartanyon were too powerful to be denied, however, swaying the would-be king to better judgement.

"We will discuss the state of this relationship after the orcs are defeated then. Until that discussion, I don't want to see you in The Dragon Keep. You are to assist in the battle and nothing more."

Desiring the last word, Arlon beckoned Sir Borin and turned his horse around. The company of knights dutifully trailed behind their mad ruler with a few even offering Gideon a nod of respect. They were proof that you didn't need to be a general to know suicidal orders when you heard them.

Gideon faced the elves behind him. "Thank you for your support, Lady Ellöria."

"The Dragorn will always have the support of the woodland folk, Master Thorn." The Lady of Ilythyra paused as another elf dipped into her ear to pass on a message. She smiled and looked at Gideon. "Reinforcements..."

Gideon happily followed Lady Ellöria to the other side of her camp, where they could look out on the eastern plains of The White Vale. It was there that they were greeted by four hundred elves in full battle armour, all lined up in perfect rows. Their appearance on the vale drew the attention of the larger camp and soon there were at least a thousand people standing by the edge, watching the elves' arrival.

"They aren't many when you consider the thousands of orcs we yet face," Ayana said in her melodic voice, "but every elf counts for five men on the battlefield and their magic makes each of them invaluable."

Gideon certainly agreed. "Along with the dragons they might just be enough to put a dent in the orcs, a dent the men of Namdhor could use to claim victory."

Lady Ellöria kept her eyes on the approaching warriors. "I would see the orcs dealt more than just a dent. The true power of elves lies in our magic, something the orcs cannot match."

Gideon turned to the Lady of Ilythyra. "What would you have them do?"

Ellöria looked up, her emerald eyes taking in the thick clouds of ash that rolled overhead. "I would have them bring light back to the world..."

CHAPTER 31
FATE-BOUND

With only a handful of chambers to search, it didn't take Inara and her parents very long to discover that Alijah was gone. The small number of rooms aside, it didn't stop the Dragorn from investigating every one of them for a second time.

Their desperate search ultimately brought them to the edge of the cave entrance, where The Adean awaited all who couldn't fly. Athis had already flown around the island and nearby cliffs, checking the rocks for any sign of Alijah's body.

"He has to have jumped," Nathaniel reasoned.

"And go where?" Inara asked the obvious question.

Reyna crouched down, her elven eyes scouring the waves below. "He grew up by the sea; he was always a good swimmer."

Inara turned away to hide her shaking head. Only a mother could say something so ridiculous. They all knew that The Lifeless Isles were too far away from The Shining Coast of Illian for anyone to swim. The surrounding islands that made up the archipelago were occupied by the young Dragorn who survived Malliath's attack, all of whom would notify her if they came across Alijah.

"What about Dragorn?" Nathaniel suggested. "The island, I mean. Could he have made it that far without a boat?"

"Possibly," Reyna replied, standing up. "They have a dense population though. Finding him there could prove more difficult than locating The Bastion."

Inara heard her parents' discussion, but her mind had begun to wander down another path, her father's words carrying more meaning than he knew. "A boat," she said absently.

Nathaniel looked out to sea then back at his daughter. "A boat?" he repeated incredulously. "You think he might have found a boat?"

"This wasn't his first visit to The Lifeless Isles," Inara explained, her mind working through her brother's most likely actions. "He might have known that we keep several boats, not far from here actually."

"Why would Dragorn have need of boats?" he asked, doubting her entire line of thinking.

"Fishing, transporting supplies from the mainland... It doesn't matter why. If he reached one of them his destination could be much farther than we think."

"Why would he leave?" Reyna had asked that question many times since waking to find her son missing.

Inara wondered if she had the answer. "Malliath... He's gone to find Malliath."

"What makes you so sure?" Her mother had the look of a desperate woman again, her worries returning tenfold.

"Because it's what I would do," Inara answered. "His bond with Malliath will be all-consuming; it always is in the beginning. You can feel their power. It draws you in so completely."

"Let's assume you're right," Nathaniel said. "Where would he go to find Malliath? No one has seen him since the battle at Namdhor."

Athis began to turn back from his patrol. *At The Bastion, Alijah protested at being brought here, but then he agreed willingly as if he wanted to be here. Why would he want to come all this way to then jump into the sea?*

Inara relived the memory of the conversation, on the steps of The Bastion. Athis was right; Alijah had gone from protesting to agreeing in the space of a few heart beats. And, only moments before that, he had been trying to commune with Malliath.

"He came with us because he knew Malliath was close by," Inara said for the benefit of her parents. "He was just using us to travel east."

There was a flicker of disappointment on the faces of both her parents, though her mother recovered faster. "Where would Malliath be, this close to The Lifeless Isles?"

"He wouldn't come anywhere near here," Nathaniel opined. "Not after his attack on the order."

"I think you're right," Inara concurred. "But he must be close enough that Alijah thought he could reach it from The Lifeless Isles."

Across their bond, Inara felt Athis look to the north, his dragon eyes taking in the islands and the larger Dragorn beyond them.

What is it? she asked him, sensing his intrigue.

There is only one place close to The Lifeless Isles that has ever been associated with Malliath the voiceless...

Inara had a look of revelation about her. "Korkanath!" she exclaimed. Seeing doubt reflected in her parents, the Dragorn explained, "It's the only place near here that Malliath might feel... I don't know, some kind of connection to."

Her father sighed, his frustration mounting. "He was enthralled to that island for a thousand years, Inara. He's also the one who burnt the school to the ground. Why would he ever return?"

Inara never thought she would feel pity for the black dragon, but the answer to her father's question could lead her to no other emotion. "Because he has nowhere else to go."

"Neither do we," Reyna added. "Alijah has a head start and Korkanath is as good a place as any to begin looking for him."

Inara looked up from the cave entrance. *Athis, come and get us.*

Nathaniel held up a hand. "*Should* we be looking for him?"

Inara would never have believed such a question could come from her father. "Why wouldn't we?" she countered.

"He's bonded with Malliath," Nathaniel stated factually. "*Shouldn't* they be left alone? Being at Malliath's side is probably the safest place in all of Verda."

"You're forgetting the part where he jumped into the ocean," Inara pointed out. "We have no idea if he's even found Malliath. He could be adrift in The Adean right now."

The cave entrance was battered by a powerful gust of wind as Athis came in to land. His sharp claws dug into the ground where so many of his ancestors had done so centuries past. A dragon's entrance was always enough to stop any conversation, the mind incapable of doing anything except marvelling at their beauty. That made Reyna's distant gaze all the more obvious.

"Mother?" Inara reached out and touched Reyna's shoulder.

Her eyes still fixed on the lapping waves below, she said, "What if we lose him to Malliath? Just as Asher warned..."

Nathaniel joined them, resting a loving hand on her other shoulder. "Asher had been to hell and back when last we spoke to him. His mind needs time to adjust. I don't think we can take everything he said literally."

As soothing as his words were, Inara could hear the doubt in his tone, though, stubborn as he was, her father would never admit that.

Reyna turned to face her husband, freeing herself of their loving touch. "Did you ever know Asher to exaggerate about anything? Our son is bonded with a dragon that no one really knows; even our oldest texts from history refer to Malliath as a shadow."

"Do you want to go to him?" Inara asked.

"I want to see him," Reyna replied. "I will know my son when I see him."

Inara couldn't argue with that. "Then we fly to Korkanath."

〜

429

BREAKING AWAY from The Lifeless Isles and Dragorn, the horizon became shrouded by a storm sweeping in from Ayda. Heavy rain pelted Korkanath and thunder roared overhead as the dark clouds spat lightning across the sky.

Athis flew low, over the tumultuous waves of The Adean, as he glided towards the rocky beach. Inara used magic to shield both herself and her parents from the sting of the lashing rain. At these speeds, those droplets of water could feel like needles cutting into the skin.

The dragon touched down on the shore and brought his wings in. The rain made it hard to discern details from the bulk of the island and the wind roared in their ears.

"Let's split up!" Inara suggested. "I'll go east, you go west!"

Her parents agreed and the trio jumped down from Athis's back, their chosen paths taking them in opposite directions.

Stay close, Athis. The Crow's spell might be broken, but I still don't trust Malliath to stay calm.

I will always be close, wingless one.

With her eternal companion returning to the sky, Inara pressed on, taking the eastern route around the island. An uneven path and sharp rocks made her journey slow, but the young Dragorn eventually came across a cave burrowed into the side of the island. It was just large enough for a dragon of Malliath's size to walk through. Also, strewn across the rocks, lay the skeletal remains of a whale, its bones gnawed and, in some cases, snapped like twigs.

Athis was quick to come down and join Inara outside the cave. *I can smell both of them,* the dragon claimed.

It might be better if you stay out here, Inara advised. *We don't know what state of mind Malliath might be in and seeing another dragon, especially one of your size, could make him feel threatened.*

You told me to stay close, Athis protested, his claws sinking into the mud beneath the rocks.

And you will be, Inara reassured. *If anything happens I'm skilled enough to stay alive until you can... assist me.*

Athis arched his head and looked down on his companion. *Assist you? If Malliath takes offence, you will need more than assistance to survive his wrath.*

Inara held up her hands. ***I just need to speak with Alijah...***

Drenched by the rain, the Dragorn left Athis outside and entered the cave with one hand resting on her Vi'tari blade. Her eyes took some time to adjust, but the general shape of the cavern was illuminated by a single crack in the top right corner. The light was poor, but it was just enough for Inara to make out Malliath's unmistakable bulk and Alijah standing in front of him.

Malliath's head snapped up and he locked his purple eyes on her. That stare was enough to root her to the spot and tighten her grip on the hilt. He was unpredictable at best, and savagely violent at his worst.

"Inara?" Alijah stepped away from Malliath's shadowy form. "I can't believe you found me."

Despite her brother's call, Inara continued her cautious approach. "Don't you remember? I could always find you."

Alijah managed half a smile, but at least that half appeared genuine. "That you could," he conceded. "Those memories don't seem like mine anymore."

Inara was so close to him now that she could see his face in detail. "Well, at least you shaved. That beard was awful..."

Alijah stroked his smooth jaw, though her attempt at humour was lost on him. "Did you bring our parents?" he asked, changing the subject.

"Yes. They're on the island, looking for you." Inara kept one eye on the dragon towering over her.

"Are they worried?" Alijah's question came with an indifferent tone, making it hard to figure out if he really cared about the answer.

"Of course they are!" Inara replied harshly. "You realise that disappearing in the middle of the night, without a word, is exactly what you did four years ago. Why would you leave without telling us?"

Alijah looked into the dark of the cavern, his thoughts his own. "I had to reach Malliath on my own."

Inara took a breath and calmed herself down. "Why on your own?"

Alijah heard the question but he responded with nothing but an empty stare. Again, Inara scrutinised her brother and found she was unable to read him.

"You don't have to do anything on your own," she told him. "We're your family. We're here for you."

There was a time, not so long ago, that such a comment would have sparked an argument between the siblings. Alijah's emotions often ruled his judgement and he was nothing if not vociferous about how he had been left behind by his family. Standing before her now, however, was a man of calm demeanour, his thoughts collected if not shared.

"I appreciate the sentiment, Inara, I really do. But I have Malliath now. You know well of the bond that exists between our kind and theirs. After you joined the Dragorn, how many times did we see each other in the first few years? I couldn't count on one hand."

Inara glanced at the dragon above her. "That was different. I had training to complete. Your bond with Malliath is... *different*." Malliath remained eerily still as he stood over them.

"*That* we can agree on," Alijah said. "Malliath and I need time, time to understand our bond. Unlike Athis or even Ilargo, he is old, ancient in fact."

"That's exactly why you need us right now," Inara insisted. "No one has ever bonded with a dragon so old. We don't know what... effects it might have on your mind."

Alijah began pacing. "I see your lips moving and hear your voice in my ear, but I know your words to be those of Asher's." Her brother tapped his temple. "There are still parts of his mind in here. I know his fears, fears he's shared with all of you it seems."

Inara swallowed hard and steadied her breath. Malliath had

quietly curled his tail around, blocking the way between her and the cave entrance.

"Even now you fear him," Alijah commented. "Do you fear me, Sister?"

Inara tore her eyes from Malliath and looked her brother in the eyes. "No." Upon reflection though, she wasn't sure she believed herself.

The light from the cave entrance was blocked as Athis slowly entered the cavern, his red scales just as dark as Malliath's now. The black dragon regarded Athis for no more than a second before looking back down at Alijah.

"Tell Athis to stop trying to communicate with him," her brother warned. "Malliath will speak through me."

I thought you were staying outside?

And now I am not, Athis simply replied.

Let's stay out of his head for now, Inara advised.

The Dragorn turned back to her brother. "He's called the voiceless one for a reason, I suppose."

Malliath huffed and adjusted his body to bring him face to face with Athis. "That's not a name he gave himself," Alijah commented quietly. "But, all the same, he has no interest in speaking to anyone but me."

Inara wasn't going to push the larger dragon. "That's fair enough. So... Does this make us all friends? You are wearing the garb of a Dragorn, after all."

Alijah looked down at his borrowed attire and straightened his jacket. "Is that what I am now? A Dragorn?"

Inara frowned, seeing that there was only one answer. "Of course you are. And," she added with a beaming smile, "you're immortal now. We get to fly side by side forever. Just like we always dreamed of."

Alijah guarded his expression. "That's what *I* dreamed of." He looked past her, to Athis. "*You* found a different dream, one that didn't include me..."

"That's not fair," Inara protested. "How many times will we go round with this? If Malliath had been there that day we both would have been bonded. We don't get to choose our fate."

Her last words caught Alijah. "Fate... You're right, of course, we don't get to choose it. But we can accept it. We can embrace that which was thrust upon us."

Inara tilted her head, her heart breaking. "Now it is I who can hear the words of another. The Crow doesn't get to say what you will do or how you should do it. Your decisions build your future, your choices your own. I don't care what he wrote ten thousand years ago and I don't care what he thinks he saw. You're my brother - I *know* you."

Inara rushed forward and clapped her hands around his smooth cheeks. Malliath growled and lowered his head threateningly, his actions provoking Athis to lurch forward and bare his fangs. Alijah, however, remained perfectly calm in his sister's embrace, his blue eyes falling into hers.

"I know you, Alijah. You're strong, even stronger now," she added, glancing at Malliath. "I know The Crow has wormed his way inside your head, but I also know you won't give in to his schemes. There's always been a great love in your heart. Love for me, for our parents, for Vighon, even Hadavad. You've only ever wanted to serve the realm, to protect it as our parents did before us."

Alijah used his thumb to wipe a single tear from Inara's cheek before pressing his hands into hers. "You are right. That's all I've ever wanted to do. And, for all The Crow's misdeeds and cruel nature, he has given me the tools to protect this realm."

Inara pulled her hands away and stepped back, her worst fears born before her. She looked up at Malliath, though the dragon's thoughts were even more guarded than her brother's. She couldn't believe that Malliath would allow The Crow's twisted teachings to guide Alijah, not when he had been a victim himself.

Alijah took a step towards her, a predator stalking towards its prey. "Father tells me that *Arlon Draqaro* is set to be the king of Namdhor, perhaps all of Illian."

Inara subconsciously stepped backward again and nodded absently. "He is."

"And the Dragorn will allow this?"

"We have no say in who wears the crown," Inara replied. "That is not our role."

"Do you know what Vighon suffered under that man? What others have suffered? How can the Dragorn stand by and let this happen?"

Inara shook her head, her brother's words increasingly alarming. "We're not letting anything *happen*, Alijah. We're at war right now. The orcs will attack again soon; *that* is our priority."

Alijah took a breath and let his eyes roam over his dark companion. "You're right; one problem at a time. Malliath will give the orcs a reason to stay underground."

Inara stood motionless, watching her brother with great intensity. "Would you do it?" she asked softly, fearful of his answer.

Understanding the truth of her question, Alijah held a moment's consideration - or at least the appearance of one. "Shouldn't I?" he replied cryptically. "Surely anyone would make a better king than Arlon Draqaro. Why not me?"

Inara swallowed the lump that formed in her throat. "Because you don't belong on the throne. We're too powerful to hold sway over the realm. That aside, consider who wants you on the throne, Brother. The Crow is not to be trusted."

"You know nothing of what you speak!" Alijah spat, his emotions emerging for the first time. "Are his methods cruel? Yes. Is the order he created unnatural? Yes. But they're all means to an end, an end that will bring about peace for all time."

"Get a hold of yourself!" Inara pleaded. "I mean your true self! The Alijah I know, the Alijah I love! Do not allow The Crow to dictate your actions nor his teachings spout words from your mouth. Be who you were meant to be: a *Dragorn*!"

435

Again, the Alijah she knew would have returned his argument with venom, the pair more than capable of arguing for hours. But any emotion that had threatened to take control of him died away, leaving him calm and collected once more. It was infuriating.

"The truth is," he began delicately, "I don't know who I am yet. I know I'm not the man you knew. I think he died in The Bastion."

Inara couldn't help the tears that streaked down her face. "Don't say that," she begged.

Alijah looked pained by her grief and he stepped close enough to put a hand on her cheek. "Whatever I am to be, I promise it will be a man you can be proud of, a brother you can love..."

Malliath relaxed and lowered his head to the ground. It was enough to make Athis withdraw his fangs from view, but Inara could still feel his anxiety.

Alijah stepped back again, though as his hand slipped from her face, Inara noticed the cuts and scars on his knuckles and fingers. They were just another reminder that he was broken in more ways than one, though Inara was helpless to think of a way to retrieve the brother she dearly missed.

"What *is* that?" Alijah said aloud, his curiosity breaking Inara's reverie.

Following her brother's gaze, she found the source of his question on a rocky outcrop not far from where they were standing. A flash of lightning caught the object with a glimmer of brilliant jade.

Athis's sight pierced the gloom and he reported, *It is a sword...*

A sword? In here?

Inara lifted her hand and cast an orb of pure light to meet the shadows. Malliath swivelled his head to protect his purple eyes from the startling light, prompting Inara to guide the orb towards the curious sword.

Alijah was faster, as always, and climbed the rocks to reach the sword first. He appeared entirely taken in by the sight of it, his eyes reflecting the jade of the steel. Inara circled around the weapon, intrigued by the way it had been plunged into the rock.

"No ordinary steel could do such a thing," she remarked.

The corner of Alijah's mouth tugged at a smile. "This sword is not ordinary," he concluded.

Crouching down, her brother ran a finger up the length of exposed blade, admiring the green colour. Inara examined the black hilt, decorated with hints of gold. She didn't like the look of it.

"Why would a sword of such fine a make be under the stone of Korkanath?"

Alijah shrugged and glanced at his companion. "Malliath doesn't recall seeing it in here."

"Then perhaps we should leave it here," Inara suggested, listening to her gut.

Her brother had other ideas. In one smooth motion, he pulled the sword free of the rock, revealing its true shape and size. Inara had seen a blade just like it, in fact an almost identical sword was currently on her hip, a claim that every Dragorn could state, including the legendary Mournblade.

"It's an elven scimitar," Alijah marvelled. He rolled his wrist and got a feel for its weight. "It's exquisite."

Inara scanned every inch of it in his hands. "It can't be..."

Alijah ceased his adoration. "It can't be what?"

Inara removed her own scimitar from her belt and held it out in front of her. Tentatively, she knocked her blade against Alijah's and witnessed a spark of multi-coloured light. Alijah held the sword at bay, confused by the flash. Inara struck the jade sword two more times, each with a little more force, and again the blades came together in a flash of multi-coloured sparks.

"What does this mean?" Alijah asked.

"It means you're holding a Vi'tari blade," she answered in disbelief.

Inara... Athis drew her attention back to him. *The sword reacted to your strikes,* he told her with serious intonation.

Inara turned back to her brother. "Impossible," she stated, wondering if she had missed the blade's reaction.

"What is it?" Alijah asked.

Inara responded with action, lashing out at Alijah with her scimitar. Three successive attacks from three different angles and Alijah deflected them all - or at least the blade did.

Her brother raised his hand in Malliath's direction, halting the dragon from lunging at either Inara or Athis. Judging by the lift in his tail, Malliath had been a heartbeat away from pouncing on one of them.

"What did you do that for?" Alijah demanded.

"I needed to see what the blade would do," Inara explained. "Did that feel like you? Did you feel in control of your actions?"

Alijah couldn't answer straight away. "Attack me again," he requested.

Inara assumed the stance of form three of the Mag'dereth and locked her eyes against her brother's, giving nothing away of her intended attack. A product of her training, the Dragorn dashed left and right before coming down on Alijah. He parried the heavy strike but she was ready with three follow-up attacks that no ordinary warrior could stand up to.

Alijah deflected, parried, and evaded every one of them. Every time their swords clashed, a flash of brilliant colour exploded from the steel of their blades.

"How did that feel?" she asked him.

"Some of it felt like me but... I could feel the sword guiding me."

Inara sheathed her weapon and held a brief consultation with Athis. The verdict wasn't positive.

"It isn't supposed to work like that," she said. "Besides the fact that there's even a Vi'tari blade in this cave, the enchantments placed upon them are unique to the wielder."

"Unique?" Alijah questioned.

"If you were to use my sword, it wouldn't guide your actions or absorb your will. It would just be as ordinary as any other sword. But, in my hands, the enchantment comes alive. That Vi'tari blade in your hands, it's—"

"Cursed!" came a call from beside Athis.

Reyna and Nathaniel stepped into the light of Inara's orb. They both looked like they had gone for a swim in The Adean. Their father kept looking at Malliath, who lay not far from Athis. He was likely feeling the same unease that Inara experienced in the black dragon's presence. Their mother, however, was captured by the green blade in her son's hand.

"That sword is cursed," she told them. "It should not be wielded by anyone."

Alijah descended to meet his parents and Inara followed, noting the sword still in his grip.

"You know of this sword?" he asked his mother.

"That's the first thing you say?" Nathaniel shot at him. "Do you have any idea how——" Reyna pressed a hand into his chest and calmed her husband before he could go on.

"Yes," she replied, "I do know of that sword. It once belonged to a Dragorn, one who opposed Valanis during The Dark War, a thousand years past. After slaying the Dragorn, Valanis took the blade and twisted the enchantment placed upon it. Using dark magic, he changed the enchantment, so that it might be wielded by any. Though, he did not gift it to just any. Valanis gave that blade to Thallan Tassariön, his general and trusted disciple."

That name triggered a memory for Inara. "Thallan? Didn't Gideon kill him at the end of the war?"

"Yes, he did. During The Battle for Velia, using Thallan's own sword against him no less."

Alijah hefted the jade weapon. "Then why is it down here?"

Reyna spared an extra moment to inspect her son. "Gideon didn't know how to destroy the blade, so he hid it. He hid it for a reason, Alijah..."

"Why? Because it can be used by anyone?"

"Exactly," Nathaniel answered. "Vi'tari blades shouldn't be wielded by just anyone; they were gifted to the Dragorn for a reason. Besides, it belonged to a maniac, who received it from a bigger maniac. Who knows how many innocent lives that thing's taken?"

Alijah clearly wasn't in a mood to give it up. "It's a powerful tool, but a tool all the same. The weapon shouldn't be judged because the wielder used it for wrong."

Reyna narrowed her eyes at her son. "It wasn't used for wrong, Alijah. It was used *by* evil for the *purpose* of evil - nothing more. It is a wicked weapon..."

"Perhaps it should be given a second chance," Alijah whispered, mostly to himself.

Inara stepped in front of her brother, drawing his eye from the blade. "You will have the opportunity to forge your own Vi'tari sword. All Dragorn make their own."

"And the secret to forging a blade as magnificent as this... it lies with the order alone?"

Inara didn't like the way he posed that particular question. "It does. We cannot allow just anyone to know of our forging techniques nor the magic we——."

"I think I'll keep it," Alijah announced over her. "After all, there is a war to fight and I can't see me finding time to forge an entire blade."

"There is no war for you to fight," Reyna insisted. As she stepped closer to her son, her eyes naturally flickered from Malliath to Alijah.

"Your mother's right," Nathaniel added. "You've already been through so much. You and... Malliath should take time to rest. On The Lifeless Isles we can——"

"I'm not going back there," Alijah cut in. "And neither is Malliath. The Crow started this war and he intended for me to finish it; so that's exactly what I'm going to do."

"At what cost?" Reyna pointedly asked. "We should avoid playing into his hands, Alijah. As you said; *he* started this war. A mind as twisted and broken as that should not be trusted."

Alijah didn't back down, his confidence resonating like never before. "The Crow will get what he deserves for his part in all of this.

Even he cannot deny the end that is coming for him. Before he meets such an end, however, we cannot ignore the plight of the north. The orcs need dealing with," Alijah looked closely at his new blade, "and I intend to *deal* with them."

Their mother dared to put herself between Alijah and Malliath. "You shouldn't go. And you definitely shouldn't go with that sword. It's a simple choice. Come with us to The Lifeless Isles and The Crow's plan means nothing, your fate your own again. But if you go north, you will be walking a path chosen for you by another. Come with us," she pleaded, taking his hand in her own. "We can do this together."

Alijah offered his mother a broad smile that didn't reach his eyes. "We are together! Can you not imagine the orcs' faces when they see the Galfreys riding into war?" He reclaimed his hand and walked past her to join Malliath. "We're flying to Namdhor. With or without you..."

Athis looked down at Inara. *You will not let him face the orcs alone. I see but one path before us.*

Inara agreed with extreme reluctance. "We go north..."

CHAPTER 32
HAREN BAIN

After decades of fighting, for both good and evil, Asher had developed an acute sense for assessing levels of threat. He knew a fight he could win when he saw it, just as he knew a fight he could lose if he was foolish enough to enter into it. Looking at the figure standing guard before the doors of Haren Bain, shrouded in a dusty black cloak, the ranger found himself struggling to gauge the level of threat it posed.

The mysterious figure stood perfectly still in the centre of the island-like platform. With its head down, there was no guessing at what was actually guarding the entrance.

"It can't be human," Vighon whispered. "It's been down here for thousands of years."

Asher agreed with the obvious statement. "Why don't you go and introduce yourself. We'll be right behind you..."

The northman rose to Asher's sarcastic challenge. "Maybe I will." As he started forward, Nemir put a strong hand on his chest and kept him where he stood.

"Do not be foolish," the elf warned. "We approach together and surround it. Should it threaten us, we kill it."

442

Asher had been hunting a variety of monsters for a long time and knew well that numbers didn't always count when the time came for slaying. Still, he was among elves and warriors all. Their presence would likely tip the scales in the party's favour.

One of the two elven warriors led the way, stepping onto the bridge first. In response, the torches that lined the bridge and the circular platform beyond came to life with light and flame. Simultaneously, Faylen's orb winked out of existence and the shrouded figure lifted its head.

As they spread out across the platform, the lone sentinel shrugged its dark cloak over the back of its pale shoulders. Asher had seen all manner of beast and monster in his time, but he had never seen a creature such as this. Shaped like a man, its skin was chalk-white, hairless, and as smooth as silk. A ragged loincloth was its only attire besides its cloak and hood, though it possessed two sword belts around its waist, each holding a pair of blades on the creature's hips.

Those four swords were not surplus to requirement, as the sentinel also had four strong arms. Its long torso was a display of muscles, including extra ones humans and elves couldn't claim. Dark and jagged nails protruded from its fingers and toes, a contrast to its smooth white skin.

Asher wasn't the last to cross the bridge, but he stopped directly in front of the sentinel. It looked back at him with completely white eyes, both devoid of detail. Judging by its mouth, which had been sewn shut, Haren Bain's guard wasn't made for bartering words.

The ranger gripped the hilt of his broadsword and the sentinel mimicked him, taking a hold of all four blades on its hips. This set the elves off, including Faylen, who quickly removed their fine scimitars and fell into battle stances. The sentinel flexed all four of its arms and brandished a sword in each hand.

Asher kept his sword in its scabbard, seeing a much faster solution. "Just use magic," he told Faylen. "Throw it into the abyss."

Faylen reached out, seeking to grip the sentinel in a spell.

Nothing happened. Nemir tried a spell of his own, then Celeqor and the others. The unnatural creature remained firm-footed, his pale eyes set on Asher.

"It's belt," Faylen warned.

The ranger gave one of the sword belts a closer examination and laid his eyes on the only thing known to sap magic. "Crissalith..." he growled.

"What in all the hells is that?" Vighon asked, his flaming sword gripped tightly in both hands.

"It cuts off our connection to magic," Faylen quickly explained, assuming her battle stance once more.

Asher had never come across the rare stones of Crissalith himself, but he remembered well the tales from Gideon and Galanör and their time in the south of Ayda. Along with the dragons, they had destroyed the only Crissalith mine known to exist. Apparently, they missed one.

"Swords it is." Asher pulled his broadsword free.

The sentinel continued to hold its ground, unnervingly calm. The companions looked from one to the other, unsure of what to expect from the four-armed guard.

"So, do we just cut its head off?" Vighon was perhaps wielding the best sword for such a job.

"That's always worked in the past." Asher stepped forward, towards the sentinel, but also towards the towering doors.

Whatever magic compelled the creature, the ranger's advance was the final straw that saw it take action against the intruders. Lunging into a deadly spin, all four of its swords extended, the sentinel flew at Asher. As one, the companions rushed in to surround Haren Bain's guard before it could chop the ranger into pieces.

Broadsword raised, Asher blocked the first of the four swords to come down on him, halting the sentinel's spin. Of course, there were three more swords ready to swing at him. The ranger parried another two but was forced to dive and roll out of the way of the fourth.

Being the closest, Vighon was the first to attack the sentinel. His fiery blade cut through the air and the creature's cloak before meeting one of its swords. Paying its smouldering cloak no heed, the sentinel turned on the northman with all four limbs and its ancient weapons spinning. Being human, Vighon was only capable of tracking so many objects moving at such speed, leaving him vulnerable to more than one biting edge of steel.

Before any fatal blow could find the northman, the elves were upon it. The sentinel kicked Vighon in the chest and sent him tumbling away, knocking Ruban over in the process. Seeing that neither was about to fall off the edge, Asher jumped back into the fray, finding his place among the fighters. The elves were lethal, working in harmonious patterns of attack. The silent guard took every cut and gash in its stride and came back at them with an unorthodox pattern of attack of its own.

One of Nemir's warriors was skewered by the sentinel's lower swords and lifted from the ground. Celeqor and Faylen dived in and plunged their scimitars into the creature's back, but it remained focused on the elf raised above it. Using its upper swords, Haren Bain's guard scissored the warrior's head off before tossing his body over the edge of the platform.

Nemir and the remaining warrior roared in anger before attacking it from both sides. The sentinel flicked one of its swords back before meeting Nemir. The captain's attack was easily blocked by three swords. That left one other. The shrouded guard thrust its fourth sword out behind it and caught the warrior in the gut. A swift kick launched him over the edge, where he would join his comrade and rest forever.

Nemir received a right hook and his head took the brunt of a hard pommel. The captain fell away, his limp body rolling towards the edge of the platform.

"Nemir!" Faylen screamed her husband's name, but she was locked in battle beside Celeqor.

Asher didn't even think as he dropped his sword and dived across the floor. The ranger caught the elf's vambrace before he disappeared over the edge, never to be seen again. He was heavy. Asher groaned and grunted as he desperately heaved Nemir upwards. He was relying on Celeqor and Faylen keeping the sentinel busy.

"Here!" Ruban dropped to his side and reached over the edge to find a purchase on Nemir. Together, they pulled him back onto the platform, though it couldn't be said to be much safer.

Faylen rolled, flipped, and spun around the sentinel while Celeqor lunged in wherever he could. Their swords clashed again and again as the fight moved in circles. Vighon, now recovered from his foot to the chest, dived back into the melee. Next to Faylen, he appeared clumsy, but always ferocious. He certainly had a technique Asher could identify with, but it didn't compare to that of an elf. Still, with one hard strike, the northman shattered one of the sentinel's swords and continued to take a chunk out of its leg.

Momentarily stunned by the loss of one of its weapons, the sentinel missed Faylen's downward strike. The High Guardian cut through one of its forearms in one clean swipe, ridding the guard of yet another weapon. Just as they looked to be gaining some kind of advantage, the sentinel jumped into the air, parried both Faylen and Vighon while simultaneously kicking Celeqor in the face. The elder skidded across the platform and impacted the solid doors.

As the guard landed, it spun around, bringing both of its swords with it. Vighon had no choice but to dive away, his reactions too slow for swordplay. Faylen met the challenge and clashed with both swords in a flurry of steel.

Asher could see the calamity that was about to take place. With every strike from the sentinel, Faylen was being pushed back to the edge of the platform. The ranger left his sword where it was and ran at the sentinel. It wasn't a graceful attack, but jumping onto its back was certainly enough to turn the creature away from Faylen.

Gripping its upper arms with his hands and wrapping one of his legs around the sentinel's only lower arm, Asher straddled it with all his strength. Vighon took advantage and came at the creature swinging his fiery blade. Another powerful kick, however, knocked the northman aside.

"Somebody kill it!" Asher yelled, his limbs entwined and useless to him now.

Faylen and Ruban came in with their swords, but the sentinel writhed with Asher on its back, making it impossible for them to strike the creature without hitting the ranger. Eventually, the guard of Haren Bain threw his head back and slammed it into Asher's face, freeing it of his hold.

No sooner did the ranger impact the floor before the sentinel took the fight to Faylen and Ruban. The squire used Vighon's enchanted shield to stay alive, but it wasn't enough to keep him on his feet after being shoved aside by two shoulders. Faylen backed off and joined Vighon, deciding that they would be better fighting side by side than challenging the guard on their own.

Asher scrambled across the platform and retrieved his broadsword, deliberately making a clatter to attract the sentinel. With the ranger on one side and Faylen and Vighon on the other, the guard was surrounded again. With one arm dripping blood from a red stump, the guard still possessed two swords and one jagged sword, broken by the northman.

"We attack it together!" Asher shouted, ready to make the dash across the platform.

The sentinel changed strategy. Instead of bracing for imminent battle, it rotated its shoulders until its black cloak was covering most of its body. It lowered its arms and used one of them to douse the licking flames that clung to the edge of his cloak.

"What's it doing now?" Vighon held his flaming sword out, the tip pointed directly at the sentinel.

The guard of Haren Bain briefly closed its eyes and with it extinguished the surrounding torches. The platform was consumed by darkness, the only light coming from Vighon's sword. Those flames, however, were not enough to keep track of the sentinel, its movements now sporadic and hidden by its cloak.

Asher moved his sword left and right, ready for the inevitable attack. His eyes darted in every direction as he tried to track the sentinel. Twice it came spinning past, revealing itself before bringing its swords to clash against his. Twice it swiped at his chest and cut across his leathers with the jagged blade. After the second strike, Asher was getting angry.

"Vighon!" Even as Asher called out to him he was reluctant to follow through with his own idea. "Sheath your sword!"

"Are you mad?" he shouted back.

"Do it!" Faylen instructed him sharply.

The northman slid his silvyr blade back into its scabbard, robbing the flames of oxygen and the companions of their only light. Pitch black settled over the entrance to Haren Bain. Asher had wanted to avoid this, fearful of his instincts taking control again, fearful of his blackouts, fearful that he would hurt more than just the sentinel...

The Nightseye elixir that would forever course through his blood came alive, the magic ignited by the absence of light. The ranger's hearing became so acute that he could hear the fabric of the sentinel's cloak dragging across its smooth skin. His skin tuned into his surroundings, becoming sensitive to the lightest of breezes that came from somewhere above the platform. He could also feel the icy aura that enveloped the sentinel as its unnatural body exuded cold.

His sense of smell was assaulted by sweat, blood, and decay, the latter coming from Haren Bain's guard. Opening his mouth, Asher could taste it all in the air. It was horribly familiar, taking him back to his time as an assassin. It was at this point he was sure he would lose control and the killer within him would take over. But it didn't...

Despite entering this predatory state, he found a focus that had escaped him since being freed of The Crow's spell. All of his senses built a crystal-clear image of his environment, attuning his muscles and reactions. He could *see* the sentinel slowly approaching, sure that it was about to complete the only job it was ever given.

Asher smiled.

As the creature came down on him with one of its swords, the ranger shifted his body just enough so that the sentinel's blade missed him by less than a hand's width. The sword dug down into the platform and the creature lurched forward, a slave to its own momentum. Asher didn't waste a second lashing out with his two-handed broadsword. The steel cut clean through the sentinel's ribs and out of the other side, splattering blood across the platform.

Ensuring he survived the counterattack, Asher immediately dived into a roll and put some distance between him and his foe.

"Asher!" Faylen called out. "We can't see anything..."

"Just stay where you are!" the ranger instructed, his blade coming up defensively.

His ears detected movement off to the side and he felt pressure against his skin as the air was displaced. Nemir was waking up...

The ranger growled and parried one blade then two before evading the jagged sword. Falling into more of a dance, Asher used the techniques he had learned in Nightfall and spun his blade around with his body, confusing the sentinel with too many potential attacks. He came out of his flurry with a single downward strike that removed another hand from the sentinel. It recoiled as the hand fell away and the jagged sword with it, but there was no sign of pain on the creature's chalk-white face.

"What's going on?" Nemir asked groggily.

"Don't move!" Faylen warned, neither able to see each other.

Asher ignored them and ducked under another attack easily seen coming by the sound of the sentinel's movements. An upward flick of his sword cut a red line up the creature's back, pushing it closer to the edge. The ranger wasn't trained to give his enemies an inch and he didn't intend to start now. He pursued the sentinel across the platform and came at it with a jumping thrust of his broadsword.

As Haren Bain's guard turned around to face him, Asher speared its chest, pushing it even farther back. Such a blow was mortal to any and all, but not Atilan's twisted pet. The ranger knew well that when striking the heart failed, there was only one other thing to do.

In a flash of steel, he whipped his sword free of its chest and chopped at the sentinel's neck with both hands gripped tightly to his hilt.

A bald head with a ragged neck flew through the air, away from its body, and disappeared over the side. Asher booted the headless body in the gut, sending it over the edge to join the rest of it for eternity.

The ranger fell to his knees, exhausted. His right leg stung in two different places and his knees protested just about everything. Thanks to the Nightseye elixir, he could hear his bones rubbing together...

"Faylen, some light."

The elf quickly responded with an orb that took off above them, bringing clarity to a blood-stained platform. Nemir found his feet and ran over to his wife. Their embrace didn't make Asher feel any better. Ruban and Vighon helped Celeqor up, the elder rubbing his sore head.

"We lost Darlyn and Orithan," Nemir lamented.

Asher felt a twinge of guilt for forgetting their names. They had both given their immortal lives for this mission, a mission he had set in motion.

"The beast is dead?" Faylen asked the ranger.

Asher nodded, unsure how long it would be before his knees were happy to take his weight again. "Let's get that door open," he suggested.

The light from Faylen's orb began to flicker. Then it began to dim.

"Do they normally do that?" Vighon asked.

Faylen looked back at Asher. "No, they don't."

The ranger forgot about his ailments and looked over the edge of the platform, a pit of dread opening within him. He couldn't see anything in the abyss. But, he could hear something. It was the distinct sound of steel crashing into rock and the mad scramble of limbs.

The sentinel was clawing its way back up...

"Get the door open, *now!*" Asher sheathed his sword and ran to help with the effort.

The door was massive and with its size came considerable weight. Even with three elves, it still required all of them to push on some part of the door. Above them, the magic of the orb continued to falter, casting them all in more shadows as the Crissalith drew closer.

Vighon bared his teeth under the exertion. "It-won't-budge!"

They could all hear the sentinel approaching now, its swords biting into the rocky column that supported the platform.

"Move aside!" Celeqor ordered.

The elder placed both of his hands over the door but never made contact with the iron. The air around his fingers became distorted and wavy with heat. It very quickly became clear that the elf was running out of magic, his connection dwindling synchronously with the fading orb. Finally, as Celeqor turned red from exertion, the door creaked and groaned. The slab of iron moved enough to offer them a glimpse of the chamber beyond.

"Push!" Asher threw all of his weight into the door.

The sentinel was so close now that the orb could no longer be sustained, drowning them all in darkness. Asher was plunged back into his heightened awareness, alerting him to the guard's imminent return. The door reluctantly scraped across the ground until there was a gap large enough for one person to slide between the edges and pass through to the other side.

"Go!" Vighon pushed Ruban through, followed by Celeqor and Faylen.

The sentinel clambered over the lip of the platform behind them, headless, but still in possession of two swords. Asher grabbed Vighon roughly by his cloak and shoved him between the doors. He might have taken a little too much satisfaction in pushing Nemir through after him.

As Haren Bain's guard charged at him, the ranger strained to keep his body between the gap. On the other side, his companions were pulling on the door to give him some relief, but the gap was closing on him.

"Asher!" Faylen screamed his name and he dived through, his feet narrowly missing the shutting door.

And shut it did. The enormous door slammed back into place as the sentinel thrust an arm through, hounding Asher. The mute guard made not a sound when it was separated from its upper arm.

Lying on the ground, his breathing ragged, Asher's senses told him the amputated limb was twitching beside his leg. He kicked it aside and rose to his feet as Faylen produced another orb to wash away his extra senses. They were all exhausted by the look of them, the elves included.

Faylen placed a hand on the ranger's shoulder. "Thank you. I saw what you did." She turned to her husband. "He saved you from certain death where I could not."

Nemir offered Asher a stoic expression. "My gratitude, Ranger."

Faylen scowled at her husband but Asher was happy to simply nod and be done with it.

Ruban slid back against the door. "I should have stayed in Namdhor..."

Their moment of reprieve was shattered when the sentinel began beating the door from the other side. Ruban yelled and dashed away with his shield raised. Requiring nothing so quaint as a brain, the creature pounded the door incessantly, though it was too solid to move even an inch.

Vighon turned to Asher. "There's another way out of here, right?"

The ranger didn't have a good answer for that. Instead, he gestured for them to follow him farther into Haren Bain, where yet more secrets awaited. Asher only hoped they weren't wielding swords...

After passing several large cages, all filled with muddy bones, the companions entered an area that stretched out into darkness, its depths beyond the light of Faylen's orb. They were naturally drawn to three large stone tables, set up in a U-shape. Beside the cages, they were the only other things that had been man-made in the whole cavern.

Whatever had decorated the tables was now scattered haphazardly over the surface and across the ground, decayed, rotten or broken. A closer inspection of the tables, under the light, showed them to be stained with dark blood.

Faylen lowered her head to look inside a half-shattered bowl, its contents long turned to dark tar. "Lady Ellöria told me what transpired in here," she said, her voice carrying far off into the cavern. "Atilan knew no bounds in his pursuit of immortality."

Asher crouched down and picked up an ancient instrument, its purpose unknown but, judging by the sharp points and crusted blood, it wasn't used for anything good. "Haren Bain is just one of the secret places Atilan used. You remember Kaliban, on the other side of Vengora? The Bastion? This is where he twisted nature."

Ruban looked back at the cages. "Were they people?"

Asher felt the pinch in his right temple. "Yes," he recalled. "Elves. This is where he turned them into orcs."

Vighon bent down and picked something up. "Using the essence of dragons," he remarked, holding up a dragon scale to the light.

Nemir looked around in disgust. "You would think a creature of such parentage would be virtuous, not violent and wicked."

"This weapon you spoke of," Celeqor pondered. "Where would we find it?"

Asher settled on the tables, where the Dragon Rider had seen the designs and the glyphs that had been etched into the table's surface. The parchments that still remained were far from legible, at least those that hadn't been torn to pieces. The glyphs were still there, however, golden and elegant in form and scribed into the stone in a perfect circle.

"The Dragon Rider came to kill Naius," Asher explained, tracing the glyphs with his finger. "He only paused because the weapon's designs caught his eye. It's here, inside the stone itself." The ranger could see the event playing out in his mind, as if he was seeing through the Dragon Rider's eyes. "His investigation was brief... Atilan was here - it was the chance they had been waiting for."

Faylen and Nemir walked around the table and all eyes turned on the ring of glyphs. "Can you recall what the designs told of the weapon's use?" Nemir asked.

Looking back at something so detailed as the writings and the drawings was painful. Asher scrunched his eyes and pushed through the spike in his head until he was looking down at the parchments, through the Dragon Rider's eyes.

"I can't translate the writing," he told them. "There are drawings." Asher tried to hold the memory over the central drawing that depicted something coming out of an orb. "It's a sphere, I think..."

"Naius did favour the design," Faylen remarked, her observation harking back to The Veil.

"I think its shape has something to do with the way the weapon works." Asher began to withdraw from the memory, easing the pain in his head. "I can see something coming out of it, but I don't know what I'm looking at - it's just a drawing."

Celeqor ushered everyone aside and delicately placed both of his hands around the glyphs. "It's a ward; though I have seen few like this one before."

"What's a ward?" Ruban asked.

"A protection spell," Asher sighed.

"Indeed," Celeqor agreed. "This one is quite sophisticated. That which we seek likely lies within the stone itself, but the spell has fused the stone back together." The elf ran his hand over the glyphs. "That's why there aren't any seams."

"Can you break through the ward?" Faylen asked.

"I can retrieve it," Celeqor assured. "But it will take time. One wrong step and the spell will fuse the stone with the weapon rather than encase it."

Something moved in the dark, silencing the group.

There was more movement, only this time it came from the other side of the cavern.

The movement preceded a low growl, which then grew to many.

"I don't think we have time." Asher pulled free his broadsword and the others mimicked him.

"What is it?" Vighon's sword was absent its flames now, the fire starved of oxygen in his scabbard.

"It could be more of those things," Ruban said in a quiet voice.

It wasn't. Asher caught sight of a pair of eyes in the dark, reflecting the light from Faylen's orb. Those eyes vanished as quickly as they appeared. It wasn't like the sentinel, though the ranger had his suspicions.

Faylen rolled over the table to join the others in the middle. "Celeqor, how long do you need?"

The elder froze, as they all did. From the darkness that stretched beyond sight, a familiar beast emerged. Its horned head twitched under the stark light of the orb and it used one of its clawed hands to shield its eyes. With pale skin and a muscled body, there was no mistaking the creature to be anything but an orc.

More eyes shone in the dark and more orcs lurked on the fringes of the light. Unlike the orcs they had encountered on the surface, these creatures were naked, their rock-like hides scratched with scars. They moved like animals, a pack closing in on their prey.

"They seem different," Ruban whispered.

"That's because they are," Vighon answered bluntly. "Look at them; they're *feral*."

"They must be the descendants of the original orcs," Faylen opined. "They must have never explored beyond The Spear."

"Who cares," Asher retorted, bringing his sword to bear. "Celeqor, break the damned ward!"

The feral orcs snapped, their collective roars filling the cavern. Out of the darkness they charged, mad with rage and a hunger for flesh. Only the boldest of their kind dared to cross into the light, though even they struggled and shielded their eyes with one hand. Asher and Vighon easily cut them down, securing their left side, while Faylen and Nemir dispatched the group attacking from the right. Even Ruban managed to kill one that jumped over the central table, filling the squire with much needed confidence.

Celeqor pored over the ring of glyphs, whispering spells under his breath. Using magic, he actually moved the engraved glyphs around the surface, rearranging them into a new order. The table, however, was reluctant to reveal its secrets.

More orcs dashed out of the dark, convinced their numbers would be sufficient to kill their prey. Asher noted that many of the beasts took no heed of his swinging sword, as if they didn't expect it to deal much damage.

After the next wave was left dead at their feet, the ranger remarked, "I don't think they've ever seen swords before."

Vighon kicked one of them over. "They just charge like mindless beasts."

More eyes glistened in the dark and feral growls accompanied them, echoing off the rock. "They might be mindless," Faylen said, "but they might number in the hundreds, maybe more."

"We're doing alright," Vighon replied with a lighter tone.

"They're predators," Nemir pointed out. "They'll soon learn and outnumber us." The elf finished by raising his hand and producing an orb of light, adding to his wife's.

Asher glanced at the elder. "Celeqor?"

"I need more time," the elf complained. "This is like a riddle in a riddle."

"It's also very old," the ranger replied, his eyes tracking the orc shadows. "Can't you just have done with the wards and rip the damned thing out?"

"Trust me, Ranger, *ancient* does not always mean *brittle*. This ward is intricate but strong. It would take something as powerful as a dragon to *break* through the magic."

A cacophonous wave of growls and roars echoed from the back the cavern, too many to count. Even Celeqor paused in his work to look into the darkness, expecting an army of orcs to wash over them.

"They're coming," Vighon warned.

Nemir turned to the ranger. "Asher, how do we get out of here?"

"You saw the passage for yourself," Asher replied. "The Dragon Rider's path is closed to us. There's only one way out..."

Vighon looked over his shoulder, to the iron doors. "We have to get past that thing again?"

The orcs were closing in, dozens upon dozens of them.

"Then let us take that path," Nemir suggested, fear in his tone. "Our chances are better against that guard than they are in here."

Asher wasn't so sure. "Celeqor?"

The elder was frantically working away again. "I need more time!"

"Asher!" Nemir hissed.

The ranger looked at Faylen instead. She nodded at him, signalling her agreement with Nemir. This wasn't how it was supposed to go...

"Alright..." Asher began to back away. "Time to get out. Celeqor, rip it out."

"I can do it," the elder insisted.

"There's no time," Asher argued, catching more orcs in his peripheral vision. "Rip it out and let's get out of here!"

The companions clustered together now, ready to make a run for the doors, where more effort would be required to pull them open. Asher could see it in his mind: the door wouldn't budge and the orcs would fall upon them in a frenzy of claws and fangs.

The orbs followed their casters, leaving Celeqor in partial darkness as he reluctantly tore himself away from the table. The elf put his hands together, then separated them with some speed. The table cracked and broke into two parts, each slab flying off into the cavern. All that remained was a single chunk of jagged stone on the ground, the weapon's casing.

"Here!" Celeqor scooped the rock up and threw it to Asher, who roughly turned Ruban around and shoved it down deep into his backpack.

"Run!" Nemir shouted, the orcs advancing in more numbers than could be counted.

The group stuck close together and ran for the doors - only Celeqor remaining apart, the last to leave. Asher stole a glance over his shoulder and witnessed the magic of elves as the elder unleashed spell after spell to keep the orcs at bay. Any who weren't blasted by the destructive forces were blinded by the flashes.

Vighon and Ruban were the first to slam into the door before immediately reversing their direction to pull on the iron slab. Nemir and Faylen added their strength while Asher dashed to the side where a pair of orcs had crept out of the dark and dared the fringes of the light.

"Asher!" Faylen called him to the door, where she and Nemir were now using magic to heave it open.

Vighon and Ruban added their physical strength and pulled on the door together. Asher sheathed his sword and found purchase beside one of the squire's hands. Before long, they were all yanking on the door while Celeqor threw his hands out in every direction, bursting orcs apart as if they were nothing more than fragile sacks of meat and gore.

As soon as the door opened an inch, the sentinel plunged one of its sword through the gap, nearly slicing Vighon's ear off. They had no choice but to slam it closed again.

Faylen turned back to shout at Celeqor. "Use the crystal!"

The elder paused his magic assault for just a moment, flashing them a concerned expression. "I only have one!" he replied, the crystal intended to open a portal to Namdhor.

"We have no choice!" Faylen yelled back. "We're going to die down here if we don't get out *now*!"

Celeqor's fingers exploded with hot white lightning that charred a group of orcs mid-run. Before the smoke could dissipate, the elder reached into his pouch and retrieved the shining crystal. He backed up until he was pressed against the rest of them, facing the approaching horde of feral orcs.

"Namdhor is too far," he told them gravely. "I cannot open a portal from here to there."

"How close *can* you get us?" Asher asked with the precious seconds they had left.

"The Iron Valley," Celeqor said hopefully. "We passed it on our way—"

"I don't care!" Asher yelled in his face. "Do it! Do it now!"

The orcs hovered by the edge of the orb's perimeter, darting backwards and forwards, afraid of the light. It was only a matter of seconds before their feral nature consumed their rationale and they charged blindly through the glow. Magic and steel wouldn't nearly be enough to see them all survive then.

"The horses!" Vighon fretted.

"Forget them!" Asher barked, bracing himself for the wave of claws.

Celeqor, his magic acutely harnessed, threw the crystal at his feet. The reaction was instantaneous. The crystal shattered on impact, unleashing its magic on a reality that couldn't stand up to it. The hard ground beneath their feet was replaced by a featureless abyss, ringed with sparks and brilliant lightning. The six companions fell through the portal and landed in a heap of limbs surrounded by snow.

Above them, the portal collapsed on itself before a single orc was able to follow them through. They were left under a dark sky and a light sprinkle of ash and snow, a world away from the depths of The Spear and the horrors of Haren Bain.

Asher scanned their environment for threats before allowing his head to fall back into the snow. He was so tired he was sure he could close his eyes and return to death, never to wake. That was certainly one of the closest calls in his life...

"Celeqor?" Faylen's concern spread among the others.

The High Guardian crawled rapidly through the snow to the elder's side. He was bleeding from the nose and ears - never a good sign among magic users. Asher had seen mages spread their magic thin before, their bodies taking the toll for using such magic. Celeqor managed to mumble some elvish words, but they were incoherent.

"He's alive!" Faylen exclaimed with relief.

Asher was glad to hear it, but he didn't join her by Celeqor's side. Instead, he grabbed Ruban by the shoulders and pointed him away so that the ranger might reach the pack on his back. He removed the rock and inspected it in the snow. One end was smooth and flat, the golden glyphs still etched into the stone. The rest was a jagged ball of solid rock...

Vighon gestured at it, his face pinched in exhaustion. "Now what do we do with it? Are you supposed to hit every single orc over the head with it?"

Asher ignored the wit. "We take it back to Namdhor."

Nemir was the first to stand up in the icy breeze. "We follow the mountains west?"

The ranger took in the sight of The Watchers, either side of The Iron Valley behind them. "It's a couple of days from here." He rose to his feet after handing the encased weapon back to Ruban. He felt a twinge in his back but it was among a plethora of aches and cuts that assaulted him.

"On *horseback*," Vighon pointed out.

"And one of us will need carrying," Faylen added, looking at Celeqor.

"Then we had better get moving..." Asher groaned.

CHAPTER 33
A HARD TRUTH

Where once the sprawling port of Dragorn was a hubbub of activity and industry, there was now only the lapping waves and the squawk of the gulls overhead. The Crow stepped off his boat, the first to find harbour in the port for some time, and surveyed the graveyards of ships and abandoned warehouses.

Sarkas looked to the west, where The Shining Coast of Illian was a distant and hazy line. Since the orcs had ravaged the mainland, there had been no one for the Dragornians to trade with, the master fishermen easily the largest source of seafood throughout all of Illian. Here and there, he spotted smaller fishing boats sailing in and out, their trading taking place inside Dragorn's high walls now.

Walking along the network of decking, The Crow was preceded by five dark mages of his order and backed by his loyal Reavers. The mages were unnecessary at this point, assigned to escort duty by Morvir - who was most certainly dead by now.

Like ghosts in the mist, sailors and fishermen, bereft of their jobs, sat on the edge of the decking with longing stares out to sea. Those that noticed Sarkas passing by held out their hands in the hope of receiving coin. The necromancer ignored them all, failing to recall a time he had ever carried coins.

Leaving the port behind, the dark mages eventually found themselves before the unwelcoming doors of Dragorn itself. Those gates had been opened a thousand years ago and not once had they been closed. Now, they were under the guard of the city watch, both on the ground and on top of the high walls. News of Illian's invasion had spread fear among the islanders, and rightly so.

They were lucky the orcs knew nothing of traversing water.

The guards protecting the gates gripped their spears and finished their conversations early as Sarkas and his ominous party approached. Luckily for them, The Crow had no intention of entering their depraved city, ruled by crime families and tyrants. Dragorn had been twisted by the humans after they assumed control in the wake of Gal Tion's Dragon War, a millennium past. Where it had once been a place for the most honourable of orders, it was now a place where monsters were made.

Fitting, Sarkas thought...

Making a left at the gates, The Crow and his entourage paid the guards no attention and, instead, followed the eastern wall of the city. The path only stretched for so long before there were rocks that required some degree of climbing. They navigated these rocks for some time until they were on the eastern edge of the island, at least three hundred feet beneath the base of the city wall.

There were more dark mages waiting for them. They stood dutifully outside the tall and pointed cave entrance, their wands drawn and aimed at three dozen workers - all taken from the city and forced into hours of excavating. Over two years, they had been replaced time and time again for fresh workers. This last batch of sorry souls looked terrified, their expressions notable even through their horrendously dirty faces.

Sarkas came to a stop in front of them, sparing a glance for the cave entrance. "Report."

One of the dark mages stepped forward and bowed his head. "My Lord Crow, we have dug free the majority of the bones and—"

"The spells?" Sarkas interrupted.

The mage swallowed his intended words and answered his master. "They have all been etched into the bones as you instructed, Lord Crow. I have overlooked them myself, *daily*, and know them to be perfect. That is, all but one..." The dark mage wet his lips. "The last spell of Astari is—"

"Known only to myself and Morvir," The Crow cut in. "Since Morvir is dead, I will finish the last spell myself." News of Morvir's death had the rest of the dark mages sharing nervous glances.

With a small voice, the mage dared to ask, "Is he to be resurrected, Lord Crow?"

"No," he answered bluntly. "And kill them," he added, nodding at the workers.

As their protests began, the dark mages turned on them with wands and staffs. The rocky shore became a site of massacre in no time, the workers helpless to defend themselves against magic. The flashing spells only continued for a few moments, the last of which struck a young man making a desperate bid towards the sea.

Before the smoke had settled, the same dark mage who had reported their progress turned back to Sarkas. "I know I talk for us all, Lord Crow, when I say we are excited to see this spell completed. It has been a hard two years but..."

The mage lost his words under the gaze of Sarkas. There was something in The Crow's eyes that gripped his throat, held his tongue, and opened a pit in his stomach.

Sarkas began to pace the entrance of the cave, placing a clear divide between himself and the dark mages. "You have all served The Black Hand with..." The Crow couldn't even bring himself to lie anymore. "Oh forget it. You have all served a false god and practised wicked deeds upon the innocent. These deeds will ensure peace for the generations to come but, in the act, you have all proven that there is no place in the new world for people of your predilections."

Seeing their confused and moronic expressions, Sarkas continued, "I am no exception. Together, we will leave this world and leave it a better place..."

With no more to say, Sarkas whipped up his wand and disarmed them all at once, casting their wands and staffs across the sand and rocks. He killed two before they scattered, just as their recent victims had. One destructive spell after another was unleashed from the tip of The Crow's ancient wand, lighting the entrance of the cave up with a multitude of colours.

The Reavers stood silently behind their master, their legendary skills not required.

When he was surrounded by even more bodies, Sarkas breathed a sigh of relief. It was all going to be over soon. He had finally reached the end of a very long journey, one that had taken him through slavery, torture, and even death. Now, under the sandy stone of Dragorn, his destiny would be fulfilled.

He was only a few steps into the cave when the diviner on his belt began to vibrate and emit a soft hum. Of course! There was one last truth to tell...

Allowing his mind to be pulled into the diviner, The Crow came face to face with King Karakulak of the orcs. The so-called God-King was just as beastly in his ethereal form as he was in reality.

"Wizard, I would have knowledge," Karakulak demanded.

"And horses would have wings," Sarkas replied sarcastically, "but we cannot all have that which we want."

The orc king bared his teeth. "The Master Dragorn invaded my ancestors' lands - an insult! You must have seen this! Why was I not told?"

"Do you fear Gideon Thorn?" Sarkas asked. "Or do you fear Mournblade?"

Karakulak sneered. "You mock me, Wizard? We have an alliance, you and I. You wanted me to bring the world of man to its knees. After Namdhor falls—"

"And *that* is why you have contacted me," The Crow interpreted.

"You want to know what I have *seen*. You want to know if the orcs will emerge victorious, as you have promised them."

"Our victory is assured!" Karakulak growled, unwilling to hear anything else.

"Then why do I detect doubt in your voice?" Sarkas countered.

The orc king narrowed his eyes. "You have seen the future, Wizard. Tell me exactly how we win, how I kill the Master Dragorn."

Finally done with his lies and deceit, Sarkas answered honestly. "Your only hope now, Karakulak of the Born Horde, is to keep taking my elixirs and prey to Gordomo that you survive the slaughter of your race."

Karakulak's face dropped. "What did you say?"

"I am trying to forge a better world, you monstrous oaf. All of Verda would become a dark and desolate place if your kind were allowed to rule."

Karakulak roared. "You lie! I will hunt you down myself, Wizard, and flay you alive! I will devour your meat and give the scraps to my garks!"

Sarkas remained perfectly calm. "Accepting the truth can be a hard thing. But take some joy from the knowledge that I have seen something beautiful emerge from the destruction of your people."

"You fiend!" the orc king bellowed. "You never had any power beyond your tricks! You have your spells and your potions, but the future is known only to me! The orcs will rule this world for all time! They will cheer my name from The Under Realm to the black sky!"

The Crow could see his elixir working just as it was designed to. Karakulak's mind was unravelling, tainted by the raw power he had been gifted. Very soon, he would be incapable of making rational decisions, a mindless monster consumed by a lust for more power.

"No, Karakulak," Sarkas said with pity, "your name will not be cheered by anyone. You have never been anything but a weapon, a weapon I created and aimed at the world of man..."

As the orc king let loose a rage-filled roar, Sarkas disconnected his mind from the diviner and returned to his body, under Dragorn. It was time to prepare for the end...

~

KARAKULAK CLENCHED his fist and broke the diviner into a hundred pieces of glass. His rage not even close to being satiated, the orc flipped the massive chest that had once imprisoned the Dragorn. He kicked it so hard it burst through the fabric of his tent and shattered on the rocks outside. Were he to destroy anything else, he would risk the integrity of the whole tent.

He seethed, the urge to kill bubbling under his skin. He would hunt The Crow to the end of the world if he had to, but he would taste that wizard's flesh!

"What have you done?" came the question from behind.

Karakulak turned around with great speed, his muscles tense and eager to explode. Seeing his mother standing in the entrance to his tent didn't make him any calmer.

The High Priestess stomped into the tent with her staff beside her. She looked down at the shards of glass and disturbed their rest with the end of her staff.

"The human has shown his true colours, then? The only question, spawn of mine, is whether the wizard's magic has doomed all of us, or just you?"

Karakulak growled. "The Crow will pay for his betrayal with his worthless life!"

His mother stamped her staff into the ground. "To what end? You are already paying the price for your unnatural alliance. Look at you!" The High Priestess pointed her jagged finger at the small chest hooked on Karakulak's belt. "You have gone down a path from which there is no return. When the truth of your *addiction* is revealed, you will have sullied our blood. We will both be sent to Gordomo in pieces..."

Karakulak heard every word but he was struggling to focus. He decided it was the elixir wearing off in his veins. He fumbled with the latches of the chest until he just removed it and placed it on the table, where he could open it with both hands. He wasn't feeling the usual drain that accompanied the fading magic, but his mind could only be described as fuzzy.

"That's right," his mother goaded, "take another swig! You could have ruled our kind without the magic! You could have been so much more! We must call off the attack! Our people cannot be led into war while your head is full of magic!"

Karakulak downed the green potion and shook his head, desperate to think clearly. "Even when the elixirs run out, victory in Namdhor will secure my reign," he stated boldly. "They believe my transformation was an act of Gordomo. You, High Priestess, will tell my people that I was blessed to destroy the world of man, that it was temporary for Gordomo's glory..."

The king looked away from his mother, his eyes struggling to bring her into focus. What was happening to him? Why wasn't his mind running circles around her? He just wanted to eat, and kill, and raze Namdhor to the ground!

"Until then," he managed, "we go to war. I will bait that stonemaw beast myself if I have to..."

Karakulak stormed out of his tent without a moment's pause for the High Priestess. He made it as far as his entourage before realising he had left his chest of elixirs behind. His plan to continue ruling after they were all gone might be plausible, but he still needed them to ensure victory in Namdhor. Turning back, he marched into his tent, past his mother, and reclaimed the chest. The High Priestess didn't even look at him, her gaze purposefully distant.

"You are no spawn of mine," she called after him.

Karakulak smiled to himself, more than happy to agree with the old wretch.

PART FOUR

CHAPTER 34
BOUND TOGETHER

F reedom. That's what this was. Alijah Galfrey had known imprisonment and torment and before that he had been chained to a life he didn't know how to navigate. But now, soaring above the world astride Malliath, he knew he was exactly where he was supposed to be.

The wind rushed through his hair, making his eyes water, and he let go of Malliath to spread his arms and take it all in. The world as gods saw it.

Freedom...

This wasn't the half-elf's first time on dragon-back, but this was definitely his first time *flying*. Leaning forward again to grip Malliath's spikes, Alijah tilted his head right, then left and watched his companion bank in the same direction. Their minds were becoming so entwined that it was impossible to tell who had really wanted to bank right and left.

Alijah smoothed his hands over Malliath's black scales, enjoying the warmth that radiated from them. With every passing second, he felt their bond strengthening, their ideals and thoughts bleeding into one. His companion's mind was powerful, a seemingly endless library of knowledge and experiences. Alijah wanted to dive in and absorb it all, to live every moment of Malliath's history.

In the hours since they departed from Korkanath, Malliath had told him that his long years of life would be too much to receive at once. There would be time for all of that, Alijah reasoned. After all, they had eternity together now.

Flying beside them, Athis carried Inara and their parents over the land. Every now and then, they would all share a brief conversation to ensure they continued in the same direction. Thankfully, the dragons had an uncanny sense of direction, which benefitted them all the more as the world was blanketed in ash clouds.

It hadn't escaped Alijah, nor Malliath, that Inara and Athis had chosen a longer route to Namdhor, one which saw them skirt around The Vrost Mountains and The Bastion. Such a path took them around to the east of the mountains and over The Black Wood and Dunwich, the most southern town in the northern realm. Heading west from there, they finally flew over The White Vale.

It was cold, to say the least. Alijah had rarely used magic throughout his life, despite half of his heritage having an affinity for it, but since bonding with Malliath the half-elf could feel a new well of magic within him. Taking advantage of his companion's natural magic, Alijah used a simple spell to keep himself warm at these dizzying heights.

Magic would also come in handy when sleep was required, but Alijah had never felt so alive astride the dragon. Sleep would have to wait. He was seeing the world from a new perspective, a dragon's perspective.

Looking to his right, he marvelled at Vengora, a weaving line of mountains that capped Illian's north and crossed the country from east to west before finding its end in a southern curve, towards Grey Stone. Alijah was taken back to his time in The Crow's company, when the necromancer told him of Erador.

On foot, he would have to leave Vengora behind, traverse the wilds of Dhenaheim, heading west, until he crossed The Whispering Mountains. Were he to cross them, he would have to contend with The Dread Wood and then the tundras of Storm's Reach. Only then would he be at the doorway to Erador, the only entrance through The Broken Mountains, following The Royal Valley.

"Erador..." The Crow had said. "That is where your journey begins..."

Alijah couldn't say what would come to pass, though right now, he had no intention of going to Erador. It was an ancient land, once ruled, and long abandoned, by humans. He couldn't imagine why his journey should begin there, a graveyard of kingdoms and Dragon Riders.

If he was indeed destined to rule, surely he would need to stay in Illian, where there were people to actually rule. Deciding that he would be better off living through events, rather than trying to interpret them and make choices accordingly, Alijah brought his thoughts in and continued to admire the world from the sky.

This was where he belonged...

Having drifted closer to the Vengoran mountains, the two dragons inevitably flew over The Selk Road, a dusky path in the snow. Following that road ever westward would take any traveller to Namdhor's mighty slope. It was on that road where both dragons caught sight of a group of people, trudging along the path without horses.

It was Malliath's sharp eyes that found Asher among the group. The black dragon had endured a forced bond with the ranger and knew him well, a fact that went both ways...

Communicating with Inara, it was immediately decided that they would change their flight paths and descend to The Selk Road. It was peculiar for Alijah to *feel* his sister's excitement across their shared bond. As convenient as it was, he couldn't say he enjoyed telepathy; it felt far too intrusive and, like Malliath, he valued his privacy.

The ranger will not touch me, Malliath stated. The dragon had no intention of making friends and least of all with the person he had been forced to share a bond with.

Don't worry, Alijah reassured, ***whatever happens, he will not accompany us. I won't allow it.***

Malliath growled low in his throat. *I do not care what you allow. If he tries to mount me I will melt his flesh from his bones...*

Alijah patted Malliath's dark scales affectionately. ***Easy, easy. We are in this together. You're not alone anymore. We must defend each other now.***

The dragon's muscles relaxed a little and his building rage faded away. They sank deeper into their bond, compounding the trust between them. Unlike Alijah, Malliath had thousands of years of solitude behind him; it would take some time before he adjusted to their new life as one.

The group, led by Asher, came to a halt at the sight of two approaching dragons. Their wings buffeted the snow and their claws shook the ground as they landed beside the road. Alijah climbed down and joined his family, though his mother ran ahead to embrace Faylen Haldör, her old mentor. It had been nearly a decade since Alijah had seen her himself. Growing up, Faylen had felt like one of the family, though she was eventually drawn away by her responsibilities in Ayda.

After Reyna released her from a tight embrace, Nathaniel followed suit, then Inara. They even greeted Nemir, Faylen's husband, with some affection. To Alijah, it felt as if he were looking through a pane of glass and viewing someone else's life. Out of some strange sense of duty and awkwardness, he was about to greet the High Guardian himself when another emerged from the group.

Vighon Draqaro!

Regardless of what had happened to him, Alijah couldn't help but grin from ear to ear seeing his best friend. They had parted ways in Vangarth, a lifetime ago it seemed. Alijah had left with Gideon and Ilargo while Vighon continued on to Grey Stone with the refugees from Lirian. So much had happened since then - a death and a rebirth for Alijah - but seeing his oldest friend was almost enough to banish it all.

Almost...

They crashed into each other, their embrace as painful as it was comforting. Alijah moved to let go but Vighon held him rooted to the spot for a moment longer. When the northman finally stepped back he cradled Alijah's face in his hands and beamed.

"It's so good to see you!" Vighon's eyes flickered to Malliath and back and his smile dropped away. "I feared the worst."

Alijah clapped him on the shoulder and glanced at the others, noting the looks they all gave Malliath. They feared him and not just because he was an enormous dragon. They feared his mind.

"You seem to have found your way without me, in the north no less." Alijah knew better than any what it meant for Vighon to be back in Namdhor.

"We have much to tell each other," Vighon said, squeezing Alijah's hand on his shoulder.

There was a part of Alijah that wanted to share everything with Vighon, as he always had. It was a small part of him, however, that couldn't stand up to the bond he now shared with Malliath, a bond that fulfilled him. Though, he couldn't deny his interest in Vighon's affairs, especially where his father, Arlon, was concerned.

"It's been too long," he finally replied, committing to nothing. "You have a new sword I see."

Vighon pulled the blade an inch from its scabbard. "Pure silvyr," he smirked.

Alijah raised an impressed eyebrow. "Why do I feel there's a good story behind it?"

"There's an even better one behind how it came to be mine." Vighon threw him a wink.

"Inara has told me some of your victories in recent weeks. What happened to the rogue I know?"

Vighon shrugged and stepped back, giving Alijah a quick inspection. "You look... different. *Stronger*. Being a Dragorn suits you."

There it was again. The assumption that he was a Dragorn because of his bond with a dragon. Alijah wanted to put his friend straight, but he knew well the power of timing as well as guarding his true thoughts and feelings. Instead of replying negatively, he simply smiled at the northman and gave him another hug. It *was* good to see him.

"Alijah..." Faylen paused, taking him in, before giving him a hug. "You look so different now." Just like Vighon, the High Guardian's eyes darted to Malliath and back.

Alijah felt nothing as he embraced her. He knew he should have felt something, anything really, but he just didn't. He hadn't gone through torment for a reunion and the world hadn't been shaped a prophecy so that he might enjoy hugs. He had a destiny to see through...

"It's good to see you," he exaggerated, his eyes roaming over Nemir, who was carrying an unconscious elf he didn't recognise.

That left only two others; a young man carrying Vighon's shield and the ranger himself. Asher was the only one who didn't look at Malliath, his intense gaze, instead, focused on Alijah. In the sights of those crystal blue eyes, the half-elf was convinced the ranger was looking inside his mind, searching for something. He offered no greeting or friendly nod; just a soul-piercing stare.

For a time, the three of them had shared a bond, each peeking inside the other's mind. They had seen things, heard things, and felt things that weren't their own. Though their unnatural bond had been broken by Inara and the Moonblade, Alijah could still feel Asher inside his head, an echo of the ranger's thoughts. The same could probably be said of Asher - an unwanted scenario as far as Alijah and Malliath were concerned.

Vighon and Inara's embrace caught Alijah's eye, tearing him away from the staring match with the ranger. Watching the two in each other's arms was like looking back into the past. Good memories began to surface, taking him back to their younger years when they had all been carefree, their fates entirely their own to decide.

How naive they had been...

After some more greetings, and the introduction of Ruban, they finally got around to asking the important questions. Alijah had wanted to instigate these questions, his concerns lying with the realm, but in the presence of Asher he felt his voice unwilling to participate. He spent most of his energy containing Malliath's contempt, reminding the dragon that Asher hadn't asked to see their thoughts or even return to the world. Malliath didn't care. The ranger had delved into his mind and taken his memories as his own - it was unforgivable.

"You have it?" Inara asked hopefully.

Vighon glanced at Asher. "Sort of..."

The ranger gestured to Ruban. "The weapon is encased in a slab of enchanted stone. We can't get it out."

"There will be time for this in Namdhor," Alijah finally spoke up. "I fear we have lingered in the vale too long, leaving the people vulnerable. The orcs won't wait for us."

"This weapon is the whole reason The Crow brought me back," Asher said gruffly.

"And he has no doubt foreseen it, and knows it will be used against the orcs," Alijah pointed out, struggling to see the ranger's eyes. "That means we *will* find a way to free it and we *will* use it to destroy the orcs."

Inara nodded in agreement. "Alijah's right; we've all been absent too long. We should return and offer our aid in the defences. Having two more dragons in the sky will likely alter any battle plans."

Nathaniel gripped his wife's shoulders and kissed her lightly on the head. "I miss the days when they used to just play hide and seek..."

Alijah wasn't in the mood for nostalgia. "We'll reach the city faster in the air. Vighon, Ruban, Nemir..." The half-elf turned his shoulders towards Malliath, inviting them onto his back.

The young squire's eyes couldn't have got any wider. "We're going on a dragon?"

Vighon turned a sour face to the dark sky. "It beats walking."

As the trio approached Malliath's neck, with Celeqor in Nemir's hands, the dragon maintained his rigid posture, making it extremely hard to reach his back. Alijah looked expectantly at his companion until those purple eyes met his own. Malliath huffed and relented, lowering his head so that the others could climb onto his back.

Since the dawn of your kind, Malliath said, *none have sat on me like a horse.*

Alijah was feeling bold towards his volatile companion. *I see now why fate has bound us together. You are of the past, your ways ancient. I am of the present, my ways relevant to the now. Together, we will find a new way of doing things, Malliath. For now, I need you to trust me, to know that I will never betray you.*

The dragon gave no protest. It was progress and Alijah was pleased with it. Their bond was a little rough around the edges, he admitted, but soon they would discover a strength that could only exist between them. It would be a strength that none would dare challenge.

Climbing onto his companion's back, he watched Asher do the same on Athis. The ranger looked at him again, a warning in his eyes this time. The true meaning behind that warning was lost on Alijah, but he knew one thing: the old assassin didn't trust him.

Were that true of anyone else, Alijah wouldn't have cared, for what could they do against him now? But he had seen enough inside Asher's head to know he was a threat to be taken seriously. With peace in mind, Alijah wouldn't abide threats in his new kingdom...

CHAPTER 35
A FOOL'S GAME

S tanding beside Ilargo in the remaining snows of The White Vale, Gideon watched the elves in the distance. Led by Lady Ellöria, they had taken themselves away from Namdhor and the sprawling camp of refugees and situated their large group on an empty plain.

They had all removed their armour and weapons, leaving them in neat rows by the tents they had abandoned. Dressed in robes and furs, they positioned themselves into a series of interlocking circles and sat down in the cold snow. Lady Ellöria was part of the smallest and most inner circle.

Walking towards him, away from the elves, was Ayana Glanduil. A master on the Dragorn council and an elf, Ayana was powerful in more ways than one. Gideon was thankful she was loyal to the order, but also to him.

"Do they have everything they need?" he asked before she reached him.

"They need only the energy of the earth itself," she answered. "They are more powerful like this."

Gideon cupped his jaw, worry lines marring his head. "Good..." he muttered.

Ayana had only to steal a glance to know he was concerned. "Alastir and Valkor have offered to assist them but I've told them they are to do nothing but rest."

"Good..." he uttered.

"You fear this won't work?" she enquired.

"I fear that five hundred elves have just left the battlefield," Gideon said, specifying his concerns. "They each count for more than one man in a fight. Now, they're just sitting in a field..."

"If this works," Ayana reminded him, "the orcs will be banished to dark once more."

Gideon looked up at the black sky. "Lady Ellöria told me this kind of spell hasn't been done for at least a century."

"That doesn't mean it won't work," Ayana insisted.

The Master Dragorn could see the orcs tunnelling under their feet every time he closed his eyes. He could see the sense in this spell, and he would never question the wisdom of Lady Ellöria, but timing was a key issue that few understood. If the orcs attacked in the next few minutes, which they could, the elves would have to rely on Namdhor's army to keep the orcs at bay until they remedied the sky.

"Has there been any word from Doran or Galanör?" Ayana asked.

There was another concern. "None," Gideon replied. "We could really do with a dwarven army arriving about now. It would also be good to know that I haven't sent three good men to their deaths..."

"The dwarves are stubborn by nature," Ayana said lightly. "I'm sure their hunt was successful, and I have no doubt that seeing an orc will enrage all of Dhenaheim."

Again, Gideon could see that it was all a matter of time, the one thing he was convinced they were all but out of.

In the hope of a distraction, he nodded at the elves in the distance. "How does this work then?"

"In theory it's simple," Ayana explained. "But magic at this level is never simple. Together, they will combine their magic, sharing it with one another in their circles. Then, when harmony is reached, they will begin to bleed the magic between the circles and build upon it. Once a limit is reached, they allow Lady Ellöria to assume control of it. This is when it becomes dangerous. That much power is life threatening."

Gideon couldn't help but think of the pools of Naius, once a source of power that damned any who entered them. "Then it's a good thing Lady Ellöria is in control," he commented.

"Indeed, her experience and age will aid her in this endeavour. However, bringing back the sun will be no simple task."

The Master Dragorn was inclined to agree. "It is a very big sky..."

"I would help," Ayana added, "but Deartanyon and I will be needed on the battlefield."

Gideon agreed. "When the time comes," he instructed her, "keep to the rear. It's going to be chaos and someone needs to stand between the orcs and the elves."

Ayana looked to protest, wishing to be on the front lines with Gideon no doubt, but her attention was drawn away from the Master Dragorn. Following her gaze, Gideon turned around to see the masses trailing down the main slope of Namdhor. Accompanying their exodus, the people of the camp began to leave their tents and move towards The King's Lake.

"What's going on now?" Gideon asked with an exasperated tone. "The orcs could attack at any minute and everyone's leaving the city."

"Worse," Ayana commented, "they're moving closer to the mountains, around the lake."

So ludicrous were their actions that Gideon could only think of one man that would give such an order. "Arlon Draqaro is going to be the end of the known world..."

"What is he doing?" Ayana took a step forward before Gideon held out his arm.

"Stay close to your kin," he said. "I will investigate."

Climbing onto Ilargo, the pair launched into the air and circled around to fly towards the city. From above, it was easy to see the flow of people as they made their way to the shore of The King's Lake.

They are amassing around the arch, Ilargo reported.

Gideon shifted his weight to look over the edge. Indeed, the people were gathering in great numbers before the massive arch that connected the slope of the city to the mighty pillar that held it up.

The King's Hollow... Gideon said with despair. ***Arlon has decided that now is the right moment to be officially crowned the king of Illian.***

He was going to wait until after the battle, Ilargo pointed out. *I thought he wanted a great victory under his belt?*

He most likely wants the history books to state that he was king during the war. He's such a fool! All of these people are vulnerable!

Gideon, the army is moving...

The Master Dragorn shifted his weight to the other side and looked out on the western plains. Several battalions were breaking away from their formations and heading for The King's Hollow.

Gideon seethed. ***He just wants as big an audience as possible...***

Ilargo glided down and landed a little farther up the shore, where he wouldn't crush anyone. Gideon jumped down, pausing for a moment before he joined the crowds. He looked back over his shoulder to see the snowy mound that covered Thraden's remains. The sight was enough to make his stomach lurch.

We will reunite them, Ilargo promised.

Just as he reached the fringes of the amassing crowds, Ilargo sensed something that drew Gideon's eyes to the east. The Master Dragorn was the only person standing still in the shuffling mob.

What is it? he asked the dragon.

Above the people, Ilargo looked to the eastern horizon with his reptilian eyes, though he was searching with his mind rather than his sharp eyes. *Athis approaches!*

Just as Gideon felt, the dragon was elated and suspiciously curious at the same time. Inara hadn't been ordered to return, her fate her own, but she had been told to take her brother to The Life-less Isles.

They are not alone, Ilargo added. *Malliath and Alijah fly with them…*

Gideon wasn't sure what to make of that news yet. He was relieved to know that Alijah was alive but Malliath was an entirely unknown quantity. At least the last time the people of the north had seen him, he was scorching orcs by the hundreds. Still, bringing both of them to an inevitable battlefield was an error in Gideon's opinion.

Can you speak to Athis yet?

No, he is still too far.

Gideon pushed his way to the very edge of the shore and made his way around the crowds to reach The King's Hollow. As he arrived, the sound of trumpets blasted the air and the people turned to see a parade of horses cutting through the masses, led by Arlon himself. Trailing behind him was the Prime Cleric of Atilan's order, the only man with the power to bestow a crown upon the head of a would-be king or queen.

As soon as you can communicate with Athis, tell them where to meet me. This whole thing is a dangerous waste of time. We need to get everyone off the vale.

Gideon took a long breath. Life had become a series of problems that needed dealing with personally and one after the other. The source of so many of those problems was about to be crowned the king of the world…

Arlon and his elaborate entourage filled the natural space that had been left under The King's Hollow. He waved to the crowds with an arrogant smile, wearing expensive clothes and a deep purple cloak lined with white fur. The people were less than enthusiastic to see their future ruler, but there were Ironsworn thugs scattered throughout *encouraging* them to be welcoming. It was the only way a man like Arlon would ever get respect.

Gideon waited until he dismounted and the horses were taken away before striding across the beach. Two Gold Cloaks stepped forward to stop him in his tracks but they quickly recognised him and parted without a word. The Master Dragorn continued to the rocky shelf where the Prime Cleric and his assistants were setting up the *stage* for the crowning.

Only Sir Borin stood between Gideon and Arlon. The giant man looked down on the Master Dragorn, his eyes shadowed inside his bucket-like helmet.

"Come to witness history have you?" Arlon called as he began his short journey up the rocky shelf.

Gideon moved to the side to see past the behemoth. "This is folly!" he yelled over the noise of the crowd. "All of these people need to get as far away from the mountains as possible!"

Arlon continued to wave at the masses, pausing only to briefly inspect his golden crown as it was passed to the Prime Cleric. "The people need this, Master Thorn!" Arlon shouted down. "Many have lost their homes, their families, their very purpose in life! They need a celebration, one which will bring them all together and unite them! My crowning is perfect timing! After today, they shall feel as one people, Illians all under the rule of one king!"

Gideon stepped closer to the natural podium. "You're playing a fool's game, Arlon!"

The Ironsworn king snapped his head down at Gideon. His disdain slowly morphed into a cruel smile and he crouched down to bring him closer to the Master Dragorn.

"I was ruling Namdhor long before that crown was mine to claim. I don't recall you minding then. Think of this as making it *official*." Arlon stood up and assumed his regal pose and waving. "Oh, and Master Thorn? From the very second that crown touches my head, you will call me *king*..."

Gideon blended back into the front row of the crowd without another word. He wanted to take Mournblade in hand and cut that crown in half. He didn't much care if it was on Arlon's head or not.

The Prime Cleric stepped forward with a large leather-bound book in his hands, the pages open. "We are gathered here today, in the year of eleven thirty-one of the Third Age, to crown Arlon, son of..." The cleric caught himself and glanced nervously at Arlon.

"I wouldn't bother mentioning it," Arlon replied quietly, waving him on.

The cleric cleared his throat. "To crown Arlon of house Draqaro!"

The Prime Cleric continued in this fashion, reading exerts from the book of Atilan's order as the long and tedious ceremony required.

Gideon kept his hand on Mournblade...

CHAPTER 36
TRACKS IN THE DEEP

D oran Heavybelly was full of nostalgia, though not the kind he enjoyed. Riding his Warhog through the ancient tunnels of Vengora, he was leading Grimwhal's army beside his brother. They had set off days ago, journeying south through the plains of Dhenaheim, an army of nearly three thousand battle dwarves and two hundred war chariots.

Sixty years ago, the son of Dorain had led this very same army across the tundra and slaughtered thousands of Hammerkegs. His last campaign. Though he had vowed to never again take the life of a fellow dwarf, he had taken no such vow in regard to leading them again.

As if reading his mind, Dakmund turned to him from astride his own Warhog. "Ye're not leadin' this army ye know. They're followin' me," he added with a thumb in his chestplate.

"I know that," Doran snapped back. "I heard father just as everyone else did. My fate is to die in battle an' hope that Grarfath takes pity on me..."

Dakmund glanced over his shoulder, checking the gap between them and the army. "Ye know he doesn' want that, don' ye?"

486

Doran wet his lips and mimicked his brother's cursory glance. "I think he'd be satisfied if I survived an' never showed me face again, aye."

"He told me abou' his plan," Dakmund continued. "Abou' me claimin' the throne upon me return..."

Doran turned to look at the axe-hammer strapped horizontally across the back of his brother's saddle. "*If* ye return," he emphasised, "it'll be with Andaljor in hand an' orc blood on ye steel. Who's goin' to deny ye the throne? The lords will offer ye great gifts an' kiss ye boots!"

Dakmund smiled. "Maybe I'll wait to clean them..."

Doran shared a short laugh with his brother before they calmed down, keeping up appearances. "It's not what I wanted for ye," he confessed. "Even father took heart in havin' a son who didn' kill other dwarves every other week. This burden should be mine, Brother..."

"Lift ye chin first-born!" Dakmund had a cheer in his voice. "This might not be the life either o' us imagined for me, but how often does the second-born get to wear the crown? Also, this entire plan has forced the clan from that ridiculous hierarchy. Don' ye get it, Doran? Now I get to really change things, make a difference where father couldn'!"

"Ye mean... Ye mean ye're not angry abou' it?"

Dakmund waved the notion away. "Don' get me wrong, I've got a lot o' hard work ahead o' me, work I could 'ave avoided had ye remained. But I'm accustomed to fightin' now, both in an' out o' the throne room."

It was baffling to hear his brother speak this way. "Ye are?" he asked astonished.

"Ye were gone for sixty years, ye dope, what do ye think I've been doin'? I'm better with a sword now than a brush. An' I know how to navigate the lords an' their lackeys. Ye jus' wait, Brother! Grimwhal is goin' to become the shinin' beacon o' what Dhenaheim could be."

That all sounded rather wonderful to the stout ranger, but he

487

more than struggled to envision it. Even if the lords put their support behind Dakmund, he still had an entire clan to bring around. How many generations had been brought up to believe in nothing else but the hierarchy?

"So... What did mother say to ye?" Dakmund enquired. "I saw her speakin' to ye before we left."

Doran could still feel his mother's hand on his cheek and see the tear in her eye. Her words, however, had been stern.

"*I have said goodbye to you far too many times,*" she had said. "*Every parting breaks my heart that much more. I fear it will shatter into pieces if your brother does not return.*" The light touch of her hand on his cheek stretched out to grip his jaw. "*Your path is your own now, Doran - you saw to that. Dakmund knows nothing but this clan. Make sure he comes back to me.*"

Doran let go of the memory and kept his eyes on the tunnel ahead. "She said if ye can' lift Andaljor than I was to wield it..." He succeeded in keeping his face straight for a few more seconds before cracking up with his brother.

"Ye're a liar, Doran Heavybelly," Dakmund accused in jest.

Doran let a moment go by. "She said goodbye."

"Oh aye? How many times is that then?"

Doran shook his head. "This time she meant it. They're lettin' me go, Dak. Father's way o' sayin' goodbye is givin' me the slimmest chance to walk away from all o' this, after the orcs are dealt with, o' course. Mother's way..." The ranger swallowed hard. "I've caused her too much pain. She has to let me go an' focus on the future. That would be ye, Brother."

Dakmund nodded along with tight lips. "When I'm king, Doran, ye will be more than welcome in me—"

Doran held up his hand. "I know, I know. But ye won't invite me, Dak; ye mustn'. Yer plans for Grimwhal are drastic enough without havin' me sittin' at yer table. There's no redemption for me in Dhenaheim an' I'm a'right with that, I've made me peace with it. Jus' promise me ye'll be a *good* king, that's all."

Dakmund sighed. "I promise, Brother."

"Right then," Doran announced with a cheerier tone, "enough o' this! I bet ye the royal coffers I kill more orcs than ye, Andaljor or no Andaljor."

"Bah!" Dakmund chuckled to himself. "Don' make bets ye can' afford, *Ranger*."

Before they could erupt in more laughter, two figures steadily came into view up ahead. The shadows melted away to reveal Galanör and Russell.

"What 'ave ye found, fellas?" Doran called.

"Ye know," Dakmund said, leaning over his Warhog, "we 'ave scouts, damn good ones too."

Doran smiled. "Not like these two ye don'."

Galanör fell in alongside Pig. "The orcs have moved on," he reported.

The son of Dorain grumbled. "I was afraid o' that..."

"They're farther south," the elf continued. "They mean to take Namdhor before invading Dhenaheim."

"That's not all," Russell chipped in. "I caught the scent of something foul, and I mean *foul*. We found some, well, I suppose they were tracks, but whatever left them is a beast we don't want to tackle down here."

"There were other tracks too," Galanör added. "Smaller, but still much larger than any of us. If I was to guess, I would say the big one is hunting the smaller ones."

Doran shrugged. "What's this got to do with the orcs, lads?"

Galanör looked to Russell and the werewolf tapped his nose. "I can smell them, the orcs. Wherever this big beastie goes, the orcs aren't far behind it."

Dakmund backhanded his brother's arm. "They're herdin' it!" he concluded.

Doran frowned. "Sounds daft to me."

Galanör shook his head. "Not if you're planning on battling dragons..."

"Show us these tracks," Dakmund commanded.

The army followed the rangers farther into Illian's foundations. The *tracks*, as Russell had called them, were more than easy enough to spot; they were so large they had formed new tunnels. Dakmund ordered the march to halt while he and Doran dismounted to investigate by torchlight.

"What could burrow through the rock like this?" Dakmund asked, perplexed by the round tunnels and their perfectly ridged surfaces.

Doran knew of only one such monster, a creature from the oldest tales of The Great War. "A stonemaw," he proclaimed.

Dakmund scratched the back of his head. "Stonemaw? From grandfather's stories?"

"They weren' stories, Dak," Doran reminded him. "They were accounts from The Great War."

"Of what beast do you speak?" Galanör questioned.

"A very big one," Doran answered, recalling the tales. "They live deep in the earth. Supposedly, if the legends are true, they burrowed the first tunnels that were later inhabited by me oldest ancestors. The orcs used them for their evil durin' the war. Rode them into battle on the surface an' let them devour dwarves by the hundreds."

Russell crouched down and sniffed the ground. "There's definitely another creature, quite a few of them I'd say."

"Likely bait," Dakmund suggested. "How else would ye guide a stonemaw? Ye can' tame 'em!"

Doran looked to the tunnel ahead and back to the waiting army behind him. "We need to press on, an' with some haste no less. There's orcs to be killin' an' we're runnin' out o' time."

"No, master dwarf," Galanör corrected. "It's Namdhor that's running out of time..."

CHAPTER 37
BY THE OLD LAWS

Situated on a towering slope and supported by a single pillar of rock, Namdhor was a marvel to behold. Approaching from the sky, there wasn't much that could distract from the magnificence of its stature on the horizon. For Vighon Draqaro, however, there was one scene that stole his attention, drawing him to the ground instead.

His stomach dropped, and not just because Malliath was making a swift descent. Curving around the base of Namdhor's slope, dark crowds were swarming The King's Hollow - that could only mean one thing.

Adding to the scene, large swathes of the army were breaking away from their formations and joining the masses. It looked like chaos from the sky. Farther south, away from the gathering crowds, Vighon discovered a strange pattern of interlocking circles in the snow. They appeared to be made of people, though they were too far away to say any more on the matter.

Adding to the strange vista that greeted them, a roaring line of fire scarred the northern land. Judging by the debris that littered the base of the flames, there had once been a row of catapults. There were no bodies scattered and no signs of a battle, leaving Vighon to wonder what had been happening in his absence.

Now easing into a gradual descent, Athis and Malliath began to glide lazily in a wide circle over the masses, so as not to frighten them. Though the dragons were widely accepted as allies, there were still many survivors from Lirian and Velia who remembered all too well that a black dragon had been instrumental in the destruction of their homes.

Both dragons flew towards the edge of The King's Lake, where Ilargo towered over the crowds. Their hulking presence alone was enough to push the crowds away from the frozen lake. A silent moment was shared between Ilargo and Malliath, their dominant natures naturally clashing. If an agreement was made, it was beyond the northman's comprehension.

Let dragons and Dragorn deal with their own business, he thought. It was up to him to see justice delivered, not just for his mother, but for everyone his father had wronged.

Vighon followed Alijah down Malliath's shoulder, aware that the dragon was so large that jumping down wasn't an option. Ruban and Nemir were close behind; the elf using magic to lower Celeqor down. Safely on the ground once more, they soon joined up with those who had arrived on Athis's back. Together, with the dragons behind them, they strode towards The King's Hollow. The crowds parted without protest, including the obvious Ironsworn among them.

The Prime Cleric stumbled over a few lines as he took in the sight of three dragons. Arlon cleared his throat and the priest repeated himself with a bolder tone. Vighon pushed through those that remained in his path until he could lock eyes with his father. It was the first time seeing him since learning the truth of his mother's murder. He once hadn't thought it possible, but he looked at Arlon now and actually hated him even more.

Gideon walked in front of the northman, breaking his focus momentarily. "Did you find it?" he asked Asher urgently.

Vighon was only partially aware of their conversation, one in which Inara became heavily involved. He became aware of another presence beside him: Alijah. It was overwhelmingly good to have his friend back by his side, but even that wasn't enough to temper Vighon's rage. He needed justice and he wouldn't be satisfied until his father's blood stained his sword.

The Prime Cleric turned another page and licked his lips. "...As tradition dictates, a king or queen is to be crowned here, under the weight of the city itself! From the time of Gal Tion, the first king of Illian, this has been the way of the north..."

Vighon kept his father's gaze, a promise in his eyes that he would undo all of his work. The longer he stood there, on the edge of the crowd, the more revulsion and contempt he felt for the man who had tormented him, forced him to do unspeakable things and, ultimately, killed his mother.

"His every breath is an insult to her," he growled, drawing a questioning look from Alijah.

The Prime Cleric looked over his shoulder and gave another priest the nod to carry the crown over. "And in the tradition of our ancestors, and in accordance with King Tion's own laws, we turn to the people!"

Arlon tore his eyes from Vighon and stared daggers at the Prime Cleric. "What?" he hissed.

The cleric could only shrug and look as small as possible. "It is tradition, your Grace..." His life still his own, the priest squared his shoulders and continued, "We turn to the people! Will you the people of the north... of *Illian*, bow to this king? Will you entrust your wellbeing, your lands, and your blood to him?"

There was a palpable silence that settled over the crowds, broken only when The Ironsworn levelled threatening hands on shoulders. The ayes came through sporadically at first, but soon caught on until the masses were in agreement that protesting their king would be a costly mistake. It was forced from almost every mouth, but the realm of man was prepared to bow to their new king in return for their lives.

It wasn't right.

Alijah gripped his sword. "They deserve better..."

Vighon agreed, but his priorities were in a different place right now. He just wanted to make Arlon pay for decades of horrendous crimes that none dared challenge him on. And in the north, where punishments were harsh, there was only way to deliver justice.

Before he knew it, the sword of the north was free of its scabbard and in his hand.

"Arlon, of house Draqaro, has the support of the people!" the Prime Cleric cheered. "Now, with the right to the throne, do any offer challenge?"

Again, Arlon turned on the priest with a promise of death in his eyes. "Challenge?" he demanded furiously.

The Prime Cleric glanced nervously at the book and swallowed hard. "It is *tradition*..."

A tight yet wicked grin spread across Arlon's face. "I think you and I require a conversation regarding *tradition*, Prime Cleric."

Both Arlon and the priest turned to look down on Vighon, who was now standing in the open space between the crowd and the rocky podium. The northman didn't even remember taking those steps to break away, but here he was with sword in hand.

His heart was beating like thunder in his chest.

The Prime Cleric's mouth dropped open and Arlon offered his son a scowl that would make most men run to the other side of the country. The people, however, were decidedly in the priest's camp of surprise and gasped at Vighon with wide eyes.

Had Vighon taken his eyes from his father, he would have noticed that everyone was looking at him.

"Do you..." The Prime Cleric adjusted his collar. "Do you offer *challenge* for the crown?"

Vighon should have screamed *no* until his lungs gave out but, instead, he pointed his fine sword at Arlon. "I offer justice for all those who have suffered under an Ironsworn rule!"

Arlon had no immediate response but to look out over the crowds. He was calculating, like always.

"You murdered her!" Vighon spat, filling the silent void that followed his proclamation.

Judging by the look on his father's face, he knew exactly what Vighon was talking about. "You are a deserter and a traitor to Namdhor!" he hurled, clawing back control. "By what right do you claim challenge?"

Vighon didn't care about any challenge. "I stand against you for those who you put in the ground! I should have done this long ago..."

Arlon bit his lip before snatching the book from the priest. He scanned the page until he found what he needed. "To challenge on the day of crowning!" he announced. "As the would-be king must seek support from the people, so too must the challenger!" Arlon was like an animal with his prey stuck in a corner. "People of Illian! Does Vighon Draqaro, a *traitor*, have your support to challenge my claim? Would you have a king who would kill his own father?"

Vighon had heard enough; there was no amount of written word that would come between him and his father. "I didn't come for any crown, I just came for you!" he barked, starting towards the podium.

Gideon rushed forward and planted a firm hand on his shoulder. "Don't," he warned, gesturing to Sir Borin and the knights that guarded Arlon. "Without a legitimate challenge, you won't even get close to him."

"Aye!" came a single call from the crowd.

Vighon turned to see Captain Garrett of the Skids. The older man stood proud on the front row and nodded at him with a wink. His vote was followed by a chorus more from the rest of the Skids, then Ruban close by. Their votes weren't nearly enough to have his challenge made legal, but their calls grew exponentially, spreading across the masses who knew of Vighon Draqaro and his flaming sword, the man who had stood between them and the orcs.

Inara's distinct voice yelled, "Aye!" and Athis and Ilargo added their roars to her vote.

This moment would have been overwhelming in every sense if Vighon knew what he had really just done. As it was, he advanced beyond Gideon and stood before his father with only one thought passing through his head: nothing would come between them now.

Arlon was visibly angered by the crowd's reaction but he managed to contain the plethora of threats that clearly dominated his thoughts. He looked down at his son with a mixture of disappointment, anger, and pity - an expression only achieved by a parent, even a terrible one.

Vighon was keen to become an orphan...

"Do you accept this challenge yourself?" the Prime Cleric asked Arlon, surprising the Ironsworn. "Or do you have a champion to fight in your stead?"

"A champion?" Vighon echoed, seeing his desired justice slipping through his fingers.

"Yes," the priest confirmed, looking from son to father. "You may each put forth a champion to fight on your behalf. It is... *tradition*," he added with audible trepidation.

A flicker of a smile flashed across Arlon's face before he took the opportunity to address the people again. "What kind of a king would I be if I began my reign by bloodying my own sword with that of my son's? I must request a champion fight my challenger and save my soul!" The Ironsworn looked down at his entourage. "Sir Borin! Will you be my champion and fight for the one who *rules* Namdhor?"

The giant stepped into the open space opposite Vighon and brandished his over-sized claymore.

The Prime Cleric turned to Vighon. "Do *you* have a champion?"

"No..." Vighon's mind could conjure no more words than that, too occupied was it with assessing the monster in front of him.

"Then you may prepare for battle!" the priest called out, setting the crowd off with renewed excitement.

Vighon gritted his teeth and stared hard at his father. "If I have to go through every one of your thugs, I will..."

Gideon pulled the northman back to the line. "We really don't need this right now," he insisted with some urgency. "We need to get everyone back!"

Vighon removed his black cloak and fur, handing it naturally to Ruban. "Someone has to make him answer for everything," he argued. "And since you aren't going to do anything, I will."

Gideon clenched his jaw and backed off as Inara took his place. "Do you know what you've just done?"

Vighon glanced at Sir Borin the Dread. "I haven't done *anything* yet." He inspected the length of his exquisite sword. "But I will."

He met Alijah's eyes but it wasn't the friend he knew looking back at him. He was quiet, unusual in itself, considering his oldest friend was about to fight to the death.

"Here." Ruban offered the northman his shield back. "I think you're going to need it..."

Vighon hefted the shield in his left hand. He had no pleasantries to offer the young man, nor anyone for that matter. He was entering into the most important fight of his life and he meant to focus on one thing and one thing only: the swing of his sword.

"Is there to be a dual?" Arlon called from the podium. "Or will you lay down your sword and bow to me?"

Vighon was about to stride back into the open space when Asher gripped him by the shoulder and turned him back. "Do you know what that is?" he asked, looking over the northman's shoulder.

"Sir Borin? He's a fiend of a witch's making. I've killed fiends before," he added boldly.

"Not like that one you haven't," Asher replied. "I saw Yelifer's work, in her room. She wasn't just a witch, she was a golem-maker."

Vighon scrunched his eyes briefly, his mind beginning to wander from the fight to come. "What's that then?"

"Look at him," Asher bade. "No man born of a woman could look like that. Sir Borin is a *golem*; a monster made of dead men. The more parts they're made of the more powerful they are. Judging by the size of him, I'd say he's made from a lot of dead men."

The northman shrugged. "You don't need to be a ranger to know he's going to be hard to kill."

"You can't kill him," Asher stated.

"Watch me," Vighon countered.

"No, I mean you can't *kill* a golem - there's nothing to kill. Only the golem-maker knows the words to destroy it and she's dead."

Vighon was becoming increasingly irritated. "Have *you* ever fought one?"

"A couple of times," the ranger answered. "The first one I dropped into a hole so deep it'll still be there to this day. The second was more powerful. I had to chop it up into pieces, box each limb up, and bury them separately."

Vighon pretended to look around. "I don't see any big holes and I left all my limb-boxes in my room." Asher was about to offer more advice when the northman held up his hand. "I'm just going to cut off his head. If he keeps going, I'll cut some more off him. Nothing is getting between me and Arlon."

Vighon turned around and met Sir Borin in the open space. To their right, Arlon and the Prime Cleric watched from the rocky podium, while to their left, the masses of Illian crammed to spectate the most exciting thing they had witnessed in a long time.

"Last chance," Arlon offered, his words sincere.

Vighon tilted his head towards the podium. "You shouldn't have killed her..."

The Prime Cleric opened his arms dramatically. "With Atilan as witness, let the challenge commence!"

Sir Borin moved with more speed than Vighon had ever witnessed in the giant. His claymore came down fast and impressively hard - a strike so sure it would have cleaved any man in half from head to groin. The northman, thankfully, wasn't standing in the same place. Rolling away, Vighon came up beside the golem and swiped with a back-handed swing. The silvyr blade sliced neatly through Sir Borin's waist, spraying the crowd with rotten gore.

They loved it.

The first strike given, the masses cheered, though whether it was bloodlust or support of Vighon was too hard to tell. Either way, Sir Borin didn't notice. The golem raised his claymore with one hand and brought it down again on Vighon. With his enchanted shield held high, the northman took the jarring blow and collapsed to his knees under the weight. He dared to glimpse over the rim of the shield before bracing again, the second strike incoming.

"Keep moving!" he heard Inara yell.

The northman did just that, scrambling to the side before a third strike landed on his shield and broke his arm. Jumping back to his feet, Vighon's shield arm felt numb and he struggled to lift it above his shoulder. There was no time, however, to assess any serious injury - Sir Borin was coming at him again.

Vighon ducked under the first swing and lashed out himself, taking a chunk from the golem's thigh. Nothing slowed the creature down. The heavy claymore came down again and again, each one missing due to the shift in the northman's shoulders. When the long blade was buried in the mud, Vighon hammered the base of the steel with his shield, hoping to knock it from the golem's grip.

It didn't.

Instead, Sir Borin grabbed the edge of Vighon's shield and flung it from the northman's arm before slamming him in the chest with a solid punch. The air exploding from his lungs, Vighon flew back and rolled through the mud, coughing and spluttering.

It was Inara and Alijah who helped him up, but it was Asher who whispered in his ear. "Golems can't swim..."

Vighon pushed through the biting pain in his chest and looked from Asher to the shoreline of The King's Lake. It was frozen solid.

Groaning, the northman pushed away from Alijah and met Sir Borin in battle once more. Without his shield now, he had no choice but to clash swords and evade where possible - there was little to be done against the golem's strength.

Manoeuvring the golem towards the lake wasn't easy. Every time he positioned himself to back up, and have Sir Borin follow him, the northman was forced to dive away to avoid losing a vital body part. For every blow the golem landed, Vighon required a two-handed hold to parry. One such blow knocked him down to one knee and the pressing claymore bit into his forehead.

He had no choice but to roll away again and search for a new angle of attack - not that it ever did much. His silvyr sword was coated in the golem's blood and gore and the ground was equally stained, yet still Sir Borin advanced.

A back hand from any creature Sir Borin's size would hurt, but a back hand from a creature wearing an iron gauntlet was almost enough to end the fight for Vighon. The world blurred into one stretch of light and before he knew it, he was face down on the ground and spitting blood.

"Get up!" he heard from everyone.

His head was so dizzy that standing up wasn't an option right now, so he settled for rolling aside. The claymore chopped into the mud where he had fallen, missing him by inches. Crouched over his blade, Vighon saw the golem's vulnerability and simply reacted, swinging his sword from his back. The silvyr blade caught Sir Borin across his bucket-like helmet and sent it flying through the air.

The crowd ceased their cheers and stared in horror at Arlon's champion. Sir Borin's face was not for the eyes of children and perhaps not even the bravest of men. His eyes were glazed grey and surround by flesh that had died decades past, surviving now through magic alone. The golem's face was a putrid colour and dissected by stitches, separating the various patches of individual's skin. His scalp was bald and marked with black tattoos, symbols that were no more than gibberish to Vighon.

A new wound was added to Sir Borin's cheek, where the sword of the north had cut through his helmet. The stitching was torn and two pieces of skin folded away from each other, revealing the muscle beneath. So shocking was the sight of him, that Vighon reclaimed his wits and staggered to his feet.

Sir Borin slowly rose to his towering height and pulled his sword from the mud. It was unclear if golems could feel anger, but that was the aura Vighon was feeling from the giant.

"Come on then," he growled at the beast. "Come on!"

The golem strode towards him and Vighon backed up, forcing the crowd to part and The King's Lake to dominate the landscape. The ice was slippery under foot, but at least it took his weight. The northman had crossed the lake as a much younger man and knew the winter ice was always thick. He began to doubt its strength, however, when Sir Borin and all his considerable weight joined him.

Be it confidence or ignorance, the golem advanced quickly on the ice. Vighon dropped and pushed his body across the ice before the first swing chopped him in half. Still sliding, he pushed himself up to his knees and turned to face his foe. Incredibly, Sir Borin was almost on top of him again. That malevolent claymore came down again with the intention of splitting the northman's skull open.

It wasn't easy on the ice, but Vighon succeeded in launching himself to the side avoiding the mortal blow. The ice audibly cracked under the golem's strike and splintered outwards from the point of the claymore like a spider's web. Still, the ice held.

Vighon sighed and scrambled to his feet, his sword ready. Their blades clashed only once and the northman was thrown back to the ice, his footing useless. Hitting the lake's hard cover was painful, eliciting a strong curse from Vighon - directed mostly at Asher and his moronic idea.

They were farther out now, some way from the shore line. There would be no help, not that Vighon would accept any. He had to be rid of the golem, an obstacle between him and his real desire.

Sir Borin lunged forward and brought his deadly claymore down on the northman. With his blade held horizontally, one hand on the silvyr, Vighon raised his weapon and intercepted the claymore. It was a heavy blow. The ice beneath his back cracked. Then the golem struck again in the same fashion, only to be blocked by the sword of the north. Again and again the creature attacked, every blow damaging the ice under them both.

Vighon viciously kicked out, hoping to break Sir Borin's knee, but the golem never faltered. Both of the northman's arms were going numb under the continued bombardment. It was only a matter of time before Arlon's champion changed tactics and attacked from a different angle.

The ice cracked again and Vighon felt the support dipping.

Sir Borin struck again.

The ice cracked some more.

The golem raised his claymore over his foul head with both hands. Vighon knew his arms didn't have it in them to keep this next blow at bay. The steel would press down, burying both itself and the sword of the north into his body. Then Arlon would get away with it all...

Vighon roared at the golem and his imminent attack. As the claymore cut through the air, the northman folded his arms and rolled to the side. Sir Borin hammered the broken ice with the strength of five men and it split through to the blisteringly cold water beneath. The event was entirely too slow for Vighon, who half-rolled back and slammed his sword onto the ice at the golem's feet.

The ice gave way.

There was no shock or surprise on Sir Borin's face as he plummeted into the depths of The King's Lake. One of his large hands reached out for the ice, but it broke away under his weight, leaving him to vanish below the dark surface.

Vighon lay back and caught his breath. Everything hurt, especially his face where the golem had back-handed him. There would be time for pain later, he told himself. Removing Sir Borin was a means to an end, his father's end...

Walking cautiously over the ice, Vighon made his way to the shore, a spectacle for all. There were no cheers for him, no hollers of congratulations. The people were in shock. Vighon assumed they had all expected him to die in that fight. If it wasn't for Asher, he probably would have. The northman was wrong, of course; his survival was not what shocked the people of Illian.

Standing before the rocky podium, haggard from battle, Vighon puffed out his chest and looked up at his father. "You're next..."

Arlon possessed an expression Vighon had never seen on his father's face before. It told of panic, a panic that wore down his outrage and left him struggling as to what to do. There had always been a fight in Arlon Draqaro but, right now, he looked on the verge of running.

Seeing that face, Vighon finally understood what Queen Yelifer had been speaking about. Arlon *was* afraid of him. The old Ironsworn was afraid of the one man - a younger and stronger version of himself - who could best him and unravel decades of planning. It was this very moment that he feared...

"Vighon Draqaro emerges the victor!" the Prime Cleric exclaimed to a shocked crowd. "In the eyes of the great Atilan and by the old laws of King Tion, I give you... OUR KING!"

Now the crowd roared.

Vighon, on the other hand, stared blankly at the priest. "Our what?" he asked, his questions drowned out by the cheering masses.

What in all the hells had he just done?

Arlon snapped. The Ironsworn pushed the priest aside and snatched a sword from the scabbard of a Gold Cloak. Vighon braced himself as his father jumped off the podium with his stolen sword angled down at him. A force, unseen by the eye, gripped Arlon mid-air and yanked him roughly to the ground with a pathetic yelp from the man.

The impact was hard and he dropped the sword in favour of cradling his body. Vighon relaxed and turned around to see Alijah's hand outstretched. He couldn't recall ever seeing his old friend use magic. Looking from Alijah to Malliath, the northman knew his closest friend wasn't the same anymore, and that scared him a little bit.

He offered the half-elf a grateful nod and turned back to his father, who was being hauled to his feet by Captain Garrett and a handful of Skids.

"You stupid fool!" Arlon spat from his knees, his arms locked behind him. "You have no idea what you've done! I disown you! You are no son of mine! Today you made an enemy you can't hope to—"

Garrett gripped Arlon by the throat. "Shut it! What would you have us do with him... *Your Grace?*"

Those last two words made Vighon feel nauseous. He stepped back from the Skids and his father, his eyes roaming aimlessly over the crowds and his friends. He hadn't done this for a crown. Justice motivated him, nothing more. The northman told himself over and over it wasn't vengeance, but he knew if he swung his sword one last time, it *would* be bloody revenge. There was a choice to be made in that moment, a choice made all the harder by the urge in his arm to bring his sword to bear.

The Prime Cleric cleared his throat from the podium and gestured to the crown residing on a plump cushion. Vighon took a long breath and swallowed the sick that desperately tried to explode forth from his stomach. He had only wanted to make his father pay.

"Your Grace?" Garrett now held a dagger to Arlon's throat. "For attacking you, his punishment is rightly death."

Vighon licked his lips. "Put him in irons," he croaked before clearing his throat. "Put him in irons," he repeated with what confidence he could muster. "And get him out of my sight."

The Skids dragged Arlon away, leaving Vighon alone in the clearing. There were mutterings from the crowd about the sword of the north in his hand and whispers of their new king. Apparently, Vighon wasn't the only person shocked by this outcome.

"Vighon," Inara said his name softly and looked to the podium, where the crown awaited him.

He could see the warm smile on her face and was drawn towards the Dragorn, lost as he was. Inara changed her smile to one of sympathy and took him by the hand and arm, gently guiding him back to the Prime Cleric. They climbed the rocky podium together, king and Dragorn side by side.

The priest of Atilan picked up his book. "We are gathered here today," he announced with a booming voice, "in the year of eleven thirty-one of the Third Age, to crown Vighon, son of... Well, I suppose it doesn't really matter," he mumbled. "We will, erm, amend that for the future. By right of challenge and support of the people, we are to crown Vighon, of house Draqaro!"

The northman stood there, dumbstruck, looking out over the thousands of cheering people, all of whom were now his *subjects*. He had no words to describe how he felt, indeed, he was somewhat numb to the whole thing.

He was the king...

He was the king of Illian!

CHAPTER 38
A KING EMERGES

L ike an ever-present observer, Asher found himself standing in a moment of history once again. How many times had he borne witness to battles of the Ages? How many kingdoms had fallen while he walked the earth? How many times had he seen tyrants defeated and heroes born?

Now, in the freezing north of the world, the ranger observed history repeat itself. Illian was returning to its roots and that of one king.

This particular ceremony would be written into history, told through song, and passed on from generation to generation for all time. The realm had stood on the brink of destruction, an inevitable conclusion under the rule of Arlon Draqaro. But then, a young man, a warrior in the eyes of the people, raised his sword and said *no*.

Asher knew he would be hearing this story in every tavern for the rest of his life. The rise of the first humble king, they would likely say. The crown given to a man who didn't want it and would claim he hadn't been fighting for it. He was perfect...

The ranger cracked a genuine smile at seeing Vighon's face - a man stunned to his core. He didn't know much about the young warrior, but he knew the northman had lived a life far simpler than any king or queen. This would change everything, and not just for Vighon, but for everyone.

"It's just like the days of old," Nathaniel commented beside him.

"What's that?" Asher asked over the cheers and applause.

"Before there were bloodlines," Nathaniel elaborated, "back when the word *noble* didn't exist. He's fought for the right and the people support him. When was the last time you saw a king be chosen by the people?"

The old knight had a point, but Asher's attention had wandered over to Alijah, the only person who wasn't beaming at their new king or celebrating. In fact, the half-elf had no readable expression at all. He stood abnormally still with his hand resting on his hilt, his eyes looking straight through Vighon.

There was nothing threatening about his stance, or even his look, but Asher knew how his mind worked, how Malliath's mind worked. Vighon's ascension wasn't part of the plan...

That should have made the ranger feel better, but it actually made his stomach lurch. The Crow had been right about everything from the moment he started spewing his visions of the future. Everything that had transpired over the last ten thousand years, including the downfall of the other kingdoms, had been to see Alijah on the throne.

So why wasn't he?

The obvious conclusion: The Crow was wrong. But Asher had spent too much time with the necromancer and seen too much to believe that. His next conclusion was far worse: Alijah would replace Vighon as king by force...

Having been inside Alijah's head, Asher couldn't see that scenario playing out. They were like brothers, closer than Alijah was with Inara.

Asher's thoughts froze under the boring eyes he could feel in the back of his head. Looking over his shoulder, Malliath was watching him intently, his purple eyes beautiful despite their promise of death. The ranger turned away from the dragon and discovered Alijah was also watching him now. All three shared a silent moment amidst the hubbub, no words required to voice the tension that existed between them.

The ceremony was suddenly interrupted when the distant cheers of the crowd were replaced by gasps. The effect rippled across the people until those under The King's Hollow were turning around to see what had cut through the ceremony.

In the silence, only Gideon's reassuring voice could be heard. "The elves..."

Asher joined the people in their wondrous gaze, the light reflecting in his eyes. The light in question was a towering column, just translucent enough to see through to the other side. The spectacular beam shot up from the ground, somewhere in the south, and pierced the dark clouds above.

It was beautiful.

The majestic sight held the gaze of all, but for a moment. The magic of the elves was ruined by another event, this time from the north.

The ground shook with a single, yet monstrously violent, tremor. The air snapped with a thundering *boom* that stretched across The White Vale, eliciting screams from the thousands gathered. The source of the explosion dominated the north as a mountain of dirt and bedrock was launched into the sky as high as the Vengoran peaks, taking the burning catapults with it and ripping the earth asunder.

The crowd immediately panicked and tried to scatter, but their packed numbers created only chaos. Beyond the people, Namdhor's army turned around and raced back to their positions.

The world was spinning out of control.

The worrying sound of splitting rock echoed inside The King's Hollow and ran up the length of the rising slope. Asher held his breath, hoping that the ancient stone would hold up.

The ground shook again when the debris, slabs of earth larger than houses, impacted the northern lands. In the distance, the Vengoran mountains failed to hold on to their blankets of snow. The avalanches were enough to conceal the sprawling forest that lined their base and fog the horizon.

"It's the orcs!" Gideon warned, gripping Mournblade in its scabbard.

Asher grabbed Ruban and tugged him to his side. "You stay close to me," he instructed, glancing at the pack on the squire's back.

"We need to free the weapon!" Vighon yelled as he jumped off the rocky podium.

"I'm open to suggestions," Asher remarked.

"Let me see it," Alijah commanded, his hand out.

Ruban removed the slab of jagged stone from his pack and lifted it for the half-elf to see. Vighon and Inara used the time to usher more people along the base of the city's foundations, pushing them south. Along with Reyna and Nathaniel, they ordered any soldier they came across to herd everyone back as far as they could. In the distance, the mountain of dirt still stained the air as the lighter debris continued to fall from the great height.

Alijah was hefting the jagged rock after inspecting the glyphs. "Perhaps a Vi'tari blade can break the stone..." Everyone took note of the jade scimitar he swept from his belt.

Gideon started forward and snatched Alijah's wrist from the air. "Where did you find that blade?"

Alijah raised a questioning eyebrow. "I don't think now is the time."

The Master Dragorn swallowed his next words and looked from the half-elf to Asher, though the ranger had little to offer. Whatever was to become of Alijah, it would have to wait until the orcs were pushed back.

Reclaiming his sword arm, Alijah threw the rock in the air and swiped with his scimitar. The enchanted weapon didn't so much as scratch the stone. As disappointing as that was, Gideon appeared far more distressed with the blade being used at all.

Faylen retrieved it from the ground and turned to Celeqor, but the elf was barely conscious. "A dragon..." she whispered. "Elder Celeqor said only something as powerful as a dragon could break through the ward."

Asher knew Faylen to be right, but the ground under their feet rumbled, distracting him. Blowing a hole in The White Vale wasn't intended to kill them all, but what followed certainly was.

"We're running out of time," he warned, looking east. The knights of Namdhor were scrambling into their formations, waiting for the orcs to emerge from the devastating hole.

The people having scattered to the south, Ilargo was able to approach the group. The emerald dragon waited for Faylen to drop the rock on the ground and step away. Then he unleashed his breath upon it. A concentrated inferno engulfed the weapon, replacing the freezing air with an intense heat.

Ilargo closed his jaw and raised his head, waiting for the smoke to clear. Asher had a bad feeling about what awaited them. Faylen crouched down and wafted the curling smoke away, revealing a perfectly intact piece of jagged stone.

"It doesn't even look hot," Vighon observed, returning with Inara and her parents.

Tentatively, Faylen touched it. "That's because it's still cold. The magic holds..."

Asher was beginning to feel as if he had let them all down. Only his confidence that The Crow wished for them to win this battle prevented him from losing all hope.

"Wait!" Inara called. "We already have something that can break wards!" The young Dragorn pulled free the Moonblade from her belt, exposing its startling glow.

The ranger stole a glance at Malliath, wondering if the dragon could still feel the sting of the Moonblade as he could. Judging by the subtle shake of his head, the ancient wyrm had no trouble recalling its bite.

With the jagged stone in one hand and the Moonblade in the

other, Inara drove the magical weapon into the flat surface, between the ring of warding glyphs. The reaction was instantaneous and the shell broke apart as if struck by wrath powder. A bronze orb, the size of a man's palm, fell to the muddy ground.

They all looked down on it until Asher picked it up and held it high. The bronze surface was unremarkable and absent a single glyph or pattern of any kind. It matched the designs Asher had seen in the Dragon Rider's memories, at least in size, though that sphere had been overlaid in a web of some kind, providing the sphere with the appearance of small uneven windows. The similarity in size aside, this sphere looked better suited to weighing paper down on some mage's desk.

"How does it work?" Gideon asked urgently.

"I have no idea," Asher confessed. "I was hoping it would be evident..."

"My king!" A group of Gold Cloaks pushed through the back of the fleeing crowds and ran to Vighon's side. "We must get you to the safety of The Dragon Keep!"

The northman looked somewhere between surprised and unimpressed. "Not this day," he replied, drawing the sword of the north. "And not this king. Fetch horses so that we might join the others before the orcs attack." The Gold Cloaks hesitated.

"Your king has spoken," Inara reminded them.

"You heard his Grace!" the captain barked. "Fetch horses at once!"

Alijah sheathed his jade scimitar. "The weapon will work," he boldly stated, making his way to Malliath. "Until then, we hit the orcs with everything we have." The black dragon welcomed his companion before the pair took off into the air.

"There isn't time to debate," Inara said. "The orcs are coming." The Dragorn squeezed her mother's shoulder before running off to join Athis.

The Gold Cloaks returned with horses in tow as the red dragon leapt into the sky, battering them with snow and ash.

511

"Perhaps we should take the weapon to the elves," Nathaniel suggested.

Gideon shook his head. "They are all needed if the sun is ever to return." The Master Dragorn turned to Asher. "The weapon is left to you, Ranger. You say The Crow brought you back to use it... Let's hope he was right."

Asher pocketed the orb into a pouch on his belt and took the reins of the nearest horse. Their collective faith in The Crow was disturbing, especially Alijah's, but Asher couldn't say it was misplaced. They were all living inside the necromancer's designs, a reality they might have to live with forever...

As Gideon was making for Ilargo, Nathaniel called out to him. They didn't have time for words now, but the old knight offered him an apologetic look and embraced him with both arms. The Master Dragorn accepted the hold and patted Nathaniel on the back affectionately. They could all feel the gentle touch of death on their shoulder, this their last time in each other's company.

"If we are to die today," Nathaniel said to him, "then we will die as friends."

Gideon replied with a coy smile. "And be remembered as heroes."

"I'll settle for survivors," Reyna finished.

Gideon nodded in agreement before making his leave astride Ilargo. Nathaniel mounted a horse and Reyna jumped on behind him, just as Nemir jumped onto Faylen's horse. Vighon was given his own, though he was busy giving instructions to his knights, ordering them ahead to various battalions to get everyone ready.

"Can I come with *you*?" Ruban asked, looking up at the ranger.

"No," Asher replied bluntly. "What you *can* do is take care of Celeqor. Get him to the elves."

The squire wasn't satisfied. "But I can fight!" he protested.

"And you will," Asher said, turning his horse to the east. "You have the hardest task of us all, Ruban Dardaris: don't let a single orc interrupt the elves and their spell. Can you do this?"

The squire licked his lips and swallowed hard. "Yes, yes I can."

"Then go about it," Asher bade, hoping he had saved the young man's life.

Now only accompanied by two Gold Cloaks, Vighon pointed his horse to the east. His eyes were fixed on the smoking hole that potted The White Vale and his jaw was set, determined. An awful lot had just been placed on his shoulders, more so than any other that Asher could claim witness to.

"Right now would be a good time to use that weapon of yours," the northman commented.

"I don't know about you," Asher replied, drawing his two-handed broadsword, "but I feel like dealing with the orcs the old-fashioned way first."

Vighon grinned. "Agreed, Ranger."

As one, companions old and new galloped across The White Vale. To the south, the people were running for the shelter of the city, though they numbered so many that the elves were still hidden behind them. Their light, however, could be concealed by nothing. If all else failed, and it might, Asher knew their spell would clear the ash and bring about the end of the orcs' attack.

To the north, the mountains sat as watchers, spectators in a battle that would determine who ruled all of Illian. Between the Namdhorian army and the mountains, a hole so big it could likely fit the entire city inside of it ruined the landscape and would for all time. The surrounding plains were littered with debris, rocks so gigantic that they would never be shifted.

After a hard ride, the companions found themselves galloping along the front line of Namdhorians. Asher could see that the spearmen had been brought to bear and the archers grouped together behind them. Whatever emerged from that hole, these men were ready to put it down.

The army didn't cheer Vighon's arrival, and why would they? He had been anointed king only minutes ago and, for many, he was just the son of a wicked man. He had only gained the support of the people because the alternative was the leader of The Ironsworn. For those among the army who did know of Vighon Draqaro, however, they had witnessed his efforts at the battle for Grey Stone and his valour during Namdhor's first invasion. His courage could not be denied nor the victories already under his belt.

Still, this battle would be the making of the young king... Or it would be the shortest reign in Namdhor's history. Asher wasn't hoping for the latter.

Accompanying Reyna and Nathaniel, Asher dismounted his horse and fell in with Faylen and Nemir, inserting themselves into the northern ranks. Among them, the ranger could see the trepidation on the men's faces; they needed something to pick them up before the battle.

Vighon had apparently detected the same atmosphere and remained astride his horse. He looked out over the men, *his* men.

"Can you feel it?" he began, his voice booming. "The very ground under our feet trembles with their approach! They would grip us with fear! They would take our hearts before they take our lives and our land! Well not this day, I say! This day, the orcs will crash upon the sons of Illian and find the end that awaits them! I do not tell you this as your... as your *king*! No! This is not a day to stand behind a king and their words! Today, we are *all* kings! This is *your* kingdom! Will the orcs take it from you?"

The army resounded with a solitary roar, a ferocious beast that would defy any foe its victory. Asher was impressed.

"We fight together now, not as the north, but as a realm! We stand together as one people! And as long as my heart beats in my chest, I will not see Illian fall to the evil of orcs! Are you with me?" Vighon raised the sword of the north over his head and the army roared once again.

Nathaniel leaned into Faylen. "Light his sword," he told her eagerly.

The elf obliged and flicked her fingers in the air, sparking the flaming spell along the length of the silvyr blade. The army doubled their roar at the sight the fiery sword, *their* fiery sword. The northman, of course, did his best not to drop the blade as it spontaneously set on fire.

The northman dismounted and slapped his horse on the rear, sending it galloping away. Without his cloak or any plated armour, Vighon looked extremely vulnerable for a king on the battlefield. Then again, the same could be said of Asher and his companions who, all but Nemir, wore hardened leathers.

Nathaniel drew his sword and turned to Asher. "It's been a long time since we faced a battle like this together."

Asher observed Reyna nocking an arrow to her enchanted bow. "Not long enough," the ranger replied with a sly smile.

As Vighon had pointed out, the ground continued to tremble beneath their feet. Asher crouched down and placed the palm of his hand to the freezing dirt. Listening to the earth was an old lesson he wouldn't likely forget, regardless of the time he had spent among the dead.

"It's moving," he stated to Faylen's dismay.

"Moving?" she echoed.

"The tremors are moving south, away from us..." Asher stood up and looked back over the army.

Above them, he could see Ilargo, Athis, Malliath, and another dragon he couldn't name. The ranger should have felt confident under their watch, but he had a feeling in his gut that had rarely been wrong and, right now, it was telling him that something terrible was about to happen, something worse than the orcs emerging from that hole.

"Spears!" Vighon bellowed, and the message was carried along the line until the Namdhorians were pointing their spears at the smoking hole. "Archers! Nock!" The sound of hundreds of arrows fitting into their bows travelled across The White Vale.

Then, the worst happened...

To the south, behind the army, a series of deafening explosions rocked the land across the length of the army. Columns of red smoke plumed into the air, masking the light from the elves. Then came the distant growls and the roars of the orcs.

"They're flanking us!" was called out from one side of the army to the other.

"Turn around!" Vighon yelled. "Pass the spears to the rear! Archers! Move to the wings!"

The orcs finally showed themselves in great numbers. They poured out of their holes with apparently no other order but to attack. They showed no signs of formation or strategy beyond their flanking manoeuvre, relying on their numbers and ferocity as always. Before long, there were at least two thousand orcs already on The White Vale and charging into the Namdhorians' rear, where the oldest and most inexperienced fighters had been placed.

Worst of all, the masses of people and the conjuring elves were all the more vulnerable; now, they had no one standing between them and the orcs. Judging by the distance that lay between The King's Hollow and the elves, Asher calculated that Ruban had yet to reach them, meaning he was likely melting into the crowds with Celeqor. Of course, that didn't make them any safer...

The tremors beneath the ranger's feet returned.

He looked down and saw a collection of small rocks vibrating. It wasn't the colliding armies, however. Pausing his charge and that of his companions, Asher looked back, towards the smoking hole that had blown The White Vale to the sky and back. The tremors increased and they all heard the ground cracking under the surface.

"What in all the hells is that?" Nathaniel's expression was similar to the feeling in Asher's gut.

From within the veil of black smoke, dozens of spiders scurried across the snow and mud, weaving between the debris. To discern them from this distance meant the beasts must be huge.

"They're boxing us in!" Reyna exclaimed.

Asher hefted his broadsword in both hands. It had been an awfully long time since he had slain a giant spider and the ranger in him was looking forward to it.

But then the hole gave birth to the real monster, one so large that the ground cracked beneath it. Shaped like a snake and covered in natural armour that plated its enormous length, the monster slithered onto The White Vale devouring spider after spider. There were no eyes to see nor a head for that matter. Where a definable head should have been was a mouth as wide and high as its hideous body. Within that terrible maw sat row after row of fangs, each as thick as a grown man.

"Move!" Asher shouted at his companions.

They sprinted to the side and dived away before the beast slammed into the back of the army. It zig-zagged left and right, its jaws consuming men by the dozen and its bulk crushing dozens more.

Asher could do nothing but pick himself up, raise his sword, and charge after it...

CHAPTER 39
THE BATTLE FOR ILLIAN

From the sky, Gideon looked down and saw his worst fears realised. The orcs were unleashed upon The White Vale in the hundreds, soon amassing to the thousands as they impacted the rear of the Namdhorian army.

That's why they were digging, he said across his bond, a bond now shared with Athis and Deartanyon.

Inara's voice carried perfectly through the dragons to Gideon's mind. *They're behind the army now. The city is unguarded!*

Ayana cut through the air astride Deartanyon. *Let us draw a line the orcs dare not cross!*

All three dragons formulated a flight path in seconds, coordinating their efforts. Gideon held on to Ilargo as the green dragon dived east, angling for the open strip of snow that separated the emerging orcs from the elves and the city. Athis was doing the same, only he approached from west, swooping over the fleeing Namdhorians as he did.

Ilargo required no instruction from Gideon and he let loose his devastating breath. The jet of fire struck the ground and streaked from east to west, a mirror of Athis who did exactly the same west to east. Before the dragons collided mid-air, they craned their necks and flew upwards, their scales only feet apart. On the ground, a wall of fire now divided the battle from the people and the elves.

Deartanyon and Ayana glided low, their wrath aimed at the emerging orcs. As the violet dragon opened his maw to deliver a fiery death, something massive slithered onto the surface of the world to the north, catching the dragon's eye. Gideon saw it too, and with the great slithering beast, he saw Namdhor's doom.

What is that? he asked his companion.

Ilargo turned towards the creature and roared. *That is an ancient beast known to my ancestors. A stonemaw! The orcs used them in The Great War against the alliance.*

The green dragon flew over the battle, searching for an angle of attack that would rid the field of such a catastrophic monster.

You can't risk burning it, Gideon warned. *It's too close to the soldiers.*

Ilargo roared again and looped around to come back at it. *Gideon, there is an orc riding on the stonemaw's back!*

It's Karakulak! Inara cried, flying over the battle with Athis.

Farther south, Deartanyon had dropped down for a second run. His explosive breath ignited the flesh of a hundred orcs and burnt the obsidian armour of dozens more. A few more attacks like that and the scales would be tipped in Namdhor's favour, but the orcs invaded with dragons in mind.

Gideon! Ayana screamed.

The Master Dragorn whipped his head to the south, fearing for her life. Giant spiders had jumped onto Deartanyon as he glided past and swarmed him and Ayana. Flashes of magic eclipsed them and spiders flew from every side of the dragon, but Ayana's power wasn't enough. Deartanyon veered south and dropped to the snow in a mighty skid, throwing Ayana from his hide. The remaining spiders scurried across his scales, searching for a place to bite him.

We're coming! Gideon yelled across the bond. *Hold on!*

No! Ayana protested. *I can handle a few spiders. Kill the stonemaw!*

Gideon hesitated where Inara did not. The young Dragorn kept to her flight path and Athis tore a red-hot line up the orcs before assaulting the stonemaw. With his wings fanned and all four claws outstretched, Athis gripped the creature's cylindrical body and heaved upwards. The stonemaw was lifted a few feet but its bulk was too heavy to be carried away from the battlefield.

Gideon! Ilargo drew his attention to the king of the orcs, who was now running up the stonemaw's exoskeleton. Karakulak was sprinting towards Athis and Inara...

Get out of there! the Master Dragorn bellowed.

The stonemaw shrieked and curled its mouth around with enough force behind it to burrow through solid rock. Athis was struck across the face by the dizzying blow, an injury he shared with Inara. The young Dragorn was hurled from his back and cast over the monster's chitinous shell, though its writhing and contorting saw her quickly rolling off the side and onto the battlefield.

Karakulak jumped off in pursuit...

Athis shook his horned head and came to his senses before his own bulk squashed the knights fighting below. The stonemaw tried to curl back around and take a bite out of his left wing, but the red dragon beat his wings and lifted off, taking him just beyond the monster's reach.

Get me down there! Gideon instructed.

Ilargo flew low, picking up orcs in all four of his claws. The dragon crushed them before releasing them to hammer more of their kin below. The stonemaw slithered around, heading towards Ilargo and eating humans and orcs alike. Their impact was assured and their speed ensured injury to both, but neither Ilargo nor Gideon cared; the beast needed putting down and Karakulak needed stopping.

Before they could meet in battle, however, another dragon flew in from the side and intercepted the stonemaw in all four claws. Ilargo swerved at the last second, avoiding the collision. Gideon looked over his shoulder to see Malliath picking the stonemaw clean from the ground with his jaws wrapped around the head-end. His dark wings flapped furiously to keep them both aloft. Being so long, the stonemaw's tail flicked at the ground, crushing knights who couldn't get away from it fast enough.

Alijah is not on Malliath's back, Ilargo observed.

Gideon turned over his other shoulder and watched Malliath carry the stonemaw west, away from the battlefield. Both apex predators, the fight was evenly matched. The dragon dropped it unceremoniously in the snow and dived down to double his assault, raking and biting at the stonemaw's natural armour. The snake-like beast coiled this way and that, making it hard for Malliath to find purchase.

Should we help? Ilargo asked between fiery breaths.

The stonemaw wrapped itself around Malliath and squeezed. The dragon's mighty roar reached across The White Vale, drowning out the battle below. His rage, however, only seemed to increase his strength and Malliath threw himself into the ground, taking the stonemaw with him. When he came back up, his jaw was clenched around the side of the monster's head, cracking its exoskeleton. The monster relented its grip and Malliath wriggled free with fire in his mouth.

Malliath can handle himself, Gideon reasoned. **Get me down there.**

～

ALIJAH FELT every one of the stonemaw's fangs rip into his body, but his mind was prepared for pain, an ally of sorts. He knew how to use it and when to ignore it. Having deliberately placed himself at the point where the orcs met the Namdhorians, he was *using it.*

So entrenched was he in the enemy's ranks that he hadn't seen a Namdhorian for some time, the knights long pushed back by the orc's surprise attack. In the thick of it, however, he was able to unleash the violent warrior The Crow had forged within him.

His new Vi'tari blade in hand, the half-elf moved like a wraith, his blade flashing green before spilling red blood across the ground. Working with the enchanted sword was akin to working with Malliath. He just had to go with the flow of its desires, while it too obeyed his wishes. Together, they were a foe the orcs couldn't contend with.

Along with his new weapon, Alijah could feel the well of magic that pulsed inside his muscles, itching to be discharged. The half-elf cast blinding light spells from his palm, permanently scarring the orcs' eyes. Those that didn't wander into stray blades were easily dispatched by Alijah's scimitar.

As Malliath exhaled his fiery breath upon the stonemaw, Alijah set free his unbridled power and cast jets of consuming flames into the horde. Lightning followed, erupting from his fingers, then ice, turning the orcs to frozen slabs. A telekinetic blast shattered obsidian and bones alike, hurling a dozen orcs into the air.

Finally, he laid eyes on the Namdhorians again. Their line had been pushed back but they were still fighting hard. It was natural to put himself between them and the orcs - where else could he be? Alijah used his inherited speed and agility to weave through the orcs and hold the ground. Wave after wave swarmed the muddy patch and wave after wave fell to his blade and magic.

"Spears!" he barked over his shoulder.

The soldiers used what precious time he could give them to angle their spears and brace. It wasn't the entire line, but ten men abreast could become the point of a spear that pierced the orcs' ranks.

One last spell, a bone-crunching wave of telekinetic energy, and the men had their opportunity to gain some ground. Alijah slipped through the gaps behind him and watched the orcs crash into the pointed spears.

"Keep pushing!" he shouted, searching for his next battle.

There were orcs behind their line: in fact, there were orcs every-where. The stonemaw had opened up wide gaps across the field, dividing the battle into patches where the orcs could slip through.

The Namdhorians hadn't been prepared for an attack like this, though no one could have predicted they would bring a stonemaw and giant spiders with them.

One such spider was scurrying through the Namdhorians, its long, pointed legs knocking them over before treading on them. Alijah broke into a sprint and skidded under the middle of its bulbous belly with his jade scimitar in hand. So fast was he that the thick blood and gore that poured out of its gaping wound splashed only over the ground. He jumped back up at the spider's back end and swiftly cut down three more orcs.

For every orc he slew, a Namdhorian soldier was saved. That's what he was supposed to be doing and this is where he was supposed to be: in the heart of it. He was the line that evil would soon learn it wasn't to cross.

Flashes of light, the discharge of spells, caught his eye. Alijah deftly climbed onto the back of an overly large orc and plunged his blade down into its head. While aloft, he surveyed the battlefield in search of the magic - there was only a handful of people in this fight who could wield magic.

As the slab of orc fell to the ground, taking Alijah with it, he glimpsed his sister leap into the air and come down on a group of orcs. He would have been content to leave her to it, being one of the most competent fighters on the battlefield, but Inara wasn't the only person he saw. The king of orcs was bearing down on her.

Alijah hadn't seen that particular orc since Velia, where he received an almost fatal beating from the king. Before that, he had watched, helpless, as Karakulak murdered Tauren on the roof of his own home. The orc king was the head of the snake, a snake The Crow had intended him to destroy.

Reclaiming his Vi'tari blade from the dead orc, he began to fight his way through the baying horde. He had a king to kill...

∾

Vighon had no thoughts of being king. He didn't consider the fate of his father, chained in irons and thrown in the dungeons. He cared little for the historic events that had transpired this very day, just as he cared little for the spectacle of the massive snake-worm that Malliath carried away.

Right now, in this very moment, there was only one thing: killing orcs. The wretched beasts were attacking again, vying for his blood, and he wasn't inclined to give them an inch.

His silvyr blade, coated in fire, sliced through obsidian armour like it wasn't even there. He also enjoyed the advantage of the flames, their light blinding the orcs who dared challenge him. Then there were those he found himself fighting beside. So skilled were they that the northman wondered if they could kill every orc by themselves.

Asher was a combination of savagery and meticulous form. His opponents were often dead before they hit the ground and those who weren't faced inevitable death from blood loss.

Nathaniel was all soldier in his technique: disciplined and brutal. He was a product of his Graycoat training. Combined with more decades of youth than any man should rightly have he was an orc's worst nightmare.

Reyna and Faylen were a blur of constant motion, as was Nemir. Their elven scimitars rang out from either side of the northman as they cut down orcs left and right. Reyna's enchanted bow made her far easier to keep track of. The arrows were launched from her bow with more power than the thundering whip of a dragon's tail. Orcs were blown apart by their impact or sent flying into others.

Faylen and Nemir had released a multitude of bright orbs, adding to their assault. Most of the orcs they came across were trying to flee the light before they realised they had nowhere to go.

There were complications to deal with at the same time, chiefly the spiders that had been chased to the surface by the giant snake-worm. With Vighon lashing out on one side of a spider and Asher on the other, the eight-legged creature was brought to its belly, where Nathaniel drove his sword into its head.

Throughout it all, Vighon could hear Ilargo and Athis doing what dragons were so feared for. They burnt everything they could. Due to the chaos of battle, however, they were unable to streak fire across the hordes because of the human lives they would claim in the process. They were stuck at the other end of battle, towards the wings, where they could torch orcs in greater numbers.

It wasn't enough...

Vighon could see nothing but orcs and giant spiders. The snake-worm had reduced the Namdhorian numbers dramatically, eating and crushing everyone in its path. Malliath had been taken out of the fight and the speed with which the orcs had infiltrated their ranks kept the other dragons at bay. Everywhere he looked, his brothers were being chopped down by orcs or ripped apart by hungry spiders.

How long could the men keep it up before the orcs gained an advantage there was no coming back from? Their only hope now lay with Lady Ellöria and the elves. If their spell worked in time, the orcs would have no choice but to flee the return of the sun. If they were too late, nightfall would be upon them and the spell would make no difference.

"Inara!" Reyna shouted her daughter's name and Vighon followed her gaze.

The young Dragorn was just visible through a brief gap in the battle. She was in the middle of it all, surrounded by enemies. Her Vi'tari blade fended off orcs on one side while her magic blasted orcs on her other side.

"Push through to her!" Nathaniel yelled, swiping his blade through an orc's midriff.

Vighon took a breath, gritted his teeth, and raised his flaming sword. Whether they would perish today or not, everything between him and Inara was about to feel the bite of his blade.

~

Asher opened his eyes to find that he was lying on his side in the mud, surrounded by charging combatants. Whether he had been struck in the face by an orc or a Namdhorian he couldn't say, but the pain in his jaw told him he had definitely been punched.

The problem was: he could remember nothing after the first swing of his sword. His killer instincts had assumed control in the heat of battle; the only part of his fractured mind that had apparently remained intact.

The ranger groaned as a variety of aches and pains exploded across his body. He cursed his own mind, wondering if he would ever reclaim control of it after having Malliath and Alijah poured inside. Those instincts, trained into the very fibres of his muscles, appeared to be his mind's safe place, where he could operate without the weight of Malliath's long life burying him under.

It couldn't go on.

Asher had no memory of the battle thus far, making him dangerous to everyone, including himself. The reality of his situation, he knew, was such that he would likely require years to reassemble his mind and find a place for the foreign memories and thoughts to live. Right now, however, on the battlefield, he didn't have years or the option of deep meditation. Now, he needed to fight with more than the mind of a feral killer.

Getting to his hands and knees, an orc burst from the fray and moved to boot him in the ribs. The ranger intercepted the leg with both hands and thrust his weight into the creature's knee, snapping it in the process. The orc fell back screaming, the opportune moment to spring and finish the job.

But Asher could feel it...

He was one aggressive action away from losing himself again. The sound of battle and roaring dragons evoked emotions in him that belonged to Malliath. As the dragon's mind bore down on him, his own mind began to retreat, relinquishing control to his instincts once more.

On his knees now, Asher looked down at his torn cloak, the sight of which sparked an idea. He quickly tore the loose strip away and said goodbye to the light, seeking some semblance of control in the dark. The battlefield assaulted his every sense, threatening to overwhelm him. The Arakesh, that always resided just under the surface, was there to employ his training.

Feeling, hearing, and tasting everything around him gave him a complete picture of his environment - now he was in control.

Asher could sense the incoming attacks from every angle, detecting the slightest of shifts in the orcs' muscles and the creak of their armour and leathers. With one hand he wielded his broadsword, always finding the orcs' weak spots where their armour was useless. With the other hand, he freed the silvyr short-sword from his back and gave his foes twice as much to fear.

Now, he was death itself...

For Inara Galfrey, there was nothing else in the world but the small island she had carved out in the middle of an ocean made from orcs. Namdhorians fought by her side and Namdhorians fell by her side, none but a Dragorn capable of surviving when surrounded on all sides.

Her right cheek was marred by three vicious cuts, given to her and Athis by the stonemaw. They stung at first, adding to the fuzzy head it had given her, but bringing her mind in line with the Vi'tari blade sharpened everything.

That edge was needed in the face of King Karakulak.

The giant orc forced its way through both enemies and allies to reach her. In its monstrous grip was a long sword made from dragon bone, a natural material so dense and durable that even her Vi'tari scimitar would struggle to break it.

Karakulak was splattered in blood, staining its pale skin. It was the only orc not wearing any armour - either a testament to its skill or its arrogance. Inara hefted her blade, deciding that she would discover the answer for herself.

The orc king barked something in its guttural language and the orcs pressing in on Inara staggered back, challenging the Namdhorians instead. The Dragorn threw out her arm and launched a fireball at the hulking orc, then another and another. Every spell flew with precision, but Karakulak was fast, its reflexes akin to an elf, and the orc evaded every one. Its strides were great, seeing it skip across the battlefield until the beast was right in front of her.

A shockwave of telekinetic energy exploded from Inara's palm and slammed into the orc's chest. It should have knocked him well off his feet and broken more than a few bones. Karakulak, however, was merely pushed back, its feet scraping along the ground. A wicked smile, followed by a growl, and the orc king was on her once more, this time its blade coming to bear.

The Dragorn couldn't ready the next spell in her mind fast enough, leaving her defence to the Vi'tari blade in her hand. The scimitar increased her grip around its hilt and thrust her arm up to bat the bone sword away. There was no time for thought after that, enslaved as she was to the rhythm of battle. Their swords attacked and parried as their bodies weaved in and out of each other.

Inara called upon every technique she knew to stay alive. Defending Karakulak's blows sent waves of pain up her arms, forcing her to rely on speed and agility to evade them. The orc was furious in its assault, showing no sign of fatigue. The king's strength was unnatural, leading Inara to one conclusion: the orc king was empowered by magic.

Magic she could combat.

The Dragorn rolled under a beheading swing and came back up with the Moonblade dagger in her free hand. On a battlefield of mud, dark armour, and blood, the magical weapon sparkled like a star. Just as she had done to Malliath, Inara had only to pierce its skin with the blade and its power would be reduced down to that of an ordinary orc. Then she would cut its wretched head off.

Karakulak roared, its eyes showing no mark of intelligence beyond base instincts. The king charged at her with its bone sword swinging wildly. She dodged left then right, careful to keep her footing as the orc pushed her back towards the fighting. Only once did the Moonblade intercept the bone sword, but that one swipe was enough to slice through the top third of the blade, enraging the orc.

Inara took her chance, seeing an opportunity to slay the beast. She dashed forward, knocking the orc's damaged sword aside with her scimitar, and leapt into the air with the Moonblade raised over her head. Her jump was perfect, the height and strength just right to ensure she buried the magical weapon in Karakulak's head.

The orc was faster.

Karakulak snatched her wrist before the Moonblade could plunge into its skull. Inara grunted as her momentum was brought to a sudden stop and she slammed into the orc's body. She didn't fall but, instead, remained in the air, held up by Karakulak. The king pulled her closer to its opening jaws, exposing its slimy fangs. Inara placed a boot in its chest and pushed away just far enough to angle her scimitar at the orc's scarred abdomen. She shoved the Vi'tari blade through to the hilt, protruding its thick back.

The orc king growled in her face, the sword in its gut barely an inconvenience. Karakulak broke her hold on the scimitar and let her body fall to the ground. A knee to the face threw Inara onto her back and sent the world spinning.

From the ground, Inara blinked hard to get the mud out of her eyes. She was greeted by Namdhorian bodies, their faces frozen in terror from their last moments. They littered the battlefield around her, their fate soon to be her own.

Karakulak yanked the Vi'tari blade from its gut and discarded it. The wound bled on both sides of the orc's body, dripping down its leg to mix with everybody else's. The king wasn't finished with her yet. Karakulak loomed over her with its broken bone sword in both hands. It had but to plunge the blade and it would send Inara and

Athis to the next place. A triumphant roar rumbled from deep in the orc's throat, victory assured.

The orc king lifted his sword and faltered on the down stroke. They could all feel it - the ground shaking. Heads started turning to the north. Inara's senses returned just enough for her to realise what the cacophonous sound was.

The dwarves of Dhenaheim had arrived!

CHAPTER 40
CLAN HEAVYBELLY

Emerging from the smoke and backed by an army of his kin, Doran entered the battlefield astride his Warhog like some hero of The Great War. They had followed the ridged tracks of the stonemaw for miles, tracking it to the source of the explosion. Now, a phalanx of dwarves charged over the lip of the hole with war cries on their lips.

Doran was beaming from ear to ear.

Russell proved he was something more than just a man as he kept up with the charging Warhogs on foot, his pick-axe in hand. Galanör couldn't boast the werewolf's speed, but he still managed to keep pace with the head of the clan. The elf looked keen to introduce Guardian and Stormweaver to the orcs - his blades had remained clean for too long.

Doran was finally in possession of real weapons, dwarf-forged steel that surpassed the human sword and axe he had used for so many years. Slung over his back was a two-handed, double-bladed war axe, the perfect weapon for chopping the heads off orcs and beasties alike. Nestled on his hip, the son of Dorain now possessed a silvyr hatchet, gifted to him in secret by his brother before they departed Grimwhal. Right now, riding into battle, Doran held a sword over his head, its edge lined in silvyr.

Beside him, Dakmund pointed to the eastern flank of the battle, then the western, sending war chariots either side. They would hound any orcs that fought on the fringes, turning them away from the battle and presenting them with enemies on both sides. It had been Doran's idea, but he had offered it to his brother to use as his own.

With the war chariots breaking away, that just left the riders of the clan to greet the orcs, and greet them they did. The Namdhorians did their best to scatter east and west, giving the Heavybellys an opening with which they could pierce the side of the battle. The orcs looked upon Doran and his clan with wide eyes, terror-stricken by the surprise attack.

Pig made a mess of the orcs too clumped together to get out of the way. The Warhog's tusks and considerable bulk shot through the horde like an arrow entering its target. Behind him, the clan fanned out, broadening the surface area of their attack. It was chaos, and there were undoubtedly human casualties - it couldn't be avoided in such a pitched battle.

Doran hacked left and right with his sword, splitting skulls and opening chest plates with every swing. The orcs were armoured, but their black obsidian might as well have been parchment when faced with silvyr-edged weapons.

Inevitably, their momentum came to a natural stop - the density of the battle impenetrable beyond a point. Doran jumped off Pig, crushing an orc beneath him, before rolling to his feet with a single message for his Warhog.

"Have fun!" he bellowed.

Pig snorted and continued with its rampage, accompanied by Dakmund's Warhog. Indeed, many of the dwarves abandoned their mounts in favour of joining the battle on foot. There was nothing quite like being in the thick of it!

So happy was Doran, that the dwarf required several minutes

of fighting before he began to realise the dire situation they were in. It didn't matter where he looked, Namdhorians were falling and every dead orc was replaced by two more. They were ferocious fighters, doing just as well with or without a weapon in their hand.

The dark sky was despairingly absent of dragons; a fact Doran was both thankful for and disheartened by. If Ilargo and his ilk were indeed flying overhead, there was a very high probability that the son of Dorain and his clan would be counted among the charred remains. The orcs had simply blended into the Namdhorian ranks with such speed that the dragons' cover was impossible.

Trying to see what positives there were, Doran decided it just meant there were more orcs for him to slay. He cut the legs out of the taller orcs, bringing them down for his finishing blows. More than once, however, he was forced to defend himself against crazed Namdhorians stuck in their battle-frenzy. It was a frenzy born of fear, Doran knew. The men were fighting for their lives and had likely come to the conclusion that they were out-matched long before the dwarves arrived.

Here and there, Warhogs crashed through, creating a bloody mess of everything and leaving a trail of destruction in their path. Doran started ushering the Namdhorians behind him, pushing them back beyond the dwarven forces in the hope of giving them a rest. It was hard to say how long any battle would go on for, but Doran knew well that a wave pattern worked best.

Hacking his way through one cluster of orcs, the son of Dorain laid eyes on his brother for the first time since they dismounted. The orcs were dropping in quick succession around Dakmund, a sight Doran was unaccustomed to. The reason for his prowess could be found in his brother's hands.

Andaljor!

With a double-headed axe on one end and a war-hammer on the other, Dakmund was a foe to avoid. The prince of Grimwhal sliced one way before quickly twisting the weapon and crushing his opponents the other way. The axe would remove legs and the hammer would break the skulls.

Hearing his mother's voice in his head, Doran fought his way to Dakmund's side and joined his brother in battle. He killed less orcs watching Dakmund's back, but for the sake of Grimwhal, he knew it was worth it.

Together, they reduced the number of orcs on the field and sent every one of them to Grarfath with Heavybelly on their lips. Doran could only hope that when their time was over on Verda's green earth, he would be allowed to join his brother in the Hall of Honour and eat at Grarfath's table.

"Havin' fun, little brother?" Doran shouted over the melee.

Dakmund caved in the head of an orc, shattering its horns in the process. "I fear we didn' bring enough," he replied gravely, his assessment harrowingly accurate.

Before Doran could offer encouragement, an orc burst through a pair of Namdhorians and launched itself at him. Unlike its kin, this orc was painted from head to toe in black and yellow, its body devoid of any armour. It was a bloody stupid way to enter a battle in Doran's opinion, but since he was currently pinned underneath the beast, he was unable to share it.

Dakmund turned to help him but quickly discovered a group of orcs had taken it upon themselves to kill him and only him, pushing him back.

The painted orc roared in Doran's face, dripping hot saliva onto his face and beard. The son of Dorain growled, dropped his sword and heaved the orc off his body just enough to sock the beast in the jaw, ridding him of its weight.

The orc, unfortunately, was quick to recover and hounded Doran before he could get to his feet. It barrelled into him, sending them both rolling across the bloody field in a tangle of limbs and punching fists. The orc, berserk in its nature, came out of the wrestle on top and immediately gripped each side of Doran's head.

What happened next was by far the most painful thing the son of Dorain had ever experienced.

He managed to displace the beast's left hand, but its right hand squeezed, forcing its thumb into Doran's left eye. The dwarf howled in pain and punched the orc relentlessly in the ribs. Ignorant to the beating, the orc maintained its hold of his head.

Doran's mind was filled with nothing except rage, the pain driving him mad. The dwarf threw all of his strength into battering the orc's arm away. Crouched over him now, the ranger reached up and snatched the orc's head, pulling it down as he lifted his head. The creature's nose broke against his forehead and it snapped its own head back, away from the source of the pain.

The son of Dorain, however, was holding onto the orc's pointed ears, both of which were ripped from its head in the process. Doran pushed the beast away and scrambled to his feet. The double-blade axe felt good in his hands, though he couldn't recall the moment he had retrieved it from his back.

Raised over his head, the axe came down on the centre of his foe's skull, splitting its head into two sides right down to the neck.

His eye hurt like hell, though there was nothing left of it to call an eye anymore. Blood dripped down his cheek and stained his blond beard red. Were the battle not so dire, he would take his time and make every single orc suffer before he ended their miserable life. As it was, he had no choice but to rejoin his brother and return to cutting the orcs down with great efficiency.

"I see ye've been makin' improvements!" Dakmund jibed, gesturing to Doran's bloody socket.

Doran swung his two-handed axe and cleaved the head from another orc. "Ye find a good dwarven woman who doesn' get weak at the knees seein' a decent battle scar!"

Dakmund laughed as he hacked two more orcs to pieces.

The battle raged on in this fashion. They would slaughter orcs beside their kin and laugh whenever they could. It was in their bones to enjoy killing orcs and enjoy it they would.

Doran couldn't say for sure how long they had been fighting for when he caught sight of two familiar faces. Galanör and Russell had stuck together, an unlikely duo given their choice of weapon. Yet, somehow, the two complemented each other, their fighting styles blending into one as they anticipated the actions of the other. They had even acquired a gathering of Namdhorian knights, all of whom had clearly decided that fighting alongside the rangers was the best way to stay alive.

A little farther beyond them, Doran noted a flaming sword diving in and out of battle. It reminded him of Vighon. The dwarf pressed on, fighting his way towards the fiery blade, his curiosity piqued. Dakmund followed him and he even drew Galanör and Russell with him. When there were finally enough orcs put down between them, they all laid eyes on the northman.

"It is ye!" Doran shouted with a grin.

Vighon slew the orc in front of him and looked down on the son of Dorain. "Where in all the hells have you been?" he asked with a coy smile.

Doran had no time to conjure a retort; there were orcs to kill. He only chopped two down before the group was dispersed by a single arrow from Reyna's bow. The elf fought side by side with Nathaniel, who guarded her back, allowing her to use her deadly bow.

"Ye're all 'ere!" Doran yelled with glee.

"Good to see you, Heavybelly!" Nathaniel cheered.

"I brought company!" Doran thumbed over his shoulder, where Grimwhal's army was blooding their steel at the orcs' expense.

"About time!" The response came from Asher, who was in the middle of putting his boot in an orc to free his broadsword from its chest.

Doran buried his axe in an orc's hip before replying. "So where's this great weapon o' yers then?"

Asher defended himself against three orcs before systematically cutting them down one by one, their skill no match for his own -

especially when blindfolded. "I'm working on it," the ranger growled.

Dakmund brought down the largest orc in their area with Andaljor's hammer denting its skull. "Are we winnin' this thing or not?"

"I'd say not!" Vighon replied, swiping his sword through an orc's midriff. "But killing him might make a difference!"

Doran and Dakmund both turned to see an orc who stood above them all. King Karakulak. The beast was still a distance away but, between them, the son of Dorain could see them closing the gap with relative ease.

"We need to reach Inara!" Reyna called over the din.

Doran became concerned when he realised the elf was still looking in Karakulak's direction. The son of Dorain jumped onto the back of the large orc brought down by Dakmund and focused on the king of orcs. To his horror, Inara was engaging the great beast and alone at that. He had heard well enough of the Dragorn Karakulak had slain...

"Well what are we fightin' 'ere for?" Doran hollered, leaping onto another orc, axe first. "Let's separate that wretched monster's head from its body!"

CHAPTER 41

REBIRTH

Gideon Thorn cut a swath through the orcs, Mournblade flashing in his hand, just as it had five thousand years ago on a battlefield just like this one. The density of the battle, so close to the centre, made it all the harder to unleash the Vi'tari blade's full potential. The density and chaos also turned Gideon around more than once, sending him farther away from Inara and Karakulak.

He needed Ilargo to fly overhead and aid his orientation, but the dragons were both occupied now in closing the holes to the south, sealing them with fire. All the while, the giant spiders harassed them, scurrying over their scales and biting them where they could. Gideon could feel the sting of those bites in more places than one.

Karakulak's distinct roar directed Gideon to the west. The Master Dragorn maintained form five of the Mag'dereth - an aggressive fighting style. His scimitar was on the attack, assaulting the orcs more than defending against them. Some even fled from the sight of his legendary sword, often running into Namdhorian blades.

There weren't many in this part of the battle, but Gideon had come across a handful of dwarves. They bore the sigil of clan Heavybelly and the Master Dragorn felt a swell of praise for Doran. He could only hope they would be enough to turn the tide...

Where's Malliath? he managed to ask between swings.

Ilargo didn't answer right away. *He is still battling the stonemaw,* the dragon finally reported.

Having seen the monster's plated hide, Gideon wasn't surprised. He decided it was a good thing in the end, believing that Malliath would likely cause more harm than good in a battle like this.

Gideon reined his thoughts in when a giant spider come thrashing through a cluster of Namdhorians in front of him. He charged at the creature with Mournblade held in both hands at shoulder height. As he reached the spider, however, there was no fight to be had.

Alijah appeared over the curve of its bulbous body and slid down towards its head, where he plunged his cursed scimitar between the spider's eyes, driving it to the ground. The half-elf didn't stop with the spider, his movements fluid and fast. The jade scimitar dashed left and right, slicing effortlessly through orcs before Alijah's hand launched a staccato of lightning at a painted berserker.

The two warriors paused, locking eyes across the melee. Alijah was covered in wounds, but Gideon guessed they were Malliath's, given to the dragon by the stonemaw. The half-elf didn't seem to care for his injuries and they certainly weren't holding him back.

It was the look in his eyes that worried the Master Dragorn. He had the look of a man possessed, as if one warrior had wiped Alijah away and replaced him entirely. Gideon had seen something similar happen to others in battle, but he had never seen it in Alijah before.

Then there was the scimitar in his hand. The last time Gideon had seen that same blade, he was hiding it in the one place he believed none would find it: Malliath's lair on Korkanath. Before that, he had seen it in the hands of Thallan Tassariön, Valanis's general and sword master. The evil elf had wielded the jade scimitar for a thousand years, using it to take innocent lives.

Cursed by Valanis himself, it didn't belong in the hands of anyone...

The heat of battle, however, was not the place to take Alijah's weapon away. Instead, Gideon did the only thing he could do: he fought by his side. Together, they cut a path through the orcs until they were in the middle of the field, where Inara and Karakulak had been duelling.

The scene was not as Gideon had last witnessed it.

The king of orcs was now surrounded by the greatest warriors in the realm. Asher swung his mighty broadsword, Doran hacked with his double-bladed axe, Vighon thrust his flaming sword, and Inara dashed in with her scimitar in one hand and the Moonblade in the other. Around them, Galanör raked at the swarming orcs with his scimitars, coupled with Russell's swinging pick-axe. Reyna and Nathaniel picked off any orcs that slipped past and were brave enough to try and help their king.

Karakulak was alone in this fight.

The orc king, however, wasn't as Gideon remembered him. Compared to his kin, Karakulak had possessed an air of intelligence about him, seen in his features and especially his eyes. Now, the orc was simply feral, lashing out in every direction with his sword of dragon bone. His pale body was streaked with blood and marred with deep wounds. It wasn't enough to slow Karakulak down though.

The orc's huge foot booted Doran in the chest and sent him flying into the fray. Karakulak accepted the biting impact of Asher's blade just to bring the ranger closer, where it could deliver a gut punch that lifted him from his feet. Karakulak roughly grabbed Asher's arm and cast him aside with a single hand before ripping the broadsword free of its bloody hip.

Vighon dragged his flaming sword down the king's back, splitting and scorching the skin all at once. Karakulak roared and backhanded the northman away, leaving only Inara to face it. The young Dragorn was exhausted by the look of her. She had been using magic where she could, adding to her physical and mental fatigue.

Gideon and Alijah rushed in as one, intercepting Karakulak's downward strike as well as impaling its side. Again, the unnatural orc absorbed its injuries and continued to lash out with the violence of an animal trapped in a corner.

Alijah cast a fireball directly into the orc's chiselled chest, pushing it back a step but no more. The charred skin gave way to muscle, a mortal wound for any but not an orc fuelled on The Crow's magic. That terrible bone sword cut through the air, hammering relentlessly at Alijah. The half-elf struck back with steel and magic, both useless against Karakulak.

Inara jumped in, giving her brother a moment's reprieve, and hacked down on Karakulak's sword arm. She was subsequently forced to drop and roll in order to avoid its devastating counterattack - a swing so strong it would have cleaved her in two.

Gideon used what magic he still harnessed to shove Inara back even farther, pushing her beyond the king's second attack. The Master Dragorn leapt in and raised Mournblade over his head to block the incoming sword. The two were locked together, pushing against each other with all their will and strength.

Karakulak was stronger.

Gideon's arms felt it first, then his back, and eventually his legs, dropping him to one knee. Karakulak growled in his face, the orc's hot breath adding to the assault. The Master Dragorn had no choice but to change his strategy and dive to the side. As he did, Mournblade flicked out not once but twice before he jumped back to his feet. The blade sliced through the orc's leg and hip, eliciting a fierce roar from the king.

Everyone pounced. Asher drove his broadsword as Doran buried his axe. Inara jumped high and impaled Karakulak's shoulder while Alijah pushed his scimitar through its ribs. This should have been the moment the king of orcs fell, its life over and its genocidal campaign with it. But it wasn't.

Somehow, against the odds and even sense itself, Karakulak dropped its sword and clawed at the warriors with his hands. Alijah was the first to be lifted into the air and hurled into the back of his father. A reaching hand over its shoulder gripped Inara and tossed her aside, leaving her at the feet of baying orcs - only her mother interceding saving her life. Doran was caught in the face by a hard knee and kicked away seconds later.

Only Asher was able to react and withdraw his sword before a skull-breaking backhand slammed into him. The ranger rolled under the attack and came up swinging again, his blade gashing a red line across Karakulak's midriff. The orc looked down at the wound and back up at Asher. Then it kicked him so hard he folded in half and skidded back through the mud until he rolled into Galanör's legs and tripped the elf up.

Gideon was still standing and he was still wielding Mournblade. His predecessor had ended The Great War five thousand years ago with the same weapon. Now he intended to do the same.

"Can you hear that echo?" the Master Dragorn called, luring the orc forward. "That's the sound of history repeating itself!" And he launched at the king with the fury of a dragon.

Snippets of thought returned to Karakulak. He could barely put his words in the right order. His emotions felt raw and powerful, controlling his actions. With every second that went by, however, he was able to understand his environment all the better.

He was on the battlefield.

He was in pain.

He was surrounded by enemies.

The God-King couldn't recall the sequence of events that had led to this moment. Images assaulted him, reminding the orc that he had ridden the stonemaw into battle. Then there was blood, and lots of it.

There were no dragons in the sky, informing the king that his original plan had worked. The orcs had attacked the Namdhorians' rear, where they were weakest. With speed and surprise, they had infiltrated the human ranks and swarmed the battlefield, preventing the dragons from eradicating them in great numbers.

This was it, surely his moment of triumph. But there were dwarves on the field, thousands of them. Where had *they* come from? And what was the beam of light in the south? Karakulak had an increasing number of questions as his senses returned.

These questions would have to wait: Gideon Thorn was standing in front of him. The Master Dragorn appeared exhausted, his shoulders hunched, his head hanging and his leathers damaged and soaked in blood. His wretched sword pointed to the ground as the last few drops of blood slipped off the end, leaving it perfectly clean.

Another moment was required for Karakulak to realise that the blood dripping from the end of that wicked sword was, in fact, his own. He looked down at his body, or what was left of it. Neither of his hands had all of their fingers, the muscle beneath his torso was exposed, the skin charred around the edges. Deep gashes decorated his once exquisite physique, some even revealing bone.

Looking back at the Dragorn, Gideon began to grow in height, his size increasing until he was equal to Karakulak. The orc suspected magic immediately until his vambraces slid from his forearms. The Dragorn wasn't getting bigger. Karakulak was shrinking. His god-like muscles and hardened bones diminished and returned to their normal size, leaving him in agony. The wounds he had received while full of The Crow's elixir demanded his attention.

Dropping to his knees, Karakulak groaned and shivered. He had to get more of the elixir! It was damaging for his mind - he believed The Crow now - but what choice did he have? The Master Dragorn was walking towards him with Mournblade in hand...

The king of orcs fumbled with the chest strapped to his belt, struggling to grip it with his ruined hands. He glanced nervously from the clasp to Gideon, praying to Gordomo for the first time in years that he would offer strength. The chest lid finally opened, its contents his only hope.

Karakulak's world fell from under him. The chest was empty. There wasn't a single vial of the luminous green elixir inside. He couldn't understand it; there had been several. Where were they?

Gideon Thorn came to stand directly in front of him, eclipsing the orc's view. In that moment, Karakulak knew exactly what had happened. The Crow had strongly advised him to appoint his mother as The High Priestess, allowing her unprecedented access to him at all times, as well as security. The wizard knew. He knew this moment would come to pass just as he knew Karakulak's mother would steal the elixirs from the chest.

The orc king wanted to kill his mother, and very slowly at that. But he knew she wasn't the one to blame for his downfall; his mother had done nothing but embrace their culture and their god as she was meant to. No, the fault lay with Karakulak himself for ever trusting The Crow and his schemes.

In this, his last moment, Karakulak enjoyed the first piece of real clarity he could recall since taking his first sip of the elixir. He was ashamed and furious all at once, but far too wounded and exhausted to take it out on anyone. All he had ever wanted was to—

GIDEON SAVOURED the defeated expression on Karakulak's face before he decapitated the wretched orc. One clean swipe - that's all it took. The king's head hit the ground with a satisfying *thud*.

Karakulak had brought Illian to its knees, altering the realm irreversibly. Yet, in the king's final seconds, bereft of The Crow's magic, Gideon had looked upon an orc like any other, though the look of revelation it had worn spoke of insight, its flaws laid bare. Still, the Master Dragorn wasn't going to feel any pity for Karakulak; the creature's death more than deserved.

Whether the warring orcs had failed to notice their leader's loss in stature and death or were too consumed by bloodlust, the battle raged on around the companions. Gideon had hoped that Karaku- lak's demise would lead many to abandon the campaign and flee. But Namdhorians were still falling...

Without a moment to spare for the victory that had just been won, every one of the warriors dived back into the fray. Gideon dispatched two who had been pushed in his direction by a dwarf wielding a large weapon with an axe on one end and a hammer on the other. The orcs fell away, absent at least one of the body parts considered to be vital, revealing Asher stumbling to his feet.

The ranger had been tangled in a heap of bodies and even when he stood he was stooped, gripping his midriff. Gideon jumped to his side and drove three orcs into a wave of Heavybellys, saving Asher from their ambush.

"You're hurt!" Gideon shouted over clashing swords.

"I've had worse," Asher grumbled, tearing the ragged blindfold from his eyes.

"Can you fight?" The Master Dragorn impaled an orc and kicked another one back.

The ranger groaned as he stretched his abdomen out. "We don't have to..."

Gideon whipped his scimitar through a gangly orc and turned to look at Asher. "What?" was all he could manage, his breath getting away from him.

"I heard it crack," Asher replied cryptically, dipping his fingers into a pouch on his belt. "The sphere. It was just a shell." The ranger removed the bronze orb from its pouch and pressed his thumb into the deep cracks and jagged holes.

Gideon wanted to desperately see what was inside the bronze shell, but the orcs refused to give him the opportunity. By the time he looked back at Asher, the ranger had discarded the broken shell and was now holding a black orb in the palm of his hand. The relic was wrapped in a metallic web, extraordinary in its design but appar- ently useless in every other regard.

"What does it do?" Gideon yelled, blocking an orc's blade from taking Asher's life.

The ranger flexed his fingers, exposing the relic to their harsh environment. "I have no idea—"

Asher's words were drowned out by a high-pitched hum emanating from the relic. Without assistance, it lifted from his hand and floated in the air, pausing a few feet above their heads. The interruption was enough to turn heads as warriors on both sides searched for the source of the dreadful sound.

Then there was light.

The small black windows, between the metallic webbing, glowed hot white and shone in every direction until the orb itself was impossible to see. Gideon averted his eyes, along with everyone around him. The closest orcs screamed in agony and shut their eyes. A few seconds later and the white light dimmed before exploding with a multitude of colours, the light increasing its reach to spread across the battlefield. It was beautiful and not at all the kind of thing expected from a weapon designed to destroy an entire species.

Regardless, the orcs saw only magic and began to flee, scattering to the wind.

Only the farthest orcs, however, succeeded in escaping the variety of colours that danced across The White Vale. For those who were trapped in the thick of the battle, there was no escaping the relic's power. Gideon watched, wondering if he was about to see thousands of orcs explode in a shower of blood and gore. Or maybe they would be disintegrated. They were dealing with the magic of Atilan, after all: anything was possible...

"Gideon..." Asher gestured to a group of orcs not far from their location.

The Master Dragorn stepped closer towards them, disbelieving of what his eyes were reporting. The orcs were all on their hands and knees, trembling in the midst of what could only be called a trans-formation.

Inara emerged from the masses with the Moonblade in hand. "What's happening to them?"

Looking around, Gideon could see that the same transformation was taking place everywhere. The orcs were screaming, their deep voices altering at an unnatural pace with every passing second. The colourful light found every crack and gap on the battlefield, resting on thousands of orcs.

The ones right in front of Gideon stopped yelling and thrust their bodies up on to their knees, as if they were drawn to the sky. Looking through the colours of light, it soon became clear that they weren't orcs anymore...

Where there had once been flesh as white as snow, there was now a variety of warmer tones shared by humans, elves, and dwarves. Their stone-like appearance was replaced with familiar soft skin. Jagged nails retracted into their fingers and their protruding knuckles smoothed out. Gone were their monstrous fangs and the sharp lines that etched their faces. Only their long hair and horns remained untouched by the relic, leaving behind a creature that could most easily be described as an elf with horns.

"What is this?" Inara whispered.

As abruptly as the relic activated, it shut down and ceased its emission. What fell to the ground was not a well-crafted sphere, however, its surface partially melted and overall shape distorted. It was of no more use now than the stones around it.

Gideon dared to approach one of the orcs as the last wisps of steam curled from its body. Along with its kin, the creature appeared exhausted after its transfiguration. Crouching down to its level, he looked over their new bodies with a closer eye. Their skin was similar to his, but they had faint scales laced throughout, their pattern as unique as their differing horns.

The orc snatched Gideon's wrist and locked eyes with the Master Dragorn. He had seen eyes like those before. In fact, he saw eyes like those every single day...

"They have the eyes of a dragon," he uttered in disbelief.

Inara and Asher joined him in front of the orcs, their hands resting on their swords. The orcs cowered in their presence, all but the orc who gripped Gideon's wrist. The creature examined him with equal curiosity.

Then it spoke.

Gideon recognised the tone of an elf and even a few elvish words, but the dialect was slightly different. He turned to Inara for any insight.

"It is elvish," she confirmed. "An older speech, but definitely elvish..."

The Master Dragorn stared back at this new creature. "You can speak elvish," he said with wonder. "Orcs don't know elvish. How do they speak it now?"

"Their ancestry is elvish," Asher posed. "Perhaps the language has been locked away in their minds for generations."

Reyna and Nathaniel pushed past a group of gawking Namdhorians. "They're definitely not orcs anymore," Reyna stated.

Gideon was entirely captured by the vibrant eyes that held him. "Then what are they?"

A single ray of sunlight pierced the sky and bathed the battlefield. Then another touched down in the west and another in the east. Above them, the ash clouds were being pulled into nothingness, like a dark blanket being torn apart. The soldiers welcomed the sun with open arms and beaming smiles. The orcs that fled the fringes of battle did not welcome it, their screams echoing across the plains.

Before any more observations could be made, the new creatures jumped up from the mud and bolted, shoving any and all aside to escape the confines of the battlefield.

"Wait!" Gideon yelled after them. "You don't have to run!"

His words were useless. Whether it was the dragon in them or the elf, they were fast and light on their feet. They weaved between the soldiers and bodies with enviable grace and agility until they were running south.

His sword still burning, Vighon was cleared a path by the Namdhorians. "They're all running in the same direction," he remarked.

"The Evermoore." Inara and Reyna named the great forest at the same time.

"They're fleeing to the woods?" Vighon pressed.

"They can feel the trees," Reyna replied wistfully. "Every elf can feel the draw of a forest that size."

Gideon moved to watch them run across The White Vale under the growing light of the returning sun. They discarded the obsidian armour that weighed them down and took no weapons with them. Only one paused and turned to look back at them: the orc Gideon had met. No one had ever seen a creature like them before, but there was no mistaking the expression this one wore. If he was representative of his new species, then they were all terribly lost and confused...

"We should help them," Inara said.

"How do we do that?" her father replied hopelessly. "They're running away from us."

"I don't know," Inara responded with frustration in her tone. "A whole new culture was just born on the battlefield. We should do *something*."

"Agreed," Vighon chipped in. "The first we'll do is give them time, let them see that we're not aggressive."

"And make sure *they're* not aggressive," Asher added.

"I doubt it," Reyna said. "That weapon was designed to undo the orcs, yes? I can't see why it would replace them with an equally aggressive species."

Doran buried his mighty axe in the mud. "I can' believe it did anythin' but scorch the lot o' 'em!"

Gideon let out a sigh of relief and let his head fall back so that the sun might warm his face. "It's over," he breathed.

As if the entire army had heard him, the Namdhorians began to cheer in patches around the battlefield. Before long, they were all cheering with their swords held high, or at least those that could hold them high.

Not far to the east, Malliath added his fearsome roar to the resounding cheer and the stonemaw flopped to the ground with a thunderous crash, its hard shell ripped open and its body shredded by dragon claws. By the look of Alijah, Malliath had taken his fair share of injuries from the ancient beast, but both of them stood tall, their wounds no bother.

In the west, Ilargo and Athis were hunting down the last of the giant spiders that sought shelter from the growing light. Through the bond, Gideon could tell that Ayana and Deartanyon were still alive, but the spiders had inflicted no small amount of damage.

Most importantly, Namdhor had remained untouched by the battle and the outcropping of rock that supported the city had survived the earth-shattering explosion that gave birth to the stonemaw.

Gideon wandered past Doran and dropped a hand on the dwarf's pauldron. "The realm owes you a debt. Your clan stopped the scales from tipping against us."

The Heavybelly was unable to answer, his words drowned out by the ruckus that erupted behind him. The men of Namdhor had swarmed Vighon and picked him up, resting him on their shoulders with renewed cheers on their lips. The northman was entirely surprised and taken aback by his championing. Gideon met his eyes and offered him a warm smile of support before raising Mournblade over his head.

"THE KING!" he bellowed.

The Namdhorian army took up the call and roared, their voices carrying across The White Vale. Vighon was taken away with it all and lifted the flaming sword of the north into the air.

Gideon couldn't believe he was standing in this particular moment. They had won, they had actually won. This wasn't the end, he knew but, right now, he was going to revel in their victory.

CHAPTER 42
THE PEOPLE'S JUSTICE

Three days of glorious sunshine and three nights of glittering stars passed over the north following the battle. For Vighon Draqaro, the days had been filled with back-breaking work, clearing The White Vale of orc bodies and making funeral pyres for the fallen sons of Namdhor. By night, however, the people celebrated.

They were the survivors of the most devastating war in over a thousand years. The celebrations were made all the better with a little dwarvish contribution. Their numbers filled out the city to near-bursting, but no one complained, drunk on relief and no small amount of ale.

Doran had told the northman that there was nothing that could create a stronger bond than fighting alongside his people. Doran had suggested that the other clans had no intentions of forming alliances with humanity, and therefore abandoned Illian to its fate rather than join them in the battle and discover any kind of unwanted unity.

Vighon was glad of the Heavybellys and most grateful for their contribution. It was daunting, however, to hear from his *advisors* - of which there were far too many - that Namdhor and Grimwhal should grow as allies under his rule. The northman had only been too happy to roll up his sleeves and help with the labour, leaving his kingly duties for another time. He only hoped that when that time came, he had wrapped his head around *being* the king.

On the morning of the fourth day, he couldn't ignore the dungeons of his own keep any longer. He waved away the servants who tried to dress him and then escort him to the dining hall. There had been many a fine item of clothing put in front of him, but the northman couldn't face wearing anything so bright... or expensive. Instead, he opted for his leathers, dark cloak, and furs.

Strapped to his belt before he left his chamber was the silvyr sword of the north. He much preferred wearing it to his crown which, thankfully, had yet to be presented to him. His coronation had been delayed, by his own command, until the city and the people had been put right: they came first.

With every hall there were knights and servants ready to bow in his presence. Vighon replied with a tight smile and a curt nod of the head, unsure what else to do. Every second of his life had become awkward and peculiar. He couldn't deny, however, the power it imbued him with. He might not have wanted the crown or the servants, but he did have them, and now he walked around with a straight back and his chin held a little higher than he was used to. It would all take some getting used to...

The way was cleared for him by his entourage of Gold Cloaks, led by Captain Garrett. They walked beside and behind the king all the way to the dungeons. It seemed rather excessive to Vighon, given their location at the top of the city.

Besides the soldiers who guarded the doors, there was another, standing a little farther up the passage.

"Ruban?" Vighon called, recognising the squire.

The young man approached and bowed his head. "Your Grace."

The northman winced. "I fear I have lost my name," he replied.

Ruban smiled. "But in its place you have gained a title."

Vighon nodded along, taking the opportunity to look over the squire. In the days since the battle, he hadn't taken the chance to bathe by the look of him. He still wore his sword on his belt and Vighon's shield over his back, lending him anything but the appearance of a squire.

"I heard you got Elder Celeqor to the elves," he remarked.

"Yes, your Grace. They were most welcoming, if all a little exhausted."

"Lady Ellöria and her kin are on my list of people to thank personally," Vighon said, wondering where he had put that list.

Ruban had no reply to that, but it was clear to see that the young man had something on his mind - why else would he have trekked up to The Dragon Keep and sought him out?

"Speak up, Dardaris," Vighon encouraged. "You've earned the right."

Ruban puffed out his chest and took a breath. "Your grace, I would like to put myself forward for the position of your squire... If you will have me?" he added quietly.

Vighon took a step back and let his eyes roam over the squire. "No," he finally answered, taking the wind out of Ruban's sails. "I feel like I have a battalion of squires and servants, most of whom believe me incapable of putting my own trousers on." The king glanced briefly over his shoulder at Garrett. "Your days as a squire have come to an end, Ruban Dardaris. I have seen something else in you. Starting this very day, you will begin training under the captain here." Garrett stepped forward with the hint of a smile on his face. "When you're ready, you will join my personal guard."

Ruban had the look of a deer caught in a hunter's sights. "Thank... Thank you, your Grace. That is an honour—"

"Stop," Vighon begged. "Every time I open my mouth someone tells me it's an honour. You'll train and you'll train hard, you hear? And you can keep the shield," he added.

"Thank you, your Grace," Ruban exclaimed again. "You have bless..." the young man caught himself. "I will train night and day until I am worthy of your—"

Vighon raised his hand. "You're doing it again. Be on your way, lad. Report to the armoury and find yourself a proper sword and leathers."

Ruban bowed his head and backed away before finally turning and leaving Vighon and all his knights. "Right..." the northman drawled. "Let's get this part over with."

Only a minute later and he was standing in front of his father, a wall of bars between them. Arlon Draqaro had lost much of the physical stature that had clung to him during his time of power. Dark rings pitted his eyes, contrasting with his pale and unshaven face. His hair, usually slicked back and immaculate, was a tangled and greasy mess. He had been allowed to retain his clothing, once searched for concealed weapons, having only his boots taken from him.

Sitting on the edge of his stained cot, Arlon leant on his knees and looked up at his son. "Finally," he croaked, "he comes to gloat. I see you've been adding to my neighbours," he observed, craning his neck to see down the hall.

Vighon didn't even bother following his father's eyes; he had seen the other cells and their Ironsworn occupants. "You over-reached," he commented quietly.

"*I* over-reached?" Arlon spat, jumping to his feet. "You were a street rat! You should be thanking me! Do you think you would be king if it wasn't for me? I spent years orchestrating this! It should be *me*!"

Vighon stepped closer to the bars. "Don't talk to me about what *should be*. My mother *should* be alive. How many more are dead and buried who *should* be alive but you ordered them otherwise? The Ironsworn are done, I tell you. Any who try to replace you will hang with the rest of them."

"Your mother *had* to die," Arlon said, shaking his head. "She was holding you back. A fisherman? No Draqaro was destined to fish for Atilan's sake! Besides, it was Cross who did the deed. Punish him."

"Cross is dead," Vighon said bluntly, taking the fire out of his father's eyes. "So are all the Ironsworn you sent after me. If I leave no other legacy than ridding the world of your lot I will die a happy man."

Arlon scrunched his face and waved the topic away. "We've all been stained by The Ironsworn. It was a hungry beast, started before my time, that turned many a good man to do evil things. Even *your* arm is not without its mark..."

Vighon subconsciously clenched his left fist, wondering if there was a spell for removing tattoos.

"Perhaps we should focus on the future?" Arlon suggested. "Focus on redemption and atonement and... that sort of thing? You will need advisors as king. Who knows the north better than I? Hmm? I could serve you? You could help me to become a better man..."

The king laughed softly to himself. "I didn't think you would."

Arlon frowned. "I would *what?*"

"Claw for life," Vighon specified. "I thought you of all people would know when he's been dealt his last hand."

Arlon slipped back from the bars. "So that's it then?" he asked with venom in his tone. "I am to be hanged like some common thief? How... *ordinary*," he added bitterly.

"No," Vighon replied. "*They* will all hang - too many demand it. But I won't start my reign by executing my father, no matter how wretched he is."

Arlon frowned. "Then what is to become of me?"

Vighon kept his eyes fixed on his father, but his words were for the knights. "Bring him."

The knights marched Arlon through the keep in chains. In the courtyard, all eyes fell on The Ironsworn leader, eager to witness the tyrant's end. Vighon said nothing but continued to walk beyond the gates and out into the city itself. At the top of the slope, with Namdhor laid out below, the king took in the fresh air beside his father.

It was overwhelming to think of it all as being his responsibility.

Before such thoughts could take a hold, Vighon turned his attention to his father, who was obviously very cold with his bare feet in the snow.

"What are we doing here, Vighon?"

The king watched the sloping street slowly begin to fill with curious people. "We're waiting," he replied ominously.

Arlon looked from his son to the gathering folk. "Waiting for what?" he asked, too tired to keep the nervousness out of his voice.

When Vighon was satisfied with the number of people watching them, he held up a key to his father. "I'm setting you free."

There wasn't an inch of Arlon's face that believed him. "What are you talking about?"

Vighon welcomed the horse brought to his side before mounting it. "I'm setting you free, Arlon. I have business to attend to in the lower town. Meet me there and I will personally free you of those chains. You have my word."

Arlon looked down at his manacled wrists and then down the main street of Namdhor. It was an awfully long way from The Dragon Keep to the lower town.

"That's a death sentence," Arlon seethed. "You might as well put the noose around my neck and have done with it!"

"You have wronged me," Vighon said from astride his horse. "But you have done far worse to the people of the north. There are many who remember well the days before you were a lord, when you wore your true face. I'm going to let the people be the judge."

"You mean executioners," Arlon corrected.

"I'm giving you a chance," Vighon told him. "Meet me in the lower town and you're free. That's more of a chance than you ever gave to anyone."

Deciding that Arlon wasn't worth another word, Vighon gave Garrett the nod to push his father on and begin what would likely be the last steps of his miserable life. The king didn't wait to see the reception that awaited The Ironsworn, choosing, instead, to press on and ride down the main slope, shortly followed by his knights.

The people he passed had a hungry look about them. Until now, they could only have dreamed of seeing Arlon Draqaro served up like this. How many of them paid illegal taxes to him? How many had lost loved ones to his schemes and greed? There wasn't a soul in Namdhor who hadn't been affected by The Ironsworn and they all wanted their pound of flesh.

Or, maybe they wouldn't. There was always a chance, however slim, that they would settle for spitting on him or throwing rotten vegetables at him.

The odds weren't in Arlon's favour...

Vighon smiled and nodded at those farther down the city, his journey impossible to miss with six Gold Cloaks in his wake. He heard his name be cheered from doorways here and there and he did his best to meet as many eyes as he could.

His destination finally reached, the king ordered his knights to stay outside. They weren't happy about the command, but Vighon assured them he would be safe in a tavern, even if it was called The Raucously Ruckus.

Without his personal guard and the attire befitting of a king, especially his crown, Vighon had assumed he could walk in and make for Galanör's room without any fuss. He was wrong. The tavern, which had remained packed in recent weeks, fell silent. So quiet was it that Vighon heard the distinct voice of Doran Heavybelly through the ceiling. Everyone had stopped what they were doing to stare at him. Then they all stood up just to bow their heads.

Vighon waved down both of his hands. "Please, please. Return to your drinks and company." Everyone looked about nervously, unsure what to do in this unorthodox situation. "The next round is on the crown!" Vighon yelled, hoping the royal coffers could afford such a thing; he had a lot to learn about his kingdom.

The tavern cheered, his words enough to put them at ease and see them return to their chairs with camaraderie. The northman gave a friendly nod to the tavern owner and signalled that he was going upstairs.

Following Doran's booming voice, Vighon soon found himself in the room he and Galanör had shared upon their arrival, a lifetime ago. The occupants of this room were unlike any other in the entire realm. That much Vighon would bet all the coin in Namdhor on.

With the exception of Alijah, the Galfreys sat together around the table in the middle of the room. Alijah himself was standing unnaturally still by the window, his hands clasped behind his back and obviously apart from everyone. Gideon Thorn shared the table with the Galfreys, his exquisite blade leaning against his chair. Russell and Galanör were both perched on a dresser with their feet on chairs. Asher was sat on the single bed with his back to the wall and his broadsword sheathed beside him. Vighon wondered if the ranger ever sat without his back to a wall...

At last, he thought, a room that remains seated when he walked in.

"Vighon!" Doran stopped pacing and opened his arms to the northman. "Or should I say, King Vighon? Eh?" The dwarf laughed heartily, sporting his new eyepatch. "I couldn' o' guessed in a thousand years it would be yerself who sat on the throne o' Illian!"

The northman replied with his awkward smile, wondering if and when he would move past it and embrace his title with confidence. "You and me both, Heavybelly." He spared Galanör a look, who had said something similar after the battle. "You wear the patch well; it suits you."

Doran ran a stubby finger over the brown leather that covered his socket. "Still stings like a bugger, let me tell ye!"

Vighon could imagine. "I spoke to your brother yesterday, Prince Dakmund."

"Aye, he said as much. The next time ye see him he'll be as kingly as yerself. Grimwhal is to be his."

"Good," Vighon agreed. "He told me that your clan has been exiled from the Dhenaheim hierarchy."

"Time will tell if that's a good thin' or a bad thin'. For now, I think it will work in Dak's favour. It'll definitely work in Namdhor's favour! Clan Heavybelly isn' a bad ally to 'ave on the other side o' Vengora."

Vighon nodded along. "I was thinking about trade."

"*You* were thinking about trade?" Inara's melodic tone was full of jest.

Vighon responded with a coy smile before returning his attention to Doran. "I have offered your kin the opportunity to stay, but they are keen to return to Grimwhal."

"Aye, Dak's got a throne to accept an' a kingdom to run. They came for orc blood an' they got it. They'll stay to see the crown put on yer head though."

Gideon raised his chin. "Has there been any sightings of..." The Master Dragon tailed off, his head tilting to the south.

"The soldiers have come to calling them Drakes," Vighon replied, clearing up the issue of naming the new species. "They've become quite the topic in the city. There's a lot of people who don't trust them, given their origins. I've already put an end to three hunting parties with their sights set on The Evermoore. I've sent scouts out but there has been no reply. With the state of everything, I can't afford to send out any more men."

Gideon turned to Galanör. "I wonder if an elven touch would be better suited to making contact..."

The elven ranger nodded in agreement. "I will talk to Lady Ellöria and the High Guardian."

That reminded Vighon. "I'm supposed to be meeting with them later today. *Who* should I address?"

Reyna displayed an amused smile. "Were we in Ayda, you would address Faylen, as the High Guardian is outranked by only the queen. However, in Illian, Lady Ellöria has been given authority by my mother, authority that Faylen will respect."

Vighon took a breath and tried to take on the details of Reyna's response. He was to address Lady Ellöria. He repeated that to himself three more times.

"I will accompany you," Galanör said reassuringly. "My kin are very interested in these Drakes."

"How so?" Nathaniel asked.

"Much like the people of the north, they have their reservations," Galanör explained. "Half elf, half dragon... All Atilan's creation. Very little has come from that man that didn't bring with it complications and this particular breed could spell doom. I believe their presence here will only bring more elves from Ayda."

"That's a good thing as far as I'm concerned," Vighon opined. "The realm has never needed their help as it does now."

"I didn't get that sense from them," Gideon added, his stare distant. "I don't think they're dangerous, to us at least."

Inara turned to look at Asher over her shoulder. "In everything that's happened since, I forgot to ask how did the weapon even work. Did you remember something on the battlefield?"

Asher shook his head. "Karakulak broke the outer shell when he kicked me."

"The orb was a shell?" Reyna clarified.

"The real weapon was inside," Asher replied. "I have no idea how or why it worked as it did..."

"There was a reason you found it encased inside a stone table," Gideon reasoned. "And why it was then hidden inside an armoured shell. Atilan must have designed it to activate in the presence of orcs. If the weapon was to be kept in the same place orcs were being created, it stands to reason that precautions would be taken to ensure they weren't unmade straight away. It had to be locked up."

Inara displayed the delighted look of revelation. "So it just had to *see* the orcs in order to work."

Asher shrugged his shoulders. "Sure..."

"We're getting a little ahead of ourselves," Alijah announced from the window, his back to them all. "A great victory has been won here. The orcs are defeated, a new species has emerged, and there is an alliance to be found in Dhenaheim... But *our* war is not over."

Doran frowned on behalf of everyone. "*Our* war? What are ye abou'?"

Alijah turned to face them, his battle wounds almost entirely healed. "The Crow remains. While he breathes, our war continues. I fear the fatalities still to come."

"You want to kill The Crow?" Inara's tone betrayed her confusion.

"We *need* to kill The Crow," Alijah exaggerated.

"Aye!" Doran agreed heartily. "The evil wretch has got it comin' a'right!"

"He isn't evil," Alijah corrected a little too quickly. "But he is *dangerous*; there's a difference."

Gideon sat up straight. "You believe he isn't finished yet?"

Alijah looked away before answering. "Before he left The Bastion, he told me we would meet again. He said that I alone would know where to find him, and that he hoped I would before it was too late."

"Too late?" Asher repeated. "That sounds ominous."

Alijah's jaw clenched and he kept his eyes off the ranger. "From our previous conversations, I would also say he has no intention of surviving this war. Whatever he's going to do next will be so devastating it will likely claim his life, and that worries me given what the realm has already gone through."

It seemed the whole room had held their breath. "And what do you think he's planning?" Gideon asked.

Alijah reached into his jacket and removed a bound scroll. "I spent some time in his chamber." The scroll was rolled out across the table, revealing a map of Illian, Ayda, and a third land Vighon had never seen before. "This map was—"

"What is *that*?" the king asked first, planting his finger on the foreign land in the west.

Alijah hesitated. "That's Erador. That's where life began, human life that is. Atilan's rule started there, though he was one of many kings to hold sway."

Vighon couldn't believe what he was hearing. "Are there any people there?"

"No," Alijah answered. "Long dead and far from our troubles. You see these symbols?"

Vighon tore his eyes from Erador and examined the red glyphs scribed over certain areas of the map. They meant absolutely nothing to him.

"It took me some time but, eventually, I remembered the translation. I hadn't seen it for a long time; it isn't a common word."

"It's the language of The First Kingdom," Gideon said, running a finger over the glyph. "So what does it say?"

Alijah looked up from the map to meet the Master Dragorn's eyes. "*Leviathan.*"

Asher shrugged. "What's a Leviathan?"

Alijah focused on the map. "Before there were humans or anything that roamed this earth on two legs, there were only Leviathans - massive beasts that could dwarf mountains. Even the dragons were young back then."

"How do you know this?" Gideon questioned.

"Malliath was there," he answered simply. "He witnessed the dragons' victory over the Leviathans, the last of which they drove into The Hox. This history wasn't lost on those of The First Kingdom; they knew Leviathans had existed before them. Digging up their remains was among Atilan's hobbies. This was *his* map."

Vighon did his best, as always, to take the great strokes of history in his stride. "Are you saying there are Leviathans..." He checked the map again. "There's one buried under Dragorn?"

"Atilan believed so. But, more importantly, The Crow believed so. I overheard a conversation in which he was told of an excavation on an island. Also, when he departed from The Bastion, he was making for a boat in Velia's harbour."

Doran held his hands up. "What exactly are we worried abou' 'ere?"

"They're necromancers," Nathaniel reminded him. "Remember

what happened the last time they found some old bones?" he added, throwing a glance at Asher.

"My bones aren't *that* old," Asher muttered.

"Ye're thinkin' he means to resurrect one o' these big beasties?"

"It's perfect," Alijah reasoned. "Dragorn is the only nation left that hasn't been wiped out by this war."

"It's also down for being a wholly lawless place," Asher pointed out. "I can't imagine the people of Dragorn fit into The Crow's peaceful vision of the future."

Vighon shared a moment with Alijah. Their eyes locked together and a palpable tension sprang up between them. This was the first time they had seen each other since the battle had started and they had yet to broach the subject of Vighon being king.

"It's enough for me," Inara said, rising from her chair.

"And me," Gideon concurred, picking up Mournblade. "I think it's time we put an end to The Black Hand, once and for all."

"We're coming too." Nathaniel rose just before Reyna followed.

Asher had nothing to add but he did pick up his broadsword and strap it to his belt, a clear indication of his intentions.

Alijah stepped back from the table. "I think it best if only those who can communicate with dragons take flight. This is a Leviathan, not some monster of the wilds."

Asher pulled his sword out an inch and inspected the steel before slotting it back into the scabbard. "The Crow has a personal guard of Reavers, all Arakesh."

"I can fight Arakesh," Alijah promptly replied.

Gideon shook his head. "Not like he can. You can fly with me."

"My bow can pierce anything," Reyna boasted, much to Alijah's chagrin.

"And I go where she goes," Nathaniel added.

Vighon opened his mouth to ensure that he was counted among them, but the northman caught his words and clamped his jaw shut. The responsibility he had hoped to escape when the war with the orcs was over came crashing down on his shoulders. He couldn't leave Namdhor now, not when there was so much to be done. It pained him to keep quiet, especially given the nature of their mission; he had been fighting The Black Hand for years beside Alijah.

"I wish I could finish this with you," he said to the half-elf. "But I—"

"Have to stay," Alijah concluded. "Of course you do. The people need their king now more than ever."

Alijah sounded sincere, but that sincerity wasn't found in his eyes. Vighon had always noted that Alijah was easy to read, his emotions and intentions often worn on his sleeve, but not now. Now, his words, tone, and body language didn't match each other as they used to.

"I would offer my pick-axe," Russell said, standing from his perch, "but monsters the size of mountains are beyond my expertise."

"I wouldn' mind takin' a crack at a new beastie..." Doran paused to swallow and lower his tone. "But dwarves weren' meant to leave the ground. Dragon-back is not where I belong."

"Agreed." Alijah's tone was a touch too harsh. "The threat we now face is beyond most in this room, perhaps all of us. If you aren't bonded to a dragon, I strongly urge you to stay."

"We're coming." Nathaniel spoke for Reyna and himself.

Asher remained stoically silent with his hand resting on his belt; he had said all that needed to be said. Vighon liked the ranger for that particular quality.

"So be it," Alijah relented. "Shall we end it then?"

Gideon strapped Mournblade to his belt. "Ilargo is almost here. Vighon, I'll have Ayana and Deartanyon stay in the north. I think their presence will help to maintain a sense of peace."

"Thank you," Vighon replied, aware that not every orc had been ensnared by Atilan's weapon.

Outside, returned to the huddle of his Gold Cloaks, Vighon watched Malliath, Ilargo, and Athis take off and climb into the pale blue sky. The northman was conflicted, believing that a king should put himself forward to protect his people, but what could he do against a Leviathan? He was just a man...

"What's all that abou'?"

Doran's question turned Vighon away from the dragons and back to the rising slope of Namdhor. There, he spotted a great mass of people parting from the main road, scattering back to their lives. In the middle of the road, abandoned by the people, was a single form lying face down. The scene was too far away to make out the gruesome details, but Vighon didn't need the details to know what had happened to his father.

"The people's justice," he replied quietly. Then he threw the key into the snow at his feet.

CHAPTER 43
BROTHERS ALWAYS

oran stood impatiently in the snow, helpless to do anything but watch his brother approach from the distance. Barring the ranger's way, four Heavybellys in full armour had intercepted his path to their ranks around The King's Lake.

He wasn't welcome.

Dakmund crunched through the snow and dismissed the soldiers with the flick of his head. They hesitated, looking back at Doran, but the prince of Grimwhal barked in their native language and sent them back in a hurry.

When they were out of earshot, he turned to his older brother. "I'm sorry abou' that. They won' tolerate yer presence off the battlefield."

Doran nodded solemnly. "I understand. I *chose* to walk away; I can' 'ave it both ways."

Dakmund flashed a glance over his shoulder before gesturing to the western shoreline of The King's Lake. "Why don' we get away from pryin' eyes an' ears..."

Along the lake, the brothers walked side by side. It was a pleasant moment for Doran. He couldn't recall them ever doing something so mundane during his time in Grimwhal.

"'ave ye got a full count o' the casualties yet?" the ranger asked.

"Not yet," Dakmund replied with grief. "The battlefield is still littered with so many..."

They passed under The King's Hollow, the supporting arch that kept all of Namdhor aloft. "Will they not look on ye with disdain for accompanyin' me?"

Dakmund peered over the lake, to his camped forces. "They'll do as they're told. At least now they will. There ain' a dwarf in Grimwhal that wouldn' stand behind the one who wielded Andaljor on the field o' battle - especially against orcs!"

Doran dropped his head. "I grew up thinkin' that would be me..."

Dakmund laughed and patted him hard on the back. "Ye never were any good at thinkin'! Fightin' is where ye've always lived. I know it were ye shame in that that drove ye to exile but, for what it's worth, I think fightin' is exactly what yer suppose' to be doin'. In Illian, ye can do that, an' ye can do it right. Killin' monsters an' helpin' folk is far more noble than anythin' ye ever did back home."

Doran did his best to wipe his eye without his brother noticing. "An' what abou' yerself?" he asked. "Are ye really goin' back to take the throne?"

"O' course I am! First thin' I'm goin' to do is start talks with the Hammerkegs. After our alliance is assured, we'll reach out to the Goldhorns an' the Brightbeards. Can ye imagine how furious King Uthrad is goin' to be when his precious hierarchy is weighted four clans to two!"

Doran stopped and turned to his brother with a brow so knitted his blond eyebrows came together as one. "Easy there! Ye makin' changes to Grimwhal is one thin', but upsettin' Silvyr Hall is an entirely different an' very dangerous thin'! Uthrad's army, combined with that o' the Stormshields, could still crush any alliance between the four o' ye. An' ye've got the lower kings to consider. They don' think like ye do, brother. They've been brought up on back-stabbin' and treachery. Ye might 'ave an alliance one day an' an enemy the next!"

Dakmund sighed. "I wish more than anythin' that I could do this with ye by me side, Brother. But I can'. I have to do this on me own, my way. I might not get it right straight away, but I've got centuries to keep tryin'. In the meantime, there's an alliance to be had with Namdhor. I like the way they chop down orcs! So do the boys! It's been a long time since we've really seen humans, an' even back in the day we had little to do with 'em. An alliance with Illian might just be enough to see Grimwhal get some real work done in Dhenaheim..."

Doran adjusted his eyepatch, unable to ignore the irritation and dull pain. "Jus' be careful, Dak. Find them that ye can trust an' assume everyone is yer enemy until proven otherwise."

"I've got mother," Dakmund reminded him. "I'm sure father will be of help to, in his own way."

The ranger could feel a twinge in his chest at the mention of his parents. He would never see them again. It wasn't that long ago that he had come to terms with that and had been living his life under that assumption. But seeing them again, talking to them... He loved his mother dearly and though he had never seen eye to eye with his father, Doran had seen another side to him now.

"Look out for 'em," Doran requested, mostly on his behalf.

Dakmund rested his hand on Doran's shoulder. "Ye 'ave me word, Brother. An' should a time come when Grimwhal is different, I will gladly welcome ye back into the clan."

Doran knew such a change would never happen, regardless of Dakmund's efforts. Still, he offered his younger brother an appreciative smile and gestured for them to continue their stroll along the shore. Their time together was limited and Doran wanted to have fonder memories of his brother than simply fighting beside him on the battlefield.

"So, how did ye find wieldin' Andaljor?" he asked, sure that he already knew the answer.

"It's goin' back on the wall is how I found it!" Dakmund complained.

Doran cracked an amused grin. "Oh aye?"

"It's balance is terrible! The hammer is far too heavy. An' it's damned cumbersome in battle. Most o' me injuries came from swingin' that bloody thin'!"

Now Doran was laughing deep in his chest, quickly followed by Dakmund. The brothers traversed most of the shoreline in this manner, transporting them both back to their youth. It was an uncertain time for Illian and Dhenaheim but, right now, Doran Heavybelly was a happy dwarf...

CHAPTER 44

BECOMING THE MONSTER

T hanks to the elves, Alijah was able to sweep through the clouds without choking on ash and Malliath was able to soar through the sky, rising and falling with the currents on his vast wings. This would have been a time to cherish, to relax and enjoy the freedom they had both fought so hard to reclaim.

But they both knew what awaited them in Dragorn.

Emerging from the cloud bank, The Adean greeted them with its seemingly endless horizon of waves. The island of Dragorn rose above those waves, a solitary block of sandy stone. Every inch of the island had been used by the Dragornians and a high wall erected around the perimeter. Unlike most kingdoms, these high walls were better for keeping the evil and the corrupt *inside*.

Apart from the farmland that ringed the inside wall of the city, the island nation was a dense collection of spires and flat-roof buildings, all of which provided narrow alleys and streets. That only left one place for something the size of a Leviathan to be found: underground.

Alijah...

The half-elf almost winced hearing Gideon's voice in his head.

He had agreed to be a part of their bond for strategy's sake, but he had specified that Malliath would be true to his title and remain voiceless - the black dragon expressed himself better with actions.

I can hear you, he replied.

You say that Malliath has faced a Leviathan before. What can we expect?

Alijah couldn't think of a more useless question. **Every Leviathan was unique. Their mentality and physical attributes were all different. They were all dangerous though, and a massive threat to anything smaller than them.**

Inara's voice flowed through their combined bond. *If The Crow's interested in this Leviathan, it's going to be more dangerous than most.*

Alijah had to agree. **We should begin searching for any signs of The Black Hand around the base of the city. If they've been excavating this thing then they're probably beneath the island. Malliath and I will fly east.**

We'll take west, Gideon said.

Malliath banked to the east and dropped their altitude, bringing them in line with the top of Dragorn's high wall. Soldiers began to flood the ramparts and man the giant ballistas that dotted the parapets. Turning his head to the right, where he could better see the island, he felt wounds that had yet to heal around his left shoulder. The stonemaw's bite had left quite the impression upon both of them.

They glided around the eastern end of the island, both searching with superior eyes. Alijah paused as he felt Malliath's thoughts rising to the surface of his own mind. It was like being picked up in a powerful wave that carried you to shore.

If a Leviathan rises, Dragorn will fall.

Alijah couldn't disagree: there was only one way an enormous monster could free itself of the foundations. This fact should have greatly disturbed the half-elf; after all, the island was densely populated. But he wasn't. All he could think about was the third lesson.

"*Sacrifice without hesitation...*" The Crow had said.

The vast majority of the island were criminals in some respect. What could they really contribute to Illian? If killing the Leviathan and defeating The Crow came at their cost, wouldn't it be worth it?

Then again, he wasn't even the king.

Those few words turned Alijah's mind upside down. He had been seconds away from ending Arlon's life himself before Vighon beat him to it. Wasn't he to become king? Wasn't that the point of his training and torment? Again, he found himself questioning The Crow, something that felt utterly wrong to him - The Crow would never lie to him.

Malliath tugged at his thoughts, bringing him back to the present where the dragon had located a cave entrance. Shaped like an arrow head, the entrance was relatively narrow. Malliath slowed down and landed in the shallows where the waves lapped against the rocks. Just beyond them, the path leading into the cave was littered with bodies. This was the place.

Alijah climbed down and refrained from communicating with the others. If The Crow was inside, he wanted to speak with him first.

Take back to the sky, he said to Malliath. ***Let them keep searching a while longer.***

Malliath glanced at the pitch black of the cave before bowing his head. *As you wish...*

A gust of wind and a splash of sea water washed over the half-elf as his companion launched into the sky. The bond between them increased with every passing moment, bringing their desires into harmony. There was still a hint of resentment from the dragon: an irritation that he was bonded at all persistently lingering between them. Alijah was confident that, given time, it would fade and they would know only the companionship of each other.

Before they could press on with the future, they had to deal with their past. Alijah gripped his Vi'tari blade, still sheathed in its scabbard, and strode into the cave. The bodies he passed were a mix of dark mages and ordinary men. He recognised the burns they all possessed as being magic in origin.

The Crow must be approaching the last of his plans if he's executing his own order.

You will kill him, Malliath replied as a matter of fact.

Killing the necromancer was certainly the logical thing to do. Alijah hadn't been lying when he told the others that The Crow was dangerous. Malliath wanted to kill him - Alijah could feel it. The dragon had no love for magic, but he had grown to truly despise it in the hands of humans. The Black Hand and the mages of Korkanath had both enslaved him to their spells, forcing him to act against his will.

Never again... Malliath hissed in his mind.

He told me that I would not be the one to bring him down. He told Hadavad the same thing. The Crow already knows who will take his life and he knows it isn't me, which tells me I don't have much time before the others arrive.

With that in mind, he made his way farther into the cave. There was a path of torches highlighting the way, guiding him into the deep. His suspicions about the Leviathan were confirmed when he came across the first fossil-like bone. It was the size of a whale and clearly only a small part of a larger skeleton. He began to notice that they were everywhere, protruding from the rocky walls. Some parts of the path required him to either duck under or climb over giant bones.

He entered a small cavern not far from the entrance and was immediately drawn to the curved bone that ran up the wall. Farther along, there were three more identical bones, all partially revealed. He was standing inside the ribcage of an enormous Leviathan...

"Impressive, no?" came The Crow's call from the other side of the cavern.

Alijah spun on his heel and withdrew his scimitar an inch from its scabbard. The necromancer, stripped to his waist, was busy carving an ancient glyph into an exposed bone using the tip of his wand. When he was finished, the wand end glowed a brilliant white and the bone was left smoking. He blew the smoke away and brushed the surface with his fingers, inspecting his work.

"What are you doing, Sarkas?" Alijah demanded, checking the shadows for any Reavers.

The wizard smiled to himself. "Sarkas... It's been an awfully long time since anyone has called me that. Nice to hear it before the end, I suppose."

"And how do you see this all ending exactly? We're standing inside a Leviathan." Alijah gestured to the glyphs. "And those are resurrection glyphs."

"You're smarter than the questions you're asking, Alijah. You know exactly what I'm going to do. You knew from the moment you picked up the map in my chamber. The questions you need to answer are: why did you go to Namdhor if you knew what was going to befall the people on this island? Why did you wait so long before telling those who could do something to stop me?"

Those questions brought a lump to Alijah's throat and he found himself unable to speak. He knew the answers, of course, but to voice them was to accept them.

"You must have thought about it on your way here," The Crow continued. "You know the people of this island have no place in your kingdom. They are the lowest of humanity, their very ideals a poison that could kill civilisation. This is the last kingdom in the dominoes, Alijah. It must fall. Only from the ashes can a new world rise, a world we both want for the people of Illian." Sarkas's tone dropped. "That's why you're going to stand there and do nothing."

The Crow turned his attention back onto the exposed bone, bringing his wand to bear. Alijah wasn't close to satisfied and he started across the puddled ground. The undead Arakesh appeared from nowhere, as if the shadows melted off them. They didn't scare him, but he wasn't ready for a fight yet and so he stopped in his tracks; he needed answers.

"Vighon Draqaro is to be crowned the king of Illian," he stated, aware that he was close to sounding like a petulant child.

"And so he will," Sarkas replied casually, his eyes on the next glyph. The Reavers, satisfied that their master wasn't being threatened, faded back into the shadows.

Alijah paid them no heed and scowled at the wizard. "I don't understand. You told me I was to be king. You told me that every day I was in that *hell*," he seethed.

"What else did I tell you?" The Crow asked.

The half-elf took a breath, thinking back to his many lessons and conversations. "That my journey would begin in Erador..."

Sarkas blew on the new glyph and wiped it down. "And it will. Your training, though vigorous, isn't nearly enough to prepare you for the duty of being the king. Your training was needed to ensure you survived the *journey* to the throne. Only on that path will you find yourself. It won't be easy but, when you come to the end, you won't just be ready to wear the crown of Illian, oh no. You will wear a crown befitting of the king who resides over all of Verda!"

Alijah took it all in his stride, his questions not answered. "What could I possibly find in Erador that will prepare me for such a fate? Long-dead kingdoms would be the last place I expect to find a *journey*."

Sarkas cocked an eyebrow. "Who said anything about it being long-dead?"

Alijah's jaw fell open as he attempted to find the words. "You... You said it was..."

The Crow shook his head. "I never told you anything of the sort. *You* arrived at that conclusion."

Alijah turned away, contemplating the revelation. He should have been able to process the information at a better speed, but the idea of there being an entire civilisation on the other side of The Hox... it was unfathomable.

"There are humans still living in Erador?"

"Quite a few, yes. Their kingdom is much older, inherited by the

575

survivors of The First War who were lucky enough not to have been in Illian during the last days. You will find them to be very different; they know nothing of magic, the old ways long forgotten."

Alijah couldn't believe it. "They've been there this whole time?"

"Shocking, isn't it? Two civilisations, separated for ten thousand years!" The Crow went back to his work on the bone. "The northern lands, beyond Dhenaheim," he continued in an unnaturally conversational tone, "are too harsh for travellers. And The Hox... Well, The Hox is an ocean twice as vast as The Adean and has long been home to the last Leviathan."

Alijah had seen that great beast in Malliath's memories and could easily imagine how it would devour ships whole. "Wait... What am *I* to do there?"

Sarkas spared him a look. "The same thing you're going to do here, the same thing you're going to do everywhere. Bring peace to the realm. They too suffer under a king, a tyrant like those before him."

Alijah couldn't wrap his head around it all. "So I'm to what? Replace this king? Rule Erador? I don't—"

"I'm sorry Alijah," Sarkas interrupted. "I can see that the training I have inflicted on you has made you somewhat reliant on me. But I'm afraid that time is over now. I have no more answers for you. Only you can decide what happens next. Go to Erador... Or don't. I leave it to you."

INARA BRACED herself as Athis came down beside Ilargo. The water splashed high into the air and the rocky beach *crunched* under his claws. Gideon and Asher had already touched down on the shore and were making their way towards the cave entrance.

"He must be inside," Reyna observed, slipping down the side of Athis's scales.

Inara spotted Malliath flying above and was inclined to agree. It had been Ilargo who first noticed the dragon had been without Alijah. Inara knew in her heart that her brother would recover from The Crow's machinations, but she didn't trust him to be alone with the necromancer...

Looking back over her shoulder, Inara had one message for Athis before entering the cave. *Be ready for anything.*

The red dragon exhaled a sharp breath. *I always am, wingless one.*

Beneath the city, the companions moved with caution and their weapons in hand. Reyna aimed her enchanted bow at every crevice and flickering shadow. It wasn't long before they were following the sound of voices, two of them - one of which definitely belonged to her brother.

Inara wasn't sure what to make of the scene they found. Under the arching bones of a giant beast, Alijah and The Crow were simply talking. The wizard was stripped down to his waist, revealing a pasty torso of scars and damaged skin. His appearance was entirely unthreatening - Inara had brought down larger foes in her time - but the ancient necromancer was wielding his wand. That alone made him dangerous.

Entering the cavern properly, it suddenly occurred to Inara that, beside Alijah, she possessed the greatest well of magic, surpassing Gideon and her mother, who was bereft of all her magic.

Gideon spearheaded their approach. "Alijah?"

The half-elf didn't answer right away, his gaze fixed on The Crow. "He means to resurrect the Leviathan."

"That I do," The Crow confirmed, entirely unbothered by their arrival. "This particular Leviathan was rather troublesome in its time. Many dragons were lost in the battle." The Crow paused as the undead Arakesh slowly slunk out of the surrounding darkness. "Atilan spent many years researching them, but I finished what he started. I categorised this one as a Cerbadon."

"We're not going to let you bring it back," Gideon stated boldly.

The Crow smirked. "It's already done. This entire island is a hub of magic thanks to the dragons who once called it home.

There's more than enough to breathe life back into these old bones..."

Reyna levelled her bow. "Enough."

Inara was barely able to track the arrow that burst forth, whistling past Gideon's arm. The Crow, however, casually shifted his shoulders as if he knew where the arrow was going to fly. The magically enhanced projectile missed its target and burrowed into the rock behind him. Inara had never seen anyone evade an arrow with such ease, especially when it had been fired by her mother.

Without missing a beat, The Crow simply said, "Kill them all."

The Reavers closed in as one, their twin blades in hand. Inara was tempted to use magic and have done with them but, after dealing with the assassins, she would face The Crow, an enemy who would require all of her strength. With that in mind, her Vi'tari scimitar went to work.

Their close-quarters quickly prevented Reyna from using her bow again. Inara and Nathaniel stepped between her and the oncoming Reavers, giving her time to withdraw her blade. The Arakesh were furious but precise in their attacks, immediately forcing the Galfreys back a step. For Inara, this was her first time fighting an assassin of Nightfall, but for her parents it was like old times. They fell in beside each other, complementing their unique styles, as they matched the dance of the Reavers.

Gideon had already cut the arm off one Arakesh and the head off another. Mournblade flashed in the torchlight, clashing and slicing with every swing. Despite his skill, the Master Dragorn was pressed back with the others and kept from The Crow.

Asher more than proved his worth, challenging three of the assassins at once. His two-handed broadsword had been sheathed, replaced by his silvyr short-sword. The ranger ducked under a killing blow and rolled across the ground to pick up a Reaver's discarded short-sword. Like them, he now wielded one in each hand and, for just a moment, Inara could see him as the assassin he had once been...

The young Dragorn rammed her scimitar into the head of her opponent and drove it to the ground. Beyond her victory, she witnessed Alijah fend off two Arakesh before decapitating a third. Inara had only a couple of seconds to watch him, but that brief glimpse was enough to reveal his new fighting style mirrored the assassins.

As disturbing as that was, nothing worried Inara more than The Crow's chanting. Throughout their battle, the necromancer had been shouting ancient words into the air. The tip of his black wand was aglow, matching the glow of the symbols etched into the large bones around them.

He was raising the Leviathan...

"We have to stop him!" she yelled over the melee.

Asher gutted one of his foes and rolled over its back with his second short-sword in his other hand. Before his feet touched the ground again, the ranger launched the weapon at The Crow, his aim true. A quick flick of his wand, however, and the wizard sent the blade spinning away.

Alijah tried next. He cut down the Arakesh in front of him and threw his arm out at the necromancer, unleashing a storm of lightning from the palm of his hand. The destructive spell slammed into an arching shield that flared around The Crow, saving his life. The half-elf pulled back his hand and readied another spell, but he was quickly set upon by more Reavers.

Gideon rushed past his next attacker and charged at the wizard with Mournblade raised over his head. The Master Dragorn succeeded in deflecting The Crow's first spell, but he didn't have it in him to repel the second. His body doubled over in the impact and he flew back across the cavern in a tumble of limbs.

Inara dispatched the assassin in front of her and ran at the necromancer. Her dash was cut short when he fired a spell her way, but she raised her free arm and erected a shield to absorb the magic. He whipped his wand at her again and again, hurling one spell after another. Inara clenched her fist and gritted her teeth.

The Crow's relentless attacks were beginning to make her arm numb, but still she continued forward, her steps in time with his spells.

The collisions against her shield were momentarily blinding, often forcing the young Dragorn to keep her eyes down. She focused on the strength of her shield and the continued motion of her feet. The closer she got the louder the wizard's words became. She had no idea how close to finishing the resurrection spell he was.

Keep going! Athis encouraged, lending her all the strength he had to give.

Inara's arm and head were shaking with the exertion. The Crow's magic was the most powerful thing she had ever stood against. Her grip increased around the hilt of the Vi'tari blade, drawing on the magic stored inside the crystal of the pommel.

It wasn't long before she couldn't hear anything except the stream of spells battering her shield and the roar that escaped her lips. A trickle of blood ran over her mouth and she tasted iron.

Keep going... Athis sounded distant now, but she could still feel the power flowing between them.

Inara thought about all the things The Crow had done to her brother and she focused that rage into one purpose. Her eyes snapped open and she thrust her scimitar forwards, through the maelstrom of clashing magic.

The flaring light disappeared. The Crow's chanting ceased. Inara's shield died away.

Looking up, her blade was almost entirely lost inside the necromancer's body. Blood ran along the scimitar and dripped to the ground. The Crow dropped his wand and Inara withdrew her blade from his abdomen. As his wand bounced on the ground, so too did the Arakesh Reavers, their existence brought to an end.

Clutching his mortal wound, The Crow's mouth twitched into a smile. "It is done..."

Despite the ringing in Inara's ears, she could hear the rock cracking around them. The glyphs etched into the Leviathan were still glowing, only now there were traces of veins and arteries growing over the bones. It was coming to life!

The Crow dropped to his knees and more blood poured from his wounds. Inara was furious. She wanted to swing her blade one last time and watch the wizard's head fly through the air as Karakulak's had.

"You can't stop it now," he croaked. "Fate will have its day..."

Inara towered over him and rested her blade across his neck. "Your schemes are at an end."

"Inara!" her mother shouted from the other side of the cavern. "We need to get out of here!"

The Crow shook his head with a soft smile. "You won't understand... until the end, Inara Galfrey."

That only enraged her all the more and she pressed the edge of her blade into his skin. "You have *lost*," she hissed.

The Crow choked on his own laugh. Then he whispered so that only she might hear his words. Inara stepped back and looked down on the wizard, her expression pulling in different directions to cope with the confusion and anger that swelled within her.

"Inara!" her father yelled urgently.

The cavern was cracking, raining a light dust over them all. The ground rumbled under their feet. The Leviathan's bones were concealed beneath muscle now, their appearance the source of the cracking rock.

The Crow turned to Alijah, off to the side. "I told you... *I* will be the monster..."

Inara met her brother's eyes and saw alarm spread across his face. "He has the Viridian Ruby!"

By the time she looked back at the dying wizard, he had removed Hadavad's ancient ruby from his pocket. Inara raised her scimitar as the ruby came to life in his hand. It flared once as her blade fell across his neck with finality. In death, the wizard's grip released the ruby, but the flare from within the gem had lifted away and disappeared into the rock beyond.

It carried The Crow's essence with it...

Alijah sheathed his blade and turned for the exit. "He's going to inhabit the Leviathan!"

"We need to get out!" Gideon warned as larger slabs began to break away from the ceiling.

Inara took one last look at The Crow, his whispered words haunting her. There was no time to dwell on them now, however, his final act of evil moments away from killing them all. She put her scimitar away and ran for Athis.

They had one last battle to fight...

ALIJAH AND MALLIATH took to the sky with Ilargo and Athis close behind. After borrowing his mother's bow and quiver, they had left his parents and the ranger by the shore - all three a hindrance to the dragons in a sky battle.

Malliath banked around to the west, putting Dragorn on their left. The city's population had no idea what was happening under their homes and businesses. Alijah could see devastating cracks run ragged up the stone walls, tripping up the soldiers on the ramparts. Inside the perimeter, the tallest spires collapsed, bringing ruin upon the narrow streets.

How big is this thing? Inara asked across their shared bond.

Alijah recalled the tooth he had seen mounted on the wall in The Crow's personal chamber. *It's going to be the biggest thing you've ever seen,* he replied honestly.

A chorus of screams erupted from the island as thousands of people scurried to the port. They filled the width of the massive gates, flooding the harbour in search of boats. Behind them, the city was falling to pieces. The very centre suddenly caved in, creating an enormous sinkhole, before it violently exploded. Tons of rock, and people, were thrown high into the air. There was so much debris that the emerging Leviathan couldn't be seen until it was almost free of its grave.

A stunned silence settled over the bond shared between the three dragons. Not even Malliath could claim to have seen a monster such as this...

The Cerbadon ascended to the island with bat-like wings stretching to cast what remained of the city in shadow. A long, pointed tail curled up and out of the hole, only to come back down and flatten more buildings and people. As it pushed through the smoke and dust, the rest of its body took shape, reminding Alijah of a dragon, only much much bigger.

Its reptilian head pointed to the heavens above and a screeching roar pierced the air. This was followed by another roar and another head. One final ear-shattering roar cracked the sky and a third head rose from the debris.

Alijah cursed under his breath.

His trepidation was quickly wiped away by the all-consuming wave that was Malliath. The black dragon was overcome with a fury that had lived inside of him for over ten thousand years. Malliath looked upon the Leviathan and knew he looked upon his most ancient enemy, as if the need to kill the monster lived in his very bones.

We need a plan of attack, Gideon urged. *A unified strategy is our best chance.*

Inara agreed. *We need to lure it away from the city!*

That won't work, Alijah told them bluntly. *The Crow is in control of it. He wants to destroy Dragorn more than he wants to swat us out of the sky.*

Gideon came back with, *Then we need a plan that will see it brought down as fast as possible.*

Alijah could feel Malliath's intentions and knew he was about to launch them at the Cerbadon. *We have a plan of attack,* he told them. *We kill it!*

Alijah! Inara's warning was lost on Alijah and he severed their bond.

The Cerbadon's heads all turned in different directions and exhaled jets of fire into the city. Its tail thrashed and swept through the eastern wall, hurling tons of stone into the air. Malliath weaved and bobbed between them all as he flew towards the beast.

Alijah was tempted to jump off and attack the Cerbadon himself, but seeing the hulking monster up close only revealed such a plan to be folly. The ancient creature was too large for anything as small as a man to do any damage. This fight was left to the dragons.

Malliath glided in behind the Cerbadon and proceeded to fly up its back, following the tail spikes until he was at the base of the three necks. The dragon continued to climb up the middle neck, banking left and right to stay in line with its movements. Malliath soon reached the head and unleashed a torrent of flames across one of its eyes.

The Cerbadon roared in agony.

Alijah almost fell from Malliath's back sheltering his ears from the deafening cry. Behind them now, the Cerbadon's face bore a smouldering crater that oozed what was left of its eye. Looking back at it, Alijah stared at the remaining scarlet eye and wondered how much of The Crow was in there.

The answer would have to remain a mystery - the Cerbadon's middle head was opening its maw of fangs. Malliath dived with all haste and they narrowly avoided the furnace that engulfed the air above them. The left and right heads took notice of them and curled their necks to angle their fire-breathing mouths.

A reprieve came in the form of Athis and Ilargo, both of whom spat fireballs at the outer heads. They entwined their flight paths, confusing the trio of heads, leading the right head straight into the middle head with enough force behind it to pierce a mountain. The Cerbadon's body staggered to the south and its four claws raked through the city.

Malliath was already on a return path that would see them come face to face with the middle head again. Throughout it all, Alijah could feel Gideon and his sister trying to reach out to him through the bond. The half-elf ignored them and nocked an arrow, his focus on the battle.

The black dragon cut through the air on the other side of the middle head, where its scarlet eye could track them. Malliath changed his direction with dramatic speed and flew directly towards its only good eye with fire in his mouth. Alijah added to the dragon's intended assault and fired his arrow.

The left head intercepted them, however, with a snapping jaw that could swallow Malliath whole. The arrow, launched from the bow with a portion of destructive magic, caught the left head in its bottom jaw, cracking one of its mighty fangs and splashing blood over its tongue.

Alijah shared his companion's irritation as they changed their direction again and avoided being eaten. This battle needed ending fast, before there was nothing left of Dragorn's population. Reluctantly, the half-elf reached out to Gideon and Inara.

Malliath and I are going to kill this thing, but we need you to keep the other heads occupied so we can get close enough!

He felt Inara's familiar confusion. *How are you going to kill it?*

Malliath hadn't told Alijah in as many words, but he just knew exactly what the dragon had in mind - and it was merciless. *Trust me,* he replied, *we're going to end this. Just keep the other heads out of our way.*

Athis and Ilargo ceased their entangled flight pattern and split up to tackle a head each. Fire streaked across the sky from both the dragons and the Cerbadon, giving the people below more opportunity to escape the city.

Malliath looped around one neck, then another before turning back in search of the best angle of attack. The middle head turned this way and that in a bid to track the dragon with its one good eye. Alijah nocked another arrow and craned his neck to see Ilargo and Athis narrowly escaping death with every flyby. Ilargo flew so close to the left head that the green dragon managed to rake his claws over the Leviathan's dark scales. They didn't leave so much as a scratch...

Alijah returned his attention to Malliath and gripped a little tighter with one hand as the dragon made a sharp ascent up the length of the central neck. It took of all Alijah's strength and dexterity to keep his arrow nocked with the other hand.

Are you sure about this? he asked, seeing the dragon's intentions laid out before him.

I was killing these things before your kind crawled out of the oceans! Malliath was all fury, a force of nature that none could withstand.

Climbing so high into the sky that they rose above the Leviathan, Malliath had but to relax his wings and see them plummet at great speed. Alijah braced himself, noting the middle head following them from below with its mouth wide open. Malliath flexed one of his wings and sent them barrelling to the side, evading the expected jet of fire.

When they came out of the roll, they were now approaching the giant head from the side harbouring the sightless eye socket. The Leviathan couldn't see them.

Alijah lifted his body up onto his knees, his muscles tensed. *Malliath...* His tone was heavy with concern.

The dragon roared in response, unwavering in his mission.

Taking into account the direction and force of the wind, Alijah aimed his bow to the left, picking an empty spot in the middle of the sky. The elf in him knew that was the exact place to release his devastating arrow.

The very second the arrow was sent on its path, Alijah had no other choice but to jump up and let his companion continue without him. There was nothing but empty air to embrace him and a mountainous fall below him. He urgently called out to Inara, reopening their bond. He could only hope now that she wasn't being chased too far by one of the Leviathan's heads.

Above him, his arrow had curved around, carried by the wind, and impacted the smoking eye socket. The magic therein exploded, blowing great chunks of debris into the air. More importantly, it opened the socket up, a hole so big a dragon could fit inside...

The ground began to consume his vision, offering him a detailed view of the ruins below and the people lying dead in the street. So much of it was burning. He called out to Inara again. Still he fell. There was only one thought that kept him calm and, as always, it was the words of The Crow: he hadn't even started his journey yet. That meant he wasn't going to die here.

Affirming his beliefs, Athis's red scales swooped under him and steadily matched his descent until he was able to find purchase on his back. The dragon flapped his wings hard and launched back into the sky before they all met the ground.

"Are you insane?" Inara yelled over her shoulder.

Alijah wanted to answer but he was forced to hold his breath. Above them, Malliath was savagely plunging his entire body inside the Leviathan's skull. Neither of them could breathe with Malliath's head submerged in blood and gore. The ancient dragon wasn't done, however.

His breath sufficiently held, Malliath finally exhaled. The Leviathan's middle head was flung back as the dragon's fire blew through what fragile membranes and muscles still separated the socket from the brain. Malliath didn't stop until the inside of the monster's head was burning, killing it instantly.

Astride Athis, Alijah was starting to panic. It didn't matter what The Crow told him when he was drowning surrounded by nothing but air. The edges of his vision were beginning to blur and the grip in his fingers loosened. Inara was saying something to him but he couldn't understand any of her words.

In an explosion of flames and smoke, Malliath dived out of the Leviathan's socket and gulped on air. Both he and Alijah could feel their lungs burning, but the air was nothing but relief. The black dragon fell for a hundred feet before flapping his wings and finding a current to glide on, his scales coated in blood.

The middle head drooped and its tongue hung lifeless between its fangs. The thick neck beneath it went limp and collapsed into the city with a mighty crash and a plume of smoke and debris. The outer heads wobbled uneasily and attempted to roar in defiance, but their voices never made more than a garble.

Alijah hung over Athis's side and followed Malliath's soaring path to the south, quickly followed by Ilargo and Gideon. Athis turned to join them, taking the group away from the tumbling Leviathan. The hulking monster staggered forwards before the left head dropped to the ground. The last head tried to take some kind of control but its single brain wasn't enough to control the body.

Together, they all watched the Cerbadon die, its beastly form filling most of the city.

Inara looked back at Alijah with a startled expression that begged a question.

Alijah glanced at Malliath beyond her and shrugged. "This wasn't his first Leviathan..."

The island was quiet now. There weren't enough people left to carry their screams into the sky. To the north, The Adean was littered with boats crammed to bursting with survivors. They would all have no choice but to head west and seek shelter on the mainland.

We should make certain they reach the shore, Inara suggested over their bond.

Agreed, Gideon replied. *Let's pick up your parents and Asher first.*

Alijah heard their brief conversation, but his sight was still fixed on the Leviathan. Smoke rose steadily from the central head until it caught the wind and drifted westward. There was nothing to be said. The victory they had gained over the beast could hardly be celebrated in the light of the massive death toll it had still caused.

For Alijah, however, it signalled the end of his training and the beginning of his journey. The Crow was dead, his bones crushed to powder beneath the city and his essence extinguished within the Leviathan. The world was suddenly wide open. With Malliath by his side, there was nothing to stop him now...

CHAPTER 45
THE WHISPER OF FATE

A new dawn greeted Inara. From the cliffs of The Lifeless Isles it was even more beautiful than any other she could remember. Warm rays washed over her face as the sun crested Ayda in the east. Breathing in the sea air, she let it all go. All the fighting. All the death. For one peaceful moment, she allowed herself to live in the past, when everything had been easy.

But then The Crow's parting words came flooding back and reality cast its dark shadow. They were living in a new world now, a world that had been ravaged by orcs, manipulated by necromancers, and forever changed by war.

How could she forget the dead? How could she let it all go? Inara Galfrey was a Dragorn - it was up to her to remember those they had lost. They were to be the light that gave people hope.

It was all so heavy, and made all the harder to carry when the pain was so close to home. Alijah had returned to her life after four years, but the cost to him was too much. Just thinking about the suffering he had endured twisted Inara's gut. She wanted to slay The Crow all over again.

Now is our opportunity, Athis said into her mind. *We can finally*

589

look to the future. There is time to help Alijah and Malliath... There is still hope.

Inara didn't have to look over her shoulder to know that her companion was walking towards her. His hot breath blew over her back before he finally came to rest beside her. As always, his presence was comforting beyond all else, but his words had missed the mark.

"I fear what is yet to come," she confessed aloud.

Athis looked down at her. *The Crow plagues your mind...*

Inara's response was on the edge of her lips when they both felt the pull from Ilargo. The green dragon was drawing everyone to him. Astride Athis, the ground was quickly left behind and the archipelago opened up around them, offering dozens of tall islands. They followed Ilargo's call to the very heart of The Lifeless Isles, where the ancient elven Dragorn had once dwelled.

Within moments, the sky was filling with dragons and their Dragorn from all over the isles. Inara held on as Athis, the largest and fastest among those in the air, dived down and flew ahead of the congregation. Angling down and around, a vast stone plateau came into view, a semi-circular slab carved out of an island's base. The stone bore ancient markings and deep grooves where the elves had left their designs.

Athis touched down with more grace than a creature of his size should be awarded. Inara slid down his side and made for the podium that rose over the plateau, where Gideon and Ilargo were waiting for everyone. Off to the side, the Dragorn caught sight of her parents and Asher. They were spectators here, regardless of their long history of heroism.

"Is something wrong, Master?"

Gideon's expression was unreadable, which only added to the mystery when he failed to answer her. Instead, they waited patiently for the plateau to fill up with the younger Dragorn. Seeing them now, Inara was thankful they were under Gideon's rule. It would have been too much to bear had they fallen in battle...

"Is this all of us?" she asked incredulously, her question mostly for herself.

Gideon sighed but maintained his composure with so many eyes on him. "Yes," he replied quietly.

There was, however, one last dragon to arrive. Malliath's approach was felt by all and their reaction was clear to see in their movements. The dragons shifted left and right to make way for his significant size, with a few even taking back to the sky in search of a nearby cliff instead. The young Dragorn warriors looked nervously from Malliath to Gideon, closely observing his own reaction.

Inara had to wonder how many before her had come within a hair's breadth of Malliath's deadly jaws or razor-sharp claws. How many had escaped death at the expense of another? Enslaved or not, they had seen the black dragon decimate their order, killing their friends without mercy. Having seen the way he killed the Leviathan, Inara didn't have to imagine the savagery they had all witnessed.

Alijah climbed down Malliath's black scales and mingled among the Dragorn, his eyes fixed on Gideon and Inara.

The Master Dragorn stepped forward. "For thousands of years, our order has gathered on this stone! From here, the Dragorn have taken shape time and time again, changing with the Ages and the people we protect!" Gideon paused and glanced at Inara. "War is inevitable! Evil will always rise to try and extinguish the light! We cannot protect the realm if we are not prepared for that evil!

"That is why we're going to train!" he announced. "And we will learn from the best! From those who have been fighting in wars for millennia! This is to be our last day in Illian!"

Inara almost started forward, her expression betraying her feelings and shock.

Gideon ignored her. "We will return!" he promised. "When we are ready! When we can defend the people against anything and not fall into darkness ourselves! We were not prepared for what befell us!" There were more than a few tentative looks thrown Alijah's way.

"That will not happen again!" Gideon continued. "When next the Dragorn rise, we will eclipse that which threatens this realm!"

The young Dragorn gathered before them fell into whispers and chatter as they shared nervous glances. "Where are we going, Master?" one was brave enough to shout out.

Gideon looked up at Ilargo. Inara had seen that look before, even expressed it herself while looking at Athis. The Master Dragorn was being bolstered by his companion.

"We are going home!" he replied. "Most of you have only seen Dragons' Reach through your bond, but two days from now, you will see it with your own eyes! As you all know, Ilargo's mother, Rainael the emerald star, and many older dragons chose to remain there after The War for the Realm! We will live among them! Learn from them! They have experiences and skills we need if we are to uphold our oath and protect Illian from harm!"

Alijah raised his chin and shouted, "Who will watch over the realm while you're in Ayda?" There were perhaps only a few gathered who registered the challenge in his tone.

All eyes shifted from Alijah to Gideon, including Inara's. "For the first time in a thousand years," he began, "Illian has one king! One *good* king!" he added. "Without rivals, there should be peace across the realm like it has never seen! The orcs have been reduced to such numbers that men alone can deal with what remains! And more elves will be sailing from Ayda as alliances grow! This might be our only opportunity to leave knowing that Illian is the safest it can be!"

"I will stay..." Inara said the words without a moment's extra thought.

"What?" Gideon turned on her.

Inara swallowed and elevated her expression from apologetic to confident. "I will stay!" she proclaimed so that all might hear her. "I will watch over the realm and guide, as I may, the new king!"

Athis didn't even flinch, aware for a split second before Inara was that she would make such a proclamation. Everything about him, from his posture to his expression, told Inara that he wholeheartedly agreed. Together, they would stand for Illian.

Gideon struggled to keep his composure. "I need you," he told her in a hushed tone.

Inara took a steadying breath. "*Illian* needs us. What rises from this war is going to be new, and ruled by an inexperienced king. I will await your return..."

Gideon clenched and unclenched his jaw before returning his attention to the crowd. "Should the realm find need of the Dragorn in our absence, *Master* Galfrey will be here! And she will call on us should the darkness return to claim the light!"

Inara clamped down on her smile - it was the first and last time any Dragorn would refer to her as master for some years.

Gideon continued his speech for a while longer, giving the young Dragorn hope that their order would have its day. In the chaos that followed everyone's dispersion, Inara drifted away and met up with her parents and Asher. They whiled the day away in each other's company, talking of what the future might hold for the alliances between Illian and Ayda now that avenues had been opened to Dhenaheim.

Reyna mostly spoke of how thrilled she was that Inara had chosen to stay behind. They ate and chatted well into the night, always wondering where Alijah was. Since the meeting, none had seen Malliath - and Alijah had remained just as hidden.

"Let them have their time," Reyna had said. "We will talk to him in the morning."

"I want to talk to him now," Inara's father had complained. "Gideon is obviously going to take him to Dragons' Reach."

"Well it will be the best place to undo The Crow's work," Reyna had countered. "Not to mention everything that's happened to Malliath."

Throughout all of their brief conversations about her brother, Inara caught glimpses of Asher, who equally caught glimpses of her.

The ranger's face told of his worries where Alijah was concerned. Then The Crow's words came back to her, weighing her down.

"Where are you going?" her mother asked as she stood up to leave the light of their fire.

"I should probably talk to Gideon. I've avoided him all day," she admitted.

"You don't have to avoid him," Nathaniel told her. "*His* decision is far rasher than your own. Besides," he added, taking a swig from his drink. "he's like family..."

Inara raised an eyebrow at her father. "I didn't think I'd hear you refer to him as family again."

Nathaniel raised his drink in the air. "Well he is. Just like all of us."

Even Asher smiled at that.

Inara bid them good night and took back to the skies astride Athis. They flew between the tall islands, taking the path that would bring them to the council's chamber and Gideon's personal quarters. Surprisingly, Malliath resided in the vast entrance to the cave. Athis had little choice but to drop Inara off and fly away in search of a better perch.

Most dragons, if not all, would bow their head at Inara and she the same in mutual respect. Malliath did no such thing. The black dragon regarded her as though she was nothing more than a passing insect.

The council chamber was illuminated up ahead, surrounded by torches that brought the stone murals to life. Gideon stood at the far end, his back to Inara, while Alijah made his way around the large table on his return to Malliath.

The siblings naturally came together. "Is everything alright?" Inara asked him.

Alijah looked from Gideon's back to her. "I have declined a position within the order," he said plainly.

Inara frowned immediately. "What? Why would you do that?"

"For many reasons," Alijah replied, clearly uninterested in

repeating them all. "Most importantly though; we simply do not belong among them. Malliath has never felt part of the order, even as far back as the Dragon Riders."

"And you?" she questioned, holding her tears at bay.

"I spent more nights than you can count looking at the stars and wishing I could be a Dragorn. But that time has passed."

Inara grabbed on to what glimmer of hope she could. "So you are to stay here? In Illian?"

It was subtle, but Alijah's muscles tensed - something he had always done as a child right before a lie left his mouth. "I cannot say for certain what the future holds for us, but we will not be staying in Illian; it has *you* now."

Inara scrutinised her brother. He hadn't lied, after all, but she knew he was holding back, omitting the exact truth of his plans.

"Don't you think you would be better staying here, with us... with *me*? I know you aren't ready to talk about it yet, but we need to be together when you are. We can face it together, Alijah. Everything The Crow did, everything that has happened to Malliath: you need us for that. Don't go through it on your own," she pleaded.

"Malliath and I haven't had the best start to our bond. We need time to understand what exists between us, what connects us. We can't do that here. There's too much bad history in Illian."

"So where will you go?" she pressed. "Ayda? You don't have to go to Dragons' Reach but you could stay with the elves. Our grand-mother would welcome both of you with open arms."

Alijah shook his head. "I'm a prince there. I need to be in a place where nobody knows me. A place where I can start again."

Inara's mind was racing as she tried to find alternatives. "Where could you go if not Illian or Ayda?" she asked, hoping to trap him in logic.

Alijah offered her a hopeful smile. "Somewhere that isn't Illian or Ayda," he replied cryptically.

Inara thought back to the map he had taken from The Crow's chamber. "Are you going to Erador?" she asked pointedly.

Alijah shrugged. "The west holds nothing but ruins."

Inara waited for a moment, giving her brother the chance to elaborate. His body language told her more than his words and she knew he was on the cusp of lying to her.

"Will you at least speak with our parents before you leave... *again*." she couldn't help herself.

Her brother didn't miss a beat. "I will, of course. Are we not to return to Namdhor, for Vighon's crowning?"

Inara tried to keep the suspicion off her face. "We were planning on returning, yes."

Alijah nodded along. "We will leave after that," he assured. "Where are our parents?" he asked casually.

Inara caught herself and discarded her suspicions for now. "They're on a beach, a mile north of here. You can't miss their fire," she added jovially.

Alijah gave her a rare smile that spoke of genuine happiness. "Father always did love a roaring fire under the stars."

Inara gripped his arm before he could walk away. "Be gentle with them. Your news will be hard on them."

Judging by her brother's expression, she couldn't tell if he believed her or not. He did, however, bow his head in acceptance of her advice. She watched him ascend Malliath's back and the pair drop away before joining Gideon in front of the farthest mural.

"He told you then," Gideon said without any greetings.

"He did."

Gideon cupped his chin. "Did he tell you where he's going?"

"No. But, if I was to guess, I'd say he's going west."

The Master Dragorn tapped his bearded chin. "Erador..." he mused.

Inara kept her eyes on the mural depicting The Great War. "Wherever he's going, his path is his own now. Hopefully, they will help each other to heal."

Gideon sighed. "And what of your path, Master Galfrey? Your

decision to stay isn't so surprising, but I fear the isolation you bring upon yourself."

Inara finally stepped away from the mural and turned to face her old mentor. "I have my parents. Besides, I'm going to be busy; there's a lot that needs doing to repair the damage wreaked by the orcs." She took a breath, struggling to read him. "*Your* decision surprised me. I never thought you would leave Illian, especially with the order in tow."

Gideon turned around and rested a hand on the chair at the head of the stone table. "It isn't forever," he reassured. "I can't risk another war with so many young. We know from elvish history that children bond to dragons far better than they would as adults. I won't send them out to die, not even for the realm. We will train. And when they're ready, we will return."

Inara could feel a swell of emotion rising within her. "I will miss you. You've guided me since I met Athis..."

Gideon gave her a warm smile. "Your days of listening to me are behind you now. How many battles have you fought? How many lives have you saved? You're already a hero among the people, Inara. I would have preferred you accompany us to Dragons' Reach, but of all those who would choose to remain, I am glad it is you. I already feel better knowing the realm is under your watch in our absence."

Inara hated any kind of compliment and pushed through it. "What if I need you?" she posed.

Gideon gestured to a small chest sitting on the edge of the table. Inara pulled back the lid and found two diviners inside.

"One for you and one for me," he said.

Inara placed the diviner inside a pouch on her belt, comforted by the ease with which she could call on her mentor. "I will do my best to uphold the principles of our order," she promised.

"I know you will," Gideon replied happily. "Vighon... *King* Vighon is lucky to have you watching out for him."

"Will you come to his crowning?"

"Of course," Gideon confirmed. "It will be a moment in history.

And," he added, "I can help escort Alastir and Valkor back with Ayana."

That pleased Inara. "Would you care to join us on the beach? Alijah is about to upset my parents and your company would be a balm."

Gideon looked to consider her offer. "I will join you shortly. There's a few things I need to put in order here first. Speaking of, I was going to place a ward over the library. If you're staying, though, I will leave it in your care. Will you keep it safe? The history of the Dragorn lies within."

"You have my word," Inara bowed her head, accepting the responsibility.

Seeing that Gideon was satisfied, she made to leave before tears found their way to the surface. Before she could walk beyond the torchlight, however, the Master Dragorn's voice filled the chamber, holding her in place.

"What did he say to you?" Gideon asked with all seriousness.

It would have been easy to assume he was talking about Alijah, but Inara knew he was referring to The Crow.

"He whispered something to you, right before the end."

Inara turned back to face her mentor. "He said..." She took a much needed breath. "He said monsters only beget monsters."

Gideon frowned and looked away. "He said the same to me, in one of the mirrors in the library. What do you think it means?"

Inara had her suspicions, a theory that twisted her gut into knots. "I don't know," she lied, falling into her fears. "I don't know..."

CHAPTER 46
THE HOUSE OF DRAQARO

Humbly knelt before the masses, Vighon opened his eyes as the crown came to rest on his head. It was light, designed for comfort so as to be worn at all times. But it felt heavy.

Under The King's Hollow, the northman stood up to the thundering cheers of the realm. Among them were his friends and greatest allies. Inara beamed at him beside her parents. Galanör clapped along with Lady Ellöria, Faylen, and the elves of Ayda and Ilythyra.

Curving around the lake, Prince Dakmund and his army of Heavybellys added their roar, their bond with Namdhor having increased with each passing day after the battle. Doran cheered him from beside Asher and Russell, both of whom appeared pleased with his new status.

His sight naturally came to rest on Alijah. His closest friend offered him a genuine smile and applauded with everyone else.

It was all so surreal. Vighon, like everyone else, had dreamt of grand things for his life, but no dream had ever been so magnificent as this. Nor had they ever been so terrifying...

599

Captain Garrett gave an order to his soldiers and one by one, across the masses, Namdhorian knights raised their banners into the air. Vighon scrutinised them, the sigil new to him. The northman couldn't help but smile at the flaming sword standing upright against a black background.

"KING VIGHON!" the Prime Cleric bellowed. "The first of his name! May the house of Draqaro henceforth be known as the house of the flaming sword!"

His announcement ushered a new wave of cheers and celebration among the people. Horns were blown from within the Namdhorian ranks and a volley of five hundred burning arrows was launched over the lake by the elves.

Lady Ellöria broke away from the crowds and ascended the rocky plateau. Her ethereal green dress made it appear as if she was gliding over the stone towards him. Carried ceremoniously in both hands, the Lady of Ilythyra presented him with the sword of the north. Only two days past, Ellöria had requested the blade remain with them until the crowning. Vighon had been reluctant to hand it over, but he and all the realm would be indebted to the elves and their magic for many years to come - the king could hardly deny any request.

"A gift for the king of Illian, on behalf of my sister, Queen Adilandra, and all my kin..."

Vighon willingly accepted his own sword back, the silvyr blade hidden within the scabbard. Ellöria gestured for him to reveal it to the people and he could see the many eager faces who were excited to see the legendary blade in their king's hand. Obligingly, the northman gripped the black hilt and slid the sword from its scabbard.

The masses cheered, and not just because the exquisite blade was held high over their king's head. As the sword had been pulled free, the length of silvyr set alight with orange flames! Vighon looked from the blade to Ellöria questioningly.

"Only the scabbard can extinguish the flames," she said over the roaring crowds.

600

Vighon admired the sword as only a warrior could. "You have my gratitude, Lady Ellöria!"

The people of Illian continued to cheer their new king, more than happy to have something to celebrate after such dark times. It took Vighon and his personal guard several hours to find their way back up the slope and into The Dragon Keep. The king had insisted on meeting as many people as possible, offering his assurances to all that great things were coming.

The bells of every church had rung out as he ascended the city and they continued to ring even now. He had been told that the people were organising at least a hundred parties that would join the very top of the city to the camps below. It meant a lot when there wasn't much to go around in the wake of such turmoil.

Inside The Dragon Keep, a huge celebratory feast was being organised by a handful of lords and ladies. Vighon cut their glee short when he ordered them to distribute the food amongst the people reducing their party to drinks and nibbles. In truth, the northman cared little for the high-borns of Namdhor - he was looking forward to having all of his companions under one roof for the night.

After Nathaniel and Gideon had given speeches and the band had taken up their merry songs, Vighon took the opportunity to speak with his friends for the first time in a few days. Upon their return, he had been told of the battle with the Leviathan - a battle of such scale that his imagination simply couldn't conjure the image. He had already sent out multiple caravans to intercept the survivors of the island nation and offer them sanctuary in Namdhor.

Seeing all the rangers clumped together with frothing ales in their hands, the king begged his pardon and walked away from some stuffy lord to share a drink with them.

"You Grace." Russell Maybury was the first to greet him and bow his head.

"You have all kept the world up on your shoulders," Vighon

replied, holding up his hand. "Some of you more than once - I will not have the rangers of the wilds bow to *me*."

Asher used his tankard to gesture at Vighon's crown. "It suits you."

The northman had forgotten he was wearing it. "It's going to take some getting used to."

"This is yer time to enjoy it, lad!" Doran reached up and heartily smacked him on the arm. "When all the parties are over, the real work begins!"

That was his opening. "Would you all accept some work if I were to offer it?"

The rangers shared curious glances. "I've never been known to refuse royalty," Asher jested.

Vighon grinned. "Good to know."

"What would you ask of us?" Galanör enquired.

Vighon checked his surroundings, aware that he was about to voice something he had yet to discuss with the lords and his advisors. "Namdhor is too small to house all of Illian. That camp is only going to get bigger and the conditions worse. I want to liberate the fallen kingdoms. I want to rebuild."

The rangers appeared impressed by the idea, if somewhat cautious. "You would rebuild Grey Stone and Velia?" Galanör questioned.

"And Lirian," Vighon replied. "The Arid Lands too. The people need somewhere to live and the land needs tending. Those cities already have foundations, infrastructure that can be rebuilt upon without too much work. If it takes the rest of my years, I *will* see the realm restored."

Asher glanced at the high-borns over Vighon's shoulder. "And who will rule these cities?"

"Provinces," Vighon corrected. "I'm not sure yet; I have a few in mind. They wouldn't be kings or queens. Maybe governors or lords or... whatever title makes them happy."

"Well, I think it's a superb plan!" Russell raised his tankard of water to the idea.

Doran shrugged. "So where do we come in to all o' this?"

"It would be foolish to assume that whatever remains of those cities isn't infested with orcs. Karakulak will likely have left some behind to ensure their dominance. I would charge all of you with expelling the orcs..."

Doran beamed. "That's funny. I was abou' to ask *ye* abou' chargin'?"

Russell shot his stout friend a sharp look. "Doran!"

"What?" Doran shrugged. "We're rangers, not Namdhorian knights!"

Vighon was quick to reply. "There would be payment, of course. I don't expect you to take on such a task without promise of coin."

"Contract accepted," Asher said with the bow of his head.

Vighon was relieved. "You will not be alone. I will assign you half a battalion. They will obey your commands."

The companions clanked their tankards together in merriment and toasted to the realm. The king continued to move from group to group, mostly in an attempt to learn who was who. In the coming days, he needed to know who he could trust and who was actually useful to him. Here and there he gave himself a break and shared a drink with a friendly face. Ruban, however, required an order from his king to partake. The young man was attired in his Namdhorian armour and golden cloak, both of which Vighon complimented.

Of course, no one ever noticed that their king had yet to take a single sip of his drink - the northman would often raise the tankard to his lips and pretend to enjoy the alcohol therein. He wanted to maintain a level head, partly because he still felt like he was in the middle of a Gobbers' nest, despite the crown on his head. There was also another part of him that couldn't settle, as if the orcs might attack again at any minute.

It was long after the sun had set, a sight long missed by the king, that he found himself talking to Gideon Thorn. The Master Dragorn's tankard was equally full and his breath absent the scent of ale. He had spoken in a hushed voice to Vighon, off to the side of the party. Given both of their titles, they were afforded privacy by the other guests and never interrupted.

Vighon did his best to maintain a calm expression upon hearing Gideon's plans for the Dragorn. The king had hoped his reign would begin with the Dragorn looking out for everyone, their presence a sign of protection across the realm. Gideon's mind wasn't to be changed, however, and his vision of what the Dragorn could truly become was inspiring. Vighon only hoped he would still be alive to see their return...

"The Age really is turning," he commented absently.

Gideon's interest was piqued. "The Age?"

Vighon threw his head to the side. "The Time Keepers or whatever they're called. They haven't made an official announcement yet; I think they're waiting for all of this to die down."

"They're declaring a new Age?"

Vighon clapped the Dragorn on the arm. "The Fourth Age is about to begin!"

Gideon smiled, though there was something more behind his expression that Vighon couldn't understand. Regardless, the Master Dragorn raised his tankard. "To the Age of the king."

The northman looked uncomfortable raising his cup. "To the... To that!"

A little while later, Vighon found his way back into the heart of the party, somewhat deflated after hearing of the Dragorns' imminent departure from Illian. He was surrounded by supporters and even people who would claim to love him, but he couldn't help feeling alone amongst them all. How was he going to do this?

His doubts were washed away by Inara Galfrey's smile; one of her many features that was always sure to disarm him and even allow him to forget the troubles that lay ahead. There were still feelings stirring inside of him, a longing for her that he couldn't quite extinguish. Seeing her now, the king knew he might never be able to deny those feelings.

"He's told you, then," she said, her blue eyes tracking Gideon across the room, where he joined Nathaniel and Reyna.

"He has," Vighon replied, unable to keep the disappointment out of his tone. "It seems I will have to say goodbye to you all over again."

Confusion flickered across Inara's face and she spared another glance at Gideon. "I'm not going with them."

Vighon's heart skipped in his chest. "You're not?" he checked, sure to keep his excitement contained.

"I'm staying in Illian," she confirmed with a tight smile. "Someone has to make sure you don't let the realm fall into ruin."

Vighon threw his head back and laughed. "Well, I'm more than glad that the burden has landed on you."

The pair fell into deep conversation, placing themselves inside a bubble in which only they existed. For a while, Vighon felt he had gone back in time to their youth, when they would sit under the trees and talk for hours, fantasising about what the future might hold. They were so far from their hopes and dreams now that it was like imagining another life that had never really existed.

It was only when the moon reached for the horizon that Vighon realised there was one person he had yet to find amid the celebrations. He had caught glimpses of Alijah throughout the night, always stalking along the edges of the chamber, never truly engaging with anyone. More than once, the king tried to share a drink with his oldest friend, but every time he got close another would get in his way and demand his time.

As pale blues and warm pinks began to spread across the night's sky, the celebrations naturally quietened down, the revellers too drunk and exhausted to continue. Reyna and Nathaniel had already retired for the night and the rangers had scattered to who knows where - only Doran remained; passed out with an empty tankard hanging between his limp fingers. Galanör and Inara were sat together, talking intently and oblivious to the fatigue that everyone else suffered. Gideon had spoken of an important errand he needed to attend to and excused himself some time ago.

It was then that Vighon realised the Master Dragorn wasn't the only person missing. He hadn't seen Alijah for many hours. When had he slipped away? He bade his personal guard to stay, reminding them that he could protect himself in his own keep. There was no sign of Alijah in the halls nor the throne room. His search could only last so long before he himself needed to find rest - there was no telling how many more days and nights of celebrations the people had in mind.

Retiring to his old quarters, the northman felt as if he had just walked away from another battlefield. He was weary to his bones and his muscles ached from previous injuries. Closing the door behind him, he could already imagine the feel of the pillow and the soft mattress beneath him. First his cloak came off, discarded on the floor, before he removed his sword belt. He didn't drop the belt, however.

Instead, he spun on his heel and withdrew the silvyr blade from the scabbard. Elvish magic gave birth to the flames and illuminated the shadowy room, as well as the figure standing by the balcony doors. Alijah's angular face didn't so much as twitch, his body completely relaxed as he leant against the stone.

Vighon took a breath and lowered his sword. "I could have run you through," he warned, struggling to find a smile at such an hour.

Alijah apparently had no problem smiling. "You could have tried," he replied coyly.

The northman was more than used to hearing his friend's arrogance, though he couldn't recall ever hearing him boast of being a better fighter, especially with a sword. "Why are you skulking around, Alijah? Do you need a room for the night?"

Alijah shook his head and his smile faded. "I just wanted to talk, away from the prying eyes and ears of the court."

Vighon sheathed his bade and the flames vanished. "Talk..." he mused. "I remember when that was so easy. When we could talk into the night and greet the dawn." The northman looked Alijah up and down, taking the measure of him. "So much has happened. To both of us," he added. "I wouldn't even know where to begin with... *talking*."

Alijah pushed away from the wall. "I think one of us asks a question and then the other responds. Or something like that."

Vighon chewed over the question that burned in his mind. "What happened to you in The Bastion?"

Alijah paused. "Ask a different question," he replied.

The northman removed the crown from his head and threw it to Alijah. "Do you want to be king?" he asked pointedly.

Alijah had caught the crown and was now inspecting it in both hands. "Do *you*?" he fired back.

"You used to be an open book," Vighon observed, a little irritation in his tone. "What happened to you, Alijah? What did The Crow do to you? Asher told us of his plan - to position you for the throne. I know he did terrible things to you. I can see it all over your—"

"Stop," Alijah commanded. He looked at the crown one last time before throwing it back to Vighon. "The throne is yours. The entire *realm* is yours. I'm not here to take that from you."

"Then what are you here for?" Vighon demanded softly. "Since you've returned I am yet to see anything of the friend I once knew. I tried desperately to find that connection, but I can see the truth in your eyes: my friend is dead." Vighon clenched his jaw but tears still welled. "I didn't want to listen to Asher, I couldn't believe it. But you're something *else* now..."

Alijah sighed. "I came to talk," he repeated with an exasperated tone. "And you shouldn't listen to anything the ranger says; he knows nothing of what he speaks. You *know* me, Vighon." Alijah stepped closer with a pleading manner. "I'm still... I'm still *me*."

Vighon narrowed his eyes, scrutinising the man before him. "Then why can't I let go of my sword?"

Alijah stepped back and looked down at Vighon's hand, gripping the hilt of his blade. "I told you; I'm not here to take anything from you." The half-elf straightened up. "I'm here to say goodbye..."

That took some of the tension out of the room. "Goodbye? You're leaving with Gideon then?"

"No," Alijah replied definitively. "I'm going away, just Malliath and me."

Vighon chastised himself. He had always listened to his gut and since engaging with Alijah, it had told him he was in danger. Yet here they were, conversing politely on the verge of farewells. Perhaps he had judged his old friend too soon and far too harshly.

"Forgive me," he begged, letting go of his sword. "I am... exhausted and overwhelmed. Why don't you stay a while longer and we can talk. We don't have to talk about The Bastion or The Crow or any of that if you don't want to. I could really use a friend right now," he added, lifting the crown.

Alijah looked away, considering the offer. "I have already said my goodbyes. If I stay, I fear I will plant a seed of hope in my parents. They are already upset enough."

"Now I know why they looked so glum during the party. What about Inara?"

Alijah shrugged. "My entire family is immortal, Vighon. We will all see each other again..."

"You're going away for a while then," Vighon concluded.

A flicker of pain crossed Alijah's face, revealing just a glimmer of the young man Vighon had loved like a brother. "I don't know how long I'll be gone for. But... you might not be here when I return."

Vighon shared that same flicker of pain. "I see," he agonised.

"Perhaps I will meet one of your many sons!" Alijah lifted his tone, but it did nothing to lift Vighon's spirits.

"I would rather you stay and see them born," Vighon preferred. "Imagine the world we could build together," he tried. "Me as the king. You and Inara as the guardians of the realm. You don't need to leave."

Alijah looked to appreciate the attempt. "This is Inara's time, just as it's yours." The half-elf moved for the balcony doors, opening them to the light of the rising sun. "All of this is in your care now, Vighon. The land, the people: they are yours to keep safe. Don't fail them, I beg you..."

Vighon's reply caught in his throat as he watched Alijah cross the small balcony and leap over the rail. The king ran to the edge with a cold fear seizing his stomach. Pressing himself to the rail, he looked over the edge just in time to see Malliath flying up towards him. Vighon instinctively drew himself backwards and tracked the black dragon who launched into the sky with Alijah on his back.

Instead of returning to the warmth of his chamber, Vighon remained on the balcony and watched Malliath fly away until he faded into the west with his oldest friend. In a matter of days, the northman felt as if he had gained the whole world and yet lost it all at the same time.

He could only hope that, no matter how old he was, one day Alijah would return and they would be reunited as the friends they once were. Until then, he sighed, there was the matter of being king to attend to...

CHAPTER 47
FAREWELLS

It was a windless day in the north, a spell of good weather the people were in much need of. It was still freezing, however, and Asher was sure to keep his green cloak about him. The ranger stood in the snow with Namdhor to his back and the elves before him. They had gathered to say farewell to Gideon and the Dragorn masters, Ayana and Alastir.

Farther north, towards the mountains, the dwarves could be seen in their great numbers. Led by Doran's brother, Dakmund, they were beginning their own journey out of Illian.

Despite the exodus, Asher could see that the people of Illian would still thrive with Vighon as their king and Inara's guardianship. Then there were the elves, who were set to return to Illian's shores in larger numbers and help where they could, especially with the mysterious Drakes.

Asher continued to watch as Gideon bid farewell to Lady Ellöria and King Vighon. There was an exchange of words between the Master Dragorn and Inara, but the ranger kept his distance from the whole thing, happy to be an observer. Gideon, however, found the ranger among the gathered and approached.

"It has been an honour to fight by your side again." Gideon bowed his head, a mark of respect he had only shown to Ellöria and Vighon.

"Hopefully," he replied, "it was for the last time."

Gideon smiled. "Hope is all we have. In our stead, I'm leaving it to Inara and the rangers of this world to keep it alive."

Asher had never been one for hope, his stock always put in action. "We will try," he promised.

That seemed to satisfy the Master Dragorn. "I'm glad you're back..."

The ranger could only respond with an appreciative nod. He still didn't know what to make of his return to life nor what it meant for his future.

After watching Gideon reduce Reyna to tears and crush Nathaniel within a tight embrace, Asher craned his neck and witnessed the end of an era. Gideon, Ayana, and Alastir all took to the sky astride their dragons and made for the east. Only Inara and Athis remained to be sentinels of red against a pale winter's day.

The farther the dragons flew the more dispersed the crowds became. Asher wandered over to Reyna and Nathaniel - he hadn't been able to speak with them since returning from The Lifeless Isles. He could still see the heartbreak in Reyna's eyes when Alijah told them he was leaving. Throughout the celebrations, they had both remained very sombre, torn between having one of their children remain behind while another disappeared.

Before he could reach them, his path was blocked by Faylen. Her beauty was startling, causing the ranger to clumsily lose track of his thoughts. Her dark hair ran over her shoulders like silk, accentuating the angular features of her pale face. Damn, he wanted to kiss her...

"Asher..." Faylen displayed just as much awkwardness around him as he did around her.

"Faylen. Will you be—"

"Are you—"

The two swallowed their words for fear of talking over the other again. At last, Faylen cleared her throat and smiled. "Are you staying in Namdhor?" she asked.

"Only for a day or so," he replied gruffly, noting Nemir's lingering presence in the distance. "Will you be staying in Illian or are you to return to Ayda?"

"I must return," Faylen said with a hint of disappointment. "As the High Guardian of Elandril, my place is by Queen Adilandra's side. There is still much to be done among my people."

Asher could only nod in agreement, unsure what else to say. If he spoke of the truth that lay in his heart he would ask her to stay with him and leave Nemir and her responsibilities behind. But such a thing could never be said aloud. Faylen was happy and that mattered so much more to Asher than anything else. To love him would only bring heartbreak; his life only a fraction of her own.

Faylen reached up and cupped his face. "You have no idea of the joy it brings knowing you have been given a second chance. You, of all people, deserve it." The elf pushed up on her toes and kissed him softly on the cheek. "Try not to mess it up and get yourself eaten by some monster..." The cheeky smile on her face was infectious.

"I'll do my best."

The ranger squeezed her hand and pulled her in for a tight embrace. He enjoyed the scent of her hair, wondering if he would ever smell it again, before reluctantly turning away in search of Reyna and Nathaniel. It was an effort not to turn back and watch Faylen return to her husband.

He found his friends talking to Inara, who was climbing up Athis's red scales as Asher approached. The Dragorn gave him a friendly nod before the dragon launched into the air.

"Is she alright?" Asher asked, aware that Inara had a tremendous amount of responsibility on her shoulders now.

"She's fine," Reyna replied confidently. "She's going to pay her respects to Arathor and Thraden."

Asher turned his head to the mountains. "Gideon was able to retrieve his body?"

"While the celebrations were in full swing," the elf explained. "Ayana helped to open a portal. They've put them together..."

Asher couldn't claim to know a lot about Dragorn tradition, but he knew they were to be put together in death. "I'm glad he was able to do that before he left."

Nathaniel was notably quiet, his gaze distant. "Did he say goodbye - Alijah?"

His son's name coaxed Nathaniel back to the moment. "He did."

"He needs time," Reyna added. "At least we know that this time."

"But we don't know *where* he's gone," Nathaniel pointed out, clearly frustrated and worried.

"Wherever it is, my love, he isn't alone. Who would dare threaten him with Malliath by his side?"

Asher averted his eyes, fearful that his feelings on the matter of Alijah and Malliath would upset his closest friends. He himself had said farewell to their son having caught up with him in the passage outside the banquet hall. They had stood in each other's way, just as the echo of their minds continued to clash inside their heads. Asher had given him a hard look.

"I've seen inside your mind," he had told him. "I know how you think. I know how Malliath thinks. *When* you return, know that I will be waiting..."

Alijah had said nothing in response, the perfect model of composure. Asher kept their brief interaction to himself and returned his attention to his friends.

"I'm sure he will be back," the ranger offered. "Illian is his home."

Reyna shot him a beaming smile that didn't reach her eyes. "Of course," she agreed, her words somewhat hollow. "In the meantime, we have to pick up the pieces and put the realm back together. Vighon has asked us to continue our roles as ambassadors with my people. In time, I'm confident we will be called upon to liaise with the dwarves of Grimwhal as well."

Nathaniel gave his first genuine smile. "If they're all as cantankerous as Doran and his brother our talks are going to be *very* interesting."

"I leave that to you," Asher replied, his grin setting them all off.

"And what does the future hold in store for you?" Reyna asked.

Asher took a long breath of the icy air. "Vighon has tasked a few of us with rooting out the orcs in the south. The quicker we can get civilisation back on track the quicker we rangers can find more work."

"Is that all there is?" Nathaniel enquired. "More work?"

Reyna turned on the ranger excitedly. "You gave us the deed to the land which we've called home. It's only right that we return it to you, now that you're—"

Asher held up his hand before talk of his resurrection came up. "I gave it to you. The land is yours. Besides," he added lightly, "the world is still full of monsters. As long as I've got the strength in my arm to swing my sword, that's what I'm going to do."

Reyna looked deep into his eyes and reached out for his hand. "You don't have to make things right anymore. You have more than atoned for your deeds as an Arakesh. You deserve some peace."

"Peace that doesn't come with death," Nathaniel added.

Reyna shot her husband a judging look. "He may speak like a fool, but his words carry wisdom, Asher. I wouldn't lose you again..."

Asher gripped her fingers. "I'm not going anywhere. If you ever need me, put up a contract with a large reward: I'll find you."

Nathaniel put his hands up. "Enough. There have been too many farewells this day. You're not leaving Namdhor today, which means you're coming with us. Somehow, Vighon Draqaro has become the king of Illian, the orcs have been defeated, and The Black Hand has been wiped out. I'd say we have at least one more night of celebrating before the world catches up with us..."

Asher laughed to himself and put his arm over Reyna's shoulder as they made their way back to the city. "Perhaps we could convince Doran to brew some of his famous ale."

Nathaniel turned to walk backwards. "If we drink so much as a drop of Doran's home-brew, the world will *never* catch up with us!"

EPILOGUE

The farther Malliath flew west, the farther Illian was left behind. For Alijah, he was leaving behind more than just the land. With every mile, he let go of his old life and embraced the unknown of what was to come, his destiny laid out before him like a blank canvas.

Sitting back, there was nothing to do but marvel at the new world as they descended beneath the clouds, revealing the foreign shoreline.

They hadn't seen land in two days, a testament to Malliath's stamina and Alijah's new-found magic. Looking from north to south, Erador stretched beyond sight, a whole new realm of untold wonders and great promise. The explorer in him was giddy with excitement, but it failed to reveal itself since that part of his previous life was buried beneath layers of discipline.

Malliath continued to glide down until he was soaring only metres over The Hox, creating a vast spray in his wake. Crossing over the beach, there was no sign of life. In fact, from the great stretch of land he had seen, there were no boats or ships docked in the shallows.

The Leviathan still hunts in these waters, Malliath told him. *Only a fool would sail The Hox.*

Alijah had looked down at the sea many times over the last two days, searching with his keen eyes for any sign of the ancient predator. Alas, he had caught no sign of the enormous beast that lurked in the depths.

Despite the lack of civilisation on land, Alijah wasn't deterred. The Crow had never lied to him.

Together, they flew over the eastern lands of Erador, weaving and gliding over green plains and rushing rivers. Memories from Malliath's past began to bleed across their bond, making Alijah feel as if he had been here before.

Look! Alijah pushed himself up and set his sights on the ground. ***That's definitely a road!***

Indeed, a dark path cut through the green pastures below, curving with the land and navigating the rivers and brooks. If Erador was truly a forgotten land, such a path would have been consumed by nature over the last ten thousand years.

Let us follow it then... Malliath suggested, his shadow rolling over the hills.

Somewhere between midday and sunset, the land opened up to a boundless plain of wonderful green. In the middle of the colossal landscape, there stood a sprawling city of tired white walls that surrounded a fortress-like palace that reached for the sky with its central spire. Alijah could imagine that it had once looked to be a splendid jewel on the lush plains.

Smoke rose from chimneys, horses and carts moved in and out via the multiple roads, and people, no bigger than ants from their height, could be seen in the farmland. To the west, sat on the open plain, was a black mass of neat rows - an army.

Erador was most certainly alive!

Alijah could feel Malliath's unease. ***They possess no magic,*** he reassured, recalling The Crow's words. ***Your might alone will make us gods to them.***

Malliath bristled. *Perhaps we should give a demonstration.*

Alijah could feel Malliath's exact intentions and knew the dragon wanted to reduce the size of their army. It would definitely send a message of some kind, but Alijah had something else in mind.

Let them see us. Take us to the main street, the one that leads to the palace in the centre.

Malliath altered his flight path and banked towards the city itself. Alijah took a moment to examine the map he had taken from The Bastion. He only unravelled it enough to see the west, where Erador dominated the ancient parchment. Judging by the surrounding landscape and the six roads he could see entering the city, he had to assume this was Valgala, Erador's capital.

Tucking the map back into his jacket, he looked ahead to see that Malliath had passed over the outer wall and was now gliding between the buildings, many of which needed a great deal of repair. The streets were filled with people and more flooded out from their homes and businesses to witness their arrival. Blue flags were hung haphazardly throughout the city, all of them emboldened with a white sigil Alijah had never seen before.

These people haven't seen a dragon in ten thousand years. They might not even know what you are.

Malliath disagreed. *The history of my kin is rich in these lands. They will know what dragons are...*

The black dragon made for the large courtyard at the base of the palace steps. A single statue, almost equal in size to Malliath, decorated the centre of the courtyard. It was a man, his identity unknown, pulling on a chain that had been wrapped around a dragon's neck. By the look of it, the stonework was very old, harking back to Erador's golden age most likely.

Maybe they do know what dragons are, Alijah relented.

Malliath's thick claws dug deep into the courtyard, his bulk clearing out the terrified on-lookers. Before Alijah had even climbed down his companion's scales, there were soldiers charging down the steps of the palace and emerging from side streets. They wielded spears, nothing but an irritation to Malliath.

Alijah casually crossed the courtyard to stand in front of Malliath, his hand resting lightly on the hilt of his scimitar. He allowed the soldiers to fill what space they could and assume their formations - it wouldn't matter.

Among them, one stepped forward. His helmet of gold was more elaborate than the others, setting him apart as someone with authority.

"You will go no farther!" he barked.

Malliath growled from behind Alijah and the soldier lost some of his nerve.

"We didn't come to start a fight," Alijah told him honestly.

The soldier looked from Alijah to Malliath and back. "Then why have you come? And with one of those?" he added, jabbing his spear in the dragon's direction.

"I wouldn't do that if I were you," Alijah warned.

The soldier should have rightly soiled himself, but he found courage from somewhere to shout, "What do you want?"

"I have come to free Erador of the shackles that chain it to the past!" Alijah announced, glancing at the horrendous statue that towered over them. "The tyranny you have lived under comes to an end this very day!"

As one, the surrounding soldiers dropped into fighting stances and levelled their spears at Alijah - it was easy to take anything he said as a threat when Malliath was standing behind him.

"Only one has to die today," Alijah advised. "You could all return to your families if you would but bow the knee."

"Kill the beast first!" the lead soldier commanded ignorantly.

Alijah sighed, pulling his Vi'tari blade free. *Try **and spare any who surrender...***

Malliath grunted, promising nothing.

What followed was far more bloodshed than Alijah wanted. He crippled and maimed where he could, sparing as many lives as possible. His green blade shattered the steel of their swords and sliced through their armour with smooth ease. Malliath unleashed his breath, smothering the courtyard in fire, smoke, and dying screams. Together, they cut through the soldiers of Valgala in a few minutes.

Malliath, however, wasn't sated by the death. He curled his tail and lashed out with such force that he broke the ancient statue into pieces, damaging an adjacent building in the process. Alijah reminded himself that the sacrifice was necessary, that a few would have to suffer before they saw the light that he brought.

Leaving Malliath behind, the half-elf ascended the steps and used magic to blow the iron doors from their hinges. Inside, he faced more resistance from those who wished to protect their poor excuse for a king. Magic was among Alijah's weapons now and he tore through the palace without sustaining a single injury. The more power he called upon the more he let Malliath into his mind and even his muscles. Killing became easy, a joy almost. In his wake was a trail of bodies that even the blind could use to follow him.

In the throne room, cathedral in its size, he found the king of Valgala. Alijah had always prided himself on being an excellent judge of character, a skill that had served him well in many a game of Galant. Scrutinising the obese man who lounged on the throne, surrounded by concubines and platters of food, he decided the king was a gluttonous fiend like so many who had held the title of king.

Were it not for the wine, which spilled out of his goblet, the king would have taken in the sight of Alijah and deduced that death had come for him. Addled as his poisoned mind was, he remained on his throne, oblivious to his retreating concubines and the dead soldier who slid off the end of Alijah's blade.

"And who might you be... *stranger*?" The king chuckled to himself. "Have you come to entertain me?"

"No," Alijah replied, his stride purposeful. "I've come to be better than you..." The Vi'tari scimitar flashed and opened the king's throat.

He fell from the throne, gargling his last words. The crown tumbled to the ground and spun around in the pooling blood. Alijah ignored the burst of screams from the women and crouched down to retrieve the jewel-encrusted head piece.

Holding it, Alijah immediately knew it wouldn't be enough. He couldn't settle for the crown of Valgala or the entirety of Erador. The fate of Alijah Galfrey had been scribed in blood ten thousand years ago, his ultimate reign inevitable.

This was only the beginning...

THE ADVENTURE CONTINUES...

THE ECHOES SAGA

THE KNIGHTS
OF ERADOR

BOOK VII

BY
PHILIP C. QUAINTRELL

PHILIP C. QUAINTRELL

———

To hear more from Philip,
including book releases and exclusive content:

WEBSITE:

Philipcquaintrell.com

FACEBOOK:

Facebook.com/philipcquaintrell

INSTAGRAM:

@philipcquaintrell.author

AUTHOR NOTES

This is not the end! Hurrah! As you've just seen on the previous page, there's more to come.

Writing 'Age of the King' then! It was both thrilling and daunting for sure. Bringing this storyline to a satisfying ending while simultaneously keeping the whole saga on track for 'The Knights of Erador' required a lot of 'staring blankly at my map' moments. I often only plan a few chapters ahead at a time, that way the story can surprise me as I go but, for this book, I actually planned out a very rough outline for about 90% of it.

This kind of had to happen for this stage of the saga as a whole though, on account of The Crow. I thought it would be super cool to have an antagonist who could see the future. I mean, why not? You can't defeat a villain who has seen how it all ends. The Crow himself, however, did find his end, regardless of what he's really accomplished. This, in part, was what I loved about him - his own demise was part of his plan!

I digressed a little there. The problem with an antagonist who can see the future is making that future actually take place. That's a hard thing to do when you prefer a more organic flow to your writing (ie, allowing characters to make choices based on their personalities and experiences and just going with it).

This ultimately meant that I had to go back and insert new Crow sections to match up with events that took place further down the line. Thankfully, this didn't happen all that much and most of the events of his foresight just happened as my sub-conscience rolled it out. Phew!

What I will say is: The Crow's ultimate plan hasn't been truly laid out yet. There's more twists and turns to come!

Now, I'm not the kind of guy who goes out in search of inspiration. I make sure I'm sat at my desk five days a week with my notes and map; that way inspiration knows where to find me! Aside from the rough chapters I planned out (as mentioned earlier) the plot itself is usually mapped out in my head in a series of beats, key scenes I suppose, rather than every little detail. I much prefer the details being filled in by the characters and their choices, many of which surprise even myself.

Speaking of those surprises, a lot of them came from the new characters. In fact, the most daunting aspect of the last three books was introducing these new characters. I'm aware of peoples' attachment to characters from the first three books, but I felt new blood was essential for moving their lives on and giving them some evolution. Despite the balancing act, I've really enjoyed bringing these new characters to life and I'm looking forward to you reading the next three books and seeing where things go (and end) for them all.

Going back to chapter one for a moment, I approached Asher's perspective with a little self-doubt. I hadn't written as Asher since the end of 'Relic of the Gods': could I still write as him? Did I still know that character inside and out? I was probably about five paragraphs in when I realised how much I had missed the old ranger! Once I started I had to make sure I returned to the other characters and storylines to actually complete the book.

Since the release of the first three books, I've received a tremendous amount of positive feedback regarding Asher. He definitely appears to be the stand-out character for everyone. He's certainly up there as my favourite; he was the first thing to be pulled out of my imagination after all. He came before the map and the names and the plot. I still have a piece of A4 paper that's titled 'Fantasy Book' and beneath it is one word: Ranger.

The old ranger aside for a moment, a new character emerged from this story that stood out to me. Vighon Draqaro! From here on out we're living in the Age of the King, Vighon's Age, and the first of his roguish name. I have no idea how much of a 'twist' it was that Vighon became the title character for this one. I say that because *I* didn't even know he was going to be king! Not until the end of 'The Fall of Neverdark', when the threads began to unravel in my plan at least. I still remember my fingers stop over the keyboard as it struck me, two books ahead of schedule, that Vighon was going to be the king of Illian.

Initially, Vighon was going to be something of an audience character - still important, but he was to be the guy who asked questions. The more I wrote about him, especially his backstory, the more I enjoyed writing as him and I eventually began to see other qualities in him, qualities that began to shine in the latter two books. Did you guys like him? Or is he, and everyone else, always going to play number two behind Asher?

Another character I haven't spoken about in a long time is Gideon Thorn. *The* Gideon Thorn! I believe it was his storyline in the first three books that left the reader with a sense of hope where many felt that despair from losing Asher. Bringing his character into the next phase of the saga was very interesting for me. Initially, I thought 'oh great! He's going to be this amazing leader/mentor with tons of wisdom and experience!'

But, then it hit me.

After I delved into his head, thirty years after I left him, I realised that he didn't have nearly as much experience as I thought. The thirst three books were certainly the making of him, but overall, that conflict was relatively brief from his perspective. Entering into a full-blow invasion, a war twice the size and scale of Valanis's return, I came to see that he had built this new order over thirty years of peace. This made his whole character even more interesting for me. Now, he had flaws and limitations.

What was more interesting was everyone's view of him, the way he was put on a pedestal above all others yet, internally, he was full of doubt and anxiety. When I started thinking from his perspective, I began to see where he had gone wrong or, at least, where he hadn't done enough. The responsibility he feels towards those of his order paired with the needs of the realm felt like the only problem he really needs to get in alignment. His decision to take the Dragorn away for a while surprised me, just as it did Inara, but it also felt right. I can't wait to see where that thread goes!

One last thing about this book -and it's a small thing. I really loved that Thallan's cursed Vi'tari blade came back! I remember Gideon hiding it under Korkanath when I was writing 'Relic of the Gods' and thinking, 'I wonder if that will ever come back into the story?' As this story unfolded and The Crow made his promise of a sword worthy of a king, I knew it had to be that scimitar. As for ALijah and his blade, we haven't seen the last of them, just as we haven't seen The Crow's legacy fulfilled to its completion yet - the last phase in the saga is going to be EPIC!

Coming soon...

Now for a little bit about myself. I don't usually write about myself personally since the books aren't about me they're about the story. Also, writing a book and setting it loose for all the world to read can leave you feeling a little vulnerable in more ways than one. So far, the only thing I'm sure you could say about me is, 'He has a big imagination!'. Well, it's certainly overactive, nay, a hungry beast that has been fed sci-fi and fantasy since three years old (thanks dad!).

When people read books it can be easy to think they're getting a piece of the author with it, as if the writer has woven some of themselves into it. I know I've put a lot of myself in The Echoes Saga - how could I not? I've been writing these stories for years now and they've changed my life.

One of the most ironic things about this saga is the twist surrounding the origin of the gods. I can see how it would be easy to believe that I don't have a faith considering I've made it clear they were never gods. In fact, I do have faith and I do attend my church regularly. I couldn't say why this particular twist came to me, but I tend to let my imagination (fiction-factory) take care of the details.

I guess it's a bit redundant to point out that I'm a geek at this point. I don't have a lot of friends with similar passions to me so I always enjoy talking with my readers when they contact me. I've always had a mind for facts concerning all things sci-fi and fantasy pop-culture (facts that don't help you in exams). So having a job where I get to make up stories all day long is a dream come true for me.

I do miss nursing (not the horrific hours though) and especially the camaraderie on every shift. Writing can be a lonely experience at times since you do the bulk of the job on your own and talking to someone about whatever you're writing can make you sound like a crazy person.

That said, I'm an introvert by nature and I love crafting these stories to share with you all. There are times when I'm writing and the world closes off, speeding time up to the point that I forget to eat or drink. I suppose that's just further proof that I love what I do.

In other 'me' news - my son is ten months old as I write this. I've already begun his Jedi training to make him into a geek worthy enough to rival his father. One day he will have to answer the big question we've all been challenged by at some point in our lives; Star Wars or Star Trek? He can prefer whatever he wants, but when it comes to Lord of the Rings or The Echoes Saga, he had better pick the latter!

I have an album on Spotify (Echoes of Fate) that lists some of the tracks I've found inspirational, so feel free to follow that as I add to it. When I'm writing, I actually listen to a writing playlist I made (it's ten hours long!). It's a combination of multiple tracks without any lyrics as I find it hard to write with someone actually singing at me. I can write without music, but I do find it to be an excellent fuel source to keep me going through certain scenes.

So, what's next? 'The Knights of Erador'! As I've mentioned before, my project following The Echoes Saga is a chronicle series about Asher and his years as a ranger. I've already penned the notes for his first four books - all self-contained stories. I can't wait for you all to get lost in his tales, but first there's a saga to finish!

As always, I would ask that you leave me a review for this book and any books of mine that you've enjoyed. I'm still self-publishing so your continued support with the stars really helps me to get the books out there, all of which cost less than a cup of coffee *anywhere*! Until the pricing is taken out of my hands, I will always aim to sell my stories at a lower cost so everyone can enjoy them.

If you don't already, please like and follow me on Facebook and Instagram where I can keep you updated on future releases and any exciting news.

Until the next time...

APPENDICES

Dwarven Hierarchy:

1. ***Battleborns*** - Ruled by King Uthrad, son of Koddun. Domain: *Silvyr Hall.*

2. ***Stormshields*** - Ruled by King Gandalir, son of Bairn. Domain: *Hyndaern.*

3. ***Heavybellys*** - Ruled by King Dorain, son of Dorryn. Domain: *Grimwhal.*

4. ***Hammerkegs*** - Ruled by King Torgan, son of Dorald. Domain: *Nimduhn.*

5. ***Goldhorns*** - Ruled by King Thedomir, son of Thaldurum. Domain: *Khaldarim.*

6. ***Brightbeards*** - Ruled by King Gaerhard, son of Hermon. Domain: *Bhan Doral.*

~

Orcish Hierarchy:

1. **The Born Horde** - Ruled by Karakulak, Chieftain of the Born Horde, Bone Lord of The Under Realm, and king of the orcs.

2. **The Berserkers** - Ruled by Chieftain Warhg the terrible.

3. **The Big Bastards** - Ruled by Chieftain Barghak the mountain-maker.

4. **The Grim Stalkers** - Ruled by Chieftain Lurg the unseen.

5. **The Fallen** - Ruled by Chieftain Orlaz the devastator.

6. **The Savage Daggers** - Ruled by Chieftain Raz-ak the swift.

7. **The Steel Caste** - Ruled by Chieftain Grul the unbearable.

8. **The Bone Breakers** - Ruled by Chieftain Dugza the marrow drinker.

9. **The Mountain Fist** - Ruled by Chieftain Golm the fiend-slayer

~

Kingdoms of Illian:

1. **Alborn** (eastern region) - Ruled by King Rayden of house Marek. Capital city: *Velia*. Other Towns and Cities: Palios, Galosha, and Barossh.

2. **The Arid Lands** (southern region) - Ruled by the elected High Council. Capital city: *Tregaran*. Other Towns and Cities: Ameeraska and Calmardra.

3. **The Ice Vales** (western region) - Ruled by King Jormund of house Orvish. Capital city: *Grey Stone*. Other Towns and Cities: Bleak, Kelp Town, and Snowfell.

4. **Orith** (northern region) - Ruled by Queen Yelifer of house Skalaf. Capital city: *Namdhor*. Other Towns and Cities: Skystead, Dunwich, Darkwell, and Longdale.

5. **Felgarn** (central region) - Ruled by King Weymund of house Harg. Capital city: *Lirian*. Other Towns and Cities: Vangarth, Wood Vale, and Whistle Town.

6. **Dragorn** (island nation off The Shining Coast to the east) - Ruled by the three crime families; the Fenrigs, the Yarls, and the Danathors.

~

Other significant locations:

Elandril (northern Ayda) - Ruled by Queen Adilandra of house Sevari. The heart of the elven nation.

The Lifeless Isles (south of Dragorn) - An archipelago and home to the dragons and the Dragorn.

Korkanath (an island east of Velia) - The most prestigious school for magic.

Stowhold (an island north of Korkanath) - The headquarters of Illian's largest bank.

Syla's Gate (south of The Arid Lands) - Entrance to The Undying Mountains.

The Tower of Dragons' Reach (south of Velia) - The meeting place for all the rulers of Illian and the Dragorn.

Ilythyra (in The Moonlit Plains) - Governed by Lady Ellöria of house Sevari. Home to a small population of elves from Elandril.

Paldora's Fall (inside The Undying Mountains) - The impact site of Paldora's Star, a well of powerful magic.

~

Significant Wars: Chronologically

The First War - Fought during The Pre-Dawn (before elvish-recorded history). King Atilan started a war with the first Dragon Riders in the hopes of uncovering their source of immortality. The war brought an end to Atilan's reign and his entire kingdom.

The Great War - Fought during the First Age, around 5,000 years ago. The only recorded time in history that elves and dwarves have united. They fought against the orcs with the help of the Dragorn, the first elvish dragon riders. This war ended the First Age.

The Dark War - Fought during the Second Age, around 1,000 years ago. Considered the elvish civil war. Valanis, the dark elf, tried to take over Illian in the name of the gods. This war ended the Second Age.

The Dragon War - Fought in the beginning of the Third Age, only a few years after The Dark War. The surviving elves left Illian for Ayda's shores, fleeing any more violence. Having emerged from The

Wild Moores, the humans, under King Gal Tion's rule, went to war with the dragons over their treasure. This saw the exile of the surviving dragons and the beginning of human dominance over Illian.

The War for the Realm - The most recent war of the Third Age, fought 30 years ago. The return of Valanis saw the world plunged back into war and the re-emergence of the Dragorn. Gideon Thorn became the first human to bond with a dragon in recorded history. Valanis was killed by the ranger, Asher, who died in their final battle.

The Northern Civil War - In the wake of The War for the Realm, the north, under the ruling city of Namdhor, was left without its king, Merkaris Tion. In the vacuum that followed, the lords and great families fell into civil war over the throne. The war lasted nearly twenty years and ended with Yelifer, of house Skalaf, seated on the throne.

Made in the USA
Las Vegas, NV
15 December 2022

62766911R00381